M000285437

WALTER DE LA MARE
SHORT STORIES
1895–1926

Walter de la Mare

SHORT STORIES
1895–1926

Edited by
GILES DE LA MARE

dlm

First published in 1996
by Giles de la Mare Publishers Limited
3 Queen Square, London WC1N 3AU

Printed in Great Britain by
Hillman Printers (Frome) Limited
All rights reserved

Designed by Ron Costley

©Literary Trustees of Walter de la Mare 1996

Walter de la Mare is hereby identified as author of
this work in accordance with Section 77 of the
Copyright, Designs and Patents Act 1988

A CIP record of this book is available
from the British Library

ISBN 1-900357-03-8 (volume I)

Giles de la Mare Publishers
would like to thank the Arts Council of England
for the grant they have kindly provided
to assist the publication of
Short Stories 1895–1926

CONTENTS

UNCOLLECTED STORIES

INTRODUCTION

When Walter de la Mare brought out his first collection of short stories called *The Riddle* in 1923 at the age of fifty, it would have been a surprise to some to discover how long he had been attracted by the genre. Few people would have guessed that his earliest published works had been stories. His first printed story, 'Kismet', had appeared in *The Sketch* in August 1895, and at least seven others had been serialized before the publication of *Songs of Childhood* in 1902. De la Mare continued writing and re-writing stories throughout the rest of his life. *The Riddle* was followed in quick succession by *Ding Dong Bell, Broomsticks* (for children), *The Connoisseur, On the Edge, The Lord Fish* (for children), and *The Wind Blows Over* in the 1920s and 1930s; and his very last major work, *A Beginning*, came out in 1955 less than a year before his death.

Apart from the *Collected Stories for Children* of 1947, he did not publish any comprehensive collection of stories comparable to the *Collected Poems* of 1942, although there were several selections from the eight main collections. The most important of these (since de la Mare was involved in the choice on both occasions) were *Stories, Essays and Poems* of 1938 published in the Everyman series and *Best Stories of Walter de la Mare* of 1942 published by Faber – who brought out all the major collections after *The Connoisseur*. The latter came out with Collins in 1926, *The Riddle* and *Ding Dong Bell* having appeared with Selwyn and Blount in 1923 and 1924, and *Broomsticks* with Constable in 1925. All in all, seventy-nine stories were published in collections, and over a score of them have never been reprinted elsewhere. The three volumes making up the first complete edition, include all these stories together with all the uncollected stories that have been found and a few unpublished ones.

De la Mare was as assiduous in serializing his stories before publication as he was in serializing his poems. Indeed, no less than sixty of the seventy-nine 'collected' stories were first published in magazines, newspapers or collections compiled by other people. When they appeared in volume form, which might be over fifty years later as happened with 'The Quincunx', they were often revised. (The interval between writing and serialization or publication in a collection could also be enormous: for example, 'A Beginning', which was published in the volume of that title in 1955, seems to have been written in about 1900, and 'The Miller's Tale', which was serialized in December 1955, was probably written about then as well.) But not all the stories that were serialized were collected. This is particularly true of the period 1895–1910 and altogether eighteen uncollected stories have so far been found. In all likelihood, de la Mare deliberately did not reprint some of them. There is, however, clear evidence that he intended to publish certain stories like 'Kismet', which was revised for publication in *A Beginning* but omitted from it at the galley-proof stage. Others may well have been forgotten in the course of time. As it is no more possible to determine the exact reasons for stories remaining uncollected than it was in the case of the poems, all the stories found have been included. They are printed in the order in which they were first serialized or published – in sections at the end of *Short Stories 1895–1926* and *Short Stories 1927–1956*.

Although a number of stories in manuscript and typescript form were discovered among de la Mare's papers, there only seemed to be good grounds for publishing four of them. Three of these had been omitted from *A Beginning* at the galley-proof stage, and the fourth was the second half of 'The Orgy: An Idyll' which was cut in two when it was published in 1930, probably because it was too long. The unpublished stories follow the uncollected ones at the end of *Short Stories 1927–1956*.

The same general arrangement has been adopted as in the *Complete Poems*. The stories have been grouped chronologically according to the volumes in which they originally appeared. *Short Stories 1895–1926* includes the first three main collections and uncollected stories from the earlier period: *Short Stories 1927–1956* the last three main collections and uncollected and unpublished stories from the later period; and *Short Stories for Children* the two children's collections. To give an indication of the order in which the stories were written or revised, a chronological list of earliest known printed versions has been included on page 495.

With one or two exceptions, the text is based on the latest printed versions worked on by de la Mare, *Stories, Essays and Poems* (1938), *Best Stories of Walter de la Mare* (1942) and *Collected Stories for Children* (1947) being the three chief sources for these apart from the eight main collections. For further details, see the Bibliographical Appendix on page 483.

The contents of the three volumes are as follows:

I SHORT STORIES 1895–1926
Stories in Collections
  The Riddle and Other Stories (1923)
  Ding Dong Bell (1924, 1936)
  The Connoisseur and Other Stories (1926)
Uncollected Stories

I am very grateful to the late Dorothy Marshall for help in tracking down uncollected stories and checking references, and to Theresa Whistler for information about early manuscript versions. The late Leonard Clark's *Checklist* for the 1956 National Book League exhibition of de la Mare books and MSS has been a useful source of information.

Giles de la Mare

ABBREVIATIONS

MAIN COLLECTIONS
R	*The Riddle and Other Stories* (1923)
DDB	*Ding Dong Bell* (1924, 1936)
Br	*Broomsticks and Other Stories* (1925)
C	*The Connoisseur and Other Stories* (1926)
OE	*On the Edge: Short Stories* (1930)
LF	*The Lord Fish* (1933)
WBO	*The Wind Blows Over* (1936)
Beg	*A Beginning and Other Stories* (1955)

OTHER COLLECTIONS
SSS	*Seven Short Stories* (1931)
SEP	*Stories, Essays and Poems* (1938)
BS	*Best Stories of Walter de la Mare* (1942)
CSC	*Collected Stories for Children* (1947)
CT	*The Collected Tales of Walter de la Mare* (1950)
SSV	*Selected Stories and Verses of Walter de la Mare* (1952)
GS	*Walter de la Mare: Ghost Stories* (1956)

uncoll	*uncollected*

STORIES
IN COLLECTIONS

THE RIDDLE
AND OTHER STORIES
(1923)

The Almond Tree[*]

My old friend, 'the Count' as we used to call him, made very strange acquaintances at times. Let but a man have plausibility, a point of view, a crotchet, an enthusiasm, he would find in him an eager and exhilarating listener. And though he was often deceived and disappointed in his finds, the Count had a heart proof against lasting disillusionment. I confess, however, that these planetary cronies of his were rather disconcerting at times. And I own that meeting him one afternoon in the busy High Street, with a companion on his arm even more than usually voluble and odd – I own I crossed the road to avoid meeting the pair.

But the Count's eyes had been too sharp for me. He twitted me unmercifully with my snobbishness. 'I am afraid we must have appeared to avoid you to-day,' he said; and received my protestations with contemptuous indifference.

But the next afternoon we took a walk together over the heath; and perhaps the sunshine, something in the first freshness of the May weather, reminded him of bygone days.

'You remember that rather out-of-the-world friend of mine yesterday that so shocked your spruce proprieties, Richard? Well, I'll tell you a story.'

As closely as I can recall this story of the Count's childhood I have related it. I wish, though, I had my old friend's gift for such things; then, perhaps, his story might retain something of the charm in the reading which he gave to it in the telling. Perhaps that charm lies wholly in the memory of his voice, his companionship, his friendship. To revive these, what task would be a burden? . . .

'The house of my first remembrance, the house that to my last hour on earth will seem home to me, stood in a small green hollow on the verge of a wide heath. Its five upper windows faced far eastwards towards the weather-cocked tower of a village which rambled down the steep inclination of a hill. And, walking in its green old garden – ah, Richard, the

[*] As printed in BS (1942). First published in *English Review*, August 1909.

crocuses, the wallflowers, the violets! – you could see in the evening the standing fields of corn, and the dark furrows where the evening star was stationed; and a little to the south, upon a crest, a rambling wood of fir-trees and bracken.

'The house, the garden, the deep quiet orchard, all had been a wedding gift to my mother from a great-aunt, a very old lady in a kind of turban, whose shrewd eyes used to watch me out of her picture sitting in my high cane chair at meal-times – with not a little keenness; sometimes, I fancied, with a faint derision. Here passed by, to the singing of the lark, and the lamentation of autumn wind and rain, the first long nine of all these heaped-up inextricable years. Even now, my heart leaps up with longing to see again with those untutored eyes the lofty clouds of evening; to hear again as then I heard it the two small notes of the yellow-hammer piping from his green spray. I remember every room of the old house, the steep stairs, the cool apple-scented pantry; I remember the cobbles by the scullery, the well, my old dead raven, the bleak and whistling elms; but best of all I remember the unmeasured splendour of the heath, with its gorse, and its deep canopy of sunny air, the haven of every wild bird of the morning.

'Martha Rodd was a mere prim snippet of a maid then, pale and grave, with large contemplative, Puritan eyes. Mrs Ryder, in her stiff blue martial print and twisted gold brooch, was cook. And besides these, there was only old Thomas the gardener (as out-of-doors, and as distantly seen a creature as a dryad); my mother; and that busy-minded little boy, agog in wits and stomach and spirit – myself. For my father seemed but a familiar guest in the house, a guest ever eagerly desired and welcome, but none too eager to remain. He was a dark man with grey eyes and a long chin; a face unusually impassive, unusually mobile. Just as his capricious mood suggested, our little household was dejected or wildly gay. I never shall forget the spirit of delight he could conjure up at a whim, when my mother would go singing up and down stairs, and in her tiny parlour; and Martha in perfect content would prattle endlessly on to the cook, basting the twirling sirloin, while I watched in the firelight. And the long summer evenings too, when my father would find a secret, a magic, a mystery in everything; and we would sit together in the orchard while he told me tales, with the small green apples overhead, and beyond contorted branches, the first golden twilight of the moon.

'It's an old picture now, Richard, but true to the time.

'My father's will, his word, his caprice, his frown, these were the tables of the law in that small household. To my mother he was the very meaning of her life. Only that little boy was in some wise independent, busy, in-quisitive, docile, sedate; though urged to a bitterness of secret rebellion at times. In his childhood he experienced such hours of distress as the years do not in mercy bring again to a heart that may analyse as well as remember. Yet there also sank to rest the fountain of life's happiness. In among the gorse bushes were the green mansions of the fairies; along the furrows before his adventurous eyes stumbled crooked gnomes, hopped bewitched robins. Ariel trebled in the sunbeams and glanced from the dewdrops; and he heard the echo of distant and magic waters in the falling of the rain.

'But my father was never long at peace in the house. Nothing satisfied him; he must needs be at an extreme. And if he was compelled to conceal his discontent, there was something so bitter and imperious in his silence, so scornful a sarcasm in his speech, that we could scarcely bear it. And the knowledge of the influence he had over us served only at such times to sharpen his contempt.

'I remember one summer's evening we had been gathering strawberries. I carried a little wicker basket, and went rummaging under the aromatic leaves, calling ever and again my mother to see the "tremenjous" berry I had found. Martha was busy beside me, vexed that her two hands could not serve her master quick enough. And in a wild race with my mother my father helped us pick. At every ripest one he took her in his arms to force it between her lips; and of those pecked by the birds he made a rhymed offering to Pan. And when the sun had descended behind the hill, and the clamour of the rooks had begun to wane in the elm-tops, he took my mother on his arm, and we trooped all together up the long straggling path, and across the grass, carrying our spoil of fruit into the cool dusky corridor. As we passed into the gloaming I saw my mother stoop impulsively and kiss his arm. He brushed off her hand impatiently, and went into his study. I heard the door shut. A moment afterwards he called for candles. And, looking on those two other faces in the twilight, I knew with the intuition of childhood that he was suddenly sick to death of us all; and I knew that my mother shared my intuition. She sat down, and I beside her, in her little parlour, and took up her sewing. But her face had lost again all its girlishness as she bent her head over the white linen.

'I think she was happier when my father was away; for then, free from anxiety to be for ever pleasing his variable moods, she could entertain herself with hopes and preparations for his return. There was a little summer-house, or arbour, in the garden, where she would sit alone, while the swallows coursed in the evening air. Sometimes, too, she would take me for a long walk, listening distantly to my chatter, only, I think, that she might entertain the pleasure of supposing that my father might have returned home unforeseen, and be even now waiting to greet us. But these fancies would forsake her. She would speak harshly and coldly to me, and scold Martha for her owlishness, and find nothing but vanity and mockery in all that but a little while since had been her daydream.

'I think she rarely knew where my father stayed in his long absences from home. He would remain with us for a week, and neglect us for a month. She was too proud, and when he was himself, too happy and hopeful to question him, and he seemed to delight in keeping his affairs secret from her. Indeed, he sometimes appeared to pretend a mystery where none was, and to endeavour in all things to make his character and conduct appear quixotic and inexplicable.

'So time went on. Yet, it seemed, as each month passed by, the house was not so merry and happy as before; something was fading and vanishing that would not return; estrangement had pierced a little deeper. I think care at last put out of my mother's mind even the semblance of her former gaiety. She sealed up her heart lest love should break forth anew into the bleakness.

'On Guy Fawkes' Day Martha told me at bedtime that a new household had moved into the village on the other side of the heath. After that my father stayed away from us but seldom.

'At first my mother showed her pleasure in a thousand ways, with dainties of her own fancy and cooking, with ribbons in her dark hair, with new songs (though she had but a small thin voice). She read to please him; and tired my legs out in useless errands in his service. And a word of praise sufficed her for many hours of difficulty. But by and by, when evening after evening was spent by my father away from home, she began to be uneasy and depressed; and though she made no complaint, her anxious face, the incessant interrogation of her eyes vexed and irritated him beyond measure.

' "Where does my father go after dinner?" I asked Martha one night, when my mother was in my bedroom, folding my clothes.

' "How dare you ask such a question?" said my mother, "and how dare you talk to the child about your master's comings and goings?"

' "But where does he?" I repeated to Martha, when my mother was gone out of the room.

' "Ssh now, Master Nicholas," she answered, "didn't you hear what your mamma said? She's vexed, poor lady, at master's never spending a whole day at home, but nothing but them cards, cards, cards, every night at Mr Grey's. Why, often it's twelve and one in the morning when I've heard his foot on the gravel beneath the window. But there, I'll be bound, she doesn't *mean* to speak unkindly. It's a terrible scourge is jealousy, Master Nicholas; and not generous or manly to give it cause. Mrs Ryder was kept a widow all along of jealousy, and but a week before her wedding with her second."

' "But why is mother jealous of my father playing cards?"

'Martha slipped my nightgown over my head. "Ssh, Master Nicholas, little boys mustn't ask so many questions. And I hope when you are grown up to be a man, my dear, you will be a comfort to your mother. She needs it, poor soul, and sakes alive, just now of all times!" I looked inquisitively into Martha's face; but she screened my eyes with her hand; and instead of further questions, I said my prayers to her.

'A few days after this I was sitting with my mother in her parlour, holding her grey worsted for her to wind, when my father entered the room and bade me put on my hat and muffler. "He is going to pay a call with me," he explained curtly. As I went out of the room, I heard my mother's question, "To your friends at the Grange, I suppose?"

' "You may suppose whatever you please," he answered. I heard my mother rise to leave the room, but he called her back and the door was shut...

'The room in which the card-players sat was very low-ceiled. A piano stood near the window, a rosewood table with a fine dark crimson work-basket upon it by the fireside, and some little distance away, a green card-table with candles burning. Mr Grey was a slim, elegant man, with a high, narrow forehead and long fingers. Major Aubrey was a short, red-faced, rather taciturn man. There was also a younger man with fair hair. They seemed to be on the best of terms together; and I helped to pack the cards and to pile the silver coins, sipping a glass of sherry with Mr Grey. My father said little, paying me no attention, but playing gravely with a very slight frown.

'After some little while the door opened, and a lady appeared. This was Mr Grey's sister, Jane, I learned. She seated herself at her work-table, and drew me to her side.

' "Well, so this is Nicholas!" she said. "Or is it Nick?"

' "Nicholas," I said.

' "Of course," she said, smiling, "and I like that too, much the best. How very kind of you to come to see me! It was to keep *me* company, you know, because I am very stupid at games, but I love talking. Do you?"

'I looked into her eyes, and knew we were friends. She smiled again, with open lips, and touched my mouth with her thimble. "Now, let me see, business first, and – me afterwards. You see I have three different kinds of cake, because, I thought, I cannot in the least tell which kind he'll like best. Could I now? Come, you shall choose."

'She rose and opened the long door of a narrow cupboard, looking towards the card-players as she stooped. I remember the cakes to this day; little oval shortbreads stamped with a beehive, custards and mince-pies; and a great glass jar of goodies which I carried in both arms round the little square table. I took a mince-pie, and sat down on a footstool nearby Miss Grey, and she talked to me while she worked with slender hands at her lace embroidery. I told her how old I was; about my great-aunt and her three cats. I told her my dreams, and that I was very fond of Yorkshire pudding, "from under the meat, you know". And I told her I thought my father the handsomest man I had ever seen.

' "What, handsomer than Mr Spencer?" she said laughing, looking along her needle.

'I answered that I did not very much like clergymen.

' "And why?" she said gravely.

' "Because they do not talk like real," I said.

'She laughed very gaily. "Do men ever?" she said.

'And her voice was so quiet and so musical, her neck so graceful, I thought her a very beautiful lady, admiring especially her dark eyes when she smiled brightly and yet half sadly at me; I promised, moreover, that if she would meet me on the heath, I would show her the rabbit warren and the "Miller's Pool".

' "Well, Jane, and what do you think of my son?" said my father when we were about to leave.

'She bent over me and squeezed a lucky fourpenny-piece into my hand. "I love fourpence, pretty little fourpence, I love fourpence better than my life," she whispered into my ear. "But that's a secret," she added, glancing up over her shoulder. She kissed lightly the top of my head. I was looking at my father while she was caressing me, and I fancied a faint sneer passed over his face. But when we had come out of the village on to the heath, in the bare keen night, as we walked along the path together between the gorse-bushes, now on turf, and now on stony ground, never before had he seemed so wonderful a companion. He told me little stories; he began a hundred, and finished none; yet with the stars above us, they seemed a string of beads all of bright colours. We stood still in the vast darkness, while he whistled that strangest of all old songs – "The Song the Sirens Sang". He pilfered my wits and talked like my double. But when – how much too quickly, I thought with sinking heart – we were come to the house-gates, he suddenly fell silent, turned an instant, and stared far away over the windy heath.

' "How weary, flat, stale – " he began, and broke off between uneasy laughter and a sigh. "Listen to me, Nicholas," he said, lifting my face to the starlight, "you must grow up a man – a Man, you understand; no vapourings, no posings, no caprices; and above all, no sham. No sham. It's your one and only chance in this unfaltering Scheme." He scanned my face long and closely. "You have your mother's eyes," he said musingly. "And that," he added under his breath, "*that's* no joke." He pushed open the squealing gate and we went in.

'My mother was sitting in a low chair before a dying and cheerless fire.

' "Well, Nick," she said very suavely, "and how have you enjoyed your evening?"

'I stared at her without answer. "Did you play cards with the gentlemen; or did you turn over the music?"

' "I talked to Miss Grey," I said.

' "Really," said my mother, raising her eyebrows, "and who then is Miss Grey?" My father was smiling at us with sparkling eyes.

' "Mr Grey's sister," I answered in a low voice.

' "Not his wife, then?" said my mother, glancing furtively at the fire. I looked towards my father in doubt but could lift my eyes no higher than his knees.

' "You little fool!" he said to my mother with a laugh, "what a sharp-shooter! Never mind, Sir Nick; there, run off to bed, my man."

'My mother caught me roughly by the sleeve as I was passing her chair. "Aren't you going to kiss me good night, then," she said furiously, her narrow under-lip quivering, "you too!" I kissed her cheek. "That's right, my dear," she said scornfully, "that's how little fishes kiss." She rose and drew back her skirts. "I refuse to stay in the room," she said haughtily, and with a sob she hurried out.

'My father continued to smile, but only a smile it seemed gravity had forgotten to smooth away. He stood very still, so still that I grew afraid he must certainly hear me thinking. Then with a kind of sigh he sat down at my mother's writing table, and scribbled a few words with his pencil on a slip of paper.

' "There, Nicholas, just tap at your mother's door with that. Good night, old fellow," he took my hand and smiled down into my eyes with a kind of generous dark appeal that called me straight to his side. I hastened conceitedly upstairs, and delivered my message. My mother was crying when she opened the door.

' "Well?" she said in a low, trembling voice.

'But presently afterwards, while I was still lingering in the dark corridor, I heard her run down quickly, and in a while my father and mother came upstairs together, arm in arm, and by her light talk and laughter you might suppose she had no knowledge of care or trouble at all.

'Never afterwards did I see so much gaiety and youthfulness in my mother's face as when she sat next morning with us at breakfast. The honey-comb, the small bronze chrysanthemums, her yellow gown seemed dainty as a miniature. With every word her eyes would glance covertly at my father; her smile, as it were, hesitating between her lashes. She was so light and girlish and so versatile I should scarcely have recognized the weary and sallow face of the night before. My father seemed to find as much pleasure, or relief, in her good spirits as I did; and to delight in exercising his ingenuity to quicken her humour.

'It was but a transient morning of sunshine, however, and as the brief and sombre day waned, its gloom pervaded the house. In the evening my father left us to our solitude as usual. And that night was very misty over the heath, with a small, warm rain falling.

'So it happened that I began to be left more and more to my own devices, and grew so inured at last to my own narrow company and small thoughts and cares, that I began to look on my mother's unhappiness almost with indifference, and learned to criticize almost before I had learned to pity. And so I do not think I enjoyed Christmas very much the less, although my father was away from home and all our little festivities were dispirited. I had plenty of good things to eat, and presents, and a picture-book from Martha. I had a new rocking-horse – how changeless and impassive its mottled battered face looks out at me across the years! It was brisk, clear weather, and on St Stephen's Day I went to see if there was any ice yet on the Miller's Pool.

'I was stooping down at the extreme edge of the pool, snapping the brittle splinters of the ice with my finger, when I heard a voice calling me in the still air. It was Jane Grey, walking on the heath with my father, who had called me having seen me from a distance stooping beside the water.

' "So you see I have kept my promise," she said, taking my hand.

' "But you promised to come by yourself," I said.

' "Well, so I will then," she answered, nodding her head. "Good-bye," she added, turning to my father. "It's three's none, you see. Nicholas shall take me home to tea, and you can call for him in the evening, if you will; that is, if you are coming."

' "Are you asking me to come?" he said moodily, "do you care whether I come or not?"

'She lifted her face and spoke gravely. "You are my friend," she said, "of course I care whether you are with me or not." He scrutinized her through half-closed lids. His face was haggard, gloomy with *ennui*. "How you harp on the word, you punctilious Jane. Do you suppose I am still in my teens? Twenty years ago, now — It amuses me to hear you women talk. It's little you ever really feel."

' "I don't think I am quite without feeling," she replied, "you are a little difficult, you know."

' "Difficult," he echoed in derision. He checked himself and shrugged his shoulders. "You see, Jane, it's all on the surface; I boast of my indifference. It's the one rag of philosophy age denies no one. It is so easy to be mock-heroic – debonair, iron-grey, rhetorical, dramatic – you know it only too well, perhaps? But after all, life's comedy, when one stops smiling, is only the tepidest farce. Or the gilt wears off and the pinchbeck tragedy shows through. And so, as I say, we talk on, being past feeling. One by one our hopes come home to roost, our delusions find themselves out, and the mystery proves to be nothing but sleight-of-hand. It's age, my dear Jane – age; it turns one to stone. With you young people life's a dream; ask Nicholas here!" He shrugged his shoulders, adding under his breath, "But one wakes on a devilish hard pallet."

' "Of course," said Jane slowly, "you are only talking cleverly, and then it does not matter whether it's true or not, I suppose. I can't say. I don't think you mean it, and so it comes to nothing. I can't and won't believe you feel so little – I can't." She continued to smile, yet, I fancied, with the brightness of tears in her eyes. "It's all mockery and make-believe; we are not the miserable slaves of time you try to fancy. There must be some way to win through." She turned away, then added slowly, "You ask me to be fearless, sincere, to speak my heart; I wonder, do you?"

'My father did not look at her, appeared not to have seen the hand she had half held out to him, and as swiftly withdrawn. "The truth is, Jane," he said slowly, "I am past sincerity now. And as for *heart* it is a quite discredited organ at forty. Life, thought, selfishness, egotism, call it what you will; they have all done their worst with me; and I really haven't the sentiment to pretend that they haven't. And when bright youth and sentiment are gone; why, go too, dear lady! Existence proves nothing but brazen inanity afterwards. But there's always that turning left to the dullest and dustiest road – oblivion." He remained silent a moment. Silence deep and strange lay all around us. The air was still, the wintry sky unutterably calm. And again that low dispassionate voice continued: "It's only when right seems too easy a thing, too trivial, and not worth the doing; and wrong a foolish thing – too dull . . . There, take care of her, Nicholas; take care of her, 'snips and snails,' you know. *Au revoir*, 'pon my word, I almost wish it was good-bye."

'Jane Grey regarded him attentively. "So then do I," she replied in a low voice, "for I shall never understand you; perhaps I should hate to understand you."

'My father turned with an affected laugh, and left us.

'Miss Grey and I walked slowly along beside the frosty bulrushes until we came to the wood. The bracken and heather were faded. The earth was dark and rich with autumnal rains. Fir-cones lay on the moss beneath the dark green branches. It was all now utterly silent in the wintry afternoon. Far away rose tardily, and alighted, the hoarse rooks upon the ploughed earth; high in the pale sky passed a few on ragged wing.

' "What does my father mean by wishing it was good-bye?" I said.

'But my companion did not answer me in words. She clasped my hand; she seemed very slim and gracious walking by my side on the hardened ground. My mother was small now and awkward beside her in my imagination. I questioned her about the ice, about the red sky, and if there was any mistletoe in the woods. Sometimes she, in turn, asked me questions too, and when I answered them we would look at each other and smile, and it seemed it was with her as it was with me – of the pure gladness I found in her company. In the middle of our walk to the Thorns she bent down in the cold twilight, and putting her hands on my shoulders, "My dear, dear Nicholas," she said, "you must be a good son to your mother – brave and kind; will you?"

'"He hardly ever speaks to mother now," I answered instinctively.

'She pressed her lips to my cheek, and her cheek was cold against mine, and she clasped her arms about me. "Kiss me," she said, "We must do our best, mustn't we?" she pleaded, still holding me. I looked mournfully into the gathering darkness. "That's easy when you're grown up," I said. She laughed and kissed me again, and then we took hands and ran till we were out of breath, towards the distant lights of the Thorns...

'I had been some time in bed, lying awake in the warmth, when my mother came softly through the darkness into my room. She sat down at the bedside, breathing hurriedly. "Where have you been all the evening?" she said.

'"Miss Grey asked me to stay to tea," I answered.

'"Did I give you permission to go to tea with Miss Grey?"

'I made no answer.

'"If you go to that house again, I shall beat you. You hear me, Nicholas? Alone, or with your father, if you go there again, without my permission, I shall beat you. You have not been whipped for a long time, have you?" I could not see her face, but her head was bent towards me in the dark, as she sat – almost crouched – on my bedside.

'I made no answer. But when my mother had gone, without kissing me, I cried noiselessly on into my pillow. Something had suddenly flown out of memory, never to sing again. Life had become a little colder and stranger. I had always been my own chief company; now another sentimental barrier had arisen between the world and me, past its heedlessness, past my understanding to break down.

'Hardly a week passed now without some bitter quarrel. I seemed to be perpetually stealing out of sound of angry voices; fearful of being made the butt of my father's serene taunts, of my mother's passions and desperate remorse. He disdained to defend himself against her, never reasoned with her; he merely shrugged his shoulders, denied her charges, ignored her anger; coldly endeavouring only to show his indifference, to conceal by every means in his power his own inward weariness and vexation. I saw this, of course, only vaguely, yet with all a child's certainty of insight, though I rarely knew the cause of my misery; and I continued to love them both in my selfish fashion, not a whit the less.

'At last, on St Valentine's Day, things came to a worse pass than ever. It had always been my father's custom to hang my mother a valentine on the handle of her little parlour door, a string of pearls, a fan, a book of poetry, whatever it might be. She came down early this morning, and sat in the window-seat, looking out at the falling snow. She said nothing at breakfast, only feigned to eat, lifting her eyes at intervals to glance at my father with a strange intensity, as if of hatred, tapping her foot on the floor. He took no notice of her, sat quiet and moody with his own thoughts. I think he had not really forgotten the day, for I found long afterwards in his old bureau a bracelet purchased but a week before with her name written on a scrap of paper, inside the case. Yet it seemed to be the absence of this little gift that had driven my mother beyond reason.

'Towards evening, tired of the house, tired of being alone, I went out and played for a while listlessly in the snow. At night-fall I went in; and in the dark heard angry voices. My father came out of the dining-room and looked at me in silence, standing in the gloom of the wintry dusk. My mother followed him. I can see her now, leaning in the doorway, white with rage, her eyes ringed and darkened with continuous trouble, her hand trembling.

' "It shall learn to hate you," she cried in a low, dull voice. "I will teach it every moment to hate and despise you as I — Oh, I hate and despise you."

'My father looked at her calmly and profoundly before replying. He took up a cloth hat and brushed it with his hand. "Very well then, you have chosen," he said coldly. "It has always lain with you. You have exaggerated, you have raved, and now you have said what can never be recalled or forgotten. Here's Nicholas. Pray do not imagine, however, that I am defending myself. I have nothing to defend. I think of no one but myself – no one. Endeavour to understand me, no one. Perhaps, indeed, you yourself – no more than — But words again – the dull old round!" He made a peculiar gesture with his hand. "Well, life is ... ach! I have done. So be it." He stood looking out of the door. "You see, it's snowing," he said, as if to himself.

'All the long night before and all day long, snow had been falling continuously. The air was wintry and cold. I could discern nothing beyond the porch but a gloomy accumulation of cloud in the twilight air, now darkened with the labyrinthine motion of the snow. My father glanced back for an instant into the house, and, as I fancy, regarded me with a kind of strange, close earnestness. But he went out and his footsteps were instantly silenced.

'My mother peered at me in a dreadful perplexity, her eyes wide with terror and remorse. "What? What?" she said. I stared at her stupidly. Three snowflakes swiftly and airily floated together into the dim hall from the gloom without. She clasped her hand over her mouth. Overburdened her fingers seemed to be, so slender were they, with her many rings.

' "Nicholas, Nicholas, tell me; what was I saying? What was I saying?" She stumbled hastily to the door. "Arthur, Arthur," she cried from the porch, "it's St Valentine's Day. That was all I meant; come back, come back!" But perhaps my father was already out of hearing; I do not think he made any reply.

'My mother came in doubtfully, resting her hand on the wall. And she walked very slowly and laboriously upstairs. While I was standing at the foot of the staircase, looking out across the hall into the evening, Martha climbed primly up from the kitchen with her lighted taper, shut-to the door and lit the hall lamp. Already the good smell of the feast cooking floated up from the kitchen, and gladdened my spirits. "Will he come back?" Martha said, looking very scared in the light of her taper. "It's such a fall of snow, already it's a hand's breadth on the window-sill. Oh, Master Nicholas, it's a hard world for us women." She followed my mother upstairs, carrying light to all the gloomy upper rooms.

'I sat down in the window-seat of the dining-room, and read in my picture-book as well as I could by the flame-light. By and by, Martha returned to lay the table.

'As far back as brief memory carried me, it had been our custom to make a Valentine's feast on the Saint's Day. This was my father's mother's birthday also. When she was alive I well remember her visiting us with her companion, Miss Schreiner, who talked in such good-humoured English to me. This same anniversary had last year brought about a tender reconciliation between my father and mother, after a quarrel that meant how little then. And I remember on this day to have seen the first fast-sealed buds upon the almond tree. We would have a great spangled cake in the middle of the table, with marzipan and comfits, just as at Christmas-time. And when Mrs Merry lived in the village, her little fair daughters used to come in a big carriage to spend the evening with us and to share my Valentine's feast.

'But all this was changed now. My wits were sharper, but I was none the less only the duller for that; my hopes and dreams had a little fallen and faded. I looked idly at my picture-book, vaguely conscious that its colours pleased me less than once upon a time, that I was rather tired of seeing them, and they just as tired of seeing me. And yet I had nothing else to do, so I must go on with a hard face, turning listlessly the pictured pages.

'About seven o'clock my mother sent for me. I found her sitting in her bedroom. Candles were burning before the looking-glass. She was already dressed in her handsome black silk gown, and wearing her pearl necklace.

She began to brush my hair, curling its longer ends with her fingers, which she moistened in the pink bowl that was one of the first things I had set eyes on in this world. She put me on a clean blouse and my buckle shoes, talking to me the while, almost as if she were telling me a story. Then she looked at herself long and earnestly in the glass; throwing up her chin with a smile, as was a habit of hers in talk. I wandered about the room, fingering the little toilet-boxes and nick-nacks on the table. By mischance I upset one of these, a scent-bottle that held rose-water. The water ran out and filled the warm air with its fragrance. "You foolish, clumsy boy!" said my mother, and slapped my hand. More out of vexation and tiredness than because of the pain, I began to cry. And then, with infinite tenderness, she leaned her head on my shoulder. "Mother can't think very well just now," she said; and cried so bitterly in silence that I was only too ready to extricate myself and run away when her hold on me relaxed.

'I climbed slowly upstairs to Martha's bedroom, and kneeling on a cane chair looked out of the window. The flakes had ceased to fall now, although the snowy heath was encompassed in mist. Above the snow the clouds had parted, drifting from beneath the stars, and these in their constellations were trembling very brightly, and here and there burned one of them in solitude, larger and wilder in its radiance than the rest. But though I did not tire of looking out of the window, my knees began to ache; and the little room was very cold and still so near the roof. So I went down to the dining-room, with all its seven candlesticks kindled, seeming to my unaccustomed eyes a very splendid blaze out of the dark. My mother was kneeling on the rug by the fireside. She looked very small, even dwarfish, I thought. She was gazing into the flames; one shoe curved beneath the hem of her gown, her chin resting on her hand.

'I surveyed the table with its jellies and sweetmeats and glasses and fruit, and began to be very hungry, so savoury was the smell of the turkey roasting downstairs. Martha knocked at the door when the clock had struck eight.

' "Dinner is ready, ma'am."

'My mother glanced fleetingly at the clock. "Just a little, only a very little while longer, tell Mrs Ryder; your master will be home in a minute." She rose and placed the claret in the hearth at some distance from the fire.

'Is it nicer warm, Mother?" I said. She looked at me with startled eyes and nodded. "Did you hear anything, Nicholas? Run to the door and listen; was that a sound of footsteps?"

'I opened the outer door and peered into the darkness; but it seemed the world ended here with the warmth and the light: beyond could extend only winter and silence, a region that, familiar though it was to me, seemed now to terrify me like an enormous sea.

' "It's stopped snowing," I said, "but there isn't anybody there; nobody at all, Mother."

'The hours passed heavily from quarter on to quarter. The turkey, I grieved to hear, was to be taken out of the oven, and put away to cool in the pantry. I was bidden help myself to what I pleased of the trembling jellies, and delicious pink blanc-mange. Already midnight would be the next hour to be chimed. I felt sick, yet was still hungry and very tired. The candles began to burn low. "Leave me a little light here, then," my mother said at last to Martha, "and go to bed. Perhaps your master has missed his way home in the snow." But Mrs Ryder had followed Martha into the room.

' "You must pardon my interference, ma'am, but it isn't right, it isn't really right of you to sit up longer. Master will not come back, maybe, before morning. And I shouldn't be doing my bounden duty, ma'am, except I spoke my mind. Just now too, of all times."

' "Thank you very much, Mrs Ryder," my mother answered simply "but I would prefer not to go to bed yet. It's very lonely on the heath at night. But I shall not want anything else, thank you."

' "Well, ma'am, I've had my say, and done my conscience's bidding. And I have brought you up this tumbler of mulled wine; else you'll be sinking away or something with the fatigue."

'My mother took the wine, sipped of it with a wan smile at Mrs Ryder over the brim; and Mrs Ryder retired with Martha. I don't think they had noticed me sitting close in the shadow on my stool beside the table. But all through that long night, I fancy, these good souls took it in turn to creep down stealthily and look in on us; and in the small hours of the morning, when the fire had fallen low they must have wrapped us both warm in shawls. They left me then, I think, to be my mother's company. Indeed, I remember we spoke in the darkness, and she took my hand.

'My mother and I shared the steaming wine together when they were gone; our shadows looming faintly huge upon the ceiling. We said very little, but I looked softly into her grey childish eyes, and we kissed one another kneeling there together before the fire. And afterwards, I jigged softly round the table, pilfering whatever sweet or savoury mouthful took my fancy. But by and by in the silent house – a silence broken only by the fluttering of the flames, and the odd far-away stir of the frost, drowsiness vanquished me; I sat down by the fireside, leaning my head on a chair. And sitting thus, vaguely eyeing firelight and wavering shadow, I began to nod, and very soon dream stalked in, mingling with reality.

'It was early morning when I awoke, dazed and cold and miserable in my uncomfortable resting-place. The rare odour of frost was on the air. The ashes of the fire lay iron-grey upon the cold hearth. An intensely clear white ray of light leaned up through a cranny of the shutters to the cornice of the ceiling. I got up with difficulty. My mother was still asleep, breathing heavily, and as I stooped, regarding her curiously, I could almost watch her transient dreams fleeting over her face; and now she smiled faintly; and now she raised her eyebrows as if in some playful and happy talk with my father; then again utterly still darkness would descend on brow and lid and lip.

'I touched her sleeve, suddenly conscious of my loneliness in the large house. Her face clouded instantly, she sighed profoundly: "What?" she said, "nothing – nothing?" She stretched out her hand towards me; the lids drew back from eyes still blind from sleep. But gradually time regained its influence over her. She moistened her lips and turned to me, and suddenly, in a gush of agony, remembrance of the night returned to her. She hid her face in her hands, rocking her body gently to and fro; then rose and smoothed back her hair at the looking-glass. I was surprised to see no trace of tears on her cheeks. Her lips moved, as if unconsciously a heart worn out with grief addressed that pale reflection of her sorrow in the glass. I took hold of the hand that hung down listlessly on her silk skirt, and fondled it, kissing punctiliously each loose ring in turn.

'But I do not think she heeded my kisses. So I returned to the table on which was still set out the mockery of our Valentine feast, strangely disenchanted in the chill dusk of daybreak. I put a handful of wine biscuits and a broken piece of cake in my pocket; for a determination had taken me to go out on to the heath. My heart beat thick and fast in imagination of the solitary snow and of myself wandering in loneliness across its untrampled surface. A project also was forming in my mind of walking over to the Thorns; for somehow I knew my mother would not scold or punish me that day. Perhaps, I thought, my father would be there. And I would tell Miss Grey all about my adventure of the night spent down in the dining-room. So moving very stealthily, and betraying no eagerness, lest I should be forbidden to go, I stole at length unnoticed from the room, and leaving the great hall door ajar, ran out joyously into the wintry morning.

'Already dawn was clear and high in the sky, already the first breezes were moving in the mists; and breathed chill, as if it were the lingering darkness itself on my cheeks. The air was cold, yet with a fresh faint sweetness. The snow lay crisp across its perfect surface, mounded softly over the gorse-bushes, though here and there a spray of parched blossom yet protruded from its cowl. Flaky particles of ice floated invisible in the air. I called out with pleasure to see the little ponds where the snow had been blown away from the black ice. I saw on the bushes too the webs of spiders stretched from thorn to thorn, and festooned with crystals of hoar-frost. I turned and counted as far as I could my footsteps leading back to the house, which lay roofed in gloomy pallor, dim and obscured in the darkened west.

'A waning moon that had risen late in the night shone, it seemed, very near to the earth. But every moment light swept invincibly in, pouring its crystal like a river; and darkness sullenly withdrew into the north. And when at last the sun appeared, glittering along the rosy snow, I turned in an ecstasy and with my finger pointed him out, as if the house I had left behind me might view him with my own delight. Indeed, I saw its windows transmuted, and heard afar a thrush pealing in the bare branches of a pear-tree; and a robin startled me, so suddenly shrill and sweet he broke into song from a snowy tuft of gorse.

'I was now come to the beginning of a gradual incline, from the summit of which I should presently descry in the distance the avenue of lindens that led towards the village from the margin of the heath. As I went on my way, munching my biscuits, looking gaily about me, I brooded deliciously on the breakfast which Miss Grey would doubtless sit me down to; and almost forgot the occasion of my errand, and the troubled house I had left behind me. At length I climbed to the top of the smooth ridge and looked down. At a little distance from me grew a crimson hawthorn-tree that often in past Aprils I had used for a green tent from the showers; but now it was closely hooded, darkening with its faint shadow the long expanse of unshadowed whiteness. Not very far from this bush I perceived a figure lying stretched along the snow and knew instinctively that this was my father lying here.

'The sight did not then surprise or dismay me. It seemed only the lucid sequel to that long heavy night-watch, to all the troubles and perplexities of the past. I felt no sorrow, but stood beside the body, regarding it only with deep wonder and a kind of earnest curiosity, yet perhaps with a remote pity too, that he could not see me in the beautiful morning. His grey hand lay arched in the snow, his darkened face, on which showed a smear of dried blood, was turned away a little as if out of the oblique sunshine. I understood that he was dead, and had already begun speculating on what changes it would make; how I should spend my time; what would happen in the house now that he was gone, his influence, his authority, his discord. I remembered too that I was alone, was master of this immense secret, that I must go home sedately, as if it were a Sunday, and in a low voice tell my mother, concealing any exultation I might feel in the office. I imagined the questions that would be asked me, and was considering the proper answers to make to them, when my morbid dreams were suddenly broken in on by Martha Rodd. She stood in my footsteps, looking down on me from the ridge from which I had but just now descended. She hastened towards me, stooping a little as if she were carrying a heavy bundle, her mouth ajar, her forehead wrinkled beneath its wispy light brown hair.

' "Look, Martha, look," I cried, "I found him in the snow; he's dead."

And suddenly a bond seemed to snap in my heart. The beauty and solitude of the morning, the perfect whiteness of the snow – it was all an uncouth mockery against me – a subtle and quiet treachery. The tears gushed into my eyes and in my fear and affliction I clung to the poor girl, sobbing bitterly, protesting my grief, hiding my eyes in terror from that still, inscrutable shape. She smoothed my hair with her hand again and again, her eyes fixed; and then at last, venturing cautiously nearer, she stooped over my father. "O Master Nicholas," she said, "his poor dark hair! What will we do now? What will your poor mamma do now, and him gone?" She hid her face in her hands, and our tears gushed out anew.

'But my grief was speedily forgotten. The novelty of being left entirely alone, my own master; to go where I would; to do as I pleased; the experience of being pitied most when I least needed it, and then – when misery and solitariness came over me like a cloud – of being utterly ignored, turned my thoughts gradually away. My father's body was brought home and laid in my mother's little parlour that looked out on to the garden and the snowy orchard. The house was darkened. I took a secret pleasure in peeping in on the sunless rooms, and stealing from door to door through corridors screened from the daylight. My mother was ill; and for some inexplicable reason I connected her illness with the bevy of gentlemen dressed in black who came one morning to the house and walked away together over the heath. Finally Mrs Marshall drove up one afternoon from Islington, and by the bundles she had brought with her and her grained box with the iron handles I knew that she was come, as once before in my experience, to stay.

'I was playing on the morrow in the hall with my leaden soldiers when there came into my mind vaguely the voices of Mrs Ryder and of Mrs Marshall gossiping together on their tedious way upstairs from the kitchen.

' "No, Mrs Marshall, nothing," I heard Mrs Ryder saying, "not one word, not one word. And now the poor dear lady left quite alone, and only the doctor to gainsay that fatherless mite from facing the idle inquisitive questions of all them strangers. It's neither for me nor you, Mrs Marshall, to speak out just what comes into our heads here and now. The ways of the Almighty are past understanding – but a kinder at *heart* never trod this earth."

' "Ah," said Mrs Marshall.

' "I knew to my sorrow," continued Mrs Ryder, "there was words in the house; but there, wheresoever you be there's that. Human beings ain't angels, married or single, and in every —"

' "Wasn't there talk of some — ?" insinuated Mrs Marshall discreetly.

' "Talk, Mrs Marshall," said Mrs Ryder, coming to a standstill, "I scorn the word! A pinch of truth in a hogshead of falsehood. I don't gainsay it even. I just shut my ears – there – with the dead." Mrs Marshall had opened her mouth to reply when I was discovered, crouched as small as possible at the foot of the stairs.

' "Well, here's pitchers!" said Mrs Marshall pleasantly. "And this is the poor fatherless manikin, I suppose. It's hard on the innocent, Mrs Ryder, and him grown such a sturdy child too, as I said from the first. Well, now, and don't you remember me, little man, don't you remember Mrs Marshall? He ought to, now!"

' "He's a very good boy in general," said Mrs Ryder, "and I'm sure I hope and pray he'll grow up to be a comfort to his poor widowed mother, if so be —" They glanced earnestly at one another, and Mrs Marshall stooped with a sigh of effort and drew a big leather purse from a big loose pocket under her skirt, and selected a bright ha'penny-piece from among its silver and copper.

' "I make no doubt he will, poor mite," she said cheerfully; I took the ha'penny in silence and the two women passed slowly upstairs.

'In the afternoon, in order to be beyond call of Martha, I went out on to the heath with a shovel, intent on building a great tomb in the snow. Yet more snow had fallen during the night; it now lay so deep as to cover my socks above my shoes. I laboured very busily, shovelling, beating, moulding, stamping. So intent was I that I did not see Miss Grey until she was close beside me. I looked up from the snow and was surprised to find the sun already set and the low mists of evening approaching. Miss Grey was veiled and dressed in furs to the throat. She drew her ungloved hand from her muff.

' "Nicholas," she said in a low voice.

'I stood for some reason confused and ashamed without answering her. She sat down on my shapeless mound of snow and took me by the hand. Then she drew up her veil, and I saw her face pale and darkened, and her clear dark eyes gravely gazing into mine.

' "My poor, poor Nicholas," she said, and continued to gaze at me with her warm hand clasping mine. "What can I say? What can I do? Isn't it very, very lonely out here in the snow?"

' " I didn't feel lonely much," I answered, "I was making a – I was playing at building."

' "And I am sitting on your beautiful snow-house, then?" she said, smiling sadly, her hand trembling upon mine.

' "It isn't a house," I answered, turning away.

'She pressed my hand on the furs at her throat.

' "Poor cold, blue hands," she said. "Do you like playing alone?"

' "I like you being here," I answered. "I wish you would come always, or at least sometimes."

'She drew me close to her, smiling, and bent and kissed my head.

' "There," she said, "I am here now."

' "Mother's ill," I said.

'She drew back and looked out over the heath towards the house.

' "They have put my father in the little parlour, in his coffin, of course; you know he's dead, and Mrs Marshall's come, she gave me a ha'penny this morning. Dr Graham gave me a whole crown, though." I took it out of my breeches pocket and showed it her.

' "That's very, very nice," she said. "What lots of nice things you can buy with it! And, look, I am going to give you a little keepsake too, between just you and me."

'It was a small silver box that she drew out of her muff, and embossed in the silver of the lid was a crucifix. "I thought, perhaps, I should see you to-day, you know," she continued softly. "Now, who's given you this?" she said, putting the box into my hand.

' "You," I answered softly.

' "And who am I?"

' "Miss Grey," I said.

' "Your friend, Jane Grey," she repeated, as if she were fascinated by the sound of her own name. "Say it now – Always my friend, Jane Grey."

'I repeated it after her.

' "And now," she continued, "tell me which room is – is the little par-lour. Is it that small window at the corner under the ivy?"

'I shook my head.

' "Which?" she said in a whisper, after a long pause.

'I twisted my shovel in the snow. "Would you like to see my father?" I asked her. "I am sure, you know, Martha would not mind; and mother's in bed." She started, her dark eyes dwelling strangely on mine. "But Nicholas, you poor lamb; where?" she said, without stirring.

' "It's at the back, a little window that comes out – if you were to come this evening, I would be playing in the hall; I always play in the hall, after tea, if I can; and now, always. Nobody would see you at all, you know."

'She sighed. "O what are you saying?" she said, and stood up, drawing down her veil.

' "But would you like to?" I repeated. She stooped suddenly, pressing her veiled face to mine. "I'll come, I'll come," she said, her face utterly changed so close to my eyes. "We can both still – still be loyal to him, can't we, Nicholas?"

'She walked away quickly, towards the pool and the little darkened wood. I looked after her and knew that she would be waiting there alone till evening. I looked at my silver box with great satisfaction, and after opening it, put it into my pocket with my crown piece and my ha'penny, and continued my building for a while.

'But now zest for it was gone; and I began to feel cold, the frost closing in keenly as darkness gathered. So I went home.

'My silence and suspicious avoidance of scrutiny and question passed unnoticed. Indeed, I ate my tea in solitude, except that now and again one or other of the women would come bustling in on some brief errand. A peculiar suppressed stir was in the house. I wondered what could be the cause of it; and began suddenly to be afraid of my project being discovered.

'None the less I was playing in the evening, as I had promised, close to the door, alert to catch the faintest sign of the coming of my visitor.

' "Run down to the kitchen, dearie," said Martha. Her cheeks were flushed. She was carrying a big can of steaming water. "You must keep very, *very* quiet this evening and go to bed like a good boy, and perhaps to-morrow morning I'll tell you a great secret." She kissed me with hasty rapture. I was not especially inquisitive of her secret just then, and eagerly promised to be quite quiet if I might continue to play where I was.

' "Well, very, *very* quiet then, and you mustn't let Mrs Marshall," she began, but hurried hastily away in answer to a peremptory summons from upstairs.

' "Almost as soon as she was gone I heard a light rap on the door. It seemed that Jane Grey had brought in with her the cold and freshness of the woods. I led the way on tiptoe down the narrow corridor and into the small, silent room. The candles burned pure and steadfastly in their brightness. The air was still and languid with the perfume of flowers. Overhead passed light, heedful footsteps; but they seemed not a disturbing sound, only a rumour beyond the bounds of silence.

' "I am very sorry," I said, "but they have nailed it down. Martha says the men came this afternoon."

'Miss Grey took a little bunch of snowdrops from her bosom, and hid them in among the clustered wreaths of flowers; and she knelt down on the floor, with a little silver cross which she sometimes wore pressed tight to her lips. I felt ill at ease to see her praying, and wished I could go back to my soldiers. But while I watched her, seeing in marvellous brilliancy everything in the little room, and remembering dimly the snow lying beneath the stars in the darkness of the garden, I listened also to the quiet footsteps passing to and fro in the room above. Suddenly, the silence was broken by a small, continuous, angry crying.

'Miss Grey looked up. Her eyes were very clear and wonderful in the candle-light.

' "What was that?" she said faintly, listening.

'I stared at her. The cry welled up anew, piteously; as if of a small remote and helpless indignation.

' "Why it sounds just like a – little baby," I said.

'She crossed herself hastily and arose. "Nicholas!" she said in a strange, quiet, bewildered voice – yet her face was most curiously bright. She looked at me lovingly and yet so strangely I wished I had not let her come in.

'She went out as she had entered. I did not so much as peep into the darkness after her, but busy with a hundred thoughts returned to my play.

'Long past my usual bedtime, as I sat sipping a mug of hot milk before the glowing cinders of the kitchen fire, Martha told me her secret...

'So my impossible companion in the High Street yesterday was own and only brother to your crazy old friend, Richard,' said the Count. 'His only brother,' he added, in a muse.

*The Count's Courtship**

It had long been our custom to muse and gossip through the summer evening twilight, and now we had lingered so late that the darkness of night had come into the room. But two, at least, of the three of us were well content so to moon on, the fitful summer lightnings shining pale on our faces as we sat at the window. As for myself, I can only confess that with every tick of the clock I had been more and more inclined to withdraw, and so give the others the opportunity and ease of my absence. But likely enough, had I done so, the Count would have bluffly recalled me, or my aunt would have roused herself from her reverie to candles and common sense.

So I held my tongue, after my aunt's example, who sat, still and erect, looking out through her glasses, her hands upon the arms of her chair, while the Count spoke seldom, and that generally in a kind of inarticulate discourse with himself.

There was plenty to busy my thoughts. The Count was evidently on the point of abandoning his long-cherished platonicism. My aunt, of late, had been far from her usual self, now brisk, now apathetic; but neither and nothing for long together. Matrimony was in the air, and I must soon be an exile. Soon, doubtless, a wife (and how capable and prudent a wife) would relieve me of my duties to my eloquent, arbitrary old friend. I had become superfluous. The most amiable of chaperons now found himself gradually converted into a tartish gooseberry. The quick lightning had but just now illumined the Count's face as he bent towards her. In his eyes was inspira-

* First published in *Lady's Realm*, July 1907.

tion. And my aunt's almost uncivil withdrawal of her hand was evidently all but the last capricious valedictory gesture to middle age and widowhood.

My aunt apparently suddenly realized this, and the hazard of keeping silent. She rose abruptly, smoothing out her silk skirts as if she had thought to herself, 'Well, that's done with.'

'I fear I was nodding, Count; I beg pardon,' she said in a rather faint voice, and behind the semblance of a yawn. 'The air's close and heavy. It seems a storm's gathering.'

We neither of us answered her.

'Richard,' she said, 'oblige me by ringing the bell.'

The Count deftly intercepted me.

'It's a waste of peace and quietness,' said he appealingly. 'Won't you sit but a few minutes longer? Who knows: not so many days may be left, with such quiet ends – the twilight, summer? Richard shall fetch you a shawl. We'll take a turn in the garden.'

'Very pretty sentiments, Count,' answered my aunt, 'but you must take pity on old bones. Upstairs must be my garden to-night. I'm tired and drowsy – it's been a hot, dusty day – and I think I'll be getting to my rest while the thunder is out of hearing.'

Soon candles gleamed on the wall; the pensive romantic twilight of evening was over. My aunt turned her face slowly, even reluctantly, I fancied, into their radiance. She looked pale, tired; and seemed disturbed and perplexed.

'I think, Richard, I'd like your arm up the stairs.' Again the Count forestalled me. 'Bless me, Count,' said my aunt in shaken, almost querulous tones, 'you'll be completely spoiling me with your – your kindness. I wouldn't rob you of your peace and quiet for all the world. There, Richard, that's it.'

She leaned a little heavily on my arm, walking slowly and deliberately. In the doorway she turned; hesitated.

'And now, good-night, my dear Count,' she said.

The Count stood, stark as a patriot, against the wall. It was not to be 'roses all the way'.

'Good-night, my dear lady,' said he.

As we slowly ascended the stairs I could hardly refrain from gently taxing my aunt with what seemed very like coquetry. Yet something in her words had set me doubting. And as I now looked sidelong at her, I fancied I could detect a gravity in her face which no mere feminine caprice could cause or explain. At her bedroom door I handed her the candle.

'I wish you could have stayed a little,' I mumbled inanely; 'he really meant it, you know. I ought to have realized that...'

She took the candle, staring vacantly into my face the while.

'I should like to see you, Richard, in about ten minutes' time,' she said. 'Step up cautiously to my room here. I shall be awaiting you. I want a few minutes' quiet, *sensible* talk – you understand?'

And with that she went in and shut the door.

'Richard, Richard,' I heard the Count's stealthy whisper at the foot of the stairs; but I made a clatter with the door handle, pretending not to have heard him.

I sat in my bedroom speculating in vain what my aunt wanted with me.

In ten minutes I tapped softly, and she herself opened the door. She was attired in a voluminous dressing-gown of scarlet flannel; her hair was loosely plaited and looped up on her shoulders, with less of grey in it than I had supposed. She shut the door after me, and rather stiffly signed to me to sit down.

'I'll trouble you, please, to speak rather softly, Richard,' she said, 'because my window is open for air, and the Count is walking in the garden.' She seated herself on a stiff bedroom chair, clasping her hands in her ample lap. 'I've called you in, my boy, to tell you that I am going to leave here tomorrow.'

I leaned forward to speak, but she peremptorily waved me back. 'Janet has ordered a cab for me; it will be at the door at eleven o'clock in the morning. My trunks – these two, just what I shall require – are packed and ready. Janet will see to the rest. And I'll ask you to be kind enough to send the others to me by the railway before the end of the week. See that they're securely locked and corded; the keys are under the clock there. What's more – I want you to take the Count for a walk early tomorrow morning, and not to return with him till luncheon, when I shall be – when I shall be, well – out of the house. Don't keep on opening your mouth, Richard; it distracts me. Then in some sort of explanation you are to tell him that his hospitality was so – so congenial to me that I hadn't the heart nor the words either – to say good-bye. Tell him I'll *write* good-bye... Is that perfectly clear, now?'

A languid breath of air gently lifted the white blind, as if to cool the flush that had spread over my aunt's cheek. Her face was inscrutable.

'What address did you say for the boxes?'

'Bless the boy! send them home.'

'Very well, Aunt Lucy,' I answered, and rose from my chair. My aunt lifted her hand, and let it fall again into her lap.

'Is there anything else?' I said.

The inscrutability of her expression angered and baffled me. She continued to look at me with an open solemnity, but as if I were a hundred miles away.

'Why do you pick and choose your words, make such a pretence,

Richard, when you might speak out?'

' "Pretence," Aunt Lucy?'

'If an old woman came in such straits to me, and I was a tolerably sensible young man like yourself, I hope and trust I'd use my wits to better purpose. I am in some anxiety. You see it. *You* are not blind. But you are saying to yourself, in your conceit and pique – "I won't ask her what it is." You think – "I'll wait for the old lady's confession; it's bound to come." I ask you candidly, is that open and manly? Is that the English frankness and chivalry we never weary of boasting about? Do you suppose that mere cleverness watched over your cradle? Do you think mere cleverness will ever win you a wife? Would – would the Count?'

Colour once more had welled into her cheeks, and her carpet-slippered foot was thrust impatiently out from beneath her dressing-gown.

'I did not suppose you wished me to intrude,' I stammered. 'You have your own reasons, I assume, for ordering me about. I assume, you had your own reasons, too, for not taking me into your confidence. I am sorry, Aunt Lucy, but I don't see what else I could have done.'

'Sit down, Richard,' she said.

'Look here, Aunt Lucy,' I interposed a little hotly, 'you ask me to speak out. You've said a good many things a fellow would resent pretty warmly from – any one else. Now let me have my say too. And I can't help it if I do offend you; or if you think I'm butting in on what doesn't concern me. I say this – it's a mean, shabby thing to treat the Count like this. You've talked and walked with him. You know what he thinks – what he feels. He's not the unfeeling simpleton you think *me*. But he can't help hoping. Now is it fair and square then to go off like this behind his back – because you daren't meet him and brave him to his face? He simply can't help himself. That's the point. I'm not blind. You can't explain and you daren't wait to be asked for an explanation. It's simply selfishness, that's what it is. And, what is worse, you don't want to go.' I blundered on and on to the grim lady, venturing much further than I had ever dreamed of doing; and then fell suddenly silent.

'In some respects, that is the truth, Richard,' she said at last, quite gently – 'I own that freely. But it's not fear or pusillanimity, and no injury, my boy. I am in the right; and yet it's true I daren't go to him and tell him so. If I lifted a finger – if, just as I am, I walked downstairs and went out and took a turn with him in the garden, on the man's arm – well, I *ask* you. What would he do?'

'He'd pop the question,' I said vulgarly and resentfully, 'and you know it. And a jolly good thing too, for both of you. What's more, you've never given him an atom of reason to suppose you wouldn't accept him.'

'I say *that's* untrue, Richard. And who asked for your views on that, pray? Be smart, sir, in better season. The Count, you say, would ask me to be his wife – what then? I am not too old; I am not too feeble; I am a practical housekeeper! and – I like the man. He'd ask me to be his wife – and then – as I walked in the garden with him, I should be stumbling and peering, pushing and poking my way. Dark to me! Whatever the happiness within. Richard, you poor blind creature, don't you see it? Can the Count marry a woman who's all but *eyeless*, who can but glimmer to-day out of what will be sightless and hopeless as that night outside, to-morrow? I have been struggling against the truth. I like being here. I like – Oh, I have stayed too long. You stupid, short-sighted men! He has seen me day after day. He has seen me go fingering on from chair to chair. Was I hiding it? Do I or do I not wear spectacles? Do they distort my eyes till I look like an owl in a belfry? Should I wear this hideous monstrosity if – you should have seen, you should have guessed.'

I put my hand on my aunt's as it lay on her knee.

'Good Lord,' I muttered, and choked into silence again.

'That's it, Richard, that's common sense,' she said, squeezing my fingers. 'It's all perfectly plain. As duty always is, thank the Lord. He wants a bright, active, capable wife – if he wants any. A blind old woman can't be that. She can't be, even if she had the heart. I'm a silly, Richard, for all my sour ways. Poor man, poor volatile generous creature. He's not quiet and stay-at-home, as his age should be. He's all capers, and fancies, and – and romance. God bless me, romance! ... And that's the end of it.'

She stayed; and we heard a light restless footfall upon the gravel beneath the window.

'I never thought I should be saying all this stuff to you; I had no such intention, Richard. But you're of my own blood, and that's something. And now off to bed with you, and not another word. Out with him at ten and back with him at twelve. And my boxes at the week's end.'

'Look here, my dear aunt — ' I began.

'You are going to tell me,' she said, 'that it's all my fancy; that my eyes are as good as yours; that I shall wreck our old friend's happiness. My dear Richard, do you suppose that my questions to the little snuff-coloured oculist were not sharp and to the point? Do you think life has not given me the courage to know that one's eyesight is at least as precious and mortal as one's heart? Do you think that an old woman, who was never idle in learning, has not by this time read through and through your old friend's warm, fickle, proud, fantastic heart? There are good things a woman can admire in a man, besides mere stubborn adoration. And the Count has most of 'em. So you see, you would have told me only what ninety-nine young men would have told me nearly as well. I think too much of you to listen to it. The hundredth for me. There, give me a kiss and go away,

Richard. I wish to retire.'

My aunt rose hastily, kissed me sharply on the cheek, hurried me out of the room, and locked the door after me.

While sitting there in her presence, I had almost failed to see the folly of the business. Her pitiless commonsense had made me an unwilling accomplice. But as I turned over our talk in my mind, I was tempted at once to betray her secret to the Count. He, too, could be resolute and rational and inflexible at need. Nevertheless, I realized how futile, how fatal the attempt might prove.

To the letter then, I determined to obey her, trusting to the Count's genius and the placability of fate for a happier conclusion. And even at that – a young man a good deal incensed with the ridiculous obligations these two elderly victims had thrust upon him found sleep that night very stubborn of attainment.

I had little expected to see my aunt at breakfast next morning; but when the Count came in from the garden, hot and boisterous, she sat waiting for him, and greeted us with her usual cheerful gravity. Only too clearly, however, my new knowledge revealed the tragic truth of her secret of the night before. She leaned forward a little on the table, gazing steadily across it, her hands wandering lightly over the cups, already half endowed with the delicacy at length to come. Never had the Count been so high-spirited, and she answered him jest for jest. Yet not one sign did she vouchsafe to assure me of our compact. She acted her part without a symptom of flinching to the end.

In a rather clumsy fashion, I fear, I at last proposed to the Count a walk over the Heath.

'An excellent suggestion, Richard,' said my aunt cordially. 'There, Count put on your hat, and take your stick, and walk off the steam. It's no use looking at *me*. I have business to attend to, so *I* can't come.'

But the Count was exceedingly unwilling to go. The garden held more charm for him, and better company. A faint groping uneasiness, too, showed itself in his features.

But my aunt would heed no scruples, no reluctances. 'When a woman wants a man out of the way, don't you suppose, Count, that she knows best?' she enquired lightly but firmly. 'Now where's your stick?'

In her eagerness she stumbled against the doorpost, and the Count caught her impulsively by the arm. Her cheek flushed crimson. For an instant I fancied that fate had indeed intervened. But the next minute the Count and I were hurried out of the house, and bound for the Heath. My aunt had herself shut the door, and, heavy with fears and forebodings, I supposed that this was the end of the matter.

It was a quiet summer morning, the sunshine sweet with the nutty and almond scents of bracken and gorse. At first, in our walk, the Count was inclined to be satirical. He scoffed at every remark I made, and scoffed at his scoffing. But at the bottom of the hollow his mood swerved to the opposite extreme. He walked, bent morosely, without raising his eyes from the grass. His only answer to every little remark I volunteered was a shrug or a grunt. His pace diminished more and more until at last he suddenly stopped, as if some one had spoken to him. And he turned his face towards home.

'What's wrong?' he said to me.

'Wrong?' said I.

'I heard your aunt calling.'

'Nonsense,' I said; 'she's two miles distant at least.'

' "Nonsense"!' said he angrily: 'I say I *heard* her calling. Am I *all* skin and bone? I'm done with the Heath.'

I remonstrated in vain. It only served to make things worse. At each word the Count's disquietude increased, he was the more obstinately bent on returning.

'Home, boy, home! I'll not be gainsaid.'

I threatened to go on alone; but the threat, I knew, was futile, and proved me at my last resource.

It was not until we were within a few yards of the house that, on turning a corner, we came in sight of the cab. With a sagacity that almost amounted to divination, the Count jumped at once to the cause of its presence there.

'What's it mean?' he hoarsely shouted, and waved his stick in the air. 'What's that cab mean, I say? What's it mean? Have you no answer, eh?' But after that one swift white glance at my face, he said no more. 'Bring that box into the house, sir,' he bawled to the cabman, 'and drive your cab to the devil.'

I followed him into the house, and the tempest of his wrath raged through it like a cloud. My aunt was not in the dining-room. Janet had fled away into the kitchen. And I suppose by this time my aunt had heard the uproar of his home-coming, for when the Count assailed her door it was secure, and she was in a stronghold.

'Mrs Lindsay! what's this mean?' he shouted. 'What have I done, that you should be leaving my house like this? Am I so far in my dotage that I must be cheated like a child? Is it open with me? You shall not go. You shall not go. I'll burn the cab first. You daren't face me, Mrs Lindsay.'

'Count, Count,' said I, 'every word – the neighbours.'

'The neighbours! the neighbours!' his scorn broke over me. 'Look to your own pottering milksop business, sir! Now, Mrs Lindsay, now!'

In envious admiration I heard my aunt open her door. For an instant there was no sound in the house.

'Count,' she said, 'I will just ask you to go quietly down to your study and remain there for five minutes. By that time I shall be ready to say good-bye to you.'

'Lucy, my dear friend,' said the Count – and all the resentment was gone out of his voice – 'I ask only one thing: you will not treat me like this?'

'Five minutes, Count, five minutes,' said my aunt.

The Count came downstairs. He paid no heed to me; went into his study and shut the door. The cabman was on the doorstep.

'Richard,' said my aunt from the loop of the stairs, 'the cabman will carry out my orders.'

I went up slowly and tapped at my aunt's door. She would not open to me.

'You have failed, Richard, that is all; a man can't do worse,' she called to me from the other side of the panels.

'He insisted, aunt,' I pleaded. 'I almost used force.'

'I don't doubt it,' she said; 'you used all the force that was in you. There, leave me now. I have other things to think about.'

'On my word of honour, believe me or not, Aunt Lucy,' I cried, 'I have done my best. "I hear her calling" – that's what he kept saying: and home he came. I would have given anything. Let me tell him. I saw his face just now. Aunt Lucy, he's an old man —'

'Listen, Richard,' she answered, and she was pressing close to the door. 'Say no more. I spoke hastily. I have thought it out; the day will pass; and all the noise and fret over. But, but – are you there, Richard?' She whispered in so low a voice that I could scarcely catch the words, 'I go because I'm tired of it all; want liberty, ease: tell him that. "Just like a woman!" say; anything that sounds best to rid him of this – fancy. Do you see? – and not a single word about the eyes. Richard! do you see? You have failed me once. I am trusting you again. That's all.'

So I went down and sat a while with my own thoughts to entertain me, in the little room with the French windows and the stuffed birds. In a few minutes I heard my aunt's footsteps descending the stairs. She was all but groping her way with extreme caution, step by step. Veil or bonnet, I know not what, had added years to her face. I had not heard the Count open his door. But in a flash I caught sight of him, on the threshold, stiff as a mute.

'Lucy,' he said, 'listen. For all that I said - for an old man's noise and fury - forgive me! That is past. My dear friend, all that I ask now is this - will you be my wife?'

My aunt's eyebrows were arched above her spectacles. She smoothed her wrinkled forehead with her fingers. 'What did you say, Count?' she said.

'I said I am sorry – beyond all words. And oh, my dear, dear lady, will you be my wife?'

'Ach – nonsense, nonsense, old friend,' said my aunt. 'And you and me so old and staid! Grey hairs. Withered sticks. From the bottom of my heart I thank you for the honour. But – why, Count, you discommode an – an old woman.' She laughed like a girl.

And she pushed her gloved hand along the wall of the passage, moving very heedfully and slowly. 'Richard, may I ask you just once more to support my poor gouty knees down these odious steps?' My aunt was speaking in a foreign tongue. The Count strode after us.

'Is this all?' said he, gazing into her face.

'God bless the man! – would he stare me out of countenance?' Her hand felt limp and cold beneath her glove. And we went out of the house into the sunlight, and descended slowly to the cab.

And that was the end of the matter. My aunt had divined the truth. Her volatile, fickle, proud, fantastic old friend moped for a while. But soon the intervention of scribbling, projects, books, and dissensions with his neighbours added this one more to many another romantic episode in his charming repertory of memories. Moreover, had my aunt chosen to return, here was a brotherly affection, flavoured with a platonic piquancy, eager to welcome, to serve, and to entertain her.

Not for many a year did I meet my aunt again. I twice ventured to call on her; but she was 'out' to me. Rumours strayed my way at times of a soured blind old woman, for ever engaged in scandalous contention with the parents of her domestics; but me she altogether ignored. And then for a long time I feared to force myself on her memory. But when the end came, and the Count was speedily sinking, some odd remembrance of her troubled his sleep. He begged me to write to my aunt, to 'ask her to come and share a last crust with an old, broken, toothless friend.' But my poor old friend died the next evening, and the last stillness had fallen upon the house before she could answer his summons.

On the day following I was sitting in the empty and darkened dining-room, when I heard the sound of wheels, and somehow divining what they portended, I looked out through the Venetian blind.

My aunt had come, as she had gone, in a hackney cab; and, refusing any assistance from the maid who was there with her, she stepped painfully down out of it, and, tapping the ground at her feet with her ebony stick, the wintry sun glinting red upon her blue spectacles as she moved, she began to climb the flight of steps alone, with difficulty, but with a vigorous assurance.

I was seized with dismay at the very sight of her. Something in her very appearance filled me with a sense of my own mere young-manliness and fatuity. I drew sharply back from the window; hesitated – in doubt whether to receive her myself, or to send for Mrs Rodd. I peeped again. She had come on slowly. But now, midway up the steps, she paused, slowly turned herself about, and stretched out her hand towards the house.

'Cabman, cabman' – her words rang against the stucco walls – 'is this the house? What's wrong with the house?'

The cabman began to climb down from his box.

'Agnes, do you hear me?' she cried with a shrill piercing horror in her voice. 'Agnes, Agnes – is the house *dark*?'

'The blinds are all down, m'm,' answered the girl looking out of the window.

My aunt turned her head slowly, and I could see her moving eyebrows arched high above her spectacles. And then she began to climb rapidly backwards down the steps in her haste to be gone. It was a ludicrous and yet a poignant and dreadful thing to see. I could refrain myself no longer.

But she was already seated in the cab before I could reach her. 'Aunt, my dear Aunt Lucy,' I said at the window, peering into the musty gloom. 'Won't you please come into the house? I have many things – a ring – books – he spoke often —'

She turned and confronted me, speechless entreaty in her blind face – an entreaty not to me, for no earthly help, past all hope of answer, it seemed; and then, with an extraordinary certainty of aim, she began beating my hand that lay upon the narrow window-frame with the handle of her ebony stick.

'Drive on, drive on!' she cried. 'God bless the man, why doesn't he drive on?' The jet butterflies in her bonnet trembled above her crimsoned brow. The cabman brandished his whip. And that was quite the end. I never saw my aunt again.

The Looking-Glass

For an hour or two in the afternoon, Miss Lennox had always made it a rule to retire to her own room for a little rest, so that for this brief interval, at any rate, Alice was at liberty to do just what she pleased with herself. The 'just what she pleased,' no doubt, was a little limited in range; and 'with herself' was at best no very vast oasis amid its sands.

She might, for example, like Miss Lennox, rest, too, if she pleased. Miss Lennox prided herself on her justice.

But then, Alice could seldom sleep in the afternoon because of her troublesome cough. She might at a pinch write letters, but they would need to be nearly all of them addressed to imaginary correspondents. And not even the most romantic of young human beings can write on indefinitely to one who vouchsafes *no* kind of an answer. The choice in fact merely amounted to that between being 'in' or 'out' (in *any* sense), and now that the severity of the winter had abated, Alice much preferred the solitude of the garden to the vacancy of the house.

With rain came an extraordinary beauty to the narrow garden – its trees drenched, refreshed, and glittering at break of evening, its early flowers stooping pale above the darkened earth, the birds that haunted there singing as if out of a cool and happy cloister – the stormcock wildly jubilant. There was one particular thrush on one particular tree which you might say all but yelled messages at Alice, messages which sometimes made her laugh, and sometimes almost ready to cry, with delight.

And yet ever the same vague influence seemed to haunt her young mind. Scarcely so much as a mood; nothing in the nature of a thought; merely an influence – like that of some impressive stranger met – in a dream, say – long ago, and now half-forgotten.

This may have been in part because the low and foundering wall between the empty meadows and her own recess of greenery had always seemed to her like the boundary between two worlds. On the one side freedom, the wild; on this, Miss Lennox, and a sort of captivity. There Reality; here (her 'duties' almost forgotten) the confines of a kind of waking dream. For this reason, if for no other, she at the same time longed for and yet in a way dreaded the afternoon's regular reprieve.

It had proved, too, both a comfort and a vexation that the old servant belonging to the new family next door had speedily discovered this little habit, and would as often as not lie in wait for her between a bush of lilac and a bright green chestnut that stood up like a dense umbrella midway along the wall that divided Miss Lennox's from its one neighbouring garden. And since apparently it was Alice's destiny in life to be always precariously balanced between extremes, Sarah had also turned out to be a creature of rather peculiar oscillations of temperament.

Their clandestine talks were, therefore, though frequent, seldom particularly enlightening. None the less, merely to see this slovenly ponderous woman enter the garden, self-centred, with a kind of dull arrogance, her louring face as vacant as contempt of the Universe could make it, was an event ever eagerly, though at times vexatiously, looked for, and seldom missed.

Until but a few steps separated them, it was one of Sarah's queer habits to make believe, so to speak, that Alice was not there at all. Then, as regularly, from her place of vantage on the other side of the wall, she would slowly and heavily lift her eyes to her face, with a sudden energy which at first considerably alarmed the young girl, and afterwards amused her. For certainly you *are* amused in a sort of fashion when any stranger you might suppose to be a little queer in the head proves perfectly harmless. Alice did not exactly like Sarah. But she could no more resist her advances than the garden could resist the coming on of night.

Miss Lennox, too, it must be confessed, was a rather tedious and fretful companion for wits (like Alice's) always wool-gathering – wool, moreover, of the shimmering kind that decked the Golden Fleece. Her own conception of the present was of a niche in Time from which she was accustomed to look back on the dim, though once apparently garish, panorama of the past; while with Alice, Time had kept promises enough only for a surety of its immense resources – resources illimitable, even though up till now they had been pretty tightly withheld.

Or, if you so preferred, as Alice would say to herself, you could put it that Miss Lennox had all her eggs in a real basket, and that Alice had all hers in a basket that was *not* exactly real – only problematical.

All the more reason, then, for Alice to think it a little queer that it had been Miss Lennox herself and not Sarah who had first given shape and substance to her vaguely bizarre intuitions concerning the garden – a walled-in space in which one might suppose intuition alone could discover anything in the least remarkable.

'When my cousin, Mary Wilson (the Wilsons of Aberdeen, as I may have told you), when my cousin lived in this house,' she had informed her young companion, one evening over her own milk and oatmeal biscuits, 'there was a silly talk with the maids that it was haunted.'

'The house?' Alice had enquired, with a sudden crooked look on a face that Nature, it seemed, had definitely intended to be frequently startled; 'The house?'

'I didn't say the *house*,' Miss Lennox testily replied – it always annoyed her to see anything resembling a flush on her young companion's cheek, 'and even if I did, I certainly *meant* the garden. If I had meant the house, I should have used the word house. I meant the garden. It was quite unnecessary to correct or contradict me; and whether or not, it's all the purest rubbish – just a tale, though, not the only one of the kind in the world, I fancy.'

'Do you remember any of the other tales?' Alice had enquired, after a rather prolonged pause.

'No, none'; was the flat reply.

And so it came about that to Sarah (though she could hardly be described as the Serpent of the situation) to Sarah fell the opportunity of enjoying to the full an opening for her fantastic 'lore'. By insinuation, by silences, now with contemptuous scepticism, now with enormous warmth, she cast her spell, weaving an eager imagination through and through with the rather gaudy threads of superstition.

'Lor, no, *Crimes*, maybe not, though blood is in the roots for all *I* can say.' She had looked up almost candidly in the warm, rainy wind, her deadish-looking hair blown back from her forehead.

'Some'll tell you only the old people have eyes to see the mystery; and some, old or young, if so be they're ripe. Nothing to me either way; I'm gone past such things. And *what* it is, 'orror and darkness, or golden like a saint in heaven, or pictures in dreams, or just like dying fireworks in the air, the Lord alone knows, Miss, for I don't. But this I *will* say,' and she edged up her body a little closer to the wall, the raindrops the while dropping softly on bough and grass, 'May-day's the day, and midnight's the hour, for such as be wakeful and brazen and stoopid enough to watch it out. And what you've got to look for in a manner of speaking is what comes up out of the darkness from behind them trees there!'

She drew back cunningly.

The conversation was just like clockwork. It recurred regularly – except that there was no need to wind anything up. It wound itself up over-night, and with such accuracy that Alice soon knew the complete series of question and answer by heart or by rote – as if she had learned them out of the *Child's Guide to Knowledge*, or the Catechism. Still there were interesting points in it even now.

'*And what you've got to look for*' — the *you* was so absurdly impersonal when muttered in that thick coarse privy voice. And Alice invariably smiled at this little juncture; and Sarah as invariably looked at her and swallowed.

'But have *you* looked for – for what you say, you know?' Alice would then enquire, still with face a little averted towards the black low-boughed group of broad-leafed chestnuts, positive candelabra in their own season of wax-like speckled blossom.

'Me? *Me?* I was old before my time, they used to say. Why, besides my poor sister up in Yorkshire there, there's not a mouth utters my name.' Her large flushed face smiled in triumphant irony. 'Besides my bed-rid mistress there, and my old what they call feeble-minded sister, Jane Mary, in Yorkshire, I'm as good as in my grave. I may be dull and hot in the head at times, but I stand *alone* – eat alone, sit alone, sleep alone, think alone. There's never been such a lonely person before. Now, what should such a lonely person as me, Miss, I ask you, or what should you either for that matter, be meddling with your Maydays and your haunted gardens for?' She broke off and stared with angry confusion around her, and, lifting up her open hand a little, she, added hotly, 'Them birds! – My God, I drats 'em for their squealin' !'

'But, why?' said Alice, frowning slightly.

'The Lord only knows, Miss; I hate the sight of 'em! If I had what they call a blunderbuss in me hand I'd blow 'em to ribbings.'

And Alice never could quite understand why it was that the normal pronunciation of the word would have suggested a less complete dismemberment of the victims.

It was on a bleak day in March that Alice first heard réally explicitly the conditions of the quest.

'Your hows and whys! What I say is I'm sick of it all. Not so much of you, Miss, which is all greens to me, but of the rest of it all! Anyhow, *fast* you must, like the Cartholics, and you with a frightful hacking cough and all. Come like a new-begotten bride you must in a white gown, and a wreath of lillies or rorringe-blossom in your hair, same pretty much as I made for my mother's coffin this twenty years ago, and which I wouldn't do now not for respectability even. And me and my mother, let me tell you, were as close as hens in a roost... But I'm off me subject. There you sits, even if the snow itself comes sailing in on your face, and alone you must be, neither book nor candle, and the house behind you shut up black abed and asleep. But, there; you so wan and sickly a young lady. What ghost would come to you, I'd like to know. You want some fine dark loveyer for a ghost – that's your ghost. Oo-ay! There's not a want in the world but's dust and ashes. That's my bit of schooling.'

She gazed on impenetrably at Alice's slender fingers. And without raising her eyes she leaned her large hands on the wall, 'Meself, Miss, meself's *my* ghost, as they say. Why, bless me! it's all thro' the place now, like smoke.'

What was all through the place now like smoke Alice perceived to be the peculiar clarity of the air discernible in the garden at times. The clearness as it were of glass, of a looking-glass, which conceals all behind and beyond it, returning only the looker's wonder, or simply her vanity, or even her gaiety. Why, for the matter of that, thought Alice smiling, there are people who look into looking-glasses, actually see themselves there, and yet never turn a hair.

There *wasn't* any glass, of course. Its sort of mirage sprang only out of the desire of her eyes, out of a restless hunger of the mind – just to possess her soul in patience till the first favourable May evening came along and then once and for all to set everything at rest. It was a thought which fascinated her so completely, that it influenced her habits, her words, her actions. She even began to long for the afternoon solely to be alone with it; and in the midst of the reverie it charmed into her mind, she would glance up as startled as a Dryad to see the 'cook-general's' dark face fixing its still cold gaze on her from over the moss-greened wall. As for Miss Lennox, she became testier and more 'rational' than ever as she narrowly watched the day approaching when her need for a new companion would become extreme.

Who, however, the lover might be, and where the trysting-place, was unknown even to Alice, though, maybe, not absolutely unsurmised by her, and with a kind of cunning perspicacity perceived only by Sarah.

'I see my old tales have tickled you up, Miss,' she said one day, lifting her eyes from the clothes-line she was carrying to the girl's alert and mobile face. 'What they call old wives' tales I fancy, too.'

'Oh, I don't think so,' Alice answered. 'I can hardly tell, Sarah. I am only at peace *here*, I know that. I get out of bed at night to look down from the window and wish myself here. When I'm reading, just as if it were a painted illustration – in the book, you know – the scene of it all floats in between me and the print. Besides, I can do just what I like with it. In my mind, I mean. I just imagine; and there it all is. So you see I could not bear *now* to go away.'

'There's no cause to worry your head about that,' said the woman darkly, 'and as for picking and choosing I never saw much of it for them that's under of a thumb. Why, when I was young, I couldn't have borne to live as I do now with just meself wandering to and fro. Muttering I catch meself, too. And, to be sure, surrounded in the air by shapes, and shadows, and noises, and winds, so as sometimes I can neither see nor hear. It's true, God's gospel, Miss – the body's like a clump of wood, it's that dull. And you can't get t'other side, so to speak.'

So lucid a portrayal of her own exact sensations astonished the girl. 'Well, but what is it, what is it, Sarah?'

Sarah strapped the air with the loose end of the clothes-line. 'Part, Miss, the hauntin' of the garden. Part as them black-jacketed clergymen would say, because we's we. And part 'cos it's all death the other side – all death.'

She drew her head slowly in, her puffy cheeks glowed, her small black eyes gazed as fixedly and deadly as if they were anemones on a rock.

The very fulness of her figure seemed to exaggerate her vehemence. She gloated – a heavy somnolent owl puffing its feathers. Alice drew back, swiftly glancing as she did so over her shoulder. The sunlight was liquid wan gold in the meadow, between the black tree-trunks. They lifted their cumbrous branches far above the brick human house, stooping their leafy twigs. A starling's dark iridescence took her glance as he minced pertly in the coarse grass.

'I can't quite see why *you* should think of death,' Alice ventured to suggest.

'Me? Not me! Where I'm put, I stay. I'm like a stone in the grass, I am. Not that if I were that old mealy-smilin' bag of bones flat on her back on her bed up there with her bits of beadwork and slops through a spout, I wouldn't make sure over-night of not being waked next mornin'. There's something in me that won't let me rest, what they call a volcano, though no more to eat in that beetle cupboard of a kitchen than would keep a Tom Cat from the mange.'

'But, Sarah,' said Alice, casting a glance up at the curtained windows of the other house, 'she looks such a quiet, *patient* old thing. I don't think I *could* stand having not even enough to eat. Why do you stay?'

Sarah laughed for a full half-minute in silence, staring at Alice meanwhile. ' "Patient"!' she replied at last, 'Oo-ay. Nor to my knowledge did I ever breathe the contrary. As for staying; you'd stay all right if that loveyer of yours come along. You'd stand anything – them pale narrow-chested kind; though me, I'm neether to bend nor break. And if the old man was to look down out of the blue up there this very minute, ay, and shake his fist at me, I'd say it to his face. I loathe your whining psalm-singers. A trap's a trap. You wait and see!'

'But how do you mean?' Alice said slowly, her face stooping.

There came no answer. And, on turning, she was surprised to see the bunchy alpaca-clad woman already disappearing round the corner of the house.

The talk softly subsided in her mind like the dust in an empty room. Alice wandered on in the garden, extremely loth to go in. And gradually a curious happiness at last descended upon her heart, like a cloud of morning dew in a dell of wild flowers. It seemed in moments like these, as if she had been given the power to think – or rather to be conscious, as it were, of thoughts not her own – thoughts like vivid pictures, following one upon another with extraordinary rapidity and brightness through her mind. As if, indeed, thoughts could be like fragments of glass, reflecting light at their every edge and angle. She stood tiptoe at the meadow wall and gazed greedily into the green fields, and across to the pollard aspens by the waterside. Turning, her eyes recognized clear in the shadow and blue-grey air of the garden her solitude – its solitude. And at once all thinking ceased.

'The Spirit is *me*: *I* haunt this place!' she said aloud, with sudden assurance, and almost in Sarah's own words. 'And I don't mind – not the least bit. It can be only my thankful, thankful self that is here. And that can *never* be lost.

She returned to the house, and seemed as she moved to see – almost as if she were looking down out of the sky on herself – her own dwarf figure walking beneath the trees. Yet there was at the same time a curious individuality in the common things, living and inanimate, that were peeping at her out of their secrecy. The silence hung above them as apparent as their own clear reflected colours above the brief Spring flowers. But when she stood tidying herself for the usual hour of reading to Miss Lennox, she was conscious of an almost unendurable weariness.

That night Alice set to work with her needle upon a piece of sprigged muslin to make her 'watch-gown' as Sarah called it. She was excited. She hadn't much time, she fancied. It was like hiding in a story. She worked with extreme pains, and quickly. And not till the whole flimsy thing was finished did she try on or admire any part of it. But, at last, in the early evening of one of the middle days of April, she drew her bedroom blind up close to the ceiling, to view herself in her yellow grained looking-glass.

The gown, white as milk in the low sunlight, and sprinkled with even whiter embroidered nosegays of daisies, seemed to attenuate a girlish figure, already very slender. She had arranged her abundant hair with unusual care, and her own clear, inexplicable eyes looked back upon her beauty, bright it seemed with tidings they could not speak.

She regarded closely that narrow, flushed, intense face in an unforeseen storm of compassion and regret, as if with the conviction that she herself was to blame for the inevitable leavetaking. It seemed to gaze like an animal its mute farewell in the dim discoloured glass.

And when she had folded and laid away the gown in her wardrobe, and put on her everyday clothes again, she felt an extreme aversion for the garden. So, instead of venturing out that afternoon, she slipped off its faded blue ribbon from an old bundle of letters which she had hoarded all these years from a school-friend long since lost sight of, and spent the evening reading them over, till headache and an empty despondency sent her to bed.

Lagging Time brought at length the thirtieth of April. Life was as usual. Miss Lennox had even begun to knit her eighth pair of woollen mittens for the annual Church bazaar. To Alice the day passed rather quickly; a cloudy, humid day with a furtive continual and enigmatical stir in the air. Her lips were parched; it seemed at any moment her skull might crack with the pain as she sat reading her chapter of Macaulay to Miss Lennox's sparking and clicking needles. Her mind was a veritable rookery of forebodings, flying and returning. She scarcely ate at all, and kept to the house, never even approaching a window. She wrote a long and rather unintelligible letter, which she destroyed when she had read it over. Then suddenly every vestige of pain left her.

And when at last she went to bed – so breathless that she thought her heart at any moment would jump out of her body, and so saturated with expectancy she thought she would die – her candle was left burning calmly, unnodding, in its socket upon the chest of drawers; the blind of her window was up, towards the houseless byroad; her pen stood in the inkpot.

She slept on into the morning of Mayday, in a sheet of eastern sunshine, till Miss Lennox, with a peevishness that almost amounted to resolution, decided to wake her. But then, Alice, though unbeknown in any really conscious sense to herself perhaps, had long since decided not to be awakened.

Not until the evening of that day did the sun in his diurnal course for a while illumine the garden, and then very briefly: to gild, to lull, and to be gone. The stars wheeled on in the thick-sown waste of space, and even when Miss Lennox's small share of the earth's wild living creatures had stirred and sunk again to rest in the ebb of night, there came no watcher – even the very ghost of a watcher – to the garden, in a watch-gown. So that what peculiar secrets found reflex in its dark mirror no human witness was there to tell.

As for Sarah, she had long since done with looking-glasses once and for all. A place was a place. There was still the washing to be done on Mondays. Fools and weaklings would continue to come and go. But give her *her* way, she'd have blown them and their looking-glasses all to ribbons – with the birds.

Miss Duveen *

I seldom had the company of children in my grandmother's house beside the river Wandle. The house was old and ugly. But its river was lovely and youthful even although it had flowed on for ever, it seemed, between its green banks of osier and alder. So it was no great misfortune perhaps that I heard more talking of its waters than of any human tongue. For my grandmother found no particular pleasure in my company. How should she? My father and mother had married (and died) against her will, and there was nothing in me of those charms which, in fiction at any rate, swiftly soften a superannuated heart.

Nor did I pine for her company either. I kept out of it as much as possible.

It so happened that she was accustomed to sit with her back to the window of the room which she usually occupied, her grey old indifferent face looking inwards. Whenever necessary, I would steal close up under it, and if I could see there her large faded amethyst velvet cap I knew I was safe from interruption. Sometimes I would take a slice or two of currant bread or (if I could get it) a jam tart or a cheese cake, and eat it under a twisted old damson tree or beside the running water. And if I conversed with anybody, it would be with myself or with my small victims of the chase.

Not that I was an exceptionally cruel boy; though if I had lived on for many years in this primitive and companionless fashion, I should surely have become an idiot. As a matter of fact, I was unaware even that I was ridiculously old-fashioned – manners, clothes, notions, everything. My grandmother never troubled to tell me so, nor did she care. And the

* As printed in BS (1942).

servants were a race apart. So I was left pretty much to my own devices. What wonder, then, if I at first accepted with genuine avidity the acquaintanceship of our remarkable neighbour, Miss Duveen?

It had been, indeed, quite an advent in our uneventful routine when that somewhat dubious household moved into Willowlea, a brown brick edifice, even uglier than our own, which had been long vacant, and whose sloping garden confronted ours across the Wandle. My grandmother, on her part, at once discovered that any kind of intimacy with its inmates was not much to be desired. While I, on mine, was compelled to resign myself to the loss of the Willowlea garden as a kind of no-man's-land or Tom Tiddler's ground.

I got to know Miss Duveen by sight long before we actually became friends. I used frequently to watch her wandering in her long garden. And even then I noticed how odd were her methods of gardening. She would dig up a root or carry off a potted plant from one to another overgrown bed with an almost animal-like resolution; and a few minutes afterwards I would see her restoring it to the place from which it had come. Now and again she would stand perfectly still, like a scarecrow, as if she had completely forgotten what she was at.

Miss Coppin, too, I descried sometimes. But I never more than glanced at her, for fear that even at that distance the too fixed attention of my eyes might bring hers to bear upon me. She was a smallish woman, inclined to be fat, and with a peculiar waddling gait. She invariably appeared to be angry with Miss Duveen, and would talk to her as one might talk to a post. I did not know, indeed, until one day Miss Duveen waved her handkerchief in my direction that I had been observed from Willowlea at all. Once or twice after that, I fancied, she called me; at least her lips moved; but I could not distinguish what she said. And I was naturally a little backward in making new friends. Still I grew accustomed to looking out for her and remember distinctly how first we met.

It was raining, the raindrops falling softly into the unrippled water, making their great circles, and tapping on the motionless leaves above my head where I sat in shelter on the bank. But the sun was shining whitely from behind a thin fleece of cloud, when Miss Duveen suddenly peeped in at me out of the greenery, the thin silver light upon her face, and eyed me sitting there, for all the world as if she were a blackbird and I a snail. I scrambled up hastily with the intention of retreating into my own domain, but the peculiar grimace she made at me fixed me where I was.

'Ah', she said, with a little masculine laugh. 'So this is the young gentleman, the bold, gallant young gentleman. And what might be his name?'

I replied rather distantly that my name was Arthur.

'Arthur, to be sure!' she repeated, with extraordinary geniality, and again, 'Arthur,' as if in the strictest confidence.

'I know you, Arthur, very well indeed. I have looked, I have watched; and now, please God, we need never be estranged.' And she tapped her brow and breast, making the Sign of the Cross with her lean, bluish forefinger.

'What is a little brawling brook', she went on, 'to friends like you and me?' She gathered up her tiny countenance once more into an incredible grimace of friendliness; and I smiled as amicably as I could in return. There was a pause in this one-sided conversation. She seemed to be listening, and her lips moved, though I caught no sound. In my uneasiness I was just about to turn stealthily away, when she poked forward again.

'Yes, yes, I know you quite intimately, Arthur. We have met *here*.' She tapped her rounded forehead. 'You might not suppose it, too; but I have eyes like a lynx. It is no exaggeration, I assure you – I assure everybody. And now what friends we will be! At times,' she stepped out of her hiding-place and stood in curious dignity beside the water, her hands folded in front of her on her black pleated silk apron – 'at times, dear child, I long for company – earthly company.' She glanced furtively about her. 'But I must restrain my longings; and you will, of course, understand that I do not complain. *He* knows best. And my dear cousin, Miss Coppin – she too knows best. She does not consider too much companionship expedient for me.' She glanced in some perplexity into the smoothly swirling water.

'I, you know,' she said suddenly, raising her little piercing eyes to mine, 'I am Miss Duveen, that's not, they say, quite the thing here.' She tapped her small forehead again beneath its sleek curves of greying hair, and made a long narrow mouth at me. 'Though, of course,' she added, 'we do not tell *her* so. No!'

And I, too, nodded my head in instinctive and absorbed imitation. Miss Duveen laughed gaily. 'He understands, he understands!' she cried, as if to many listeners. 'Oh, what a joy it is in this world, Arthur to be understood. Now tell me,' she continued with immense nicety, 'tell me, how's your dear mamma?'

I shook my head.

'Ah,' she cried, 'I see, I see; Arthur has no mamma. We will not refer to it. No father, either?'

I shook my head again and, standing perfectly still, stared at my new acquaintance with vacuous curiosity. She gazed at me with equal concentration, as if she were endeavouring to keep the very thought of my presence in her mind.

'It is sad to have no father,' she continued rapidly, half closing her eyes; 'no head, no guide, no stay, no stronghold; but we have, O yes, we have another father, dear child, another father – eh? . . . Where . . . Where?'

She very softly raised her finger. 'On high,' she whispered, with extra-ordinary intensity.

'But just now,' she added cheerfully, hugging her mittened hands together, 'we are not talking of Him; we are talking of ourselves, just you and me, *so* cosy, *so secret!* And it's a grandmother? I thought so, I thought so, a grandmother! O yes, I can peep between the curtains, though they do lock the door. A grandmother – I thought so; that very droll old lady! *Such* fine clothes! Such a presence, oh yes! A grandmother.' She poked out her chin and laughed confidentially.

'And the long, bony creature, all rub and double' – she jogged briskly with her elbows, 'who's that?'

'Mrs Pridgett,' I said.

'There, there,' she whispered breathlessly, gazing widely about her. 'Think of that! *He* knows; *He* understands. How firm, how manly, how undaunted! . . . *One* t?'

I shook my head dubiously.

'Why should he?' she cried scornfully. 'But between ourselves, Arthur, that is a thing we *must* learn, and never mind the headache. We cannot, of course, know everything. Even Miss Coppin does not know everything' – she leaned forward with intense earnestness – 'though I don't tell her so. We must try to learn all we can; and at once. One thing, dear child, you may be astonished to hear, I learned only yesterday, and that is how exceed-ingly *sad* life is.'

She leaned her chin upon her narrow bosom pursing her lips. 'And yet you know they say very little about it...They don't *mention* it. Every moment, every hour, every day, every year – one, two, three, four, five, seven, ten,' she paused, frowned, 'and so on. Sadder and sadder. Why? why? It's strange, but oh, so true. You really can have no notion, child, how very sad I am myself at times. In the evening, when they all gather together, in their white raiment, up and up and up, I sit on the garden seat, on Miss Coppin's garden seat, and precisely in the middle (you'll be kind enough to remember that?) and my *thoughts* make me sad.' She narrowed her eyes and shoulders. 'Yes and frightened, my child! Why must I be so guarded? One angel – the greatest *fool* could see the wisdom of that. But billions! – with their fixed eyes shining, so very boldly, on me. I never prayed for so many, dear friend. And we pray for a good many odd things, you and I, I'll be bound. But there, you see, poor Miss Duveen's on her theology again – scamper, scamper, scamper. In the congregations of the wicked we must be cautious! . . . Mrs Partridge and grandmamma, so nice, *so* nice; but even that, too, a *little* sad, eh? She leaned her head questioningly, like a starving bird in the snow.

I smiled, not knowing what else she expected of me; and her face became instantly grave and set.

'He's right; perfectly right. We must speak evil of *no* one. *No* one. We must shut our mouths. We — ' She stopped suddenly and, taking a step leaned over the water towards me, with eyebrows raised high above her tiny face. 'S–sh!' she whispered, laying a long forefinger on her lips. 'Eavesdroppers!' She smoothed her skirts, straightened her cap, and left me; only a moment after to poke out her head at me again from between the leafy bushes. 'An assignation, no!' she said firmly, then gathered her poor, cheerful, forlorn, crooked, lovable face into a most wonderful contraction at me, that assuredly meant – 'But, *yes!*'

Indeed it was an assignation, the first of how many, and how few. Sometimes Miss Duveen would sit beside me, apparently so lost in thought that I was clean forgotten. And yet I half fancied it was often nothing but feigning. Once she stared me blankly out of countenance when I ventured to take the initiative and to call out good morning to her across the water. On this occasion she completed my consternation with a sudden, angry grimace – contempt, jealousy, outrage.

But often we met like old friends and talked. It was a novel but not always welcome diversion for me in the long shady garden that was my privy universe. Where our alders met, mingling their branches across the flowing water, and the kingfisher might be seen – there was our usual tryst. But, occasionally, at her invitation, I would venture across the stepping-stones into her demesne; and occasionally, but very seldom indeed, she would venture into mine. How plainly I see her, tip-toeing from stone to stone, in an extraordinary concentration of mind – her mulberry petticoats, her white stockings, her loose spring-side boots. And when at last she stood beside me, her mittened hand on her breast, she would laugh on in a kind of paroxysm until the tears stood in her eyes, and she grew faint with breathlessness.

'In all danger,' she told me once, 'I hold my breath and shut my eyes. And if I could tell you of every danger, I think, perhaps, you would understand – dear Miss Coppin...' I did not, and yet, perhaps, very vaguely I did see the connection in this rambling statement.

Like most children, I liked best to hear Miss Duveen talk about her own childhood. I contrived somehow to discover that if we sat near flowers or under boughs in blossom, her talk would generally steal round to that. Then she would chatter on and on: of the white sunny rambling house, somewhere, nowhere – it saddened and confused her if I asked where – in which she had spent her first happy years; where her father used to ride on a black horse; and her mother to walk with her in the garden in a crinolined gown and a locket with the painted miniature of a 'divine' nobleman inside it. How very far away these pictures seemed!

It was as if she herself had shrunken back into this distant past, and was babbling on like a child again, already a little isolated by her tiny infirmity.

'That was before — ' she would begin to explain precisely, and then a criss-cross many-wrinkled frown would net her rounded forehead, and cloud her eyes. Time might baffle her, but then, time often baffled me too. Any talk about her mother usually reminded her of an elder sister, Caroline. 'My sister, Caroline,' she would repeat as if by rote, 'you may not be aware, Arthur, was afterwards Mrs Bute. *So* charming, *so* exquisite, *so* accomplished. And Colonel Bute – an officer and a gentleman, I grant. And yet ... But no! My dear sister was *not* happy. And so it was no doubt a blessing in disguise that by an unfortunate accident she was found *drowned*. In a lake, you will understand, not a mere shallow noisy brook. This is one of my private sorrows, which, of course, your grandmamma would be horrified to hear – horrified; and which, of course, Partridge has not the privilege of birth even to be informed of – *our* secret, dear child – with all her beautiful hair, and her elegant feet, and her eyes no more ajar than this; but blue, blue as the forget-me-not. When the time comes, Miss Coppin will close my own eyes, I hope and trust. Death, dear, dear child, I know they *say* is only sleeping. Yet I hope and trust *that*. To be sleeping wide awake; oh no!' she abruptly turned her small untidy head away.

'But didn't they shut *hers*? I enquired.

Miss Duveen ignored the question. 'I am not uttering one word of blame,' she went on rapidly; 'I am perfectly aware that such things confuse me. Miss Coppin tells me not to think. She tells me that I can have no opinions worth the mention. She says, "Shut up your mouth". I must keep silence then. All that I am merely trying to express to you, Arthur, knowing you will regard it as sacred between us – all I am expressing is that my dear sister, Caroline, was a gifted and beautiful creature with not a shadow or vestige or tinge or taint of confusion in her mind. *Nothing*. And yet, when they dragged her out of the water and laid her there on the bank, looking — ' She stooped herself double in a sudden dreadful fit of gasping, and I feared for an instant she was about to die.

'No, no, no,' she cried, rocking herself to and fro, 'you shall *not* paint such a picture in his young, innocent mind. You *shall* not.'

I sat on my stone, watching her, feeling excessively uncomfortable. 'But what *did* she look like, Miss Duveen?' I pressed forward to ask at last.

'No, no, no,' she cried again. 'Cast him out, cast him out. *Retro Sathanas!* We must not even *ask* to understand. My father and my dear mother, I do not doubt, have spoken for Caroline. Even I, if I must be called on, will strive to collect my thoughts. And that is precisely where a friend, you, Arthur, would be so precious; to know that you too, in your innocence, will be helping me to collect my thoughts on that day, to save our dear Caroline from Everlasting Anger. That, that! Oh dear: oh dear!' She turned on me a face I should scarcely have recognized, lifted herself trembling to her feet, and hurried away.

Sometimes it was not Miss Duveen that was a child again, but I that had grown up. 'Had now you been your handsome father – and I see him , O, so plainly, dear child – had you been your father, then I must, of course, have kept to the house . . . I must have; it is a rule of conduct, and everything depends on them. Where would Society be *else*? she cried, with an unanswerable blaze of intelligence. 'I find, too, dear Arthur, that they increase – the rules increase. I try to remember them. My dear cousin, Miss Coppin, knows them all. But I – I think sometimes one's *memory* is a little treacherous. And then it must vex people.'

She gazed penetratingly at me for an answer that did not come. Mute as a fish though I might be, I suppose it was something of a comfort to her to talk to me.

And to suppose that is *my* one small crumb of comfort when I reflect on the kind of friendship I managed to bestow.

I actually met Miss Coppin once; but we did not speak. I had, in fact, gone to tea with Miss Duveen. The project had been discussed as 'quite, quite impossible, dear child' for weeks. 'You must never mention it again.' As a matter of fact I had never mentioned it at all. But one day – possibly when their charge had been less difficult and exacting, one day Miss Coppin and her gaunt maid-servant and companion really did go out together, leaving Miss Duveen alone in Willowlea. It was the crowning opportunity of our friendship. The moment I espied her issuing from the house, I guessed her errand. She came hastening down to the waterside, attired in clothes of a colour and fashion I had never seen her wearing before, her dark eyes shining in her head, her hands trembling with excitement.

It was a still, warm afternoon, with sweet-williams and linden and stocks scenting the air, when, with some little trepidation, I must confess, I followed her in formal dignity up the unfamiliar path towards the house. I know not which of our hearts beat the quicker, whose eyes cast the most furtive glances about us. My friend's cheeks were brightest mauve. She wore a large silver locket on a ribbon; and I followed her up the faded green stairs, beneath the dark pictures, to her small, stuffy bedroom under the roof. We humans, they say, are enveloped in a kind of aura; to which the vast majority of us are certainly entirely insensitive. Nevertheless, there was an air, an atmosphere as of the smell of pears in this small attic room – well, every bird, I suppose, haunts with its presence its customary cage.

'This,' she said, acknowledging the bed, the looking-glass, the deal washstand, 'this, dear child, you will pardon; in fact, you will not see. How could we sit, friends as we are, in the congregation of strangers?'

I hardly know why, but that favourite word of Miss Duveen's, 'congregation', brought up before me with extreme aversion all the hostile hardness and suspicion concentrated in Miss Coppin and Ann. I stared at the queer tea things in a vain effort not to be aware of the rest of Miss Duveen's private belongings.

Somehow or other she had managed to procure for me a bun – a saffron bun. There was a dish of a grey pudding and a plate of raspberries that I could not help suspecting (and, I am ashamed to say, with aggrieved astonishment), she must have herself gathered that morning from my grandmother's canes. We did not talk very much. Her heart gave her pain. And her face showed how hot and absorbed and dismayed she was over her foolhardy entertainment. But I sipped my milk and water, sitting on a black bandbox, and she on an old cane chair. And we were almost formal and distant to one another, with little smiles and curtseys over our cups, and polished agreement about the weather.

'And you'll strive not to be sick, dear child,' she implored me suddenly, while I was nibbling my way slowly through the bun. But it was not until rumours of the tremendous fact of Miss Coppin's early and unforeseen return had been borne in on us that Miss Duveen lost all presence of mind. She burst into tears; seized and kissed repeatedly my sticky hands; implored me to be discreet; implored me to be gone; implored me to retain her in my affections, 'as you love your poor dear mother, Arthur,' and I left her on her knees, her locket pressed to her bosom.

Miss Coppin was, I think, unusually astonished to see a small strange boy walk softly past her bedroom door, within which she sat, with purple face, her hat strings dangling, taking off her boots. Ann, I am thankful to say, I did not encounter. But when I was safely out in the garden in the afternoon sunshine, the boldness and the romance of this sally completely deserted me. I ran like a hare down the alien path, leapt from stone to stone across the river; nor paused in my flight until I was safe in my own bed-room, and had – how odd is childhood! – washed my face and entirely changed my clothes.

My grandmother, when I appeared at her tea-table, glanced at me now and again rather profoundly and inquisitively, but the actual question hovering in her mind remained unuttered.

It was many days before we met again, my friend and I. She had, I gathered from many mysterious nods and shrugs, been more or less confined to her bedroom ever since our escapade, and looked dulled and anxious; her small face was even a little more vacant in repose than usual. Even this meeting, too, was full of alarms; for in the midst of our talk, by mere chance or caprice, my grandmother took a walk in the garden that afternoon, and discovered us under our damson tree. She bowed in her dignified, aged way. And Miss Duveen, with her cheeks and forehead the colour of her petticoat, elaborately curtseyed.

'Beautiful, very beautiful weather,' said my grandmother.

'It is indeed,' said my friend, fixedly.

'I trust you are keeping pretty well?'

'As far, ma'am, as God and a little weakness of the heart permit,' said Miss Duveen. 'He knows all,' she added, firmly.

My grandmother stood silent a moment.

'Indeed He does,' she replied politely.

'And that's the difficulty,' ventured Miss Duveen, in her odd, furtive, friendly fashion.

My grandmother opened her eyes, smiled pleasantly, paused, glanced remotely at me, and, with another exchange of courtesies, Miss Duveen and I were left alone once more. But it was a grave and saddened friend I now sat beside.

'You see, Arthur, all bad things, we know, are best for us. Motives included. That comforts me. But my heart is sadly fluttered. Not that I fear or would shun society; but perhaps your grandmother... I never had the power to treat my fellow-creatures as if they were stocks and stones. And the effort not to notice it distresses me. A little hartshorn might relieve the *palpitation*, of course; but Miss Coppin keeps all keys. It is this shouting that makes civility such a task.'

'This shouting' – very faintly then I caught her meaning, but I was in no mood to sympathize. My grandmother's one round-eyed expressionless glance at me had been singularly disconcerting. And it was only apprehension of her questions that kept me from beating a retreat. So we sat on, Miss Duveen and I, in the shade, the day drawing towards evening, and presently we walked down to the water-side, and under the colours of sunset I flung in my crumbs to the minnows, as she talked ceaselessly on.

'And yet,' she concluded, after how involved a monologue, 'and yet, Arthur, I feel it is for your forgiveness I should be pleading. So much to do; such an arch of beautiful things might have been my gift to you. It is here,' she said, touching her forehead. 'I do not think, perhaps, that all I might say would be for your good. I must be silent and discreet about much. I must not provoke' – she lifted her mittened finger, and raised her eyes – 'Them,' she said gravely. 'I am tempted, terrified, persecuted. Whispering, wrangling, shouting: the flesh is a grievous burden, Arthur; I long for peace. Only to flee away and be at rest! But,' she nodded, and glanced over her shoulder, 'about much – great trials, sad entanglements, about much the Others say, I must keep silence. It would only alarm your innocence. And that I will never, *never* do. Your father, a noble, gallant gentleman of the world, would have understood my difficulties. But he is dead ...Whatever that may mean. I have repeated it so often when Miss Coppin thought that I was not – dead, dead, dead, dead. But I don't think that even now I grasp the meaning of the word. Of you, dear child, I will never say it. You have been life itself to me.'

How generously, how tenderly she smiled on me from her perplexed, sorrowful eyes.

'You have all the world before you, all the world. How splendid it is to be a Man. For my part I have sometimes thought, though they do not of course intend to injure me, yet I fancy, sometimes, they have grudged me *my* part in it a little. Though God forbid but Heaven's best.'

She raised that peering, dark, remote gaze to my face, and her head was trembling again. 'They are saying now to one another – *"Where is she? where is she? It's nearly dark, m'm, where is she?"* O, Arthur, but there shall be no night *there*. We must believe it, we must – in spite, dear friend, of a weak horror of glare. My cousin, Miss Coppin, does not approve of my wishes. Gas, gas, gas, all over the house, and when it is not singing, it roars. You would suppose I might be trusted with but just my own one bracket. But no – Ann, I think – indeed I fear, sometimes, has no —' She started violently and shook her tiny head. 'When I am gone,' she continued disjointedly, 'you will be prudent, cautious, dear child? Consult only your heart about me. Older you must be . . . Yes, certainly, he must be older,' she repeated vaguely. 'Everything goes on and on – and round!' She seemed astonished, as if at a sudden radiance cast on an old and protracted perplexity.

'About your soul, dear child,' she said to me once, touching my hand, 'I have never spoken. Perhaps it was one of my first duties to keep on speaking to you about your soul. I mention it now in case they should rebuke me when I make my appearance there. It is a burden; and I have so many burdens, as well as pain. And at times I cannot think very far. I *see* the thought; but it won't alter. It comes back, just like a sheep – *"Ba-aa-ah"*, like that!' She burst out laughing, twisting her head to look at me the while. 'Miss Coppin, of course, has no difficulty; gentlemen have no difficulty. And this shall be the occasion of another of our little confidences. We are discreet?' She bent her head and scanned my face. 'Here,' she tapped her bosom, 'I bear his image. My only dear one's. And if you would kindly turn your head, dear child, perhaps I could pull him out.'

It was the miniature of a young, languid, fastidious-looking officer which she showed me – threaded on dingy tape, in its tarnished locket.

'Miss Coppin, in great generosity, has left me this,' she said, polishing the glass on her knee, 'though I am forbidden to wear it. For you see, Arthur, it is a duty not to brood on the past, and even perhaps, indelicate. Some day, it may be, you, too, will love a gentle girl. I beseech you, keep your heart pure and true. This one could not. Not a single word of blame escapes me. I own to my Maker, *never* to anyone else, it has not eased my little difficulty. But it is not for us to judge. Whose office is that, eh?' And again, that lean small forefinger, beneath an indescribable grimace; pointed gently, deliberately, from her lap upward. 'Pray, pray,' she added, very violently, 'pray, till the blood streams down your face! Pray, but rebuke not. They all whisper about it. Among themselves,' she added, peering out beneath and between the interlacing branches. 'But I simulate inattention, I simulate...' The very phrase seemed to have hopelessly confused her. Again, as so often now, that glassy fear came into her eyes; her foot tapped on the gravel.

'Arthur,' she cried suddenly, taking my hand tightly in her lap, 'you have been my refuge in a time of trouble. You will never know it, child. My refuge, and my peace. We shall seldom meet now. All are opposed. They repeat it in their looks. The autumn will divide us; and then, winter; but, I think, no spring. It is so, Arthur, there is a stir; and then they will hunt me out.' Her eyes gleamed again, far and small and black in the dusky pallor of her face.

It was indeed already autumn; the air golden and still. The leaves were beginning to fall. The late fruits were well-nigh over. Robins and tits seemed our only birds now. Rain came in floods. The Wandle took sound and volume, sweeping deep above our stepping stones. Very seldom after this I even so much as saw our neighbour. But I chanced on her again one still afternoon, standing fixedly by the brawling stream, in a rusty-looking old-fashioned cloak, her scanty hair pushed high up on her forehead.

She stared at me for a moment or two, and then, with a scared look over her shoulder, threw me a little letter, shaped like a cock-hat, and weighted with a pebble stone, across the stream. She whispered earnestly and rapidly at me over the water. But I could not catch a single word she said, and failed to decipher her close spidery handwriting. No doubt I was too shy, or too ashamed, or in a vague fashion too loyal, to show it to my grandmother. It is not now a flattering keepsake. I called out loudly I must go in; and still see her gazing after me, with a puzzled, mournful expression on the face peering out of the cloak.

Even after that we sometimes waved to one another across the water, but never if by hiding myself I could evade her in time. The distance seemed to confuse her, and quite silenced me. I began to see we were ridiculous friends, especially as she came now in ever dingier and absurder clothes. She even looked hungry, and not quite clean, as well as ill; and she talked more to her phantoms than to me when once we met.

The first ice was in the garden. The trees stood bare beneath a pale blue sunny sky, and I was standing at the window, looking out at the hoar-frost, when my grandmother told me that it was unlikely that I should ever see our neighbour again.

I stood where I was, without turning round, gazing out of the window at the motionless ghostly trees, and the few birds in forlorn unease.

'Is she dead, then?' I enquired.

'I am told,' was the reply, 'that her friends have been compelled to have her put away. No doubt, it was the proper course. It should have been done earlier. But it is not our affair, you are to understand. And, poor creature, perhaps death would have been a happier, a more merciful release. She was sadly afflicted.'

I said nothing, and continued to stare out of the window.

But I know now that the news, in spite of a vague sorrow, greatly relieved me. I should be at ease in the garden again, came the thought – no longer fear to look ridiculous and grow hot when our neighbour was mentioned, or be saddled with her company beside the stream.

Selina's Parable*

On the wide wooden staircase that led up to her big sea-windy bedroom in the old house in which Selina was staying was a low, square window. For Selina, every window in her small private world had a charm, an incantation all its own. Was it not an egress for her eye to a scene of some beauty, or life, or of forbiddingness; was it not the way of light; either her own outward, or the world's inward? This small window in particular beguiled Selina, because, kneeling there (it was of too narrow a frame to permit a protracted standing or stooping) she looked out of it, and down from it, upon a farmyard. Selina knew farmyards that more seductively soothed her aesthetic sense – farmyards of richer ricks, of solider outbuildings, of a deeper peace. But since this farmyard, despite its litter and bareness, was busy with life – dog in kennel, chicken, duck, goose, gander and goslings, doves, a few wild birds, some even of the sea, an occasional horse and man – contemplation of it solaced her small mind, keeping it gently busy, and yet in a state narrowly bordering on trance.

Selina was dark and narrow-shouldered, with eyes of so intense a brown that, when the spirit that lurked behind them was absorbed in what they gazed on, they were like two small black pools of water. And one long, warm, languorous afternoon she found herself kneeling once again at the low staircase window even more densely engrossed than usual. Towards

* As printed in *The Nap and Other Stories* (1936). First published in *New Statesman*, 1 November 1919.

the bottom of the farmyard, perhaps twenty paces distant, stood a low stone barn or little granary, its square door opening blackly into the sunlight upon a flight of, maybe, ten rough and weed-tousled stone steps. Beyond its roof stretched the green dreaming steeps of the valley. From outside this door, it was the farmer's wont, morning and evening, to feed his winged stock.

On this particular afternoon the hour was but hard on four. Something unusual was afoot. Selina watched the farmer ponderously traverse the yard, and, in his usual stout Alexander-Selkirkian fashion, ascend into the granary. Surely not thus unseasonably to dispense the good grain, but for some purpose or purposes unknown – unknown at least to Selina.

Neverthless, all his chickens, such is faith, instinct, habit, and stupidity, had followed close upon his heels, and were now sleekly and expectantly clustered in mute concourse upon the steps and on the adjacent yardstones, precisely like an assemblage of humanity patiently waiting to be admitted into the pit of a theatre or into the nave of a church.

There was a dramatic pause. The sun shone on. The blue seemed to deepen. A few late-comers flurried in from the by-ways and hedges. The rest of the congregation was steadfast – with just a feverish effort apparent here and there of some one jealous individual to better her position at the expense of those more favourably situated. Then, after a prolonged interval, the square door was reopened, and the farmer emerged, empty-handed and apparently unconscious of the expectant assemblage awaiting him. Without so much as a glance of compassion or even of heed, he trod heavily down the stone steps through the assembled hens, careless to all appearance whether his swinging, cumbrous boots trod the more eager underfoot, and – wonder of wonders! – he left the door behind him, and at its very fullest gape.

Selina sighed: the happiest of sighs, that of expectation and forbidden delight. It was as if the commissionaire of the theatre or the gaitered archdeacon of the cathedral had simply betrayed his edifice, and its treasures, to the mob. God bless me, thought Selina, they'll go in and help themselves!

Only one moiety of this brilliant speculation of Selina's was to be proved justified. Led by a remarkably neat jimp blue-black Leghorn hen, deliciously feminine and adventurous, churchwarden's helpmeet if ever there was one, the whole feathered mob, as if under the gesture of a magician, with an instantaneous and soundless ingurgitation of appetite and desire, swept upward and in. Threescore hens at least were there, the appropriate leaven of cocks, two couple of ducks, three doves, a few predatory wildings, while the little cluster of geese on the outskirts outstretched their serpentine necks and hissed.

Selina, transfixed there in a felicity bordering upon rapture, watched. Like Athene above the plains of Troy, she gathered in her slim shoulders as if to swoop. What was happening within, beyond that strange square of velvety afternoon darkness? The rapine, the orgy, the indiscriminate gorge? Alas, no! Whether or not the marauders had discerned or even so much as descried the fatted bags of oats and maize and wheat that were undoubtedly shelved within that punctual hostel, Selina could not guess. This only was perfectly plain – that the concourse was now dejectedly emerging, dispirited and unfed. One by one, in ruffled groups, peevish, crestfallen, damped, the feathered congregation by ones and twos and threes reappeared, trod, or hopped, or fluttered down the shallow familiar disenchanted steps, the ducks, too, dumb and ignoble, the cocks simulating indifference or contempt, the wildings – as wild as ever.

When Selina, still agape, came to herself, the farmyard was much as usual – dispersed clusters of huffed, short-memoried and dusting fowl, a pacing cock, the dog, head on paws, still asleep, doves in comparatively dispassionate courtship on the roof, duck and drake guzzling in that unfathomable morass of iniquity known as the duck pond.

'Came to herself' – for Selina's was a type of mind that cannot but follow things up (as far as ever she could go); it was compelled, that is, by sheer natural impulse, to spin queer little stories out of the actual, and even, alas, to moralize.

'Why,' she mused, 'poor hen-brained things, they came to be fed. Always when the farmer opened the door and went in, grain, the bread of life, came out. Always. And he, surely, being a more or less generous creature, capable at *any* moment of magnanimity, and not, gracious goodness, a cold and bloated cynic, since one must at least *think* the best of what is and may be, why, of course, they simply could not *but* go in, as they did, and, to say the least of it, just see for themselves. You surely can't impiously raid the *given*. Morning, and possibly afternoon, the poor creatures as best their natural powers allow, reward the farmer for his benefactions. A little indirectly, perhaps, but surely you wouldn't expect the poor things to reason that he gives – well, what he does give – solely for gain, that his bounty is sheer profiteering, that it is their eggs, their poor carcases, or their positive offspring he is after, for his own – well, to them – immeasurably barbarous purposes.

'Suppose with avid beak (a little magnified, of course) they surge in one day and carry off his last squalling baby – that puffy little Samuel – from his cradle. Suppose they do. It will serve him right: it will be tit for tat. They had believed in him – that was the point. Now they won't: they *can't* – at least not for ten minutes. Though they are always hungry. Yes, they had climbed up, lured on by sheer indifference masquerading as generosity, in the heat of the day, too, and that peculiarly slim and jimp black Leghorn pullet in particular, only to discover – nothing, just cool inner darkness and odoriferous vacancy. Even a horny, fussy old verger would at least have shooed them out again, have told them that they had made a mistake, that there wasn't any extra thing "on" of that kind – no *confirmation* service, you know.' And Selina fleetingly smiled, narrow cheek, delicate lip, and black abstracted eye.

'How very like poor human beings,' she went on, pursuing her small privy thoughts, slipping down, as she did so, from kneeling to sitting, and automatically readjusting the tortoiseshell comb in her dark hair; 'punctually they go to church (some of them), not attempting to guess, or not capable, I suppose, of really *knowing*, what for; but confident that the bishop or rector or somebody will be in the pulpit and that they will be fed.

'And then comes a day...Now what *is* the difference,' mused Selina, contemplatively narrowing her inward gaze, 'what is the real difference between Farmer Trepolpen and God, and between that fussy, forward – still she was adventurous – little Leghorn, who must lay the most delicious little cream-coloured eggs, and Me? Surely no: He cannot want me (He cannot expect me to go to church and praise and pray) simply for the sake of my wretched little hard-boiled bits of goodness. Does He really only think of us twice in twenty-four hours, like the tides, like matins and evensong, as – well, as I think of Him?

'And if in between-whiles He did think of me or I of Him, isn't there any inexhaustible store of heavenly manna which my trussed-up soul – and I suppose the others – though I wouldn't mind the doves and the sea-gull or ... Oh dear, oh dear!'

Selina stared softly on, down the sunlit and intensely still staircase into the shadow. 'Of course,' began again that still small voice within in faraway tones, 'it's not quite like that, it's *not* on all fours. It's a bigger dream than that. If they, silly cackling creatures, mercifully don't know what that carnivorous old egg-hunter is after, I'm pretty certain he doesn't know eventually himself. Merely keeping them alive: though that's something. But not the other. Anyhow, suppose, just suppose *not*. Suppose there's someone, a kind of unseen circumspectious spirit, kneeling crunched-up there at a little square staircase window. Oh, ever so happy and dreamy and sorrowful and alone, and not in the least muddle-minded – omniscient, I *suppose*, though that, of course, must be omni – omni-sensitive, too – just staring down in sheer joy and *interest* at the farmer, and the sunshine, and the valley, and the yard, and the hens, and that delicious filthy duck-pond and – and the Atlantic, absolutely all *Its*, and...What wouldn't I...?'

But at that moment, and only just in time to dissever the philosophical net in which poor Selina's soul was definitely strangling, a whiff of hot baked 'splitters' wafted itself up the staircase, and Selina with an exclamatory 'Lawks!' and a thin flying hand flung up once more to her tortoiseshell comb, remembered her tea.

Seaton's Aunt*

I had heard rumours of Seaton's aunt long before I actually encountered her. Seaton, in the hush of confidence, or at any little show of toleration on our part, would remark, 'My aunt', or 'My old aunt, you know', as if his relative might be a kind of cement to an *entente cordiale*.

He had an unusual quantity of pocket-money; or, at any rate, it was bestowed on him in unusually large amounts; and he spent it freely, though none of us would have described him as an 'awfully generous chap'. 'Hullo, Seaton,' we would say, 'the old Begum?' At the beginning of term, too, he used to bring back surprising and exotic dainties in a box with a trick padlock that accompanied him from his first appearance at Gummidge's in a billycock hat to the rather abrupt conclusion of his schooldays.

From a boy's point of view he looked distastefully foreign with his yellowish skin, slow chocolate-coloured eyes, and lean weak figure. Merely for his looks he was treated by most of us true-blue Englishmen with condescension, hostility, or contempt. We used to call him 'Pongo', but without any much better excuse for the nickname than his skin. He was, that is, in one sense of the term what he assuredly was not in the other sense, a sport.

Seaton and I, as I may say, were never in any sense intimate at school; our orbits only intersected in class. I kept deliberately aloof from him. I felt vaguely he was a sneak, and remained quite unmollified by advances on his side, which, in a boy's barbarous fashion, unless it suited me to be magnanimous, I haughtily ignored.

We were both of us quick-footed, and at Prisoner's Base used occasionally to hide together. And so I best remember Seaton – his narrow watchful face in the dusk of a summer evening; his peculiar crouch, and his inarticulate whisperings and mumblings. Otherwise he played all games slackly and limply; used to stand and feed at his locker with a crony or two until his 'tuck' gave out; or waste his money on some outlandish fancy or other. He bought, for instance, a silver bangle, which he wore above his left elbow, until some of the fellows showed their masterly contempt of the practice by dropping it nearly red-hot down his neck.

---

* As printed in BS (1942). First published in *London Mercury*, April 1922.

It needed, therefore, a rather peculiar taste, and a rather rare kind of schoolboy courage and indifference to criticism, to be much associated with him. And I had neither the taste nor, probably, the courage. None the less, he did make advances, and on one memorable occasion went to the length of bestowing on me a whole pot of some outlandish mulberry-coloured jelly that had been duplicated in his term's supplies. In the exuberance of my gratitude I promised to spend the next half-term holiday with him at his aunt's house.

I had clean forgotten my promise when, two or three days before the holiday, he came up and triumphantly reminded me of it.

'Well, to tell you the honest truth, Seaton, old chap —' I began graciously: but he cut me short.

'My aunt expects you,' he said; 'she is very glad you are coming. She's sure to be quite decent to *you*, Withers.'

I looked at him in sheer astonishment; the emphasis was so uncalled for. It seemed to suggest an aunt not hitherto hinted at, and a friendly feeling on Seaton's side that was far more disconcerting than welcome.

We reached his aunt's house partly by train, partly by a lift in an empty farm-cart, and partly by walking. It was a whole-day holiday, and we were to sleep the night; he lent me extraordinary night-gear, I remember. The village street was unusually wide, and was fed from a green by two converging roads, with an inn, and a high green sign at the corner. About a hundred yards down the street was a chemist's shop – a Mr Tanner's. We descended the two steps into his dusky and odorous interior to buy, I remember, some rat poison. A little beyond the chemist's was the forge. You then walked along a very narrow path, under a fairly high wall, nodding here and there with weeds and tufts of grass, and so came to the iron garden-gates, and saw the high flat house behind its huge sycamore. A coach-house stood on the left of the house, and on the right a gate led into a kind of rambling orchard. The lawn lay away over to the left again, and at the bottom (for the whole garden sloped gently to a sluggish and rushy pond-like stream) was a meadow.

We arrived at noon, and entered the gates out of the hot dust beneath the glitter of the dark-curtained windows. Seaton led me at once through the little garden-gate to show me his tadpole pond, swarming with what (being myself not in the least interested in low life) seemed to me the most horrible creatures – of all shapes, consistencies, and sizes, but with which Seaton was obviously on the most intimate of terms. I can see his absorbed face now as, squatting on his heels he fished the slimy things out in his sallow palms. Wearying at last of these pets, we loitered about awhile in an aimless fashion. Seaton seemed to be listening, or at any rate waiting, for something to happen or for someone to come. But nothing did happen and no one came.

That was just like Seaton. Anyhow, the first view I got of his aunt was when, at the summons of a distant gong, we turned from the garden, very hungry and thirsty, to go in to luncheon. We were approaching the house, when Seaton suddenly came to a standstill. Indeed, I have always had the impression that he plucked at my sleeve. Something, at least, seemed to catch me back, as it were, as he cried, 'Look out, there she is!'

She was standing at an upper window which opened wide on a hinge, and at first sight she looked an excessively tall and overwhelming figure. This, however, was mainly because the window reached all but to the floor of her bedroom. She was in reality rather an undersized woman, in spite of her long face and big head. She must have stood, I think, unusually still, with eyes fixed on us, though this impression may be due to Seaton's sudden warning and to my consciousness of the cautious and subdued air that had fallen on him at sight of her. I know that without the least reason in the world I felt a kind of guiltiness, as if I had been 'caught'. There was a silvery star pattern sprinkled on her black silk dress, and even from the ground I could see the immense coils of her hair and the rings on her left hand which was held fingering the small jet buttons of her bodice. She watched our united advance without stirring, until, imperceptibly, her eyes raised and lost themselves in the distance, so that it was out of an assumed reverie that she appeared suddenly to awaken to our presence beneath her when we drew close to the house.

'So this is your friend, Mr Smithers, I suppose?' she said, bobbing to me.

'Withers, aunt,' said Seaton.

'It's much the same,' she said, with eyes fixed on me. 'Come in, Mr Withers, and bring him along with you.'

She continued to gaze at me – at least, I think she did so. I know that the fixity of her scrutiny and her ironical 'Mr' made me feel peculiarly uncomfortable. None the less she was extremely kind and attentive to me, though, no doubt, her kindness and attention showed up more vividly against her complete neglect of Seaton. Only one remark that I have any recollection of she made to him: 'When I look on my nephew, Mr Smithers, I realize that dust we are, and dust shall become. You are hot, dirty, and incorrigible, Arthur.'

She sat at the head of the table, Seaton at the foot, and I, before a wide waste of damask tablecloth, between them. It was an old and rather close dining-room, with windows thrown wide to the green garden and a wonderful cascade of fading roses. Miss Seaton's great chair faced this window, so that its rose-reflected light shone full on her yellowish face, and on just such chocolate eyes as my schoolfellow's, except that hers were more than half-covered by unusually long and heavy lids.

There she sat, steadily eating, with those sluggish eyes fixed for the most part on my face; above them stood the deep-lined fork between her eyebrows; and above that the wide expanse of a remarkable brow beneath its strange steep bank of hair. The lunch was copious, and consisted, I remember, of all such dishes as are generally considered too rich and too good for the schoolboy digestion – lobster mayonnaise, cold game sausages, an immense veal and ham pie farced with eggs, truffles, and numberless delicious flavours; besides kickshaws, creams and sweetmeats. We even had a wine, a half-glass of old darkish sherry each.

Miss Seaton enjoyed and indulged an enormous appetite. Her example and a natural schoolboy voracity soon overcame my nervousness of her, even to the extent of allowing me to enjoy to the best of my bent so rare a spread. Seaton was singularly modest; the greater part of his meal consisted of almonds and raisins, which he nibbled surreptitiously and as if he found difficulty in swallowing them.

I don't mean that Miss Seaton 'conversed' with me. She merely scattered trenchant remarks and now and then twinkled a baited question over my head. But her face was like a dense and involved accompaniment to her talk. She presently dropped the 'Mr', to my intense relief, and called me now Withers, or Wither, now Smithers, and even once towards the close of the meal distinctly Johnson, though how on earth my name suggested it, or whose face mine had reanimated in memory, I cannot conceive.

'And is Arthur a good boy at school, Mr Wither?' was one of her many questions. 'Does he please his masters? Is he first in his class? What does the reverend Dr Gummidge think of him, eh?'

I knew she was jeering at him, but her face was adamant against the least flicker of sarcasm or facetiousness. I gazed fixedly at a blushing crescent of lobster.

'I think you're eighth, aren't you, Seaton?'

Seaton moved his small pupils towards his aunt. But she continued to gaze with a kind of concentrated detachment at me.

'Arthur will never make a brilliant scholar, I fear,' she said, lifting a dexterously burdened fork to her wide mouth...

After luncheon she preceded me up to my bedroom. It was a jolly little bedroom, with a brass fender and rugs and a polished floor, on which it was possible, I afterwards found, to play 'snow-shoes'. Over the washstand was a little black-framed water-colour drawing, depicting a large eye with an extremely fishlike intensity in the spark of light on the dark pupil; and in 'illuminated' lettering beneath was printed very minutely, 'Thou God Seest ME', followed by a long looped monogram, 'S.S.', in the corner. The other pictures were all of the sea; brigs on blue water; a schooner overtopping chalk cliffs; a rocky island of prodigious steepness, with two tiny sailors dragging a monstrous boat up a shelf of beach.

'This is the room, Withers, my poor dear brother William died in when a boy. Admire the view!'

I looked out of the window across the tree-tops. It was a day hot with sunshine over the green fields, and the cattle were standing swishing their tails in the shallow water. But the view at the moment was no doubt made more vividly impressive by the apprehension that she would presently enquire after my luggage, and I had brought not even a toothbrush. I need have had no fear. Hers was not that highly civilized type of mind that is stuffed with sharp, material details. Nor could her ample presence be described as in the least motherly.

'I would never consent to question a schoolfellow behind my nephew's back,' she said, standing in the middle of the room 'but tell me, Smithers, why is Arthur so unpopular? You, I understand, are his only close friend.' She stood in a dazzle of sun, and out of it her eyes regarded me with such leaden penetration beneath their thick lids that I doubt if my face concealed the least thought from her. 'But there, there,' she added very suavely, stooping her head a little, 'don't trouble to answer me. I never extort an answer. Boys are queer fish. Brains might perhaps have suggested his washing his hands before luncheon; but – not my choice, Smithers. God forbid! And now, perhaps, you would like to go into the garden again. I cannot actually see from here, but I should not be surprised if Arthur is now skulking behind that hedge.'

He was. I saw his head come out and take a rapid glance at the windows.

'Join him, Mr Smithers; we shall meet again, I hope, at the tea-table. The afternoon I spend in retirement.'

Whether or not, Seaton and I had not been long engaged with the aid of two green switches in riding round and round a lumbering old grey horse we found in the meadow, before a rather bunched-up figure appeared, walking along the field-path on the other side of the water, with a magenta parasol studiously lowered in our direction throughout her slow progress, as if that were the magnetic needle and we the fixed Pole. Seaton at once lost all nerve and interest. At the next lurch of the old mare's heels he toppled over into the grass, and I slid off the sleek broad back to join him where he stood, rubbing his shoulder and sourly watching the rather pompous figure till it was out of sight.

'Was that your aunt, Seaton?' I enquired; but not till then.

He nodded.

'Why didn't she take any notice of us, then?'

'She never does.'

'Why not?'

'Oh, she knows all right, without; that's the dam awful part of it.' Seaton was one of the very few fellows at Gummidge's who had the ostentation to use bad language. He had suffered for it too. But it wasn't, I think, bravado. I believe he really felt certain things more intensely than most of the other fellows, and they were generally things that fortunate and average people do not feel at all – the peculiar quality, for instance, of the British schoolboy's imagination.

'I tell you, Withers,' he went on moodily, slinking across the meadow with his hands covered up in his pockets, 'she sees everything. And what she doesn't see she knows without.'

'But how?' I said, not because I was much interested, but because the afternoon was so hot and tiresome and purposeless, and it seemed more of a bore to remain silent. Seaton turned gloomily and spoke in a very low voice.

'Don't appear to be talking of her, if you wouldn't mind. It's – because she's in league with the Devil.' He nodded his head and stooped to pick up a round flat pebble. 'I tell you,' he said, still stooping, 'you fellows don't realize what it is. I know I'm a bit close and all that. But so would you be if you had that old hag listening to every thought you think.'

I looked at him, then turned and surveyed one by one the windows of the house.

'Where's your *pater*?' I said awkwardly.

'Dead, ages and ages ago, and my mother too. She's not my aunt even by rights.'

'What is she, then?'

'I mean she's not my mother's sister, because my grandmother married twice; and she's one of the first lot. I don't know what you call her, but anyhow she's not my real aunt.'

'She gives you plenty of pocket-money.'

Seaton looked steadfastly at me out of his flat eyes. 'She can't give me what's mine. When I come of age half of the whole lot will be mine; and what's more' – he turned his back on the house – 'I'll make her hand over every blessed shilling of it.'

I put my hands in my pockets and stared at Seaton; 'Is it much?'

He nodded.

'Who told you?' He got suddenly very angry, a darkish red came into his cheeks, his eyes glistened, but he made no answer, and we loitered listlessly about the garden until it was time for tea ...

Seaton's aunt was wearing an extraordinary kind of lace jacket when we sidled sheepishly into the drawing-room together. She greeted me with a heavy and protracted smile, and bade me bring a chair close to the little table.

'I hope Arthur has made you feel at home,' she said as she handed me my cup in her crooked hand. 'He don't talk much to me; but then I'm an old woman. You must come again, Wither, and draw him out of his shell. You old snail!' She wagged her head at Seaton, who sat munching cake and watching her intently.

'And we must correspond, perhaps.' She nearly shut her eyes at me. 'You must write and tell me everything behind the creature's back.' I confess I found her rather disquieting company. The evening drew on. Lamps were brought in by a man with a nondescript face and very quiet footsteps. Seaton was told to bring out the chess-men. And we played a game, she and I, with her big chin thrust over the board at every move as she gloated over the pieces and occasionally croaked 'Check!' – after which she would sit back inscrutably staring at me. But the game was never finished. She simply hemmed me in with a gathering cloud of pieces that held me impotent, and yet one and all refused to administer to my poor flustered old king a merciful *coup de grâce*.

'There,' she said, as the clock struck ten – 'a drawn game, Withers. We are very evenly matched. A very creditable defence, Withers. You know your room. There's supper on a tray in the dining-room. Don't let the creature over-eat himself. The gong will sound three-quarters of an hour *before* a punctual breakfast.' She held out her cheek to Seaton, and he kissed it with obvious perfunctoriness. With me she shook hands.

'An excellent game,' she said cordially, 'but my memory is poor, and' – she swept the pieces helter-skelter into the box – 'the result will never be known.' She raised her great head far back. 'Eh?'

It was a kind of challenge, and I could only murmur: 'Oh I was absolutely in a hole, you know!' when she burst out laughing and waved us both out of the room.

Seaton and I stood and ate our supper, with one candlestick to light us, in a corner of the dining-room. 'Well, and how would you like it?' he said very softly, after cautiously poking his head round the doorway.

'Like what?'

'Being spied on – every blessed thing you do and think?'

'I shouldn't like it at all,' I said, 'if she does.'

'And yet you let her smash you up at chess!'

'I didn't let her!' I said indignantly.

'Well, you funked it, then.'

'And I didn't funk it either,' I said; 'she's so jolly clever with her knights.' Seaton stared at the candle. 'Knights,' he said slowly. 'You wait, that's all.' And we went upstairs to bed.

I had not been long in bed, I think, when I was cautiously awakened by a touch on my shoulder. And there was Seaton's face in the candlelight – and his eyes looking into mine.

'What's up?' I said, lurching on to my elbow.

'*Ssh!* Don't scurry,' he whispered. 'She'll hear. I'm sorry for waking you, but I didn't think you'd be asleep so soon.'

'Why, what's the time, then?' Seaton wore, what was then rather unusual, a night-suit, and he hauled his big silver watch out of the pocket in his jacket.

'It's a quarter to twelve. I never get to sleep before twelve – not here.'

'What do you do, then?'

'Oh, I read: and listen.'

'Listen?'

Seaton stared into his candle-flame as if he were listening even then. 'You can't guess what it is. All you read in ghost stories, that's all rot. You can't see much, Withers, but you know all the same.'

'Know what?'

'Why, that they're there.'

'Who's there?' I asked fretfully, glancing at the door.

'Why, in the house. It swarms with 'em. Just you stand still and listen outside my bedroom door in the middle of the night. I have, dozens of times; they're all over the place.'

'Look here, Seaton,' I said, 'you asked me to come here, and I didn't mind chucking up a leave just to oblige you and because I'd promised; but don't get talking a lot of rot, that's all, or you'll know the difference when we get back.'

'Don't fret,' he said coldly, turning away. 'I shan't be at school long. And what's more, you're here now, and there isn't anybody else to talk to. I'll chance the other.'

'Look here, Seaton,' I said, 'you may think you're going to scare me with a lot of stuff about voices and all that. But I'll just thank you to clear out; and you may please yourself about pottering about all night.'

He made no answer; he was standing by the dressing-table looking across his candle into the looking-glass; he turned and stared slowly round the walls.

'Even this room's nothing more than a coffin. I suppose she told you – 'It's all exactly the same as when my brother William died' – trust her for that! And good luck to him, say I. Look at that.' He raised his candle close to the little water-colour I have mentioned. 'There's hundreds of eyes like that in this house; and even if God does see you, He takes precious good care you don't see Him. And it's just the same with them. I tell you what, Withers, I'm getting sick of all this. I shan't stand it much longer.'

The house was silent within and without, and even in the yellowish radiance of the candle a faint silver showed through the open window on my blind. I slipped off the bedclothes, wide awake, and sat irresolute on the bedside.

'I know you're only guying me,' I said angrily, 'but why is the house full of – what you say? Why do you hear – what you *do* hear? Tell me that, you silly fool!'

Seaton sat down on a chair and rested his candlestick on his knee. He blinked at me calmly. 'She brings them,' he said, with lifted eyebrows.

'Who? Your aunt?'

He nodded.

'How?'

'I told you,' he answered pettishly. 'She's in league. You don't know. She as good as killed my mother; I know that. But it's not only her by a long chalk. She just sucks you dry. I know. And that's what she'll do for me; because I'm like her – like my mother, I mean. She simply hates to see me alive. I wouldn't be like that old she-wolf for a million pounds. And so' – he broke off, with a comprehensive wave of his candlestick – 'they're always here. Ah, my boy, wait till she's dead! She'll hear something then, I can tell you. It's all very well now, but wait till then! I wouldn't be in her shoes when she has to clear out – for something. Don't you go and believe I care for ghosts, or whatever you like to call them. We're all in the same box. We're all under her thumb.'

He was looking almost nonchalantly at the ceiling at the moment, when I saw his face change, saw his eyes suddenly drop like shot birds and fix themselves on the cranny of the door he had left just ajar. Even from where I sat I could see his cheek change colour; it went greenish. He crouched without stirring, like an animal. And I, scarcely daring to breathe, sat with creeping skin, sourly watching him. His hands relaxed, and he gave a kind of sigh.

'Was *that* one?' I whispered, with a timid show of jauntiness. He looked round, opened his mouth, and nodded. 'What?' I said. He jerked his thumb with meaningful eyes, and I knew that he meant that his aunt had been there listening at our door cranny.

'Look here, Seaton,' I said once more, wriggling to my feet. 'You may think I'm a jolly noodle; just as you please. But your aunt has been civil to me and all that, and I don't believe a word you say about her, that's all, and never did. Every fellow's a bit off his pluck at night, and you may think it a fine sport to try your rubbish on me. I heard your aunt come upstairs before I fell asleep. And I'll bet you a level tanner she's in bed now. What's more, you can keep your blessed ghosts to yourself. It's a guilty conscience, I should think.'

Seaton looked at me intently, without answering for a moment. 'I'm not a liar, Withers; but I'm not going to quarrel either. You're the only chap I care a button for; or, at any rate, you're the only chap that's ever come here; and it's something to tell a fellow what you feel. I don't care a fig for fifty thousand ghosts, although I swear on my solemn oath that I know they're here. But she' – he turned deliberately – 'you laid a tanner she's in bed, Withers; well, I know different. She's never in bed much of the night, and I'll prove it, too, just to show you I'm not such a nolly as you think I am. Come on!'

'Come on where?'

'Why, to see.'

I hesitated. He opened a large cupboard and took out a small dark dressing-gown and a kind of shawl-jacket. He threw the jacket on the bed and put on the gown. His dusky face was colourless, and I could see by the way he fumbled at the sleeves he was shivering. But it was no good showing the white feather now. So I threw the tasselled shawl over my shoulders and, leaving our candle brightly burning on the chair, we went out together and stood in the corridor.

'Now then, listen!' Seaton whispered.

We stood leaning over the staircase. It was like leaning over a well, so still and chill the air was all around us. But presently, as I suppose happens in most old houses, began to echo and answer in my ears a medley of infinite small stirrings and whisperings. Now out of the distance an old timber would relax its fibres, or a scurry die away behind the perishing wainscot. But amid and behind such sounds as these I seemed to begin to be conscious, as it were, of the lightest of footfalls, sounds as faint as the vanishing remembrance of voices in a dream. Seaton was all in obscurity except his face; out of that his eyes gleamed darkly, watching me.

'You'd hear, too, in time, my fine soldier,' he muttered. 'Come on!'

He descended the stairs, slipping his lean fingers lightly along the balusters. He turned to the right at the loop, and I followed him barefooted along a thickly carpeted corridor. At the end stood a door ajar. And from here we very stealthily and in complete blackness ascended five narrow stairs. Seaton, with immense caution, slowly pushed open a door, and we stood together, looking into a great pool of duskiness, out of which, lit by the feeble clearness of a night-light, rose a vast bed. A heap of clothes lay on the floor; beside them two slippers dozed, with noses each to each, a foot or two apart. Somewhere a little clock ticked huskily. There was a close smell; lavender and eau de Cologne, mingled with the fragrance of ancient sachets, soap, and drugs. Yet it was a scent even more peculiarly compounded than that.

And the bed! I stared warily in; it was mounded gigantically, and it was empty.

Seaton turned a vague pale face, all shadows: 'What did I say?' he muttered. 'Who's – who's the fool now, I say? How are we going to get back without meeting her, I say? Answer me that! Oh, I wish to God you hadn't come here, Withers.'

He stood audibly shivering in his skimpy gown, and could hardly speak for his teeth chattering. And very distinctly, in the hush that followed his whisper, I heard approaching a faint unhurried voluminous rustle. Seaton clutched my arm, dragged me to the right across the room to a large cup-board, and drew the door close to on us. And, presently, as with bursting lungs I peeped out into the long, low, curtained bedroom, waddled in that wonderful great head and body. I can see her now, all patched and lined with shadow, her tied-up hair (she must have had enormous quantities of it for so old a woman), her heavy lids above those flat, slow, vigilant eyes. She just passed across my ken in the vague dusk; but the bed was out of sight.

We waited on and on, listening to the clock's muffled ticking. Not the ghost of a sound rose up from the great bed. Either she lay archly listening or slept a sleep serener than an infant's. And when, it seemed, we had been hours in hiding and were cramped, chilled, and half-suffocated, we crept out on all fours, with terror knocking at our ribs, and so down the five narrow stairs and back to the little candle-lit blue-and-gold bedroom.

Once there, Seaton gave in. He sat livid on a chair with closed eyes.

'Here,' I said, shaking his arm, 'I'm going to bed; I've had enough of this foolery; I'm going to bed.' His lips quivered, but he made no answer. I poured out some water into my basin and, with that cold pictured azure eye fixed on us, be-spattered Seaton's sallow face and forehead and dabbled his hair. He presently sighed and opened fish-like eyes.

'Come on!' I said, 'Don't get shamming, there's a good chap. Get on my back, if you like, and I'll carry you into your bedroom.'

He waved me away and stood up. So, with my candle in one hand, I took him under the arm and walked him along according to his direction down the corridor. His was a much dingier room than mine, and littered with boxes, paper, cages, and clothes. I huddled him into bed and turned to go. And suddenly, I can hardly explain it now, a kind of cold and deadly terror swept over me. I almost ran out of the room, with eyes fixed rigidly in front of me, blew out my candle, and buried my head under the bedclothes.

When I awoke, roused not by a gong, but by a long-continued tapping at my door, sunlight was raying in on cornice and bedpost, and birds were singing in the garden. I got up, ashamed of the night's folly, dressed quickly, and went downstairs. The breakfast room was sweet with flowers and fruit and honey. Seaton's aunt was standing in the garden beside the open french window, feeding a great flutter of birds. I watched her for a moment, unseen. Her face was set in a deep reverie beneath the shadow of a big loose sun-hat. It was deeply lined, crooked, and, in a way I can't describe, fixedly vacant and strange. I coughed politely, and she turned with a prodigious smiling grimace to ask how I had slept. And in that mysterious fashion by which we learn each other's secret thoughts without a syllable said, I knew that she had followed every word and movement of the night before, and was triumphing over my affected innocence and ridiculing my friendly and too easy advances.

We returned to school, Seaton and I, lavishly laden, and by rail all the way. I made no reference to the obscure talk we had had, and resolutely refused to meet his eyes or to take up the hints he let fall. I was relieved – and yet I was sorry – to be going back, and strode on as fast as I could from the station, with Seaton almost trotting at my heels. But he insisted on buying more fruit and sweets – my share of which I accepted with a very bad grace. It was uncomfortably like a bribe; and, after all, I had no quarrel with his rum old aunt, and hadn't really believed half the stuff he had told me.

I saw as little of him as I could after that. He never referred to our visit or resumed his confidences, though in class I would sometimes catch his eye fixed on mine, full of a mute understanding, which I easily affected not to understand. He left Gummidge's, as I have said, rather abruptly, though I never heard of anything to his discredit. And I did not see him or have any news of him again till by chance we met one summer afternoon in the Strand.

He was dressed rather oddly in a coat too large for him and a bright silky tie. But we instantly recognized one another under the awning of a cheap jeweller's shop. He immediately attached himself to me and dragged me off, not too cheerfully, to lunch with him at an Italian restaurant nearby. He chattered about our old school, which he remembered only with dislike and disgust; told me cold-bloodedly of the disastrous fate of one or two of the older fellows who had been among his chief tormentors; insisted on an expensive wine and the whole gamut of the foreign menu; and finally informed me, with a good deal of niggling, that he had come up to town to buy an engagement-ring.

And of course: 'How is your aunt?' I enquired at last.

He seemed to have been awaiting the question. It fell like a stone into a deep pool, so many expressions flitted across his long, sad, sallow, un-English face.

'She's aged a good deal,' he said softly, and broke off.

'She's been very decent,' he continued presently after, and paused again. 'In a way.' He eyed me fleetingly. 'I dare say you heard that – she – that is, that we – had lost a good deal of money.'

'No,' I said.

'Oh, yes!' said Seaton, and paused again.

And somehow, poor fellow, I knew in the clink and clatter of glass and voices that he had lied to me; that he did not possess, and never had possessed, a penny beyond what his aunt had squandered on his too ample allowance of pocket-money.

'And the ghosts?' I enquired quizzically.

He grew instantly solemn, and, though it may have been my fancy, slightly yellowed. But 'You are making game of me, Withers,' was all he said.

He asked for my address, and I rather reluctantly gave him my card.

'Look here, Withers,' he said, as we stood together in the sunlight on the kerb, saying good-bye, 'here I am, and – and it's all very well. I'm not perhaps as fanciful as I was. But you are practically the only friend I have on earth – except Alice . . . And there – to make a clean breast of it, I'm not sure that my aunt cares much about my getting married. She doesn't say so, of course. You know her well enough for that.' He looked sidelong at the rattling gaudy traffic.

'What I was going to say is this: Would you mind coming down? You needn't stay the night unless you please, though, of course, you know you would be awfully welcome. But I should like you to meet my – to meet Alice; and then, perhaps, you might tell me your honest opinion of – of the other too.'

I vaguely demurred. He pressed me. And we parted with a half promise that I would come. He waved his ball-topped cane at me and ran off in his long jacket after a bus.

A letter arrived soon after, in his small weak handwriting, giving me full particulars regarding route and trains. And without the least curiosity, even perhaps with some little annoyance that chance should have thrown us together again, I accepted his invitation and arrived one hazy midday at his out-of-the-way station to find him sitting on a low seat under a clump of 'double' hollyhocks, awaiting me.

He looked preoccupied and singularly listless; but seemed, none the less, to be pleased to see me.

We walked up the village street, past the little dingy apothecary's and the empty forge, and, as on my first visit, skirted the house together, and, instead of entering by the front door, made our way down the green path into the garden at the back. A pale haze of cloud muffled the sun; the garden lay in a grey shimmer – its old trees, its snap-dragoned faintly glittering walls. But now there was an air of slovenliness where before all had been neat and methodical. In a patch of shallowly dug soil stood a worn-down spade leaning against a tree. There was an old decayed wheelbarrow. The roses had run to leaf and briar; the fruit-trees were unpruned. The goddess of neglect had made it her secret resort.

'You ain't much of a gardener, Seaton,' I said at last, with a sigh of relief.

'I think, do you know, I like it best like this,' said Seaton. 'We haven't any man now, of course. Can't afford it.' He stood staring at his little dark oblong of freshly turned earth. 'And it always seems to me,' he went on ruminatingly, 'that, after all, we are all nothing better than interlopers on the earth, disfiguring and staining wherever we go. It may sound shocking blasphemy to say so; but then it's different here, you see. We are further away.'

'To tell you the truth, Seaton, I *don't* quite see,' I said; 'but it isn't a new philosophy, is it? Anyhow, it's a precious beastly one.'

'It's only what I think,' he replied, with all his odd old stubborn meekness. 'And one thinks as one *is*.'

We wandered on together, talking little, and still with that expression of uneasy vigilance on Seaton's face. He pulled out his watch as we stood gazing idly over the green meadows and the dark motionless bulrushes.

'I think, perhaps, it's nearly time for lunch,' he said. 'Would you like to come in?'

We turned and walked slowly towards the house, across whose windows I confess my own eyes, too, went restlessly meandering in search of its rather disconcerting inmate. There was a pathetic look of bedraggledness, of want of means and care, rust and overgrowth and faded paint. Seaton's aunt, a little to my relief, did not share our meal. So he carved the cold meat, and dispatched a heaped-up plate by an elderly servant for his aunt's private consumption. We talked little and in half-suppressed tones, and sipped some Madeira which Seaton after listening for a moment or two fetched out of the great mahogany sideboard.

I played him a dull and effortless game of chess, yawning between the moves he himself made almost at haphazard, and with attention elsewhere engaged. Towards five o'clock came the sound of a distant ring, and Seaton jumped up, overturning the board, and so ended a game that else might have fatuously continued to this day. He effusively excused himself, and after some little while returned with a slim, dark, pale-faced girl of about nineteen, in a white gown and hat, to whom I was presented with some little nervousness as his 'dear old friend and schoolfellow'.

We talked on in the golden afternoon light, still, as it seemed to me, and even in spite of our efforts to be lively and gay, in a half-suppressed, lack-lustre fashion. We all seemed, if it were not my fancy, to be expectant, to be almost anxiously awaiting an arrival, the appearance of someone whose image filled our collective consciousness. Seaton talked least of all, and in a restless interjectory way, as he continually fidgeted from chair to chair. At last he proposed a stroll in the garden before the sun should have quite gone down.

Alice walked between us. Her hair and eyes were conspicuously dark against the whiteness of her gown. She carried herself not ungracefully, and yet with peculiarly little movement of her arms and body, and answered us both without turning her head. There was a curious provocative reserve in that impassive melancholy face. It seemed to be haunted by some tragic influence of which she herself was unaware.

And yet somehow I knew – I believe we all knew – that this walk, this discussion of their future plans was a futility. I had nothing to base such scepticism on, except only a vague sense of oppression, a foreboding consciousness of some inert invincible power in the background, to whom optimistic plans and love-making and youth are as chaff and thistledown. We came back, silent, in the last light. Seaton's aunt was there – under an old brass lamp. Her hair was as barbarously massed and curled as ever. Her eyelids, I think, hung even a little heavier in age over their slow-moving, inscrutable pupils. We filed in softly out of the evening, and I made my bow.

'In this short interval, Mr Withers,' she remarked amiably, 'you have put off youth, put on the man. Dear me, how sad it is to see the young days vanishing! Sit down. My nephew tells me you met by chance – or act of Providence, shall we call it? – and in my beloved Strand! You, I understand, are to be best man – yes, best man! Or am I divulging secrets?' She surveyed Arthur and Alice with overwhelming graciousness. They sat apart on two low chairs and smiled in return.

'And Arthur – how do you think Arthur is looking?'

'I think he looks very much in need of a change,' I said.

'A change! Indeed?' She all but shut her eyes at me and with an exaggerated sentimentality shook her head. 'My dear Mr Withers! Are we not *all* in need of a change in this fleeting, fleeting world?' She mused over the remark like a connoisseur. 'And you,' she continued, turning abruptly to Alice, 'I hope you pointed out to Mr Withers all my pretty bits?'

'We only walked round the garden,' the girl replied; then, glancing at Seaton, added almost inaudibly, 'it's a very beautiful evening.'

'*Is* it?' said the old lady, starting up violently. 'Then on this very beautiful evening we will go in to supper. Mr Withers, your arm; Arthur, bring your bride.'

We were a queer quartet, I thought to myself, as I solemnly led the way into the faded, chilly dining-room, with this indefinable old creature leaning wooingly on my arm – the large flat bracelet on the yellow-laced wrist. She fumed a little, breathing heavily, but as if with an effort of the mind rather than of the body; for she had grown much stouter and yet little more proportionate. And to talk into that great white face, so close to mine, was a queer experience in the dim light of the corridor, and even in the twinkling crystal of the candles. She was naïve – appallingly naïve; she was crafty and challenging; she was even arch; and all these in the brief, rather puffy passage from one room to the other, with these two tongue-tied children bringing up the rear. The meal was tremendous. I have never seen such a monstrous salad. But the dishes were greasy and over-spiced, and were indifferently cooked. One thing only was quite unchanged – my hostess's appetite was as Gargantuan as ever. The heavy silver candelabra that lighted us stood before her high-backed chair. Seaton sat a little removed, his plate almost in darkness.

And throughout this prodigious meal his aunt talked, mainly to me, mainly *at* him, but with an occasional satirical sally at Alice and muttered explosions of reprimand to the servant. She had aged, and yet, if it be not nonsense to say so, seemed no older. I suppose to the Pyramids a decade is but as the rustling down of a handful of dust. And she reminded me of some such unshakable prehistoricism. She certainly was an amazing talker – rapid, egregious, with a delivery that was perfectly overwhelming. As for Seaton – her flashes of silence were for him. On her enormous volubility would suddenly fall a hush: acid sarcasm would be left implied; and she would sit softly moving her great head, with eyes fixed full in a dreamy smile; but with her whole attention, one could see, slowly, joyously absorbing his mute discomfiture.

She confided in us her views on a theme vaguely occupying at the moment, I suppose, all our minds. 'We have barbarous institutions, and so must put up, I suppose, with a never-ending procession of fools – of fools *ad infinitum*. Marriage, Mr Withers, was instituted in the privacy of a garden; *sub rosa,* as it were. Civilization flaunts it in the glare of day. The dull marry the poor; the rich the effete; and so our New Jerusalem is peopled with naturals, plain and coloured, at either end. I detest folly; I detest still more (if I must be frank, dear Arthur) mere cleverness. Mankind has simply become a tailless host of uninstinctive animals. We should never have taken to Evolution, Mr Withers. "Natural Selection!" – little gods and fishes! – the deaf for the dumb. We should have used our brains – intellectual pride, the ecclesiastics call it. And by brains I mean – what do I mean, Alice? – I mean, my dear child,' and she laid two gross fingers on Alice's narrow sleeve, 'I mean courage. Consider it, Arthur. I read that the scientific world is once more beginning to be afraid of spiritual agencies. Spiritual agencies that tap, and actually float, bless their hearts! I think just one more of those mulberries – thank you.

'They talk about "blind Love",' she ran on derisively as she helped herself, her eyes roving over the dish, 'but why blind? I think, Mr Withers, from weeping over its rickets. After all, it is we plain women that triumph, is it not so – beyond the mockery of time. Alice, now! Fleeting, fleeting is youth, my child. What's that you were confiding to your plate, Arthur? Satirical boy. He laughs at his old aunt: nay, but thou didst laugh. He detests all sentiment. He whispers the most acid asides. Come, my love, we will leave these cynics; we will go and commiserate with each other on our sex. The choice of two evils, Mr Smithers!' I opened the door, and she swept out as if borne on a torrent of unintelligible indignation; and Arthur and I were left in the clear four-flamed light alone.

For a while we sat in silence. He shook his head at my cigarette-case, and I lit a cigarette. Presently he fidgeted in his chair and poked his head forward into the light. He paused to rise, and shut again the shut door.

'How long will you be?' he asked me.

I laughed.

'Oh, it's not that!' he said, in some confusion. 'Of course, I like to be with her. But it's not that. The truth is, Withers, I don't care about leaving her too long with my aunt.'

I hesitated. He looked at me questioningly.

'Look here, Seaton,' I said, 'you know well enough that I don't want to interfere in your affairs, or to offer advice where it is not wanted. But don't you think perhaps you may not treat your aunt quite in the right way? As one gets old, you know, a little give and take. I have an old godmother, or something of the kind. She's a bit queer, too... A little allowance; it does no harm. But hang it all, I'm no preacher.'

He sat down with his hands in his pockets and still with his eyes fixed almost incredulously on mine. 'How?' he said.

'Well, my dear fellow, if I'm any judge – mind, I don't say that I am – but I can't help thinking she thinks you don't care for her; and perhaps takes your silence for – for bad temper. She has been very decent to you, hasn't she?

' "Decent"? My God!' said Seaton.

I smoked on in silence; but he continued to look at me with that peculiar concentration I remembered of old.

'I don't think, perhaps, Withers,' he began presently, 'I don't think you quite understand. Perhaps you are not quite our kind. You always did, just like the other fellows, guy me at school. You laughed at me that night you came to stay here – about the voices and all that. But I don't mind being laughed at – because I know.'

'Know what?' It was the same old system of dull question and evasive answer.

'I mean I know that what we see and hear is only the smallest fraction of what is. I know she lives quite out of this. She *talks* to you; but it's all make-believe. It's all a "parlour game". She's not really with you; only pitting her outside wits against yours and enjoying the fooling. She's living on inside on what you're rotten without. That's what it is – a cannibal feast. She's a spider. It doesn't much matter what you call it. It means the same kind of thing. I tell you, Withers, she hates me; and you can scarcely dream what that hatred means. I used to think I had an inkling of the reason. It's oceans deeper than that. It just lies behind: herself against myself. Why, after all, how much do we really understand of anything? We don't even know our own histories, and not a tenth, not a tenth of the reasons. What has life been to me? – nothing but a trap. And when one sets oneself free for a while, it only begins again. I thought you might understand; but you are on a different level: that's all.'

'What on earth are you talking about?' I said contemptuously, in spite of myself.

'I mean what I say,' he said gutturally. 'All this outside's only make-believe – but there! what's the good of talking? So far as this is concerned I'm as good as done. You wait.'

Seaton blew out three of the candles and, leaving the vacant room in semi-darkness, we groped our way along the corridor to the drawing-room. There a full moon stood shining in at the long garden windows. Alice sat stooping at the door, with her hands clasped in her lap, looking out, alone.

'Where is she?' Seaton asked in a low tone.

She looked up; and their eyes met in a glance of instantaneous under-standing, and the door immediately afterwards opened behind us.

'*Such* a moon!' said a voice, that once heard, remained unforgettably on the ear. 'A night for lovers, Mr Withers, if ever there was one. Get a shawl, my dear Arthur, and take Alice for a little promenade. I dare say we old cronies will manage to keep awake. Hasten, hasten, Romeo! My poor, poor Alice, how laggard a lover!'

Seaton returned with a shawl. They drifted out into the moonlight. My companion gazed after them till they were out of hearing, turned to me gravely, and suddenly twisted her white face into such a convulsion of con-temptuous amusement that I could only stare blankly in reply.

'Dear innocent children!' she said, with inimitable unctuousness. 'Well, well, Mr Withers, we poor seasoned old creatures must move with the times. Do you sing?'

I scouted the idea.

'Then you must listen to my playing. Chess' – she clasped her forehead with both cramped hands – 'chess is now completely beyond my poor wits.'

She sat down at the piano and ran her fingers in a flourish over the keys. 'What shall it be? How shall we capture them, those passionate hearts? That first fine careless rapture? Poetry itself.' She gazed softly into the gar-den a moment, and presently, with a shake of her body, began to play the opening bars of Beethoven's 'Moonlight' Sonata. The piano was old and woolly. She played without music. The lamplight was rather dim. The moonbeams from the window lay across the keys. Her head was in shadow.

And whether it was simply due to her personality or to some really occult skill in her playing I cannot say; I only know that she gravely and deliberately set herself to satirize the beautiful music. It brooded on the air, disillusioned, charged with mockery and bitterness. I stood at the window; far down the path I could see the white figure glimmering in that pool of colourless light. A few faint stars shone, and still that amazing woman behind me dragged out of the unwilling keys her wonderful grotesquerie of youth and love and beauty. It came to an end. I knew the player was watching me. 'Please, please, go on!' I murmured, without turning. '*Please* go on playing, Miss Seaton.'

No answer was returned to this honeyed sarcasm, but I realized in some vague fashion that I was being acutely scrutinized, when suddenly there followed a procession of quiet, plaintive chords which broke at last softly into the hymn, 'A Few More Years Shall Roll'.

I confess it held me spellbound. There is a wistful, strained plangent pathos in the tune; but beneath those masterly old hands it cried softly and bitterly the solitude and desperate estrangement of the world. Arthur and his lady-love vanished from my thoughts. No one could put into so hackneyed an old hymn tune such an appeal who had never known the meaning of the words. Their meaning, anyhow, isn't commonplace.

I turned a fraction of an inch to glance at the musician. She was leaning forward a little over the keys, so that at the approach of my silent scrutiny she had but to turn her face into the thin flood of moonlight for every feature to become distinctly visible. And so, with the tune abruptly terminated, we steadfastly regarded one another; and she broke into a prolonged chuckle of laughter.

'Not quite so seasoned as I supposed, Mr Withers. I see you are a real lover of music. To me it is too painful. It evokes too much thought...'

I could scarcely see her little glittering eyes under their penthouse lids.

'And now,' she broke off crisply, 'tell me, as a man of the world, what do you think of my new niece?'

I was not a man of the world, nor was I much flattered in my stiff and dullish way of looking at things by being called one; and I could answer her without the least hesitation.

'I don't think, Miss Seaton, I'm much of a judge of character. She's very charming.'

'A brunette?'

'I think I prefer dark women.'

'And why? Consider, Mr Withers; dark hair, dark eyes, dark cloud, dark night, dark vision, dark death, dark grave, dark DARK!'

Perhaps the climax would have rather thrilled Seaton, but I was too thick-skinned. 'I don't know much about all that,' I answered rather pompously. 'Broad daylight's difficult enough for most of us.'

'Ah,' she said, with a sly inward burst of satirical laughter.

'And I suppose,' I went on, perhaps a little nettled, 'it isn't the actual darkness one admires, it's the contrast of the skin, and the colour of the eyes, and – and their shining. Just as,' I went blundering on, too late to turn back, 'just as you only see the stars in the dark. It would be a long day without any evening. As for death and the grave, I don't suppose we shall much notice that.' Arthur and his sweetheart were slowly returning along the dewy path. 'I believe in making the best of things.'

'How very interesting!' came the smooth answer. 'I see you are a philosopher, Mr Withers. H'm! "As for death and the grave, I don't suppose we shall much notice that." Very interesting... And I'm sure,' she added in a particularly suave voice, 'I profoundly hope so.' She rose slowly from her stool. 'You will take pity on me again, I hope. You and I would get on famously – kindred spirits – elective affinities. And, of course, now that my nephew's going to leave me, now that his affections are centred on another, I shall be a very lonely old woman... Shall I not, Arthur?'

Seaton blinked stupidly. 'I didn't hear what you said, Aunt.'

'I was telling our old friend, Arthur, that when you are gone I shall be a very lonely old woman.'

'Oh, I don't think so;' he said in a strange voice.

'He means, Mr Withers, he means, my dear child,' she said, sweeping her eyes over Alice, 'he means that I shall have memory for company – heavenly memory – the ghosts of other days. Sentimental boy! And did you enjoy our music, Alice? Did I really stir that youthful heart?... O. O, O,' continued the horrible old creature, 'you billers and cooers, I have been listening to such flatteries, such confessions! Beware, beware, Arthur, there's many a slip.' She rolled her little eyes at me, she shrugged her shoulders at Alice, and gazed an instant stonily into her nephews's face.

I held out my hand. 'Good night, good night!' she cried. 'He that fights and runs away. Ah, good night, Mr Withers; come again soon!' She thrust out her cheek at Alice, and we all three filed slowly out of the room.

Black shadow darkened the porch and half the spreading sycamore. We walked without speaking up the dusty village street. Here and there a crimson window glowed. At the fork of the high-road I said good-bye. But I had taken hardly more than a dozen paces when a sudden impulse seized me.

'Seaton!' I called.

He turned in the cool stealth of the moonlight.

'You have my address; if by any chance, you know, you should care to spend a week or two in town between this and the – the Day, we should be delighted to see you.'

'Thank you, Withers, thank you,' he said in a low voice.

'I dare say' – I waved my stick gallantly at Alice – 'I dare say you will be doing some shopping; we could all meet,' I added, laughing.

'Thank you, thank you, Withers – immensely,' he repeated.

And so we parted.

But they were out of the jog-trot of my prosaic life. And being of a stolid and incurious nature, I left Seaton and his marriage, and even his aunt, to themselves in my memory, and scarcely gave a thought to them until one day I was walking up the Strand again, and passed the flashing gloaming of the second-rate jeweller's shop where I had accidentally encountered my old schoolfellow in the summer. It was one of those stagnant autumnal days after a night of rain. I cannot say why, but a vivid recollection returned to my mind of our meeting and of how suppressed Seaton had seemed, and of how vainly he had endeavoured to appear assured and eager. He must be married by now, and had doubtless returned from his honeymoon. And I had clean forgotten my manners, had sent not a word of congratulation, nor – as I might very well have done and as I knew he would have been pleased at my doing – even the ghost of a wedding present. It was just as of old.

On the other hand, I pleaded with myself, I had had no invitation. I paused at the corner of Trafalgar Square, and at the bidding of one of those caprices that seize occasionally on even an unimaginative mind, I found myself pelting after a green bus, and actually bound on a visit I had not in the least intended or foreseen.

The colours of autumn were over the village when I arrived. A beautiful late afternoon sunlight bathed thatch and meadow. But it was close and hot. A child, two dogs, a very old woman with a heavy basket I encountered. One or two incurious tradesmen looked idly up as I passed by. It was all so rural and remote, my whimsical impulse had so much flagged, that for a while I hesitated to venture under the shadow of the sycamore-tree to enquire after the happy pair. Indeed I first passed by the faint-blue gates and continued my walk under the high, green and tufted wall. Hollyhocks had attained their topmost bud and seeded in the little cottage gardens beyond; the Michaelmas daisies were in flower; a sweet warm aromatic smell of fading leaves was in the air. Beyond the cottages lay a field where cattle were grazing, and beyond that I came to a little churchyard. Then the road wound on, pathless and houseless, among gorse and bracken. I turned impatiently and walked quickly back to the house and rang the bell.

The rather colourless elderly woman who answered my enquiry informed me that Miss Seaton was at home, as if only taciturnity forbade her adding, 'But she doesn't want to see *you*.'

'Might I, do you think, have Mr Arthur's address?' I said.

She looked at me with quiet astonishment, as if waiting for an explanation. Not the faintest of smiles came into her thin face.

'I will tell Miss Seaton,' she said after a pause. 'Please walk in.'

She showed me into the dingy undusted drawing-room, filled with evening sunshine and with the green-dyed light that penetrated the leaves overhanging the long french windows. I sat down and waited on and on, occasionally aware of a creaking footfall overhead. At last the door opened a little, and the great face I had once known peered round at me. For it was enormously changed; mainly, I think, because the aged eyes had rather suddenly failed, and so a kind of stillness and darkness lay over its calm and wrinkled pallor.

'Who is it?' she asked.

I explained myself and told her the occasion of my visit.

She came in, shut the door carefully after her, and, though the fumbling was scarcely perceptible, groped her way to a chair. She had on an old dressing-gown, like a cassock, of a patterned cinnamon colour.

'What is it you want?' she said, seating herself and lifting her blank face to mine.

'Might I just have Arthur's address?' I said deferentially, 'I am so sorry to have disturbed you.'

'H'm. You have come to see my nephew?'

'Not necessarily to see him, only to hear how he is, and, of course, Mrs Seaton, too. I am afraid my silence must have appeared...'

'He hasn't noticed your silence,' croaked the old voice out of the great mask; 'besides, there isn't any Mrs Seaton.'

'Ah, then,' I answered, after a momentary pause, 'I have not seemed so black as I painted myself! And how is Miss Outram?'

'She's gone into Yorkshire,' answered Seaton's aunt.

'And Arthur too?'

She did not reply, but simply sat blinking at me with lifted chin, as if listening, but certainly not for what I might have to say. I began to feel rather at a loss.

'You were no close friend of my nephew's, Mr Smithers?' she said presently.

'No,' I answered, welcoming the cue, 'and yet, do you know, Miss Seaton, he is one of the very few of my old schoolfellows I have come across in the last few years, and I suppose as one gets older one begins to value old associations...' My voice seemed to trail off into a vacuum. 'I thought Miss Outram', I hastily began again, 'a particularly charming girl. I hope they are both quite well.'

Still the old face solemnly blinked at me in silence.

'You must find it very lonely, Miss Seaton, with Arthur away?'

'I was never lonely in my life,' she said sourly. 'I don't look to flesh and blood for my company. When you've got to be my age, Mr Smithers (which God forbid), you'll find life a very different affair from what you seem to think it is now. You won't seek company then, I'll be bound. It's thrust on you.' Her face edged round into the clear green light, and her eyes groped, as it were, over my vacant, disconcerted face. 'I dare say, now,' she said, composing her mouth, 'I dare say my nephew told you a good many tarra-diddles in his time. Oh, yes, a good many, eh? He was always a liar. What, now, did he say of me? Tell me, now.' She leant forward as far as she could, trembling, with an ingratiating smile.

'I think he is rather superstitious,' I said coldly, 'but, honestly, I have a very poor memory, Miss Seaton.'

'Why?' she said. '*I* haven't.'

'The engagement hasn't been broken off, I hope.'

'Well, between you and me,' she said, shrinking up and with an immensely confidential grimace, 'it has.'

'I'm sure I'm very sorry to hear it. And where is Arthur?'

'Eh?'

'Where is Arthur?'

We faced each other mutely among the dead old bygone furniture. Past all my analysis was that large, flat, grey, cryptic countenance. And then, suddenly, our eyes for the first time really met. In some indescribable way out of that thick-lidded obscurity a far, small something stooped and looked out at me for a mere instant of time that seemed of almost intolerable pro-traction. Involuntarily I blinked and shook my head. She muttered some-thing with great rapidity, but quite inarticulately; rose and hobbled to the door. I thought I heard, mingled in broken mutterings, something about tea.

'Please, please, don't trouble,' I began, but could say no more, for the door was already shut between us. I stood and looked out on the long-neglected garden. I could just see the bright weedy greenness of Seaton's tadpole pond. I wandered about the room. Dusk began to gather, the last birds in that dense shadowiness of trees had ceased to sing. And not a sound was to be heard in the house. I waited on and on, vainly speculat-ing. I even attempted to ring the bell; but the wire was broken, and only jangled loosely at my efforts.

I hesitated, unwilling to call or to venture out, and yet more unwilling to linger on, waiting for a tea that promised to be an exceedingly comfort-less supper. And as darkness drew down, a feeling of the utmost unease and disquietude came over me. All my talks with Seaton returned on me with a suddenly enriched meaning. I recalled again his face as we had stood hang-ing over the staircase, listening in the small hours to the inexplicable stir-rings of the night. There were no candles in the room; every minute the autumnal darkness deepened. I cautiously opened the door and listened, and with some little dismay withdrew, for I was uncertain of my way out. I even tried the garden, but was confronted under a veritable thicket of foliage by a padlocked gate. It would be a little too ignominious to be caught scaling a friend's garden fence!

Cautiously returning into the still and musty drawing-room, I took out my watch, and gave the incredible old woman ten minutes in which to reappear. And when that tedious ten minutes had ticked by I could scarcely distinguish its hands. I determined to wait no longer, drew open the door and, trusting to my sense of direction, groped my way through the corridor that I vaguely remembered led to the front of the house.

I mounted three or four stairs and, lifting a heavy curtain, found myself facing the starry fanlight of the porch. From here I glanced into the gloom of the dining-room. My fingers were on the latch of the outer door when I heard a faint stirring in the darkness above the hall. I looked up and became conscious of, rather than saw, the huddled old figure looking down on me.

There was an immense hushed pause. Then, 'Arthur, Arthur,' whispered an inexpressibly peevish rasping voice, 'is that you? Is that you, Arthur?'

I can scarcely say why, but the question horribly startled me. No conceivable answer occurred to me. With head craned back, hand clenched on my umbrella, I continued to stare up into the gloom, in this fatuous confrontation.

'Oh, oh,' the voice croaked. 'It is *you*, is it? *That* disgusting man!... Go away out. Go away out.'

At this dismissal, I wrenched open the door and, rudely slamming it behind me, ran out into the garden, under the gigantic old sycamore, and so out at the open gate.

I found myself half up the village street before I stopped running. The local butcher was sitting in his shop reading a piece of newspaper by the light of a small oil-lamp. I crossed the road and enquired the way to the station. And after he had with minute and needless care directed me, I asked casually if Mr Arthur Seaton still lived with his aunt at the big house just beyond the village. He poked his head in at the little parlour door.

'Here's a gentleman enquiring after young Mr Seaton, Millie,' he said. 'He's dead, ain't he?'

'Why, yes, bless you,' replied a cheerful voice from within. 'Dead and buried these three months or more – young Mr Seaton. And just before he was to be married, don't you remember, Bob?'

I saw a fair young woman's face peer over the muslin of the little door at me.

'Thank you,' I replied, 'then I go straight on?'

'That's it, sir; past the pond, bear up the hill a bit to the left, and then there's the station lights before your eyes.'

We looked intelligently into each other's faces in the beam of the smoky lamp. But not one of the many questions in my mind could I put into words.

And again I paused irresolutely a few paces further on. It was not, I fancy, merely a foolish apprehension of what the raw-boned butcher might 'think' that prevented my going back to see if I could find Seaton's grave in the benighted churchyard. There was precious little use in pottering about in the muddy dark merely to discover where he was buried. And yet I felt a little uneasy. My rather horrible thought was that, so far as I was concerned – one of his extremely few friends – he had never been much better than 'buried' in my mind.

The Bird of Travel*

We had been talking of houses – their looks and ways and influences. What shallow defences they were, we agreed, even for the materialist, with their brittle glass, and baked clay bricks; and what mere fungi most of them. Worse still – the dreadful species that isn't haunted *at all*, not even by the graces or disgraces of its inmates – mere barracks deaf to life and insensitive even to the weathers of heaven. A cherry-eyed little man of the name of Bateson, I remember, told us of a house he had known that had year by year gently and furtively shifted itself a few feet down its valley towards the sea. A full green mile to go. He said it was the property of a family so fair of skin and hair as to be almost albinos – but still, a happy one.

Somebody capped this with the ancient yarn of Lord Montberris, who built a new wing to his family edifice every year, till the estate was utterly ruined. Whereupon he set fire to the place in the vain hope of getting rid of its Devil *that* way. And at last a quaint old creature whose name I have forgotten, but who, so I was told, had been something of a versifier in his younger days, told us the following rather pointless story, about a house called the Wood.

'I must have been scarcely in my first breeches,' he began, rubbing his hand down his face, as if he was sleepy, 'when I first heard of the old house called the Wood. We lived then – my own people I mean – some few miles distant from it as the crow flies. There was a remote kinship with its inmates – people of a restless blood and with a fair acreage of wild oats to their credit. A quarrel, a mild feud of the Montague and Capulet order, had

* First published in *Lady's Realm*, October 1908.

separated us; and – well, we rarely mentioned them; their name was seldom heard. But an old relative of my mother's who lived with us in those days used to tell us about the house, warning us, in that peculiarly enticing fashion old people have, not to tempt Providence in that direction. Let but its evil genius squawk once in our young ears – we might never come back. That kind of thing.

'The consequence was that while we were still mere infants, my younger sister and I – she in a dark green tartan frock, I remember – set out one early morning, fully intending to see or hear the strange Bird that was reported to haunt its chaces and its glades. What if it did instil into us the wander-lust? It was just what we wanted – Seven League Boots. We hoped – with beating hearts – even to sprinkle a grain or two of salt on its tail!

'But we never pushed as far as the house itself, nor even into the denser woods amongst which it lay. We sat in the sun-glazed buttercups and ate our dinner, and, I think, forgot our errand beneath the blossoming may-trees.

'Later, I tried the same experiment alone. It was winter then. Deep snow lay on the ground, and I pushed on through the woods until I was actually in sight of the upper windows of the house. Dusk was beginning to thicken – its strange thievish blur creeping across the whiteness of the snow. Presently, I found myself in a sort of walk or alley between a high hedge of yew and beech. And as I stood there, hesitating whether to go on or to turn back, a figure – a child of about my own age – appeared at its further end. She was dressed, I remember, in a cloak with a hood – crimson, I think, and carried a muff.

'At that very instant, as our young eyes met across the wintry air, the last of the evening's robins broke into its tiny, shrill, almost deafening peal of notes. And fled. What is it in such moments that catches the heart back, and stamps them on the memory as if they were tidings of another world? Neither of us stirred. A little snow fell from the vacant twig.

The scarcely visible, narrow, and, to my young eyes, strangely beautiful face gazed on at me. I might even then have realized that we were fated some day to meet again. But even if I had, I should hardly have surmised it would prove as eventlessly.

'Then I was shy – a gawkish boy. Moreover, I was on forbidden ground. I naturally fancied, too, any such distant cousin might resent my being there – a stranger and uninvited. With a curious drag of my body in the dead silence that had followed the song, I began a tuneless sort of airy whistling, turned on my heel and crunched off in the snow. When in the white darkening alley I cast back this phantom creature a thief-like glance out of the corner of my eye, she had vanished.

'I don't suggest that this incident left much impression on me – though I remember every detail of it to this day. Then Life called me away; and it

was at least a score or so of years afterwards, while wandering one afternoon in the neighbourhood of my old home again, that I chanced on a
finger-post pointing and stooping towards a thicket of trees beyond a
grassy lane, and marked "To the Wood".

'I had seen something of the world by then, and without excessive satisfaction. The old story came back to mind. It linked up two selves rather
crudely severed. I dropped a friendly nod at the post and turned off in its
direction. The path – a pretty soggy one after the heavy summer rains – led
through neglected preserves, and after walking for half an hour or so, I
came out into a kind of clearing. And there amid the serene quietude of its
remarkably dense woods was the long, low house.

'Its walls, once grey, were now densely mantled with greenery – rose,
jasmine, wistaria. It showed, however, little trace of age or change. An
unusual silence hung over its scene. No smoke, or sign of occupancy;
indeed, all but one of the windows within view were shuttered. I doubt if
the Ancient Mariner's spectral barque more eloquently expressed desertion
and vacancy.

'For a few minutes I leaned over a decrepit gate, my eyes roving to and
fro across the wide stone façade. The whole place looked as if it had settled
its eyelids and composed its mouth for a protracted and stagnant sleep. I
have heard of toads being found immured but yet alive in the virgin rock
of a coal mine: it looked like that. At last I made my way up the weedy
path, and, at the back of the house, where even yet a few hardy human
vegetables contested the soil with Nature's wildings, I discovered a door on
the latch.

'I tapped and listened; tapped and listened again; and, as if it were Echo
herself, some hidden thrush's rapping of a snail's shell against its sacrificial
stone was my only answer. Then, at a venture, I pushed open the door,
stepped in, and making my way along a narrow passage, entered a little
morning room whose air was burdened with a faint odour as of sweetish
mildew – long-faded flowers perhaps. A piano stood where the window
might best illuminate the singer, and a few pictures in water-colour hung on
the low walls. A volume of music lay open on the table: It was Gounod's
"How Beautiful Upon the Mountains".

'I passed from room to room, and from an attic window surveyed many
acres – versts, one might say – of the tree-tops – of the motionless woods.
And there my mind lapsed into a sort of daydream. So closely familiar
seemed all around me that I even began to doubt my own memory. The
chests and cupboards, the posied carpets on the uneven floors, the faint
nosegays of the wall-paper – surely one couldn't so instantly "recognize",
so to speak, objects seen for the first time. And yet – well, most rare human
experience is like that.

'One talks of the *years* of childhood: centuries would be a better word. The sense of this familiarity, this recognition – was only the sharper, the more wistful (to use an old-fashioned word) for the fact that the house was vacant, except for the faces upon its walls. Through narrow crannies sunshine had sucked the brightness of their colours from tapestry and curtain. The she-spider had woven and withered in her snares; and a legionary dust, like fine gold, floated and whirled in a beam of the declining sun, when I drew the shutter.

'I spent the next hour or so that remained of daylight in roaming the woods, half-elated, half-ashamed at my trespass, descending into every hollow, ascending every steep, but, nowhere surprised any secret, and nowhere confronted hint of ghost of man or beast. Indeed, so shut in was the house by its trees that from no point of vantage, so far as I could discover, could one command any glimpse of the country beyond the valley. It had been built in a bowl of verdure and foliage. And for those who had occupied it, rumour of the world must have been carried by the winds across the hills, unheeded in this hollow.

'And then, while I was slowly returning towards it once more, under the still, reddish, evening sky, suddenly I heard thrice repeated an extraordinary call. It pierced my mind like an arrow. It almost absurdly startled me – like the shrilling of a decoy, as if my own name had been called in a strange or forgotten tongue.

'Of English birds, the blackcap, perhaps, sings with a vestige of that wild and piercing sweetness. Imagine such a voice twenty times more vigorous suddenly breaking in upon that evening silence – falling on from note to note as if some unearthly traveller were summoning from afar his strayed dog on the hillside!

'Yet it was evidently a bird that had screamed, for presently after, as I stood hotly, attentively listening, I saw mount nobly into the deep blue air and wheel into the darker thicket a bird of the form and wing of a kestrel, but much larger – its plumage of an almost snowy whiteness, and of a flight inexpressively serene.

'I heard no more his cry, though I listened long; nor did I set eyes on the bird again, either then, or afterwards: though the woods were motionless and so silent the gloaming it seemed as if the world had swooned.

'I was ridiculously elated with my adventure. Had I not now encountered the veritable Bird of Travel, which childish legend had credited with such fabulous powers? Here was the deserted house, and still echoing in my heart that cry, the lure, as of some innocent Banshee. Who, I wondered, had last heard the call in the green spring, and felt leap and kindle insatiable desire. The past slid back. I was a child again; looking up into the withered old face of my childhood:

' "But is it *true*, grandmamma? Please tell us, is it *true*?" '

' "True, my dears? Why I myself perfectly well remember Hamilton and Paul when they were boys not so very many years older than yourselves. I remember, too, my father telling me how, one autumn evening, while he and these two friends of his were returning with their guns and spaniels through the woods, the bird had flown out screaming above their heads. *He* stopped up his ears. *He* had his work to do. But the other two lads watched it in the air, drinking in its forbidden song. Nothing anyone could say could restrain them then. Poor fellows! – fine handsome fellows. And now, Hamilton lies far away, unburied amid the Andes, and Paul drowned in the Straits of Magellan."

'It didn't matter how far the old lady wandered from her theme of this family's destiny, and of their house, and of this ominous bird, she invariably concluded her narrative with this faint, high trembling *refrain* – "And now, Hamilton lies far away, unburied amid the Andes, and Paul drowned in the Straits of Magellan." '

'O *Keith of Ravelston, the sorrows of thy line!*'

'So ran the ancient story. And had I not that very afternoon returned the painted gaze of these young gentlemen? It seems to me, too, though you may build pretty strongly in this world, even the most substantial of us must depart in time. All the long annals of this family, anyhow, were a record of unrest, of fruitless (or worse) venture, of that absurd nomad instinct – travellers to whom had come eventually, far from home, the same practised, inevitable guide. Well, there are some of us who prefer the kind of travel that can be enjoyed in an armchair!

'I had cast one last full look behind me and was returning by the path I have mentioned, cumbered with weeds and brambles, when I looked up from out of my thoughts, and saw approaching me a lady. A bright chill half-moon had now risen in the twilight above the woods, and I could see her face distinctly in its thin radiance. The brows were high and narrow (for she was carrying her hat in her hand), the nose was long, like the noses in some old Italian pictures; the chin firm, yet rounded to a point.

'I could see her plainly in the silverish dusk-light: and yet, oddly enough, for a moment no flash of recognition told me who she was. And then I knew. She eyed me sharply and fully, almost arrogantly, a dark flush in her cheeks, and bowed. I apologized as best as I could for my intrusion. I reminded her of the former neighbourhood and acquaintance of our families; and told her of my childish curiosity to explore the woods, yes, and confessed to having heard the wondrous phoenix, and confronted its victims.

'She listened with face slightly averted, and now turned with a lively smile. "You have guessed right," she said, "the portraits are of my great-uncles; and I am the child you – but evidently you don't remember that...

So please say no more. How I love those pictures – those two outlandish brilliant faces. A bad painter may be a queerly telling artist."

'She glanced into my eyes with a peculiar smile on her lips. "You see, nowadays, so far as my own family is concerned, I am the last," she continued. "So you will realize how welcome even the remotest of cousins must be! Of all these years – all those births and deaths, and births again – there is not one left of us in this world here except me." She glanced up under the half-moon with shining eyes, almost as if in apology, yet still, as if in boast.

' "And are you a traveller, too?" I questioned.

'She beckoned me to follow her back by the way I had come.

' "A traveller? No indeed. Not I. Our bright particular genius has always refused to meddle the least bit with me. I used to lie awake half the night long, summer and winter too, in hope to be exiled. That was years and years ago; the mad 'teens. But deep, deep down, perhaps, I feared my own desire. I cannot tell you – this place is rooted in my heart. It *is* me. Here, only, I seem to catch at the meaning of being alive at all. It is a little lodge, and yonder winds the mysterious avenue. I'll wait. Forgive such nonsense; but it is that incessant expectation – *incessant*; boxes packed and corded, as it were, the door ajar. It is *that* I hunger for – for then . . . And this quiet – it is always silent in these woods. The winds and storms go over us, you see, like the waters in the book of Job. I never remember it when I am away, – this curious quiet even beneath the hollow tumult of a gale far overhead – without an almost unendurable shudder of longing. Shall I ever cease if I begin to talk of it? But now I see that with that longing, that greed – far, far beyond the greed of the little girl I used to be even for ices and macaroons (and would you believe it, to see a ghost!) – it was like keeping a wild beast without meat, to deny my poor heart its native air. Better dead than dying. It was an extraordinary home-coming – this very morning. I was alone. I got back early, soon after daybreak, and opened a window to the first rose of dawn. I cannot tell you the *voracity* of it all: the dew, the depth, and the immortal usualness.

' "And now – well, really it is *very* delightful – though an hour ago I should have madly resented such an idea – it *is* delightful to have found so old an unknown friend waiting me – and one remembered so well."

'She laughed out, when I tried to excuse myself for so dull a memory.

' "That's because you are a poet, Mr —" she said. "You see, I know all about you; and you, nothing about me! I have noticed it again and again. People with imagination are almost indecently bereft of the common feelings. And now, will you please sit on this bench while I make some tea for us both. It's all I can offer. I shan't be long But stuff your fingers into your ears. He screams at night too! Now which was the door I left unfastened?"

'I sat there – where she had left me. The moon slid on, casting her shadows. A few late moths ghosted about me in and out of her beams. It might have been a dream. I might have been thousands of years old. Strange, that. Strange. Why, I might have been in another world...But never mind that.

'Well, my unconventional hostess returned in a few minutes, and we sat sipping our tea on the little balcony in the mild autumnal night.

'And as we sat we talked – as fancy led; she in a rather high-pitched voice, and with curious half-gestures. It seemed as if she thought always with arrow on the string and bow bent – a bow which a dull world had invariably reminded her to slacken. Her eyes were extraordinarily dark and lustrous in the shadow of that thin clear light, revealing, it seemed, a curious exaltation of spirit at this sudden and strange return to solitude and to her old home. She exulted in her solitude, and had not the least misgiving at the thought of staying indefinitely in the house.

' "It won't be for long," she repeated. "They have patched and tortured and experimented, and at last I am done. They've as good as told me so now, the poor dear, scientific creatures. Surely it is not surrender when the wound is mortal and the enemy is – that one. But *enemy*! What shallow, stuffy nonsense *that* is! We have handed down our restless memories, the old forlorn absurdities, father to son and son again, and now I am, well, just the last echo of the refrain before the end. 'Ah, Elizabeth,' mother used to laugh at me in the old days when we were a happy family in the Wood, 'he will sing to you too in due season.' Probably she meant a far tamer fowl. In her heart of hearts she hated the wander-taint, as you may imagine. And yet – she herself at last couldn't resist it. We are wayfaring men one and all and *my* journey will be better than dreams."

'There was a peculiar sidelong movement of her head, as she said this; she was stooping a little, busied over the tea-things. With teapot poised in one thin narrow hand, she suddenly turned on me.

' "Shall I tell you why? Shall I?" Again that curious movement, and I fancied for an instant that she was about to cry. "It is because *I* am coming back."

'For an instant or two I did not catch her meaning; then, with that odd warmth and confusion within one's very body which any unforeseen reference to death inevitably brings, I muttered a few of the familiar clichés. "Besides," I added, "look at me. Surely this face is nearer the sight of death than yours. You cannot see your own in this moonlight. Shall we have a wager on it? And pay – when at last we meet again? For good? Come, now."

' "Yes, but you see," she replied eagerly, "it's all very well to talk about happy reunions. Where? Call it a condition of mind; whose? Surely that which found the very bones of its delight here? Do you remember what Catherine says in *Wuthering Heights*? But there, never mind, when *my* bird wings free, I know its resting place. I *know* it. You see? The ones that have gone – they changed little; but strangely and instantaneously. And now they thrid some finer air, have rarer senses, and their tap is heard on walls of the mind that are scarcely there, so tenuous they are. Not that I want proof. And such proof! I *know* it. And when your time comes, I give you my invitation now. What *is* that old phoenix of ours? Do you suppose we could snare him, cage him; tie him to a perch? Isn't he in our very minds? How then? Could we be else than wanderers? May we be forgiven for this futile waste of its powers."

'I suppose I was a little taken aback by this outpouring. For she leaned her face into her hands and laughed.

' "Just 'hysteria,' you are thinking," she said suddenly, looking up at me from them. I sat in the shadow now, so perhaps my face was not too clearly visible.

' "But what *is* this coming back?" I stupidly questioned.

' "Oh, but you don't understand," she cried, turning breathlessly on me. "It is here now. And then, shall I not see? shall I not know? and probably before the very last of these leaves is fallen? Oh, how I detest the sentimentality they talk; fobbing us off with their precious stones and golden harps. Symbols if you like, but beyond any poor earthly spirit's hope or desire. If we humans have *climbed* to where we are – though I don't believe it – by way of the happy and innocent animals, do you suppose we are going to suddenly jump half-a-dozen stories instead of ascending on and on and on? What is space but the all I am? What is time but the all I was and shall be? I cannot express myself, but if you could hear the roaring of the fire *here,* you would not be wanting any words. Never in the whole of my reading, in the whole queer skein of things called my life – never have I encountered a single human being who expressed a tenth of the sheer delight of sharing – well, say, just that bit of garish moon in this tiny bowl of the world's greenery. 'Blind,' 'ungrateful,' 'worms of earth,' no word in the language could express our fatuity. *Then* I shall be free...But there, it's time, as the old Scottish ballad says, you were awa'. And it's time, as some less anonymous poet says, I sought my couch. I confess I hated the very sight of you when I saw you trespassing in my woods. Another hereditary taint. But you have forgiven me...and I will walk a little distance with you on your way."

'Well, I confess, her vehemence had stirred up my sluggish mind a good deal more even than had the bird before her. I followed her all but in silence. We came to a kind of alley, its yew hedge long untended, though the light of the moon pierced through upon its sward.

'She paused, her face averted. "And now" – she said, "goodbye, for this life. Yours that way; mine this. And may all that is meant by heaven be with you."

'I did as I was bid. Silence crept in upon me – an entire world – like a dangerous flood. The grass was hoar with a moonlight almost as white as snow. The years seemed to melt away like a dream, and, as I turned, seeing her there still waiting, I realized that she herself must have devised this echo of our first and only other meeting. The strange rapt face looked curiously unreal. With queer contrary thoughts in my mind, I gazed across at her, not more trustful of my eyes perhaps in that uncertain light than I had been of my ears earlier in the evening. She did not stir. All perfectly still things seem to have a look of agelessness and of the eternal. And then – I turned on my heel, and when, now no longer a shy awkward silly boy, I looked back as of old and for the last time; again it was in vain. She was gone...'

So this, it appeared was all. This was the story of 'The Wood'! We others glanced a little uncomfortably at one another, I remember, at this crisis in the evening's talk – a poet's story in sober earnest: incoherent, obscure, unreal, unlifelike, without an ending.

'And the Bird?' cried one of us, maybe a little more 'fatuous' than the rest. The old man was at that moment beckoning to the Club waiter, and appeared not to have noticed the question. And nobody, it seemed, had either the stupidity or the courage to add, 'And what, pray, are *you* waiting for?'

*The Bowl**

It was one autumn evening – in the month of October, I think, for I can just remember that the thin gold and tawny beechleaves were still floating down in the garden in the hazy sunshine, and that already a fire burned in the grate to cheer the colder twilights, when first my very young eyes fell in wonder upon Mrs Orchardson's silver bowl. Perhaps it had always been there, and always as conspicuous. But it was then, I am sure, that I first noticed it. It stood on the sideboard beside a cut-glass decanter reflecting the ruddy colour of its wine in the smooth cheeks of its two laughing Cupids. It had handles, two pendant rings as plain in workmanship as the buckle on a child's shoe. I stood and stared up at it, as young eyes will at any such magical object. There was a sort of secret jollity in the very look of it – an air to blow bubbles in, cool as an orchard, or as the half-hidden valleys of a summer cloud.

I was astonished at it, entranced by it; longed to touch and handle it, and

* As printed in *The Nap and Other Stories* (1936).

even felt, I verily believe, a kind of covetousness and an envy of the friend whose bowl it was. And if I had been a jackdaw of equal proportions to myself, I should certainly have carried it off to hide in the chimney or hole in the wall, wherever my nest might be. As it was, I at least carried off a very vivid remembrance of it in my mind – which, fortunately, in a world hedged about with a superfluity of *Don'ts*, is not a felony.

Anyhow, when one dark rainy morning the sharp need came for *something* of this kind, it was I who thought of the bowl, which, after all, could contain almost as much Jordan water as could the freestone font in St Barnabas's, and was twenty times more beautiful.

All through the night, while I had been placidly asleep, I learned at my lonely breakfast, my friend Mrs Orchardson's little baby had been simply burning like a coal at death's door. It was a most interesting and enthralling piece of news. And I'm not so sure that I did not speculate how it was that, in my long nocturnal journeyings in the wilds of dreamland, I had not heard its wailing cries as it, too, a much smaller spirit, ran along into the shadowy valley. For after all, abstractions like death are for a child little more than a vague and menacing something in a dream.

Mrs Orchardson's baby had, of course, been sickening for some little time past. I had been angry and jealous more than once because it had been the cause of my seeing very little of her, and of my being entertained a good deal less than I thought proper on so short a visit. I could remember well enough its little blue-eyed puckered face and slatey-blue eyes, with an expression in them too, almost as dull as slate. Indeed, one morning, not long before – an unusually hot morning for October – she and I and it had sat on a rug in the garden together under the elms. A few withered wild flowers still showed in the grass, I remember, with nothing but their swollen seed vessels left of their summer.

And I had noticed too, how peculiar a shiningness had come into Mrs Orchardson's grey eyes when she talked to her baby. Yet anxiety kept her forehead frowning even while she was smiling, as she stared down into its small ugly wizened face. I didn't think it was in the least a pretty baby, and was vexed at its persisting in being ill.

These last few days, indeed, I had been left almost entirely to myself, with nobody to say a word to, except Esther, the parlourmaid – a sandy-coloured woman with a thick down on her face – and now and then to Mrs Orchardson's cook, who had a way of speaking to me as if I were a kind of clockwork image incapable of even hearing her words. 'And how is the poor little infant this morning?' I asked her once, mimicking the old doctor. She looked at me as if I were a snake in the grass – as no doubt I was.

But to come back to the silver bowl again. I had finished my bread and milk, had for the third time shooed away the cat from getting on to the table, and now sat staring through the long rainy window with my spoon in my mouth, when the door opened, and Mrs Orchardson put her face in at it. It was grey, almost like wet chalk, and her eyes were so sharp and far-off-looking that she seemed scarcely to be aware of me at all. She was certainly looking at me, and yet as if through me, and with almost as horrified an expression as if she could see the very bones in my body. And then suddenly she came in, almost fell down on her knees beside my chair, clasped me round, and hid her face in my lap. 'O, Nick, Nick, you poor lonely thing,' she said, sobbing, 'she is worse, much, much worse. She is dying.'

'Oh, dear!' I said in a mournful voice, 'oh, dear!'

'So you will just try,' she went on hurriedly, as if she were saying something that at any moment might be forgotten, 'you will just try to be quiet and happy by yourself. It won't be long; not very long.' She paused, and I sat on as still as the loaf of bread on the table. She did not seem even to be breathing. But in a minute or two she lifted her wet face from my pinafore, and was looking entirely different from herself. I should hardly have recognized her – and yet she was quite calm, though her cheeks were almost like clay and her eyes as if they had fallen a little back into her head. 'And now, you see,' she added, as if not to me at all, 'Mr Cairns is coming to christen her, to make her God's little child. As you are, Nick.'

'Isn't it going to be taken to church, then?' I said in a sepulchral voice.

'No,' she answered, listening, but not to me.

'But why?' I said in disappointment. She put her hands to my cheeks, cupping my chin in them, and simply looking at me.

'But,' I said wriggling away, 'there's no font here; there *must* be a font like as at church.' I frowned, looking at her a little scornfully out of the corner of my eye. 'It won't be much good if you don't. At least that's what Esther says.'

She only shook her head, still gazing at me, and listening. '*I* know!' I said, 'will that big silver bowl on the sideboard do for a font, Mrs Orchardson? It's a very big bowl!'

She smiled at me brightly.

'Why, of course, you strange creature, that will do beautifully... And now —' She got up, and stood looking for a moment out of the window, as if she had forgotten my presence altogether. 'In all this loveliness!' she almost whispered, though all that she could see was just an ordinary wet morning...

Dr Sharp would not return again for an hour, so there were only Mrs Orchardson, and Esther, and Mr Cairns in the bedroom besides myself and the baby. The cook, I heard, wouldn't come, because she was afraid of being upset. That seemed silly to me. When I went into the room, a little square table already stood between the fire and the sunshine, and it was covered with a linen napkin with a fringe. On this were burning two tall white candles in silver sticks; and in the midst was the bowl with a little water in it which by tiptoeing I could just manage to see. I stared between surprise and dismay at Mr Cairns when he came in in his surplice. He seemed to be a person absolutely different from the two Mr Cairns I knew already – the one a smiling but rather silly-smiling elderly man in his old clerical clothes in the Vicarage garden; the other, of course, looking almost artificial, as he stood intoning the service in church.

Having blown out the candles, and placed them on the dressing table he signed to us to stand up, myself being between Mrs Orchardson and Esther, and the baby lying still and scarlet and open-eyed and without a single sound in Mrs Orchardson's arms. Once I remember, as he leaned over towards her, Mr Cairns's surplice brushed my cheek with its peculiar dry perfume of cambric. And when he dipped his fingers into the bowl I saw the water-butterflies jig on the ceiling.

He did not seem to have noticed that I was there, though for a moment or two his glasses blazed on me like lanterns when he fronted the window. He took the little baby in his great hands. It had begun to cry then. But its crying was more like a very, very old woman's than a natural baby's, and the fingers it spread out in the air an instant were like white match-sticks, they were so thin and shrunken. I smiled at it and made a grimace to please it, but it looked at me like purple glass, as if it was not there to see me or to be amused.

When the service was done, Mr Cairns stooped down and kissed the baby, and he looked a very old man indeed; and yet when he stood up again and had taken off his stole and surplice, he was exactly the same as when I had seen him reading in his garden.

'My dear, dear lady, you must not grieve over-much,' he said to Mrs Orchardson, at the door of the bedroom, 'He knows His lambs, all His lambs. And He is merciful.'

He leant his chin, and smiled towards me with a curious wrinkle on his face. His brown eyes reminded me of berries. They were full of kindness, even though the look in them was not very attentive. I whispered to Esther, asking if I might be allowed to carry the silver bowl downstairs again. And all she gave me was a sharp shake of the head and a greenish look, because I don't think she liked to say no while Mr Cairns was in hearing. He must have heard what I said, because he put his fingers on my hair and smiled at me again, so that I had to go downstairs in front of him, and I think he must have told Mrs Orchardson meanwhile what to do with the bowl and the water.

In the hall he talked for a minute or two in secret with Esther. 'In that case send the little boy to me, then,' I heard him say. 'Mrs Cairns will be at home. Poor tiny lamb! To think it must have suffered like you and me!'

Esther shut her fair-lashed eyes a moment as if to show it would be a mercy
if the baby did die, and then opened them again very stern and mournfully
when she saw me watching her.

Yet in my heart of hearts I was perfectly sure that Mrs Orchardson's little baby would *not* die. I cannot tell whence this assurance came. It may
have been the fruit of a child's natural intuition; or even of his exquisite
eyesight – experienced, as it would seem, to see through, and not only on
the surface. But for one thing, I had all along felt a firm belief in the in-
herent virtue of the bowl, and was contemptuous of Esther for shutting her
eyes like that. It seemed impossible that the clear shallow water in its
shadowy deeps should not wash all taint of sickness away. Besides, *I* had
thought of it.

This, I think, was the reason why I flatly refused to accept Mr Cairns's
invitation to go to the Rectory, when Esther told me to do so. I knew perfectly well she wouldn't be able to make me go against my will while the
baby was so ill. At last she gave a furious empty toss with my grey wool
scarf that she was carrying in her hand, and looked at me as if no tongue
could express her hatred.

'And don't you feel *no* pity for that poor suffering mite upstairs, you
obstinate boy?' she asked me in a low compressed voice. I merely stared at
her without answering, and she had to turn her eyes away.

'He don't even know the meaning of the word!' she said, and shut the
door of the dining-room after her as if she hoped its wood would stick for
ever after to the lintel. But I did not mind her temper. Presently she came in
again, looking even angrier and whiter than before.

'Is this the time for building and Noah's-Arking,' she almost shouted in
my ear as I sat on the hearth rug; 'is *this* the time? – when that poor little
innocent is rattling its very life out over your head?'

I looked no further up at her than at the tray in her hand. 'You little
imp!'

'I suppose when it gets well, it will have to be christened all over again,
properly, won't it?' I inquired. I knew she was staring at me, and hating me
for not caring what she said.

'Where' – she gasped, almost losing herself in her rage – 'where you pick
up such evil heathenish notions from I can't think. Not from *this* house.
There's not a speck of sin left in the whole of that infant's body now; not a
speck. And if you had gone to that kind Mr Cairns as he arst, he would
have *told* you so.'

'I didn't want to go, and Mrs Orchardson wouldn't have tried to make
me.' The blood seemed to rise up in my body and I could hear my own
voice growing more insolent and trumpeting every moment. 'What's more,
Miss Esther, I don't believe a bit in your old holy water. It isn't *going* to die,

and even if you hope it will, it won't. And you're treading on one of my animals.'

At that she deliberately kicked down the fort I was building with her foot.

'You are a little devil incarnate; that's what you are,' she screamed at me, if one can scream without raising one's voice. 'A little devil. You ought never to have been allowed in a Christian house. It's Tophet and the roaring flames that you're bound for, my young man. You've *murdered* that poor mite. You mark my words!'

I was so much enraged at this that I hit at a little bulge in her boot with one of my bricks.

'You're a beast,' I bawled at her in a voice no louder than her own. 'You're a filthy beast. And I don't mind where I go, so long as *you* aren't there. Not a – not a *dam.*'

Her face was so close to mine in its hatred that I saw her eyes change, and her lips stiffen, as if she was afraid. 'You wait, Master Nicholas; you wait! For that vile horrid word! You wait! The master shall hear of that.'

I laughed at her sneeringly. 'I dare you to say it to him. He wouldn't care; he thinks you're a stupid hairy woman. And *I* think you're *hateful.*' She lifted her hand and shut her eyes. 'O, my God,' she said, 'I can't stand it,' and all but ran out of the room.

When she was gone – with the inside of my stomach feeling as if it were on fire – I climbed the stairs to my bedroom, and, boots and all, flung myself down on the white quilt of the bed.

Nothing happened. The house remained in silence. A flying shower rattled on the window pane, and then the sun returned and shone grey and golden in the raindrops. And I hated everything I looked at. I thought how I would kill Esther; and how I would kick her body when she was dead.

But gradually the furnace within me began to die down, my 'thoughts' wandered away, and my eyelids were drooping into a drowse when I heard a muffled sound of footsteps to and fro, to and fro, ascending from the bedroom immediately beneath me, and I remembered the baby. And suddenly a dark shivering horror turned me to ice, and there, as I lay, I prayed to be forgiven for having been myself, and implored God to let me take its sufferings or to die instead of it. So I lay; flat on my stomach, and prayed.

The afternoon had now grown a little darker in the room, and in a while after this, I must have emptily fallen asleep. For the next thing I remember is finding a cold arm round me in the dregs of the dusk and lips close to my face softly whispering and murmuring, their soft warm breath on my cheek.

'Guess, Nick! Guess!' said that soft, thrilling voice, when I stirred a little nearer. 'Guess!'

I put back my head, and by staring close could just see the light from the window reflected in Mrs Orchardson's eyes. A curious phosphorescence was there too; even her skin seemed very faintly to shine.

'Why,' I said, 'she's much better.'

At which those eyes gazed through the narrow air between us as incredulously as if at an angel. 'You knew it; you *knew* it? You precious holy thing! And all this while you have been brooding up here by yourself. What can I say? How can I tell you? Oh, Nick, I shall die of happiness.'

She squeezed herself closer to me in the vacant space on the bed, clasping me round – her shoulders shaking with what just for a minute I thought was laughing.

'I never *can* say how, Mrs Orchardson;' I managed to murmur after a long pause; 'but I was quite sure, you know. I don't think grown-up people understand.'

'And I don't, either,' she said with a little hysterical laugh. 'Indeed, indeed I don't. But there –' she raised her face, sat up, put her hands to her hair, and smiled down on me. I too scrambled up; and could see her plainly now as if by a thin mist-like light from her own body. 'Bless me, Nick, I have made your hair all wet with crying. God bless you, my dear. It was all you; all you.'

She sat in silence a moment, but not as if she was thinking. Then suddenly she breathed, and lifted her head. 'And now I must go, and we mustn't make the teeniest tiniest little crick of a sound. She is asleep. Follow me down – just two shadows. And don't, Nick, *don't* let me vanish away.'

'Will everything,' I asked her when we were safely downstairs; 'will everything be just as ordinarily again now, Mrs Orchardson?'

'You have *missed* me, you dear thing?' she asked, glancing over her shoulder, in the glaring light that now stretched down on us. She was kneeling at the sideboard.

'Esther never says a word, except to make me hate her,' I replied. 'So, of course, most what she says about me is true. So I think now that the baby's quite better, Mrs Orchardson, I had better go home again. Even Mr Cairns wouldn't let me carry the bowl downstairs. And if it hadn't been for that...'

The blue of her eyes shone across at me like bits of the sky seen through a window. They opened wider and wider. 'But, Nick, my *dear!*' she cried at last, clear and small as a bird. 'I hadn't a notion that you had been unhappy. Indeed, indeed I hadn't. Blind selfish creature that I am. He is shaking, poor darling. He is absolutely worn out!'

And at that I could refrain my self-righteousness and self-commiseration no longer. I ran over to her, bowed myself double beside her on the floor, and sobbed 'as if my heart would break'.

The Three Friends*

The street was narrow; yet, looking up, the two old friends, bent on their accustomed visit, could discern – beyond a yellow light that had suddenly shone out into the hushed gloom from an attic window – the vast, accumulated thunderclouds that towered into the darkening zenith.

'That's just it,' continued Mr Eaves, more emphatically, yet more confidentially, 'it isn't my health, Sully. I'm not so much afraid of my health. It's – it's my...' He took off his hat and drew his hand over his tall, narrow head, but pushed on no further towards the completion of his sentence.

Mr Sully eyed him stonily. 'Don't worry then,' he said. 'Why worry? There's worry enough in the world, old sport, without dreaming about it.'

'I know,' said Mr Eaves; 'but then, you see, Sully —' They had paused at the familiar swing-door, and now confronted one another in the opaque, sultry silence. And as Mr Sully stood for an instant in close contact with his old crony in the accentuated darkness of the mock-marble porch, it was just as if a scared rabbit had scurried out of Mr Eaves's long white face.

'Look here,' Mr Sully exclaimed with sudden frivolity, 'we'll ask Miss Lacey'; and was followed by his feebly protesting companion into the bar.

The long black stuffed bench and oblong mahogany table, darkened here and there by little circular pools of beer, stood close against the wall, and Mr Sully began to divulge his friend's confidences even before Miss Lacey could bring them their glasses. A commissionaire sat in the further bar, nodding over an old newspaper; and Mr Eaves kept his eyes fixed on his oblong lurching head, while he listened, fascinated and repelled, to his friend's facetiousness.

'Now, supposing, Miss Lacey, my dear,' began Mr Sully shrewdly, half-closing his eyes as if to gloss over his finesse, 'supposing a young man, a nice, curly-headed young man – just about our old friend's age here' – Miss Lacey, with a kind of arch and sympathetic good nature, leaned a large, dark head to glance at Mr Eaves – 'supposing a nice young gentleman – just as it might be our old friend himself here – came, like an innocent, to entrust to your blessed bosom a secret – a sacred secret: what would you do?'

'Lor' bless me, Mr Sully, sir, is that all you was coming to! A secret? Why, keep it, to be sure; and not the first time neether.' Miss Lacey advanced to the bar, black, precise and cheerful, with the two small, thick glasses in her hand.

* As printed in *The Picnic and Other Stories* (1941). First published in *Saturday Westminster Gazette*, 19 April 1913.

'Good,' said Mr Sully, with an almost professional abandon. 'Good. *So far.* But step number two; supposing, my dear, you couldn't for the life and love of you *help* him in his little difficulty – dependent on his secret, let's say – what then?'

'Why, I'd keep it all the more,' cried Miss Lacey brightly.

'A woman's answer, Eaves; and none the worse for that,' said Mr Sully. 'But on the other hand, supposing you were a practical' – he paused with the little water-jug hovering an inch or two above his friend's glass – 'supposing you were a practical, unromantic old blackguard like me – why, you'd go and tell it to the first lovely blooming creature that came along.' He eyed her steadily yet jocosely. 'And that's why I'm going to tell it to you, my dear!'

'How you do tease, to be sure!' said Miss Lacey. 'He's a real tease, isn't he, Mr Eaves?'

Mr Sully's eyes suddenly sobered with overwhelming completeness. He pointed coldly with his stick. 'He's been dreaming of hell,' he said.

Mr Eaves, on his part, withdrew large, weak, colourless eyes from the uneasy head of the commissionaire, and turned them on Miss Lacey. She glanced at him swiftly, then stooped, and took up a piece of sewing she had laid down on her wooden chair, in the little out-of-the-way bar.

'I don't approve of such subjecs,' she said, 'treated frivolous.'

'Gracious goodness, Eaves,' said Mr Sully, 'she says "frivolous". Hell – "frivolous"!'

'Why,' said Miss Lacey lucidly, 'I'm not so green as I look.'

'Well, you couldn't look younger, if being young's to be green,' said Mr Sully; 'and as sure, my dear, as that was a flash of lightning, it – it's the real thing.'

When the faint but cumulative rumble of thunder that followed had subsided, Miss Lacey seemed to have withdrawn her attention. Mr Sully edged slowly round on his feet and faced his friend. 'You old skeleton at the feast! You've alarmed the poor child,' he said.

Miss Lacey spoke without raising her eyes, bent closely on her needle. 'Not me,' she said; 'but I don't hold with such ideas.'

'Tell her yourself,' said Mr Sully to his friend; "tell her yourself; they never *will* believe *me*."

Mr Eaves shook his head.

'Why not?' said Mr Sully.

'God bless me,' said Mr Eaves, with sudden heat, 'I'm old enough to be her father.'

Miss Lacey looked up over her sewing. 'You'd scarcely believe *me*,' she said mysteriously; 'but there was a young gentleman down Charles Street, where I used to be, that had dreams – well, there, shocking! Nobody but me had the patience to listen to him. But you can't give all your attention to one customer, can you? He,' she cast a curious glance into the shadows brooding over the commissionaire – 'he got up out of his bed one night, just as you or me might – he was living in private apartments, too – struck a match, so they said, and cut his throat. Awful. From ear to ear!' Her thimbled finger made a demure half-circuit of the large pearls of her necklace.

Mr Sully gazed roundly. 'Did he, though? But there, you see,' and he leant in great confidence over the counter, 'Mr Eaves here doesn't shave!'

Mr Eaves smiled vaguely, half-lifting his stick, as if in coquettish achnowledgement of his friend's jest.

'No, no, old friend,' he said, 'not that, not that, I hope.'

'Gracious goodness,' said Mr Sully cordially, 'he mustn't take it to heart like that. A dream's a dream.'

'Why, of course, it is,' said Miss Lacey. 'You ought to take more care of yourself, sir; didn't he, Mr Sully?'

Mr Eaves gazed dispassionately, and yet with some little dignity, in the isolation of attention he had evoked. He turned slowly towards the bar, and stooped a little – confidentially. 'Not once, not twice,' he said ruminatingly, 'but every blessed night. Every blessed night.'

Miss Lacey eyed him with searching friendliness.

'Tell her,' said Mr Sully, walking slowly and circumspectly to the door, and peeping out through the cranny into the darkened street.

Mr Eaves put his empty glass deliberately upon the counter, drew his hand slowly across his mouth and shook his head. 'It's nothing to tell, when you come to that. And...' he nodded a questioning head towards the solitary occupant of the other bar.

'Oh, fast; bless you,' said Miss Lacey. 'As reg'lar as clockwork – you'd hardly believe it.'

'He'll break his neck, some day,' remarked Mr Sully tersely, 'with that jerking.'

'You see, my dear,' continued Mr Eaves trustfully, 'I don't mind my old friend, Mr Sully, making a good deal of fun at my expense. He always has: eh, Sully? But he doesn't *see*. You don't *see*, Sully. There the thing is; and truth all over it. Facts are facts – in *my* belief.'

'But fire and brimstone, and suchlike; oh no!' said Miss Lacey with a dainty little shudder. 'I can't credit it, reelly; oh no! And poor innocent infants, too! You may think of me what you like, but nothing'll make me believe *that*.'

Mr Sully looked over his shoulder at Mr Eaves. 'Oh, that,' said his old friend, 'was only Mr Sully's fun. *He* says it's Hell. *I* didn't. My dream was only – *after*; the state after death, as they call it.'

'I see,' said Miss Lacey, lucidly, summoning all her intelligence into her face.

Mr Eaves leaned forward, and all but whispered the curious tidings into her ear. 'It's – it's just the same,' he said.

'The same?' echoed Miss Lacey. 'What?'

'The same,' repeated the old man, drawing back, and looking out of his long, grey, meaningless face at the little plump, bright, satiny woman.

'Hell?' breathed Miss Lacey.

' "The state after death",' called Mr Sully, still peering into the gloom – and stepped back rather hurriedly in the intense pale lilac illumination of a sudden flickering blaze of lightning.

Thunder now clanged directly overhead, and still Mr Eaves gazed softly yet earnestly into nothingness, as if in deep thought.

'Whatever you like to call it,' he began again steadily pushing his way, 'that's how I take it. I sit with my wife, all just the same; cap and "front" and all, just the same; gas burning, decanter on the table, books in the case, marble clock on the mantelpiece, just the same. Or perhaps I'm walking in the street, just the same; carts and shops and dogs, all just the same. Or perhaps I'm here, same as I might be now; with Sully there, and you there, and him there,' he nodded towards the commissionaire. 'All just the same. For ever, and ever, and ever.' He raised his empty glass to his lips, and glanced almost apologetically towards his old friend. 'For ever, and ever,' he repeated, and put it down again.

'He simply means,' said Mr Sully, 'no change. Like one of those blessed things on the movies; over and over again, click, click, click, click, click; you know. I tell him it's his sentence, my dear.'

'But if it's the same,' Miss Lacey interposed, with a little docile frown of confusion, 'then what's different?'

'Mark me, Eaves, my boy,' cried Mr Sully softly at the door; 'it's the ladies for brains, after all. That's what they call a poser. "What's different", eh?'

Mr Eaves pondered in a profound internal silence in the bar. And beyond the windows, the rain streamed steadily in a long-drawn gush of coolness and peace. 'What's *different*?' repeated Mr Sully, rocking infinitesimally on his heels.

'Why,' said Mr Eaves, 'it seems as if there *I* can't change either; can't. If you were to ask me how I know – why, I couldn't say. It's a dream. But that's what's the difference. There's nothing to come. *Now*: why! I might change in a score of ways; just take them as they come. I might fall ill; or Mrs Eaves might. I might come into some money; marry again. God bless me, I might *die*! But there, that's all over; endless; no escape; nothing. I can't even die. I'm just meself, Miss Lacey; Sully, old friend. Just meself, for ever, and ever. Nothing but me looking on at it all, if you take me – just what I've made of it. It's my' – his large pale eyes roved aimlessly – 'it's just what Mr Sully says, I suppose; it's my sentence. Eh, Sully? wasn't that it?

My sentence?' He smiled courageously.

'Sentence, oh no! Sentence? You!' cried Miss Lacey incredulously. 'How could you, Mr Sully? Sentence! Whatever for, sir?'

Mr Eaves again glanced vaguely at the sleeper, and then at his friend's round substantial shoulders, rigidly turned on him. He fixed his eyes on the clock.

'You've never done no *harm*, Mr Eaves!' cried Miss Lacey, almost as if in entreaty.

'You see,' said the old gentelman, glancing over his shoulder, 'it isn't what you do: so I seem to take it.' Mr Sully half turned from the door, as if to listen. 'It's what you are,' said Mr Eaves, as if to himself.

'Why, according to that,' said Miss Lacey, in generous indignation, 'who's safe?'

A day of close and tepid weather followed the storm. But it was on the evening of the next day after that – an evening of limpid sunshine and peace, the sparrows chirping shrilly in the narrow lights and shadows of the lane, that Mr Sully came in to see Miss Lacey.

She was alone: and singing a little quiet tune to herself as she went about her business. He shook his head when she held up two glasses; and raised just one forefinger.

'He's dead,' he said.

'Oh, no!' cried Miss Lacey.

'This morning . . . in his sleep.' He gazed at her with an unusual – with a curiously fish-like concentration.

'Poor, poor gentleman,' said Miss Lacey. 'He *was* a gentleman, too; and no mistake. Never a hard word for nobody; man, woman, or child. A kind good gentleman – always the same. But it's shocking. Well, well. But how dreadfully sudden, Mr Sully, sir!'

'Well, I don't know,' said Mr Sully almost irritably. 'And if so, where's the change?' His round shoulders seemed with slight effort almost to shrug themselves.

'Goodness gracious,' Miss Lacey cried, 'you don't mean – you don't mean to think – you don't say it's true? What he was telling us, Mr Sully?'

'I'm not so sure,' her visitor replied vaguely, almost stubbornly. 'Where else, after all, knowing all that, why, where else *could* he go?'

'Mr Eaves, Mr Sully? Him? oh, no!'

Mr Sully, in the intense clear quiet of the bar, continued to stare at her in a manner something like that of an over-glutted vulture. He nodded.

Miss Lacey's kind brown eyes suddenly darkened as if with a gust of storm. 'But, then, what about *us*?' she cried piteously, and yet with the tenderest generosity.

'Well,' said Mr Sully, opening the door, and looking out into the sunny evening air, 'if you ask me, that's merely a question of time.'

Lispet, Lispett and Vaine*

Maunders's little clear morning town was busy with dogs and tradesmen and carriages. It wore an almost child-like vivacity and brightness, as if overnight it had been swept and garnished for entranceable visitors from over the sea. And there – in the blowy sunshine, like some grotesque Staffordshire figure on a garret chimney-piece – there, at the street corner, sat so ludicrous an old man that one might almost have described him as mediæval.

A peak cap, of a slightly marine, appearance, was drawn down over his eyes. Beneath it, wisps of grey hair and a thin beard helplessly shook in the wind; and before him stood a kind of gaping wallet, of cracked American cloth, held yawningly open by its scissor-legs.

From this receptacle, ever and again, he extracted a strand of his dyed bast, or dubiously rummaged in its depths for his scissors. Whereupon he would gingerly draw the strand between his lips – a movement that positively set one's teeth on edge – and at the same moment he would cast a bleared, long, casual glance first down the street to his right – High Street; and then up the street to his left – Mortimer Street; as the bast drew him round.

I had watched him awhile from under the canvas window-blind of Lister Owlett's, the Curio Shop, in which my friend Maunders was chaffering with a dark sardonic-looking man over a piece of Sheffield plate, and, at last, with that peculiar mixture of shame, compassion, amusement, and horror which such ineffectual (though possibly not unhappy) beings produce on one, I had crossed the road and had purchased an absurd little doll bast marketing basket. Oddly, too, *after* I had actually selected my specimen, and had even paid its price, the queer remote old creature had insisted on my taking a rather more ornate example of his wares...

'You know, Maunders,' I said, when we were a hundred yards or so beyond the old gentleman's pitch, 'this thing isn't at all badly made. The pattern is rather pretty, and there's a kind of useless finish to it. There's still something to be said for the amateur. Anyhow, Bettie will like it.'

Maunders turned his long, large, palish face of his and looked at me

* First published in *Yale Review,* January 1923.

with his extraordinary eyes. For the ninety-ninth time at least I noticed that their faint blue and his necktie's azure called each to each, as deep calls to deep.

'Amateur!' he echoed blandly, though a peculiar fixity of attention had gathered into his gaze; 'why, that old gentleman is the last of – of the Lispets.' He turned his head away – a queer-shaped, heavy head – and added: 'Quite the last.'

'Lispets, Maunders; what are they?'

"My dear K —, believe me,' said Maunders almost mincingly, 'not everything is a jest. You must now have trodden the streets of this small town at least a dozen times. The Works – what remains of them – are not seven miles off. And yet, here you are, pleasantly fluting that you have lived a life of such obscurity as never to have heard of Lispet, Lispett and Vaine's. It's an affectation. I can scarcely forgive you. Nor will Henrietta.'

He was – as usual – gently thrusting-out before him his handsome malacca cane in a manner which frequently persuaded approaching pedestrians that he was blind. And he repeated *sotto voce,* and as if out of an ocean of reflection, ' "Lispet, Lispett and Vaine; Mercers to Their Majesties..." I wish I could remember exactly how the old title went. In latter times, I mean.'

'Who were "their Majesties," then?'

' "Their Majesties"?' said Maunders. 'Oh, mere kings and queens. In the Firm's heyday they were, of course, the crowned heads of practically the whole barbaric globe. But what is history – mummified fact; desiccated life; the irretrievable. You are merely one of the crowd who care not tuppence for such things. The present generation – with its Stores and Emporiums and Trusts and "Combines" – is blind to the merest inkling of what the phrase Merchant Prince implies. We are not even conscious of irony in little Tommy Tucker's *Nation of Shopkeepers.* Other times, better manners. The only "entirely honest merchant" of late years – so far as I have definitely heard – is bones in Shirley graveyard. Still, the Lispet tradition was not one of mere honesty.'

'What, then,' said I.

'Well, in the first place,' replied Maunders, sliding me a remote ruminative glance, 'it rambles back almost to prehistoric times. You may hunt down the aboriginals of the Firm for yourself, if you feel so inclined. They appear to have been Phoenicians. Tyre, maybe, but I gather non-Semitic. Some remote B.C. glasswork in the Egyptian galleries of the British Museum bears their "mark" – two inverted V's with a kind of P between. There are others – a cone "supported by" two doves; a running hound, a crescent moon, and a hand – just a slim, ungrasping hand. Such marks have been discovered, they say, woven into mummy linen, into Syrian embroidery, Damascus silks, and tapestry from the Persian Gulf.

'The priestesses of Astaroth, according to Bateson, danced in gauze of L.
L. & V.'s handiwork. They exploited the true bombyx ages before Ptolemy;
their gold thread gleamed on the Ark of the Covenant; and it was fabric of
their weaving in which the Queen of Sheba marvelled before Solomon. The
shoes of his apes, sewn-in with seed pearls and splinters of amethyst were
— But what's the good of chattering on like this? I'm not,' groaned
Maunders with a muffled yawn, 'I'm not a perambulating encyclopaedia.
Some old pantaloon of a German, long before Bateson, burrowed in true
German fashion into the firm's past. You may go to bed with his book, if
you like – this very night. And then, of course, there are one or two of their
old ledgers and curios in the local museum. But I'm not an antiquarian. My
only point is that the past even of a soapboiler is none the worse for being
the distant past. What's more, they knew in those days that objects are only
of value when representative of subjects. Has it never occurred to you (no,
I suppose not) that the Wisest's apes, ivory, and peacocks were symbolical?
The apes representing, of course —'

'*Of course*,' I interruped hurriedly. 'But what I'm after, Maunders, is
something faintly resembling matter-of-fact. These Lispet people – what is
really their history? Subsequent, I mean, to the Apocrypha on which you
have already drawn. Honestly, that pathetic old guy with the pouch of bast
at the corner rather interested me.'

' "Drawn on!" he says,' drawled Maunders. 'When I have not even
distantly referred to Joseph's Coat, or that she-devil Jezebel's head-dress, or
to the Grand Khan, or to the Princess Assinimova, or to the tanned Barbary
kid cuirass of steel and emeralds in which Saladin met his end. A Firm that,
apart from clients celebrated in Holy Writ, once happily wrote off bad
debts incurred with such customers as Semiramis, Sappho, Paris, and the
Arch – or, as we amused moderns suppose, the exceedingly arch – Druids,
might well boast – though it didn't – not only of its repute but also of its
catholicity.

'No, no'; he mooned slowly about him. 'Your precious old "matter-of-
fact"! As if you were a clerk in unholy orders, as if you bought your boots
in Scotland Yard, as if you were a huckster of hardware. By all means you
shall have the facts. But for heaven's sake – for heaven's sake, precocious
K —, be careful with them. A friend of mine (an earnest man) was once
given a fact, and it exploded – in his bathroom.'

Dangling the last-of-the-Lispet's little basket on my forefinger, I awaited
the facts.

'The point is,' Maunders murmured on, 'what of the slightest interest to
you can there be to say of a firm that is now dust, and that followed a tradition which in these days would within six months clap its partners into

Bedlam or the Bankruptcy Court? You must confess that that kind of sweet reasonableness, hardly less than the modern variety, is at last death to any decent humanity. At long last, maybe. And how divine a decay! Anyhow, there they were – and there, too, are the ruins of them, edging the smooth sloping crest of Adderley Hill, on the other side of the town. Henrietta shall take you there tomorrow, if you're a polite guest. She loves to expatiate on that kind of rubble – the Failures.

'Still, try to imagine it, my dear K —, in its green and early days. A long range of low buildings, part half-timbered Tudor, with a few wombed-in bits of thirteenth- and fourteenth-century work, and a fringe of excellent eighteenth-century – weathered and lovely moulded brick. In its prime it must have been a ravishing sight, with its hanging sign of faded blue and gold, its walls and thatch, and shingles, cobbled alleys and water-conduits, worn and mellow with the peace of a thousand thousand sunsets, the mosses and rain-stains and frost-flowerings of centuries of autumns and winters – just England's history, moral and actual, in antique stone and gable and mullion.

'That's as it may be. I have no wish to exaggerate. There is no particular virtue in mere age – except to the imagination. Still, your mere "facts" are something I suppose. The fact that they were spinning silk – here in England – before the Conqueror came over. The fact that they were world-renowned glovers long before Elizabeth's time. The fact that their Egyptian cotton must have been abob on the Mediterranean when Lancashire, please God, was a verdant solitude, and *your* forefathers, my poor dear, were gadding about in woad.

'They had their foreign agents, of course, netting in handiwork from all over the globe, on which they themselves set the final seal. I won't labour the point. All I suggest is that you should ask a Bond Street dealer to supply you with a Persian rug of L. L. & V. workmanship. But avoid the First of April for the enterprise. And yet, do you know, there was really nothing at the root of them but – well, a kind of instinct: to keep themselves clean. Animals share it. That, and the pride with which a single virtue darkens and suffocates a man if he isn't for ever toiling to keep its growth under. The one secret of their stability, of their being, and, in times past, of their success, was simply this – that nothing they should, would, or could ever conceivably offer for sale need disturb for a breath of a sob or the weight of a dewdrop the ashes of their sleeping forefathers in Adderley Church-yard. The like of which their forefathers had done by *their* forefathers.

'Why, if the ancient Hebrew Jews bequeath the very droop of their noses, why shouldn't an old English "House" bequeath its tradition? They believed – not Athanasian fashion but in their insides, so to speak – they believed in that perfect quality and consummate workmanship which, naturally, only exorbitant prices can assure. Exorbitant prices, mind you, not profits. They valued their fair fame. Only what was good enough for a Lispet could hope to satisfy a partner who spelt his name with two t's, and only what satisfied a Lispett left unashamed the conscience of a Vaine.

'In plain Anglo-Saxon, the whole thing in decent practical moderation was merely the positive forecast of a Utopian dream. If ever you pass that way, rest for a moment at the mouth of the Well at the World's End. And drink, pretty creature. Perhaps you will discover a cone supported by two doves scrawled on the bottom of its bronze bucket.'

'Perhaps,' I echoed, as cheerfully as possible.

'At an extreme, of course, this tradition became the very devil. I don't say they made any claim to be gentry, or that they refused any kind of exalted alliance if nicely and unostentatiously proffered. There's an old tale of one of their apprentices who went sightseeing in the fourteenth century. Among other little romantic adventures, he hunted the Unicorn, got a siren with child, fought a demon in Babylon, and bartered tiaras with the reigning Pope in Avignon – very much at that precise moment at a loose end.

'Still a tale's only a tale, though none the worse for that. You want naked facts – a most indecorous variety; and one of them is that during the nearer centuries the three families riotously intermarried, making the green one red, as the poet says. They were self-sufficient – like Leonardo. Except, of course, that they were artists only in the sense that they designed and distributed objects of flawless craftsmanship; while he was a consummate craftsman only by degree of his supreme art. And that was – or was not – between himself and the infinite, so to speak.'

'I love your "so-to-speaks," Maunders.'

'It's very nice of you,' said Maunders. 'But what I really want to say is that gradually the "standing" of the Firm lost everything in the nature of the precarious. Then, enter Beelzebub. Their only conceivable corruption could come from within, in one or two forms, putrefaction or petrifaction. Well, you shall see. In their earlier annals they can never so much as have tasted temptation to sink to trade devices. Progress, on the other hand, was practically denied to them. Their monopoly was the only one to be had for the asking – their integrity.

'I am not joking. Their wares were as innocent of guile and as beautiful as the lilies of the field. All they needed for mere prosperity was the *status quo*. Does Nature? The high and mighty sought them out for precisely the same reason as a young man with imagination pursues that Will-o'-the-Wisp called Beauty. Have you ever noticed how different a respect one has for an *advertised* article and for an article whose virtues have been sweetly absorbed into one's soul?

'Compare, for instance, a cottage loaf with *foie gras*; or the Mr Anon of the Scottish Ballads with Sappho; or Lord Loveaduck's "brilliance" with Gamma in Leo. Lispet, Lispett and Vaine would have as gladly catalogued their goods as have asked for references. Advertise! Why, a lady might as well advertise her great-grandmother's wig. They were merchants of the one true tradition. Their profits were fees. Their arrogance was beyond the imagination of a Tamburlaine, and their – what shall we call them? – their principles were as perennial as the secret springs of the Oceans. It was on similar principles that Satan sold the fruit to Mother Eve.'

'I see,' said I. 'If one *can*, Maunders – through a haze of contradictions.'

'You cannot see,' said Maunders. 'But that is simply because your modern mind is vitiated by the conviction that you just *pay* a tradesman to sell you a decent article, that you can with money buy quality. You can't. L. L. & V. merely graciously *bestowed* on their customers the excellence of their wares, of their "goods" in the true old meaning of the term – a peculiar something in the style and finish which only the assurance of their history and their intentions – their ideals, if you like – made possible.

'Good heavens, man, isn't there a kind of divination between one's very soul and a thing decently made – whether it's a granite Rameses, or a Chelsea porringer? The mere look of a scarf or a snippet of damask or of lawn, or of velvet, a stomacher or a glove of L. L. & V. make is like seeing for the first time a bush of blowing hawthorn or a nymph in a dell of woodruff, when, say, you are nine. Or, for the last, when you are nine-and-ninety.'

'My dear Maunders,' I smiled benignly. 'What on earth are you talking about? I have always supposed that speech was intended to disclose one's meaning. Nymphs!'

'Well,' replied Maunders, imperturbably shoving his "Sheffield" candlestick at last into his slate-covered greatcoat pocket; 'I merely mean that there is a kind of goodness in good work. It confers a sort of everlasting youth. Think of the really swagger old boys we call the masters. What do you actually get out of them? The power to be momentarily immortal, that's all. But that's beside the point. What I wanted to tell you about – and you are a poor receptacle – is, of course, the firm's inevitable degradation. I have kept you pining too long. First they petrified, and then the stone began to rot away. The process must of course have been very gradual. It was Anthony Lispett who at the same time finished it off, and who yet – at least according to *my* notion of the thing, though Henrietta does not agree – and who yet redeemed the complete contraption.

'He must have come into the firm when he was a comparative youngster, say nineteen, towards the end of the eighteenth century. Needless to say, not a single one of the partners, not at least to my knowledge, ever went to a university or any fallalery of that kind. They held aloof from alien ideals. Their "culture" was in their history and in their blood; and not a

Methuselah's lifetime could exhaust even a fraction of that. They had no ambitions; did not mix; kept to themselves. Their ladies made their own county society – sparrowhawk-nosed, sloping-shouldered, high-boned, fair-haired beauties for the most part. It was an honour to know them; to be known by them; a privilege – and one arrogantly reserved, to be among their "customers". They were Lispet, Lispett and Vaine.

'Well, this Anthony seems to have been something of an exotic leaven. From the beginning, he was two-thirds himself, *plus*, if you like, three thirds a Lispett. There is a portrait of him in his youth – an efflorescent Georgian dandy, whiskers, *hauteur*, eyebrows all complete; a kind of antique Beau Brummel. No doubt the old boys squinted askew at him out of their spectacles, no doubt they nodded at each other about him over their port. No doubt their good ladies pursed their mouths at him over their teacups.

'But they could no more resist the insidious growth of the creature than Jack's mother could have held down the sprouting beanstalk. He was clearly the fruit of breeding-in, and of a kind of passive vain-gloriousness, as you will see when Henrietta exhibits the Family Tree.

'Old John Vaine Lispet Lispett had married his first cousin Jemima Lispett, and Anthony, it seems, was their only child. There is a story that old John himself in his youth had – well, gossip is merely gossip, and gossamer's merely gossamer, however prolific it may be. And, whether or not, there is no doubt that Anthony in his boyhood had made an attempt to run away. They picked him up seven miles from the coast – half-starved and practically shoeless. He must have been off to Tyre or Damascus, or something of that kind. One knows how one's worm may turn.

'Poor child – just that one whiff of freedom, and he was back once more, gluing his nose, beating his fledgling plumes, against an upper window of the house on the hill. The whole thing, top to bottom, was a kind of slavery, of course. The firm had its own Factory Laws.

'No "hand", for example was allowed to wear, at least within sight of those windows, any fabric not of the firm's weaving. No hand ever came into direct contact with one of the partners. There was a kind of hereditary overseer – a family of the name of Watts. Every hand, again, was strictly forbidden to starve. If he or she misbecame himself or herself, instant dismissal followed; and a generous pension.

'So drastic was the relation between the valley-village and the hill that for upwards of two hundred and fifty years, only one hand *had* so misbecome herself. She had smiled a little smile one spring morning out of her little bottle-glass casement above her loom at the middle-aged Vaine; and she drew her pension for six months! They say she drowned herself in the Marshes. It is as if you went and hanged yourself for having too short a nose.'

'I cannot see the analogy,' said I.

'No,' said Maunders, 'but your Maker would – the Jehovah that blessed the race of the vulture that sold me this old replica of a candlestick. Can't you understand that her smile was a natural thing (just out of herself), and that he was a kind of sacrosanct old Pharaoh? The discipline was abominable according to our sentimental modern notions. But then, the perquisites were pretty generous.

'The long and the short of it was that every single one of the firm's employees was happy. They were happy in the only sense one *can* be truly happy – in service. Corruptions have swarmed in now, but in the old days the village in the valley must have been as beautiful as a picture of this green old world hung up in the forecourt of Paradise.

'It had houses contemporary with every wing of the Works on the hilltop. Its wages were for the most part the only decent wages one can accept. They were in *kind*. What, I ask you, in the sight of heaven is the fittest payment to John Keats for a sonnet – a thousand guineas or a plume of your little Elizabeth's golden fuzz?

'I don't want to sentimentalize. J.K. had to live, I suppose (though why, we may be at loggerheads to explain). But what is porridge without cream, and what is cream if you loathe the cow? I ask you, my dear K., is not a living wage simply one that will keep the *kind* of life it represents fully alive?

'Give them the credit, then. L. L. & V. kept their hands positively blossoming with life. I don't mean they theorized, Marx is merely the boiled-up sentiment of a civilization gone wrong. They weren't philanthropists. Nor am I, please heaven. The quality of the L. L. & V. merchandise ensured quality in their hands. Where we walk now – this macadamized road – was once a wood of birches and bluebells. Can you even imagine its former phantom denizens to have been knocked-kneed or under-hung?'

'Perhaps not,' said I, 'but are you intending to imply that the "phantom denizens," as you call them, manufacture the bluebells?'

Maunders made an indescribably guttural noise in his throat.

'What I am saying,' he replied, 'is that the village was as lovely a thing to see and live and laugh and love and dream in as were the bodies of the human beings that occupied it. *Their* stock, too, had climbed from grace to grace. They enjoyed a recognizable type of beauty. The girls were as fair-skinned as a plucking of apricots, with hair of a spidery fine silkenness, and eyes worthy of their veiling. Just Nature's mimicry, I suppose; like an Amazonian butterfly, or the praying mantis or – or the stick caterpillar.

'I can see them – and so could you, if you had the eyes – I can see them dancing in the first of early moonlight, or bathing in what, prior to the human spawning of tin cans and old boots, was a stream crystal as Pharpar. I can see them sallying out and returning on their chattering to-and-fro in the morning dews and the greying twilight. No set hours; only a day as long or as short as love of its task could make it. What indeed is breeding, my dear K —, but the showing forth of a perfectly apt and peculiar excellency? Just fitness for its job. Puma, pelican, Patagonian papalja, pretty Poll.'

'What is a papalja, Maunders?' I inquired.

'I don't know,' said Maunders, 'But imagine them – with whatever effort is necessary – ascending and descending that hill-side through their Fruit Walk! It is about the nearest approach to any earthly vision I can achieve of Jacob's ladder. Give even your abominable old London a predominant L. L. & V. – well, *then*, but not till then, you may invite me to the Mansion House for its annual November 9th. But there, I'm not an iconoclast.'

'I wish, Maunders,' said I, 'you would at your leisure re-read *Unto this Last*; and that you would first make the ghost of an attempt to tell a decent story. What was the Fruit Walk?'

The Town's puddly, petrol-perfumed, outlying streets were still busy with pedestrians – nurses and perambulators, children in woollen gaiters, and young ladies with red hair. It was, therefore, almost as difficult to keep abreast with Maunders as it was to follow his obscure meanderings.

'Oh, the Fruit Walk,' he muttered, staring vacantly through a dairyman's window at an earthenware green-and-grey pelican with a fish in its bill. 'The Fruit Walk was merely the cherries and quinces and crab-apples and damsons that had been planted in rosy, snowy, interlacing, discontinuous quincunx fashion; half circling and straggling over and down the green mounting and mounded hill to the very edge of the quarry. Not a miserable avenue, of course, but a kind of to-and-fro circuitous chace between village and Works. Once, your eyes might actually have seen that divine chimneyed cluster, tranquil as an image in water, on the dark emerald hilltop in the dying, gaudy sunset. And, shelving down, that walk in bloom! One might almost assume that L. L. & V. weather habitually haunted the scene. Things do react on one another, you know; and Nature wears fourteenth-century sleeves.'

'Oh, for pity's sake, Maunders, let's get back to Anthony. What about Anthony?'

Maunders, softly striding along like an elephant in his flat square-toed shoes, appeared to be pondering.

'Well,' he began slowly, 'the "what-about" of Anthony covers a rather wide field. I fancy, do you know, there was a tinge of Traherne in his composition. The beau was only the chrysalis stage. Of course it was Blake's era. I fancy Anthony sowed pretty early his wild oats. There are many varieties, and his were mainly of the mind.

'He was not, I venture to add, to make things *quite* clear to you, either a marrying or an un-marrying man. And, of course, like all instinctive creatures with a never-waning fountain of life in them, he shed. Some of us shed feathers, some fur, some innocence, some principles, and all shed skin – the seven year's spring-cleaning, you know, that leaves the house in the flooding May-day sunlight a little bit dingier that it was before.

'Well, Anthony seems to have shed what one mistakes for artificialities. He shed his ringlets, his foppish clothes, his pretences of languor, his dreamy superiority. He shed his tacit acceptance of the firm's renown, and so discovered his own imagination. Only in the "tip-toppers" do intellect and imagination lie down together, as will the lion and the lamb.

'Then, of course, he seems gradually or suddenly to have shed the L. L. & V. pride and arrogance. He must have begun to think. All these centuries, please remember, the firm had been gradually realizing why, actually *why*, their stuff was super-excellent in the eyes of humanity. And that – Oh, I don't know; but to realize that, perhaps, is to discount its merits elsewhere. Anthony, on the other hand, had come to realize, in his own queer vague fashion, that one's only salvation is to set such eyes squinting. And yet, not of set and deliberate purpose. He was not a wit. Art, my dear, dear K —, whatever you may like to say, *is* useless; unless one has the gumption to dissociate use from materialism.'

'I was not aware,' said I, 'that I had said anything. You mean, I suppose, that a man has only to realize that his work is excellent for it to begin to lose its virtue. Like beauty, Maunders, and the rouge-pot and powder-puff? Still, I prefer Anthony to trade ethics. What did the rest of them do?'

'What I was about to tell you,' replied Maunders mildly, 'is that Anthony had bats in his belfry. Not the vampire variety; just *extra*-terrestrial bats. He was "queer". Perhaps more in him that in most of us had come from elsewhere. And the older he grew the more the hook-winged creatures multiplied. No doubt the Firm would have edged him out if it had been practicable. No doubt the young hedge-sparrows would edge out the squab-cuckoo, if that were manageable. But it was not. Anthony was double-dyed, a Lispett with two t's, and it would have been *lèse majesté*, domestic high-treason, to acknowledge to the world at large that he was even eccentric.

'Well, there he was, a smallish man, with short-growing hair, a little like Thothmes II, to judge from his portrait – a man of extraordinary gifts in his craft, of an exquisite sensibility to quality and design, but seldom, I imagine, at the Board Meetings. Often, it seems, he used to ramble off into the country. He appears to have especially hated a sort of Frenchiness that had crept into the firms' wares. But much worse than mooning about to soak in Englishness again, he would ramble off into the country of his *mind*, and there you need to have a faint notion of where you are before you can safely go any further. It's difficult, of course, to know exactly what his broodings were. But the story goes that he would complete his nocturnal pilgrimages by climbing up before daybreak into one of the fruit-trees on the hill, a magnificent mulberry – to see the sun, I suppose; to "look down" as far as possible on the Works; to be up among the morning birds, like the old man in the limerick.'

'An odd bat, that,' I interposed.

'There he would squat,' continued Maunders imperturbably, 'poor old creature, peering out of the leaves, the rose of dawn on his face, as when it lightened Blake's. And presently, the angels up from the valley would pass by, singing and laughing, to their work. A pretty sight it must have been, with their young faces and pure colours and nimble practised gestures. For, mind you, it was still a happiness to be one of the hands in the firm – as compared, at any rate, with being a grimy paw elsewhere. Only at long last would *they* become aware of the glowing gloom in the heads. Not merely were the brains of the firm tending in one direction and the members remaining more or less static in another, but things outside were beginning to change. The god of machinery was soon to spout smoke and steam from his dismal nostrils, and man to learn the bright little lesson that not only necessities, but even luxuries, can be the cheaper if they are manufactured a gross at a time.'

'Yes,' said I; 'there he would squat; and then?'

'Then,' breathed Maunders, 'one morning, one shafted scarlet morning, it seems he saw – well, I cannot say what exactly he did see. No hand anyhow, but a light-embodied dream. A being lovelier than any goddess for whom even an L. L. & V. in the service of the Sorceress of Sidon could have been moved from bowels of superstitious horror to design sandals. A shape, a fleetingness, a visitant – poor old Bat-in-the-Belfry – evoked by a moment's aspiration and delight out of his own sublime wool-gatherings. And so this ageing creature, this extra-Lispetted old day-dreamer, fell in love – with a non-entity.'

'My dear Maunders; pause,' I said. 'In mere self-respect! How could such an occurrence as that have been recorded in the Firm's annals? No; no.'

'Weren't there letters?' sighed Maunders, turning suddenly on me, malacca cane in air. 'Wasn't there a crack-brained diary? Haven't you a vestige of old-fashioned and discredited gumption? Wait till I have finished, and let your sweet-smelling facts have a show. Ask Henrietta. I say,' he repeated stubbornly, 'that between the dawn and the daytime, down out of his broad foliage, the hill-side in indescribable bloom, this old meandering Query, this half-demented old Jack-o'-Dreams saw a Vision, and his heart went the same way as long since had gone his head. Haven't I told you he was what the dear old evolutionists, blind to the inexhaustible graces of creation, esteem a *sport*?

'The Family Tree had blossomed out of season, for the last time, jetting

its dwindling virtue into this final, queer, anomalous bloom; rich with nec-
tarous bane. It had returned upon itself. 'Tis the last rose of Summer that
sighs of the Spring. "Ah, yes, but did the vision see *him*?" – you are sneering to yourself.

'And to that I reply: I don't know. Do they ever? Or is it that only certain
long-suffering eyes can afford them the hospitality of becoming visible?
Anyhow, *I* see her. And in a fashion that is not only the bliss but the very deuce
of solitude. Ignore its bidding, K —, and we are damned. Oh yes, I know. The
inward eye is all very well. I know it. But to share that experience with these
outward groping orbs, I'd – well, I'd gladly go bankrupt. Ask Henrietta.'

'What happened then?'

'This happened. The wool-gathering wits flocked back and golden-
fleeced him. One might almost say he became equally astute and extravagant. As a matter of fact, of course, only willing and selfless service can
bring every human faculty to bear.' Maunders sighed. 'He sent a cheque
for a thousand guineas or so to a Dutch bulb-farm, and planted the hill-
walk with tulips, April-blue scyllas and *narcissi poetici. Narcissi poetici!*
He tapped an earth-bound spring and set up fauns and dryads, amoretti
and what not, spouting subterranean water. He built a shrine of alabaster
– with an empty niche.

'It appeared to be mere scatter-brained fooling. Still, it was in a sense in
the L. L. & V. tradition, and his partners appear to have let him have a free
hand. Don't forget their even then almost illimitable resources. They'd far
far rather – even the strict-whiskered Vaine of the period, who in unhap-
pier circumstances might have sat for the typical alderman – they'd infinitely rather he exhibited his peculiarities within their sphere, so to speak,
than bring them to mockery before the world at large.'

'I see.'

'They hadn't till then perhaps baldly recognized the world at large,
except as a hot-bed of prehistoric or sycophantic customers. And they
never – not for an instant – even surmised his depredations would prove
active from *within*. None the less, like some secret serpent, spawn of the
forgotten fabulous, he was in fact gnawing at the very vitals of the
tradition. Let me put it bluntly, in terms which even you, my dear K —, will
appreciate. Anthony Lispett had "gone balmy" on his Vision. She – and
therefore he – was "beside *himself*".

'I do not suggest that he mixed her up with his superannuating old *cor-
pus vile*; nothing vulgar to talk of, and tragic to think of, in that sort. He
merely lived on from that daybreak dream to dream with but one desire in
his poor cracked old cranium – to serve her idea. Aren't we, all of us, myth-
makers? Grins not the Lion at the Unicorn? Does not the soapboiler
bedizen our streets with Art – and "atmosphere"? Anthony's myth was from

elsewhere – neither from his stomach, his pocket, his reputation, his utilitarian morals, nor his brains. That was all. And as he served her, I suppose, he found himself cherubically treading yet more secretly and inwardly her hesperidean meads.'

I glanced at Maunders in some dismay. 'How?'

'Well,' said he, 'it is not easy to divine how exactly Anthony began his malpractices. But clearly, since he was perpetually haunted by this illusion of a divine, unearthly stranger, a sort of Athene haunting his hill, his one desire could not but be to set the Works working for *her*. He could bide his time. He could be quiet and gradual. Anyhow, we know the event, though we can't say precisely how it evolved.

'One may assume, I suppose, that he would steal to and fro among the nocturnal looms and presses and vats and dyeing rooms, and, ten times more richly gifted by his insane inspiration than he was even by nature, that he just doctored right and left. He would experiment night after night with the firm's materials in the raw. Worse, he rationed himself in his tree-gazing; and climbed to his leafy perch only during certain conjunctions of the planets. Mere circumstances seem to have waited on him, as did the sun on Joshua.

'But the Lispet and the Vaine of this time were nothing but hidebound old bachelors – intent only on saving the face of convention. The last Double-T died the day after the site of the shrine was decided on. There was no young blood in the firm. And with an almost diabolical ingenuity Anthony seems to have executed only the orders of such clients as wanted the firm's very finest and rarest handiwork. Even those, of course, who coveted or could afford only the commoner materials were already beginning to dwindle in numbers.

'The other customers he kept waiting, or insulted with questions, or supplied with more delicate and exquisite fabrics than they required.

'The story goes that a certain Empress renowned for her domestic virtues commanded a trousseau for yet another royal niece or what not. A day or two before the young woman's nuptials, and weeks late, arrived silks and tissues and filigrees spun out of some kind of South American and Borneo spider silk, such as only a nymph could wear. My dear K —, it nearly hatched a European War. That particular Court was little but a menagerie of satyrs.

'Countesses and such-like soliciting "fives" and "fours" in gloves, and "ones" in stockings, might still faintly hope to be accommodated; and even then their coveted wares were a tight fit. For a while the firm seems to have survived on the proceeds from merchandise intended for grown-ups which your cosmopolitan Croesuses snapped up for their children. At second-hand, of course, since few of them could extort a "reference" to the firm for love or even for money.

'Henrietta has a few bits of embroideries and silk of the time. Perhaps she will show them to you. Even a human craft can reflect a divine disaster. And the linens! – of a quality that would derange the ghost of an Egyptian embalmer.

'Even worse, Anthony seems to have indulged an extraordinary sense of propriety. He would lavish L. L. & V. urbanities on some sylph of an actress who had no more morals in the usual acceptation of the term than a humming bird, and flatly returned fabulous cheques (with the order) to old protégés of the firm merely convicted of fortune-making, or of organized "philanthropy", or of "bettering the conditions" of their fellow-creatures. He seems to have hated the virtuous for their own sake alone.

'In short, he grew madder and madder, and the custom, the good-will, even the reputation of the firm melted like butter in the sun. The last Lispet followed the last Double-T – expired of apoplexy in the counting-house, and was sat on by the coroner. The reigning Vaine turned religious and was buried in a sarcophagus of Portland stone under the foundations of the Unitarian Chapel which he himself had laid in the hope perhaps to lay the L. L. & V. devil at the same time.

'The hands dwindled, died out, dropped away, or even emigrated to the paws. Only a few with some little competence and an impulsive fund of gratitude and courtesy worked on for a master of whom because they loved him, they asked the paltriest wages. The Fruit Walk mutinied into a thicket; the fountains choked themselves with sighing and greened with moss; the tulips found a quieter Nirvana in mere leaf. And Anthony made at last no pretence even of patronizing the final perishing flower of the firm's old clientele.

'He trafficked in a kind of ludicrous dolls' merchandize – utterly beautiful little infinitesimals in fabrics worth a hundred times their weight in rubies. So ridiculous a scandal had the "business" at last become that when its few scoffing creditors for old sake's sake sold it up, not a single bid was made for the property. It is in ruins now. Consult Ezekiel. Or Henrietta.

'I have no wish to sentimentalize; I am not a cynic or a philosopher. Yet I slide my eyes back to that narrow hilled-in strip of sea-coast whence once rose walled Tyre and Sidon, Arvard and Jebail, and – well, I merely remind myself that the Rosetta Stone is but a hornbook of the day before yesterday's children of men. Things *do* as a matter of fact seem to rot of their own virtue – inverted, so to speak. It's not likely to occur again. I mean, not for some time. The Town was almost apologetic. Democracy rarely runs to extremes – unless one may so describe the guillotine. But I am no politician. Enough of that. Even transatlantic visitors are now rare.'

Maunders and I were standing together by this time under the laurels and bay-trees, not of his own planting, beside his garden railings; he with his bulging, pale-blue eyes – and his sham candlestick branching out of his pocket; and I – well, irritated beyond endurance.

'Good heavens, Maunders,' I exclaimed, 'the stuff you talk! But one would not mind that so much if you could spin a decent yarn. You haven't even told me what became of the Belfry. Was he *nothing* but bats at last?'

'Old Anthony?' he murmured softly. 'Why, there is nothing in that. He lived on – for years – in the Works. You could see his burning candle from the valley, even on nights of full moon. And, of course, some gay imbecile set the story about that the whole lovely abandoned, derelict place was haunted. Twangling strings and vanishing faces, and a musing shape at a remoter window, her eyes reflecting a scene which only an imagination absolutely denuded of commonsense could hope or desire to share with her. After all, one does ignore the ghost until it is well out of the body. Ask Henrietta.'

'But, Maunders,' I called after him.

Too late: his shapeless slouching slate-grey body with its indescribable hat and malacca cane had vanished among the "evergreens", and the only answer I received was the dwindling rumour of my own expostulatory voice among their leaves – 'Maunders...'

Strange to say, it was in this moment of helplessness that I discovered that my little bast basket was gone. When? How? For an instant I hesitated – in pure cowardice. It was a quarter past one, and Mrs Maunders, a charming and active hostess, if a little of a martinet, disapproved of unpunctual guests. But only for an instant. The thought of Bettie's fair, glad little face decided me; and I set out to retrace my footsteps in search of the lost plaything. Alas, in vain.

The Tree*

Encased in his dingy first-class railway carriage, the prosperous Fruit Merchant sat alone. From the collar of his thick frieze greatcoat stuck out a triangular nose. On either side of it a small, bleak, black eye gazed absently at one of the buttons on the empty blue-upholstered seat opposite to him. His breath spread a fading vapour in the air. He sat bolt upright, congealed in body, heated in mind, his unseeing eye fixed on that cloth button, that stud.

There was nothing else to look at, for his six narrow glass windows were whitely sheeted with hoar-frost. Only his thoughts were his company, while the coach, the superannuated coach, bumped dully on over the metals. And

---

* First published in *London Mercury,* October 1922.

his thoughts were neither a satisfaction nor a pleasure. His square hard head under his square hard hat was nothing but a pot seething with vexation, scorn, and discontent.

What had invited him out so far, in weather so dismal, on a line so feebly patronized? Anger all but sparkled in his mind as he considered the intention of his journey, and what was likely to be the end and outcome of it. Twelve solid yet fleeting years divided him from his last encounter with his half-brother – twelve *cent per cent* years – shipload on shipload of exotic oranges and lemons, pineapples, figs, and blushing pomegranates. At this very moment three more or less seaworthy ocean tramps were steaming across the watery channels of the world laden with cargoes of which he was the principal consignee. He stretched out his legs, crossed his feet. He was a substantial man. There was nothing fantastic about *him*.

To put on airs when you couldn't afford them; to meet a friendly offer with rank ingratitude; to quarrel with the only relative on earth who had kept you out of the workhouse – he had sworn never to set foot in the place again. Yet – here he was: and nothing but a fool for his pains. Having washed his hands of the whole silly business, he should have kept them washed. Instead of which he thrust them deeper into his capacious pockets and wondered to heaven when his journey was to come to an end.

No, it was with no charitable, no friendly, no sentimental motive that he was being glided joltingly on. A half-brother – and particularly if he owes you a hundred pounds and more – need not be even fractionally a being one smiles to think of for the sake of auld lang syne. There was nothing in common between the two of them except a father now twenty-five years in his grave and a loan that would never be repaid.

That was one galling feature of the situation. There was another. In plain print and in his own respectable morning newspaper the Fruit Merchant had chanced but a week or two ago on the preposterous fact that a mere woodcut of a mere 'Bird and Flower,' initialled P. P., had fetched at Christie's ninety-seven guineas. Ninety-seven guineas; sixty-eight crates of excellent Denia oranges at thirty shillings a crate. What the devil! His small eyes seemed to congest and yet at the same time to protrude from their sockets.

'P. P.'! – perfect pest; paltry poser; plaguey parasite. And yet – hardly a parasite. You couldn't with a term like that dish a half-brother who hadn't sent you a single word of greeting for twelve solid fleeting prosperous years. Even if he did owe you a hundred pounds. Even if he hadn't the faintest wish to remind you of the fact. Not that the Fruit Merchant *wanted* his hundred pounds. He wasn't a debt collector. He wasn't even vindictive. It was the principle of the thing.

For if half-an-hour's silly scratching over a little lump of wood could fetch you £101 17s., about twenty-nine and a half minutes would bring in a round hundred. And there were more birds and more flowers in that infernal tree than Noah could have found room for in his Ark. The tree! – the very thought of it swept a pulsating cloud of rage over the Fruit Merchant's eyes. Cool, quiet insolence – he could have forgiven that, and could almost have forgotten it. But the faintest recollection of the tree, and of the talk under it, never failed to infuriate him. It infuriated him now almost beyond endurance, simply because he knew, in the secrecy of his thoughts, that *this* was the decoy which was dragging him on these fifty-three interminable miles on a freezing hideous country afternoon.

The tree: never in all his life had he met with such an exhibition of sheer, stark, midsummer madness. And yet with every inch of his journey the recollection grew on him. He couldn't get it out of his head. Curiosity, resentment, vindictiveness, a cold creeping cunning – a score of conflicting emotions zigzagged to and fro in his mind. He glared through them at the walls of his cage. But worst outrage of all was the creeping realization – and his body stiffened at the thought – that he was even now, and perhaps even a little more than ever, afraid of the tree. When you finally deal with a relative and a bloodsucker who has been a pest to you all your life, the one thing you do not look for is an interference of that kind.

He could not deny it, the tree had impressed him. Ever since that first swimming stare at it, the moment he thought of his brother, of the country, even of his boyhood – there it was. It had impressed him so much that the upholstered button had now completely disappeared, and he seemed to be actually in the presence of it again. He saw it as vividly as if its image hung there before his very eyes in the slightly self-warmed air of his solitary compartment. The experience filled him with so sudden a flood of aversion and resentment that the voice of the guard chaunting the name of his destination reached him only just in time to set him frantically pulling down his frozen window and ejecting himself out of the train.

One hasty glance around him showed that he was the sole traveller to alight on the frosted timbers of the obscure little station. A faint rosiness in the west foretold the decline of the still wintry day. The firs that flanked the dreary passenger-shed of the platform stood burdened already with the blackness of coming night.

He was elderly, he was obese, his heart was none too sound, at least as compared with his head. Yet if he intended to catch the last train home, he had scarcely a couple of hours in which to reach his half-brother's wretched little house, to congratulate him on his guineas, to refuse to accept repayment of his loan, to sneer at his tree, and to return to the station.

A bark at a weedy young porter in mittens, with mouth ajar over his long teeth, sent him ambling off for a conveyance. The Fruit Merchant stood under the shed in his frieze coat and square hard hat and watched the train glide out of the station. The screech of its engine, horning up into the windless air, had exactly expressed his own peculiar sentiments.

There was not a living being in sight whereon to breathe a curse. Only himself, a self he had been vaguely cursing throughout his tedious journey. The frozen landscape lay white in the dying day. The sun hung like the yolk of an egg above the still horizon. Some menace in the very look of this sullen object hinted that P. P. might long since have crossed the bourne from which no belated draft on any earthly bank had ever been known to transpire.

The thought diverted into ruggeder channels the current of the talk which he had intended to engage in with his half-brother. In other words, he would give the silly fool a bit of his mind. The fact was, their last quarrel – if anything so one-sided could be called a quarrel – had tinctured the Fruit Merchant's outlook on the world a good deal more densely than he would until now have confessed. A frown settled above the sullen eyes.

No living creature, no sound stirred the air. The fair country lay cold as if in a swoon. Like a shallow inverted saucer a becalmed sky curved itself over the unbroken quiet of the fields. His broad cleft chin thrust into his muffler, his hands into his capacious pockets, the stranger to these parts stood waiting, just stood there, with his small black eyes staring desolately out of his clothes. Why, you might just as well be marooned in a foreign land, or on a stage – sinister, cold, vacant, and not a single soul in the audience. At the sound of wheels and hoofs he coughed as if in uncontrollable indignation; and turned smartly on his heels...

With a gesture of disdain the Fruit Merchant sourly thrust a shilling into the weedy porter's immense knuckled hand and mounted into the cab. At his onset the whole square fusty interior leaned towards him like an extinguisher over the stub of a candle. The vehicle disgraced the universe. Even the man on the box resembled some little cautious and obscure animal that had been dug up out of the earth. When given his direction his face had fallen into an indescribable expression beneath its whiskers: an expression, it appeared, which was its nearest approach to a smile.

'And don't spare your – horse,' had barked his fare, slamming the rickety door behind him.

A railway carriage even of the most antique description, when its glass is opaque with rime, is a little less like a prison cell than a four-wheeled cab. For which reason, perhaps, as the vehicle ground on beneath the misty leafless elms, the frigid air was allowed to beat softly in from the open window upon its occupant's slightly impurpled face.

And still on and on, now here, now there, memory retrieved for the sombre shape within it every incident of his last experience on this self-same road. It had been summertime – June. He had been twelve years younger, a good gross of years less prosperous, and not perhaps quite so easily fanned into a peculiar helpless state of rage.

Indeed, his actual meeting with his half-brother at the little white garden gate had been almost friendly. So friendly that it would hardly have been supposed they were in any way unpleasingly related to one another, or that the least responsibility of each to each could have caused any kind of festering recrimination. Not that P. P. was even then the kind of person one hastens to introduce to one's friends. You not only never knew how he would look or what he would say. You weren't even certain what he might do. A rolling stone that merely fails to gather moss is a harmless object by comparison with one that appears to gather momentum. And even the most trifling suggestion, not so much of eccentricity as of an alien and crooked gleam in the eye, is apt to make the most respectable company a little uneasy.

Not that the two half-brothers had ever discussed together their aims and intentions and ideas about life; their desires or motives or hopes, or aversions or apprehensions or prejudices. The Fruit Merchant had his fair share of most of these human incentives, but he also had principles, and one of them was to keep his mouth shut.

They had met, had shaken hands, had exchanged remarks on the weather. Then P. P., in his frayed jacket and slippers, with his meagre expressionless face, had aimlessly led off his visitor into the garden, had aimlessly dropped a few distant remarks about their common past; and then, surrounded as they were by the scenery, scents, and noises of summer, had pushed his knotted hands into his trousers pockets, and fallen silent; his grey, vacant eyes fixed on the tree. The Fruit Merchant had tried in vain to break the silence, to shrug his way out of it. He also could only stand and stare up and up – at the tree.

Solitary, unchallenged, exotic in its station all but at the foot of the broken-hedged, straggling garden, it rose to heaven, a prodigious spreading ascendant cone, with its long, dark, green, pointed leaves. It stood, from first springing branch to apex, a motionless and somnolent fountain of flowers.

If his half-brother had taken the Fruit Merchant into a dingy little greenhouse and had shown him an ailing plant that with care, water, and guano had been raised from some far-fetched seed – well, that might have been something to boast about. He himself was in the trade. He knew a Jaffa orange from a mandarin. The stuff has to *grow*, of course; and he was broad-minded enough to approve of rural enterprise. Giant Mangolds and Prize Pumpkins – they did no harm. They encouraged the human vegetable. But the...

At last he had come to his senses and had peered fretfully about him.

The garden was a waste, the hedges untrimmed, a rank lusty growth of weeds flaunted their flowers at the sun. And this tree – it must have been flourishing here for centuries past, a positive eyesore to any practical gardener. P. P. couldn't even put a name to it. Yet by the fixed idiotic dreamy look on his face you might have supposed it was a gift from heaven; that, having waved his hands about like those coloured humbugs with the mango, the thing had sprung up by sheer magic out of the ground.

Not that the Fruit Merchant had denied that it was unique. He had never seen, nor would he ever want to see, its double. The sun had beaten down upon his head; a low, enormous drone filled the air; the reflected light dazed his eyes. A momentary faintness had stolen over him as he had turned once more and glanced again into his half-brother's long bony face – the absent eyes, the prominent cheek, the greying hair dappled with sunlight.

'How do you *know* it's unique?' he had asked. 'It may be as common as blackberries in other parts of the country – or abroad. One of the officers on the *Catamaran* was telling me...'

'I don't know,' his half-brother had interrupted him, 'but I have been looking at trees all my life. This resembles all, reminds me of none. Besides, I'm not going abroad – at least for the present.'

What had he meant by that? The Fruit Merchant hadn't inquired; had merely stood there in the flowers and grasses, blinking up once more into the spreading branches, almost involuntarily shaking his head at the pungent sweetness that hung dense and sickly in the air. And the old familiar symptoms began to stir in him, as he now sat jolting on in his cab – symptoms which his intimates would have described in one word: fuming.

He was not denying it, not he – the tree had been remarkable as trees go. For one thing, it bore two distinct kinds and shapes of blossom. The one circular and full and milky in a dark cuplike calyx, with clusters of scarlet-tipped pistils; the other a pale yellow oval, three-petalled, with a central splash of orange. He had surreptitiously squeezed a couple of the fallen flowers into his pocket-book, had taken them out at his office in the Borough the next morning to show them to the partner he had afterwards advantageously bought out of the business, only to find them black, slimy, and unrecognizable, and to be laughed at for his pains.

'What's the use of the thing?' he had next inquired of his half-brother in a gross voice. 'Is it edible?' At which, with the faint smile on his face that had infuriated the Fruit Merchant even as a boy, the other had merely shrugged his shoulders.

'Why not try it on the pigs?'

'I don't keep pigs.'

Keep pigs, indeed; there wasn't the faintest symptom that he would ever be able to keep himself!

'Well, aren't there any birds in these parts?' It had been a singularly false move.

'It has brought its own,' had been his half-brother's muttered retort.

There was no denying it – at least so far as the Fruit Merchant's small ornithological knowledge went. At that very moment birds of a peculiarly vivid green sheeniness were hovering and dipping between the deep blue of the sky and the mountainous blossoming. Little birds, with unusually long attenuated bills, playing, fluttering, lisping, courting, and apparently sucking the heady nectar from the snowy and ivory cups, while poised like animate gems on the wing. He had again opened his mouth, but his half-brother had laid a lean tingling hand on his sleeve. 'Listen!' he said.

Half-stifled, jetting, delirious bursts of song twinkled, belled, rose, eddied, overflowed from the tented depths of the tree, like the yells and laughter of a playground of children suddenly released for an unexpected half-holiday. Listen, indeed! The noise of the creatures was still echoing in his ears as he sat there bulkily swaying, his eyes fixed on the pallid, gliding hedgerow from his fusty cab.

P. P. had not positively claimed that every single chorister in the chorus was an exotic visitant. He had gone further. He had gently bent down a low-lying fan of leaves and bloom, and not content with exhibiting one by one living specimens of a little spotted blue iridescent beetle, a horned kind of cock-chafer, and a dappled black-and-yellow-mottled ladybird – all of them following their lives in these surroundings; he had also waved a lean hand in the direction of a couple of gaudy butterflies intertwining in flight down the slope of the garden, had pointed out little clumps of saffron and sky-blue flowers, and a rank, ungainly weed with a cluster of black helmet-shaped florets at its tips, asserting that they were as rare – as unprecedented – in those parts as the tree itself.

'You don't mean to say because the thing's brought its own vermin that it's any the better for that? Lord, we can do that in the fruit trade.'

'It's brought me,' said the other, mooning meanwhile in the opposite direction.

'And where do you raise your pertatoes and artichokes and scarlet runners? It looks to me like a dam waste of soil.'

The wandering greenish-grey eyes had rested for a moment on the puffy contemptuous face a few inches beneath them without the faintest symptom of intelligence. Empty eyes, yet with a hint of danger in them, like a bright green pool of water in a derelict quarry. 'You shall have a basket of the fruit; if you'll risk it. It never really ripens – queer-looking seeds.'

'You eat it yourself, then?'

The eyes slid away, the narrow shoulders had lifted a little. 'I take things as they come.' It was precisely how he had afterwards taken the cheque.

Seated there, on either side of the deal table, in the bare, uncarpeted, uncurtained living-room of the cottage over a luncheon of bread and dry cheese and onions, with the reflected light of the tree on his half-brother's face, the talk between the two of them had gradually degenerated into an altercation.

At length the Fruit Merchant, with some little relief, had completely lost his temper. A half empty jam-pot buzzing with bees was no more appetizing an object because the insects were not of the usual variety. He had literally been stung into repeating a few semi-fraternal truths.

To submit to being half-starved simply because nobody with money to waste would so much as look at your bits of drawings; to sit there dream-ily grinning at a tree in your back-garden, twenty times more useless because there wasn't its like for miles around, even *if* there wasn't; to be content to hang like a bloodsucker on the generosity of a relative half-blood and half-water – well, he had given P. P. a bit of his mind.

The Fruit Merchant instinctively drew a cold fat hand down his face as a more and more precise recollection of the subsequent scene recurred to him. Mere silence can be insulting, and there was one thing about his half-brother – worse than all the rest of his peculiarities put together – that had never failed to reduce him to a feverish helplessness: his eyes. They didn't see you even when they were fixed on you across a couple of feet of deal board. They saw something else; and with no vestige of common courtesy.

And those hands – you could swear at a glance that they had never done a single honest day's work in their owner's lifetime. Every sight of them had made it easier for the Fruit Merchant to work himself up into a blind refreshing rage. The cottage had fairly shaken to his abuse. The raw onions had danced under his fist on the table. And twining in and out between his roarings and shoutings had meandered on that other low, groping, dis-passionate voice – his brother's.

He had found his own place; and there he intended to remain. Rather than sit on a stool in a counting-house writing invoices for crates of oranges and pineapples he would hang himself from the topmost branches of the tree. You had your own life to lead, and it didn't matter if you died of it. He was not making any claims. There was nothing the same in this world for any two individuals. And the more different everything was, the more closely you should cling to the difference.

Oh, yes, he had gone on, it was mere chance, or whatever you liked to call it, that had brought him here; a mere chance that the tree had not even been charged for in the rent. There it was, and it would last him his life-time; and, when that was over, he wouldn't complain. He had wagged his skimpy beard, a pencil between his fingers. No, he wouldn't complain if they just dug a hole in the garden and shovelled his body in under the grass within reach of the rootlets. What's your body? – 'They'll buy me all right when I'm safely dead. Try it – it's a fair speculation.'

'Try what?' The Fruit Merchant's countenance had suddenly set like a gargoyle in cast-iron.

His half-brother had nodded towards a dingy portfolio that stood leaning against a half-empty bookcase. And at that his guest had laid about him with a will. 'So that's the kind of profit you are hoping to make out of your blighted old bee-bush? That's your profit? *That's* your fine airs – your miserable scribblings and scragglings.'

He had once more slammed down his fat fist on the table and delivered his ultimatum. 'See here, I give you a hundred pounds, here and now. There's no claim on me, not a shred. We don't even share the same mother, even if we share the same dad. You talk this abject rubbish to me. You have never earned a decent penny in your life. You never will. You are a fool and a loafer. Go to the Parish; and go for good. I'm sick of it, d'ye hear? – sick of it. You sit there, whiffling that I haven't eyes in my head, that I don't know black from white, that you'd rather hang your miserable carcase in your wretched old tree than take a respectable job. Well, hang it there – it won't break the branches if this is the only kind of meal you can give a visitor! I'm done with you. I wash my hands of you. Do you hear?'

He had – inaccurately – pantomimed the operation, sweeping over the jam-pot as he did so, and now drew in his breath – a cold breath, too; as, with eyes fixed on the ever-lightening hedgerows beyond his oblong window, he remembered the renewed red-hot stab of pain that had transfixed the ball of his thumb.

It recalled him instantaneously to his surroundings. Scrambling up from his seat he ejected his head out of the cab into the open. 'Whoa, there! Whoa, I say: I'm getting out.'

The horse was dragged up on to its haunches, the cab came to a stand-still, and, to the roaring suspirations of the animal, the Fruit Merchant alighted on the tinkling ice of a frozen wayside puddle of water. He turned himself about. Time and the night had not tarried during his journey. The east was a blaze of moonlight. The moon glared in the grey heavens like a circular flat little window of glass.

'Wait here –' the Fruit Merchant bade his cabman in the desolation. 'You've pretty near shaken the head off my body.'

The cabman ducked his own small head in reply, and saluted his fare with a jerk of his whip. 'You won't be long,' he sang out between his whiskers.

'What did he mean by that?' was the Fruit Merchant's querulous question to himself as he mounted the few remaining yards of by-lane towards the crest of the slope. He was tired and elderly and cold. A pathetic look, one almost of sadness, came into his face. He pushed up his muffler and coughed. There replied the faintest echo from the low copse that bordered the lane. Grass, crystalled with hoar-frost, muffled his footsteps. What had he meant by that? repeated self to self, but not as if expectant of an answer.

When well out of sight of the cabman and his vehicle beneath the slope of the hill, the Fruit Merchant paused and lifted his eyes. League beyond league beneath him, as if to the confines of the world, the countryside spread on – frost-beclad meadow, wood and winding lane. And one sole house in sight, a small, tumbledown, lightless, huddling cottage, its ragged thatch and walls chequered black with shadow and dazzling white with wash of moonshine. And there – lifting itself into the empty skies, its twigs and branches sweeping the stars, stood, as if in wait for him, the single naked gigantic tree.

The Fruit Merchant gazed across at it, like an obese minute Belial on the ramparts of Eden. He had been fooled, then; tricked. He might have guessed the fatuity of his enterprise. He *had* guessed it. The house was empty; the bird had flown. Why for a single instant had he dreamed otherwise? Simply because all these years he had been deceived into believing there was a kind of honesty in the fellow. Just that something quixotic, stupid, stubborn, dense, dull, demented which – nothing but lies, then.

That bee in his bonnet, that snake in his grass: nothing but lies. There was no principle by which you could judge a man like that; and yet – well, after all, he was like anybody else. Give him a taste of the sweets of success, and his boosted solitude, his contempt for the mere decencies of life, his pretended disgust at men more capable and square-headed than himself had vanished into thin air. There were fools in the world, he had now discovered, who would pay ninety-seven guineas for a second- or third-hand scrabble of a drawing. 'Right you are; hand over the dibs, and I am off!'

A scornful yet lugubrious smile stole over the Fruit Merchant's purplish features. He would be honest about it; he positively enjoyed acknowledging when a rival had bested him over a bargain. He would even agree that he had always nursed his own little superstitions. And now all that fine silly talk – sheer fudge. He had been himself childish fool enough to be impressed by it; yes, and to have been even a little frightened by – a tree.

He eyed it there – that gaunt, prodigious weed; and then, with one furtive glance over his round shoulder towards the crest of the slope behind which lay his way of escape from this wintry landscape and from every memory of the buffoon who had cheated him, he slowly descended the hill, pushed open the broken gate, and entered the icy untended garden.

Once more he came to a standstill in his frieze coat, and from under the brim of his hard hat stared up into the huge frigid branches. There is a supple lift and ease in the twigs of a tree asleep in winter. Green living buds are everywhere huddling close in their drowsy defences. Even the Fruit Merchant could distinguish between the dreaming and the dead, or, at any rate, between the unripe and the rotten.

And as he looked, two thoughts scurried like rats out of the wainscot of his mind. An unprecedented foreboding descended on him. These lean shrunken twigs, these massive vegetable bones – the tree was dead. And up there – he shifted rapidly to and fro in order to secure an uninterrupted view of a kind of huddling shape up aloft there, an object that appeared to be stooping crazily forward as if on a similar quest in respect to himself.

But, no. He took a deep breath. The muffled knocking against the wall of his head ceased. He need not have alarmed himself: an optical illusion. Nothing.

The tree *was* dead. That was clear – a gaunt, black, sapless nightmare. But the ungainly clump and shape, hoisted midway among its boughs was not a huddling human body. It was only yet another kind of derelict parasite – withered mistletoe. And that gentle spellican-like rattling high overhead was but the fingering of a faint breeze in the moonlight; clacking twig against twig.

Maybe it would have simplified matters if — But no need to dwell on that. One corpse at a time was enough for any man on a night like this and in a country as cheerless as the plains of Gomorrah. A phrase or two out of his familiar bills of lading recurred to the Fruit Merchant's mind – 'the act of God'. There was something so horrific in the contorted set of the branches outthrust in ungainly menace above his head that he was reminded of no less a depravity than the devil himself. Thank the Lord, his half-brother had *not* remembered to send him a parcel of the fruit.

If ever poison showed in a plant, it haunted every knot and knuckle of this tree. Judgment had overtaken it – the act of God. That's what came of boasting. That's what came of idling a useless life away in a daydream at other people's expense. And now the cunning bird was flown. The insult of his half-brother's triumph stabbed the Fruit Merchant like a sword.

A sudden giddiness, the roar as of water, caused in part no doubt by the posture of his head, again swept over him, reverberated in his ears. He thrust a cautious hand into the breast of his coat and lowered his eyes. They came to a stay on the rugged moonlit bole. And there, with a renewed intensity of gaze, they once more fixed themselves.

The natural living bark of the tree had been of a russet grey, resembling that of the beech. Apart from a peculiar shimmeringness due to the frost that crystalled it over, and as the skin of a dead thing, that bark now suggested the silveriness of leprosy. So far, so good. But midway up the unbranched bole, at the height of five to six feet from the ground, appeared a wide peculiar cicatrice. The iridescent greyness here abruptly ended. Above it stretched a clear blank ring of darker colour, knobbed over, in and out, with tiny sparkling clusters of fungi.

The Fruit Merchant stole in a pace or two. No feat of the inhuman this. Cleanly and precisely the thick rind of the tree must some time since have been cut and pared away in a wide equal ring; a ring too far from the ground to have been the work of pigs or goats, too smooth and sharp-edged to have been caused by the gnawings of cattle. It was perfectly plain; the sap-protecting skin of the thing had been deliberately cut and hacked away. The tree had been murdered. High in the moonlit heavens it gloated there: a victim.

Not until then did the Fruit Merchant stealthily turn and once more survey his half-brother's house. The slow and almost furtive movement of his head and shoulders suggested that the action was involuntary. From this garden side the aspect of the hovel was even more abject and disconsolate. Its one ivy-clustered chimney-stack was smokeless. The moonbeams rained softly and mercilessly on the flint walls, the boarded windows, the rat-and-bird-ravaged thatch.

Only a spectre could be content with such a dwelling, and a guilt-stricken wretch at that. Yet without any doubt in the world the house was still inhabited. For even now a slender amber beam of light leaned out at an obtuse angle from some crevice in the shuttering wood into the vast bath of moonshine.

For a moment the Fruit Merchant hesitated. He could leave the garden and regain his cab without nearing the house. He could yet once more 'wash his hands'. Certainly, after sight of the maniac's treacherous work on his unique God-given tree he hadn't the faintest vestige of a desire to confront his half-brother. Quite the reverse. He would far rather fling a second hundred pounds after the first than be once more contaminated by his company. There was something vile in his surroundings.

In shadows black as pitch, like these, any inconceivably evil creature might lie in covert. If the tree alive could decoy an alien fauna to its succulent nectar, the tree dead might well invite even less pleasing ministrations. Come what come would, he was prepared. It might startle him; but he was dead-cold already; and when your whole mind is filled with disgust and disquiet there is no room for physical fear. You merely want to shake yourself free – edge out and be off.

Nevertheless, the human intruder in this inhuman wilderness was already, and with infinite caution, making his way towards the house. On a pitch-black night he might have hesitated. Hadn't venomous serpents the habit of stealing for their winter slumber into the crannies and hollows of fallen wood? Might not even the lightest northern zephyr bring down upon his head another vast baulk of timber from the withered labyrinth above? But so bright was the earth's lanthorn, so still the starry sky, that he could hear and even see the seeds from the humbler winter weeds scattering out from their yawning pods, as, with exquisite care, he brushed on through the tangling growths around him.

And having at length closely approached the walls, standing actually within a jutting shadow, he paused yet again and took a deep breath into his body before, gently lifting himself, he set his eye to the crevice from which poured out that slender shaft of light.

So artificially brilliant was the room within – by comparison with the full moonlight of the Fruit Merchant's natural world without – that for an instant or two he saw nothing. But he persevered, and after a while his round protruding eye found itself master of at least half the space on the other side of the shutters. Stilled through and through, his fingers clutching the frosted sill, he stood there half suspended on his toes, and as if hypnotized.

For scarcely more than a yard distant from his own there stooped a face – his half-brother's: a face to haunt you to your dying day. It was surmounted by a kind of nightcap, and was almost unrecognizable. The unfolding of the hours of twelve solitary years had played havoc with the once-familiar features. The projecting brows above the angular cheekbones resembled polished stone. The ears stood out like the vans of a bat on either side above the corded neck. The thin unkempt beard on the narrow jaw brushed the long gnarled hand that was moving with an infinite tedious care on the bare table beneath it.

Motionlessly the hanging paraffin lamp poured its radiance upon this engrossed cadaverous visage, revealing every line and bone, hollow and wrinkle.

Nevertheless its possessor, this old man, shrunken and hideous in his frame of abject poverty, his arms drawn close up to his fallen body, worked sedulously on and on. And behind and around him showed the fruit of his labours. Pinned to the scaling walls, propped on the ramshackle shelf above his fireless hearthstone, and even against the stale remnant of a loaf of bread on the cracked blue dish beside him, was a litter of pictures. And everywhere, lovely and marvellous in all its guises – the tree. The tree in May's showering loveliness, in summer's quiet wonder, in autumn's decline, in naked slumbering wintry grace. The colours glowed from the fine old rough paper like lamps and gems.

There were drawings of birds too, birds of dazzling plumage, of flowers and butterflies, their crimson and emerald, rose and saffron seemingly shimmering and astir; their every mealy and feathery and pollened boss and

petal and plume on fire with hoarded life and beauty. And there a viper
with its sinuous molten scales; and there a face and a shape looking out of
its nothingness such as would awake even a dreamer in a dream.

Only three sounds in that night-quiet, and these scarcely discernible,
stirred in the watcher's ear: the faint shrill sing-song of the flame of the
lamp, the harsh wheezy breath of the artist, and a faint scuttling as of rats
or mice. This austere and dying creature must have come in at last from the
world of nature and mankind a long time ago. The arm that had given the
tree its quietus had now not the strength to lift an axe. Yet the ungainly fingers toiled assiduously on.

The Fruit Merchant, spying in on the old half-starved being that sat
there, burning swiftly away among his insane gewgaws, as nearly broke out
crying as laughing. He was frightened and elated; mute and bursting with
words. The act of God! Rather than even remotely resemble that old scarecrow in his second childhood pushing that tiny-bladed knife across the
surface of a flat of wood, he would — . An empty and desolate look stole
into the gazing eye.

Not that he professed to understand. He knew nothing. His head was
completely empty. The last shred of rage and vindictiveness had vanished
away. He was glad he had come, for now he was going back. What little of
the present and future remained would soon be the past. He, too, was
ageing. *His* life also was coming to an end. He stared on – oh, yes. And not
even a nephew to inherit his snug fat little fortune. Worldly goods, shipload
on shipload – well, since he could not take them away with him, he would
leave them behind. He would bequeath them to charity, to the W.F.M.P.A.
perhaps; and he would make a note of the hundred pounds.

Not in malice; only to leave things business-like and in order; to do your
duty by a greedy and ungrateful world even though you were soon to be
washing your hands of that, too. All waste, nothing but waste. But he
thanked the Lord he had kept his sanity, that he was respected; that he
wasn't in the artificial fruit trade – the stuff your grandmother belled under
glass. He thanked the Lord he wasn't foul to look at; foul probably to
smell; and a poison even to think about.

Yet still he peeped on – this old Tom, though at no Lady Godiva. 'They'
would buy right enough – there was no doubt of that. Christie's would
some day be humming with the things. He didn't deny the old lunatic that.
He knew a bird when he saw it – even on paper. Ninety-seven guineas: at
that rate there was more money swimming about in this pestilent hovel
than ever even he himself could lay his practised hands on.

And there were fools in plenty – rich, dabbling, affected, silly fools –
dillytanties, you called 'em – who would never know that their lying, preposterous P. P. had destroyed the very life of the tree that had given its all

for him. And why? And why? The Fruit Merchant was almost tempted to burn down the miserable cabin over his half-brother's head. Who could tell? . . . A gust of wind stirred in the bedraggled thatch, feebly whined in the keyhole.

And at that moment, as if an angry and helpless thought could make itself audible even above the hungry racketing of mice and the melancholic whistling of a paraffin lamp – at that moment the corpse-like countenance, almost within finger-touch on the other side of the table, slowly raised itself from the labour of its regard, and appeared to be searching through the shutter's cranny as if into the Fruit Merchant's brain. The glance swept through him like an avalanche. No, no. But one instantaneous confrontation, and he had pushed himself back from the impious walls as softly as an immense sack of hay.

These were not eyes – in that abominable countenance. Speck-pupilled, greenish-grey, unfocused, under their protuberant mat of eyebrow, they remained still as a salt and stagnant sea. And in their uplifted depths, stretching out into endless distances, the Fruit Merchant had seen regions of a country whence neither for love nor money he could ever harvest one fruit, one pip, one cankered bud. And blossoming there beside a glassy stream in the mid-distance of far-mountained sward – a tree.

In after-years an old, fat, vulgar, and bronchitic figure, muffled up in a pathetic shawl, would sometimes be seen seated in a place of honour, its hard square hat upon its thick bald skull, within positive reach of the jovial auctioneer's ivory hammer. To purchase every 'P. P.' that came into the market was a dream beyond even a multi-millionaire's avarice. But small beetles or grubs or single feathers drawn 'from the life' were within scope of the Fruit Merchant's purse. The eye that showed not the faintest vestige of reflected glory from the orange of the orange, the gamboge of the lemon, or the russet bronze of the pomegranate – in their crated myriads – would fitfully light up awhile as one by one, and with reiterated grunts of satisfaction, he afterwards in the secrecy of his home consigned these indifferent and 'early' works of art to the flames.

But since his medical man had warned him that any manifestation of passion would almost unquestionably prove his ultimate manifestation of anything, he steadily avoided thinking of the tree. Yet there it remained, unexorcizable, ineradicable, in his fading imagination.

Indeed, he finally expired in the small hours one black winter's morning, and as peacefully as a child, having dreamed that he was looking through a crevice into what could not be hell, but might be limbo or purgatory, the place of departed spirits. For there sat his half-brother, quite, quite still. And all around him, to be seen, haunted gay and painted birds and crystal flowers and damasked butterflies; and, as it were, sylphs and salamanders, shapes of an unearthly beauty. And all of them strangely, preternaturally still, as if in a peepshow, as if stuffed.

Out of the Deep

The steely light of daybreak, increasing in volume and intensity as the east grew larger with the day, showed clearly at length that the prodigious yet elegant Arabian bed was empty. What might tenderly have cradled the slumbers of some exquisite Fair of romance now contained no human occupant at all. The whole immense room – its air dry and thin as if burnt – was quiet as a sepulchre.

To the right of the bed towered a vast and heavily carved wardrobe. To the left, a lofty fireplace of stone flanked by its grinning frigid dogs. A few cumbrous and obscure oil paintings hung on the walls. And, like the draperies of a proscenium, the fringed and valanced damask curtains on either side the two high windows, poured down their motionless cataract of crimson.

They had been left undrawn over night, and yet gave the scene a slight theatricality, a theatricality which the painted nymphs disporting them-selves on the ceiling scarcely helped to dispel.

Not that these coy and ogling faces suggested any vestige of chagrin at the absence of the young man who for some weeks past had shared the long nights with them. They merely smiled on. For, after all, Jimmie's restless head upon the pillow had never really been in harmony with his pompous inanimate surroundings – the thin high nose, like the beak of a small ship, between the fast-sealed lids and narrow cheekbones, the narrow bird-like brow, the shell of the ear slightly pointed. If, inspired by the distant music of the spheres, the painted creatures had with this daybreak broken into song, it would certainly not have been to the tune of 'Oh Where, and Oh Where is My Little Dog Gone?' There was even less likelihood of Jimmie's voice now taking up their strains from out of the distance.

And yet, to judge from appearances, the tongue within that head might have been that of an extremely vivacious talker – even though, apart from Mrs Thripps, its talk these last few days had been for the most part with himself.

Indeed, as one of his friends had remarked: 'Don't you believe it. Jimmie has pots and pots to say, though he don't say it. That's what makes him such a dam good loser.' Whether or not; if Jimmie *had* been in the habit of conversing with himself, he must have had odd company at times.

Night after night he had lain there, flat on his back, his hands crossed on his breast – a pose that never failed to amuse him. A smooth eminence in the dark, rich quilt about sixty inches from his chin indicated to his attentive eye the points of his toes. The hours had been heavy, the hours had been long – still there are only twelve or so of utter darkness in the most tedious of nights, and matins tinkles at length. Excepting the last of them – a night, which was now apparently for ever over – he had occupied this majestic bed for about six weeks, though on no single occasion could he have confessed to being really at home in it.

He had chosen it, not from any characteristic whim or caprice, and certainly not because it dominated the room in which his Uncle Timothy himself used to sleep, yes, and for forty years on end, only at last to expire in it. He had chosen it because, when its Venetian blinds were pulled high up under the fringed cornice, it was as light as a London April sky could make it; and because – well, just one single glance in from the high narrow doorway upstairs had convinced him that the attic in which he was wont to sleep as a small boy was simply out of the question. A black heavy flood of rage swept over him at sight of it – he had never before positively realized the abominations of that early past. To a waif and stray any kind of shelter is, of course, a godsend, but even though this huge sumptuous barrack of a house had been left to him (or, rather, abandoned to him) by his Uncle Timothy's relict, Aunt Charlotte, Jimmie could not – even at his loosest – have been described as homeless.

Friendless rather – but that of his own deliberate choice. Not so very long ago, in fact, he had made a clean sweep of every single living being, male or female, to whom the term friend could, with some little elasticity, be applied. A little official affair, to put it politely, eased their exit. And then, this vacant hostel. The house, in fact (occupied only by a caretaker in the service of his aunt's lawyers) had been his for the asking at any time during the last two or three years. But he had steadily delayed taking possession of it until there was practically no alternative.

Circumstances accustom even a young man to a good many inconveniences. Still it would have been a little too quixotic to sleep in the street, even though his Uncle Timothy's house, as mere 'property', was little better than a white and unpleasing elephant. He could not sell it, that is, not *en masse*. It was more than dubious if he was legally entitled to make away with its contents.

But, quite apart from an extreme aversion to your Uncle Timothy's valuables in themselves, you cannot eat, even if you can subsist on, articles of *virtu*. Sir Richard Grenville – a hero for whom Jimmie had every respect – may have been accustomed to chewing up his wine-glass after swigging off its contents. But this must have been on the spur of an impulse, hardly in obedience to the instinct of self-preservation. Jimmie would have much preferred to balance a chair at the foot of his Uncle's Arabian bed and salute the smiling lips of the painted nymphs on the ceiling. Though even that experiment would probably have a rather gritty flavour. Still, possession is nine points of the law, and necessity is the deadly enemy of convention. Jimmie was unconscious of the faintest scruples on that score.

His scruples, indeed, were in another direction. Only a few days ago – the day, in fact, before his first indulgence in the queer experience of pulling the bell – he had sallied out with his Aunt Charlotte's black leather dressing bag positively bulging with a pair of Bow candlesticks, an illuminated missal, mutely exquisite, with its blues and golds and crimsons, and a tiny old silver-gilt bijouterie box. He was a young man of absurdly impulsive aversions, and the dealer to whom he carried this further consignment of loot was one of them.

After a rapid and contemptuous examination, this gentleman spread out his palms, shrugged his shoulders, and suggested a sum that would have caused even a more phlegmatic connoisseur than his customer's Uncle Timothy to turn in his grave.

And Jimmie replied, nicely slurring his r's, 'Really Mr So-and-so, it is impossible. No doubt the things have an artificial value, but not for me. I must ask you to oblige me by giving me only half the sum you have kindly mentioned. Rather than accept *your* figure, you know, I would – well, perhaps it would be impolite to tell you what I would prefer to do. *Dies irae, dies illa,* and so on.'

The dealer flushed, though he had been apparently content to leave it at that. He was not the man to be easily insulted by a good customer. And Jimmie's depredations were methodical. With the fastidiousness of an expert he selected from the rare and costly contents of the house only what was light and portable and became inconspicuous by its absence. The supply he realized, though without any perceptible animation, however recklessly it might be squandered, would easily last out his lifetime.

Certainly *not.* After having once made up his mind to accept his Uncle Timothy's posthumous hospitality, the real difficulty was unlikely to be a conscientious one. It was the attempt merely to accustom himself to the house – the hated house – that grew more and more arduous. It falsified his hope that, like other experiences, this one would prove only the more piquant for being so precarious. Days and moments quickly flying – just his one funny old charwoman, Mrs Thripps, himself, and the Past.

After pausing awhile under the dingy and dusty portico, Jimmie had entered into his inheritance on the last afternoon in March. The wind was fallen; the day was beginning to narrow; a chill crystal light hung over the unshuttered staircase. By sheer force of a forgotten habit he at once ascended to the attic in which he had slept as a child.

Pausing on the threshold, he looked in, conscious not so much of the few familiar sticks of furniture – the trucklebed, the worn strip of Brussels carpet, the chipped blue-banded ewer and basin, the framed illuminated texts on the walls – as of a perfect hive of abhorrent memories.

That high cupboard in the corner from which certain bodiless shapes had been wont to issue and stoop at him cowering out of his dreams; the crab-patterned paper that came alive as you stared; the window cold with menacing stars; the mouseholes, the rusty grate – trumpet of every wind that blows – these objects at once lustily shouted at him in their own original tongues.

Quite apart from themselves, they reminded him of incidents and experiences which at the time could scarcely have been so nauseous as they now seemed in retrospect. He found himself suffocatingly resentful even of what must have been kindly intentions. He remembered how his Aunt Charlotte used to read to him – with her puffy cheeks, plump ringed hands, and the moving orbs of her eyes showing under her spectacles.

He wasn't exactly accusing the past. Even in his first breeches he was never what could be called a nice little boy. He had never ordered himself lowly and reverently to any of his betters – at least in their absence. Nevertheless, what stirred in his bosom as he gazed in on this discarded scene was certainly not remorse.

He remembered how gingerly and with what peculiar breathings, his Uncle Timothy used to lift his microscope out of its wooden case; and how, after the necessary manipulation of the instrument, he himself would be bidden mount a footstool and fix his dazzled eye on the slides of sluggish or darting horrors of minute magnified 'life'. And how, after a steady um-aw-ing drawl of inapprehensible instruction, his uncle would suddenly flick out a huge silk pocket handkerchief as a signal that little tongue-tied nervous boys were themselves nothing but miserable sluggish or darting reptiles, and that his nephew was the most deplorable kind of little boy.

Jimmie remembered, too, once asking the loose bow-shaped old gentleman in his chair if he might himself twist the wheel; and his Uncle Timothy had replied in a loud ringing voice, and almost as if he were addressing a public meeting: 'Um, ah, my boy, I say No to that!' He said No to most things, and just like that, if he vouchsafed speech at all.

And then there was Church on Sundays; and his hoop on weekdays in the Crescent; and days when, with nothing to do, little Jimmie had been wont to sit watching the cold silvery rain on the window, the body he was in slowly congealing the while into a species of rancid suet pudding. Mornings too, when his Aunt Charlotte would talk nasally to him about

Christianity; or when he was allowed to help his uncle and a tall, scared parlourmaid dust and re-arrange the contents of a cabinet or bureau. The smell of the air, the check duster, the odious *objets d'art* and the ageing old man snorting and looking like a superannuated Silenus beside the neat and frightened parlourmaid – it was a curious thing; though Death with his louring grin had beckoned him off: there he was – alive as ever.

And when amid these ruminations, Jimmie's eyes had at last fixed themselves on the frayed, dangling cord that hung from the ceiling over the trucklebed, it was because he had already explored all that the name Soames had stood for. Soames the butler – a black-clothed, tub-bellied, pompous man that might have been his Uncle Timothy's impoverished first cousin or illegitimate step-brother: Soames: Soames.

Soames used frequently to wring Jimmie's then protuberant ears. Soames sneaked habitually; and with a sort of gloating piety on his drooping face, was invariably present at the subsequent castigation. Soames had been wont to pile up his plate with lumps of fat that even Destiny had never intended should consort with any single leg of mutton or even sirloin of beef – jelly-like, rapidly cooling *nuggets* of fat. And Soames invariably brought him cold rice pudding when there was hot ginger roll.

Jimmie remembered the lines that drooped down from his pale long nose. The sleek set of his whiskers as he stood there in his coat-tails reflected in the glass of the sideboard, carving the Sunday joint.

But that slack green bell-cord! – his very first glimpse of it had set waggling *scores* of peculiar remembrances. First, and not so very peculiarly, perhaps, it recalled an occasion when, as he stood before his Aunt's footstool to bid her Good-night, her aggrieved pupils had visibly swum down from beneath their lids out of a nap, to fix themselves and look at him at last as if neither he nor she, either in this or in any other world, had ever so much as seen one another before. Perhaps his own face, if not so puffy, appeared that evening to be unusually pasty and pallid – with those dark rings which even to this day added vivacity and lustre to his extremely clear eyes. And his Aunt Charlotte had asked him why he was such a cowardly boy and so wickedly frightened of the dark.

'You know very well your dear Uncle will not permit gas in the attic, so there's no use asking for it. You have nothing on your conscience, I trust? You have not been talking to the servants?'

Infallible liar, he had shaken his head. And his Aunt Charlotte in return wagged hers at him.

'It's no good staring in that rebellious, sullen way at me. I have told you repeatedly that if you are really in need of anything, just ring the bell for Soames. A good little boy with nothing on his conscience *knows* that God watches over him. I hope you are at least trying to be a good little boy.

There is a limit even to your Uncle's forbearance.'

It was perfectly true. Even bad little boys might be 'watched over' in the dead of night, and as for his Uncle Timothy's forbearance, he had discovered the limitations of that fairly early in life.

Well, it was a pity, he smiled to himself, that his Aunt Charlotte could not be present to see his Uncle Timothy's bedroom on that first celebration of their prodigal nephew's return. Jimmie's first foray had been to range the house from attic to cellar (where he had paused to rest) for candlesticks. And that night something like six dozen of the 'best wax' watched over his heavy and galvanic slumbers in the Arabian bed. Aunt Charlotte, now rather more accustomed to the dark even than Jimmie himself, would have opened her eyes at *that*.

Gamblers are naturally superstitious folk, he supposed; but that was the queerest feature of the whole thing. He had not then been conscious of even the slightest apprehension or speculation. It was far rather a kind of ribaldry than any sort of foreboding that had lit up positive constellations of candles as if for a Prince's – as if for a princely Cardinal's – lying-in-state.

It had taken a devil of a time too. His Uncle Timothy's port was not the less potent for a long spell of obscure mellowing, and the hand that held the taper had been a shaky one. Yet it had proved an amusing process too. Almost childish. Jimmie hadn't laughed like that for years. Certainly until then he had been unconscious of the feeblest squeamish inkling of anything – apart from old remembrances – peculiar in the house. And yet – well, no doubt even the first absurd impulsive experiment that followed *had* shaken him up.

Its result would have been less unexpected if he hadn't made a point and almost a duty of continually patrolling the horrible old vacant London mansion. Hardly a day had lately passed – and there was nothing better to do – but it found him on his rounds. He was not waiting for anything (except for the hour, maybe, when he would have to wait no more). Nevertheless, faithful as the sentinel on Elsinore's hoary ramparts, he would find himself day after day treading almost catlike on from room to room, surveying his paradoxical inheritance, jotting down a list in a nice order of the next 'sacrifices', grimacing at the Ming divinities, and pirouetting an occasional long nose at the portraits on the walls.

He had sometimes had a few words – animated ones, too – with Mrs Thripps, and perhaps if he could have persuaded himself to talk 'sensibly,' and not to gesticulate, not to laugh himself so easily into a fit of coughing, she would have proved better company. She was amazingly honest and punctual and quiet; and why to heaven a woman with such excellent qualities should customarily wear so scared a gleam in her still, colourless eyes, and be so idiotically timid and nervous in his company, he could not imagine.

She was being paid handsome wages anyhow; and, naturally, he was aware of no rooted objection to other people helping themselves; at least if they managed it as skilfully as he did himself. But Mrs Thripps, it seemed, had never been able in any sense at all to help herself. She was simply a crape-bonneted 'motherly' creature, if not excessively intelligent, if a little slow in seeing 'points'. It was, indeed, her alarm when he asked her if she had happened to notice any young man about the house that had irritated him – though, of course, it was hardly fair not to explain what had given rise to the question. That was perfectly simple. It was like this —

For years – for centuries, in fact – Jimmie had been, except in certain unusual circumstances, an exceedingly bad sleeper. He still hated sleeping in the dark. But a multitude of candles at various degrees of exhaustion make rather lively company when you are sick of your Uncle Timothy's cellar. And even the best of vintage wines may prove an ineffectual soporific. His, too, was a wretchedly active mind.

Even as a boy he had thought a good deal about his uncle and aunt, and Soames, and the house, and the Rev Mr Grayson, and spectres, and schoolmasters, and painted nymphs, and running away to sea, and curios, and dead silence, and his early childhood. And though, since then, other enigmas had engaged his attention, this purely automatic and tiresome activity of mind still persisted.

On his oath he had been in some respects and in secret rather a goody-goody little boy; though his piety had been rather the off-spring of fear than of love. Had he not been expelled from Mellish's almost solely for that reason? What on earth was the good of repeatedly thrashing a boy when you positively knew that he had lied merely from terror of your roaring voice and horrible white face?

But there it was; if there had been someone to talk to, he would not have talked so much to himself. He would not have lain awake thinking, night after night, like a rat in a trap. Thinking was like a fountain. Once it gets going at a certain pressure, well, it is almost impossible to turn it off. And, my hat! what odd things come up with the water!

On the particular night in question, in spite of the candles and the mice and the moon, he badly wanted company. In a moment of pining yet listless jocosity, then, he had merely taken his Aunt Charlotte's advice. True, the sumptuous, crimson, pleated silk bell-pull, dangling like a serpent with a huge tassel for skull over his Uncle Timothy's pillow, was a more formidable instrument than the yard or two of frayed green cord in the attic. Yet they shared the same purpose. Many a time must his Uncle Timothy have stretched up a large loose hand in that direction when in need of Soames's nocturnal ministrations. And now, alas, both master and man were long since gone the way of all flesh. You couldn't, it appeared, pull bells in your coffin.

But Jimmie was not as yet in his coffin, and as soon as his fingers slipped down from the smooth pull, the problem, in the abstract, as it were, began to fascinate him. With cold froggy hands crossed over his beautiful puce-patterned pyjamas, he lay staring at the crimson tassel till he had actually seen the hidden fangs flickeringly jet out at him.

The effort, then, must have needed some little courage. It *might* almost have needed a tinge of inspiration. It was in no sense intended as a challenge. He would, in fact, rather remain alone than chance summoning – well, *any* (once animate) relic of the distant past. But obviously the most practical way of proving – if only to yourself – that you can be content with your own reconnaissances in the very dead of night, was to demonstrate to that self that, even if you should ask for it, assistance would not be forthcoming.

He had been as fantastic as that. At the prolonged, pulsating, faint, distant tintinnabulation he had fallen back on to his pillow with an absurd little quicket of laughter, like that of a naughty boy up to mischief. But instant sobriety followed. Poor sleepers should endeavour to compose themselves. Tampering with empty space, stirring up echoes in pitch-black pits of dark-ness is scarcely sedative. And then, as he lay striving with extraordinary fervour not to listen, but to concentrate his mind on the wardrobe, and to keep his eyes from the door, that door must gently have opened.

It must have opened, and as noiselessly closed again. For a more or less decent-looking young man, seemingly not a day older than himself was now apparent in the room. It might almost be said that he had insinuated himself into the room. But well-trained domestics are accustomed to move their limbs and bodies with a becoming unobtrusiveness. There was also that familiar slight inclination of the apologetic in this young man's pose, as he stood there solitary in his black, in that terrific blaze of candle-light. And for a sheer solid minute the occupant of the Arabian bed had really stopped thinking.

When indeed you positively press your face, so to speak, against the crystalline window of your eyes, your mind is apt to become a perfect vac-uum. And Jimmie's first rapid and instinctive 'Who the devil...?' had remained inaudible.

In the course of the next few days Jimmie was to become familiar (at least in memory) with the looks of this new young butler or valet. But first impressions are usually the vividest. The dark blue-grey eyes, the high nose, the scarcely perceptible smile, the slight stoop of the shoulders – there was no doubt of it. There was just a flavour, a flicker, there, of resemblance to himself. Not that he himself could ever have cut as respectful and respectable a figure as that. And the smile! – the fellow seemed to be rumi-nating over a thousand dubious, long-interred secrets, secrets such as one may be a little cautious of digging up even to share with one's self.

His face turned sidelong on his pillow, and through air as visibly transparent as a sheet of glass, Jimmie had steadily regarded this strange bell-answerer; and the bell-answerer had never so much as stirred his frigid glittering eyes in response. The silence that hung between them produced eventually a peculiar effect on Jimmie. Menials as a general rule should be less emphatic personally. Their unobtrusiveness should surely not emphasize their immanence. It had been Jimmie who was the first to withdraw his eyes, only once more to find them settling as if spellbound on those of his visitor.

Yet, after all, there was nothing to take offence at in the young man's countenance or attitude. He did not seem even to be thinking-back at the bell-puller; but merely to be awaiting instructions. Yet Jimmie's heart at once rapidly began to beat again beneath his icy hands. And at last he made a perfectly idiotic response.

Wagging his head on his pillow, he turned abruptly away. 'It was only to tell you that I shall need nothing more to-night,' he had said.

Good heavens. The fatuity of it! He wanted, thirsted for, scores upon scores of things. Aladdin's was the cupidity of a simpleton by comparison. Time, and the past, for instance, and the ability to breathe again as easily as if it were natural – as natural as the processes of digestion. Why, if you were intent only on a little innocent companionship, one or two of those nymphs up there would be far more amusing company than Mrs Thripps. If, that is, apart from yearning to their harps and viols, they could have been persuaded to scrub and sweep. Jimmie wanted no other kind of help. There is a beauty that is but skin-deep.

Altogether it had been a far from satisfactory experience. Jimmie was nettled. His mincing tones echoed on in his mind. They must have suggested that he was unaccustomed to menservants and bell-pulls and opulent surroundings. And the fellow had instantly taken him at his word. A solemn little rather agreeable and unservile inclination of the not unfriendly head – and he was gone.

And there was Jimmie, absolutely exhausted, coughing his lungs out, and entirely incapable of concluding whether the new butler was a creature of actuality or of dream. Well, well, well: that was nothing new. That's just how things do take one in one's weak moments, in the dead of night. Nevertheless, the experience had apparently proved sedative. He had slept like an infant.

The morning found him vivacious with curiosity. He had paused to make only an exceedingly negligent toilet before beginning his usual wanderings about the house. Calm cold daylight reflection may dismiss almost any nocturnal experience as a dream, if, at any rate, one's temperature in the night hours is habitually above the norm. But Jimmie could not, or would not, absolutely make up his mind. So clear a picture had his visitant imprinted on his memory that he even found himself (just like a specialist sounding a patient in search of the secret ravages of phthisis) – he had even found himself stealthily tapping over the basement walls – as if in search of a concealed pantry! A foolish proceeding if one has not the least desire in the world to attract the attention of one's neighbours.

Having at length satisfied himself in a rather confused fashion that whatever understudy of Soames might share the house with him in the small hours, he must be a butler of the migratory order, Jimmie then began experimenting with the bells. Mounted on a kitchen chair, cornice brush in hand, he had been surprised by Mrs Thripps, in her quiet boots, as he stood gently knocking one by one the full eighteen of the long, greened, crooked jingle row which hung open-mouthed above the immense dresser.

She had caught him in the act, and Jimmie had once more exercised his customary glib presence of mind.

'They ought to be hung in a scale, you know. Oughtn't they, Mrs Thripps? Then we could have "Home, sweet Home!" and a hunting up and a hunting down, grandsires and treble bobs, and a grand maximus, even on week days. And if we were in danger of any kind of fire – which *you* will never be, we could ring them backwards. *Couldn't* we, Mrs Thripps? Not that there's much quality in them – no medieval monkish tone or timbre in *them*. They're a bit mouldy, too, and one can't tell t'other from which. Not like St Faiths's! One would recognize that old clanker in one's shroud, wouldn't one, Mrs Thripps? Has it ever occurred to you that the first campanologist's real intention was not so much to call the congregation, as to summon – well – what the congregation's after?'

'Yes, sir,' Mrs Thripps had agreed, her watery grey eyes fixed largely on the elevated young man. 'But it don't matter which of them you ring; I'll answer *hany* – at least while I'm in the house. I don't think, sir, you rest your mind enough. My own boy, now; *he's* in the Navy...'

But with one graceful flourish Jimmie had run his long-handled brush clean east to west along the clanging row. 'You mustn't,' he shouted, 'you shouldn't. Once aboard the lugger, they are free! It's you *mothers*...' He gently shook his peculiar wand at the flat-looking little old woman. 'No, Mrs Thripps; what I'm after is he who is here, *here! couchant, perdu, laired,* in these same subterranean vaults when you and I are snug in our nightcaps. A most nice-spoken young man! *Not* in the Navy, Mrs Thripps!'

And before the old lady had had time to seize any one of these seductive threads of conversation, Jimmie had flashed his usual brilliant smile or grimace at her, and soon afterwards sallied out of the house to purchase a further gross or two of candles.

Gently and furtively pushing across the counter half a sovereign – not as a douceur, but merely as from friend to friend – he had similarly smiled back at the secretive-looking old assistant in the staid West End family-grocer's.

'No, I didn't suppose you *could* remember me. One alters. One ages. One deals elsewhere. But anyhow, a Happy New Year to you – if the next ever comes, you know.'

'You see, sir,' the straight-aproned old man had retorted with equal confidentiality, 'it is not so much the alterations. They are what you might call un-cir-cum-ventible, sir. It's the stream, sir. Behind the counter here, we are like rocks in it. But even if I can't for the moment put a thought to your face – though it's already stirring in me in a manner of speaking, I shall in the future, sir. You may rely upon that. And the same, sir, to you; and many *of* them, I'm sure.'

Somehow or other Jimmie's vanity had been mollified by this pleasing little ceremoniousness; and that even before he had smiled yet once again at the saffron young lady in the Pay Box.

'The truth is, my dear,' he had assured himself, as he once more ascended into the dingy porch, 'the truth *is* when once you begin to tamper, you won't know where you are. You won't, really.'

And that night he had lain soberly on, in a peculiar state of physical quiescence and self-satisfaction, his dark bright eyes wandering from nymph to nymph, his hands folded over his breast under the bedclothes, his heart persisting in its usual habits. Nevertheless, the fountain of his thoughts had continued softly to plash on its worn basin. With ears a-cock, he had frankly enjoyed inhaling the parched, spent, brilliant air.

And when his fingers had at last manifested the faintest possible itch to experiment once more with the bell-pull, he had slipped out of bed, and hastily searching through a little privy case of his uncle's bedside books, had presently slipped back again, armed with a fat little copy of *The Mysteries of Paris,* in its original French.

The next day a horrible lassitude descended upon him. For the better part of an hour he had stood staring out of the drawing-room window into the London street. At last, with a yawn that was almost a groan, and with an absurdly disproportionate effort, he turned himself about. Heavily hung the gilded chandeliers in the long vista of the room; heavily gloomed the gilded furniture. Scarcely distinguishable in the obscurity of the further wall stood watching him from a mirror what might have appeared to be the shadowy reflection of himself. With a still, yet extreme aversion he kept his eyes fixed on this distant nonentity, hardly realizing his own fantastic resolve that if he did catch the least, faint independent movement there, he would give Soames Junior a caustic piece of his mind...

He must have been abominably fast asleep for hours when, a night or two afterwards, he had suddenly awakened, sweat streaming along his body, his mouth stretched to a long narrow O, and his right hand clutching the bell-rope, as might a drowning man at a straw.

The room was adrowse with light. All was still. The flitting horrors between dream and wake in his mind were already thinning into air. Through their transparency he looked out once more on the substantial, the familiar. His breath came heavily, like puffs of wind over a stormy sea, and yet a profound peace and tranquillity was swathing him in. The relaxed mouth was now faintly smiling. Not a sound, not the feeblest, distant unintended tinkling was trembling up from the abyss. And for a moment or two the young man refrained even from turning his head at the soundless opening and closing of the door.

He lay fully conscious that he was not alone; that quiet eyes had him steadily in regard. But, like rats, his wits were beginning to busy themselves again. Sheer relief from the terrors of sleep, shame of his extremity and weakness, a festering sense of humiliation – yes, he must save his face at all costs. He must put this preposterous spying valet in his place. Oddly enough, too, out of the deeps a peculiar little vision of recollection had inexplicably obtruded itself into consciousness. It would be a witticism of the first water.

'They are dreadfully out of season, you know,' he began murmuring affectedly into the hush, 'dreadfully. But what I'm really pining for is a bunch of primroses...A primrose by the river's brim... *must* be a little conservative.' His voice was once more trailing off into a maudlin drowsiness. With an effort he roused himself, and now with an extremely sharp twist of his head, he turned to confront his visitor.

But the room was already vacant, the door ajar, and Jimmie's lids were on the point of closing again, sliding down over his tired eyes like leaden shutters which no power on earth could hinder or restrain, when at the faintest far whisper of sound they swept back suddenly – and almost incredibly wide – to drink in all they could of the spectacle of a small odd-looking child who at that moment had embodied herself in the doorway.

She seemed to have not the least intention of returning the compliment. Her whole gaze, from out of her fair flaxen-pigtailed face, was fixed on the coarse blue-banded kitchen bowl which she was carrying with extreme care and caution in her two narrow hands. The idiots down below had evidently filled it too full of water, for the pale wide-petalled flowers and thick crinkled leaves it contained were floating buoyantly nid-nod to and fro as she moved – pushing on each slippered foot in turn in front of the other, her whole mind concentrated on her task.

A plain child, but extraordinarily fair, as fair as the primroses themselves in the congregation of candle-light that motionlessly flooded the room – a narrow-chested long-chinned little creature who had evidently outgrown her strength. Jimmie was well accustomed to take things as they come; and his brief sojourn in his uncle's house in his present state of health had already enlarged the confines of the term 'thing'. Anyhow, she was a relief from the valet.

He found himself, then, watching this new visitor without the least trace of astonishment or even of surprise. And as his dark eyes coursed over the child, he simply couldn't decide whether she most closely 'took after' Soames Junior or Mrs Thripps. All he could positively assure himself of was just the look, 'the family likeness'. And that in itself was a queerish coincidence, since whatever your views might be regarding Soames Junior, Mrs Thripps was real enough – as real, at any rate, as her scrubbing-brush and her wholesome evil-smelling soap.

As a matter of fact, Jimmie was taking a very tight hold of himself. His mind might fancifully be compared to a quiet green swarming valley be-tween steep rock-bound hills in which a violent battle was proceeding – standards and horsemen and smoke and terror and violence – but no sound.

Deep down somewhere he really wanted to be 'nice' to the child. She meant no ill; she was a demure far-away harmless-looking creature. Ages ago... On the other hand he wished to heaven they would leave him alone. They were pestering him. He knew perfectly well how far he was gone, and bitterly resented this renewed interference. And if there was one thing he detested, it was being made to look silly – 'I hope you are trying to be a good little boy?... You have not been talking to the servants?' That kind of thing.

It was, therefore, with mixed feelings and with a tinge of shame-faced-ness that he heard his own sneering, toneless voice insinuate itself into the silence; 'And what, missikins, can I do for you?... *What*, you will under-stand; not *How*?' The sneer had degenerated into a snarl.

The child at this had not perceptibly faltered. Her face had seemed to lengthen a little, but that might have been due solely to her efforts to deliver her bowl without spilling its contents. Indeed she actually succeeded in so doing, almost before Jimmie had time to withdraw abruptly from the little gilt-railed table on which she deposited the clumsy pot. Frock, pigtail, red hands – she seemed to be as 'real' a fellow creature as you might wish to see. But Jimmie stared quizzically on. Unfortunately primroses have no scent, so that he could not call on his nose to bear witness to his eyes. And the congested conflict in the green valley was still proceeding.

The child had paused. Her hands hung down now as if they were accustomed to service; and her pale blue eyes were fixed on his face in that exasperating manner which suggests that the owner of them is otherwise engaged. Not that she was looking *through* him. Even the sharpest of his 'female friends' had never been able to boast of that little accomplishment. She was looking into him; and as if he occupied time rather than space. Or was she, sneered that weary inward voice again, was she merely waiting for a tip?

'Look here,' said Jimmie, dexterously raising himself to his elbow on the immense lace-fringed pillow, 'it's all very well; you have managed things quite admirably, considering your age and the season, and so on. But I didn't ask for primroses, I asked for violets. That's a very old trick – very old trick.'

For one further instant, dark and fair, crafty and simpleton face communed, each with each. But the smile on the one had fainted into a profound childlike contemplation. And then, so swift and imperceptible had been his visitant's envanishment out of the room, that the very space she had occupied seemed to remain for a while outlined in the air – a nebulous shell of vacancy. She must, apparently, have glided *backwards* through the doorway, for Jimmie had assuredly not been conscious of the remotest glimpse of her pigtail from behind.

Instantly on that, the stony hillside within had resounded with a furious clangour – cries and shouts and screamings – and Jimmie, his face bloodless with rage, his eyes almost blind with it, had leapt out of the great bed as if in murderous pursuit. There must, however, have been an unusual degree or so of fever in his veins that night so swift was his reaction. For the moment he was on his feet an almost unendurable self-pity had swept into possession of him. To take a poor devil as literally as that! To catch him off his guard; not to give him the mere fleck of an opportunity to get his balance, to explain, to answer back! Curse the primroses.

But there was no time to lose.

With one hand clutching his pyjamas, the other carrying the bowl, he poked forward out of the flare of the room into the cold lightlessness of the wide stone staircase.

'Look here,' he called down in a low argumentative voice, 'look here, You! You can cheat and you can cheat, but to half strangle a fellow in his sleep, and then send him up the snuffling caretaker's daughter – No, No ...Next time, you old makebelieve, we'd prefer company a little more – a little more *congenial*.'

He swayed slightly, grimacing vacantly into the darkness, and listening to his speech as dimly as might a somnambulist to the distant roar of falling water. And then, poor benighted creature, Jimmie tried to spit, but his lips and tongue were dry, and that particular insult was spared him.

He had stooped laboriously, had put down the earthenware bowl on the Persian mat at the head of the staircase, and was self-congratulatorily re-welcoming himself into the scene of still lustre he had dared for that protracted minute to abandon, when he heard as if from beneath and behind him a kind of lolloping disquietude and the sound as of a clumsy-clawed, but persistent animal pushing its uncustomary awkward way up the soap-polished marble staircase.

It was to be tit for tat, then. The miserable ménage had let loose its menagerie. That. They were going to experiment with the mouse-cupboard-and-keyhole trickery of his childhood. Jimmie was violently shivering; his very toes were clinging to the mat on which he stood.

Swaying a little, and casting at the same time a strained whitened glance round the room in which every object rested in the light as if so it had rested from all eternity, he stood mutely and ghastly listening.

Even a large bedroom, five times the size of a small boy's attic, affords little scope for a fugitive, and shutting your eyes, darkening your outward face, is no escape. It had been a silly boast, he agreed – that challenge, that 'dare' on the staircase; the boast of an idiot. For the 'congenial company' that had now managed to hoof and scrabble its way up the slippery marble staircase was already on the threshold.

All was utterly silent now. There was no obvious manifestation of danger. What was peering steadily in upon him out of the obscurity beyond the door, was merely a blurred whitish beast-like shape with still, passive, almost stagnant eyes in its immense fixed face. A perfectly ludicrous object – on paper. Yet a creature so nauseous to soul and body, and with so obscene a greed in its motionless piglike grin that with one vertiginous swirl Jimmie's candles had swept up in his hand like a lateral race of streaming planets into outer darkness.

If his wet groping fingers had not then encountered one of the carved pedestals of his uncle's bedstead, Jimmie would have fallen; Jimmie would have found, in fact, the thing's physical level.

Try as he might, he had never in the days that followed made quite clear in his mind why for the third time he had not made a desperate plunging clutch at the bell rope. The thing *must* have been Soames Junior's emissary, even if the bird-faced scullery maid with the primroses had not also been one of the 'staff.'

That he had desisted simply in case she should herself have answered his summons and so have encountered the spurious animal as she mounted the dark staircase seemed literally too 'good' to be true. Not only was Jimmie no sentimentalist, but that particular kind of goodness, even in a state of mind perfectly calm and collected, was not one of his pleasanter characteristics.

Yet facts are facts – even comforting ones. And unless his memory was utterly untrustworthy, he had somehow – somehow contrived to regain his physical balance. Candelabrum in hand, he had actually, indeed, at last emerged from the room, and stooped his dark head over the balusters in search of what unaccountably had *not* awaited his nearer acquaintance. And he had – he must have – flung the substantial little blue-banded slop-basin, primroses and all, clean straight down in the direction of any kind of sentient target that happened to be in its way.

'You must understand, Mrs Thripps,' he had afterwards solemnly explained, 'I don't care to be disturbed, and particularly at night. All litter should, of course, be immediately cleared away. That's merely as things go in a well-regulated household, as, in fact, they *do* go. And I see you have replaced the one or two little specimens I was looking over out of the cabinet on the staircase. Pretty things, too; though you hadn't the advantage of being in the service of their late owner – my uncle. As *I* was. Of course, too, breakages cannot be avoided. There, I assure you, you are absolutely free. Moth and rust, Mrs Thripps. No; all that I was merely enquiring about at the moment is that particular pot. There was an accident last night – primroses and so on. And one might have expected, one might almost have sworn, Mrs Thripps, that at least a shard or two, as the Psalmist says, would have been pretty conspicuous even if the water *had* completely dried away. Not that I heard the smash, mind. I don't go so far as that. Nor am I making any insinuations *whatever*. You are the best of good creatures, you are indeed – and it's no good looking at me like Patience on a monument; because at present life is real and life is earnest. All I mean is that if one for a single moment ceases to guide one's conduct on reasonable lines – well, one comes a perfectly indescribable cropper, Mrs Thripps. Like the pot.'

Mrs Thripps's grey untidy head had remained oddly stuck out from her body throughout this harangue. 'No, sir,' she repeated once more. 'High and low I've searched the house down, and there isn't a shadder of what you might be referring to, not a shadder. And once more, I ask you, sir; let me call in Dr Stokes. He's a very nice gentleman; and one as keeps what should be kept as close to himself as it being his duty he sees right and proper to do. Chasing and racketing of yourself up and down these runs of naked stairs – in the dead of night – is no proper place for you, sir, in *your* state. And I don't like to take the responsibility. It's first the candles, then the bells, and then the kitching, and then the bason; I know what I'm talking about, sir, having lost two, and one at sea.'

'And suppose, my dear,' Jimmie had almost as brilliantly as ever smiled; 'suppose we are all of us "at sea." What then?'

'Why then, sir,' Mrs Thripps had courageously retorted, 'I'd as lief be at the bottom of it. There's been as much worry and trouble and making two ends meet in *my* life not to make the getting out of it what you'd stand on no ceremony for. I say it with all decent respect for what's respectful and proper, sir; but there isn't a morning I step down those area steps but my heart's in my mouth for fear there won't be anything in the house but what can't answer back. It's been a struggle to keep on, sir; and you as generous a gentleman as need be, if only you'd remain warm and natural in your bed when once there.'

A little inward trickle of laughter had entertained Jimmie as he watched the shapeless patient old mouth utter these last few words.

'That's just it, Mrs Thripps,' he had replied softly. 'You've done for me far more effectively than anyone I care to remember in my insignificant little lifetime. You have indeed.' Jimmie had even touched the hand bent like the claw of a bird around the broom-handle. 'In fact, you know – and I'm bound to confess it as gratefully as need be – they are *all* of them doing for me as fast as they can. I don't complain, not the least little bit in the world. All that I might be asking is, How the devil – to put it politely – how the goodness gracious is one to tell which is which? In my particular case, it seems to be the miller that sets the wind: not, of course, that he's got any particular grain to grind. Not even wild oats, you funny old mother of a youthful mariner. No, no, no. Even the fact that there wasn't perhaps any pot after all, you will understand, doesn't positively prove that neither could there have been any primroses. And before next January's four months old we shall be at the end of yet another April. At least —' and a sort of almost bluish pallor had spread like a shadow over his face – 'at least you will be. All of which is only to say, dear Madam, as Beaconsfield remarked to Old Vic, that I am thanking you *now*.'

At which Mrs Thripps immediately fell upon her knees on her house-maid's pad and plunged her hands into her zinc pail – only instantly after to sit back on her heels, skinny hands on canvas apron. 'All I says, sir, is, We go as we go; and a nicer gentleman, taking things on the surface, I never worked for. But one don't want to move too much in the Public Heye, sir. Of all the houses below stairs I've worked for and all alone in I don't want to charnst on a more private in a manner of speaking than this. All that I was saying, sir, and I wouldn't to none but you, is the life's getting on my nerves. When that door there closes after me, and every day drawing out steady as you can see without so much as glancing at the clock – I say, to myself, Well, better that pore young gentleman alone up there at night, cough and all, than *me*. I wouldn't sleep in this house, sir, not if you was to offer me a plateful of sovereigns... Unless, sir, you *wanted* me.'

On reflection Jimmie decided that he had cut almost a gallant figure as he had retorted gaily – yet with extraordinary sobriety: 'You shall have a whole dishful before I'm done, Mrs Thripps – with a big scoop in it for the gravy. But on my oath, I assure you there's absolutely nothing or nobody in this old barn of a museum except you and me. Nobody, unless, of course, you will understand, one happens to pull the bell. And that we're not likely to do in broad daylight. Are we, Mrs Thripps?' Upon which he had hastily caught up his aunt's handbag and had emerged into a daylight a good deal bleaker if not broader than he could gratefully stomach.

For a while Jimmie had let well alone. Indeed, if it had been a mere matter of choice, he would far rather have engaged in a friendly and jocular conversation of this description with his old charwoman than in the endless monologues in which he found himself submerged on other occasions. One later afternoon, for instance, at half-past three by his watch, sitting there by a small fire in the large muffled drawing room, he at length came definitely to the conclusion that some kind of finality should be reached in his relations with the Night Staff in his Uncle Timothy's.

It was pretty certain that *his* visit would soon be drawing to a close. Staying out at night until he was almost too exhausted to climb down to the pavement from his hansom – the first April silver of dawn wanning the stark and empty chimney-pots – had proved a dull and tedious alternative. The mere spectator of gaiety, he concluded, as he stared at the immense picture of the Colosseum on his Uncle Timothy's wall, may have as boring a time as must the slaves who cleaned out the cages of the lions that ate the Christians. And snapping out insults at former old cronies who couldn't help their faces being as tiresome as a whitewashed pigsty had soon grown wearisome.

Jimmie, of course, was accustomed to taking no interest in things which did not interest him; but quite respectable people could manage that equally well. What fretted him almost beyond endurance was an increasing inablity to keep his attention fixed on what was really *there,* what at least all such respectable people, one might suppose, would unanimously agree was there.

A moment's fixture of the eyes – and he would find himself steadily, steadily listening, now in a creeping dread that somewhere, down below, there was a good deal that needed an almost constant attention, and now in sudden alarm that, after all, there was absolutely nothing. Again and again in recollection he had hung over the unlighted staircase listening in an extremity of foreboding for the outbreak of a rabbit-like childish squeal of terror which would have proved – well, *what* would it have proved? My God, what a world! you can prove nothing.

The fact that he was all but certain that any such intolerably helpless squeal never *had* wailed up to him out of its pit of blackness could be only a partial consolation. He hadn't meant to be a beast. It was only his facetious little way. And you would have to be something pretty piggish in pigs to betray a child – however insubstantial – into the nausea and vertigo he had experienced in the presence of that unspeakable abortion. The whole thing had become a fatuous obsession. If, it appeared, you only remained solitary and secluded enough, and let your mind wander on in its own sweet way, the problem was almost bound to become, if not your one and only, at least your chief concern. Unless you were preternaturally busy and preoccupied, you simply couldn't live on and on in a haunted house without being occasionally reminded of its ghosts.

To dismiss the matter as pure illusion – the spectral picturing of life's fitful fever – might be all very well; that is if you had the blood of a fish. But who on earth had ever found the world the pleasanter and sweeter a place to bid good-bye to simply because it was obviously 'substantial', whatever *that* might mean? Simply because it did nothing you wanted it to do unless you paid for it pretty handsomely; or unless you accepted what it proffered with as open a hospitality as Jimmie had bestowed on his pilgrims of the night. Not that he much wanted – however pressing the invitation – to wander off out of his body into a better world, or, for that matter, into a worse.

Upstairs under the roof years ago Jimmie as a small boy would rather have died of terror than meddle with the cord above his bed-rail – simply because he knew that Soames Senior was at the other end of it. He had hated Soames; he had merely feared the nothings of his night hours. But, suppose Soames had been a different kind of butler. There must be almost as many kinds as there are human beings. Suppose his Uncle Timothy and Aunt Charlotte had chosen theirs a little less idiosyncratically; what then?

Well, anyhow, in a sense, he was not sorry life had been a little exciting these last few weeks. How odd that what all but jellied your soul in your body at night or in a dream, might merely amuse you like a shilling shocker in the safety of day. The safety of day – at the very cadence of the words in his mind, as he sat there in his aunt's 'salon', his limbs huddled over Mrs Thripps's fire, Jimmie's eyes had fixed themselves again. Again he was listening. Was it that, if you saw 'in your mind' *any* distant room or place, that place must actually at the moment contain you – some self, some 'astral body'? If so, wouldn't, of course, you *hear* yourself moving about in it?

There was a slight whining wind in the street outside the rainy window that afternoon, and once more the bright idea crossed Jimmie's mind that he should steal upstairs before it was dark, mount up onto the Arabian bed and just cut the bell-pull – once for all. But would that necessarily dismiss the Staff? Necessarily? His eye wandered to the discreet S of yet another bell-pull – that which graced the wall beneath the expansive white marble chimney-piece.

He hesitated. There was no doubt his mind was now hopelessly jaundiced against all bell-ropes – whether they failed to summon one to church or persisted in summoning one to a six-foot hole in a cemetery. His Uncle Timothy lay in a mausoleum. On the other hand he was properly convinced that a gentleman is as a gentleman does, and that it was really 'up to you' to treat *all* bell-answerers with decent courtesy. No matter who, when, where. A universal rule like that is a sheer godsend. If they didn't answer, well, you couldn't help yourself. Or rather, you would have to.

This shivering was merely physical. When a fellow is so thin that he can almost hear his ribs grind one against the other when he stoops to pick up a poker, such symptoms must be expected. There was still an hour or two of daylight – even though clouds admitted only a greyish light upon the world, and his Uncle Timothy's house was by nature friendly to gloom. That house at this moment seemed to hang domed upon his shoulders like an immense imponderable shell. The flames in the chimney whispered, fluttered, hovered, like fitfully-playing, once-happy birds.

Supposing if, even against his better judgment, he leaned forward now in his chair and – what was infinitely more conventional and in a sense more proper than summoning unforeseen entities to one's bedside – supposing he gave just one discreet little tug at that small porcelain knob; what would he ask for? He need ask nothing. He could act. Yes, if he could be perfectly sure that some monstrous porcine caco-demon akin to the shapes of childish nightmare would come hoofing up out of the deeps at his behest – well, he would chance it. He would have it out with the brute. It was still day.

It was still day. But, maybe, the ear of pleasanter visitors might catch the muffled tinkle? In the young man's mind there was now no vestige of jocularity. In an instant's lightness of heart he had once thought of purchasing from the stiff-aproned old assistant at his Aunt Charlotte's family grocer's, a thumping big box of chocolates. Why, just that one small bowl in *famille rose* up there could be bartered for the prettiest little necklet of seed pearls. She had done her best – with her skimpy shoulders, skimpier pigtail and soda-reddened hands. Pigtail! But no; you might pull real bells: to pull dubiously genuine pigtails seemed now a feeble jest. The old Jimmie of that kind of facetiousness was a thing of the past.

Apart from pigs and tweeny-maids, what other peculiar emanations might in the future respond to his summonings, Jimmie's exhausted imagination could only faintly prefigure. For a few minutes a modern St Anthony sat there in solitude in the vast half-blinded London drawing-room; while shapes and images and apparitions of memory and fantasy sprang into thin being and passed away in his mind. No, no.

'Do to the Book; quench the candles;
Ring the bell. *Amen, Amen.*'

– he was done with all that. Maledictions and anathemas; they only tangled the hank.

So when at last – his meagre stooping body mutely played on by the flamelight – he jerked round his dark narrow head to glance at the distant mirror, it must have been on the mere after-image, so to speak, of the once quite substantial-looking tweeny-maid that his exhausted eyes thirstily fixed themselves.

She was there – over there, where Soames Junior had more than once taken up his obsequious station. She was smiling – if the dusk of the room could be trusted that far; and not through, but really *at* Jimmie. She was fairer than ever, fairer than the flaxenest of nymphs on his uncle's ceiling, fairer than the saffronest of young ladies in the respectablest of family grocers, fairer even than —

Jimmie hung on this simple vision as did Dives on the spectacle of Lazarus in bliss. At once, of course, after his very first sigh of relief and welcome, he had turned back on his lips a glib little speech suggesting forgiveness – Let auld acquaintance be forgot; that kind of thing. He was too tired even to be clever now. And the oddest of convictions had at once come into his mind – seemed almost to fill his body even – that she was waiting for something else. Yes, she was smiling as if in hope. She was waiting to be told to go. Jimmie was no father. He didn't want to be considerate to the raw little creature, to cling to her company for but a few minutes longer, with a view to returns in kind. No, nothing of all that. 'Oh, my God; my God!' a voice groaned within him, but not at any unprecedented jag or stab of pain.

The child was still waiting. Quite quietly there – as if a shadow, as if a secret and obscure ray of light. And it seemed to Jimmie that in its patient face hung veil upon veil of uncountable faces of the past – in paint, stone, actuality, dream – that he had glanced at or brooded on in the enormous history of his life. That he may have coveted, too. And as well as his rebellious features could and would, he smiled back at her.

'I understand, my dear,' he drew back his dry lips to explain. 'Perfectly. And it was courtesy itself of you to look in when I didn't ring. I *didn't*. I absolutely put my tongue out at the grinning old knob...But no more of that. One mustn't talk for talking's sake. Else, why all those old Trappists ...though none of 'em such a bag-of-bones as me, I bet. But without jesting, you know...'

Once more a distant voice within spoke in Jimmie's ear. 'It's important'; it said. 'You really must hold your tongue – until, well, it holds itself.' But

Jimmie's face continued to smile.

And then suddenly, every vestige of amusement abandoned it. He stared baldly, almost emptily at the faint inmate of his solitude. 'All that I have to say,' he muttered, 'is just this: – I have Mrs Thripps. I haven't absolutely cut the wire. I wish to be alone. But *if* I ring, I'm not *asking*, do you see? In time I may be able to know what I want. But what is important now is that no more than that accursed Pig were your primroses 'real', my dear. You see things *must* be real. And now, I suppose,' he had begun shivering again, 'you must go to – you must go. But listen! listen! We part friends!'

The coals in the grate, with a scarcely audible shuffling, recomposed themselves to their consuming.

When there hasn't been anything there, nothing can be said to have vanished from the place where it has not been. Still, Jimmie had felt infinitely colder and immeasurably lonelier when his mouth had thus fallen to silence; and he was so empty and completely exhausted that his one apprehension had been lest he should be unable to ascend the staircase to get to bed. There was no doubt of it: his ultimatum had been instantly effective. The whole house was now preternaturally empty. It was needless even to listen to prove that. So absolute was its pervasive quietude that when at last he gathered his bones together in the effort to rise, to judge from the withering colour of the cinders and ashes in the fireplace, he must have been for some hours asleep; and daybreak must be near.

He managed the feat at last, gathered up the tartan travelling shawl that had tented in his scarecrow knees, and lit the only candle in its crystal stick in his Aunt Charlotte's drawing-room. And it was an almost quixotically peaceful though forebodeful Jimmie who, step by step, the fountain of his thoughts completely stilled, his night-mind as clear and sparkling as a cavern bedangled with stalagmites and stalactites, climbed laboriously on and up, from wide shallow marble stair to stair.

He paused in the corridor above. But the nymphs within – Muses, Graces, Fates, what not – piped in vain their mute decoy. His Uncle Timothy's Arabian bed in vain summoned him to its downy embraces. At the wide-open door he brandished his guttering candle in a last smiling gesture of farewell: and held on.

That is why when, next morning, out of a sounding slanting shower of rain Mrs Thripps admitted herself into the house at the area door, she found the young man, still in his clothes, lying very fast asleep indeed on the truckle-bed in the attic. His hands were not only crossed but convulsively clenched in that position on his breast. And it appeared from certain distressing indications that he must have experienced a severe struggle to refrain from a wild blind tug at the looped-up length of knotted whip-cord over his head.

As a matter of fact it did not occur to the littered old charwoman's mind to speculate whether or not Jimmie had actually made such a last attempt. Or whether he had been content merely to wait on a Soames who might, perhaps, like all good servants, come when he was wanted rather than when he was called. All her own small knowledge of Soameses, though not without comfort, had been acquired at second-hand.

Nor did Mrs Thripps waste time in surmising how Jimmie could ever have persuaded himself to loop up the cord like that out of his reach, unless he had first become abysmally ill-content with his small, primitive, and belated knowledge of campanology.

She merely looked at what was left of him; her old face almost comically transfixed in its appearance of pity, horror, astonishment, and curiosity.

The Creatures*

It was the ebbing light of evening that recalled me out of my story to a consciousness of my whereabouts. I dropped the squat little red book to my knee and glanced out of the narrow and begrimed oblong window. We were skirting the eastern coast of cliffs, to the very edge of which a plough-man, stumbling along behind his two great horses, was driving the last of his dark furrows. In a cleft far down between the rocks a cold and idle sea was soundlessly laying its frigid garlands of foam. I stared over the flat stretch of waters, then turned my head, and looked with a kind of sudden-ness into the face of my one fellow-traveller.

He had entered the carriage, all but unheeded, yet not altogether unresented, at the last country station. His features were a little obscure in the fading daylight that hung between our four narrow walls, but apparently his eyes had been fixed on my face for some little time.

He narrowed his lids at this unexpected confrontation, jerked back his head, and cast a glance out of his murky glass at the slip of greenish-bright moon that was struggling into its full brilliance above the dun, swelling uplands.

'It's a queer experience, railway-travelling,' he began abruptly, in a low, almost deprecating voice, drawing his hand across his eyes. 'One is cast into a passing privacy with a fellow-stranger and then is gone.' It was as if

* First published in *London Mercury*, January 1920.

he had been patiently awaiting the attention of a chosen listener.

I nodded, looking at him. '*That* privacy, too,' he ejaculated, 'all that!' My eyes turned towards the window again: bare, thorned, black, January hedge, inhospitable salt coast, flat waste of northern water. Our engine-driver promptly shut off his steam, and we slid almost noiselessly out of sight of sky and sea into a cutting.

'It's a desolate country,' I ventured to remark.

'Oh, yes, "desolate,"' he echoed a little wearily. 'But what frets me is the way we have of arrogating to ourselves the offices of judge, jury, and counsel all in one. As if this earth . . . I never forget it – the futility, the presumption. It *leads* nowhere. We drive in – into all this silence, this – this "forsakenness", this dream of a world between her lights of day and night time. We desecrate. Consciousness! What restless monkeys men are.' He recovered himself, swallowed his indignation with an obvious gulp. 'As if,' he continued, in more chastened tones – 'as if that other gate were not for ever ajar, into God knows what of peace and mystery.' He stooped forward, lean, darkened, objurgatory. 'Don't we *make* our world? Isn't that our blessed, our betrayed responsibility?'

I nodded, and ensconced myself, like a dog in straw, in the basest of all responses to a rare, even if eccentric, candour – caution.

'Well,' he continued, a little weariedly, 'that's the indictment. Small wonder if it will need a trumpet to blare us into that last "Family Prayers". Then perhaps a few solitaries – just a few – will creep out of their holes and fastnesses, and draw mercy from the merciful on the cities of the plain. The buried talent will shine none the worse for the long, long looming of its napery spun from dream and desire.

'Years ago – ten, fifteen, perhaps – I chanced on the queerest specimen of this order of the "talented". Much the same country, too. This' – he swept his glance out towards the now invisible sea – 'this is a kind of dwarf replica of it. More naked, smoother, more sudden and precipitous, more "forsaken", moody. Alone! The trees are shorn there, as if with monstrous shears, by the winter gales. The air's salt. It is a country of stones and emerald meadows, of green, meandering, aimless lanes, of farms set in their clefts and valleys like rough time-bedimmed jewels, as if by some angel of humanity, wandering between dark and daybreak.

'I was younger then – in body: the youth of the mind is for men of a certain age; yours, maybe, and mine. Even then, even at that, I was sickened of crowds, of that unimaginable London – swarming wilderness of mankind in which a poor lost thirsty dog from Otherwhere tastes first the full meaning of that idle word "forsaken". "Forsaken by whom?" is the question I ask myself now. Visitors to my particular paradise were few then – as if, my dear sir, we are not all of us visitors, visitants, revenants, on earth, panting for time in which to tell and share our secrets, roving in search of the marks that shall prove our quest not vain, not unprecedented, not a treachery. But let that be.

'I would start off morning after morning, bread and cheese in pocket, from the bare old house I lodged in, bound for that unforeseen nowhere for which the heart, the fantasy aches. Lingering hot noondays would find me stretched in a state half-comatose, yet vigilant, on the close-flowered turf of the fields or cliffs, on the sun-baked sands and rocks, soaking in the scene and life around me like some pilgrim chameleon. It was in hope to lose my way that I would set out. How shall a man find his way unless he lose it? Now and then I succeeded. That country is large, and its land and sea marks easily cheat the stranger. I was still of an age, you see, when my "small door" was ajar, and I planted a solid foot to keep it from shutting. But how could I know what I was after? One just shakes the tree of life, and the rare fruits come tumbling down, to rot for the most part in the lush grasses.

'What was most haunting and provocative in that far-away country was its fleeting resemblance to the country of dream. You stand, you sit, or lie prone on its bud-starred heights, and look down; the green, dispersed, tree-less landscape spreads beneath you, with its hollows and mounded slopes, clustering farmstead, and scatter of village, all motionless under the vast wash of sun and blue, like the drop-scene of some enchanted playhouse centuries old. So, too, the visionary bird-haunted headlands, veiled faintly in a mist of unreality above their broken stones and the enormous saucer of the sea.

'You cannot guess there what you may not chance upon, or whom. Bells clash, boom, and quarrel hollowly on the edge of darkness in those breakers. Voices waver across the fainter winds. The birds cry in a tongue unknown yet not unfamiliar. The sky is the hawks' and the stars'. *There* one is on the edge of life, of the unforeseen, whereas our cities – are not our desiccated, jaded minds ever continually pressing and edging further and further away from freedom, the vast unknown, the infinite presence, picking a fool's journey from sensual fact to fact at the tail of that he-ass called Reason? I suggest that in that solitude the spirit within us realizes that it treads the outskirts of a region long since called the Imagination. I assert we have strayed, and in our blindness abandoned — '

My stranger paused in his frenzy, glanced out at me from his obscure cor-ner as if he had intended to stun, to astonish me with some violent heresy. We puffed out slowly, laboriously, from a 'halt' at which in the gathering dark and moonshine we had for some while been at a standstill. Never was wedding-guest more desperately at the mercy of ancient mariner.

'Well, one day,' he went on, lifting his voice a little to master the resounding heart-beats of our steam-engine – 'one late afternoon, in my goal-less wanderings, I had climbed to the summit of a steep grass-grown cart-track, winding up dustily between dense, untended hedges. Even then I might have missed the house to which it led, for, hair-pin fashion, the track here abruptly turned back on itself, and only a far fainter footpath led on over the hill-crest. I might, I say, have missed the house and – and its inmates, if I had not heard the musical sound of what seemed like the twangling of a harp. This thin-drawn, sweet, tuneless warbling welled over the close green grass of the height as if out of space. Truth cannot say whether it was of that air or of my own fantasy. Nor did I ever discover what instrument, whether of man or Ariel, had released a strain so pure and yet so bodiless.

'I pushed on and found myself in command of a gorse-strewn height, a stretch of country that lay a few hundred paces across the steep and sudden valley in between. In a V-shaped entry to the left, and sunwards, lay an azure and lazy tongue of the sea. And as my eye slid softly thence and upwards and along the sharp, green horizon line against the glass-clear turquoise of space, it caught the flinty glitter of a square chimney. I pushed on, and presently found myself at the gate of a farmyard.

'There was but one straw-mow upon its staddles. A few fowls were sunning themselves in their dust-baths. White and pied doves preened and cooed on the roof of an outbuilding as golden with its lichens as if the western sun had scattered its dust for centuries upon the large slate slabs. Just that life and the whispering of the wind: nothing more. Yet even at one swift glimpse I seemed to have trespassed upon a peace that had endured for ages; to have crossed the viewless border that divides time from eternity. I leaned, resting, over the gate, and could have remained there for hours, lapsing ever more profoundly into the blessed quietude that had stolen over my thoughts.

'A bent-up woman appeared at the dark entry of a stone shed opposite to me, and, shading her eyes, paused in prolonged scrutiny of the stranger. At that I entered the gate and, explaining that I had lost my way and was tired and thirsty, asked for some milk. She made no reply, but after peering up at me, with something between suspicion and apprehension on her weather-beaten old face, led me towards the house which lay to the left on the slope of the valley, hidden from me till then by plumy bushes of tamarisk.

'It was a low grave house, grey-chimneyed, its stone walls traversed by a deep shadow cast by the declining sun, its dark windows rounded and uncurtained, its door wide open to the porch. She entered the house, and I paused upon the threshold. A deep unmoving quiet lay within, like that of water in a cave renewed by the tide. Above a table hung a wreath of wild flowers. To the right was a heavy oak settle upon the flags. A beam of sunlight pierced the air of the staircase from an upper window.

'Presently a dark, long-faced gaunt man appeared from within, contemplating me, as he advanced, out of eyes that seemed not so much to fix the intruder as to encircle his image, as the sea contains the distant speck of a ship on its wide blue bosom of water. They might have been the eyes of the blind; the windows of a house in dream to which the inmate must make something of a pilgrimage to look out upon actuality. Then he smiled, and the long, dark features, melancholy yet serene, took light upon them, as might a bluff of rock beneath a thin passing wash of sunshine. With a gesture he welcomed me into the large dark-flagged kitchen, cool as a cellar, airy as a belfry, its sweet air traversed by a long oblong of light out of the west.

'The wide shelves of the painted dresser were laden with crockery. A wreath of freshly-gathered flowers hung over the chimney-piece. As we entered, a twittering cloud of small birds, robins, hedge-sparrows, chaffinches fluttered up a few inches from floor and sill and window-seat, and once more, with tiny starry-dark eyes observing me, soundlessly alighted. I could hear the infinitesimal *tic-tac* of their tiny claws upon the slate. My gaze drifted out of the window into the garden beyond, a cavern of clearer crystal and colour than that which astounded the eyes of young Aladdin.

'Apart from the twisted garland of wild flowers, the shining metal of range and copper candlestick, and the bright-scoured crockery, there was no adornment in the room except a rough frame, hanging from a nail in the wall, and enclosing what appeared to be a faint patterned fragment of blue silk or fine linen. The chairs and table were old and heavy. A low light warbling, an occasional *skirr* of wing, a haze-like drone of bee and fly – these were the only sounds that edged a quiet intensified in its profundity by the remote stirrings of the sea.

'The house was stilled as by a charm, yet thought within me asked no questions; speculation was asleep in its kennel. I sat down to the milk and bread, the honey and fruit which the old woman laid out upon the table, and her master seated himself opposite to me, now in a low sibilant whisper – a tongue which they seemed to understand – addressing himself to the birds, and now, as if with an effort, raising those strange grey-green eyes of his to bestow a quiet remark upon me. He asked, rather in courtesy than with any active interest, a few questions, referring to the world, its business and transports – *our* beautiful world – as an astronomer in the small hours might murmur a few words to the chance-sent guest of his solitude concerning the secrets of Uranus or Saturn. There is another, an inexplorable side to the moon. Yet he said enough for me to gather that he, too, was of that small tribe of the aloof and wild to which our cracked old word "for-saken" might be applied, hermits, lamas, clay-matted fakirs, and such-like; the snowy birds that play and cry amid mid-oceanic surges; the living of an oasis of the wilderness; which share a reality only distantly dreamed of by the time-driven thought-corroded congregations of man.

'Yet so narrow and hazardous I somehow realized was the brink of fellow-being (shall I call it?) which we shared, he and I, that again and again fantasy within me seemed to hover over that precipice Night knows as fear. It was he, it seemed, with that still embracive contemplation of his, with that far-away yet reassuring smile, that kept my poise, my balance. "No," some voice within him seemed to utter, "you are safe; the bounds are fixed; though hallucination chaunt its decoy, you shall not irretrievably pass over. Eat and drink, and presently return to 'life'." And I listened, and, like that of a drowsy child in its cradle, my consciousness sank deeper and deeper, stilled, pacified, into the dream amid which, as it seemed, this soundless house of stone now reared its walls.

'I had all but finished my meal when I heard footsteps approaching on the flags without. The murmur of other voices, distinguishably shrill yet guttural even at a distance, and in spite of the dense stones and beams of the house which had blunted their timbre, had already reached me. Now the feet halted. I turned my head – cautiously, even perhaps apprehensively – and confronted two figures in the doorway.

'I cannot now guess the age of my entertainer. These children – for chil-dren they were in face and gesture and effect, though as to form and stature apparently in their last teens – these children were far more problematical. I say "form and stature", yet obviously they were dwarfish. Their heads were sunken between their shoulders, their hair thick, their eyes discon-certingly deep-set. They were ungainly, their features peculiarly irregular, as if two races from the ends of the earth had in them intermingled their blood and strangeness; as if, rather, animal and angel had connived in their creation.

'But if some inward light lay on the still eyes, on the gaunt, sorrowful, quixotic countenance that now was fully and intensely bent on mine, emphatically that light was theirs also. He spoke to them; they answered – in English, my own language, without a doubt: but an English slurred, bro-ken, and unintelligible to me, yet clear as bell, haunting, penetrating, pining as voice of nix or siren. My ears drank in the sound as an Arab parched with desert sand falls on his dried belly and gulps in mouthfuls of crystal water. The birds hopped nearer as if beneath the rod of an enchanter. A sweet continuous clamour arose from their small throats. The exquisite colours of plume and bosom burned, greened, melted in the level sun-ray, in the darker air beyond.

'A kind of mournful gaiety, a lamentable felicity, such as rings in the cadences of an old folk-song, welled into my heart. I was come back to the borders of Eden, bowed and outwearied, gazing from out of dream into dream, homesick, "forsaken".

'Well, years have gone by,' muttered my fellow-traveller deprecatingly, 'but I have not forgotten that Eden's primeval trees and shade.

'They led me out, these bizarre companions, a he and a she, if I may put it as crudely as my apprehension of them put it to me then. Through a broad door they conducted me – if one who leads may be said to be conducted – into their garden. Garden! A full mile long, between undiscerned walls, it sloped and narrowed towards a sea at whose dark unfoamed blue, even at this distance, my eyes dazzled. Yet how can one call that a garden which reveals no ghost of a sign of human arrangement, of human slavery, of spade or hoe?

'Great boulders shouldered up, tessellated, embossed, powdered with a thousand various mosses and lichens, between a flowering greenery of weeds. Wind-stunted, clear-emerald, lichen-tufted trees smoothed and crisped the inflowing airs of the ocean with their leaves and spines, sibilating a thin scarce-audible music. Scanty, rank, and uncultivated fruits hung close their vivid-coloured cheeks to the gnarled branches. It was the harbourage of birds, the small embowering parlour of their house of life, under an evening sky, pure and lustrous as a water-drop. It cried "Hospital" to the wanderers of the universe.

'As I look back in ever-thinning nebulous remembrance on my two companions, hear their voices gutturally sweet and shrill, catch again their being, so to speak, I realize that there was a kind of Orientalism in their effect. Their instant courtesy was not Western, the smiles that greeted me, whenever I turned my head to look back at them, were infinitely friendly, yet infinitely remote. So ungainly, so far from our notions of beauty and symmetry were their bodies and faces, those heads thrust heavily between their shoulders, their disproportioned yet graceful arms and hands, that the children in some of our English villages might be moved to stone them, while their elders looked on and laughed.

'Dusk was drawing near; soon night would come. The colours of the sunset, sucking its extremest dye from every leaf and blade and petal, touched my consciousness even then with a vague fleeting alarm.

'I remember I asked these strange and happy beings, repeating my question twice or thrice, as we neared the surfy entry of the valley upon whose sands a tiny stream emptied its fresh waters – I asked them if it was they who had planted this multitude of flowers, many of a kind utterly unknown to me and alien to a country inexhaustibly rich. "We wait; we wait!" I think they cried. And it was as if their cry woke echo from the green-walled valleys of the mind into which I had strayed. Shall I confess that tears came into my eyes as I gazed hungrily around me on the harvest of their patience?

'Never was actuality so close to dream. It was not only an unknown country, slipped in between these placid hills, on which I had chanced in my ramblings. I had entered for a few brief moments a strange region of consciousness. I was treading, thus accompanied, amid a world of welcoming and fearless life – oh, friendly to me! – the paths of man's imagination, the kingdom from which thought and curiosity, vexed scrutiny and lust – a lust it may be for nothing more impious than the actual –had prehistorically proved the insensate means of his banishment. "Reality", "Consciousness": had he for "the time being" unwittingly, unhappily missed his way? Would he be led back at length to that garden wherein cockatrice and basilisk bask, harmlessly, at peace?

'I speculate now. In that queer, yes, and possibly sinister, company, sinister only because it was alien to me, I did not speculate. In their garden, the familiar was become the strange – "the strange" that lurks in the inmost heart, unburdens its riches in trance, flings its light and gilding upon love, gives heavenly savour to the intemperate bowl of passion, and is the secret of our incommunicable pity. What is yet queerer, these beings were evidently glad of my company. They stumped after me (as might yellow men after some occidental quadruped never before seen) in merry collusion of nods and wreathed smiles at this perhaps unprecedented intrusion.

'I stood for a moment looking out over the placid surface of the sea. A ship in sail hung phantom-like on the horizon. I pined to call my discovery to its seamen. The tide gushed, broke, spent itself on the bare boulders, I was suddenly cold and alone, and gladly turned back into the garden, my companions instinctively separating to let me pass between them. I breathed in the rare, almost exotic heat, the tenuous, honeyed, almond-laden air of its flowers and birds – gull, sheldrake, plover, wagtail, finch, robin, which as I half-angrily, half-sadly realized fluttered up in momentary dismay only at *my* presence – the embodied spectre of their enemy, man. Man? Then who were these? . . .

'I lost again a way lost early that morning, as I trudged inland at night. The dark came, warm and starry. I was dejected and exhausted beyond words. That night I slept in a barn and was awakened soon after daybreak by the crowing of cocks. I went out, dazed and blinking into the sunlight, bathed face and hands in a brook nearby, and came to a village before a soul was stirring. So I sat under a thrift-cushioned, thorn-crowned wall in a meadow, and once more drowsed off and fell asleep. When again I awoke, it was ten o'clock. The church clock in its tower knelled out the strokes, and I went into an inn for food.

'A corpulent, blonde woman, kindly and hospitable, with a face comfortably resembling her own sow's, that yuffed and nosed in at the open door as I sat on my stool, served me with what I called for. I described – not without some vanishing shame, as if it were a treachery – my farm, its whereabouts.

'Her small blue eyes "pigged" at me with a fleeting expression which I failed to translate. The name of the farm, it appeared, was Trevarras. "And did you see any of the Creatures?" she asked me in a voice not entirely her own. "The Creatures?" I sat back for an instant and stared at her; then realized that Creature was the name of my host, and Maria and Christus (though here her dialect may have deceived me) the names of my two gardeners. She spun an absurd story, so far as I could tack it together and make it coherent. Superstitious stuff about this man who had wandered in upon the shocked and curious inhabitants of the district and made his home at Trevarras – stranger and pilgrim, a "foreigner", it seemed, of few words, dubious manners, and both uninformative.

'Then there was something (she placed her two fat hands, one of them wedding-ringed, on the zinc of the bar-counter, and peered over at me, as if I were a delectable "wash"), then there was something about a woman "from the sea". In a "blue gown", and either dumb, inarticulate, or mistress of only a foreign tongue. She must have lived in sin, moreover, those pig's eyes seemed to yearn, since the children were "simple", "naturals" – as God intends in such matters. It was useless. One's stomach may sometimes reject the cold sanative aerated water of "the next morning", and my ridiculous intoxication had left me dry but not yet quite sober.

'Anyhow, this she told me, that my blue woman, as fair as flax, had died and was buried in the neighbouring churchyard (the nearest to, though miles distant from, Trevarras). She repeatedly assured me, as if I might otherwise doubt so sophisticated a fact, that I should find her grave there, her "stone".

'So indeed I did – far away from the elect, and in a shade-ridden northwest corner of the sleepy, cropless acre: a slab, scarcely rounded, of granite, with but a name bitten out of the dark rough surface, "*Femina Creature*".'

The Riddle*

So these seven children, Ann and Matilda, James, William and Henry, Harriet and Dorothea, came to live with their grandmother. The house in which their grandmother had lived since her childhood was built in the time of the Georges. It was not a pretty house, but roomy, substantial, and square; and a great cedar tree outstretched its branches almost to the windows.

When the children were come out of the cab (five sitting inside and two beside the driver), they were shown into their grandmother's presence. They stood in a little black group before the old lady, seated in her bow-window. And she asked them each their names, and repeated each name in her kind, quavering voice. Then to one she gave a work-box, to William a jack-knife, to Dorothea a painted ball; to each a present according to age. And she kissed all her grand-children to the youngest.

'My dears,' she said, 'I wish to see all of you bright and gay in my house. I am an old woman, so that I cannot romp with you; but Ann must look to you, and Mrs Fenn too. And every morning and every evening you must all come in to see your granny; and bring me smiling faces, that call back to my mind my own son Harry. But all the rest of the day, when school is done, you shall do just as you please, my dears. And there is only one thing, just one, I would have you remember. In the large spare bedroom that looks out on the slate roof there stands in the corner an old oak chest; aye, older than I, my dears, a great deal older; older than my grandmother. Play any-where else in the house, but not there.' She spoke kindly to them all, smil-ing at them; but she was very old, and her eyes seemed to see nothing of this world.

And the seven shildren, though at first they were gloomy and strange, soon began to be happy and at home in the great house. There was much to interest and to amuse them there; all was new to them. Twice every day, morning and evening, they came in to see their grandmother, who every day seemed more feeble; and she spoke pleasantly to them of her mother, and her childhood, but never forgetting to visit her store of sugar-plums. And so the weeks passed by...

It was evening twilight when Henry went upstairs from the nursery by himself to look at the oak chest. He pressed his fingers into the carved fruit and flowers, and spoke to the dark-smiling heads at the corners; and then, with a glance over his shoulder, he opened the lid and looked in. But the chest concealed no treasure, neither gold nor baubles, nor was there any-

---

* As printed in CSC (1947). First published in *Monthly Review*, February 1903.

thing to alarm the eye. The chest was empty, except that it was lined with silk of old rose, seeming darker in the dusk, and smelling sweet of pot-pourri. And while Henry was looking in, he heard the softened laughter and the clinking of the cups downstairs in the nursery; and out at the window he saw the day darkening. These things brought strangely to his memory his mother who in her glimmering white dress used to read to him in the dusk; and he climbed into the chest; and the lid closed gently down over him.

When the other six children were tired with their playing, they filed into their grandmother's room for her good-night and her sugar-plums. She looked out between the candles at them as if she were uncertain of something in her thoughts. The next day Ann told her grandmother that Henry was not anywhere to be found.

'Dearie me, child. Then he must be gone away for a time,' said the old lady. She paused. 'But remember, all of you, do not meddle with the oak chest.'

But Matilda could not forget her brother Henry, finding no pleasure in playing without him. So she would loiter in the house thinking where he might be. And she carried her wooden doll in her bare arms, singing under her breath all she could make up about it. And when one bright morning she peeped in on the chest, so sweet-scented and secret it seemed that she took her doll with her into it – just as Henry himself had done.

So Ann, and James, and William, Harriet and Dorothea were left at home to play together. 'Some day maybe they will come back to you, my dears,' said their grandmother, 'or maybe you will go to them. Heed my warning as best you may.'

Now Harriet and William were friends together, pretending to be sweethearts; while James and Dorothea liked wild games of hunting, and fishing, and battles.

On a silent afternoon in October, Harriet and William were talking softly together, looking out over the slate roof at the green fields, and they heard the squeak and frisking of a mouse behind them in the room. They went together and searched for the small, dark hole from whence it had come out. But finding no hole, they began to finger the carving of the chest, and to give names to the dark-smiling heads, just as Henry had done. '*I know!* let's pretend you are Sleeping Beauty, Harriet,' said William, 'and I'll be the Prince that squeezes through the thorns and comes in.' Harriet looked gently and strangely at her brother but she got into the box and lay down, pretending to be fast asleep, and on tiptoe William leaned over, and seeing how big was the chest, he stepped in to kiss the Sleeping Beauty and to wake her from her quiet sleep. Slowly the carved lid turned on its noiseless hinges. And only the clatter of James and Dorothea came in sometimes to recall Ann from her book.

But their old grandmother was very feeble, and her sight dim, and her hearing extremely difficult.

Snow was falling through the still air upon the roof; and Dorothea was a fish in the oak chest, and James stood over the hole in the ice, brandishing a walking-stick for a harpoon, pretending to be an Esquimau. Dorothea's face was red, and her wild eyes sparkled through her tousled hair. And James had a crooked scratch upon his cheek. 'You must struggle, Dorothea, and then I shall swim back and drag you out. Be quick now!' He shouted with laughter as he was drawn into the open chest. And the lid closed softly and gently down as before.

Ann, left to herself, was too old to care overmuch for sugar-plums, but she would go solitary to bid her grandmother good-night; and the old lady looked wistfully at her over her spectacles. 'Well, my dear,' she said with trembling head; and she squeezed Ann's fingers between her own knuckled finger and thumb. 'What lonely old people, we two are, to be sure!' Ann kissed her grandmother's soft, loose cheek. She left the old lady sitting in her easy chair, her hands upon her knees, and her head turned sidelong towards her.

When Ann was gone to bed she used to sit reading her book by candle-light. She drew up her knees under the sheets, resting her book upon them. Her story was about fairies and gnomes, and the gently-flowing moonlight of the narrative seemed to illumine the white pages, and she could hear in fancy fairy voices, so silent was the great many-roomed house, and so melli-fluent were the words of the story. Presently she put out her candle, and, with a confused babel of voices close to her ear, and faint swift pictures before her eyes, she fell asleep.

And in the dead of night she rose out of her bed in dream, and with eyes wide open yet seeing nothing of reality, moved silently through the vacant house. Past the room where her grandmother was snoring in brief, heavy slumber, she stepped lightly and surely, and down the wide staircase. And Vega the far-shining stood over against the window above the slate roof. Ann walked into the strange room beneath as if she were being guided by the hand towards the oak chest. There, just as if she were dreaming it was her bed, she laid herself down in the old rose silk, in the fragrant place. But it was so dark in the room that the movement of the lid was indistinguishable.

Through the long day, the grandmother sat in her bow-window. Her lips were pursed, and she looked with dim, inquisitive scrutiny upon the street where people passed to and fro, and vehicles rolled by. At evening she climbed the stair and stood in the doorway of the large spare bedroom. The ascent had shortened her breath. Her magnifying spectacles rested upon her nose. Leaning her hand on the doorpost she peered in towards the glimmering square of window in the quiet gloom. But she could not see far, because her sight was dim and the light of day feeble. Nor could she detect the faint fragrance as of autumnal leaves. But in her mind was a tangled skein of memories – laughter and tears, and children long ago become old-fashioned, and the advent of friends, and last farewells. And gossiping fitfully, inarticulately, with herself, the old lady went down again to her window-seat.

The Vats*

Many years ago now – in that once upon a time which is the memory of the imagination rather than of the workaday mind, I went walking with a friend. Of what passed before we set out I have nothing but the vaguest recollection. All I remember is that it was early morning, that we were happy to be in one another's company, that there were bright green boughs overhead amongst which the birds floated and sang, and that the early dews still burned in their crystal in the sun.

We were taking our way almost at haphazard across country; there was now grass, now the faintly sparkling flinty dust of an English road, underfoot. With remarkably few humans to be seen, we trudged on, turning our eyes ever and again to glance laughingly, questioningly, or perplexedly at one another's, then slanting them once more on the blue-canopied countryside. It was spring, in the month of May, I think, and we were talking of Time.

We speculated on what it was, and where it went to, touched in furtive tones on the Fourth Dimension and exchanged 'the Magic Formula'. We wondered if pigs could see time as they see the wind, and wished we could recline awhile upon those bewitching banks where it grows wild. We confessed to each other how of late we had been pining in our secret hearts for just a brief spell of an *eternity* of it. Time wherein we could be and think and dream all that each busy, hugger-mugger, feverish, precipitate twenty-four hours would not allow us to be or to think or dream. Impracticable, infatuate desire! We desired to muse, to brood, to meditate, to embark (with a buoyant cargo) upon that quiet stream men call reverie. We had all but forgotten how even to sleep. We lay like Argus of nights with all our hundred eyes ajar.

There were books we should never now be able to read; speculations we

* As printed in BS (1942). First published in *Saturday Westminster Gazette*, 16 June 1917.

should never be able to explore; riddles we should never so much as hear put, much less expounded. There were, above all, waking visions now past hoping for; long since shut away from us by the stream of the hasty moments – as they tick and silt and slide irrecoverably away. In the gay folly of that bright morning we could almost have vowed there were even other 'selves' awaiting us with whom no kind of precarious tryst we had ever made we had ever been faithful to. Perhaps they and we would be ready if only the world's mechanical clocks would cease their trivial moralizings.

And memories – surely they would come arrowing home in the first of the evening to haunts serene and unmolested, if only the weather and mood and season and housing we could offer were decently propitious. We had frittered away, squandered so many days, weeks, years – and had saved so little. Spendthrifts of the unborrowable, we had been living on our capital – a capital bringing in how meagre an 'interest' – and we were continually growing poorer. Once, when we were children, and in our own world, an hour had been as capacious as the blue bowl of the sky, and of as refreshing a milk. Now its successors haggardly snatched their way past our sluggard senses like thieves pursued.

Like an hour-glass that cannot tell the difference between its head and its heels; like a dial on a sunless day; like a time-piece wound-up – wound-up and bereft of its pendulum; so were we. Age, we had hideously learned, devours life as a river consumes flakes of the falling snow. Soon we should be beggars, with scarcely a month to our name; and none to give us alms.

I confess that at this crisis in our talk I caught an uncomfortable glimpse of the visionary stallions of my hearse – ink-black streaming manes and tails – positively galloping me off – wreaths, glass, corpse and all, to keep their dismal appointment with the grave: and even at that, abominably late.

Indeed, our minds had at length become so profoundly engaged in these pictures and forebodings as we paced on, that a complete aeon might have meanwhile swept over our heads. We had talked ourselves into a kind of oblivion. Nor had either of us given the least thought to our direction or destination. We had been following not even so much as our noses. And then suddenly, we 'came to'. Maybe it was the unwonted silence – silence unbroken even by the harplike drone of noonday – that recalled us to ourselves. Maybe the air in these unfamiliar parts was of a crisper quality, or the mere effect of the strangeness around us had muttered in secret to our inward spirits. Whether or not, we both of us discovered at the same instant and as if at a signal, that without being aware of it, and while still our tongues were wagging on together on our old-fashioned theme, we had come into sight of the 'Vats'. We looked up, and lo! – they lay there in the middle distance, in cluster enormous under the cloudless sky: and here were we!

Imagine two age-scarred wolf-skinned humans of prehistoric days paddling along at shut of evening on some barbarous errand, and suddenly from a sweeping crest on Salisbury Plain descrying on the nearer horizon the awful monoliths of Stonehenge. An experience resembling that was ours this summer day.

We came at once to a standstill amid the far-flung stretches of the unknown plateau on which we had re-found ourselves, and with eyes fixed upon these astonishing objects, stood and stared. I have called them Vats. Vats they were not; but rather sunken Reservoirs; vast semi-spherical primeval Cisterns, of an area many times that of the bloated and swollen gasometers which float like huge flattened bubbles between earth and heaven under the sunlit clouds of the Thames. But no sunbeams dispread themselves here. They lay slumbering in a grave, crystal light, which lapped, deep as the Tuscarora Trough, above and around their prodigious stone plates, or slats, or slabs, or laminae; their steep slopes washed by the rarefied atmosphere of their site, and in hue of a hoary green.

As we gazed at them like this from afar they seemed to be in number, as I remember, about nine, but they were by no means all of a size. For one or two of the rotundas were smaller in compass than the others, just as there may be big snails or mushrooms in a family, and little ones.

But any object on earth of a majesty or magnitude that recalls the pyramids is a formidable spectacle. And not a word passed between us, scarcely a glance, as with extreme caution and circumspection we approached – creeping human pace by pace – to view them nearer.

A fit of shivering came over me, I recollect, as thus advantaged I scanned their enormous sides, shaggy with tufts of a monstrous moss and scarred with yard-wide circumambulations of lichen. Gigantic grasses stooped their fatted seedpods from the least rough ledge. They might be walls of ice, so cold their aspect; or of a matter discoverable only in an alien planet.

Not – though they were horrific to the *eye* – not that they were in themselves appalling to the soul. Far rather they seemed to be emblems of an ineffable peace; harmless as, centuries before Noah, were the playing leviathans in a then privy Pacific. And when one looked close on them it was to see myriads of animated infinitesimals in crevice and cranny, of a beauty, hue and symmetry past eye to seize. Indeed, there was a hint remotely human in the looks of these Vats. The likeness between them resembled that between generations of mankind, countless generations old. Contemplating them with the unparalleled equanimity their presence at last bestowed, one might almost have ventured to guess their names. And never have I seen sward or turf so smooth and virginally emerald as that which heaved itself against their Brobdingnagian flanks.

My friend and I, naturally enough, were acutely conscious of our minuteness of stature as we stood side by side in this unrecorded solitude, and, out of our little round heads, peered up at them with our eyes. Obviously their muscous incrustations and the families of weeds flourishing in their interstices were of an age to daunt the imagination. Their ancestry must have rooted itself here when the dinosaur and the tribes of the megatherium roamed earth's crust and the pterodactyl clashed through its twilight – thousands of centuries before the green acorn sprouted that was to afford little Cain in a fallen world his first leafy petticoats. I realized as if at a sigh why smiles the Sphinx; why the primary stars have blazed on in undiminishing midnight lustre during man's brief history and his childish constellations have scarcely by a single inch of heaven changed in their apparent stations.

They wore that air of lively timelessness which decks the thorn, and haunts the half-woken senses with the odour of sweet-brier; yet they were grey with the everlasting, as are the beards of the patriarchs and the cin-dery craters of the moon. Theirs was the semblance of having been lost, forgotten, abandoned, like some foundered Nereid-haunted derelict of the first sailors, rotting in dream upon an undiscovered shore. They hunched their vast shapes out of the green beneath the sunless blue of space, and for untrodden leagues around them stretched like a paradisal savanna what we poor thronging clock-vexed men call Silence. Solitude.

In telling of these Vats it is difficult to convey in mere words even a frac-tion of their effect upon our minds. And not merely our minds. They called to some hidden being within us that, if not their coeval, was at least aware of their exquisite antiquity. Whether of archangelic or daemonic construc-tion, clearly they had remained unvisited by mortal man for as many cen-turies at least as there are cherries in Damascus or beads in Tierra del Fuego. Sharers of this thought, we two dwarf visitors had whispered an instant or so together, face to face; and then were again mute.

Yes, we were of one mind about that. In the utmost depths of our imag-inations it was clear to us that these supremely solitary objects, if not pos-itively cast out of thought, had been abandoned.

But by whom? My friend and I had sometimes talked of the divine Abandoner; and also (if one can, and may, distinguish between mood and person, between the dream and the dreamer) of It. Here was the vacancy of His presence; just as one may be aware of a filament of His miracle in the smiling beauty that hovers above the swaying grasses of an indecipherable grave-stone.

Looking back on the heatless and rayless noonday of those Vats, I see, as I have said, the mere bodies of my friend and me, the upright bones of us, indescribably dwarfed by their antediluvian monstrosity. Yet within the lightless bellies of these sarcophagi were heaped up, we were utterly assured (though *how*, I know not) floods, beyond measure, of the waters for which our souls had pined. Waters, imaginably so clear as to be dense, as if of melted metal more translucent even than crystal; of such a tenuous purity that not even the moonlit branches of a dream would spell their reflex in them; so costly, so far beyond price, that this whole stony world's rubies and sapphires and amethysts of Mandalay and Guadalajara and Solikamsk, all the treasure-houses of Cambalech and the booty of King Tamburlane would suffice to purchase not one drop.

It is indeed the unseen, the imagined, the untold-of, the fabulous, the forgotten that alone lies safe from mortal moth and rust; and these Vats – their very silence held us spellbound, as were the Isles before the Sirens sang.

But how, it may be asked. No sound? No spectral tread? No faintest summons? And not the minutest iota of a superscription? None. I sunk my very being into nothingness, so that I seemed to become but a shell receptive of the least of whispers. But the multitudinous life that was here was utterly silent. No sigh, no ripple, no pining chime of rilling drop within. Waters of life; but infinitely still.

I may seem to have used extravagant terms. My friend and I used none. We merely stood in dumb survey of these crusted, butt-like domes of stone, wherein slept *Elixir Vitae*, whose last echo had been the Choragium of the morning stars.

God knows there are potent explosives in these latter days. My friend and I had merely the nails upon our fingers, a pen-knife and a broken pair of scissors in our pockets. We might have scraped seven and seventy score growths of a Nebuchadnezzar's talons down to the quick, and yet have left all but unmarked and unscarred those mossed and monstrous laminae. But we had tasted the untastable, and were refreshed in spirit at least a little more endurably than are the camel-riders of the Sahara dream-ridden by mirage.

We knew now and for ever that Time-pure *is*; that here – somewhere awaiting us and all forlorn mankind – lay hid the solace of our mortal long-ing; that doubtless the Seraph whose charge is the living waters will in the divine hour fetch down his iron key in his arms, and – well, Dives, rich man and crumb-waster that he was, pleaded out of the flames for but one drop of them. Neither my friend nor I was a Dives then, nor was ever likely to be. And now only I remain.

We were Children of Lazarus, ageing, footsore, dusty and athirst. We smiled openly and with an extraordinary gentle felicity at one another – his eyes and mine – as we turned away from the Vats.

DING DONG BELL
(1924, 1936)

*Lichen**

Ther cam a privee theef, men clepeth Deeth,
That in this contree al the peple sleeth,
And with his spere he smoot his herte a-two,
And wente his wey with-outen wordes mo...

Except for one domed and mountainous cloud of snow and amber, the sky
was blue as a child's eyes, blue as the tiny chasing butterflies which looped
the air above our shimmering platform – bluer far, in fact, than my new silk
sunshade. I just sat and basted my travel-wearied bones in the sunshine;
and thanked heaven for so delicious a place to be alive in.

It was, I agree, like catching sight of it in hungry glimpses through a
rather dingy window. There had been frequent interruptions. First had
come a goods train. It had shunted this way, it shunted that. Its buffers
crashed; its brakes squealed; its sheep baa-ed, and its miserable, dribbling
cattle, with their gleaming horns, stared blindly out at us under their long
eyelashes in a stagnant dumb despair.

When that had gone groaning on its way, a 'local' – a kind of nursery
train – puff-puffed in on the other side. And then we enjoyed a Strauss-like
interlude of milk-cans and a vociferous Sunday school excursion – the
scholars (merely tiny tots, many of them) engaged even on this weekday in
chaunting at intervals the profoundest question man can address to the
universe: 'Are we downhearted? No!'

These having at last wandered off into a dark-mouthed tunnel, the
noonday express with a wildly-soaring crescendo of lamentation came
sweeping in sheer magnificence of onset round its curve, roared through the
little green empty station – its windows a long broken faceless glint of sunlit glass – and that too vanished. Vanished!

A swirl of dust and an unutterable stillness followed after it. The skin of
a banana on the platform was the only proof that it had come and gone.

---

* As printed in SEP (1938). First published in *Lady's Realm*, September 1907. See also 'De
Mortuis', Uncollected Stories, p.444, which has epitaphs in common.

Its shattering clamour had left for contrast an almost helpless sense of peace. 'Yes, yes!' we all seemed to be whispering – from the Cedar of Lebanon to the little hyssop in the wall – 'here we all are; and still, thank heaven, safe. *Safe*.'

The snapdragons and sweet-williams burned on in their narrow flint-bordered bed. The hollow of beautiful verdure but a stone's throw beyond the further green bank, with its square bell-tower and its old burial stones, softly rang again with faint trillings. I turned instinctively to the old gentleman who was sharing the hard, 'grained', sunny bench with me, in sure and certain hope of his saying Amen to my relief. It was a rather heedless impulsiveness, perhaps; but I could not help myself – I just turned.

But no. He tapped the handle of his umbrella with gloved fingers. 'As you will, ma'am,' he said pettishly. 'But *my* hopes are in the past.'

'I was merely thinking,' I began, 'the contrast, you know; and now – how peaceful it all is.'

He interrupted me with a stiff little bow. 'Precisely. But the thought was sentimental, ma'am. You would deafen us all to make us hear. You tolerate what you should attack – the follies, vexations, the evils which that pestilent monster represents; haste, restlessness, an impious money-grubbing. I hate the noise; I hate the trespass; the stench; the futility. Fifty years ago there wasn't a sound for leagues about us but the wind and the birds. Few came; none went. It was an earthly Paradise. And over there, as you see, lay its entry elsewhither. Fifty years ago you could have cradled an infant on that old tombstone yonder – Zadakiel Puncheon's – and it would have slept the sun down. Now, poor creature, his ashes are jarred and desecrated a dozen times a day – by mechanisms like *that*!'

He flicked a gaudy bandana handkerchief in the direction the departing dragon had taken – a dragon already leagues out of sight and hearing.

'But how enchanting a name!' I murmured placatingly. 'Zadakiel Puncheon! It might have come out of Dickens, don't you think – a godfather of Martin Chuzzlewit's? Or, better still, Nathaniel Hawthorne.'

He eyed me suspiciously over his steel spectacles. 'Well, Dickens, maybe. But Hawthorne: I admit him reluctantly; a writer, with such a text to his hand that — And how many, pray, of his fellow-countrymen ever read him; and how many of *them* pay heed to him?'

'But surely,' I interposed hastily, 'think of St Francis, of Madame Guyon, of – of all the mystics! Or even of the cities where, you know, Lot...just the five righteous...Besides, even though Hawthorne didn't preach – well, hard *enough*; even if *no* one reads him, we can't blame Dickens – we've no right to do that. *Surely*!' I had grown quite eloquent – and scarlet.

He waved me blandly aside. 'I blame nobody, my dear young lady. Mine are merely old-fashioned opinions; and I have no wish to enforce them.

Nor even to share them. My *views*, I mean' – he whisked me a generous little bow – 'not these few sunny minutes. They indeed are a rare privilege. No, I loved old things when I was a child; I love them now. I despise nothing simply because the Almighty has concealed its uses. I see no virtue in mere size, or in mere rapidity of motion. Nor can I detect any particular preciousness in time "saved", as you call it, merely to be wasted.'

The gay handkerchief flicked these sentiments to the heavens as if in contemptuous challenge of the complete Railway Companies of the Solar System, and dismayed with the burden of my responsibility, I gazed out once more into the bird-enchanted, shadowy greenland – whispering its decoy to us immediately on the other side of its low stone wall.

A brief silence fell. There seemed suddenly to be nothing left to talk about. The old gentleman peered sidelong at me an instant, then thrust out a cramped-up hand, and lightly touched my sleeve.

'I see you don't much affect my old-fashioned tune, ma'am. But such things will not pester you for long. Most of my school have years since set out on the long vacation. Soon they'll be packing me off too; and not a soul left to write my epitaph...

'Here lies old bones;
Sam Gilpin once.

'How'll that do, heh?' He rocked gently on his gingham. ' "Sam Gilpin once..." But that's gone too,' he added, as if he were over-familiar with the thought.

'But I *do* understand, perfectly,' I managed to blurt out at last. 'And I agree. And it's hateful. But we can't help ourselves! You see we *must* go on. It's the – the momentum; the sheer impetus.'

He openly smiled on me. 'Well, well, well!' he said. '*Must* go on, eh? And soon, too, must I. So we're both of a mind at last. And that being so, I wish I could admit you into my museum over yonder. It is my last resource. I spend a peaceful hour in it whenever I can. Hardly a day passes just now but I make my pilgrimage there – between (to be precise, my dear young lady) – between the 7.23 *up* and the 8.44 *down*.'

'And there are epitaphs?' I cried gaily, with that peculiar little bell-peal in the voice, I'm afraid, which one simply cannot avoid when trying to placate infants, the ailing, and the aged.

'Ay, epitaphs,' he repeated. 'But very few of *this* headlong century. The art is lost; the spirit's changed. Once the living and the dead were in a good honest humour with one another. You could chisel the truth in, even over a lifelong crony's clay. You could still share a jest together; one on this side of the grave, one on that. But now the custom's gone with the mind. We are too mortal solemn or too mortal hasty and shallow.

'Why, over there, mark ye' – he pointed the great fat-ferruled stump of his umbrella towards the half-buried tombstones once more – 'over *there*, such things are as common as buttercups. And I know most of 'em by heart. My father, ma'am, was the last human creature laid to rest in that graveyard. He was a scholar of a still older school than I – and that's next quietest to being in one's grave. I remember his tree there when it sighed no louder than a meadow brook. Shut your eyes now of a windy evening, and it might be the Atlantic. There they lie. And I'll crawl in somewhere yet, like the cat in the adage – out of this noisy polluted world!' A little angry cloud began to settle on his old face once more.

'And there's two things else make it an uncommon pleasant place to rest in – a little brawling stream, that courses along upon its southern boundary, and the bees and butterflies and birds. There's rare plantage there, and it attracts rare visitors – though not, I am grateful to say, the human biped. No.'

Yet again a swallow swooped in from the noonday blue in a flight serene and lovely as a resting moonbeam. Somewhere behind the peculiar fretwork with which all railway directors embellish their hostels it deposited its tiny bundle of flies in squawking mouths out of sight though not out of hearing, and, with a flicker of pinion, was out, off, away again, into the air.

My old gentleman had not noticed it. He was still gently fuming over the murdered past: still wagging his head in dudgeon in his antique high hat.

'But I had no idea,' I ventured to insinuate at last, 'there were ever many really original epi —'

'I am not expectant of "ideas" nowadays, ma'am,' he retaliated. 'We don't think: we plot. We don't live: we huddle. We deafen ourselves by shouting. "There is no *peace*, saith my God..." and I'll eat my hat, if He did not mean for the blind worms as well as "for the wicked".'

He stooped forward to look into my face. 'Smile you may, ma'am,' he went on a little petulantly, patting his emphasis once more on the yellowed ivory handle of his umbrella, 'you know there is *not*. But there, they too had their little faults. They were often flints to the poor; merciless to the humble:

> 'No Voice to scold;
>   No face to frown;
> No hand to smite
>   The helpless down:
> Ay, Stranger, here
>   An Infant lies.
> With worms for
>   Welcome Paradise.

'*That's* there, I grant ye; to commemorate what they called a charity brat; that's there, and it was true to the times.'

His voice had completely changed in his old-fashioned recitation of the little verses; he declaimed them with oval mouth, without gesture, and yet with a kind of half-timid enthusiasm.

'And then,' he continued, 'there's little Ann Hards:

'They took me in Death dim,
    And signed me with God's Cross;
Now am I Cherub praising Him
    Who but an infant was.

'And not many yards distant is a spinster lady who used to live in that old Tudor house whose chimney-stacks you can see there above the trees. She was a little "childish", poor creature, but a gentle loving soul – Alice Hew:

'Sleep sound, Mistress Hew!
Birds sing over you:
The sweet flowers flourish
Your own hands did nourish;
And many's the child
By their beauty beguiled.
They prattle and play
Till night call them away;
In shadow and dew:
Sleep sound, Mistress Hew!'

I leant forward in the warm ambrosial air. It seemed I could almost read the distant stones myself in its honey-laden clearness. 'Please, please go on – if it does not tire you. How I wish I could venture in! But there goes the station master – the "Station Master"! Isn't *that* medieval enough? And I *suppose* there'll be no time!'

'Right once more: the bull's-eye once more,' he retorted in triumph. 'No time; and less eternity. Think of it: I must have been fifty years on this world before those young eyes of yours were even opened. And was the spirit within *you* in a worse place then than this, think ye? And for the fifty years that you, perhaps, have yet to endure, shall I be in a worse, think ye?' A queer zestful look had spread over his features; and once again he lifted his voice, decanting the next lines as if in praise of some old vintage port:

'All men are mortal, and I know 't;
As soon as man's up he's down;

> Here lies the ashes of Thomas Groat,
> Gone for to seek his Crown.

'I knew Groat's nephews. "Old Tom" he used to be called; and by the wags, "Unsweetened". In three years they drank down the money that he had taken fifty to amass. He died of a stroke the night before my father was born – with a lighted candle and a key in his hand. Going to bed, ma'am.

'Then there's old Sammie Gurdon's. Another character – twenty stone to the ounce; redder than his own Christmas baron of beef; with a good lady to match. But the inn's pulled down now, and a chocolate-coloured jail has been erected over its ruins they call an hotel. And his son's dead too:

> 'Maybe, my friend, thou'rt main athirst,
>   Hungry and tired, maybe:
> Then turn thy face by yon vane, due west;
>   Trudge country miles but three;
> I'll warrant my son, of the "Golden Swan",
>   Will warmly welcome thee.

' "Golden Swan"! You should see it to-day ma'am. "Ugly Duckling" would be nearer the mark! And now, if you'll take advantage of this elegant bench a moment' – he proffered a trembling and gallant hand – 'you may just espy the sisters. See, now' – he had climbed up beside me – 'there's their cypresses, and, in the shade beneath, you should catch sight of the urns. Terra-cotta, ma'am; three. Do you see 'em? Three.'

I gazed and I gazed. And at last nodded violently.

'Good!' he cried. 'And thus it runs.' He traced with his umbrella in the air, over the inscription, as it were:

> 'Three sisters rest beneath
>   This cypress shade,
> Sprightly Rebecca, Anne,
>   And Adelaide.
> Gentle their hearts to all
>   On earth, save Man;
> In Him, they said, all Grief,
>   All Wo began.
> Spinsters they lived, and spinsters
>   Here are laid;
> Sprightly Rebecca, Anne,
>   And Adelaide.

'And their nieces and grandnieces have gone on saying it – with worse manners – until one's ashamed to look one's own cat in the face. But that's neither here nor there. To judge from their portraits, mind ye, they were a rather masculine trio. And Nature prefers happy mediums. I'm not condemning them, dear young lady. God forbid; I'm no Puritan. But — '

'That reminds me,' I interposed hastily, 'of an epitaph in my own little churchyard – Gloucestershire: it's on a wife:

'Here lies my wife,
Susannah Prout;
She was a shrew
I don't misdoubt:
Yet all I have
I'd give, could she
But for one hour
Come back to me.'

'A gem! a gem! my dear young lady,' cried my old gentleman – as if he had himself remained a bachelor solely by accident; 'and that reminds *me* of one my dear Mother never tired of repeating:

'Ye say: We sleep.
But nay, We wake.
Life was that strange and chequered dream
For the waking's sake.

'And *that* reminds me of yet another which I chanced on – if memory does not deceive me – in one of the old city churches – of London: ah, twenty years gone or more:

'Here lieth Nat Vole,
Asleep now, poor Soul!
'Twas one of his whims
To be telling his dreams,
Of the Lands therein seen
And the Journeys he'd been!
La, if now he could speak,
He'd not listeners seek!'

'And who wrote *that*, I wonder?'

'Ah,' he echoed slyly, '"Who killed Cock Robin?" Dickie Doggerel, maybe – his mark! But what I was going to tell you concerns yet another spinster; also of this parish. Names are no matter. She was a wild, dark-eyed solitary creature, and in the wisdom of the Lord had a tyrant for a father. Even in the nursery – generally a quiet enough little mite – when once she had made up her mind, there was no gainsaying her. And she had a peculiar habit – a rooted instinct – my dear young lady, when she was crossed, of flinging herself flat on her face on the floor. Quite silent, mind ye – like one of those corpse-mimicking insects. Nothing would move her, while she could claw tight to anything at hand.

'However trivial the cause – perhaps a mere riband in her hair – that was the result. In a word, as we used to say when we were boys, she shammed dead. Of course, as the years went by, these fits of stubborn obstinacy were less frequent. All went pretty well for a time, until her very wedding-day – bells ringing, guests swarming, almond-blossom sprouting, bridesmaids blooming – all of a zest. And then and there, fresh from her maid, she flung herself flat on her face once more. Refused to speak, refused to stir. Her father stormed; her aunts cajoled; her old nurse turned on the watering-cart.' My old gentleman grimly chuckled. 'No mortal use at all. The lass was adamant.

'And fippety-foppety Mr Bridegroom, whom I never cared much for sight or scent of, must needs smile and smile and return home to think it over. From that moment her father too fell mum. They shared the same house, the same rooms, the same table – but mute as fish. And either for want of liberty or want of company, the poor young thing fell into what they used to call a decline. And then she died. And the old despot buried her, laying her north to south, and face downward in her coffin.'

'Face downward!' I exclaimed.

'Face downward,' he echoed, 'as by rights our sprightly three over yonder should have been buried, being all old maids. And she, poor soul, scarce in her twenties...And for text: "*Thou* art thy mother's daughter."'

'Autres temps, autres moeurs,' I ventured, but feeling uncommonly like a piping wren meanwhile.

'Ah, ah, ah!' laughed my old gentleman; 'I have noticed it!...And now, perhaps you may be able to detect with those young eyes of yours a little old tombstone set under that cypress yonder...Too far? Too "dark", eh?...Well, that's a sailor's; found wellnigh entirely fish-eaten in the Cove yonder – under Cheppelstoke Cliff. And pretty much to the point it is. Let – me – see. Ay, thus it goes.' He argued it out with his gloved forefinger for me:

'If thou, Stranger, be John Virgin, then the
Corse withinunder is nameless, for the Sea
so disfigured thy Face, none could tell
whether thou were John Virgin or no:

'Ay, and whatever name I bore
I thank the Lord I be
Six foot in English earth, and not
Six fathom in the sea.

'Good English sense, that, with a bay-leaf of Greek and a pinch of Irish
to keep it sweet. He was the ne'er-do-well son of an old miller, so they say,
who ground for nothing for the poor. So that's once upon a time too! But
there, ma'am, I'm fatiguing you...'

'Please, please go on,' I pleaded hurriedly. 'What's that curious rounded
stone rather apart from the others, with the ivy, a little up the hill?' We had
resumed our seats on the hard varnished bench, as happy as lovebirds on a
perch. My old gentleman evidently enjoyed being questioned.

'What, Fanny's? That's Fanny Meadows's, died of a consumption, poor
lass, 1762 – May 1762:

' "One, two three" —
O, it was a ring
Where all did play
The hours away,
Did laugh and sing
Still, "One, two, three,"
Ay, even me
They made go round
To our voices' sound:
'Twas life's bright game
And Death was "he".
We laughed and ran
Oh, breathlessly!
And I, why, I
But a maid was then,
Pretty and winsome,
And scarce nineteen;
But 'twas "One – two – three;
And – out goes she!"'

His aged, faded eyes, blue as a raven's, narrowed at me an instant; and
the queerest glimpse, almost one of anxiety, came into his face. He raised
his head, as if to smile the reminder away, and busily continued. 'Now
come back a little, along this side. A few paces beyond, under the horn-
beam, lies Ned Gunn, a notorious poacher in these parts – though the
ingrate's forgotten his dog:

'Where be Sam Potter now?
Dead as King Solomon.
Where Harry Airte I knew?
Gone, my friend, gone.
Where Dick, the pugilist?
Dead calm – due East and West.
Toby and Rob and Jack?
Dust every one.
Sure, they'll no more come back?
No: nor Ned Gunn.

'Not that there would be many to welcome him if he did. And next him lies a curmudgeonly old fellow of the name of Simpson, who lived in that old yellow stone house you may have seen beyond the meadows. He was a kind of caretaker. Many's the time he chased me when I was a lad for trespassing there:

' "Is that John Simpson?"
"Ay, it be."
"What was thy age, John?"
"Eighty-three."
"Was't happy in life, John?"
"Life is vain."
"What then of death, friend?"
"Ask again."

'And that, my dear young lady, is wisdom at any age; though Simpson himself, mind ye, couldn't mumble at last a word you could understand, having no teeth in his head. And yet another stranger is rotting away under an oblong of oak a pace or two beyond Simpson. I don't mean he was strange to the locality' – he gazed full at me over his spectacles – 'not at all – I knew him well; though by habit he was a silent close-mouthed man, with a queer dark eye. I mean he was strange to this World. And *he* wrote his own epitaph:

'Dig not my grave o'er deep
Lest in my sleep
I strive with sudden fear
Toward the sweet air.

'Alas! Lest my shut eyes
Should open clear

To the depth and the narrowness —
Pity my fear!

'Friends, I have such wild fear
Of depth, weight, space;
God give ye cover me
In easy place!

'Not that they favoured him much on that account! It's a hard soil. And
next *him*, with snapdragons shutting their mocking mouths at you out of
every crumbling cranny, is Tom Head. A renowed bell-ringer in his day:

'I rang yon bells a score of years:
Never a corse went by
But they all said – bid old Tom Head
Knoll the bell dolesomely:
Ay, and I had a skill with the rope
As made it seem to sigh.

'Now I must tell you there was an old gentleman lived here before my
time – and his name is of no consequence – who had a fancy for com-
memorating those who would otherwise have left scanty remembrances
enough behind them. Some I have already made mention of. Here's
another. Nearly every village, you must know, my dear young lady, has its
half-wit, but not every village graveyard. And where this one's bush is, they
call Magpie Corner. Let me see now...' My old gentleman made two or
three false starts here; but at last it ran free.

'Here lieth a poor Natural:
The Lord who understandeth all
Hath opened now his witless eyes
On the Green Fields of Paradise.

'Sunshine or rain, he grinning sat:
But none could say at who or what.
And all misshapen as he were,
What wonder folk would stand and stare?

'He'd whistle shrill to the passing birds,
Having small stock of human words;
And all his company belike
Was one small hungry mongrel Tyke.

'Not his the wits ev'n joyed to be
When Death approached to set him free —
Bearing th' equality of all,
Wherein to attire a Natural

'But there goes the signal! And we've scarce time for the midget.'

A strange old green porter shuffled out from his den into the sunshine. A distant screech, like the crow of a ghostly pheasant, shrilled faintly out of the distance. I had suddenly grown a little tired; and hated the thought of the journey before me. But my arbitrary old gentleman cared for none of these things.

He gave me his 'midget' leisurely, academically, tenderly:

'Just a span and half a span
From head to heel was this little man.
Scarcely a capful of small bones
Raised up erect this Midget once.
Yet not a knuckle was askew;
Inches for feet God made him true;
And something handsome put between
His coal-black hair and beardless chin.
But now, forsooth, with mole and mouse,
He keeps his own small darkened house.'

He paused an instant, and laid lightly two gloved, mysterious fingers on my arm.

'She's coming,' he almost whispered. 'There's her white wool against the blue.' He nodded towards the centipede-like creature creeping over the greenness towards us. 'We are all mythologists – and goddesses! We can't avoid it and – and' – he leaned closer and clucked the words under the very brim of my hat – 'it's called Progress. Veil then those dark eyes just once of a morning, ma'am; and have a passing thought for Sam Gilpin. We shall meet again; the unlikeliest like with like. And this must be *quite* the last. Just beside a little stone sill of water in that corner' – once more the iron-ferruled stump was pointed towards the tombs – 'where the birds come to drink, is the figure of a boy standing there, in cold stone, listening. How many times, I wonder, have I scurried like a rabbit at twilight past his shrine? And yet, no bones there; only a passing reminder:

'Finger on lip I ever stand;
    Ay, stranger, quiet be;
This air is dim with whispering shades
    Stooping to speak to thee.

What do we make of that, eh?'

He sprang up, his round glasses blazing in the sun. 'Well, well! Smiles be *our* finis, ma'am. And God bless you for your grace and courtesy... Drat the clumsy fellow!'

But it was I who 'passed on' – into the security of a 'compartment' filled with two fat commercial-looking gentlemen asleep; a young lady in goggles smoking a cigarette; a haggard mother with a baby and a little boy in velveteen trouserettes and a pale blue bow who was sucking a stick of chocolate, and a schoolboy swinging his shoes, learning geography, and munching apples. A happy human family enough.

I joined them as amiably as the heat allowed. And my last gliding glimpse of the tranquil little country station – burning sweet-william, rioting rose – descried my old gentleman still on his bench; still in his tall hat; still leaning on his gingham; a kind of King Canute by the sad sea waves of Progress, tapping out his expostulations and anathemas, though now to his own soul alone.

'Benighted'*

> As for us two, lest doubt of us yee have,
> Hence far away we will blindfolded lie...

We surveyed one another a little ruefully in the starry air – and it is many years ago now, that quiet evening – then turned once more to the darker fields around us.

'Yes,' she said; 'there isn't the least doubt in the world. We are lost. Irretrievably. Before that owl screeched there seemed to be just a remote chance for us... But now: not a house, not a living being in sight.'

'Not one,' I said.

'Not even Mrs Grundy,' she said, and sighed. 'Poor dear – she has sipped her posset, tied on her nightcap, and gone to bed.'

Baa! cried a faintly lachrymose voice out of the stony pasture beyond the rough flint wall.

'It's all very well to say "Baa",' she replied, accepting the challenge. 'But it makes us all, you see, look a little sheepish.' There was silence: we trudged on.

Nights of summer-time remain warm with day, and are seldom more

* First published in *Pall Mall Magazine*, July-December 1906.

than veiled with a crystalline shadowiness which is not darkness, but only the withdrawal of light. Even at this midnight there was a radiance as of pale blue glass in the north, though east to west stretched the powdery myriads of the Milky Way. Honeysuckle, bracken, a hint of hay, and the faint, aromatic scent of summer lanes saturated the air. The very darkness was intoxicating.

'I could walk on like this for ever,' I managed to blurt out at last.

'Those "for evers"!' mocked a quiet voice.

The lane ran deeper and gloomier here. Beneath heavy boughs thick with leaves gigantic trees were breathing all around us. The vast, taciturn silence of night haunted the ear; yet little furtive stirring sounds kept the eyes wide open. Once more we paused, standing stock still together.

'Let's just go on up – a little way,' I pleaded. 'There *might* be a house. You look so sleepy – and so lovely – my dear. A sort of hawk-like look – with that small head in this dim blur; even though your eyes *are* full of dreams.'

She laughed and turned away. 'Not sleepy, only a little drugged. And oh, if only I could be lovely *enough*!

We did go up, and presently, out from under the elms. And we came to many houses, low and squat and dark and still – roofing the soundest of all sleepers. We gazed slowly from stone to stone, from tiny belfry to distant Vega.

'Well, there they are,' I said. 'And they appear to have been there for some little time. What a silence!'

'Why, so!' she answered. 'And such is life, I suppose – just the breaking of it.'

'And you forgive me?'

'I try.'

'I could have sworn we were on the right road.'

' "She trusted in him, and there was none to deliver her!" But of course,' she said, 'the road *is* right. There is no other way than the way once taken. And especially this. Besides, my dear, I don't mind a bit; I don't indeed. It's still, and harmless, and peaceful, and solitary. We are all alone in the world. Let's sit down in there and talk.'

So we entered the old graveyard by its tottering gateway and seated ourselves on a low flat tombstone, ample enough in area for the Sessions of all the Sons of Israel.

The wakefulness of long weariness had overtaken us. The dark air was translucently clear, sprinkling its cold dew on all these stones and their overshadowing boughs. We ravenously devoured the fragments left over after our day's march. And we talked and talked, our voices sounding small and hollow even to ourselves, in this heedful solitude. But at last we too fell silent; for it began to be cold, and that hour of the night was coursing softly by us when a kind of unhumanity seems to settle on the mind, and words lose the meanings they have by day; just as the things of day may be transformed by night – ranging themselves under the moon like phenomena of another world.

'I wonder,' I said at last, 'when we – or just you, or I, come to a place like this: I wonder, shall we forget – be forgotten – do you think? Nearly all these must be.'

'In time,' she answered.

'Yes, in time; perhaps. Not exactly "forget", though – but remember; with all the hopelessness, the helpless burning and longing gone. Isn't that it?'

'I wonder,' she said gravely. 'Life's an abominably individual thing. We just *live* on our friends.'

'And what would you say about me – if you had to? On my stone, I mean? *Before* forgetting me?'

But her face gave no sign that she had heard so fatuous a question. I somehow refrained the sigh that offered itself.

'Let's see – if we can – what *they* did,' I suggesed instead.

So, no moon yet shining, I took out my matchbox and counted out its contents into her left hand.

'Twenty-one,' I said dubiously. 'Not *too* many for so much to do!'

'Riches!' she replied. 'You see, even if we have to use two for a tombstone, that would be ten altogether, and a little stone over. And surely there should be, say, *three* epitaphs among them. I mean, apart from mere texts. It's a little odd you know,' she added, peering across the huddled graves.

'What's odd?'

'Why, that there are likely to be so few worth reading – with such lots to say.'

'Not so very odd,' I said. 'Your Mrs Grundy hates the sight of them. They frighten her.'

'Well, I don't somehow think,' she answered, peering through the shadowiness at me, 'I don't somehow think anybody else ever was here but you and me. It's between real and dream – like Mrs Grundy herself.'

I held out my hand; but she smiled and would give me no proof. So we began our scrutiny, first stooping together over the great stone that had seated us to supper. And all that it surrendered for our reward was the one vast straddling word – 'M. O. R. S.'

The dark, flat surface was quite unbroken else. The flame (screened between the shell of my hands) scarcely illumined its margins. The match languished and fell from my fingers.

' "Mors", she spelt it out. 'And what does Mors mean?' inquired that oddly indolent voice in the quiet. 'Was it his name, or his initials, or is it a charm?'

'It means – well, sleep,' I said. 'Or nightmare, or dawn, or nothing, or – it might mean everything.' I confess, though, that to my ear it had the sound at that moment of an enormous breaker, bursting on the shore of some unspeakably remote island; and we two marooned.

'Well, that's one,' she said. ' "MORS": how dull a word to have so many meanings! You men are rather heavy-handed, you know. You think thinking helps things on. I like that Mors. He was a gentleman.'

I stared blankly into the darkness; and my next match flared in vain on mouldering illegibility. The third lasted us out, however, stooping side by side, and reading together:

> Stranger, where I at peace do lie
> Make less ado to press and pry!
> Am I a Scoff to be who did
> Life like a stallion once bestride?
> Is all my history but what
> A fool hath – soon as read – forgot?
> Put back my weeds, and silent be.
> Leave me to my own company!

We hastened to do as we were bid, confronted by phantom eyes so dark and piercing, and groped our way over a few markless grassy mounds to the toppling stone of 'Susannah Fry, who after a life grievous and disjointed, fell asleep in a swoon':

> Here sleep I,
> Susannah Fry,
> No one near me,
> No one nigh:
> Alone, alone
> Under my stone,
> Dreaming on,
> Still dreaming on:
> Grass for my valance
> And coverlid,
> Dreaming on
> As I always did.
> 'Weak in the head?'
> Maybe. Who knows?
> Susannah Fry
> Under the rose.

Under the rose Susannah lay indeed – a great canopy of leaves and sweetness looming up palely in the night darkness. 'That's six,' I said, turning away from a tomb inscribed with that prosaic rendering of 'Gather ye rosebuds' – 'Take care lest ye also be called early'; and the victim a Jeremiah of seventy-two! The tiny flame spluttered and hissed in the dewy grass.

But our seventh rewarded us:

> Here lies my husbands; One, Two, Three:
> Dumb as men ever could wish to be.
> As for my Fourth, well, praise be God
> He bides for a little above the sod.
> But his wits being weak and his eyeballs dim,
> Heav'n speed at last I'll wear weeds for him.
> Thomas, John, Henry, were these three's names
> And to make things tidy, I adds his – James.

'If it would not in the least prejudice matters, might I, do you think, be Thomas?' I said. 'The unsuspecting?'

She laughed out of the darkness. 'The pioneer!' she said. 'Hope on.'

Our next two matches burned over a stone which only the twisted roots of a rusty yew tree had for a little while saved from extinction. The characters were nearly extinct on its blackened lichenous surface:

> Here restes yᵉ boddie of one
> Chrystopher Orcherdson.
> Lyf he lived merrilie;
> Nowe he doth deathlie lie:
> All yᵉ joye from his brighte face
> Quencht in this bitter place.
> With gratefull voice then saye,
> Not oures, but Goddes waye!

With grateful voice I counted out yet another six of the little store left into a hand cold and dim. And we took it in turn to choose from among the grassy mounds and stones. Two matches were incontinently sacrificed: one to a little wind from over the countryside, smelling of Paradise; and one to a bramble that all but sent me crashing on to the small headstone of the 'Shepherd', whose mound was a positive mat of fast-shut bindweed flowers. Oddly enough, their almond-like smell became more perceptible in the vague light we shed on them.

A Shepherd, Ned Vaughan,
'Neath this Tombstone do bide,
His Crook in his hand,
And his Dog him beside.
Bleak and cold fell the Snow
On Marchmallysdon Steep,
And folded both sheepdog
And Shepherd in Sleep.

Our next two matches gleamed on a tomb raised a little from the ground, with a damp-greened eyeless head on each panel that must once have been cherubim:

Here rest in Peace Eliza Drew and James Hanneway
  whom Death haplessly snatched from Felicity.
Eliza and James in this sepulchre tarry
Till God with His trumpet shall call them to marry.
Then Angels for maids to the bride shall be given,
And loud their responses shall echo in Heaven.
And e'en though it be that on Paradise Plains
A wife is no wife; spinster spinster remains;
These twain they did tarry so long to be wed
They might now prefer to stay happy instead.
Howe'er it befall them, Death's shadows once past,
They'll not laugh less sweetly who learn to laugh last.

And we spent two more on a little old worn stone couched all askew, and nearly hidden in moss:

Poor Sam Lover,
Now turf do cover;
His Wildness over.

It was obviously a sacred duty to clear at least of sow-thistles and nettles the grave of one once loved so kindly. 'There! Sam Lover,' exclaimed a rather breathless voice at last, ' "nettles shall not sting this year".'

And at that moment the first greenish pallor of the fast-waning and newly-risen moon peered out on us from between the yews.

Distant and companionable, cock answered cock across the drowsy acres. But even when it had ascended a little into its brightness the moon shone but wanly, casting the greyest of faint shadows from the fretted spire over the tombs of a Frenchman, Jules Raoul Dubois, and the Virgin on his left hand.

> Here sleeps a Frenchman: Would I could
> Grave in his language on this wood
> His many virtues, grace and wit!
> But then who'd read what I had writ?
> Nay, when the tongues of Babel cease,
> One word were all sufficient – Peace!

Thick English grasses waved softly over him beyond the faint moonlight, and covered as deeply the grave of one left nameless:

> Blessed Mary, pity me.
> Who was a Virgin too, like Thee;
> But had, please God, no little son
> To shower a lifetime's sorrows on.

Just a message out of nothingness, for the words summoned no picture, scarcely even the shadow of a human being, into the imagination. Not so those over which the last of our twenty-one battled feebly against the moon:

> J.T.
> Here's Jane Taylor.
> Sweet Jane Taylor,
> Dark,
> Wild,
> Dear Jane Taylor.

Silence, dense as the milky mist that wreathed the neighbouring water-meadows, now enwrapt us. Cold and cheerless, we sat down once more to await the coming of the dawn. And it was the sun's first clear beams, putting to shame all remembrance of night, that, slanting in palest gold, lit up for us a little odd stone at our feet, almost hidden in brambles:

> Be very quiet now:
> A child's asleep
> In this small cradle,
> In this shadow deep!

Words have strange capricious effects. *Now*, it was as if I could actually recall in memory itself the infant face in its white frilled cap – icily still, stonelike.

And then I raised my eyes and looked into the face of the living one beside me. Hers were fixed as if absently on the broken inscription, the curved lids fitting them as closely as its calyx the rose. The face was cold and listless; her hands idle in her lap. It was as though the beauty of her face were lying (like a mask) dead and forgotten, the self within was so far away.

A thrush broke into song, as if from another world. Conscious at last of my silence perhaps, she slowly lifted her head into the gilding sunshine. And as if with a shrug of her slender shoulders, 'Now for the rest of our lives,' she said.

Strangers and Pilgrims*

To me, who find,
Reviewing my past way, much to condemn,
Little to praise, and nothing to regret,
(Save some remembrances of dream-like joys
That scarcely seem to have belonged to me)
If I must take my choice between the pair
That rule alternately the weary hours,
Night is than day more acceptable; sleep
Doth, in my estimate of good, appear
A better state than waking; death than sleep:
Feelingly sweet is stillness after storm,
Though under covert of the wormy ground!

William Wordsworth

It was later even than Mr Phelps had supposed. But now his day was nearly over. Not an arduous, and perhaps a rather vacant day, spent as it had been like thousands of its forerunners between his three-roomed cottage – resembling at this season a mound of flowers more than a house – and the great church. Lank and ascetic, in his old many-buttoned cassock, ponderous key in hand and the heavy door yawning behind him, he had paused as was his habit in the southern porch to lift his eyes towards the smooth, low, bright-green hills that rose beyond it. Dotted with dwarfed and scattered thorn-trees and bushes of juniper in their mounded hollows, they lay there – mantled with light and colour. They were his constant companions, unchanging and serene.

Shadows in the oblique sunshine were now encroaching upon them.

* Added in 1936 edition of *Ding Dong Bell*. First published in *Yale Review*, March 1936.

High in the vault of the blue air a few gulls were circling; the plaintive sweet call of a peewit fell faintly on his ear. And behold, one solitary human figure was descending the rough cart-track towards the church. Mr Phelps had at once fixed his eyes on this unlikely fellow-creature.

Head bowed down, he came slowly, steadily, ploddingly on; now treading the grass between the wheel-ruts, and now stumbling into the ruts themselves, though he raised no dust into the gilding evening light. Like all ancient buildings, the old church attracted an odd assortment of visitors; but few – at least so late in the day– came from this direction: that of the sea. Mr Phelps kept his quarry closely in view. For a moment, but only for a moment, his cautious but discerning soul had uncharitably debated whether or not he could be perfectly sober.

It was as yet no more than on the fringe of the holiday season, and little opportunity had recently been offered him for descanting on the glories of the edifice in his charge – a privilege of which he never wearied. This individual, however, had no trace of the holiday-maker in his aspect. From head to foot he was in black. And yet, the verger, long practised in these little matters, had at once decided that he was not in holy orders. He was the better pleased to think so. Laymen make the more docile listeners. And you might be excessively odd, yet orthodox. At this moment there could be no question of the odd. 'In the name of God,' the old man heard himself muttering, 'and who can this be?'

Unwilling to be caught resembling a spider in wait for a fly, he withdrew a few paces into the church, and in this seclusion kept an ear cocked beyond it. At length the iron latch of the lych-gate had clicked. Peering out, he still kept watch. The stranger had paused before a vast palisaded vault, but rather as if to make certain that he was alone than to read what was inscribed on its panels. Indeed, as he came on, his face had oddly contracted at the discovery that the heavily-hinged door within the porch was a few inches ajar. He hesitated again – like an animal wary of a trap. It was Mr Phelps's opportunity.

'Good evening, sir,' he said, sallying out pleasantly. 'And a very beautiful evening it is!'

The stranger became completely motionless, as motionless as some animal or insect 'shamming dead'. The deep-set inward eyes under his black hat-brim seemed to be slightly asquint, so fixed was his scrutiny. A prolonged murmuration had ebbed away into silence in the sunlit calm of the evening – the placid breaking of a seventh wave along the low beach beyond the hill – a sigh as of time itself in the quiet.

'Is this St Stephen's, Langridge?' came at length the inquiry – but in tones so mumbled and muffled that Mr Phelps had detected no motion in the questioner's mouth.

He smiled urbanely; but, he *knows* it is Langridge, was the conviction that had swiftly flitted through his mind. 'Indeed, yes, sir; this is Langridge. The village you'll find is only a few minutes' distance, beyond the trees round the bend of the road; and *this* is St Edmund's, King and Martyr.' With but a lift of a forefinger he had indicated the great beautiful stone church behind him.

'You may perhaps, sir, have already noticed in the niche above our heads the crossed arrows and the crowned head – with open mouth – between the fore-paws of the wolf. And as you may be aware, the body of the saintly King was not discovered and reattached to the head until some fifty years afterwards – after he was martyred, sir. A pitiless affair. There is a scrap of old glass too in the vestry showing him one among a happy group of the halt and the lame – and all of them *carrying* their crutches!'

The loose creaseless trousers were powdered with dust; the dark hands hung squat and swollen from their cuffs. Owing in part to his having spent so many years within walls and in part to a bilious constitution, the verger's lean ecclesiastical countenance was somewhat tallowy in hue. His visitor's might have been modelled out of wax. The lips had lost their red, his eyes resembled little flat agates beneath their heavy lids – the eyelids, one might conjecture, of one so wearied out with this world's travailings that they could never be surfeited enough with sleep. It was a face burdened with a profound secretiveness. Only an extreme solitude surely could have produced the appearance of so dark a lethargy. And yet, no countryman, Mr Phelps had concluded; possibly a lay-reader, though he hardly thought so.

'I was just about to lock up, sir. The key, as you see, is in my hand. But if you had anything in particular in view? . . .'

The stranger withdrew his glance from the time-pocked dismembered stone head that graced the porch and slowly eyed him. He drew in his lips. 'As a matter of fact,' he said, and as if he were repeating a lesson, 'I am – and have been for some time – in search of . . . of an inscription. But I agree; yes, it is growing late. And you must be gone?' He raised his head as though to measure the advance of darkness with his eyes, but stealthily, one by one, surveyed instead the grinning row of gargoyles that jutted out above the weathered groining of the windows, then glanced back at the track he had recently descended.

'Why, yes, sir, but that's of no account,' Mr Phelps assured him. ' "At length it ringeth to evensong," as the old rhyme says, but I should be very glad to give you any assistance in my power. We are not, as you can see, *short* of inscriptions – inside or out! In fact our population here must now far exceed what is left in the village yonder. In these days, sir, we cannot even make good our losses. All sheep, and few lambs. There will presently, I sometimes say, be nobody and nothing left but me and the church! If you would give me the name, or even as much as the year and place, there might be no difficulty. In late summer we have visitors from all parts of the world, most merely from hearsay, but a good sprinkling of them hunting up ancestors, coats of arms, pedigrees and so forth. Anything for deep-laid English roots, sir; and no wonder. There was a party from the United States of America, a very talkative lady, sir, who I myself tracked down only a few weeks ago to 1616 – the year of the lamented death, you will remember, of the poet William Shakespeare. And highly gratified she was.'

The stranger appeared to have listened, but made no comment. You would hardly associate him just now, mused the verger, with the heraldic. There are individuals who in spite of copious hints at a private history suggest neither roots nor pedigree. This one, indeed, to judge from his appearance, might himself be one of his more recent ancestors – the slack ill-fitting black clothes, the elastic-sided boots, the shield-shaped cravat decked with a garnet pin, the shapeless black-banded hat. They reminded Mr Phelps of an enlarged and tinted photograph of his own father which graced the chimney-piece of his crowded little sitting-room. He had been posed by the genial photographer of the county town standing in his Sunday best beside a canvas depicting a large urn – a rather funereal effect.

In this case the funereal seemed to have been carried to an extreme. The verger – dust in hand – had helped to officiate at many 'interments' in his day, but never before had he encountered a human being so eloquent of mourning. His black was almost dazzling in its intensity – as dazzling as the dark outer blue of the Atlantic. On glancing away for an instant a faintly green after-image was left within the eye. Only guilty sorrow has a blackness as much bereft of light; and despair one as dense. And the more repeatedly Mr Phelps examined the stranger before him the less he could make of him, except that he resembled a receptacle which however much you might pour into it in the way of information, you could never hope to brim. Still, any listener was better than none; he must craftily play his catch, and hope for the best.

With a mild sacerdotal gesture he invited his visitor to follow him in. 'Perhaps,' he explained ingenuously, 'we might first take a glance at the interior. As you see, sir, we have some uncommonly fine Norman work – early Norman, some of it, too. Before the Conqueror, they say; though there seems to be no end to their disputings. And that, sir, is a unique angel roof in the chapel yonder. There are only three, I am told, to match it in these islands. The rood-screen has been carefully restored but not re-coloured; and we are proud of our pews; the poppyheads are very little damaged. Them old high pews may have had their abuses, sir – sleeping, snoring, and children monkeying – but rush chairs with Norman I never could away with. Our brasses, too. Mostly in Latin of course; but you will find the English in the pamphlet. If, that is,' he added gallantly, 'you should require it. In fact, as I often repeat, we are packed from crypt to belfry with the Past. Yes, sir; and with all due respect, I might say that this church has become a second home to me. Indeed, believe it or not, I can detect the presence of a stranger in it even before I've either seen or heard him.'

This particular stranger's eyes had meanwhile settled vacantly on a slab of grey marble which had been inset in the stone of the wall opposite to him. It was surmounted by the flat square head of a cherub, but the words beneath it must at this distance have been completely indecipherable.

'The "Past",' he repeated dully, as if the meaning of the word were no longer worth even the effort of speech. 'Yes. And yet... The truth is, there *is* no past. There is only what is here now. For all that,' he added, his flat husky tones sinking almost into inaudibility, 'I must, even recently, have read over hundreds – I say, hundreds of inscriptions.'

'Indeed, sir?' said the verger tactfully. 'And I see you have already detected one which attracts practically every visitor that comes along; especially our female visitors.'

He rapidly sidled his way between the pews, and in a tenoring voice, a little throaty but not unpleasing, intoned aloud:

> 'Here lies – how sad that he is no more seen –
>   A child so sweet of mien
> Earth must with Heaven have conspired to make him.
>   As wise a manhood, 'tis said,
>   Promised his lovely head;
>   As gentle a nature
>   His every youthful feature.
> But now no sound, no word, no night-long bird –
> Not even the daybreak lark can hope to awake him.'

'Not even the daybreak lark,' he repeated, and paused to look back. 'Why, sir, in the spring, as you might well guess, there's scarcely a minute of the day without its circling skylark over these quiet hills; and no doubt it has always been so.' His visitor was continuing to listen. 'But "youthful" notwithstanding, sir, if this little lad had lived up to now, he would be *one-hundred-and-twenty-four* years of age! And that is a fact, seeing him so young in the mind's eye, that never fails to strike me as pathetic. I agree it's nothing to the point,' he added, after yet another glance at his listener, 'since it is the age that we die at we remain – at least in memory. Tidings sad enough, sir, for the old and infirm. Still, you cannot put an old man back into his youth again, however much he may covet it.'

'It's the human way,' Mr Phelps's visitor had huskily interposed, as if he were unaccustomed to the sound of his own voice. 'But what is age? No more than a mask; even if what is done is done for ever. The cocoon may perish, but not the deathless worm. You said "the Past"; but it's the same thing. Its all is all *we* have.'

The verger had discovered little coherency in these remarks; but he was intent, however, not on receiving but on giving. 'Certainly, sir,' he agreed. 'And here, though six and thirty years divide them, another child lies buried; and he was only seven. Not that at such an age he can have known what he would be missing.' Again he spared his visitor's eyesight.

> 'Here lies a strangely serious child,
> Called on earth Emmanuel.
> Never to laughter reconciled,
> This day-long peace must please him well;
> He must, forsooth, in secret keep
> Smiling – that he is so sound asleep.

'Yet you'll notice, sir, solemn-soever a child as he may have been, the stone-cutter has notwithstanding put in here – and here – and here – the usual and common toys of children – a rattle, a nursery trumpet, a top and so forth; pretty no doubt in intention, sir, but still wide of the mark. And *there*, close adjacent,' he rapidly continued, as if to stifle an incipient interruption, 'a weeping willow, as you see, spreading its stony leaves and branches from summit to base of the complete memorial stone. That's where' – he pointed – '*that* one's mother lays, and the child beside her. Not, as I take it, the father, sir. Though why, I cannot tell you. There may have been good reasons; or bad.

> 'Are thou a widow? Then, my Friend,
> By this my tomb a moment spend,
> To breathe a prayer o'er these cold stones
> Which house-room give to weary bones.
> And may God grant, when thou so lie,
> Dust of thy loved one rest nearby!

'Widow or not, I always say, *that* is a supplication it's hard to pass entirely unheeded, sir. They lie so near, what remains of them, and yet so seldom in memory's sight.' With no more than a fleeting glance out of his watery grey eye, the verger had led the way on; like a dog on a familiar scent. 'Now this,' he was explaining, his lean forefinger laid on a tablet flush with the wall, and no more than half the size of a pocket handkerchief, 'this is our smallest and shortest – a tailor's; though he'd have small trade here now, I fancy, if he came back! Of the name of Hackle, William Hackle. They say he was a one-eyed old man – like his implement, sir.

> 'Here's an old Taylour, rest his eye:
> Needle and thredde put by.

'And it couldn't have been put shorter. Next we have Silas Dwight – the memorial only; the remains themselves having been interred outside. Not that that need have been intended for any slight on them, sir. There are many no doubt who would prefer the open. According to our records he was choirmaster here for seventeen years, so the horn spoken of is mainly what they call a figure of speech.' His voice rose a little to do justice to his theme:

> 'Though hautboy and bassoon may break
> This ancient peace with, Christians, Wake!
> We should not stir, nor have, since when
> God rest you, merry Gentlemen!
> He of the icy hand us bid,
> And laid us 'neath earth's coverlid.
> Yet oft did Silas Dwight, who lies
> Under this stone, in cheerful wise
> Make Chancel wall and roof to ring
> With Christmas Joys and Wassailing;
> And still, maybe, may wind his horn
> And stop out shrill, This Happy Morn.

'The days here spoken of, as you may recollect, sir, were those before the church organs, at least in village churches, fine as ours may be. And speaking for myself, though the instrument you see yonder, three manuals, cost us a thumping sum of money, I like the old single fiddles and clarinets better than the yowling and bumbling of the stops and pedals. All depends, of course,' he had lowered his voice into the confidential, 'on who's handling them; but, no matter who, I never did care much for the clatter – nor for the notion of the lad, neither, cracking his nuts behind her and blowing her up.'

The stranger had rather belatedly met his glance. It was encouragement enough. 'Now here, sir,' the verger, eager as a schoolboy, had shuffled across to the south aisle again, 'here, talking of age, we have our Parr. Not, I must warn you, the famous Thomas, who outlived ten kings of England and begot a child, sir, so the story goes, when he was twenty years over his century. Which, I may add, is nothing much to boast of by comparison with some of these old patriarchs mentioned in the Scriptures. No, *our* Parr –

William – departed this life three days *short* of his century; a sad vexation, I have no doubt, to his relatives, sir, wishful to be bruiting him abroad. I've heard tell of some old Greek who did the same, but his name escapes me. Well, sir, so much for William Parr. And his lettering's so cut, you'll notice, on his "decent and fair Marble" as I've seen it described, that it's easiest to read sideways, though for my part I could manage it upside down! This is how it goes:

> 'He that lies here was mortal olde,
> All but a hundred, if truth be told.
> His pinpricke eyes, his hairless pate,
> Crutch in hand, his shambling gaite —
> All spake of Time: and Time's slow stroke,
> That fells at length the stoutest Oke.
> Of yeares so many now he is gone
> There's nought to tell except this stone.
> His name was Parr: decease did he
> In Seventeen Hundred Sixty Three.'

The old verger had once more intoned the lines aloud, since the stranger had remained where he had left him. 'Outside,' he added, 'a yard or so beyond this wall, in fact, there is a similar inscription, and one that strikes nearer home; at least to me, sir. I'll show you the stone itself in a few minutes; but this is how that runs:

> 'Three score years I lived; and then
> Looked for to live another ten.
> But he who from the Hale and Quick
> Robs the pure Oile that feeds the Wick
> Chanced my enfeebled frame to mark —
> Hence, this unutterable Darke.

'Which is only to declare, sir, that there is more than one way of looking at the same occurrences in life – a point by your leave to which we will return later. In the meantime, sir, if you please, would you step this way?'

Even Mr Phelps had paused a moment to give dramatic effect to his next exhibit. 'The tomb now before us,' he announced, 'is reputed, sir, to be the finest specimen of sepulchral art we have. Not only in St Edmund's, but in these parts. And not merely that, neither. The medicos tell me – gentlemen, I mean, learned in such things – that there is not a single bone in the human anatomy missing in this skeleton here – of the finest alabaster. It represents, as you see, the figure of Death, scythe over shoulder, lantern in hand;

though, as I've heard say, he can as often manage his private business in the dark. Sir Willoughby Branksome was quondam owner, sir, of the old Manor House beyond the village – a family going back into mediaeval times – and the house was built much about the same period as the roof over our heads.'

The stranger had drawn nearer, and was emptily surveying the ornate details of the tomb.

> Alas! Alack!
> We come not back.
> Adieu! and Welladay!
> Yet, if we could,
> No wise man would;
> What more is left to say?

'Considering the cost and the sculpture work, I must confess,' remarked the verger, 'that *that* has a disappointing ring; at least to my ear, sir. Words and effigy don't rightly match. Besides, as you can see for yourself, counting the two rows of them there, he left nine ungrown children behind him, not including the smallest already gone, and holding a skull in her infant hands. Ten, sir, must be a burden to any mother. Quality, or otherwise. And she did well by some of them, too; as you can see by the marbles to either hand – a countess there, and a Lord Admiral here. The truth is, times change. What is common human nature in one age is unbefitting levity in another.' He turned for a word of approval, and so met for an instant the direct leaden lustreless gaze of his companion in the church. 'Here, for example,' he hastened on, 'is such doggerel as no chisel would be allowed to cut on sacred walls in these days – a Henry the Eighth in private life. And yet, are we any more conscionable of the *facts*?

> 'Here rests in peace, Rebecca Anne,
> Spouse of Job Hodson, Gentleman.
>
> Here also Henrietta Grace,
> Destined to lie in this same place.
>
> And Jane, who three brief years of life
> Did bear the honoured name of wife.
>
> Here also Caroline (once Dove).
> And him, the husband of the above.

'And that, sir, is a standing example, as I have heard our good Bishop himself declare, of God's plenty!'

Daylight had been steadily draining out of the church, and dusk seeping in. The last hues of the sunset had long since vanished from the stone walls beyond the dog-toothed arcade of the clerestory windows. A small indistinct shape had begun soundlessly flitting to and fro beneath the timbers of the roof overhead. The great church, cold, serene, motionless as if frozen, was preparing itself for the night.

Visitors to it – ignorant, frivolous, inquiring, learned, indifferent, were all in Mr Phelps's daily round. Never had he encountered one so frigid and irresponsive. There hung too about him a vague hint of the earthy; as if he might have slept overnight in a cellar. Was he intelligent enough – that tallow-flat face – to have followed what had been said? Or was perhaps the gentleman a little hard of hearing? Or was he merely humouring his cicerone, passing the time away, until he could get about his own private business? A word or two of inquiry, Mr Phelps was well aware, might at once set him on the right track. Nevertheless he refrained from uttering it. Patience no doubt would at last be its own reward, even if the sands of day were ebbing low.

'If only, sir,' he remonstrated, with a disarming smile, 'you had happed in on me a few minutes earlier, I could have shown you our crypt. There's many who visit us solely for that purpose. But it's beyond hours already now, and down there it must be long ago pitch dark. What's more, the rector has a mortal dread of fire.' He held his head sidelong a little, and a childishly naïve and deprecating smile descended into the furrows of his long jaw as he added – 'both here, and hereafter. Besides, we should have no light left for the churchyard.'

With the faintest indication of a gesture the other seemed to intimate that there was no necessity for haste, that time was of no concern to him, and a church as pleasant a lodging for the night as any. He had sluggishly followed the verger into the bell-chamber under the west tower, glancing up narrowly, as he did so, at the slack ropes looped dangling through the holes in its ceiling.

'Now here, sir,' said Mr Phelps, coming to a standstill again, 'is what was in my mind to speak of a moment or two ago. Some four or five summers since, not to put too fine a point on it, there came here a grey-faced, stunted little old brat of a man – and I had my misgivings the moment I set eyes on him – who first listened me out, and then, quite deliberately, sir, told me to my face that all I had been repeating was nothing but *holy hocum*: his very words. "I don't give that for your old stones and bones," he said, and spat on the floor. Now in my humble estimation, sir, that man's was the soul of nothing short of a maniac's. He had gone bad, and the devil had entered into him. I gave him a look, sir: I led him to that door, without a word more uttered: and I shook the dust of him from off my feet.

'That's one side, one extreme of the story. On the other; that we mortals should dread the tomb – that's only natural. And it's when we are nearing the end that what may be called the real takes on another colour, sir. You look at those about you and can't any more so surely rely on what they *are*, if you take me. As once you could. There is so thin a crust, sir, in a manner of speaking, between being awake and asleep – very fast asleep indeed. A sip of a doctor's drug, and not only the lantern goes out but everything it shone on. I had that experience myself not more than a month or two since – only a decayed tooth, sir: outer darkness, and then the awakening. If that *comes*. It is like as if we were treading a flat fall of untrodden snow and suddenly it is thin ice – cat ice, as we used to call it when we were boys – and we are gone. Not, mind you, that the waters of death, however cold they may be, are not – well, the waters of life. Faith is faith. What then do you conjecture must the infidel think of finding statements in stone in a Christian church which are sheer contrary to its own beliefs? Not that I should be repeating this to *every* visitor. That would be neither meet nor proper; besides, few would care. But even in this small parcel of ground around us here we have no fewer than five dimetrically different views on the subject – dimetrically different. Here, for one, is the grave of a child named Blackstone, Timothy Blackstone, who, as we read for ourselves, "was borne a Weakling and lived but to be three years old". But what is said of him? –

> 'O Death, have care
> Only a Childe lies here.
> A fear-full mite was he,
> My last-born, *Timothy*.
> Shroud then thy grewsome face,
> When thou dost pass this place;
> Lest his small ghoste should see,
> And weep for me!

'The ghost of a *child*, sir, mark you, and a very young child. And no doubt it is his mother who is speaking, or one who is speaking *for* his mother. And yet, poor lamb, he is considered as being still frightened and still forsaken – at evils that were long, long ago all safely over!'

The stranger had raised his hand again, had turned with mouth ajar, as if to expostulate. 'One moment, sir, if you please,' cried Mr Phelps. 'Cheek by jowl with it, as you see, we have "O. A." – no more than the initials, and the years, 1710 – 1762 – and this!

'Who: and How: and Where: and When –
Tell their stones of these poore men.
Grudge not then if one be bare
Of Who, and How, and When, and Where.

Such is nought to them who sigh
Still with their last breath, Why?

'That's *another* way of looking at the riddle, and, I grant you, in our low
moments there's a good deal to be said for the "Why". But what I am bearing towards, if you follow me, is whether we are not already edging into
the neighbourhood of the heathen, sir? And yet, mark you – light itself by
comparison – here's another, clean contrary to both:

'Son of man, tell me,
Hast thou at any time lain in thick darkness,
Gazing up into a lightless silence,
A dark void vacancy,
Like the woe of the sea
In the unvisited places of the ocean?
And nothing but thine own frail sentience
To prove thee living?
Lost in this affliction of the spirit,
Did'st thou then call upon God
Of his infinite mercy to reveal to thee
Proof of his presence –
His presence and love for thee, exquisite creature
    of his creation?
To show thee but some small devisal
Of his infinite compassion and pity, even
    though it were as fleeting
As the light of a falling star in a dewdrop?
Hast thou? O, if thou hast not,
Do it now; do it now; do it now!
Lest that night come which is sans sense,
    thought, tongue, stir, time, being,
And the moment is for ever denied thee,
Since thou art thyself as I am.

'While here again, sir, beneath the very soles of our feet,' he tapped the stone with the capless toe of his shoe, 'here we have Richard Halladay, and a very fine piece of lettering, I allow – though a few words, as you see, have been worn flat by the bell-ringers' treadings, sir.' He glossed the inscription as he read:

> 'Each in place as God did 'gree
> Here lie all ye Bones of me.
> But what made them walke up right,
> And, cladde in Flesh, a goodly Sight,
> One of hostes of Living Men —
> Ask again – ask again!

'And last this, which, being human, we all can share. It was, sir, my poor dear mother's favourite of them all:

> 'O onlie one, Fare-well!
> Love hath not words to tell
> How dear thou wert, and art,
> To an emptie heart.'

He had paused before attempting the last line. 'But now, sir,' he went rapidly on, 'to continue my argument. We all feel and realize *that* when the grief is on us. But what I am asking myself is what one of these Moho-metans or suchlike, heretics as we call them, would think of so much of the contradictory, sir, in so little space! The fact is, when it comes to a question of truth – and, "What *is* Truth?" said Pontius Pilate – it's as if each and every one of us had his own private compass. From birth, sir. The needle pointing not due north, mark you, never that, but a few hairsbreadths or more short of it. As life goes on, now this way it veers, now that; and the most we can do as it seems to me, is to see that it doesn't jam.'

A little breathless, a fresh apprehension transfixing his pale face, he paused a moment – his own needle havering rather more widely than usual – as if to let this reflection sink in. Mr Phelps's stranger had at last found voice again.

'You forget,' he was saying, 'that every syllable inscribed on these walls was put there by the living. None *by*, but only *of* the dead. Better, a thousand times, I agree, a single word of pity and forgiveness than – nothing at all. As for any attempt to return, a mere child could have little occasion for it. But these others – do *they*, do you suppose, never come back?' The last few hollow, challenging, half-stifled words had rung out oddly in the silence of the church – and far more exclamatorily than Mr Phelps's pleasant tenoring.

Back, back, back, had quietly fainted away the echo – as if indeed the masons of the ancient building when fitting stone to stone had childishly so adapted its acoustics as to ensure a device of which the Elizabethan drama- tists and the old poets never wearied. A long pause followed. But the set black eyes in the expressionless face were still apparently expecting an answer. The verger thrust his hand into his cassock pocket, drew out an immense handkerchief, and replaced it. He temporized.

'I agree, sir,' he smiled inquiringly, 'that the dead cannot compose their own epitaphs! They might make queer, ay, and moving reading if they did. The riddle to *me* is what sort of question you could put to such a one as Lazarus as you'd most wish to have answered, as would *assure* the point. But taking *your* question merely as it is put, I would not deny the possibil- ity of such occurrences. God forbid. One may become aware of what is unusual, yet not know. You would be astonished, sir, how even the hopping of a bird, or the skirring of a withered leaf in the draught over the stones, will sound out in these walls when I'm alone here. And it's seldom so late. Nor would I deny that now and again I have fancied that other occu- pants...' His glance fixed on his visitor, a temporary confusion had spread over his mind, and he failed to complete his sentence. 'But, there; the human eye, sir, can be a great deceiver!'

'That indeed is so,' the low insistent voice rejoined, 'but there may be those who prefer *not* to be seen?'

The verger disliked being cornered, but he had sat under many preachers.

'The points as I take it, sir, are these. First,' he laid forefinger on fore- finger, 'the number of those gone as compared with ourselves who are still waiting. Next, there being no warrant that what is seen – if seen at all – is wraiths of the departed, and not from elsewhere. The very waterspouts out- side are said to be demonstrations of that belief. Third and last, another question: What purpose could call so small a sprinkling of them back – a few grains of sand out of the wilderness, unless, it may be, some festering grievance; or hunger for the living, sir; or duty left undone? In which case, mark you, which of any of us is safe?'

His visitor lifted a heavy head and looked at him. 'But the living them- selves,' he said, 'have instincts, hidden impulses, are driven, beaten, incited on to what may at last appear the unevadable. Then why not *they*? What proof is there...only "duty"? They might, no more than the living, be aware of any purpose, yet be compelled to pursue it. And assuredly,' he hes- itated, 'if, at the end, there had been extreme trouble and – horror.'

The harsh screaming of the swifts coursing in the twilight beyond the leaded windows before they retired into the heavens to sleep out the night upon the wing, was for the moment the only comment on these remarks.

'Well, sir,' said Mr Phelps uneasily at last, 'I confess you press me close.

But we are still no nearer what you had in mind, and I must be locking up. Perhaps you would care to take a glance at a few of the stones in the churchyard, if there is light enough left? But, first,' he added, with a little bow of old-fashioned courtesy, 'and I trust I haven't been detaining you, sir; would you very kindly put your name in our Visitors' Book?'

The well-worn volume stood on a table by itself. He set it open at the current page, and himself dipped the pen into the inkpot. His visitor accepted the pen, paused, and, without again raising his heavy eyes, stooped over the book.

Mr Phelps politely retired, drew open the great door, and his visitor, rather reluctantly, it seemed, and still as far as space permitted keeping his distance, presently edged out and preceded him into the churchyard. From their haunts in the green hills came yet again the sweet and sorrowful cry of the peewits. The air in the porch, after the stony chill within, struck warm on the cheek, and mild as new milk, laden faintly with the earth-sweet fragrance of the hills and the remote freshness of the sea. The evening star in the tarnished gold of the west shone liquid and solitary. The verger feasted his eyes a moment on this quiet scene.

It was as if he had half-forgotten but had now retrieved it, after some dark passage of the mind. An unusual sense of fatigue, mind and body, had stolen over him, and he was relieved that his catechism was over. Few visitors volunteered many questions. If they did, they were questions expected, easy to answer – concerning dates, styles, uses, rituals and so forth. He regretted now, but only because he was unwontedly tired, that he had not a moment ago seized his opportunity to bid this stranger Godspeed. He was none the less astonished to discover on issuing from the porch that he had already vanished. Since he was nowhere within sight, he cannot but have made his way round the east end of the church. Had this, he mused a little forlornly, been merely with the notion of evading the customary tip?

He could recall many such hints of human nature – pious and prosperous pilgrims absent-mindedly debating if perhaps sixpence would be enough. To describe as sardonic any smile on so mild, horse-resembling and pensive a face as the verger's would be absurd. In his own small way he was an artist. Tips were not his sole incentive. Besides, his comfortable little balance in the Savings Bank needed no refreshing, not at this late day. He could, then, easily afford this faint grin of amusement. 'The horseleach hath two daughters, crying Give, give!'

No, it was the *gaucherie*, the unfriendliness that piqued the old man. And not merely that, something else, less easy to describe. Should he let him go, or be after him? This was not his first visit to the church – of that he was convinced. Then why pretend it? Had the stranger hoped to find himself alone there? For what purpose? Now that Mr Phelps was no longer

listening to his own voice – perhaps his favourite occupation – hitherto
unheeded impressions had begun to coagulate in his mind.

Clothes, manner, gait, speech – never in his long experience had any
specimen of a human being embodied so many peculiarities. And there was
yet another, pervading all the rest, but more elusive. The verger was a confirmed dreamer. His office, perhaps, and his daily surroundings accounted
for a more active night-life. In this he was apt to have strange experiences
– to find himself surveying vast shelves of sloping rocks, the sea, enormous
buildings, their bells ringing, but not to summon humanity within their
walls. At this very moment – wideawake though he had supposed himself
to be – he might have issued from such a dream. The body sometimes seems
as precarious as if it had but just been put on. And now, quite another suspicion had struck across his mind. Was this man – was he – quite *sane*?
That taciturnity, the vigilance, the dark, fixed, lightless eye, the galvanic
gestures, the evasiveness. No; to put it crudely, it would be as well to see
him safely off the premises.

He hastened away, the hem of his iron-black cassock rustling over the
grass as, in spite of his sixty-odd years, he stepped nimbly across the inter-
vening mounds. And though he was half prepared to find no trace of his
visitor, there was nothing unexpected in that visitor's appearance when, on
skirting the outer walls of the Lady Chapel, he set eyes on him again. He
was standing in engrossed contemplation of yet another tombstone, and
evidently unaware that he was observed.

Solitary thus in this dusky green on the colder north side of the high old
ecclesiastical mansion, and motionless as an image in a waxwork show, he
looked, if not exactly more real, at least more conspicuously actual than
anything around him. It was almost as though he had dressed up to simulate a certain part on the stage of life, and had overdone it. But perhaps Mr
Phelps himself was now overdoing it a little! He was at any rate taking
liberties, and had no intention of playing the spy. He coughed discreetly.
But his visitor had either not heard this announcement, or had taken no
notice of it. He had remained unmoved, peering, as if shortsightedly, at the
defaced inscription at his feet, one which Mr Phelps could easily have
repeated to him, word-perfect:

> He who hath walked in darkest night,
> Stars and bright moon shut out from sight,
> And Fiends around him cruel as sin,
> Finds welcome even the coldest Inn.

With no more than a slow unsteady movement of his head, he presently
turned aside to the stone of Susanna Harbert, 'Spinster of this Parish':

Let upon my bosom be
Only a bush of Rosemary;
Even though love forget, its breath
Will sweeten this ancient haunt of Death.

But if any bush had ever been planted there, it was gone. Instead, a delicate forest of summer grasses and a few wild flowers concealed the flattened mound.

'You will pardon me breaking in, sir,' interposed the verger, but drawing no nearer, 'there are very few inscriptions in this part of the churchyard; it is seldom visited. If you would give me even so much as a name to go by, it *might* be, sir, within my recollection. I have been here for many years. But the stone itself will almost certainly be on the south side.'

The stranger, looking, as Mr Phelps afterwards put it to himself, more like a copy of a human being than ever, continued for some moments merely to gaze at him; but not as if there were any activity of speculation behind his fixed eyes. 'The name?' he repeated at last, as if he had drawn the word cold and dripping out of some unfathomable well of memory. 'The name was Ambrose Manning...It was said he had made away with himself. It was said...' But nothing further came.

'Ah!' ejaculated the verger in unfeigned dismay...'And the date, sir, perhaps?'

'1882.'

'Well, in that case,' was the hesitant reply, 'we *are* on the right side.' The syllables he had heard, though they had been uttered in so low and lifeless a voice, were now being called, whispered, echoed in every chamber of the old man's memory. Where, where, had he seen, heard, that name before? 'You see,' he was explaining, 'at that time, and perhaps even now, his remains would not so much as have entered the church; not *felo de se*, sir. The whole service, a special one, would be at the grave's side. There was one, I recollect, many years ago, the rain pouring in torrents, and a heavy sea running. But,' he added, as if in apology, 'not *fifty* years ago!'

By this time he was thoroughly wearied of his task. He had been ill-advised to linger so long – this craving for *any* listener. His one desire was to get back to his cottage and to the cold supper that was awaiting him. Nevertheless he was still reluctant to leave such a visitor at large and to his own devices in the precincts of the church. Only two grave-stones, however, now remained between him and freedom; he would at any rate wait them out. They leaned slightly askew under a much-lopped but still hardy old yew tree, one of them encrusted from summit to base with a thin, pale mantling of grey and green.

Traveller, forbear
To brood too secretly on what is here!
Death hath us in his care.
There is no Fear.
But thou, in life – Oh, but I thee implore,
Stray thou amidst these dangerous shades no more!

Mr Phelps was observing his visitor with some anxiety. He looked like a man upon the verge of a trance, a cataleptic, a somnambulist. 'I have never *myself*,' he told him, 'been aware of any "danger" here. And, as you your-self pointed out but a few minutes since, though I confess the thought had never occurred to me, not in that shape, sir – it is the *living* who are speaking to us from these stones – not the dead. Or at least, those who were living at that time. And last,' he went on, since no response had been vouchsafed to him, 'there's this.' He emphasized the word, in a tone of finality, pointing with his finger. 'But it's "N. F." – as you see, sir; and so the initials don't suit with the names you mentioned. A very tragic case, too – for more than one; as I remember hearing when a boy:

'Here lies the Self-Dishonoured Body of N. F. who
perished miserably by his own Hand on October 31 in
the year of our Lord 1875.

See now, if thou have any heed
For thine own soul, now hence make speed!
Here in this waste of briar and thorn
Sojourns one hungry and forlorn,
Self-murdered, unassoiled, unshriven,
Haunting these shades twixt Earth and Heaven.
O get thee gone; no biding make;
Lest the Unsleeping find the Wake!'

The stranger (having as it appeared digested these words also), with a peculiar motion of the head, again glanced gently around him, then lifted his colourless face towards the dimly gilded hands of the clock in the church tower. Whereupon, the bells within, as if in response to a silent invitation, chimed out the hour – that of compline. Perplexed, even vexed at this taci-turnity and poor fellowship, Mr Phelps remarked a little coldly that 'this' was 'the nearest way out'. But again to unlistening ears, for his visitor with no more than a last furtive and empty yet concentrated glance at him, had turned aside, and was already making his way under the dark trees towards a stile which gave egress to a plank bridge over a brook, and so to the hills beyond.

Mr Phelps watched him until he had vanished – not merely from sight, but as if the dense motionless foliage had swallowed him up. There was not a sigh of wind to stir the flowering grasses. The waters of the brook in their narrow ravine were singing a quiet tune; a corncrake was calling in the meadows beyond the low stone wall. All was as it had ever been. The verger turned about at length and paced slowly back to the south porch. Should he or should he not re-enter the church? Should he postpone what he had in mind until the morning? He was aware of a distaste to linger any more. And yet...

He adjusted the key, stepped across the threshold into the darkened building, paused, drew to the heavy door behind him, paused again, then deliberately locked it. Having lit a stub of candle, which in its brass dish-shaped holder he took from a cupboard in the vestry, he unlocked a small iron safe and laid the burial book on the table. The gilt of its title – *Register of Burials*; *Church of St Edmund*; *Langridge* – had nearly faded from out of its covers. Having adjusted his eyeglasses on the extremity of his long stooping nose, he stood there in the stony silence, the radiance of the candle striking up into his long face, etching in with black shadow the lines upon it, chiefly of kindliness, long service and curiosity. Then with a wetted finger he slowly turned over the leaves until he came to January 1, 1882.

After that he drew his finger steadily down each of the following few pages in turn until he came to November 4. Memory had not deluded him; at least not wholly. '*November 4. Ambrose Manning,*' he read. Nothing more than that, and even this had proved to be erroneous. A thin line in red ink had been drawn through both names, and in another hand there followed a scrawled – 'Nothing known. Not buried here.'

Mr Phelps – his eyebrows mounted high on his conical bare forehead – continued for a few moments to scrutinize the entry: he could recall no other example of the kind. How many years had it been since he had chanced on it? 'H'm, not buried here,' he muttered to himself. 'Strange... Why not, then...? And where?'

'Where?' an excessively faint voice from nowhere had muttered as if in reply. Scrupulous servant of habit that he was, though a little jarred, he put back the book into the iron chest, locked it, and, cupping the lighted candle with his bony fingers, made his way out of the vestry. The Visitors' Book lay open, as he had left it, on its narrow table, the pen beside it, now dry. Mr Phelps glanced down at the scribbled page. The latest entry on it was the signature of Helen Jane Wilkinson (Mrs) of 1a Portsea Terrace, High Wycombe. His last visitor then, taking advantage of his own courtesy, had merely pretended to write his name. There was no reason to suppose that he could have forgotten it!

The verger's grey eyes wandered vacantly over the scribbled page. He felt a trifle cold, empty, anxious and oppressed. And as he stood pondering, momentarily severed and estranged as it seemed for the first time in all these years from the beloved, familiar building in his charge, a faint sound arrested his attention. A sound that was no more than a whisper, as of a minute clot of plaster falling from the roof onto the flags beneath. He jerked his head sidelong towards the door that he had but a few minutes before locked behind him.

He held his breath to listen again; then, puffing out his candle-end, crept to the cranny of the door, remaining there as motionless for a while as a cat at a mouse's hole. Slowly and stealthily at length he pushed the key into the lock, turned it in the oiled wards, and drew open the door. But no. The sound he had heard can have been no more than a mere fancy. The ancient porch stood empty; the southern sky now framed beyond it was studded with a few brightening stars. He was unutterably relieved; and yet not wholly so. A hitherto unheeded misgiving was gnawing in his mind. Poor creature – he was debating within himself; this man had come to him hungry, famished, it seemed, for help, and had gone away unsatisfied. He realized now that he had swallowed an extreme distaste for his visitor only in order to indulge his own love of talking. Yet, even at the worst there had been nothing of active evil in that mask of a human face, only an animal-like patience and obstinacy, clay-cold, impassive. No signal of hope either, or of comradeship; only the sediment of an unspeakable obsession. He might have been searching for years. But why?

Nor had it occurred to the verger, he ruminated mutely, to offer his belated visitor even so much as a glass of cold water. A few words of comfort, of reassurance – *they* would not necessarily have been cold. And – least commendable perhaps of all motives – you never can tell when you may not be needing them yourself.

Winter*

All the other gifts appertinent to man, as the malice of
this age shapes them, are not worth a gooseberry...

Any event in this world – any human being for that matter – that seems to wear even the faintest cast or warp of strangeness, is apt to leave a disproportionately sharp impression on one's senses. So at least it appears to me.

* See also 'De Mortuis', Uncollected Stories, p.444, which has epitaphs in common.

The experience lives on secretly in the memory, and you can never tell what trivial reminder may not at some pregnant moment bring it back – bring it back as fresh and living and green as ever. That, at any rate, is my experience.

Life's mere ordinary day-by-day – its thoughts, talk, doings – wither and die away out of the mind like leaves from a tree. Year after year a similar crop recurs: and that goes too. It is mere débris; it perishes. But these other anomalies survive, even through the cold of age – forsaken nests, everlasting clumps of mistletoe.

Not that they either are necessarily of any use. For all we know they may be no less alien and parasitic than those flat and spotted fungi that rise in a night on time-soiled birch trees. But such is their power to haunt us. Why else, indeed, should the recollection of that few moments' confrontation with one who, I suppose, must have been some sort of a 'fellow-creature' remain so sharp and vivid?

There was nothing much unusual in the circumstances. I must have so met, faced, passed by thousands of human beings: many of them in almost as unfrequented places. Without effort I can recall not one. But this one! At the first unexpected premonitory gloom of winter; at sight of any desolate stretch of snow; at sound at dusk of the pebble-like tattling of a robin; at call, too, of a certain kind of dream I have – any such reminder instantly catches me up, transports me back. The old peculiar disquietude possesses me. I am once more an unhappy refugee. It is a distasteful experience.

But such things are difficult to describe – to share. Date, year are, at any rate, of no account; if only for the reason that what impresses us most in life is independent of time. One can in memory indeed live over again events in one's life even twenty years or more gone by, with the same fever of shame, anxiety, unrest. Mere time is nothing.

Nor is now the actual motive of my journey of any consequence. At the moment I was in no particular trouble. No burden lay on my mind – nothing, I mean, heavier than that of being the kind of self one is – a fret common enough in these late days. And though my immediate surroundings were unfamiliar, they were not unusual or unwelcome, since, like others who would not profess to be morbid, I can never pass unvisited either a church of any age or its yard.

Even if I have but a few minutes to spare I cannot resist hastening in to ponder awhile on its old glass and brasses, its stones, shrines, and monuments. Sir Tompkins This, Lord Mount Everest That – one reads with a curious amusement the ingenuous bygones of their blood and state. I have sometimes laughed out. And queer the echo sounds in a barrel roof. And perhaps an old skimpy verger looks at you, round a pillar. Like a bat.

In sober fact this human pomposity of ours shows a little more amiably against any protracted background of time – even a mere two centuries of it. There is an almost saturnine vanity in the sepulchral – 'scutcheons, pedigrees, polished alabaster cherubim and what not. You see it there – like a scarcely legible scribbling on the wall. – well, on this occasion it was not any such sacred interior I was exploring, but a mere half-acre of grave-stones huddling under their tower, in the bare glare of a winter's day.

It was an afternoon in January. For hours I had been trudging against a bitter winter wind awhirl with snow. Fatigue had set in – that leaden fatigue when the body seems to have shrunken; while yet the bones keep up a kind of galvanic action like the limbs of a machine. Thought itself – that capricious deposit – had ceased for the time being. I was like the half-dried mummy of a man, pressing on with bent head along an all but obliterated track.

Then, as if at a signal, I looked up; to find that the snow had ceased to fall: that only a few last, and as if forgotten, flakes were still floating earthwards to their rest in the pallid light of the declining sun.

With this breaking of the clouds a profounder silence had fallen upon the dome-shaped summit of the hill on which I stood. And at its point of vantage I came to a standstill awhile, surveying beneath me under the blue-ing vacancy of the sky, amidst the white-sheeted fields, a squat church tower, its gargoyles stooping open-mouthed – scarcely less open-mouthed than the frosted bells within. The low mounded wall that encircled the place was but just perceptible, humped with its snow. Its yews stood like gigantic umbrellas clotted with swansdown; its cypresses like torches, fringed, crested, and tufted with ash.

No sound broke the frozen hush as I entered the lych-gate; not a figure of man or beast moved across that far-stretching savanna of new-fallen snow. You could have detected the passage of a fly. Dazzling light and gem-clear coloured shadow played in hollow and ripple. I was treading a virgin wilderness, but one long since settled and densely colonized.

In surroundings like these – in any vast vacant quiet – the senses play uncommonly queer tricks with their possessor. The very air, cold and ethereal and soon to be darkened, seemed to be astir with sounds and shapes on the edge of complete revelation. Such are our fancies. A curious insecure felicity took possession of me. Yet on the face of it the welcome of a winter churchyard is cold enough; and the fare scanty!

The graves were old: many of them recorded only with what nefarious pertinacity time labours and the rain gnaws. Others befrosted growths had now patterned over, and their tale was done. But for the rest – some had texts: 'I am a Worm, and no Man'; 'In Rama was there a Voice heard: Lamentation and Weeping'; 'He knoweth the Way that I take'. And a few still bore their bits of doggerel:

> Stranger, a light I pray!
> Not that I pine for day:
> Only one beam of light —
> To show me Night!

That struck me as a naïve appeal to a visitor not as yet in search of a roof 'for when the slow dark hours begin', and almost blinded for the time being by the dazzle of the sunlight striking down on these abodes around him!

I smiled to myself and went on. Dusk, as a matter of fact, is *my* mind's natural illumination. How many of us, I wonder, 'think' in anything worthy of being called a noonday of consciousness? Not many: it's all in a mirk, without arrangement or prescience. And as for dreaming – well, here were sleepers enough. I loafed on – cold and vacant.

A few paces further I came to a stand again, before a large oval stone, encircled with a blunt loop of marble myrtle leaves embellishing the words:

> He shall give His angels charge over thee,
> To keep thee in all thy ways.

This stone was clasped by two grotesque marble hands, as if he who held it knelt even now behind it in hiding. Facing north, its lower surface was thickly swathed with snow. I scraped it off with my hands:

> I was afraid,
> Death stilled my fears:
> In sorrow I went,
> Death dried my tears:
> Solitary too,
> Death came. And I
> Shall no more want
> For company.

So, so: the cold alone was nipping raw, and I confess its neighbour's philosophy pleased me better: i.e., it's better to be anything animate than a dead lion; even though that lion be a Corporal Pym:

> This quiet mound beneath
> Lies Corporal Pym.
> He had no fear of death;
> Nor Death of him.

Or even if the anything animate be nothing better than a Logge:

> Here lies Thomas Logge – a Rascally Dogge;
> A poor useless creature – by choice as by nature;
> Who never served God – for kindness or Rod;
> Who, for pleasure or penny, – never did any
> Work in his life – but to marry a Wife,
> And live aye in strife:
> And all this he says – at the end of his days
> Lest some fine canting pen
> Should be at him again.

Canting pens had had small opportunity in this hillside acre: and the gentry of the surrounding parts, like those of most parts, had preferred to lie inside under cover – where no doubt Mr Jacob Todd had prepared for many of them a far faster and less starry lodging:

> Here be the ashes of Jacob Todd,
> Sexton now in the land of Nod.
> Digging he lived, and digging died,
> Pick, mattock, spade, and nought beside.
> { Here oft at evening he would sit
> { Tired with his toil, and proud of it;
> { Watching the pretty Robins flit.
> Now slumbers he as deep as they
> He bedded for yᵉ Judgement Day.

Mr Todd's successor, it seemed, had entrusted him with a little protégée, who for a few years – not quite nine – had been known as Alice Cass:

> My mother bore me:
> My father rejoiced in me:
> The good priest blest me:
> All people loved me:
> But Death coveted me:
> And free'd this body
> Of its youthful soul.

For youthful company she had another Alice. A much smaller parcel of bones this – though in sheer date upwards of eighty years her senior:

Here lyeth our infant, Alice Rodd;
She were so small,
Scarce aught at all,
But a mere breath of Sweetness sent from God.

Sore we did weepe; our heartes on sorrow set.
Till on our knees
God sent us ease:
And now we weepe no more than we forget.

Tudor roses had been carved around the edge of her stone – vigorously and delicately too, for a rustic mason. Every petal held its frozen store. I wandered on, restlessly enough, now that my journey was almost at an end, stooping to read at random; here an old broken wooden cross leaning crookedly over its one legible word 'Beloved'; here the great, flat, seventeenth-century vault of Abraham Devoyage, 'who was of France, and now, please God, is of Paradise'; and not far distant from him some Spanish exile, though what had brought such a wayfarer to these outlandish parts, heaven alone could tell:

Laid in this English ground
A Spaniard slumbers sound.
Well might the tender weep
To think how he doth sleep —
Strangers on either hand —
So far from his own land.
O! when the last Trump blow,
May Christ ordain that so
This friendless one arise
Under his native skies.
How bleak to wake, how dread a doom,
To cry his sins so far from home!

And then Ann Poverty's stone a pace or two beyond him:

Stranger, here lies
Ann Poverty;
Such was her name
And such was she.
May Jesu pity
Poverty.

A meagre memorial, and a rather shrill appeal somehow in that vacancy. Indeed I must confess that this snowy waste, these magpie stones, the zebra-like effect of the thin snow-stripings on the dark tower beneath a leaden winter sky suggested an influence curiously pagan in effect. Church sentiments were far more alien in this scene of nature than beneath a roof. And after all, Nature herself instils into us mortals, I suppose, little but endurance, patience, resignation; despair – or fear. That she can be entrancing proves nothing.

On the contrary, the rarer kinds of natural loveliness – enormous forests of flowering chestnuts, their league-long broken chasms sonorous with cataracts and foaming with wild flowers; precipitous green steeps – quartz, samphire, cormorant – plunging a thousand fathoms into dark gulfs of emerald ocean – such memories hint far rather at the inhuman divinities. This place, too, was scarcely one that happy souls would choose to haunt. And yet, here was I...in a Christian burial ground.

But then, of course, one's condition of spirit and body must be taken into account. I was exhausted, and my mind like a vacant house with the door open – so vacant by now that I found I had read over and over the first two or three lines of Asrafel (or was it Israfel?) Holt's blackened inscription without understanding a single word; and then, suddenly, two dark eyes in a long cadaverous face pierced out at me as if from the very fabric of his stone:

> Here is buried a Miser:
> Had he been wiser,
> He would not have gone bare
> Where Heaven's garmented are.
> He'd have spent him a penny
> To buy a Wax Taper;
> And of Water a sprinkle
> To quiet a poor Sleeper.
> He'd have cried on his soul,
> 'O my Soul, moth & rust! —
> What treasure shall profit thee
> When thou art dust?'
> '*Mene, Tekel, Upharsin*!'
> God grant, in those Scales,
> His Mercy avail us
> When all Earth's else fails!

'...Departed this life May the First 1700'. Two long centuries dead, seraphic Israfel! Was time nothing to him either?

'Now withered is the Garland on the...' the fragment of old rhyme chased its tail awhile in the back of my mind, and then was gone.

And I must be going. Winter twilight is brief. Frost was already glittering along the crisping surface of the snow. A crescent moon showed silvery in the sun's last red. I made her a distant obeisance. But the rather dismal sound of the money I rattled in my pocket served only to scare the day's last robin off. *She* – she paid me no heed.

Here was the same old unanswerable question confronting the traveller. 'I have no Tongue,' cried one from his corner, 'and Ye no Ears.' And this, even though nearby lay Isaac Meek, who in certain features seems easily to have made up for these deficiencies:

> Hook-nosed was I; loose-lipped. Greed fixed its gaze
> In my young eyes ere they knew brass from gold.
> Doomed to the blazing market-place my days,
> A sweating chafferer of the bought, and sold.
> Frowned on and spat at, flattered and decried,
> One only thing man asked of me – my price.
> I lived, detested; and forsaken, died,
> Scorned by the Virtuous and the jest of Vice.
> And now behold, you Christians, my true worth!
> Step close: I have inherited the Earth.

I turned to go – wearied a little even of the unwearying. Epitaphs in any case are only 'marginal' reading. There is rarely anything unusual or original in such sentiments as theirs. Up to that moment (apart from the increasing cold) this episode – this experience – had been merely that of a visitor ordinarily curious, vulgarly intrusive, perhaps, and one accustomed to potter about among the antiquated and forgotten.

No: what followed came without premonition or warning. I had been stooping, for the last time, my body now dwarfed by the proximity of the dark stone tower. I had been reading all that there was to be read about yet another forgotten stranger; and so rapidly had the now north-east wind curdled the air that I had been compelled to scrape off the rime from the lettering with numb fingertips. I had stooped (I say) to read:

> O passer-by, beware!
> Is the day fair? —
> Yet unto evening shall the day spin on
> And soon thy sun be gone;
> Then darkness come,
> And this, a narrow home.

Not that I bid thee fear:
Only, when thou at last lie here,
Bethink thee, there shall surely be
Thy Self for company.

And with its last word a peculiar heat coursed through my body. Consciousness seemed suddenly to concentrate itself (like the tentacles of an anemone closing over a morsel of strange food), and I realized that I was no longer alone. But – and of this I am certain – there was no symptom of positive *fear* in the experience. Intense awareness, a peculiar physical, ominous absorption, possibly foreboding; but not actual fear.

I say this because what impressed me most in the figure that I now saw standing amid that sheet of whiteness – three or four grave-mounds distant on these sparse northern skirts of the churchyard – what struck me instantly was the conviction that to him I myself was truly such an object. Not exactly of fear; but of unconcealed horror. It is not, perhaps, a pleasing thing to have to record. My appearance there – dark clothes, dark hair, wearied eyes, ageing face, a skin maybe somewhat cadaverous at that moment with fasting and the cold – all this (just what my body and self looked like, I mean) cannot have been much more repellent than that of scores and scores of men of my class and means and kind.

I was merely, that is, like one of the 'Elder Ladies or Children' who were bidden (by Mr Nash's Rules of the Pump Room in Bath in 1709) be contented 'with a second bench ... as being past, or not come to, Perfection'.

None the less, there was no doubt of it. The fixed open gaze answering mine suggested that of a child confronted with a fascinating but repulsive reptile. Yet so strangely and arrestingly beautiful was that face, beautiful with the strangeness I mean of the dreamlike, with its almost colourless eyes and honey-coloured skin, that unless the experience of it had been thus sharply impressed, no human being could have noticed the emotion depicted upon its features.

There was not the faintest faltering in the steady eyes – fixed, too, as if this crystal graveyard air were a dense medium for a sight unused to it. And so intent on them was I myself that, though I noticed the slight trembling of the hand that held what (on reflection) appeared to resemble the forked twig which 'diviners' of water use in their mysteries, I can give no account of this stranger's dress except that it was richly yet dimly coloured.

As I say, my own dark shape was now standing under the frowning stonework of the tower. With an effort one of its gargoyles could have spilt heaven's dews upon my head, had not those dews been frozen. And the voice that fell on my ear – as if from within rather than from without – echoed cold and solemnly against its parti-coloured stone:

'Which is the way?'

Realizing more sharply with every tardy moment that this being, in human likeness, was not of my kind, nor of my reality; standing there in the cold and snow, winter nightfall now beginning to lour above the sterile landscape; I could merely shake a shivering head.

'Which is yours?' sang the tranquil and high yet gentle voice.

'There!' I cried, pointing with my finger to the pent-roofed gate which led out on to the human road. The astonishment and dread in the strange face seemed to deepen as I looked.

'But I would gladly...' I began, turning an instant towards the gloomy snow clouds that were again gathering in the north – 'I would gladly...' But the sentence remained unfinished, for when I once more brought my eyes back to this confronter, he was gone.

I agree I was very tired; and never have I seen a more sepulchral twilight than that which now overspread this desolate descent of hill. Yet, strange though it may appear, I knew then and know now that this confrontation was no illusion of the senses. There are hours in life, I suppose, when we are weaker than we know; when a kind of stagnancy spreads over the mind and heart that is merely a masking of what is gathering beneath the surface. Whether or not, as I stood looking back for an instant before pushing on through the old weathered lych-gate, an emotion of intense remorse, misery, terror – I know not – swept over me. My eyes seemed to lose for that moment their power to see aright. The whole scene was distorted, awry.

THE CONNOISSEUR
AND OTHER STORIES
(1926)

*Mr Kempe**

It was a mild, clammy evening; and the swing-door of the tap-room stood wide open. The brass oil-lamp suspended from the rafter had not yet been lit; a small misty drizzle was drifting between the lime-washed walls and the over-arching trees on the further side of the lane; and from my stool at the counter I could commune, as often as I felt inclined, with the wild white eye of the Blue Boar which fleered in at the window from the hanging sign.

Autumnal scents, failing day, rain so gentle and persistent – such phenomena as these have a slightly soporific effect on the human consciousness. It is as though its busy foreground first becomes blurred, then blotted out; and then – the slow steady sweep of the panorama of dream that never ceases its strange motioning. The experience is brief, I agree. The footlights, headlights, skylights brighten again: the panorama retires!

Excluding the landlady, who occasionally waddled in from her dusky retreat behind the bar, there were only three of us in the tap-room – three chance customers now met together for the first time: myself; a smallish man with an unusually high crown to his head, and something engagingly monkey-like in his face; and a barrel-shaped person who sat humped up on a stool between us in an old shooting-jacket and leather leggings, his small eyes set close together on either side a red nose.

I had been the last to put in an appearance, but had not, it seemed, damped anything in the nature of a conversation. Such weather does not conduce to it. But three may be some sort of company where two is none; and what, at last, set us more or less at our ease was an 'automatic machine' that stood in the corner of the tap-room under a coloured lithograph of Shotover, the winner of the Derby in 1882. It was a machine of an unusual kind since it gave its patronizers nothing tangible for their penny – not even their ladylove on a slip of cardboard, or a clinging jet of perfume.

It reminds me now of the old Miracle Plays or Moralities. Behind its glass it showed a sort of grotto, like a whited sepulchre, with two

* First published in *London Mercury* and *Harper's Magazine*, November 1925.

compartments, over which descended the tresses of a weeping willow. You slipped a penny into the slot, and presently a hump-backed mommet in a rusty-black cowl jerked into view from the cell on the left. He stood there a moment in the midst – fixedly looking at you: then decamped into the gloom again.

But this was if your luck was out – or so I assumed. If it was in, then a nymph attired in skirts of pink muslin wheeled out of the flowery bower on the eastern side; and danced a brief but impassioned *pas seul*.

My three pennies had brought me one fandango from the latter and two prolonged scrutinies from the former – a proportion decided on, no doubt, by the worldly-wise manufacturer of the machine. But this was not all. In intention at least he must have been a practical optimist. For if the *nymph* responded to your penny, you were invited to slip yet another coin into another slot – but before you could count ten. This galvanized the young lady into a giddy pursuit of the numbskull in the black hood – a pursuit, however, which ended merely in the retirement of them both behind the scenes.

The man in leggings had watched my experiments with eyes almost as motionless as plums in a pudding. It was my third penny that had wooed out the nymph. But the 'grandfather's clock' in the corner had ticked loudly at least five times before I managed to insert a fourth. It was a moment of rapt – of an aching – excitement. What teeming passion showed itself in that wild horseplay behind the glass! And then, alas, the machinery ceased to whirr; the clock ticked on; the faint rustle of the drifting rain sounded once more at the open door; I returned to my stool; and the landlady retired into her den.

'Bang goes fourpence,' I remarked a little sheepishly. 'Still, mine was about the right average, I suppose.'

The man in the leather leggings – as if the problem were not for *his* solution – at once turned his little eyes towards our companion in the corner, whose face was still wreathed with the friendliest of grimaces at my efforts.

'Well, now,' he took me up, 'I'm not so sure. In my view, that minx there sidles out too often. Most young men and more old ones would be content with once in six. I would myself. It's our credulity. We live on hopes, however long they may be deferred. We *live*, as you might say; but how many of us learn? How many of us want to make sure?' He paused for an answer: his small eyes fixed in his face. 'Not one in a million,' he decided.

I stole another look into the narrow darkness of the Young Lady's Bower.

'Oh,' he interrupted, 'I wasn't thinking merely of the "eternal feminine", as they call it. That's only one of the problems; though even an answer to that might be interesting. There's Free Will, for example; there's Moral Responsibility; and such little riddles as where we all come from and where we are going to. Why, we don't even know what we are – in ourselves, I mean. And how many of us have tried to find out?'

The man in leggings withdrew his stare and groped out a hand towards his pint-pot. 'Have you?' he enquired.

The dark-eyed, wizened face lit up once more with its curiously engaging smile. 'Well, you see, I was once a schoolmaster, and from an official point of view, I suppose, it is part of the job. To find answers, I mean. But, as you'll agree, we temporize; we compromise. On the other hand, I once met quite by chance, as we call it, a man who had spent I should guess a good many years on that last problem. All by himself, too. You might almost describe it as a kind of pilgrimage – though I'm not anxious to repeat it. It was my turn for a lesson.'

'And what was *his* solution?' I enquired.

'Have you ever been to Porlock – the Weir?' the little man enquired.

I shook my head.

'I mention Porlock,' he went on, 'because if you had ever been there, the place I'm thinking of might perhaps call it to mind. Though mine was on a different scale – a decidedly different scale. I doubt, for example, if it will ever become one of those genial spots frequented by week-end tourists and *chars-a-banc*. In the days I'm speaking of – twenty years or more ago – there wasn't even the rudiments of an inn in the place. Only a beershop about half the size of this tap-room, with a population to match – just a huddle of fishermen's cottages tucked in under the cliff.

'I was walking at the time, covering unfamiliar ground, and had managed to misread my map. My aim had been to strike into a cliff-path that runs more or less parallel with the coast; but I had taken the wrong turn at the cross-roads. Once astray, it seemed better manners to keep on. How can you tell what chance may have secreted in her sleeve, even when you don't put pennies in slots?

'I persuaded an old lady to give me tea at one of the cottages, and asked my way. Visitors were rare events, it seemed. At first she advised me to turn back; I couldn't do better than that. But after further questioning, she told me at last of a lower cliff track or path, some miles apparently this side of the one I had in view. She marked it out for me with her rheumaticky old forefinger on the table-cloth. Follow this path far enough, I gathered, it would lead me into my right road at last.

'Not that she suggested my making the attempt. By no means. It was a matter of seven miles or more. And neither the natives of the village nor even chance visitors, it seemed, were tempted to make much use of this particular route.'

'Why not?' enquired the man in leggings, and immediately coughed, as if he had thought better of it.

'That's what I am coming to,' replied the schoolmaster – as though he had been lying in wait for the question. 'You see my old lady had volunteered her last piece of information with a queerish look in her eyes – like some shy animal slipping into cover. She was telling me the truth, but not, I fancied, the whole truth.

'Naturally I asked what was wrong with the path; and was there anything of interest on the way or at the end of it – worth such a journey? Once more she took a long slow look at me, as if my catechism were rather more pressing than the occasion warranted. There *was* a something marked on the map, she had been given to understand – "just an old, ancient building, like".

'Sure enough there was: though unfortunately long wear of the one I carried had not only left indecipherable more than an Old English letter or two of any record of it, but had rubbed off a square half-mile or so of the country round about it.

'It was proving a little irksome to draw Truth out of her well, and when innocently enough I asked if there was any one in charge of the place, the old lady was obviously disconcerted. She didn't seem to think it needed being taken charge of; though she confessed at last that a house "not nearly so old, sir, you will understand", stood nearby, in which lived a gentleman of the name of Kempe.

'It was easier sailing now that we had come to Mr Kempe. The land, it appeared, including the foreshore – but apart from the chapel – had been in his family since the beginning of time. Mr Kempe himself had formerly been in the church – Conformist or otherwise – and had been something of a traveller, but had returned home with an invalid wife many years before.

'Mrs Kempe was dead now; and there had been no children, "none, at least, as you would say grew up to what might be called living". And Mr Kempe himself had not only been ailing for some little time, but might, for all my informant knew apparently, be dead himself. Nevertheless, there was still a secretive look in the faded eyes – almost as if she believed Mr Kempe had discovered little methods of his own against the onsets of mortality! Anyhow, she couldn't tell; nobody ever went that way now, so far as she was aware. There was the new road up above. What's more, tidings of Mr Kempe's end, I gathered, however solitary, would not exactly put the village into mourning.

'It was already latish afternoon; and in that windless summer weather walking had been a rather arduous form of amusement. I was tired. A snowy low-pitched upper-room overlooking the sea was at my disposal if I wanted it for a night or two. And yet, even while I was following this good soul up her narrow staircase, I had already decided to push on in the direction of Mr Kempe. If need be, I would come back that evening. Country people are apt to be discreet with strangers – however open in appearance.

Those shrewd old eyes – when at least they showed themselves – had hinted that even with an inch to the mile a map-maker cannot exhaust a country-side. The contours, I had noticed, were unusual. Besides, Mr Kempe was not less likely to be interesting company because he was a recluse!

'I put down five shillings on account for my room, and the kindly old creature laid them aside in an ornament on her mantelpiece. There they lie still, for all I know. I have never reclaimed them.'

The man in leggings once more turned his large, shapeless face towards the schoolmaster, but this time he made no audible comment.

'And did you find Mr Kempe?' I enquired.

The schoolmaster smiled, looking more like a philanthropic monkey than ever. 'I set out at once: watched by the old lady from her porch, until, with a wave of my hand for adieu, I turned out of the village street, and she was hidden from sight. There was no mistaking the path – even though it led off over a stile into a patch of stinging-nettles, and then past a boggy goose-pond.

'After a few hundred yards it began to dip towards the shore, keeping more or less level with the sea for a mile or so until it entered a narrow and sandy cove – the refuge even in summer of all sorts of flotsam and sea-rubbish; and a positive maelstrom, I should imagine, when the winter gales sweep in. Towards the neck of this cove the wheel-marks in the thin turf faded out, and the path meandered on for a while beside a brook and under some fine ash trees, then turned abruptly to the right, and almost due north. The bleached bows of a tarred derelict boat set up on end and full of stones – *The Orion* – was my last touch with civilization.

'It was a quiet evening; the leaves and grasses shone green and motion-less, the flowers standing erect on their stalks under the blue sky, as if carved out of wax. The air was uncommonly sweet, with its tang of the sea. Taking things easy like this, it was well worth while to be alive. I sat down and rested, chewing a grass-stalk and watching the friendly lapping sea. Then up and on.

'After about an hour's steady walking, the path began once more to ascend. It had by now led shorewards again, though I was softly plodding on out of sight and all but out of sound of the tide. Dense neglected woods rose on either side of me, and though wherever the sun could pierce in there were coverts in plenty, hardly a cry of insect or bird stirred the air. To all intents I might have been exploring virgin country. Now and again indeed the fallen bole of a tree or matted clumps of bramble, briony, and traveller's joy compelled me to make a widish detour. But I was still steadily ascending, and the view tended at length to become more and more open; with here and there a patch of bright green turf and a few scrub bushes of juniper or sprouting tamarisk.

'Shut in as I had been, until this moment it had been difficult to guess how far above me the actual plateau lay, or precisely how far below, the sea – though I had caught distant glimpses now and again of its spreading silver and the far horizon. Even at this point it would have been flattery to call the track a path. The steeper its incline, the more stony and precarious became one's footing. And then at last I rounded the first of a series of bluffs or headlands, commanding a spectacular view of the coast behind me, though nothing of what lay in front.

'The tiny village had vanished. About a hundred and fifty feet beneath the steep on whose margin I was standing – with a flaming bush of gorse here and there, and an occasional dwarf oak as grey as silk in the evening light – the incoming tide gently mumbled its rocks, rocks of a peculiar patchy green and black.

'I took another look at my map, enjoyed a prolonged "breather", and went on. Steadily up and inward now and almost due north-west. And once more untended thickets rose dense on either side, and the air was oppressed with a fragrance sickly as chloroform. Some infernal winter tempest or equinoctial gale must have lately played havoc here. Again and again I had to clamber over the bole or through the head-twigs of monster trees felled by the wind, and still studded with a few sprouting *post-mortem* pale-green buds. It was like edging between this world and the next.

'Apart, too, from the gulls with their saturnine gabbling, and flights of clanging oyster-catchers on the rocks below, what birds I saw were birds of prey: buzzards and kestrels chiefly, suspended as if by a thread from space, their small heads stooping between their quivering wings. And once I overheard what I took to be the cough of a raven to its mate. About twenty minutes afterwards, my second bluff hove into sight. And I paused for a while, staring at it.

'For ordinary purposes I have a fairly good head. And yet I confess that before venturing further I took a prolonged look at this monster and at the faint patternings of the path that lay before me, curving first in, then out, along and across the face of the cliff, and just faintly etching its precipitous surface as it edged out of sight. It's a foolish thing perhaps to imagine oneself picked out clean against the sky on a precipitous slope – if, that is, you mean to put the fancy into action. You get a sort of double-barrelled view of your mortal body crouching there semi-erect, little better than a framework of bones.

'Not that there was as yet any positive risk or danger. The adventure would have been child's play, no doubt, even for an amateur mountaineer. You had only to pick your way, keeping a sharp eye on the loose stones, and – to avoid megrims – skirting round the final curve without pausing to look up or to look down. A modest man might possibly try all fours. Still, after that, it did not surprise me to remember that visitors to these parts had usually preferred some other method of reaching the road and country up above. Pleasure may be a little *over*-spiced with excitement.'

'Steep, eh?' ejaculated the man in leggings.

'Yes, steep,' replied the schoolmaster; 'though taken as mere scenery,' he continued, 'there was nothing to find fault with. Leagues and leagues of sea stretched out to the vague line of the horizon like an immense plate, mottled green and blue. A deep pinkish glow, too, had begun to spread over the eastern skies, mantling up into heights of space made the more abysmal in appearance by wisps of silver cirrus.

'Now and again I lay back with my heels planted on what was left of the path, and rested a moment, staring up into that infinity. Now and again I all but decided to go back. But sheer curiosity to see the mysterious hermitage of which I had heard, and possibly the shame of proving myself yet another discredited visitor, lured me on. Solitude, too, is like deepening water to a swimmer: that also lures you on. Except for an occasional bloated, fork-tailed, shrimp-like insect that showed itself when a flake of dislodged stone went scuttering down into the abyss below, I was the only living creature abroad. Once more I pushed cautiously forward. But it was an evil-looking prospect, and the intense silence of the evening produced at last a peculiar sense of unreality and isolation. My universe seemed to have become a mere picture – and I out of place in it. It was as if I had been mislaid and forgotten.

'I hung by now, I suppose, about two or three hundred feet above the sea; and maybe a hundred or so beneath the summit of the wall which brushed my left elbow. Wind-worn boulders, gently whispered over by saplings of ash or birch, jutted shallowly here and there above and below me. Marine plants lifted their wind-bitten flowers from inch-wide ledges on which their seeds had somehow found a lodging. The colours mirrored in sky and water increased in brilliance and variety as the sunset advanced, though here was only its reflection; and the flat ocean beneath lapped soundlessly on; its cream-like surf fringing here and there the very base of the cliff, beneath which, like antediluvian monsters, vast rocks lay drowsing. I refrained from examining them too closely.

'But even if – minute intrusive mote that I was, creeping across that steep of wall – even if I had been so inclined, there was little opportunity. Though for centuries wind, frost and rain had been gnawing and fretting at the face of the cliff, sure foothold and finger-hold became ever more precarious. An occasional ringing reverberation from far below suggested, too, that even the massive bulk of rock itself might be honeycombed to its foundations. What once had been a path was now the negation of one. And the third prodigious bluff towards which I presently found myself slowly, almost mechanically, advancing, projected into space at a knife-like angle; cut sharp in gigantic silhouette against the skies.

'I made a bewildering attempt to pretend to be casual and cheerful – even to whistle. But my lips were dry, and breath or courage failed me. None the less I had contrived to approach within twenty yards or so of that last appalling precipice, when, as if a warning voice had whispered the news in my ear, I suddenly realized the predicament I was in. To turn back now was impossible. Nor had I a notion of what lay on the further side of the headland. For a few instants my bones and sinews rebelled against me, refusing to commit themselves to the least movement. I could do no more than cling spasmodically with my face to the rock.

'But to hang there on and on and wither like an autumnal fly was out of the question. One single hour of darkness, one spinning puff of wind, would inevitably dislodge me. But darkness was some hours distant; the evening was of a dead calm; and I thanked my stars there was no sun to roast and confuse me with his blaze and heat. I thanked my stars – but where would my carcase be when those stars began to show themselves in the coming night? All this swept through my mind in an instant. Complete self-possession was the one thing needful. I realized that too. And then a frightful cold came over me; sweat began to pour off my body; the very soul within me became sick with fear.

'I use the word soul because this renewed nausea was something worse than physical. I was a younger man then, and could still in the long run rely on nerve and muscle, but fear turns one's blood to water – that terror of the spirit, and not merely of the mind or instinct. It bides its moment until the natural edges off into – into the unknown.

'Not that Nature, as we call her, even in the most congenial surroundings, is the sort of old family nurse that makes one's bed every morning, and tucks one up with a "God bless you" overnight. Like the ants and the aphides and the elvers and the tadpoles, she produces us humans in millions; leaving us otherwise to our own devices. We can't even guess what little stratagems for the future she may be hiding up her sleeve. We can't even guess. But that's a mere commonplace. After all, so far as we can prove, she deserves only a small "n" to her name.

'What I'm suggesting is merely that though she appeared to have decoyed me into this rat-trap with all her usual artlessness, she remained a *passive* enemy, and what now swathed me in like a breath of poison – as, with face, palms, knees and belly pressed close against the rock, I began once more working softly on from inch-wide ledge and inch-deep weed, my tongue like tinder, my eyes seeming to magnify every glittering atom they tried to focus – was the consciousness of some power or influence beyond Nature's. It was not so much of death – and I actually with my own eyes *saw* my body inertly hurtling to its doom beneath – that I was afraid. What terrified me beyond words to express was some positive presence here in a more desperate condition even than I. I was being waylaid.

'When you come to such a pass as this, you lose count of time. I had become an automaton – little better than a beetle obeying the secret dictates of what I believe they call the Life-Urge; and how precisely I contrived to face and to circumnavigate that last bit of precipice, I cannot recall. But this once done, in a few minutes I was in comparative safety. I found myself sluggishly creeping again along a path which had presently widened enough to allow me to turn my face outwards from the rock, and even to rest. And even though the precipice beneath me was hardly less abrupt and enormous, and the cliff-face above actually overhung my niche, for the time being I was out of physical danger. I was, as they say, my own man again; had come back.

'It was high time. My skull seemed to have turned to ice; I was wet through; my finger-nails were split; my hands covered with blood; and my clothes would have disgraced a tramp.

'But all trace of fear had left me, and what now swept my very wits away in this almost unendurable reaction was the sheer beauty of the scene that hung before my eyes. Half reclining, not daring yet to stir, my outstretched hands clasping two knobs of rocks, my eyeballs gently moving to and fro, I sat there and feasted on the amazing panorama spread out before me; realizing none the less that I was in the presence of something – how can I express it? – of something a little different from, stranger and less human than – well, our old friend Nature.

'The whole face of this precipice was alight with colour – dazzling green and orange, drifts of snow and purple – campion, sea-pink, may-weed, samphire, camomile, lichen, stonecrop, with fleshy and aromatic plants that I knew not even the names of, sweeping down drift beyond drift into a narrow rock-bound tranquil bay of the darkest emerald and azure, and then sweeping up once more drift beyond drift into the vault of the sky, its blue fretted over as if by some master architect with silvery interlacings, a scattered feather-like fleece of vapour.

'The steady cry too, possibly amplified by echo, of the incoming tide reached me here once more; a whisper and yet not toneless. And on and on into the distance swept the gigantic coast line, crowned summit to base with its emerald springtide woods.

'Still slightly intoxicated as I was by the terror and danger in which I had been, and which were now for the moment past and gone, I gave myself ample opportunity to rest and to drink in this prodigious spectacle. And yet, as I lay there, still at a dizzy altitude, midway between sea and sky but in perfect safety, the odd conviction persisted, that though safe, I was not yet secure. It was as if I were still facing some peril of the mind, and absurd and irrational though it may sound there was a vague disquieting hint within me of disappointment – as if I had lost without realizing it a unique opportunity. And yet, all this medley of hints and intuitions was wholly subsidiary to the conviction that from some one point in all this vacancy around me a steady devouring gaze was fixed on me – that I was being watched.'

Once more our hard-headed friend fidgeted uneasily on his stool.

'It sounds absurd, I agree,' the schoolmaster caught him up. 'Simply because, apart from the seabirds and the clouds, I had been and was still the only moving object within view. The sudden apparition of me crawling around that huge nose of rock must have been as conspicuous as it was absurd. Besides, myriads of concealed eyes in the dense forest towering conically up on the other side of the narrow bay beneath me, and looming ever more mistily from headland to headland towards the north and west, could have watched my every movement. A thousand arrows from unseen archers concealed on the opposing heights might at any instant have trans-fixed me where I lay. One becomes conscious, too, of the sort of empty settled stare which fixes an intruder into such solitudes. It is at the same time vacant, enormous and hostile.

'But I don't mean that. I still mean something far more definite – and more dangerous, too, than that; and I keep to it even if this precise memory may have been affected by what came after. For I was soon to learn that in actual fact I *was* being watched; and by as acute and unhuman a pair of eyes as I have ever seen in mortal head.

'With infinite caution I rose to my feet again at last, and continued my journey. The path grew steadily easier; soil succeeded to bare rock, and this must not very long before, I discovered, have been trodden by other human feet than mine. There were marks of hobnails between its tussocks of grass and moss and thrift.

'It presently descended a little, and then in a while, from out of the glare of the evening, I found myself entering a broader and heavily-shaded track leading straight onwards and tunnelling inland into the woods. It was, to my amazement, close on eight o'clock, and too late to dream of turning back, even if I could have persuaded myself to face again the experience of the last half-hour. Yet whatever curiosity might say for itself, I felt a pecu-liar disinclination to forge ahead. The bait had ceased to be enticing.

'I paused once more under the dismal funnel of greenery in which I found myself staring at the face of my watch, and then had another look at the map. A minute or two's scrutiny assured me that straight ahead was my only possible course. And why not? There was company ahead. In this damp soil the impressions of the hob-nailed shoes showed more clearly.

Quite recently those shoes must have come and gone along this path on three separate occasions at least. Mine had been a rather acutely solitary excursion, and yet for the life of me I had not the smallest desire to meet the maker of those footprints.

'In less than half an hour, however, I came to a standstill beneath "the old, ancient building, like" that had once been marked on my map. And an uncompanionable sight it was. Its walls lay a little back from the green track in what appeared to be a natural clearing, or amphitheatre, though at a few yards' distance huge pines, in shallow rising semi-circles, hemmed it in. In shape it was all but circular; and must once no doubt have been a wayside hermitage or cell. It was of stone and was surmounted by a conical roof of thick and heavy slabs, at the south side of which rose a minute bell-cote, and towards the east a stunted stone cross, with one of its arms broken away.

'The round arched door – its chevron edging all but defaced – refused to open. Nothing was to be seen in the gloom beyond its gaping keyhole. There was but one narrow slit of window, and this was beyond my reach. I could not even guess the age of this forbidding yet beautiful thing, and the gentleman – as I found afterwards – who had compiled the local guide-book had omitted to mention it altogether. Here and there in its fabric decay had begun to show itself, but clumsy efforts had been made at repair.

'In that deep dark verdurous silence, unbroken even by drone or twitter, the effect of those walls in their cold minute simplicity was peculiarly impressive. They seemed to strike a solemn chill into the air around them – those rain-stained senseless stones. And what looked like a kind of derelict burial-ground to the south side of it only intensified its sinister aspect. No place surely for when the slow dark hours begin.

'The graves were very few in number, and only one name was decipherable on any of the uncouth and half-buried headstones. Two were mere mounds in the nibbled turf. I had drawn back to survey once more from this new aspect the walls beyond, when – from one instant to the next, so to speak – I became aware of the presence of Mr Kempe. He was standing a few paces distant, his gaze in my direction – as unexpected an apparition as that of Banquo in *Macbeth*. Not even a robin could have appeared with less disturbance of its surroundings. Not a twig had snapped, not a leaf had rustled.

'He looked to be a man of about sixty or more, in his old greenish-black half-clerical garb, his trousers lapping concertina-like over immense ungainly boots. An antiquated black straw hat was on his head. From beneath it grey hair flowed out a little on either side the long colourless face with its straggling beard. His eyes were clear as water – the lids unusually wide apart – and they had the peculiarity, perceptible even at this distance, of not appearing to focus what their attention was fixed upon. That attention was fixed upon me as a matter of fact, and, standing as I was, with head turned in his direction, we so remained, closely regarding one another for what seemed to be a matter of hours rather than of moments.

'It was I who broke the silence with some affectedly-casual remark about the weather and the interestingness of the relic that stood, something like a huge mushroom of stone, nearby. The voice that sounded in answer was even more astonishing than Mr Kempe himself. It seemed to proceed from a throat rusty from want of use, and carried a kind of vibrant glassy note in it, like the clash of fine glass slightly cracked. At first I could not understand what he said. The sound of it reminds me now of Alexander Selkirk when his rescuers found him in Juan Fernandez. They said he spoke his words by halves, you'll remember. So did Mr Kempe. They sounded like relics of a tongue as ancient as the unknown hermit's chapel beside which we had met.

'Still, I was myself as nervous as a cat. With all his oddities – those wide, colourless eyes, those gestures, that over-loud voice, there was nothing hostile, nothing even discourteous in his manner, and he did not appear to be warning me off as a trespasser. Indeed the finger wagging at me in the air was clearly beckoning me on. Not that I had any keen inclination to follow. I preferred to go on watching him, and attempted to mark time by once more referring to the age and architecture of the chapel – asked him at last pointblank if it were now too late to beg the courtesy of a glance inside.

'The evening light momentarily brightened above the dark spreading tops of the pines and struck down full on this queer shape with its engrossed yet vacant face. His eyes never faltered, their pin-prick pupils fixed in their almost hueless irises. Reflected thus, I seemed to be an object of an extremely limited significance – a mere speck floating in their intense inane. The eyes of the larger cats and the hawk tribe have a similar effect; and yet one could hardly assert that their prey has no significance for *them*!

'He made no attempt to answer my questions, but appeared to be enquiring, in turn, how I had contrived to invade his solitude; what I wanted, in short. I was convinced none the less that he was deceiving me. He knew well how I had come: for, of course, meeting as we had, only one way had been possible – that from the sea.

'It might be impolitic to press the matter. I merely suggested that my journey had not been "roses all the way", that I must get back to the world above before nightfall; and once more gave him to understand my innocent purpose – the desire to examine this curious relic. His gaze wandered off to the stone hermitage, returned, and then as if in stealth, rested an instant intently on my hands. Otherwise he remained perfectly motionless: his long knotted fingers hanging down out of the sleeves of a jacket too short for his gaunt body – and those ineffable clumsy, rusty boots.

'The air in this green niche of the bay was stagnant with the scent of foliage and flowers; and so magically dark and clear it was as though you were in the presence of a dream. Or of a dreamer indeed – responsible not only for its beauty, but also for its menacing influence on the mind. All this, however, only convinced me the more of the necessity to keep my attention steadily fixed on the figure beside me. There was a something, an aura, about him difficult to describe. It was as if he himself were a long way off from his body – though that's pure nonsense, of course. As the phrase goes – he was not *all there*. Once more his eyes met mine, and the next thing that occurred to me was that I had never seen a human countenance that betrayed so desperate a hunger. But for what? It was impossible to tell.

'He was pressing me to follow him. I caught the word "key"; and he at once led the way. With a prolonged reluctant look behind me – that anti-quated cell of stone; those gigantic pines; the few sinking mounds clad in their fresh green turf – I turned in my tracks; and the glance he cast at me over his shoulder was intended, I gathered, as a smile of encouragement.

'The straggling gabled house to which he conducted me, with its low tower and smokeless chimneys now touched with the last cold red of sun-set, was almost more windows than wall. The dark glass of their casements showed like water in its discoloured sides. Beyond it the ravine ascended ever more narrowly, and the house rested here in this green gap like a mummy long since deserted by its ghost.

'We crossed a cobbled courtyard, and Mr Kempe preceded me up a wooden flight of stairs into a low-ceiled room with one all but ivy-blinded window, and, oddly enough, a stone floor. Except for the space where hung the faded portrait of what appeared to be a youngish woman, her hair dressed in ringlets, bookshelves covered the walls. Books lay hugger-mugger everywhere, indeed: on the table, on the chairs, on the floor, and even piled into the chimney of the rusty grate. The place was fusty with their leather bindings, and with damp.

'They had evidently been both well used and neglected. There was little opportunity to get the general range of their titles – though a complete row of them I noticed were in Latin – because some vague intuition compelled me to keep my attention fixed upon my host. He had motioned me to a chair, and had seated himself on another that was already topped with two or three folios. It must have been even at midday a gloomy room; and owing to its situation it was a dark house. The door having admitted us, stood open; beyond it yawned the silent staircase.'

At this the schoolmaster paused; the landlady of the Blue Boar had once more emerged, and, like one man, we shamefacedly pushed our three glasses across the counter.

'And what happened then?' I enquired.

At this the man in leggings slightly turned his tortoise-like head in my direction, as if its usual resort was beneath a shell.

The schoolmaster watched the shape of the landlady till it had vanished into the dusk beyond. 'Mr Kempe began talking to me,' he said. 'Rapidly and almost incoherently at first, but gradually slowing down till I could understand more or less what he was saying. He was explaining, a little unnecessarily as I fancied, that he was a recluse; that the chapel was not intended for public worship; that he had few visitors; that he was a scholar and therefore was in need of little company but his books. He swept his long arm towards these companions of his leisure. The little light that silted through the window struck down across his tousled head, just touching his brow and cheekbones as he talked. And then in the midst of this harangue he suddenly came to an end, and asked me if I had been sent there. I assured him that I had come of my own free will, and would he oblige me before we returned to the chapel, with a glass of water. He hesitated.

' "Water?" he repeated. "Oh, water?" And then with a peculiar gesture he crossed the room and shut the door after him. His boots beat as hollowly on the stairs as sticks on a tom-tom. I heard the creaking of a pump-handle, and in a moment he reappeared carrying a blue-lined cup without a handle. With a glance at the portrait over my head, I drank its ice-cold contents at a gulp, and pushed the cup in between two dogs-eared books.

' "I want to get back to the road up above," I explained.

'This seemed to reassure him. He shut his mouth and sat gazing at me. "Ah! The road up above!"

'Then, "Why?" he suddenly almost bawled at me, as if I were sitting a long way off. His great hands were clasped on his angled knees, his body bolt upright.

' "Why what?"

' "Why have you come here? What is there to spy out? This is private property. What do you do – for a living? What's the use of it all?"

'It was an unusual catechism – from stranger to stranger. But I had just escaped an unpleasant death, and could afford to be indulgent. Besides, he was years and years older than I. I told him that I was a schoolmaster, on vacation, not thinking it necessary to add that owing to a small legacy I was out of a job at the time. I said I was merely enjoying myself.

' "Enjoying yourself! And you teach!" he cried with a snap of his jaw. "And what do you teach? Silly, suffocating lies, I suppose; or facts, as you prefer to call them." He drew his hand down his long colourless face, and I stole a glance towards the door. "If human beings *are* mere machines, well and good," he went on. "But supposing, my young friend, they are not mere machines? Supposing they have souls in their bodies; what then?

Supposing *you* have a soul in your body: what then? Ay, and the proof; the proof!"'

The schoolmaster's face puckered up once more into a genial smile.

'I won't attempt,' he went on, 'to repeat word for word the talk I had that evening. I can give only the gist of it. But I had stumbled pretty abruptly, you'll notice, on Mr Kempe's King Charles's head. And he presented me with it on a charger. He was possessed, I gathered, by one single aim, thought and desire. All these years of his "retirement" had apparently been spent in this one quest – to *prove* man's possession of a "Soul". Certain doubts in my mind sprang up a little later in the evening, but it was clear from the beginning that in pursuit of this he had spared neither himself nor the wife that was gone. It was no less clear that he was entirely incapable of what better brains, no doubt, would have considered a scientific treatment of his theme.

'He thrust into my hand a few chapters of a foolscap manuscript that lay on the table – a fly-blown murky pile of paper at least eighteen inches high. Never have I seen anything to which the term "reading-*matter*" seemed more appropriate. The ink was faded on the top page; it was stained as if with tea. This work was entitled briefly, "The Soul" – though the sub-title that followed it would not have disgraced the author of the "Anatomy".

'I could follow no more than a line or two at a time of the crazy handwriting. The pages were heavily interscored, annotated and revised, not only in pencil but in violet and in red ink. A good part of it appeared to be in Latin and Hebrew, and other inactive tongues. But turning them over at haphazard I caught such page-headings as "Contemplation"; "Dreams"; "Flagellation"; "Cadaver"; "Infancy". I replaced the sheets a little gingerly on the table, though one mustn't, of course, judge of the merits of a work by the appearance of it in MS.

'The desolation of its author's looks and his abruptness of manner thinned away awhile as he warmed to his subject. But it was not so much his own sufferings in the cause as the thought of what Mrs Kempe's last few years on earth must have been to her, that made me an attentive listener. Hers must indeed have proved a lingering death. He had never left her side, I gathered, for weeks at a time, except to tend his patch of garden, and to prepare their niggardly meals. And as her body had wasted, poor soul, his daily inquisition, his daily probings had become ever more urgent and desperate.

'There was no doubt in the world that this afflicted old man had loved his wife. The softening of the vacant inhuman eyes as he told me of that last deathbed colloquy was enough to prove that. Maybe it was in part because of this affection that mere speculation had sharpened into what they call an *idée fixe*. Still, I hardly think so. More probably the insidious germ had shared his cradle. And after all, some degree of conviction on the subject is not out of place in men of his cloth. He had abandoned his calling indeed, he was assuring me, solely as a proof of his zeal!

'He showed me also one or two late photographs of Mrs Kempe – taken with his own antiquated camera, and "developed" maybe in this very room. Soul indeed! There was little else. The face murkily represented in them wore a peculiar remote smile. The eyes had been hollowly directed towards the round leather cap of the machine. And so fallen were the features, now fading away on the discoloured paper, they might as well have been the presentment of a ghost.

'What precise proofs he had actually demanded of this companion of his hermitage I cannot even guess. And what proofs might he still be pleading for, pursuing? Evidently none as yet had satisfied his craving. But it was at least to his credit that his own personal experiments – experiments on himself, I mean – had been as drastic. In one of them I had unwittingly shared. For the cliff path, I discovered, had long been his constant penance. A cat-like foot was concealed beneath those Brobdingnagian boots. His had been the hand that had not only helped Nature protect her fastnesses, but had kept off all but one or two occasional stragglers as fatuous as myself.

'It had been his haunt, this path – day and night. He questioned the idle heavens there. In the face of a peril so extreme the spirit wins almost to the point of severance from its earthly clay. Night and a half-moon and the northern constellations – I could at least in fancy share his vigils there. Only an occasional ship ventures into sight of that coast, but almost any day, it seemed, during these last few years a good spyglass might have discerned from its decks a human shape facing the Infinite from that appalling eyrie.

'Both delusions and illusions, too, are rapid breeders. Which of the two, I wondered – still wonder – was *this* old man's conviction – the conviction, I mean, that one is likely to be more acutely conscious of the spirit within when the body is suspended, as it were, from the lintel of death's door. What dreams may come in such circumstances every practical psychologist no doubt would merely pooh-pooh. Still, after all, Mr Kempe had been something of a pioneer in this inquest. He had not spared himself. He could not live by faith, it seemed. He must indeed again and again have come uncommonly near dying in the pursuit of it.

'He had fasted moreover, and was now little more than a mere frame of bones within his outlandish clothes. Those boots of his – they kept forcing themselves on my attention – a worse fit than any worn by some homesick desperate soldier clambering "over the top" in the Great War. They stuck in my mind.

' "You don't seem to realize – you folk out there don't seem to realize" he suddenly began shouting at me, "that nothing in this world is of the slightest importance compared with a Yes or No to what I ask. If we are nothing more than the brutes that perish – and no sign ever comes from them, I may tell you – then let us perish, I say. Let fire descend from Heaven and shrivel us up. I care not in what cataclysm of horror. I have passed them all. I am suggesting no blasphemy. I make no challenge; no denial – merely a humble plodder, my dear sir. But no! Nothing. Nothing. Nothing. Not a word." He lifted himself out of his chair, opened the door, looked out and came back again.

' "I disapprove" – he brandished his outspread fingers at me – "I disapprove absolutely of peering and prying. Your vile pernicious interferences with the natural mysteries which we as humanity inherited from the old Adam – away with them! I declare I am a visitor here. I declare that this" – he swept his hand down his meagre carcase, – "this is my mere tenancy. All that I seek is the simplest proof. A proof, that would not so much as stay a pulse-beat in the vile sceptics that give their wretched lives to what they call Science.

' "I am not even a philosopher," he ejaculated. "I am here alone, a way-faring man and a fool. Alone – in the face of this one supreme mystery. And I need aid!" His voice ceased; he threw out his hands and sat there emptily gazing at me.

'And so he continued. Now he would lift himself out of his chair and prowling from shelf to shelf, scanning at but an inch or two distant the titles of their contents, would thrust volume after volume into my hands for evidence, accompanying his clumsy motions with peevish and broken comments impossible to follow. I was presently surrounded with these things as with a surf.

'Then he would once more seat himself, and embark on a protracted harangue with that cracked disused voice rising steadily until it broke in a discordant screech of argument.

' "Almighty God," he yelled at me, "you sit there, living, breathing, a human being; and the one justification of this hideous masquerade left uncertain." He flung his hand into the air. "What right has he even to share the earth with me!" he shouted into the quiet.

'Then once more there followed as swift a return to silence, to self-possession – that intent devouring stare. One at least knows oneself to be something objective in any chance-encountered pair of human eyes. In his, as I have said already, I appeared to have no material existence whatsoever. Mr Kempe might have been surveying, talking to, his own shadow. It was peculiarly disconcerting.

'After yet another such outburst he had for a moment lain back in his chair as if exhausted. And I was so intent in my scrutiny of him that a second or two went by before I sprang forward to pick up the few dingy photographs that had fallen out of his hand on to the grimy patch of carpet beneath. But he himself had stooped even more abruptly, and our skulls collided together with a crack that for the moment all but dazed me.

'But the eye moves almost as swiftly as the mind, and the collision had not been hasty enough to prevent my snatching a glimpse of one or two of them, photographs of which neither this widower nor his wife had been the original. I drew back appalled – their details fixed in my mind as if etched there by a flash of lightning. And, leaving him to gather up his further evidences as best he could, I instantly found myself edging towards the door. Those squalid oblongs of cardboard were easily concealed in his immense palm. He pawed them together as clumsily as a bear might combs of honey; then slowly raised his grey dishevelled head, and met my eyes.

'I paused. "You have had other visitors at times?" I queried as mildly as my tongue would allow.

' "What visitors, young man, do you mean, may I ask?" An extraordinary change had come into his voice – a flatness, an obsequiousness. The ingratiating tones were muffled, as if he could hardly trust himself to speak. For a while I could only gape in reply.

' "Like myself," I blurted out at last. "Visitors who come to – well, out of sheer curiosity. There's the other route, I suppose?"

'My one desire just then was to keep my thoughts about Mr Kempe rational and within bounds. To make a monster of him would be merely to lose my head once more as I had already lost it on that afternoon's journey. None the less I was now looking at him through the after-image of those chance-seen photographs. They were a disturbing medium. The body of a human being who has fallen from a great height is not pleasing and pacifying to look at even though for a while its owner may have survived the fatality. There were others, too; and yet, it was less his photographs than the amateur photographer that had set my teeth on edge. He looked so old and so helpless – like an animal, as I say, enslaved by – and yet incapable of obeying – some heaven-sent instinct. That terrifying, doglike despair!

'But then, open your newspaper any fine morning of your life, and which is the more likely to greet you on the news-page: the innocent young lady in the pink gauze petticoats over there, or that old figure of fun in the monk's cowl?'

The tortoiselike shape of the man in leggings once more stirred on its stool. But this time his little eyes were turned in my direction.

'How did you manage to get out at last?' I enquired of the schoolmaster.

'Well,' he said, 'all this time Mr Kempe had been watching me as circumspectly as I had been watching him, but as if, too, he were uncertain how many paces distant from him I stood. Then once more voice and manner changed. He feigned to be reassured. "It has been a wonderful day," he remarked, with the dignity of an old retired scholar whose dubious fortune it has been to entertain a foreign prince; "a wonderful day. And my only regret is that I was unprepared for the occasion; that I have so poor a hospitality to offer. You may have had an exceedingly painful experience this afternoon. Why, my dear sir, in the absence of mind that comes over me once I embark on this hobby of mine, I haven't even asked you to wash your hands."

'Almost involuntarily I glanced down at them. Like Macbeth's they needed the invitation. But I must confess I preferred this old minister when he was not talking to me as if I were an imbecile child in a Sunday School. Besides, I knew perfectly well that – whether from that tumbling watch-tower of his, or from some hiding-place in the woods – there had been one intent witness of that experience. I thrust my hands into my pockets out of his sight.

' "If you will await me here a moment,' he went on – and his utterance began to thicken again, "I will get the key to the chapel – a remarkable, even unique example of its order. There was a well, too, in former times, and even archeologists have failed to agree about its date. They used to come; they used to come: and would argue, too. Why I can *prove* it is in parts at least not later than the ninth century. And the interior... but, dear me, it will soon be dark; and – no – you mustn't think of leaving the house to-night. I need company; I *need* it." He poked forward at me again, while yet furtively and rapidly edging towards the door.

'With a peculiar disinclination to come into the very slightest contact with his person, I had to dodge out of his way to allow him to pass, and attempted to do so without appearing to show like a visitor who has strayed by mischance into the cage of a dangerous animal in some zoological garden. The old grey tousled head turned not an inch upon its heavy angular shoulders as he passed me; but in the dimming light of the window I caught a glimpse of the wide sea-like eyes intently fixed on me – like lifeless planets in the waste of space.

'Even a young man may have intimations of the fool he is about to prove himself. Intimations, I mean, that come too late. Before the cumbrous door had closed behind him, I was listening for the sound of the key being turned in the lock. I didn't even wait to try the handle, but tiptoed as rapidly as possible over the heaped-up books on the floor towards the window. It was one of dingy oblong panes, and the hasp was broken. The drop beneath its sill – to any one at least who had reached the house by the less easy way of the two roads – was almost as easy as getting into bed. It would land me some ten feet below on a heap of vegetable rubbish. But the hinges of the window had been allowed to rust, and the wood to shrink and swell with the changing seasons.

'Not a sound had followed the locking of the door, and unless Mr Kempe had disencumbered his feet of their boots, he was at that moment collecting his wits immediately outside of it. I tiptoed across once more. "Please don't let me be any trouble," I bawled. "I could come again another time."

'The next instant I was back at the window, listening. The answer boomed down at me at last from some room above. But I could distinguish no words – merely a senseless babble. It would be indiscreet, it seemed, to hesitate any longer. I seized a frowsy cushion and with all my force thrust it against the rotten frame of the window. It flew open with but one explosive crack. I was prepared for it. Once more I paused. Then after a last hasty glance round that dismal laboratory, its scattered books, fusty papers, blackened ceiling, broken lamp – and that one half-obliterated portrait of the gentle apologetic faded young woman on the wall, I clambered soundlessly on to the sill, and dropped. The refuse below was thoroughly rotten; not a twig snapped.

'The moment I touched ground I regretted this ignominious exit. There was I, a young man – thirty to forty years at least the junior of Mr Kempe – a young man who, whether or not possessed of a soul, was at least fairly capable in body. Surely I might have ventured! – life has more riddles than one. But I did not pursue these thoughts far. The very look and appearance of the house as I glanced up at the window out of which I had descended so abruptly, its overhanging gable, its piebald darkened walls rising towards the first stars under the last of twilight – it was hardly less unhappy and unpleasing company than its tenant.

'I groped my way beyond its purlieus as quickly and silently as I could, mounted a low wall and was already in the woods. By luck I had caught a glimpse of the Plough straddling above the chimneys, so I knew my north, and edged off upwards and westwards for some little distance under the motionless trees before I came to a halt.

'The house was now out of sight, its owner once more abandoned to his own resources, and researches. And I was conscious of no particular desire to return to examine the interior of the small stone chapel nor the inscriptions on the few headstones which memoralized those who had been longest slumbering in the ground nearby.

'Possibly I was not the only visitor who had bidden the recluse in this valley so unmannerly a farewell. I cannot at any rate imagine anyone simpleton enough to venture back even in response to the sound of hysterical weeping that came edging across the silence of the woods.'

'D'ye mean that old man was *crying*?' queried our friend in leggings.

The drizzle in the lane outside the Inn had plucked up courage as daylight ebbed, and had increased to a steady downpour. He had to repeat his question.

'I mean,' said the schoolmaster a little acidly, 'exactly what I say. I am nothing much of a traveller, or perhaps I could tell you what resemblance the noise of it had to the cajolings of a crocodile.'

'My God!' coughed the other derisively. With this he seemed to have finally made up his mind, and lurched heavily off his stool. And without even so much as a 'good-night' to our landlady, he betook himself out of the bar.

Except for the noise of the rain a complete silence followed his departure.

'And you never went back?' I ventured presently. 'Or – or spoke about the matter?'

'I mean, do you see,' said the schoolmaster, 'I acted like a fool. I should have taken Mr Kempe simply on his face value. There was nothing to complain about. He hadn't *invited* me to come and see him. And it was hardly his fault, I suppose, if an occasional visitor failed to complete so precarious a journey. I wouldn't go so far as that. He was merely one of those would-be benefactors to the human race who go astray; get lost, ramble on down the wrong turning. *Qua* pioneer, I ask,' he rapped his fingers on the pewter of the counter, 'was he exceptional?' He was arguing with himself, not with me.

I nodded. 'But what was your impression – was *he* sure – Mr Kempe? Either way?'

'The Soul?'

'Yes,' I echoed, 'the Soul.'

But I repeated the word under my breath, for something in the sound of our voices seemed to have attracted the attention of the landlady. And, alas, she had decided to light up.

The solemnity of man's remotest ancestors lay over the schoolmaster's features. 'I can't say,' he replied. 'I am not certain even if he was aware how densely populated his valley appeared to be – to a chance visitor, I mean. What's more, to judge from the tones of his voice, he had scarcely the effect of a single personality. There were at least three Mr Kempes present that evening. And I haven't the faintest wish in the world to meet any one of them again.'

'And afterwards? Was it comparatively easy finding your way – on to the new cliff road?'

'Comparatively,' said the schoolmaster. 'Though it took time. But nights are fairly short in May, even in country as thickly wooded as that.'

I continued to look at him without speaking; yet another unuttered question on my lips.

To judge from the remote friendly smile he just blinked at me, he appeared to have divined it, though it produced no direct answer. He got down from his stool, looked at his empty glass – and for the first time I noticed he was wearing mittens over his small bluish hands. 'It's getting late,' he said, with an eye fixed vacantly once more on the automatic machine in the corner of the tap-room. There was no denying it; nor that even the musty interior of the Blue Boar looked more hospitable than the torrential darkness of the night outside.

How strange is man. The spectacle depressed me beyond words – as if it had any more significance than that for its passing hour a dense yet not inbeneficent cloud was spread betwixt this earth of ours and the faithful shining of the stars.

But I did not mention this to the schoolmaster. He seemed to be lost in a dark melancholy, his face a maze of wrinkles. And beyond him – in a cracked looking-glass – I could see his double, sitting there upon its stool. I was conscious that in some way I had bitterly disappointed him. I looked at him – my hand on the door-handle – waiting to go out...

Missing*

It was the last day of a torrid week in London – the flaming crest of what the newspapers call a *heat wave*. The exhausted inmates of the dazzling, airless streets – plate-glass, white stone, burnished asphalt, incessant roar, din, fume and odour – have the appearance at such times of insects trapped in an oven of a myriad labyrinthine windings and chambers; a glowing brazen maze to torture Christians in. To have a *mind* even remotely resembling it must be Satan's sole privilege!

I had been shopping; or rather, I had been loafing about from one department on to another in one of the huge 'stores' in search of bathing-drawers, a preventative of insect bites, and a good holiday 'shocker', and had retired at last incapable of buying anything – even in a world where pretty well everything except peace of mind can be bought, and sold. The experience had been oppressive and trying to the temper.

Too hot, too irritable even to lunch, I had drifted into a side street, and then into a second-hand bookshop that happened still to be open this idle Saturday afternoon; and having for ninepence acquired a copy of a book on psycho-analysis which I didn't want and should never read, I took refuge in a tea shop.

In spite of the hot-water fountain on the counter it was a degree or two cooler in here, though even the marble-top tables were tepid to the touch.

* As printed in BS (1942), but also including a manuscript alteration made by de la Mare in his copy of C (1926).

Quiet and drowsy, too. A block of ice surmounted the dinner-wagon by the counter. The white clock face said a quarter to three. Few chairs were now occupied; the midday mellay was over. A heavy slumbrousness muffled the place – the flies were as idle as the waitresses, and the waitresses were as idle as the flies.

I gave my order, and sat back exhausted in a listless vacancy of mind and body. And my dazed eyes, having like the flies little of particular interest to settle on, settled on the only fellow reveller that happened to be sitting within easy reach. At first glimpse there could hardly be a human being you would suppose less likely to attract attention. He was so scrupulously respectable, so entirely innocent of 'atmosphere'. Even a Chelsea psychic would have been compelled to acknowledge that this particular human being had either disposed of his aura or had left it at home. And yet my first glimpses of him had drawn me out of the vacuum into which I had sunk as easily as a cork is drawn out of an empty bottle.

He was sitting at a table to the left, and a little in front of me. The glare from the open door and the gentler light from the cream-blinded shop window picked out his every hair and button. It flooded in on him from the sparkling glittering street, focused him, 'placed' him, arranged him – as if for a portrait in the finest oils for next year's Academy. Limelight on the actor-manager traversing the blasted heath is mere child's play by comparison.

Obviously he was not 'the complete Londoner' – though that can hardly be said to be a misfortune. On the other hand, there was nothing rural, and only a touch or so of the provincial, in his appearance. He wore a neat – an excessively neat – pepper-and-salt tweed suit, the waistcoat cut high and exhibiting the points of a butterfly collar and a triangle of black silk cravat slipped through a gold mourning ring. His ears maybe were a little out of the mode. They had been attached rather high and flat on either side of his conical head with its dark, glossy, silver-speckled hair.

The nose was straight, the nostrils full. They suggested courage of a kind; possibly, even, on occasion, bravado. He looked the kind of man, I mean, it is well to keep out of a corner. But the eyes that were now peering vacantly down that longish nose over a trim but unendearing moustache at the crumbs on his empty plate were too close together. So, at least, it seemed to me. But then I am an admirer of the wide expressive brow – such as our politicians and financiers display. Those eyes at any rate gave this spruce and respectable person just a hint, a glint of the fox. I have never heard, though, that the fox is a dangerous animal even in a corner; only that he has his wits about him and preys on geese – whereas my stranger in the tea shop had been refreshing himself with Osborne biscuits.

It was hot. The air was parched and staled. And heat – unless in Oriental regions – is not conducive to exquisite manners. Far otherwise. I continued to watch this person, indolently speculating whether his little particularities of appearance did not match, or matched too precisely. Those ears and that cravat, for example; or those spruce-moustached nostrils and the glitter of the close-neighbouring eyes. And why had he brought to mind a tightly-packed box with no address on it? He began to be a burden, yet I could not keep my eyes away from him – nor from his hands. They were powerful and hairy, with large knuckles; and now that they were not in use he had placed them on his knees under the dark polished slab of his marble table. Beneath those knees rested his feet (the toes turned in a little) in highly-polished boots, with thickish soles and white socks.

There is, I agree, something peculiarly vulgar in thus picking a fellow-creature to pieces. But even Keats so dissected Miss Brawne; and even when he was in love with her: and it was certainly not love at first sight between myself and this stranger.

Whether he knew it or not, he was attaching himself to me; he was making his influence felt. It was odd, then, that he could remain so long unconscious of so condensed a scrutiny. Maybe that particular nerve in him had become atrophied. He looked as if a few other rather important nerves might be atrophied. When he did glance up at me – the waitress having appeared with my tea at the same moment – there was a far-away startled look in his bleak blue-black eyes – as if he had been called back.

Nothing more; and even at that it was much such a look as had been for some little time fixed on the dry biscuit crumbs in his empty plate. He seemed indeed to be a man accustomed to being startled or surprised into vigilance without reason. But having seen me looking at him, he did not hesitate. He carefully took up his hat, his horn-handled and gold-mounted umbrella, and a large rusty scaling leather bag that lay on a chair beside him; rose; and stepping gently over with an almost catlike precision, seated himself in the chair opposite to mine. I continued to pour out my tea.

'You will excuse me troubling you,' he began in a voice that suggested he could sing tenor though he spoke bass, 'but would you kindly tell me the number of the omnibus that goes from here to King's Cross? I am a stranger to this part of London.'

I called after the waitress: 'What is the number of the bus,' I said, 'that goes from here to King's Cross?'

'The number of the bus, you say, that goes from here to King's Cross?'

'Yes,' I said, 'to King's Cross.'

'I'm sure *I* don't know,' she said. 'I'll ask the counter.' And she tripped off in her silk stockings and patent leather shoes.

'The counter will know,' I assured him. He looked at me, moving his lips over his teeth as if either or both for some reason had cause to be uneasy.

'I am something of a stranger to London altogether,' he said, 'and I don't usually come these ways: it's a novelty to me. The omnibuses are very convenient.'

'Don't you? Is it?' I replied. 'Why not?' They were rather point-blank questions (and a gentleman, said Dr Johnson, does not ask questions) but somehow they had slipped out as if at his pressing invitation.

He looked at me, his eyes seeming to draw together into an intenser focus. He was not exactly squinting, but I have noticed a similar effect in the eyes of a dog when its master is about to cry 'Fetch it!'

'You see,' he said, 'I live in the country, and only come to London when I seem to need company – badly, I mean. There's a great contrast between the country and this. All these houses. So many strange faces. It takes one out of oneself.'

I glanced round at the sparsely occupied tables. A cloud apparently had overlaid the sun, for a dull coppery glow was now reflected from the drowsy street. I could even hear the white-faced clock ticking. To congratulate him on his last remark would hardly have been courteous after so harmless an advance. I merely looked at him. What kind of self, I was vaguely speculating, would return into his hospitality when he regained his usual haunts?

'I have a nice little place down there,' he went on, 'but there's not much company. Lonely: especially now. Even a few hours makes all the difference. You would be surprised how friendly a place London can be; the people, I mean. Helpful.'

What can only be described as a faint whinny had sounded in his voice as he uttered that 'helpful'. Was he merely to prove yet another of those unfortunate travellers who have lost the return halves of their railway tickets? Had he marked me down for his prey!

'It is not so much what they say,' he continued, laying his hand on the marble table; 'but just their being about, you know.' I glanced at the heavy ring on its third finger and then at his watch-chain – woven apparently of silk or hair – with little gold rings at intervals along it to secure the plait. His own gaze continued to rest on me with so penetrating, so corkscrew-like an intensity, that I found myself glancing over my shoulder in search of the waitress. She however was now engaged in animated argument with the young lady at the pay-desk.

'Do you live *far* from London?' I ventured.

'About seventy miles,' he replied with an obvious gulp of relief at this impetus to further conversation. 'A nice old house too considering the rent, roomy enough but not too large. Its only drawback in some respects is there's nothing near it – not within call, I mean; and we – I – suffer from the want of a plentiful supply of water. Especially now.'

Why so tactless a remark on this broiling afternoon should have evoked so vivid a picture of a gaunt yellow-brick building perched amid sloping fields parched lint-white with a tropical drought, its garden little more than a display of vegetable anatomies, I cannot say. It was a house of a hideous aspect; but I confess it stirred my interest. Whereupon my stranger, apparently, thought he could safely glance aside; and I could examine him more at leisure. It was not, I have to confess, a taking face. There was a curious hollowness in its appearance. He looked like the shell of a man, or rather, like a hermit crab – that neat pepper-and-salt tweed suit and so on being a kind of second-hand accumulation on his back.

'And of course,' he began again, 'now that I am alone I become' – he turned sharply back on me – 'I become more conscious of it.'

'Of the loneliness?' I suggested.

Vacancy appeared on his face, as if he had for the instant stopped thinking. 'Yes,' he replied, once more transfixing me with those bleak close eyes of his, 'the loneliness. It seems to worsen more and more as the other slips away into the past. But I suppose we most of us have much the same experience; just of that, I mean. And even in London . . .'

I busied myself with my tea things, having no particular wish at the moment to continue the conversation. But he hadn't any intention of losing his victim as easily as all that.

'There's a case now here in the newspaper this morning,' he went on, his glance wandering off to a copy of the *Daily Mail* that lay on the chair next the one he had just vacated. 'A man not much older than I am – "found dead". Dead. The only occupant of quite a good-sized house, I should judge, at Stoke Newington – though I don't know the place personally. Lived there for years on end without even a charwoman to do for him – to – to work for him. Still even there there was some kind of company, I suppose. He could look out of the window; he could hear people moving about next door. Where I am, there isn't another house in sight, not even a barn, and so far as I can see, what they call Nature doesn't become any the more friendly however long you stay in a place – the birds and that kind of thing. It may get better in time; but it's only a few months ago since I was left quite like this. When my sister died.'

Obviously I was hooked beyond hope of winning free again until this corkscrew persistent creature had had his way with me. The only course seemed to be to get the experience over as quickly as possible. It is not easy, however, to feign an active sympathy; and mention of his dead sister had produced in my mind only a faint reflex image of a dowdy lady no longer young in dingy black. Still, it was an image that proved to be not very far from the actuality.

'Any close companionship like that', I murmured, 'when it is broken is a tragic thing.'

He appeared to have seen no significance in my remark. 'And you see, once there were three of us. Once. It never got into the papers – at least not into the London papers, except just by mention, I mean.' He moistened his lips. 'Did you ever happen to come across a report about a lady, a Miss Dutton, who was "missing"?'

It was a pretty stupid question, for after all, few human beings are so gifted as to be able to recall the names even of the protagonists in genuine *causes célèbres*. To bear in mind every sort of Miss Dutton whose disappearance would be referred to only in news-snippets borrowed by the Metropolitan press from the provincial, would be rather too much of a tax even for those interested in such matters. I sipped my tea and surveyed him as sagaciously as possible; 'Not that I can actually recall,' I said. 'Miss – Dutton? It isn't a very uncommon name. You knew her?'

'Knew her!' he repeated, placing his hands on his knees and sitting stiffly back in his chair, his eyes unflinchingly fixed on mine. 'She lived with us a matter of two years or more. It was us she left. It was my house she was missing from. It caused quite a stir in the neighbourhood. It was the talk of the countryside. There was an Inquiry; and all that.'

'How long ago?'

'Pretty near a year ago. Yes; a year yesterday.'

'Do you mean the Inquiry, or when Miss Dutton disappeared?'

'The Inquiry,' he replied in a muffled fashion, as if a little annoyed at my want of perspicacity. 'The other was – oh, a month or more before that.'

The catechism was becoming a rather laborious way of extracting a story, but somehow its rudiments had begun to interest me. I had nothing to do. To judge from the look of the street, the quicksilver in the thermometer was still edging exquisitely upwards. I detested the thought of emerging into that oven. So apparently did my companion, unless the mere sound of his voice seemed to him better entertainment than, say, the nearest 'picture palace' – where at least one would be out of sight and it would be dark.

'I should have thought,' I began again in a voice as unconcerned as I could manage, 'that living as you do, a stir in the neighbourhood would not much matter, though I agree that the mystery itself must have mattered a good deal more. That of course must have been a great shock to you both.'

'Ay,' he said, with a gleam in his eye, 'but that's just what you Londoners don't seem to understand. You have your newspapers and all that. But in most ways you don't get talked about much. It's not so in the country. I guarantee you might be living right in the middle of the Yorkshire Moors and yet, if it came to there being anything to keep their tongues wagging, you'd know that your neighbours were talking of you, and what about, for miles around. It gets across – like those black men's drums one hears about in West Africa. As if the mere shock of the thing wasn't enough! What I feel about it is that nowadays people don't seem to show any sympathy, any ordinary feeling with – with those in such circumstances; at least, not country people. Wouldn't you say yourself,' he added, with feline rapidity, 'that if *you* were reported as missing it would be rough luck if nobody cared?'

'I don't quite see what you mean,' I replied. 'I thought you said that the disappearance of your friend made a stir in the neighbourhood.'

'Yes; but they were not thinking so much of *her* as of the cause of it.'

We exchanged a long glance, but without much addition to my own small fund of information. 'But surely,' I ventured, that must depend upon where she was supposed to have disappeared *to*?'

'That,' he replied, 'they never knew. We couldn't find out not one iota about it. You've no idea' – he drew his hands down over his face as if to clear away a shadow from his eyes – 'you've no idea. Since she has gone I feel almost sometimes as if she can never have been real. *There*, but not real; if you understand me. I see her; and then the real thing goes again. It never occurred to me, that.'

'The psychologists would tell us something about that.'

'The what?' he asked sharply.

'Oh, those who profess to explain the workings of the mind. After all, we can't definitely say whether that teapot there is real – what it is in itself, I mean. And merely to judge from its looks,' I added, 'one might hope it was a pure illusion.'

He looked hard at the teapot. 'Miss Dutton was a very well-preserved woman for her age,' he said. 'And when I say "not real", it's only in a manner of speaking, I mean. I've got her portrait in the newspaper in my pocket-book. That ought to prove her real enough. I never knew any one who was more "all there", as they say. She was a good friend to me – I have every reason to remember her. She came along of her own free will – just a chance meeting. In Scarborough, as a matter of fact. And she liked the comforts of a home after all those hotels and boarding-houses.'

In the course of these ruminating and mournful remarks – and there was unmistakable 'feeling' in his tones – he was rather privily turning over the contents of an old leather pocket-book with an inelastic black band. He drew out a frayed newspaper cutting and put it down on the table beside the teapot.

'Looking at that, you wouldn't be in much doubt what Miss Dutton was in herself, now, would you? You'd recognize her,' he raised his eyes, 'if she were – if you met her, I mean, in these awful streets? I would myself.'

It was impossible to decide whether this last remark was ironical, triumphant, embittered, or matter-of-fact; so I looked at Miss Dutton. She was evidently a blonde and a well-preserved woman, as my friend had intimated; stoutish, with a plump face, a plump nose, infantile blue eyes, frizzy hair, and she wore (what a few years ago were old-fashioned and are now new-fashioned) long ear-rings.

It was curious what a stabilizing effect the ear-rings produced. They resembled the pole Blondin used to carry as he tripped across his rope over the Niagara Falls. Miss Dutton was looking out of her blurred image with a sort of insouciance, gaiety, 'charm', the charm that photographers aim at but rather seldom convey. Destiny, apparently, casts no retrospective shadow. I defy anybody to have found the faintest hint in that aware, vain, commonplace, good-natured face which would suggest Miss Dutton was ever going to be 'missed' – missed, I mean, in the sense of becoming indiscoverable. In the other sense her friends would no doubt miss her a good deal. But then boarding-houses and hotels are the resorts rather of acquaintances than of friends.

The owner of the newspaper snippet was scrutinizing the gay, blurred photograph with as much interest as I was; though to him it was upside-down. There was a queer foolish look on his face, a little feline, perhaps, in its sentimentality.

I pushed back the cutting across the marble table and he carefully re-interred it in his pocket-book. 'I was wondering,' he rambled on as he did so, 'what you might have thought of it – without prejudice, so to speak, if you had come across it – casually-like; in the newspaper, I mean?'

The question was not quite so simple as it sounded. It appeared as if my new acquaintance were in wait for a comment which he himself was eager to supply. And I had nothing much to say.

'It's difficult, you know, to judge from prints in newspapers,' I commented at last. 'They are usually execrable even as caricatures. But she looks, if I may say so, an uncommonly genial woman: feminine – and a practical one, too. Not one, I mean, who would be likely to be missing, except on purpose – of her own choice, that is.' Our eyes met an instant. 'The whole business must have been very disturbing, a great anxiety to you. And, of course, to Miss... to your sister, I mean.'

'My name,' he retorted abruptly, shutting his eyes while a bewildering series of expressions netted themselves on his face, 'my name is Bleet.'

'Miss Bleet,' I added, glancing at the pocket into which the book had by now disappeared, and speculating, too, why so preposterous an *alias* should have occurred to apparently so ready a tongue.

'You were saying "genial",' he added rapidly. 'And that is what they all agreed. Even her only male relative – an uncle, as he called himself, though I can swear she never mentioned him in that or in any other capacity. She hadn't always been what you might call a happy woman, mind you. But they were bound to agree that those two years under my care – in our house – were the happiest in Miss Dutton's life. We made it a real home to her.

She had her own rooms and her few bits of furniture – photographs, what-nots and so on, quite private. It's a pretty large house considering the rent – countrified, you know; and there was a sort of a new wing added to it fifty years or more ago. Old-fashioned, of course – open fireplace, no bath, enormous kitchen range – swallows coal by the bushel – and so on – very inconvenient but cheap. And though my sister was not in a position to supervise the housekeeping, there couldn't be a more harmless and affectionate creature. To those, that is, who were kind to her. She'd run away from those who weren't – just run away and hide. I must explain that my poor sister was not quite – was a little weak in her intellects – from her childhood. It was always a great responsibility. But as time went on,' he drew his hand wearily over his face, 'Miss Dutton herself very kindly relieved me of a good deal of that. You said she looked a practical woman; so she was.'

His narrative was becoming steadily more personal, and disconcerting. And yet – such is humanity – it was as steadily intensifying in interest. A menacing rumble of thunder at that moment sounded over the street, and a horse clattered down with its van beyond the open door. My country friend did not appear to have noticed it.

'You never know quite where you are with the ladies,' he suddenly ejaculated, and glanced piercingly up – for at that moment our waitress had drawn near.

'It's a 'Ighteen,' she said, pencil on lip, and looking vacantly from one to the other of us.

' "Ighteen",' echoed her customer sharply; 'what's that? Oh the omnibus. You didn't say what you meant. Thank you.' She hovered on, check-book in hand. 'And please bring me another cup of coffee.' He looked at me as if with the intention of duplicating his order. I shook my head. 'One cup, then, miss; no hurry.'

The waitress withdrew.

'It looks as if rain was coming,' he went on, and as if he were thirsting for it as much as I was. 'As I was saying, you can never be quite sure where you are with women; and, mind you, Miss Dutton was a woman of the world. She had seen a good deal of life – been abroad – Gay Paree, Monte Carlo, and all that. Germany before the war, too. She could read French as free and easy as you could that mennoo there. Paper-bound books with pictures on them, and that kind of thing.' He was looking at me, I realized, as if there were no other way of intimating the particular kind of literature he had in mind.

'I used to wonder sometimes what she could find in us, such a lonely place; no company. Though, of course, she was free to ask any friends if she wanted to, and talked of them too when in the mood. Good class, to judge from what she said. What I mean is, she was quite her own mistress. And I must say there could not be more good humour and so on than what she showed my poor sister. At least, until later. She'd talk to her as if conversing; and my sister would sit there by the window, looking back at her and smiling and nodding just as if she were taking it all in. And who knows, perhaps she was. What I mean is, it's possible to have things in your head which you can't quite put into so many words. It's one of the things I look for when I come up to London: the faces that could tell a story though what's behind them can't.'

I nodded.

'I can assure you that before a few weeks were over she had got to be as much at home with us as if we had known her all our lives. Chatty and domesticated, and all that. And using the whole house just as if it belonged to her. All the other arrangements were easy, too. I can say now, and I said it then, that we never once up to then demeaned ourselves to a single word of disagreement about money matters or anything else. A woman like that, who has been all over the continent, isn't likely to go far wrong in that. I agree the terms were on the generous side; but then, you take me, so were the arrangements.

'She asked herself to raise them when she had been with us upwards of twelve months. But I said "No". I said, "A bargain's a bargain, Edna" – we were "Edna" and "William" to one another, by then, and my sister too. She was very kind to my poor sister; got a specialist up all the way from Bath – though for all his prying questions he did nothing, as I knew he wouldn't. You can't take those things so late. Mind you, as I say, the business arrangements were not all on one side. Miss Dutton liked things select and comfortable. She liked things to go smoothly; as we all do, I reckon. She had been accustomed to smart boarding-houses and hotels – that kind of thing. And I did my level best to keep things nice.'

My stranger's face dropped into a rather gloomy expression, as if poor humanity had sometimes to resign itself to things a little less agreeable than the merely smooth and nice. He laid down his spoon, which he had been using with some vigour, and sipped his coffee.

'What I was going to explain,' he went on, rubbing at his moustache, 'is that everything was going perfectly easy – just like clockwork, when the servant question came up. My house, you see, is on what you may call the large side. It's old in parts, too. Up to then we had had a very satisfactory woman – roughish but willing. She was the wife, or what you might just as well call the widow, of a sailor. I mean he was one of the kind that has a ditto in every port, you know. She was glad of the place, glad to be where her husband couldn't find her, even though the stipulation was that her wages should be permanent. That system of raising by driblets always leads to discontent. And I must say she was a fair tyrant for work.

'Besides her, there was a help from the village – precious little good *she* was. Slummocky – and *stupid*! Still, we had got on pretty well up to then, up to Miss Dutton's time, and for some months after. But cooking for three mouths is a different thing to two. Besides, Miss Dutton liked her meals dainty-like: a bit of fish, or soup occasionally, toast-rack, tantalus, serviettes on the table – that kind of thing. But all that came on gradual-like – the thin edge of the wedge; until at last, well, "exacting" wasn't in it.

'And I must say,' he turned his wandering eye once more on mine, 'I must say, she had a way of addressing menials which sometimes set even my teeth on edge. She was a lady, mind you – though what *that* is when the breath is out of your body it's not so easy to say. And she had the lady's way with them – those continental hotels, I suppose. All very well in a large establishment where one works up against another and you can call them names behind their backs. But our house wasn't an establishment. It wouldn't do there: not in the long run, even if you had an angel for a general, and a cook to match.

'Mind you, as I say, Miss Dutton was always niceness itself to my poor sister: never a hard word or a contemptuous look – not to her face nor behind her back, not up to then. I wouldn't have tolerated it either. And you know what talking to a party that can only just sit, hands in lap, and gape back at you means, or maybe a word now and then that doesn't seem to have anything to do with what you've been saying. It's a great affliction. But servants were another matter. Miss Dutton couldn't demean herself to them. She lived in another world. It was, "Do this"; and "Why isn't it done?" – all in a breath. I smoothed things over, though they got steadily worse and worse, for weeks, and weeks, ay, months. It wore me to a shadow.

'And one day the woman – Bridget was her name – Irish, you know – she flared up in earnest and gave her, as they say, as good as she got. I wasn't there at the time. But I heard afterwards all that passed, and three times over – on the one side at least. I had been into the town in the runabout. And when I came home, Mrs Tantrums had packed up her box, got a gig from the farm, and was gone for good. It did me a world of harm, that did.

'Pretty well upset, I was too, as you can imagine. I said to Miss Dutton, "Edna," I said, "all I am saying is, was it necessary to go to such extremes? Not," I said, "mind you, Edna, that she was all sugar and honey even to me. I knew the wrong side of her mouth years before *you* appeared on the scene. What you've got to do with such people is – to manage – be firm, keep 'em low, but manage. It isn't commonsense to cut off your tongue to spite your teeth. She's a woman, and Irish at that," I said, "and you know what to expect of them."

'I was vexed, that's a fact, and perhaps I spoke rather more sharply than need have been. But we were good friends by that time: and if honest give-and-take isn't possible between friends, where are you? I ask you. There was by that time too, nothing left over-private between us, either. I advised her about her investments and so on, though I took precious good care not to be personally involved. Not a finger stirring unless she volunteered it first. That all came out too. But it was nothing to do with me, now, was it, as man to man, if the good lady took a fancy into her head to see that my poor sister was not left to what's called the tender mercies of this world after my death?

'And yet, believe me, they fixed on that, like leeches. My hell, they did! At the Inquiry, I mean. And I don't see how much further their decency could have gone if they had called it an Inquest; and...'

Yet another low (almost gruff) volley of thunder interrupted his discourse. He left the sentence in the air; his mouth ajar. I have never met any one that made such active use of his chin in conversation, by the way, as Mr Bleet did. It must have been exceedingly fatiguing. I fancy he mistook just then the expression on my face for one of inquiry. He leant forward, pushing down towards me that long hairy finger on the marble table-top.

'When I say "tender mercies",' he explained, 'I don't mean that my sister would have been left penniless, even if Miss Dutton or nobody like her had come into the house. There was money of my own too, though, owing to what I need not explain' – he half swallowed the words – 'not much.' He broke off. 'It seems as if we are in for a bit of a thunderstorm. But I'd sooner it was here than down my way. When you're alone in the house you seem to notice the noise more.'

'I fancy it won't be much,' I assured him. 'It will clear the air.'

His eyes opened as if in astonishment that any mere act of nature could bring such consolation.

'You were saying,' I exclaimed, 'that you lost your maid?' He glanced up sharply. 'Though of course,' I added hastily, 'you mustn't let me intrude on your private affairs.'

'Not at all; oh, not at all,' he interrupted with relief. 'I thought you said, "lost my head". Not at all. It makes all the difference to me – I can assure you – to be able to go over it like this. Friendly like. To get a listener who has not been fed up on all that gossip and slander. It takes some living down, too. Nothing satisfies them: nothing. From one week's end to another you can't tell where they'll unearth themselves next.'

It was becoming difficult to prevent a steadily growing distaste for my companion from showing itself in my face. But then self-pity is seldom ingratiating. Fortunately the light where we sat was by now little better than dusk. Indeed, to judge from the growing gloom in our tea-shop, the heavens at this moment were far from gracious. I determined to wait till the rain was over. Besides, though my stranger himself was scarcely winning company, and his matter was not much above the sensational newspaper order, the mere zigzagging of his narrative was interesting. Its technique, I mean, reminded me of the definition of a crab: 'The crab is a little red ani-mal that walks backwards.'

'The fact is,' he went on, 'on that occasion – I mean about the servant – Miss Dutton and I had words. I own it. Not that she resented my taking the thing up in a perfectly open and friendly way. She knew she had put me in a fair quandary. But my own private opinion is that when you are talking to a woman it's best not to bring in remarks about the sex in general. A woman is herself or nothing, if you follow me. What she thinks is no more than another skin. Keep her sex out of it, and she'll be reasonable. But no further. As a matter of fact, I never argue with ladies. But I soon smoothed that over. It was only a passing cloud. And I must say, considering what a lady she *was*, she took the discomforts of having nothing but a good-for-nothing slattern in the house very generously, all things considered.

'Mind you, I worked *myself*, fit for any couple of female servants: washed up dishes, laid the table, kept the little knick-knacks going. Ay, and I'd go into the town to fetch her out little delicacies: tinned soups and peaches, and suchlike; anything she might have a taste to. And I taught her to use the runabout for herself, though to hear her changing gear was like staring ruin in the face. A gallon of petrol to a hank of crimson silk – that kind of thing. Believe me, she'd go all those miles for a shampoo-powder, or to have tea at a tea-shop – though you can't beat raw new-laid eggs and them on the premises. They got to know her there. She was a rare one for the fashions: scarves and motor-veils, and that kind of thing. But I never demurred. It wasn't for me to make objections, particularly as she'd do a little shopping on the housekeeping side as well, now and then. Though, mind you, she knew sixpence from a shilling, and particularly towards the last.

'What was the worst hindrance was that my poor sister seemed to have somehow come to know there were difficulties in the house. I mean that there had begun to be. You don't know how they do it; but they do. And it doesn't add to your patience, I grant, when what you have done at one moment is done wrong over again the next. But she meant well, poor creature: and scolding at her only made things worse. Still, we got along happily enough for a time, until' – he paused once more with mouth ajar – 'until Miss Dutton took it into her head to let matters come to a crisis. Now judging from that newspaper cutting I showed you, what would you take the lady's age to be? Allowing, as you might say, for all that golden hair?'

It was an indelicate question. Though why the mere fact that Miss

Dutton was now missing should intensify its indelicacy, it is not easy to say.

'Happiness makes one look younger than one really is,' I suggested.

He gaped at me, as if in wonderment that in a world of woe he himself was not possessed of a white beard as long as your arm.

' "Happiness?" ' he echoed.

'Yes, happiness.'

'Well, what I mean is, you wouldn't say she was in the filly class; now, would you? High-spirited, easy-going, and all that; silly, too, at times: but no longer young. Not in her heyday, I mean.'

I pushed my empty cup aside and looked at him. But he looked back at me without flinching, as if indeed it was a pleasant experience to be sharing with a stranger sentiments so naïve regarding 'the fair sex'.

'Mind you, I don't profess to be a young man either. But I can assure you on my word of honour, that what she said to me that evening – I was doing chores in the kitchen at the time, and she was there too, arranging flowers in a vause for supper; she had a dainty taste in flowers – well, she asked me why I was so unkind to her, so unresponsive, and – it came on me like a thunderbolt.'

As if positively for exemplification, a violent clap of thunder at that moment resounded overhead. The glasses and crockery around us softly tinkled in sympathy. We listened in silence to its reverberations dying away across the chimney-tops; though my companion seemed to be taking them in through his mouth rather than through his ears. His cheek paled a little.

'That's what she asked me, I say. And I can tell you it took me on the raw. It was my turn to flare up. We had words again: nothing much, only a storm in a tea-cup.' Instead of smiling at the metaphor in the circumstances, he seemed astonished, almost shocked, at its aptitude. But he pushed on boldly.

'And then after I had smoothed things over again, she put her cards on the table. Leap Year, and all that tomfoolery, not a bit of it! She was in dead earnest. She told me what I had guessed already, that she had scarcely a friend in the world. Never a word, mind you, of the Colonel – interloping old Pepper-face! She assured me, as I say, she hadn't not only a single relative, but hardly a friend; that she was, as you might say, alone in life, and – well, that her sentiments had become engaged. In honour bound I wouldn't have breathed this to a living soul who knew the parties; but to a stranger, if I may say so, it isn't quite the same thing. What she said was – in the kitchen there, and me in an apron, mind you, tied round me – doing chores – she said – well, in short, that she wanted to make a match of it. She had taken a fancy to me, and was I agreeable.' There was no vanity in his face; only a stark unphilosophical astonishment. He seemed to think that to explain all is to forgive all; and was awaiting my concurrence.

'You mean she proposed marriage,' I interrupted him with needless pedantry, and at once, but too late, wished the word back. For vestiges of our conversation had evidently reached the counter. Our waitress, still nibbling her pencil, was gazing steadily in our direction. And for some obscure reason this heat that we were sharing with the world at large, combined with this preposterous farrago, was now irritating me almost beyond endurance. The fellow's complacency was incredible.

I beckoned to the young woman. 'You said this gentleman's bus to King's Cross was an Eighteen, didn't you?'

'Yes, 'Ighteen,' she repeated.

'Then would you please bring him an ice.'

Mr Bleet gazed at me in stupefaction; a thick colour had mounted into his face. 'You don't mean to say,' he spluttered, 'that *I* made any such mention of such a thing. I'm sure I never noticed it.'

My impulse had been nothing more than a protest against my own boredom and fatigue; but the way he had taken it filled me with shame. What would the creature's state of mind be like if his memory was as untrustworthy as that? The waitress retired.

It's so devilishly hot in here,' I explained. 'And even talking is fatiguing in this weather.'

'Ay,' he said in a low voice. 'It is. But you aren't having one yourself?'

'No, thank you,' I said, 'I daren't. I can't take ices. Indigestion – it's a miserable handicap...You were saying that at the time of Miss Dutton's proposal, you were in the kitchen.'

There was a pause. He sat looking foolishly at the little glass dishful of ice-cream: as surprising a phenomenon apparently as to an explorer from the torrid zone earth's northern snows must first appear. There was a look upon his face as if he had been 'hurt', as if, like a child, at another harsh word he might burst out crying.

'I hardly know that it's worth repeating,' he said at last lamely. His fine resonant voice had lost its tone. 'I suppose she intended it kindly enough. And I wouldn't say I hadn't suspected which way the wind was blowing: Willie this, and Willie that. I've always been William to them that know me, except Bill at school. But it was always Willie with her; and a languishing look to match. Still, I never expected what came after that. It took me aback.

'There she was, hanging on my every word, looking volumes, and me not knowing what to say. In a way too, I was attached to her. There were two sides to her, I allow that.' He turned away but not, it seemed, in order to see the less conspicuous side more clearly. 'I asked her to let me think things over, and I said it as any gentleman would. "Let me think it over, Edna," I said. "You do me honour," I said. Her hand was on my arm. She was looking at me. God being my witness, I tried to spare her feelings. I eased it over, meaning it all for the best. You see that little prospect had no more than occurred to me. Married life wasn't what I was after. I shouldn't be as old as I am now – and unmarried, I mean – if that had been so. It was uncomfortable to see her carrying on like that: too early. But things having come to such a pass, well, as you might say, we glided into an under-standing at last. And with what result? Why...she made it an occasion for putting her foot down all the way round. And hadn't I known it of old?'

He looked at me searchingly, with those dog-bright eyes, those high-set ears, as if to discover where precisely I now was in relation to his confidences.

'She took the reins, as they say. All in good temper for the most part; but there was no mistaking it. Mistress first and Mrs after, in a manner of speaking. But when it came to speaking sharply to my poor sister on a matter which you wouldn't expect even a full-witted person to be neces-sarily very quick about at the uptake – I began to suspect I had made a mis-take. I knew it then: but forewarned isn't always forearmed. And mistakes are easier to make than to put right. It had gone too far...'

'If you really don't want that ice, I can easily ask the waitress to take it away,' I assured him, if only to bring back that wandering empty eye from the reverie into which he seemed to have fallen. Or was it that he was merely absorbed in the picture of the rain-drenched street that was reflected in the looking-glass behind my chair?

'Thank you,' he said, taking up the spoon.

'And Miss Dutton left you at last. Did she tell you she had any intention of going?'

'Never,' he asseverated. 'Not a word. No, not a single word. And if you *can't* explain it, well then, why go on trying? I say. Not at this late day. But you might as well argue with a stone wall. The heat had come by then. Last summer, you know: the drought. Not the great drought, I mean – but round our parts in particular. The whole place was dried up to a tinder; cracks in the clay; weeds dying; birds gone. Even the trees flagging: and the oaks half eaten up by caterpillars already. Meantime, I don't know how it was – unless, perhaps, the heat – but there had been another quarrel. They never got *that* out of me at the Inquiry, though; I can tell you. And that was patched up, too. I apologized because she insisted. But she had hurt me; she had hurt my feelings. And I couldn't see that marriage was going to be a very practical experiment on those lines. But she came round; and con-sidering what an easy woman of the world she looks like in that photo-graph, you wouldn't have guessed, would you, that crying, weeping, I mean, was much in her way? I found that out, too. Fatiguing.

'And it didn't suit her, either. But she was what they call a woman made for affection. And I mean by *that*,' he broke in emphatically, 'she liked to monopolize. She wasn't a sharer. We were badly in want of a servant our-selves by that time, as you may imagine. Going from bad to worse, and me with a poisoned thumb, opening tins. But *she* was in want of servants still more. She wanted me. Husbands often are nothing much better. What's more, I don't wish to say anything against the – against her now; but for the life of me I can't see any reason why she should have gone so far as to insult me. And not a week since we were like birds on one roost. To insult me, mind you, with my poor sister there, listening by!

'But I had learned a bit by then. I held my tongue, though there was plenty of things to say in reply if I could have demeaned myself to utter them. Plenty. I just went on looking out of the window, easing myself with my foot – we were in the drawing-room at the time – and the very sight of the dried-up grass and the dead vegetables, and the sun pouring down out of the sky like lava from a volcano would have been enough in themselves to finish off most people's self-restraint. But as I say, I just stood there thinking of what I might have said, but saying nothing – just let her rant on.

'Why, for instance, do you suppose she had made out weeks before that her investments were bringing in twice as much as they really did? Why all that stuff about Monte Carlo and that lady from America when it was only Boulogne and what they call a *pension*, which in plain English is nothing more than lodgings? Mind you,' he said, as if to intercept the remark I had no intention of making, 'mind you, I agree there *was* a competence, and I agree that, apart from a silly legacy to the Home for Cats and Dogs and that Belgian knacker trade, she had left all there was to leave to my sister – and long before what I told you about just now. I saw that in black and white. It was my duty. That was all settled. On the other hand, how was I to know that she wouldn't change her mind; that she hadn't been paving the way, as you may call it? And why had she deliberately deceived me? I thought it then, and I think it now, more than ever – considering what I have been through. It wasn't treating me fairly, and particularly before she was in a position when things couldn't be altered, so to speak, as between husband and wife. Stretch it too far, and...'

Owing to the noise of the rain – and possibly in part to his grammar – it was only with difficulty that I could now follow what the creature was mumbling. I found my attention wandering. A miniature Niagara at least eighteen inches wide was at this moment foaming along the granite gutter while the rain in the middle of the street as it rebounded above the smoking asphalt was lifting into the air an exquisite mist of spray. I watched it enthralled; it was sweet as the sight of palm-trees to my tired hot eyes, and its roar and motion lulled me for a moment or two into a kind of hypnotic trance. When I came back to myself and my trivial surroundings, I found my companion eyeing me as if he had eagerly taken advantage of these moments of oblivion.

'That's the real thing,' he said, as if to humour me, beckoning with his thumb over his shoulder. 'That rain. But it's waste on only stones.' He eyed it pensively, turning his head completely round on his narrow shoulders to do so. But only for a moment. He returned to the business in hand as promptly as if we gossipers had been called to order by the Chairman of a Committee.

'Now it says in that report there, which you have just been reading, that Miss Dutton had not been seen after she left Crowstairs that afternoon of the 3rd of July. That's what it says – in so much print. And I say that's a lie. As it came out later on. And it doesn't make it any truer being in print. It's inaccurate – proved so. But perhaps I ought to tell you first exactly how the whole thing came about. Things get so confused in memory.' Once more he wearily drew his hand over his face as if to obliterate even the memory itself. 'But – quite apart from the others – it's a relief to get things clearer even in one's own mind. The fact is, the whole thing was over between us a day or two before. As I say, after the last little upset which I told you about, things were smoothed out again as usual. At least on her side, though there was precious little in which I was really myself at fault. But my own belief is that she was an hysterical woman. What I mean is, she didn't need anything to make a fuss about; to fire up over. No foundation except just her own mood and feelings. I never was what they call a demonstrative person; it isn't in our family. My father himself was a schoolmasterish kind of man. "It hurts me more than it hurts you"; that kind of man. And up to the age of ten I can honestly say that I never once heard my mother answer him back. She felt it, mind you. He thrashed me little short of savage at times. She'd look on, crying; but she kept herself in. She knew it only made matters worse; and she died when I was twelve.

'Well, what I think is this – that Miss Dutton made a mistake about me. She liked comfort. Breakfast in bed; slippers at night; hot water to wash in; that kind of thing. I'll go further: she was meant for luxury. You could see it in her habits. If she had been twice as well off, she'd have wanted three times as many luxuries: lady's maid, evening dress, tea-gowns, music in the drawing-room – that sort of thing. And maybe it only irritated her when she found that I could keep myself in and just look calm, whatever she did or said. Hesitate to say whatever came into her mind? – not she! – true or untrue. Nor actual physical violence, either. Why months before, she threw a vause full of flowers at me: snowdrops.'

The expression on his face suddenly became fixed, as if at an unexpected recollection.

'I am not suggesting,' he testified earnestly, 'considering – considering what came after, that I bear her any grudge or malice on account of all that. All I mean is that I was pressed and pushed on to a point that some would say was beyond human endurance. Maybe it was. But what I say is, let', his voice trembled, 'bygones be bygones. I will say no more of that. My point is that Miss Dutton, after all, was to be, as they say, a bird of passage. There had been a final flare up and all was over between us. Insult on insult she heaped on me. And my poor sister there, in her shabby old black dress, peering out at us, from between her fingers, trembling in the corner like a dumb animal. She had called her in.

'And me at my wits' end, what with the servant trouble and the most cantankerous and unreasonable lot of tradespeople you could lay hands on, north or south. I can tell you, I was pretty hard pressed. They dragged all that up at the Inquiry. Oh, yes, bless you. Trust 'em for that. Once it's men against man, then look to it. Not a *public* Inquiry, mind you. No call for that. And I *will* say the police, though pressing, and leaving no stone unturned in a manner of speaking, were gentlemen by comparison. But such things leak out. You can't keep a penny-a-liner from gabbing, and even if there had been nothing worse to it they'd have made my life a hell upon earth.

'Nothing worse to it? How do you mean?'

His glance for the instant was entirely vacant of thought. 'I mean,' he said stubbornly, after a moment's hesitation, 'the hurt to my private feelings. That's what I mean. I can hear her now. And the first thing I felt after it was all over, was nothing but relief. We couldn't have hit it off together, not for long: not after the first few weeks, anyhow. Better, I say, wash your hands of the whole thing. I grant you her decision had left me in a nasty pickle. As a matter of fact, she was to go in a week, and me to clear up the mess. Bills all over the place – fresh butter, mind you, olives, wine, tinned mock turtle – that kind of thing; and all down to my account. What I feel is, she oughtn't to have kept on at me like that right up to the last. Wouldn't you have thought, considering all things, any woman with an ounce of common sense – not to speak of common caution – would have let sleeping dogs lie?'

He was waiting for an answer.

'What did her uncle, the Colonel, say to that?'

'Oh, him,' he intimated with an incredible sneer. 'In the Volunteers! I was speaking as man to man.'

'And she didn't even wait the two or three days, then?'

'It was the 3rd of July,' he repeated. 'After tidying things up for the day – and by that time, mind you, every drop of water had to be brought in buckets across the burnt-up fields from a drying-up pond half a mile away. But it was done. I did it. After finishing, I say, all the rest of the morning chores, I was sitting there thinking of getting a snack of lunch and then what to do next, when I heard a cough – her door had opened; and then her footstep on the stairs – slippers.' He held up that hairy forefinger of his as if at an auction, and he was speaking with extreme deliberation as if, with eyes and senses fixed on the scene, he were intent to give me the exactest of records in the clearest of terms. 'And I said to myself, "She's coming! and it's all to begin again!" I said it; I knew it. "And face it out? ... then – me?" ' He shook his head a little like a cat tasting water, but the eyes he showed me were like the glazed windows of an empty shop. 'No, I made myself scarce. I said to myself: "Better keep your distance. Make yourself scarce; keep out of it." And heaven help me I had been doing my best to forget what had passed the night before and to face what was to come. And so – I went out.

'It was early afternoon: sultry, like now. And I wandered about the fields. I must have gone miles and never met a soul. But if you ask me to say where, then all I can say is: Isn't one field the living image of another? And what do you see when your mind isn't there? All round Winstock way – lanes, hedges, cornfields, turnips – tramp and tramp and tramp. And it was not until about seven o'clock that evening that I got back again. Time for supper. I got out the crockery and – and raked out the fire. No sign of nobody, nor of my sister either – though there was nothing in that: she had a habit of sitting up at her bedroom window, and looking out, just with her hands in her lap. And the house as still as a – as still as a church.

'I loafed about a bit in the kitchen. Call *her*? Well, hardly! There was plenty to do. As usual. The supper, and all that. The village woman had left about eleven that morning – toothache. She owned to it. Not that that put me about. I can cook a boiled egg and a potato well enough for most Christians. But hot meals – meals for – well, anyhow, there was nothing hot that evening. It was about seven-thirty by then, I suppose; and I was beginning to wonder. Then I thought I'd go out in the yard and have a look at the runabout – an old Ford, you know – I hadn't had time then for weeks to keep it decent. When I got to the shed, there was a strange cat eating up some fish-bones; and when I looked in, it was gone.'

'You mean the Ford?'

'Yes, the Ford. There wasn't a sign of it. That froze me up, I can tell you, for there had been gipsies about a day or two before. I rushed into the house and called out up the stairs, "Edna! Edna! Are you there? The Ford's gone." No answer. I can tell you I was just like a frenzied man. I looked in the drawing-room – teapot and cup on a tray but empty: just sunshine streaming in as if nothing had happened. Then I looked into her little parlour: boudoir, she called it. Nothing doing. Then I went upstairs and tapped on her bedroom door. "Miss Dutton," I said, "have you seen anything of the Ford? It's gone." And then I looked in. That was the queer thing about it. They all said that. That it never occurred to me, I mean, that she was not in the car herself. But what I say is – how can you think of everything before you say it, and wasn't it I myself that *said* I had said it?

'Anyhow, I looked in: I suppose a man can do *that* in his own house and his car gone from under his very nose! And believe me, the sight inside was shocking. I'm a great stickler myself for law and order, for neatness, I mean. I had noticed it before: it irritated me. In spite of all her finery, she was never what you would call a tidy woman. But that room beat every-thing. Drawers flung open, dresses hugger-mugger, slippers, bags, bead-work, boxes, gimcracks all over the place. But not a sign of her. I looked – everywhere. She wasn't there, right enough. Not – not a sign of her. She was gone. And – and I have never seen her since.'

The rain was over, and the long sigh he uttered seemed to fill the whole tea shop as if it were a faint echo of the storm which had ceased as suddenly as it had begun. The sun was wanly shining again, gilding the street.

'You at once guessed, I suppose, the house had been broken into, while you were out?'

He kept his eyes firmly on mine. 'Yes,' he said. 'That's what I thought – at first.'

'But then, I think you said a minute or two ago that Miss Dutton *was* actually seen again?'

He nodded. 'That's just it,' he said, as if with incredulous lucidity. 'So you see, the other couldn't have been. The facts were against it. She was seen that very evening,' he said, 'and driving my Ford. By more than one, too. Our butcher happened to be outside his shop door; no friend of mine either. It was a Saturday, cutting up pieces for the 4d. and 6d. trays, and he saw her going by: saw the number too. It was all but broad daylight, though it's a narrow street. It was about seven then, he said, because he had only just wound his clock. There she was; and a good pace too. And who could be surprised if she looked a bit unusual in appearance? It's exactly what you'd expect. You don't bolt out of a house you have lived in com-fortable for two or three years as neat as a new pin.'

'What was wrong with her?'

'Oh, the man was nothing better than a fool, though promptitude itself when it came to asking a good customer to settle up. He said he'd have hardly recognized her. There, in my car, mind you, and all but broad daylight.'

'But surely,' I said as naturally as possible, 'even if it is difficult some-times to trace a human being, it is not so easy to dispose of a car. Wasn't that ever found?'

He smiled at me, and in a more friendly way than I should have deemed possible in a face so naturally inexpressive.

'You've hit the very nail on the head,' he assented. 'They did find the car – on the Monday morning. In fact it was found on the Sunday by a young fellow out with his sweetheart, but they thought it was just waiting – picking flowers, or something. It had been left inside a fir-copse about a couple of hundred yards from a railway station, a mile or so out of the town.'

'Just a countryfied little railway station, I suppose? Had the porter or anybody noticed a lady?'

'Countryfied – ay, maybe: but the platform crowded with people going to and fro for their week's marketing, besides a garden party from the Rectory.'

'The platform going into the town?'

'Yes, that's it,' said my friend. 'Covering her tracks.'

At that moment I noticed one of our waitress's bright-red 'Eighteens' whirling past the tea-shop door. It vanished.

'She had had a letter that morning – postmark Chicago,' the now far-too-familiar voice edged on industriously. 'The postman noticed it, being foreign. It's my belief *that* caused it. But mind you, apart from that, though I'm not, and never was, complaining, she'd treated me, well — ' But he left the sentence unfinished while he clumsily pushed about with his spoon in the attempt to rescue a fly that had strayed in too far in pursuit of his sweet cold coffee. He was breathing gently on the hapless insect.

'And I suppose, by that time, you had given the alarm?'

'Given the alarm?' he repeated. 'Why?'

The sudden frigidity of his tone confused me a little. 'Why,' I said, 'not finding Miss Dutton in the house, didn't you let anybody know?'

'Now my dear sir,' he said, 'I ask you. How was *I* to know what Miss Dutton was after? I wasn't Miss Dutton's keeper; she was perfectly at liberty to do what she pleased, to come and go. How was *I* to know what she had taken into her head? Why, I thought for a bit it was a friendly action considering all things, that she should have borrowed the car. Mind you, I don't say I wasn't disturbed as well, her not leaving a word of explanation, as she had done once before – pinned a bit of paper to the kitchen table – "Yours with love, Edna" – that sort of thing. Though that was when everything was going smooth and pleasant. What I did first was to go off to a cottage down the lane and inquire there. All out, except the daughter in the wash-house. Not a sight or sound of car or Miss Dutton, though she did recollect the honk of a horn sounding. "Was it my horn?" I asked. But they're not very observant, that kind of young woman. Silly-like. Besides, she wasn't much more than a child.'

'And your sister: where actually was she, after all?'

He looked at me as if once more in compliment of my sagacity.

'That, I take it – to find and question *her*, I mean, was a matter of course. I went up to her room, opened the door, and I can hear myself actually saying it now: "Have you seen anything of Edna, Maria?"

'It was very quiet in her room – stuffy, too, and for the moment I thought she wasn't there; and then I saw her – I detected her there – crouching in the farthest corner out of the light. I saw her white face turn round, it must have been covered up. "Where's Edna, Maria?" I repeated. She shook her head at me, sitting there beyond the window. I could scarcely see her. And you don't seem to have realized that any kind of direct or sudden question always confused her. It didn't seem she understood what I was saying. In my belief it was nothing short of brutal the way they put her through it. I mean that Colonel, as he calls himself. Over and over and over again.

'Well, we weren't in any mood for food, as you may guess, when eight, nine, went by – and no sign of her. At last it was no use waiting any longer; but just to make sure, I went over to the farm two miles or so away – a little off the road, too, she must have taken to the town. We were still pretty friendly there. It was about half-past nine, I suppose, and they had all gone to bed. The dog yelled at me as if it was full moon and he had never seen me before. I threw a handful of gravel up at the old man's window, and I must say, considering all things, he kept his temper pretty well. Specially as he had seen nothing. Nothing whatever, he said.

' "Well," I said, speaking up at him, and they were my very words, "I should like to know what's become of her." He didn't seem to be as anxious as I was – thought she'd turn up next morning. "That kind of woman knows best what she's about," he said. So I went home and went to bed, feeling very uneasy. I didn't like the feel of it, you understand. And I suppose it must have been about three or four in the morning when I heard a noise in the house.'

'You thought she had come back?'

'What?' he said.

'I say, you thought she had come back?'

'Yes, of course. Oh yes. And I looked out of my bedroom door over the banisters. By that time there was a bit of moonlight showing, striking down on the plaster and oilcloth. It was my sister, with an old skirt thrown over her nightgown. She was as white as a sheet, and shivering.

' "Where have you been, Maria?" I asked her in as gentle a voice as I could make it. The curious thing is, she understood me perfectly well. I mean she answered at once, because often I think really and truly she did understand, only that she couldn't as quickly as most people collect her wits as they say.

'She said, mumbling her words, she had been looking for her.

' "Looking for who?" I said, just to see if she had taken me right.

' "For her," she said.

' "For Edna?" I asked. "And why should you be looking for Edna this time of night?" I spoke a little more sternly.

'She looked at me, and the tears began to roll down her face.

' "For God's sake, Maria, why are you crying?" I said.

' "Oh," she said, "she's gone. And she won't come back now."

'I put my arm round her and drew her down on to the stairs. "Compose yourself," I said to her, "don't shiver and shake like that." I forgot she had been standing barefoot on the cold oilcloth. "What do you mean, Gone? Don't take on so. Who's to know she won't come back safe and sound?" I am giving you the words just as they came out of our mouths.

' "Oh," she said, "William, you know better than me – I won't say anything more. Gone. And never knowing that I hadn't forgotten how kind she was to me!"

' "Kind, my girl!" I said. "Kind! In good part, maybe," I said, "but not surely after what she said to you that day?"

'But I could get nothing more out of her. She shrank up moaning and sobbing. She had lost herself again, her hair all draggled over her eyes, and she kept her face averted from me, and her shoulders were all humped, shaking under my hands – you know what women are. So I led her off to her room and made her as comfortable as I could. But all through the night I could hear her afterwards when I went to listen, and talking too.

'You can tell I was by now in a pretty state myself. That was a long night for me. And what do you think: when I repeated that conversation to the Colonel, and the Inspector himself standing by, he as good as told me he didn't believe me. "Friendly questions"! I could have wrung his nose. But then by that time my poor sister couldn't put two words together, he bawled at her so; until even the Inspector said it was not fair on her, and that she wouldn't be any use, anyhow, whatever happened.'

Once again there fell a pause in my stranger's disjointed story. He took two or three spoonfuls in rapid succession of his half-melted ice-cream. Even though the rain and the storm had come and gone, the air was not appreciably cooler, or rather it was no less heavy and stagnant. Our waitress had apparently given us up as lost souls, and I glanced a little deprecatingly at the notice, 'No gratuities', on the wall.

'How long did the drought last after that?' I inquired at last.

'The drought?' said my friend. 'The questions you ask! Why, it broke that very night. Over an inch of rain we had in less than eight hours.'

'Well, that, at any rate, I suppose, was something of a comfort.'

'I don't see quite why,' he retorted.

'And then you informed the police?'

'On the Sunday.' He took out a coloured silk handkerchief from the pocket of his neat pepper-and-salt jacket, and blew his nose. It is strange how one can actually anticipate merely from the general look of a man such minute particulars as the trumpeting of a nose. Strange, I mean, that all the parts and properties of human beings seem to hang so closely together, as if in positive collusion. Anyhow, the noise resounded through the glass-walled marbled room as sharp as a cockcrow.

'Well,' he said, 'that's where I stand. Looking at me, you wouldn't suppose perhaps that everything that a man wants most in this world has been destroyed and poisoned away. I had no call perhaps to be confiding in a mere stranger. But you couldn't credit the relief. I have nothing left now. I came up here to lose myself in the noise – so shocking quiet it is there, now. But I have to go back – can't sleep much, though: wake up shouting. But what's worst is the emptiness: it's all perished. I don't want anything now. I'd as lief die and have done with it, if I could do it undriven. I've never seen a desert, but I reckon I know what the inside of one's like now. I stop thinking sometimes, and get dressed without knowing it. You wouldn't guess that from my appearance, I dare say. But once begin living as you feel underneath living *is*, where would most of us be? They have hounded me on and they've hounded me down, and presently they'll be sealing me up, and me never knowing from one day to another what news may come of – of our friend. And my sister gone and all.'

'She isn't "missing" too, I hope?' As I reflect on it, it was a vile question to have put to the man. I don't see how anything could have justified it. His face was like a burnt-out boat. The effect on him was atrocious to witness. His swarthy cheek went grey as ashes. The hand on the marble table began to tremble violently.

'Missing?' he cried. 'She's *dead*. Isn't *that* good enough for you?'

At this, no doubt because I was hopelessly in the wrong, I all but lost control of myself.

'What do you mean?' I exclaimed in a low voice. 'What do you mean by speaking to me like that? Haven't I wasted the better part of a Saturday afternoon listening to a story which, if I cared, I could read in your own county newspaper? What's it all to me, may I ask? I want to have nothing more to do with it – or you either.'

'You didn't say that at the beginning,' he replied furiously, struggling to his feet. 'You led me on.'

'Led you on, by God! What do you mean by such a piece of impudence? I say I want nothing more to do with you. And if that's how you accept a kindness, take my advice and keep your troubles to yourself in future. Let your bygones *be* bygones. And may the Lord have mercy on your soul.'

It was a foul outburst, due in part, I hope, to the heat; in part to the suffocating dehumanizing foetor which spreads over London when the sun has been pouring down on its bricks and mortar as fiercely as on the bones and sands of some Eastern mud village.

My stranger had sat down again abruptly, had pushed his ice away from him and covered his face with his hands. His shoulders were jumping as if with hiccups. It was fortunate perhaps that at the moment there was no other eater in the café. But the waitresses were clustered together at the counter. They must have been watching us for some little time. And the manageress was there, too, looking at us like a scandalized hen over her collar through her pince-nez. We were evidently causing a disturbance – on the brink of a 'scene'. A visionary placard flaunted across my inward eye: *Fracas in a Restaurant.*

I too sat down, and beckoned peremptorily to the young lady who had been so attentive about the bus.

'My bill, please,' I said – 'this gentleman's and mine.' And then, foolishly, I added, 'It's hot, isn't it?'

She made no reply until, after damping her lead pencil, she had added up her figures and had handed me between her finger-tips the mean scrap of paper. Then she informed me crisply, in fastidious Cockney, that some people seemed to find it hotter than most, and that it was past closing time, and would I please pay at the desk.

My accomplice had regained a little of his self-restraint by now. He put out a wavering hand and took up his hard felt hat. It was almost incredible that so marked a change should have come over so insensitive a face in that brief space of time. Its touch of bravado, its cold clear stare as of a watchful dog, even the neatness of it, had disappeared. He looked ten years older – lost and abandoned. He put out his other hand for the check. It was a curious action for a man with an intense closeness – if not meanness – clearly visible on his features. 'I should prefer, if you don't mind, to pay my bill myself,' he said.

'Not at all,' I replied brusquely. 'It was my ice-cream. I must apologize for having been so abrupt.'

He tried to smile; and it was like the gleam of a sickly evening sunshine after heavy winter rain.

'It's broken me: that's all I can say,' he said. 'What I say is, you read such things in the newspapers, but you don't know what they mean to them as are most concerned. I don't see how you can. But anyhow, I *can* pay my way.'

I hesitated. A furious contest – dim spread-eagled figures silhouetted, as it were, against a background of utter black – seemed to be proceeding in some dream in my mind, a little beyond actual consciousness. 'Well,' I blurted, 'I hope time will make things better. I can guess what I should feel like myself in similar circumstances. If I were you, I should...' But at sight of him, the words, I am thankful to say, faded out before I could utter them.

'If I were you' – how easy! But how is that metamorphosis conceivable?

He looked at his hat; he looked at his ice-cream, now an insipid mush; he looked anxiously and searchingly at the table – marked over with the hieroglyphics of dark ugly marble. And at last he raised his eyes – those inexpressive balls of glass – and looked at me. He changed his hat from his right to his left hand, and still looking at me, hesitated, holding the empty hand out a little above the table. Then turning away, he drew it back.

I pretended not to have noticed the action. 'There should be another Eighteen in a few minutes,' I volunteered. 'And I think I noticed a stopping-place a few yards down.'

Nevertheless I couldn't for the moment leave him there – to the tender mercies of those censorious young waitresses in their exquisitely starched caps. 'I am going that way,' I said. 'Shall I see you into it?'

'It's the heat,' he said. 'No, thank you. You have been a...'

With a gasp I repelled as well as I could the distaste for him that was once more curdling as if with a few drops of vinegar my very blood. What monsters of hatred and uncharitableness we humans can be! And what will *my* little record look like, I wonder, when the secrets of all hearts are opened?

It seemed for the time being as though the whole of my right arm had become partially paralysed. But with an effort I put out my hand at last; and then he, too, his – a large green solitaire cuff-link showing itself against his wristband as he did so. We shook hands – though I doubt if a mere fleshly contact can express much while the self behind it is dumb with instinctive distaste.

Besides, the effect on him even of a friendly action as frigid as this was horribly disconcerting. It reminded me of ice pitted and crumbling in a sudden thaw. He seemed to have been reduced to a state of physical and spiritual helplessness as if by an extremity of emotion, or by a drug. It was nauseating. It confused me and made me ashamed and miserable. I turned away abruptly; paid our bill at the desk, and went out. And London enveloped me.

The Connoisseur *

PARK STREET

It was a narrow discreet street, and, in this late evening twilight, all but deserted. There had been rain, bringing with it an earthy fragrance from the not far distant park, and small clear puddles of water filled the hollows of the paving-stones. Clumsily picking his way between them, St Dusman came shuffling along between the houses to keep a rather belated tryst. He paused now and again to examine the numbers on the fanlights, and at last halted, at No. 13, where he stood for a few moments peering in over the spearheaded palisade that guarded its area. As yet the curtains of the shallowly curved window abutting on the street had not been drawn nor its shutters closed.

From a candelabrum on a lacquer Chinese table in the midst of the room, electric tapers cast their beams upon the exquisite objects that stood around them. This sharp metallic light bathed ivory and porcelain, the wax-like flowers in their slim vase, the few pictures, as if they were the sacred relics of a shrine.

The old creature's eyes gazed vaguely through their magnifying spectacles at this scene of still life, then groped onward towards the figure of a man, as yet apparently in his early thirties, who now stood in the doorway, slim, sleek, dark – as if for foil to the very vase on the table with its pale green leaves and flowers. His neat head was stooping forward and inclined a little towards his left shoulder, for at that moment with intense interest and vigilance he was vainly endeavouring to see the old man out there in the darkening street as clearly as St Dusman could see him.

The old man hesitated no longer. With the aid of its wrought steel handrail he mounted the three shallow steps of the outer door, under its narrow shell-shaped porch, and rapped softly with his knuckles on the panel. The stranger himself hastened to open it, though for an instant or two he seemed to have paused with fingers on its catch, and after the briefest scrutiny of the face of his visitor from penetrating green-grey eyes, led him, almost as though surreptitiously, into the very room which the saint had surveyed from without. And he himself drew their curtains over the windows.

'You may not have been expecting me, Mr Blumen?' said the old man

---

* First published in *Two Tales*, Bookman's Journal, London, July 1925, and *Yale Review*, July 1925. Two sections of the story called 'The Seven Valleys' and 'En Route' that were omitted in C (1926) and then restored in *Collected Tales* (New York, 1950), probably with de la Mare's approval, have been restored here, too.

courteously, still a little breathless. 'Although, indeed, I am a little late. My friends detain me at times. And this is my last errand for the day.'

Mr Blumen's eyes were now steadily fixed on his visitor's face. 'I must confess,' he replied, 'that I was *not* expecting you. Not, I mean, to-night.'

'But you had not entirely forgotten me?' the old man pressed him whimsically. 'You have now and then given a passing thought to me? I leave footprints outside.'

Mr Blumen smiled, at least with his lips. 'You bring back at least one old memory – an experience often repeated when I was a small boy – in Bath, you know. The experience, I mean, of being "called-for". Now and then, for there are many kinds of parties, it was a relief, a positive god-send.'

There was just a hint of the formal in this rapid and not unfriendly speech. It had been uttered too in a lowish voice, though, even at that, the characteristic slight lisp and blurred r's had been detectable.

The old saint peered up at the young man over his thick-glassed spectacles. 'I can well understand it,' he said at last. 'It meant returning home. Ours is a longer journey, Mr Blumen.'

The dark eyes had sharpened. 'It *has* a goal, then?'

'Surely!' replied the old man. 'Were you uncertain even of that? Not,' he added candidly, 'not that the metaphor carries us quite all the way. Lassitude follows after most races; and what are called goals and prizes may be disappointing. But what – if I may venture – suggested to you that any journey in this world, in any precise meaning of the word, has an *end*?'

'Well,' replied Mr Blumen, 'there are many philosophies, and one may listen to all without being persuaded to accept any.'

'But hardly without divining any – just on one's own account?' returned the old man, almost as if he were smilingly bent on coaxing a secret out of a child. 'Wouldn't that be a little unfair to the mere facts of the case? Now I'll be bound, Mr Blumen, when you were a small boy, you must have dreamed now and then? So far at least you were conscious of circles within circles – and without – so to say?'

There was remarkably little of the childish in the keen, ashen face confronting him. The dark, large-pupilled eyes had wandered almost stealthily from point to point of the objects around them, every one of which seemed now to be flashing secret signals one to the other in this motionless creek of air.

'Well possibly,' replied Mr Blumen. 'But even a pessimist would agree that it is as well to make the best one can of the one "circle" – without vexing oneself too much with shallow and futile speculations concerning any other. And optimists; well —' a slight shrug of the narrow shoulders completed the sentence. 'I must be quite candid, though. I am unconscious of the least wish in the world to bid adieu to what they call "things as they are" – to things, that is, as they appear to me to be. I realize, none the less, that you have obligations. And – thank you for fulfilling them so considerately.'

At this, the old man folded one hand over the other under his loose sleeves, sighed, and quietly seated himself on the edge of a chair that stood nearby. 'Thank *you*, Mr Blumen,' he said; 'I will enjoy a moment's needed rest.'

'Forgive me,' cried the other hastily, turning as he spoke towards the tiny sideboard – riding there in the offing, as it were, of this bright inward pool of silence, with its delicate cargo of Venetian glass and wine.

But his visitor pleasantly waved this little courtesy aside. 'To tell you the truth, Mr Blumen,' he explained, 'and you are exceedingly tolerant, I haven't the head for it. And though I am familiar with our route – almost excessively familiar – we shall still need our combined cold wits to face it out. You were saying "things as they are" – a stimulating phrase enough in itself. Still, I have no very close knowledge of what you call the world; apart, I mean, from my daily duties. May I assume that "things as they are" now surround us?' The aged eyes peered carefully and cautiously once more through their thick glasses. 'That is so? Please, then, tell me why you are disinclined to leave them. You have seen a good deal of them?'

Mr Blumen drew in his underlip as if to moisten it with his tongue. He paused; in search of words. 'Well,' he ventured at last, 'partly, I suppose, because of those weeds of superstitious fear planted in one's mind when one is young; partly because life *can* be uncommonly entertaining; and partly because I dislike leaving what I have spent a good many years making my own.'

'Making your own!' echoed the gentle old voice a little drily; though there was a twinkle in its owner's eye. 'But you will not be ceasing to *think* when we make a start. And surely it is only thoughts, hopes, desires, dreams, and so on that you can really claim as having been made your own.

'In a sense,' agreed his quarry. 'But then I'm no Platonist, either. One's friends, one's pursuits, one's possessions' – he made a little gesture with his right hand that till that moment had been reposing in his pocket – 'surely they are the very proofs of one's *self* that one hungers for. Not of course that they can be permanent; or need be.'

'Friends are friends,' said the old man. 'I can understand that. But possessions? I take it, Mr Blumen, that you would include in that category what I see around me. Perhaps you would tell me why you value them so highly. Were there not things less perishable to possess; things that of their own nature would be less inclined to bid *you* good-bye? That old image of Kuan Yin over there, for example, is she any the more or less a symbol than the very ferocious onion-green dragon displaying his tail on that pot yonder? Better both in the imagination, don't you think, Mr Blumen, than – well, round one's neck? Besides, earth-time is fleeting. Was it ever, do you feel, worth while to do more than merely borrow its energies, apart from much else; and be grateful?'

'To whom?' Mr Blumen blurted.

'That is a question,' retorted the old man serenely, hugging his hands a little closer under their wide sleeves – 'that is a question which it would take rather more earth-time than you and I have at our disposal just now to answer.'

The shoulders beneath the neat dinner-jacket slightly lifted themselves. 'We don't always expect answers to our questions,' he said.

'Well now, see here,' said the old man, and he vigorously readjusted his spectacles on the bridge of his broad and rather stumpy nose. 'There are many similar things to these in every house in every neighbouring street, are there not? Is it just the sense of possession that is the charm? Or of being possessed?'

'Things *similar*, perhaps,' smiled Mr Blumen indulgently. 'But I need hardly suggest to an adept like yourself that many of the specimens around us at this moment are practically unique. And do you mean to imply, sir, that the beauty and rarity of a thing amount to nothing in what perhaps – whether expressed in earth-time or otherwise – you would agree to call the long run?'

'Come, come,' said the old man, 'surely rarity is the reward of a mere acquisitiveness? While as for beauty; indeed, Mr Blumen, in my humble office – a little arduous, too, at times, if I may confess it – there is not much leisure for beauty. Still, I think you will agree that what you and I mean by the word, and so far as we are personally concerned, it depends solely upon the eyes in our heads. And we have a good many, you know. With the exception, too, of the rare flowers on your table – specimens, I suspect, which would hardly be recognized even by their less remote ancestors – everything here, I notice, is – what shall we call it – of human workmanship.'

'They are works of art,' agreed Mr Blumen. 'They represent years of human skill, human delight, and human devotion and desire. What have you against them? For that matter what has *he* against them who has so punctually provided me with your company this evening?'

A very sober countenance now scrutinized Mr Blumen – and the old man, as if to suit posture to face, seemed to have composed himself even more heavily in his chair. He gazed hard, but made no answer; then turned his head and almost cautiously surveyed the objects around him as one by one they met his eye.

All the *familles* were there: *noire*, *verte*, and *rose*; each of them signally represented by elegant ambassadors, only the more amiable and acceptable for their extreme age. On half a dozen varieties of gods, on fabulous heroes and monsters renowned in old tales, and on exquisite Tanagra figures, and shapes of beast, bird, and fable, made small in priceless images of stone, earthenware, porcelain, enamel, ivory, metal, alighted his gentle glance. The faintly greenish glass on table and sideboard, like colourless and heatless crystal flame, lifted its burden of gimcracks, sweetmeats, and liqueurs, a few inches aloft.

The rugs beneath the old man's mud-stained feet by far excelled in blended colour and design the minute French masterpieces in paint, and the worn, dimmed tapestry that here and there relieved the delicate gilt of the walls and of the few chairs. A smiling cherub disguised as Father Time stood on tiptoe with uplifted scythe above the minute gilt clock, ticking out Mr Blumen's envious moments upon the carved chimney-piece. The fragile peace around him and his visitor indeed was so tenuous it seemed that at any moment it might explode, and shatter itself into its component atoms. When the old man's voice again broke the silence, it was positively as if he himself had shattered in sheer actuality some crystal image lifting itself into the still, elastic air.

'You would, I believe, Mr Blumen, be surprised,' that voice was murmuring gently, 'you would be surprised at the range of humanity that lies reflected around us. Here and there our company – and, as you well know, whatever a man does is to some extent a mirror of what he is: here and there (and forgive me for confessing it) that company, I say, is detestable to the last degree. You will be well rid of it. There are poisons that enter by the eye as well as in the blood. What is even worse – except for that moth searching the shadows over there, whose presence no doubt is explained by my poor company – I perceive here no faintest sign of life. Of life, I mean, here and now.'

A thin dark cloud had mounted into Mr Blumen's pallid face. 'If you had consented to delay your visit even by half an hour,' he retorted, with a contemptuous gesture towards the two chairs drawn up to the table, 'your last remark would hardly have been to the point.'

'Do not misdoubt me,' replied his visitor courteously. 'I have no very acute intelligence. But I have heard the rumours of busy domestic sounds from below; and I detect preparations for a visitor. But I meant by life a happy freedom of the spirit rather than mere amusement of the body. A life *delighted* in.'

'A pet canary, perhaps?' But the voice was almost too tired to be insolent.

'Why not indeed?' replied the old man, 'if you took a lively pleasure in it. Still, cages remain cages; and you yourself would agree with me that heart and soul you yourself are something of a recluse. And this I gather is your hermitage. And I have seldom in a pretty wide experience of such things seen a cage more elaborate. You are content with it?'

Mr Blumen stared a little heavily into the face of his visitor. 'If you know anything of the society in this neighbourhood, and if you mean that I enjoy solitude, then I am in complete agreement with you.'

'So would any chrysalis be,' said his visitor almost gaily. 'I grieve with all my heart that you are compelled to resign things you have grown to care for – hoarded, Mr Blumen; that it is now too late, I mean, to have *given* them away.'

Mr Blumen laid a gentle hand upon the corner of the chimney-piece. For an instant their ashen wax-like lids descended over his green-grey eyes.

'And now,' went on his visitor gently, rising to his feet, 'that last taxi-cab has passed out of hearing. There is more than half a moon to-night over Whinnimoor. It is time for us to be off.'

SASURAT

The soft white glare of snow fringed the crests of the mountains that surrounded the tortuous valley beneath them. Blossoming trees and coloured drifts of flowers mounted up almost to their frozen margin. The sun ascending into the dark blue vault of the sky, though it was but an hour or two after break of day, cast beams so fierce upon their flanks that the lawn-like mists were already swirling in the heat, showering their dew on leaf and flower and rock.

St Dusman had made his way into the valley in the small hours, and now sat drowsing on a stone beside which roared a torrent of green water. He had removed his sandals in order to lave his feet in the coldness, and now it would appear as if every flame-plumed bird in the thickets around him, and every puffing breath of wind that came wandering across the precipitous gorges, were inviting the spirit of the old man to return to the world, to slip out of sleep and waken again. With mouth agape, however, he nodded on. Flies and butterflies of innumerable dyes flashed and fluttered in the empty air around him. Fish of hardly less brave a livery sported with fin and tail over the coloured stones that tessellated the bed of the stream that flowed beside him.

Two or three hundred feet above, at the foot of one of the lower peaks glittering in the sunrays with rainbow flashes from its exposed face of rock and quartz, a mountain leopard now stole into view, lifting its gentle head into the sunshine. With twitching brows and whiskers, it sniffed the morning air, while its amber eyes rested for a moment upon the stooping figure of the old man crouched up and motionless in sleep far beneath him. With a faint uneasy mew, it then lifted its gaze upwards towards a pair of eagles circling in the enormous cavity of the now starless heavens. Then curling its narrow beautiful body upon the sward under the rocky wall of the mountain, it couched with head on paws, and composed itself to sleep.

It was the scream of a parrakeet that pierced through the old man's dreams at last. His eyes opened, he raised his head and looked around him. Where all had been dark with the gloom of night was now radiant with day. He rose to his feet and shuffled towards a huge spreading tree from amid whose swaying branches of foliage, almost brushing the ground beneath them with their blooms, he could wait and watch unseen. Resting his hand upon a smooth bough of the tree a little above his head, he contemplated the scene around him.

A smile spread over his seamed, weather-worn old face as his eyes roved to and fro. For twenty or thirty paces distant from him on a smooth drift of sward stood, as it were, a low small arbour woven of dried grass and rushes, and roofed with patches of moss and coloured feathers even. No bigger than a beehive though it was, it showed as conspicuous on the turf as a green oasis in the wilderness, or an isle of coral rising gently with its palms and tamarisks from out of the sea.

Some small creature, it was evident, had diligently collected together for its pleasure a few of the more sparkling and garish objects that lay within reach – muscous growths, for example, that flourished only in the denser and darker thickets of the surrounding forest, the bark of a silvery shrub that ventured nearest of all on the hilltops to the never melting snows, a fossil shell or two. While scattered about the rounded entrance to the arbour lay bright pebbles, bright 'everlasting' flowers, scraps of quartz, and what appeared to be flakes of a shining metal.

The old man sighed, though he did not stop smiling, as he feasted himself on these simple artifices and awaited the appearance of the hidden designer. The hours of eternity are no longer than those of time. Contrariwise, a century of earth's seasons may be in thought but as transitory as the colours of a rainbow. But, whatever his ruminations might be, St Dusman made no attempt to suppress the look of humorous compassion that now wrinkled his face at this showing of yet another renewed attempt to make a haven in the wilderness.

He had not very long to wait. For sunbeams had but just gilded the fringe of the water in its cold rocky channel, when there came a sudden scurry of wings from above his sheltering tree, and there alit on the very stone that had been his nocturnal stool, a bird.

From claw to crest it reared itself about eighteen inches from its resting-place, and in plumage was of a uniform saddish green, though tinged at the extremities of its primaries and of its tail feathers with a dull cinnamon, its breast deepening to a faint shot purple towards the belly.

With dipping and sidling head it surveyed the minute surrounding plateau, showing in its quick movements a faint unease as if its senses were dimly aware of strange and dangerous company. So translucent was the surrounding air that even at this distance the old man could mark the silvery rim to the iris of its eye, and could count the horned, outspread claws that clutched the stone. He had long since descried too, even to the delicate markings of its rosettes, the leopard apparently sleeping away its vigil on the height above.

The bird that had thus alighted on the stone nearby, appeared to be in quest of company. It bowed and becked now a little this way, now a little that; it stretched and sleeked a wing until every speck on its neutral-patterned feathers displayed itself in the sun. Then crouching lower and amorously into its soft plumage, with stealthy movements it twisted its neck upon its shoulders until its beak, as if in maternal joy and quietude, lay gently upon its bosom. The old man smiled at the realization that while this last gesture had come straight from nature's teaching, what had preceded it seemed to have been learned by mimicry and to have been practised with reluctance.

A slight stir within the arbour now caught his attenion. Instantly the visitor on the stone drew herself down and sped swiftly into cover behind and beneath the boulders that lay along the margin of the stream. Many minutes passed. The sun swept upward into the heavens, rejoicing in his strength. By infinite degrees the shadows cast by mountain peak and crest moved in a vast curve like the hands of an enormous timepiece. At faintest touch of their chill in its lair the leopard had stirred, lifted and stretched itself, and after one swift glance over the scene spread out beneath it, had vanished from sight, as if in obedience to a secret cue.

And now from out the pitch-black arch of its nesting-place, issued into the blazing glare of the morning a creature compared with whom the visitor to its domains was but as a handmaid in the train of the Queen of Sheba compared with King Solomon in all his glory. Its crested head was of molten gold – a gold which swam and rippled down towards its folded wings into a lively green seen only in rare mosses and in the shallows of the oceans. Green, blue, and purple then mingled their beauty. The wing tips were black as soot; the tail coverts, interrupted with snow, resembled them; while above them, arched over its back, flowed upwards two paler shafts terminating in a lyre-shaped pattern of hues almost indistinguishable the one from the other, as they glinted, flashed, and melted in the sun.

This lordly creature, having surveyed a moment the surrounding day, trod delicately onwards to its bathing-place; and after a while returned once more to preen itself amid the odd riches which it had collected and strown in devices recognizable only by itself, around its arbour. And not until now stole out again its humble infatuated visitor.

The old man almost laughed outright to see the disdain with which his lordship refused to recognize his visitor's presence there. Indolently, methodically he continued his exquisite toilet. While she, poor creature, as if now utterly ashamed of her former wiles, cowered half in shadow, half in sun, gently observing him. 'O Lucifer, Son of the Morning,' muttered the old man – beads of sweat, in spite of the sheltering branches above him glistening on his bald pate, 'O Lucifer, Son of the Morning, by pride fell the Angels.'

Sheer curiosity seemed at last to overcome her as she drew a little nearer to watch the adored one rearrange his treasury. Now one shell, then another, a fragment of quartz or of glinting metal, he lifted with his beak and disposed in place. There appeared to be singularly little method in his peculiar hobby, for as often as not he returned to its former place in the pattern what but a moment or two before he had with extreme deliberation deposited elsewhere. Possibly some outlying province of his bird-like mind and attention was concerned with his faithful visitor. But not the faintest ripple of neck or plume betrayed it. His complete heed seemed to be solely for his pretty collection.

'How strange it is,' thought the old man, 'that even in the simplest of her creatures nature consistently endeavours to reach the least bit further than she can stretch.' There was something almost human in the queer devices these creatures of the same kin and kind were exhibiting, though neglect and contempt were steadily reducing the unwanted one to her own sovran and instinctive self. She rose out of the shadow, displayed once more an indolent wing, and emitted from her throat a curious, bubbling, guttural note.

And apparently, as if at last in heed of her entreaties, her disdainful idol had suddenly thrust forward his golden head; every feather on his body seeming to bristle and roughen itself as he stared. Yet even this could be but small comfort to her meekness and vanity, for his silver-lined eyes were now fixed not upon herself but a few paces beyond her.

There was a deathly pause. For an instant or two the small lovely universe around them, snow-masked mountain-top to brawling stream, seemed to have been swept up in a soundless swoon. Then, as if at a signal, three sentient objects flashed into movement, so rapid as to be individually indistinguishable.

With a mighty whirr of wing, scattering with its talons as it rose the shells and pebbles strown around it, the Bird of the Arbour flashed into the air; and the crouching leopard leapt towards its prey.

Distracted an instant by the foe swooping to attack it, the beast swerved in its leap, missing by a few inches its assured victim, succeeding merely in tearing out a few dull feathers from her wing. She screamed piteously as she fled, then turned too late to observe what had befallen. Plunging with beak and claw, the master of the arbour had cowed for a moment her assailant. The leopard crouched snarling, with lashing tail, defending its eyes against plunging beak and claw. Then suddenly, and with one lightning buffet of its paws, it leapt into the air, and smote its aggressor down.

St Dusman drew his roughened hand over his forehead; and seizing his staff issued out from his retreat towards the fray. If he had intended to intervene to any purpose in what was passing, he had come too late. After one glimpse of this advancing Strangeness, the leopard with cringing body turned swiftly and fled.

The old man approached the wounded and dying bird, which feebly endeavoured to beat off his advances. He raised it gently in his arms, and carrying it back into the shadow of its arbour, laid it down among its treasures. The creature's dimming eye gazed vacantly on these vanishing possessions.

'Poor soul, poor soul,' the old man whispered. Then hastening down to the stream, he dipped the hem of his outer garment into the water and returning, squeezed out a few drops into its yawning bill.

Strange changes of hue seemed to be chasing, like wind over wheat, across its miraculous plumage. Its glazing eye was fixed, hardly in terror now, but in mute hopeless entreaty, upon the old man's face.

'There, there, my dear,' he said, as if an old bachelor of a hundred generations had somehow learned to croon to a hurt child. 'There, there, my dear; it's only time to be whispering adieu again. The longer the journey the more numerous the inns. And perhaps a moment or two's rest in each.'

But as he watched its quickening pangs the old man suddenly rebuked himself for his stupidity in not reminding himself that other comfort – tenderer than any human heart could offer – was near at hand. He lifted his eyes and searched the surrounding thickets. It was not yet too late. The carcase of the creature beneath his hands was not yet wholly insensitive. And having moistened once again the pointed tongue within its beak, the old man rose to his feet and shuffled off as quick as his old bones would allow, down into the ravine where brawled the mountain river.

Nor while the morning hours lasted did he attempt to look behind him. He merely sat there lost in reverie.

And since the tongues of the water kept up an incessant roar and babblement, no faintest murmur of the plaintive farewells behind him told whether, like the fabulous swan, the Bird of the Arbour sings only at the approach of death.

KOOTOORA

Even the keenest eye slowly and circumspectly directing its gaze in as remote an ambience as it could command from any one of the blackened crests that lifted themselves fifteen to twenty feet like the billows of a frozen sea on this Plain of Kootoora, would have discerned no sign of life. Minute slender steel-coloured midges, it is true, their burnished wings like infinitesimal flakes of mica beating the arid air, their horn-shaped snouts curved beneath their many-prismed eyes, drifted in multitudinous clusters in every hollow. They might be animate ashes.

Specks even more minute circling at ethereal altitudes above the vast crater of distant Ajubajao betokened the haunt of some species of vulture, though what meat nourished them more substantial than the air in which they circuited there was nothing to show.

Their towering vans commanded, however, an immense range of scene, and they long since must have descried from so dizzying a coign, a tiny erect shape scrambling toilsomely from out of the east towards the centre of this wild and hideous plateau. From crest to crest of the parched savanna of lava, now pausing to recover his breath and to survey what lay before him, now sliding and swaying into the yawning hollow beneath him; clambering to his feet when some unnoticed obstacle or more dangerous glissade had sent him sprawling; he pushed steadily on.

In his pertinacity, in the serene indomitableness of his age-raddled countenance he resembled no less a personage than the first Chinese patriarch, Bodhidharma, as – muffled in his mantle – he is depicted crossing the Yangtze river, his broad soles poised upon a reed.

For this very reason, maybe, the vultures of Ajubajao wheeled no nearer. Or it may be that a pilgrim or traveller who of his own free will, or at the promptings of a bizarre romance, or in service of some incalculable behest, dares the confines of a region as barren as this, quickly dissipates whatever pleasant juices his body may contain. Or it may be some inscrutable intuition in those carrion-fed brains had revealed that destiny had him in keeping beneath her brazen wing. Abject and futile creature though he appeared to be, he came undeviatingly on.

Its last filmy wreaths of sulphurous smoke had centuries before ceased to wreathe themselves from Ajubajao's enormous womb. Leagues distant though its cone must be, its jagged outlines were sharply discernible, cut clean against that southern horizon. The skies shallowly arching the plain of lava that flowed out annularly from its base in enormous undulations, league on league until its margin lay etched and fretted against the eastern heavens – this low-hung firmament was now of a greenish pallor. In its midst the noonday's sun burned raylessly like a sullen topaz set in jade.

But utterly lifeless though the plain appeared to be, minute susurrations were occasionally audible, caused apparently by scatterings of lava dust lifted from their hollows on heated draughts of air. These gathering in volume, raised at last their multitudinous voices into a prolonged hiss, a sustained shrill sibilation as if the silken fringes of an enormous robe were being dragged gently across this ink-black Sahara.

As they subsided once more, drifting softly to rest, a faint musical murmur followed their gigantic sigh, like that of far-distant drums and dulcimers from a secret and hidden borderland. Then this also ceased, and only the plaintive horns of the midges and the scurry of beetles scuttling beneath their shards to and fro in their haunts in the crevices of the lava broke the hush.

In a deep angular hollow of the nearest of these lava dunes, lay basking a serpent, flat of head and dull of eye, its slightly rufous skin mottled and barred in faintest patternings of slate and chocolate. So still she lay, her markings might appear to be but the vein of an alien stone or metal imbedded in the lava. But now and again, at the dictate of some inward whim, her blunted tail arched itself an inch or two above the floor of its black chamber, emitting a hollow and sinister rattling – as if in admonishment or endearment of the brood of her young that lay drowsing in an apparently inextricable knot of paler colouring nearby.

The hours of Kootoora's morning glided on, revealing little change except an ever increasing torridity, until the thin air fairly danced in ecstasy – like an exquisitely tenuous gas boiling in a pot – above every heat-laved arch and hollow. The skies assumed a yet paler green, resembling that of verdigris, and deepening towards the north to a dull mulberry. Strange tremors now shook the air, and thicker-crusted though its skin might be than any leviathan, a sinister insecurity haunted the plain. Here took its walks that spectre, danger, but more appallingly bedizened than in any other region of the earth.

Sluggish stirrings, the warning of some obscure instinct, in the serpent's blood now quickened her restlessness, though the lidless eyes set in that flat and obtuse head betrayed no glimmerings of intelligence or fear. She drew in closer to her brood and again and yet again her rattle drummed sullenly in the heat. A sound alien from any experience that had ever been hers in these familiar haunts had broken the silence. It was the footstep of approaching fear.

Writhing swiftly beneath and towards the face of the lava incline, wherein a black splash marked the crannied entrance of her secret chamber, she swept aside the fragments of dried skin which she had sloughed in bygone years. An increasing movement in the lively tangle behind her showed that her last insistent summons had been heeded. One by one her restless younglings disentangled their coils from the general knot, and slid noiselessly into cover. But a few yet remained, semi-torpid, and, as her inscrutable wits warned her, in imminent danger beneath the glare of the sun, when suddenly the presence and influence of a human shape struck down across the lava wall; and the diffused purple shadow cast by the rayless sun lay over its hollow.

The body that caused it was invisible to the serpent. But her rattle sounded unceasingly, as with groping coils she turned now this way, now that, in endeavour to repel this menace to her solitude and her young's safety. Rearing herself at last in a blind fury of terror and anguish, with blunt head and flickering tongue she struck again and again, not at the dreadful human gently surveying her out of his smiling yet anguished face, as draggled, parched, and half-fainting he watched her every movement, but merely at the insensitive shadow that overhung her lair.

The hollow desperate thumping of her slenderly boned head knocking its own knell grew fainter. But the last of her brood had made its way into safety before, bruised and bleeding, it drooped motionless in the dust. At this the old man scrambled down into the hollow. It had been an arduous journey for what might seem so trivial an errand, but there was no symptom of impatience in his gestures as, having moistened with spittle the ball of his thumb, he gently smeared the muzzle of his victim.

Then he too bent his head, heedless of the still feebly flickering tongue, and seemed to be whispering into the creature's sense some far-brought message of his own.

And, yet again, from across the parched precipitous flanks of Ajubajao, moved, as it were, a vast suspiration of wind, sulphurously hot, of a dense suffocating odour, bestirring in its course the hovering multitudes of the midges, and driving before it a thin cloud of lava dust, as the wind drives shadow across the flats of a sea. Yet again that insidious whispering filled the quiet; and the remote dulcimers tattooed their decoy.

The saint crouched low, hooding as best he could beneath his mantle his eyes, mouth, and nostrils against the smothering, skirring particles. A minute whirlpool of air came dancing like a host of dervishes into the she-serpent's hollow. Lifting the dried scaly fragments of her discarded skin, it dispersed them here, there, everywhere, in its minute headlong rout...

THE SEVEN VALLEYS

The Rest House at the mouth of the Seventh Valley was made of a supple withy woven together layer above layer, with a shell-shaped thatch roofing it in. Seen from a distance this smiling morning, perched amid the green undulations surrounding it, it had the appearance of a beehive. For these withies or osiers, as they dry in that temperate air, fade from their first willow grey-green into a gleaming bronze. Sprouting out of the thatch, too, bloomed and flourished whole families of minute plants, their round-budded clusters showing like the heads of some congregation of insects engaged in prayer.

It was the only dwelling completely within view, rising above the sward on which it stood some thirty yards within the mouth of the valley, the sides of which yawned smoothly wider and wider until they narrowed again towards the entry of the Sixth. Beyond that, yet again – further away than it looked in this translucent atmosphere – tapered into the stillness the summit of yet another Rest House. And so on and on, as it would seem, valley by valley, to the very gates themselves.

The shelving hollow of the nearer expanse was of a tranquil yet lively green. The close turf moulded itself over these verdant contours as delicately as the bloom on the cheek of a sleeping baby or a plum. Clumps, here and there, of a low blossoming tree, its fragrance rilling and wreathing into shallows of sweetness upon the still air, alone interrupted its surface. While in drifts of sapphire blue, over which now hovered and fluttered hosts of a narrow-winged silver butterfly, shimmered like a diapered carpet the myriads of yet another tiny-statured flower.

Winding their way between them, skirting always as near as possible each grove in turn, green paths, faintly patterning the darker green around them, converged like the outspread claws of a gigantic bird, towards the Rest House, the two westernmost of them dipping suddenly out of sight into azure space, as if here they plunged into an abyss of air.

Little traffic, it would appear, could occasion tracks so faint. Up and inward, beyond the Rest House indeed, the broader track was fainter yet; while, bordering it closely in a clean straight line, descended yet another, shallowly printed over with the gallopings of innumerable hoofs.

At a few paces distant from the Rest House, on a rough wooden seat sat the young man Cuspidor. 'A humble office,' had smiled his old friend, 'merits a humble name. Not all the saints, you will find, have endearing manners. The eager hunter has only his quarry in mind. He does not pause to examine every small chit-chat bird that scolds at him from a bush. Others of the saints, my son, discern only too keenly. The modest syllables of the name you now possess may therefore bring a trace of indulgence into their scrutiny. That of shoe-cleaner of the Seventh Valley may appear to be a humble occupation. It is an unworthy one, however, only if one pay regard not to the wearer but merely to the worn.'

Cuspidor, though little else than a mere mortal, had been fairly content with his new office. But he sometimes pined for more company and even for rather more work. Saints only of the First Hierarchy, he had been told, had occasion to traverse in turn each of the Seven Valleys. Of these by far the greater number made no stay in the Seventh, and had no need of his ministrations. And even of the First Hierarchy there were many Orders.

'So, too, of the stars, my son,' St Dusman had explained. 'Those which to our groping eyes appear the dimmest, may so appear not because they are of inferior splendour but because they are the more remote.'

Cuspidor indeed had little need to complain of undue courtesies. Wayfarers who were bound only for the nearer Valleys, to await such biddings as might reach them there, frequently passed on their way with downcast head as if lost in reverie, and without so much as lifting their eyes to glance at the shoe-cleaner and his hostel, or even at the galloping messengers that, like drifts of sunbeams in a forest, swept past them across the turf, bound on errands the goal and purpose of which even the farthest-travelling of the saints themselves seemed content to be ignorant.

Cuspidor had no clock. But he possessed a little wit, and had set up on end a switch of wood, and had cut out on the turf a circle round it, marked at intervals with a XII, a III, a VI and a IX. And though he had no clear notion of what exact quantity of time consisted his day, he had some clumsy notion of the number of the days themselves, as they glided like flowing water through the weeds of his consciousness.

Much else, apart from realization of those days, so glided. Even irrevocable dreams may leave behind them in the mind of the dreamer the empty shell of their being; and Cuspidor was as vaguely aware of events and experiences beyond his comprehension as a fish in the shallows of the ocean may be aware of the outskirts of the continents that fringe it in. His duties though menial were light. He kept watch upon the paths from dawn till twilight: and then no more. After nightfall – though in this region only a deep emerald dusk, thinning to a crystalline radiance above the remoter valleys, succeeded the placid glory of the day – after nightfall any belated traveller must knock, and Cuspidor must rise from his bed to bid him welcome, and to prepare the guest room. No visitor made a prolonged stay, and few, any.

Having come to where the shoe-cleaner stood awaiting him with downcast eyes beside his bench, the pilgrim would rest first one foot, then another, on the wooden block prepared for the purpose. And the young man, having unlatched them, would remove shoes or sandals, scrape off into the hollow beneath whatever foreign matter, dust or mud, still adhered to their under-surface, set them out of the sun, and have them ready when their owner next appeared, bent on his outward journey.

Some little practice had resulted in what was by now almost conspicuous evidence of Cuspidor's labours. A few paces behind the hostel, where stood his beehives and grew his grain and fruit, lay a heap of refuse. It was his little private record of the saints' wayfarings – as well as of his own industry. Even a casual eye might have fastened in amazement on the medley of elements represented there: minute stones of a lustre that must surely have once been precious to *some* discerning eye; fine-coloured sands unlike any Earth or her sister planets can afford; scraps of what resembled ivory, infinitesimals of an endless variety, objects far past their present owner's sagacity to give a name to, or even to recognize, lay scattered and buried in this heap.

While still unaccustomed to his duties and by means of a rough sieve which he had plaited out of fibre from the bark of his fruit trees, Cuspidor had spent his leisure hours in separating the coarser objects in this heap into kinds. The brighter these were in mere light and colour the more they charmed his eye, though of their origin and value he was entirely ignorant. Next, what was rare and strange delighted him. But here, too, he fumbled in ignorance. And he had at last wearied of the pursuit altogether, confining his attention solely to an ivory-coloured dust which, he discovered, if scraped together without any other admixture and kneaded with a little water or spittle, could be converted into a smooth, plastic clay. And this he had taught himself to model rudely into whatever shape chanced to take his fancy. If but a word or a smile were bestowed on his workmanship, it was ample reward. And as he made more progress he was as content with none.

With a lump of this far-fetched clay on his knee, a pointed twig between his fingers, and his body bent almost double, he now sat this fresh morning, completely engrossed in yet another such attempt. It was proving one, however, of infinitely greater difficulty than any that had preceded it. That very daybreak, as he had first stirred in sleep, there had risen in dream into his imagination a phantasmal face of a beauty beyond any that he remembered to have seen in actuality. And yet how strangely familiar it seemed. It had outlasted the dream that gave it birth, haunting his mind, and it now hung before his very eyes, gazing intently out of its fairness as if at the same time happy in his company and grieved at the faintness of his recognition.

Lest it should at any instant vanish as swiftly into the nothing out of which it had appeared, Cuspidor, intent on his clay, had forgotten his shoe-cleaning, the saints, the very place wherein he sat. He kneaded and moulded and graved and smoothed – his tongue showing its tip the while between his lips; a frown between his wide young brows as if his destiny itself, his very peace and being hinged upon his success. So woefully absorbed had he become in this peculiar occupation that it was not the old man's footstep on the sward, but St Dusman's voice, as he stood peering over his shoulder, that suddenly brought him back to himself.

The old saint must for some little while past have been drawing near the shoe-cleaner in full view – as soon indeed as he had emerged out of the abyss on the path by which he usually approached the Rest House. Nor was he the only living creature now in sight. A sudden heat coursed through Cuspidor's body when, having lifted his eyes at his greeting, he discovered already midway up the Sixth Valley, and proceeding on his journey, the figure of one whose raiment showed by its markings that he was no less sacred a personage than a Saint of the Third Order.

'Your flesh may well creep, my son,' said the old man gently, 'but by good fortune he needed nothing of you. We made our greetings as he passed me, and I see that he has returned from regions innocent altogether of the metamorphoses of what we may call the tangible and the superfluous. But be wary. There are saints of his hierarchy who strike as swiftly as a thunderbolt.'

The shoe-cleaner with trembling hands – due in part to the strain of his work and in part to recognition of the peril he had escaped – gazed after the bent and tottering shape now steadily receding from sight. His mouth was shut now; and the phantasmal face had vanished like clouded moonlight from a pool.

'And what are you after this morning, my son? Tired of your pretty baubles?'

The voice was kindly as ever, and as ever seemed to evoke from hidden chambers in the shoe-cleaner's mind the ghosts of memories, rather than memories themselves. He rose to his feet and bowed to the old man; still grasping in his hand the orb of kneaded clay, which had stubbornly refused to become more than a clumsy and distasteful symbol of what had haunted his mind.

'If it please you, Master, a wondrous dream visited me this morning.'

'Then be sure you were sleeping fitfully and in some longing, and you were not alone,' replied the old man.

The intent narrow eyes in the clean-cut mobile face beneath his own slid round in survey of the verdurous slopes beneath and above them. For Cuspidor only the phantoms of serenity now had their dwelling here. The Saint of the Third Order had by this time entered the immense bottle-shaped approach to the Sixth Valley. And the continual ventriloquial silver twittering in the skies above his own of a company of small hovering birds that tenanted this tranquil wilderness was the only sound and sight of life. A shadow spread over his features as he groaned rather than sighed.

'Weary already?' insisted the old man.

'It seemed it was a dream,' was the answer, 'that would last on into the day. And now it is gone.'

'And you were endeavouring, I see,' the saint retorted, 'to fashion it out of mud.'

'It is a marvellously easy clay to the fingers, at any rate,' said the young man. 'And if only I had the skill I could prove it.'

'Let me see,' said St Dusman.

The young shoe-cleaner thrust out his hand over an up-bent elbow, poising his earthen lump in his right palm. And by some secret device of the light that gently flooded the green meadow which stretched in tranquil amplitude around them, there appeared in his crude model a trace of something a little closer to his hope in its markings than the young man had first detected. After a moment or two the old man pushed his spectacles (whose rims even in this rare air showed symptoms of rust) above his eyes, and scrutinized the lump a second time.

'This then was in the image of your dream?' he enquired. 'Why immure in what so soon perishes that which in imagination might remain as fresh as its original?'

The shoe-cleaner frowned and flung his lump of clay to the ground. 'Why, Master, there is more than one way even of cleaning shoes. It is the best that gives the most pleasure: even though it takes the most pains.'

The old man's eyes were of the dimmest blue – far paler than any flower dropped from Dis's wagon, or even than those which sprinkled their spices like dew in this celestial air. The attention in them now fined itself to a needlepoint, on which, say the sages, thousands upon thousands and many thousands of angels may find an easy footing.

'You have happiness in your work then, Mr shoe-cleaner?' he enquired pleasantly.

A queer crisscross expression mapped its way into the young man's face. The keenness as of a bird, the guile as of a serpent, the alert fixedness as of some long-experienced adept of a craft showed in it; and all of them in the service, so to speak, of an almost childlike smile. 'What amuses me,' he said, 'is that a wayfarer that came yesterday, after watching me awhile stooping over my work here – bending his look on me, as you will understand, just round the rim of his sandal – gave me this.'

He held up for St Dusman's inspection a slender stem of ivory expanding into a narrow spoon-like groove. 'He must have noticed my miserable "lumps of mud," ' he explained. 'And there was nothing on *his* feet but a scraping of gold-dust.'

'I know him,' said St Dusman. 'It was St Antioch. Can you describe your dream in words, my son?'

The narrow eyelids fell, the hands fumbled. 'If I could see it in actuality in the air before me,' muttered a low voice, 'I should be happy for ever.'

'Well, well, well,' nodded the old man solemnly. 'Once again, and yet again... You are choosing, I fear, a very long circuit before you will have the opportunity of sharing the experience of standing, as did St Antioch yesterday, amused at the shoe-cleaner with a pretty knack in his craft. Nevertheless, time is made of eternity, and happiness, my son, is but of a moment; and that moment lost in an oblivion of loving kindness.'

PRINCE AHMAT NAIGUL

The gloom of night lay over the dense forests that spread themselves like a pall over the face of the earth on either side of the high road – that immeasurable causeway from north of the Great River for countless leagues to the sea. The skies above their motionless crests were fiery with stars. Immediately in front of the horsemen indeed, who were now rapidly approaching along the dim white benighted track on their many-days' journey from the northern mountains to the Winter Palace that reared its walls and cupolas upon the precipitous banks of the river, stood (rivalling each the other) above the distant fret of trees, and but a few degrees apart, silver Venus and the flaming Dog-Star.

The horsemen – the scarlet of their head-dresses and their cloaks scarcely discernible in this dense dusk – rode so far in advance of the cavalcade which was following after them that the dust they raised in passing had already floated to rest again before its leaders came into sight.

Under a milk-cupped, leaf-tressed, umbrella-like tree at the edge of the curved dip which the gigantic highway made at this point in its course, owing to the waters of a brackish lake which stretched itself out like a silver dragon in the uttermost glooms of the forest, sat a leper. Forbidden by law to show his shape in village or city, keeping his slender hold on life as best he could, he was a wanderer and a vagrant, dependent on the charity of chance wayfarers. Yet his marred face, glimmering faintly beneath this black canopy of boughs as if with a phosphorescence of its own, was in spite of its hideousness benign with magnanimity and peace. His empty dish – formed out of the shell of an immense nut whose kind hung in huge clusters, like slumbering groups of monkeys, amid one of the forest trees nearby – lay empty beside him. He had composed his emaciated limbs in an attitude of contemplation. But his bleared eyes were now fixed on the torches and lanthorns of the approaching cavalcade, as its horsemen and broad-wheeled coaches came sweeping towards his screened retreat along the road.

The skies were still and windless, sharing as it seemed awhile the quiet of boundless space. Even above the swelling tumult raised by the travellers in their journey, the leper marked the melancholy chantings of the night-birds in the branches above his head and in the thickets around him. Scared by scent and rumour of these human invaders as they approached, the cowering beasts of the forest had long since retired into their further fast-nesses, though the bolder of them paused to gaze stealthily out at the leashed hounds, the hooded hawks, the intent or sleeping faces of the con-voy, and its living lovely treasure as it swept on its way.

The crackling torch-flames and coloured lanthorns now flung mean-while a brilliant and moving cloud of luminosity above the causeway; bridle, harness, lance, scabbard, and spur glittered amid the brilliant colourings of the throng.

It was the Prince Ahmat Naigul, returning with his bride after the feasting and festivities of their marriage-rites. Coach after coach, burdened with the grandees of his court and retinue – some gently slumbering as they reclined on the low, shallow, cushioned seats within, others chattering and making merry, their eyes gleaming restlessly in the light flung into the dim recesses within their small wheeled houses from the torches of the horse-men that flanked each vehicle in turn – lumbered heavily by, grinding the powdered flint of the highway into dust yet finer. It seemed this living stream between these darkened walls would never cease.

None the less, there came an interval at last in its garish onset. Then yet another squadron followed after, their milk-white cloaks drawn back over the crimson and silver of their silken undervests to the cruppers of long-maned horses of the colour of old ivory, their head-dresses surmounted with bejewelled plumes of stiff-spined feathers. They rode in silence, spear in hand, the personal bodyguard of Prince Ahmat Naigul himself, whose coach, lightly swaying on its heavy springs and fashioned of dark wood, ivory and silver, now drew near, drawn by its eight ink-black Tartary draught-horses, their outlandish outriders muffled to the eyes this summer evening in tippets of sable.

The leper rose shivering to his feet, and muffling with his hand the deep-cut copper bell that swung suspended by a hempen cord about his middle, he advanced to the edge of the highway.

And within the royal coach, her head at a gentle angle against its swan-white cushions, Ahmat Naigul's princess lay asleep. About her brow was a green circlet of leaves of the everlasting Ooneetha tree. Her hair hung down on either side her quiet head in braided plaits, dangling upon her slender shoulders and thence upon the smooth inlaid feathers of the hooded cloak that enwrapped her, itself patterned in a linked soft loveliness after the fashion of the same tree. Her face resembled in its quietude and fairness the twilight of an evening in May, and she reclined in profound slumber, the orange doublet and cuirass of the dark Prince beside her shining like still sheaves of flame against her snow.

His eyes were fixed intently upon the gently moving darkness of the forest that skirted the high road, but ever and again his gaze returned to rest upon the dreaming one beside him. And with bare hand holding his jewelled glove, he would, as it were, make to stroke the feathered folds of her cloak, and then, gently drawing it back, refrain, once more resuming his scrutiny of the vast silence that compassed them in.

At that instant, the gently rocking coach in which he sat lurched slightly on its leathern springs, as if the mettlesome horses that drew it had swerved at some unexpected sight or sound. A challenging voice broke into the hush. The wheels slowly ceased to revolve; then came to rest in the dust. With a sharp turn of his head, the Prince stooped forward in the warm gloom of the carriage, and peered out of the window. Delicate shafts of light from the moon that every moment was riding higher into the vacancy of the sky, struck diagonally across, silvering the motionless wall of trees that bordered this bend of the high road.

Full in this flooding radiance, shell in hand, his once white rags dingy and blotched, stood the leper, his matted hair falling lank on either side his half-disfeatured face. The glass-clear pupils beneath the half-closed and fretted lids, were steady in their regard, and were fixed not on the Prince, not apparently on any single object within the shadow of the coach, but as if in contemplation far beyond it. Nevertheless, the first clear glimpse of this whited wayside figure seemed to turn Ahmat Naigul's body to stone. He desisted even from breathing, nor dared to glance behind him into the shadow, lest the eyes that had been so gently slumbering were now wide agape. And yet the terror that had suddenly assailed a heart at least as courageous as that of any beast that prowled the forests around him had sprung solely from instinct. Such dreadful shows of God's providence as this mendicant were none too rare, even in a country magnanimously governed.

A profound foreboding darkened his mind as in the twilight reflection of the dust and foliage of the wayside Prince Ahmat Naigul now turned to scrutinize his bride. Their lids lay gently on her rounded eyes, though above them the pencilled brows were lifted as if in a faint and delicious astonishment. A rose-like flush had risen into her cheek; her lips were a moth's-wing apart. The feathered cloak – needled together of down from the plumage of the swans that haunt the still green creeks of the Great River – almost imperceptibly rose and fell above the quiet breast. No dream even, unless a dream of peace, haunted the spirit within.

Stealthily as a serpent the Prince lifted himself to his feet and stepped down out of the carriage. A tense silence now lay over this loop of the great highway. All tongues had fallen still, and though curiosity had turned not one head by a hair's-breadth in his direction, the complete cavalcade was arrested as if at a secret word of command. It might have been the assemblage of a dream.

With a word to the horseman that now stood dismounted in the dust a little behind the royal coach, Prince Ahmat Naigul passed on, preceded by the leper, and at a few paces distant came to a pause and confronted him.

The wolf of disease had all but gnawed away the nose. The cheek was sunken, the coarse hair hung limp and matted over the eroded ears. The hand that held the bowl to his breast shimmered as if it were inlaid with the scales of a fish, while the other grasped tight its copper bell as if with the talons of a bird. None the less, the glass-like eyes beneath their withering lids continued to gaze out as if in reverie. And not only humility, but an inward gentleness and peace, like that burthening the sails of an incoming ship in a squalid haven, shed their influences from this appalling shape. As in a lamp fashioned out of the coarsest horn, a gentle flame seemed to be burning from within the emaciated physiognomy.

Amid the folds of Ahmat Naigul's dimmed orange and scarlet, the jewels glowed softly in the moonlit atmosphere. His narrow head was flung back a little as if his nostrils were in doubt of the air they breathed. Poverty, it has been recorded, is a gift of the Infinite. And the Prince made a slight obeisance as he drew a ring from his finger and advancing a pace nearer dropped it into the leper's bowl.

'A voice within,' he muttered, 'tells me that life is brief. I am prepared, Sorrowful One, and of your mercy would be thankful to follow at once.'

The leper inclined his head a little towards the Prince, but his eyes remained unstirring.

'How knowest thou,' the parched lips gasped, 'how knowest thou the message has come for *thee*? Brief though the hour may be, it has its meed of minutes. Empty your mind of all but its most secret memories; have you peace at last?'

'Is rest possible where happiness dwells?' returned Ahmat Naigul.

'Only where rest is is happiness. Your journeyings have brought you here. Nor is it my bidding to call you yet away.'

'Who then?' answered the thread-like voice, as the hand beneath the cloak groped upwards towards the dagger concealed beneath it.

'I have your alms,' said the leper; 'and now, if, as it seems, your highness's will is to lead while others follow, our one and only need is that we exchange the kiss of peace.'

And it seemed to the Prince as he stooped forward, resting his trembling hands upon the leper's shrivelled shoulders, that the infinitely aged face

beneath his eyes might be that of Death, so utterly serene it was. But no
dreadful horror of mortal malady now showed itself. Even the holes, where
nostrils as sweet with health as his should be, were now dark casements
commanding a secret country; and the narrowed eyes above them were as
windows lit with such sunlight as springs reflected from untrodden snows.
And as if Ahmat Naigul had sipped of some potent syrup, consciousness
lost count for one instant of eternity of time and space. Memories as of a
myriad lifetimes swept pleasantly before his eyes.

He drew back at last, and there broke upon his ear, loud as the clang of
a temple gong, the clink of a horseman's silver bridle. And even yet the
leper had not bent his eyes in his direction. Releasing his bell from his grasp
and letting it swing soundlessly above the dust, the leper stooped, and
having groped, hoarsely breathing, with his fingers in the dust, raised himself up once more and thrust out from his body his dried-up palm, at angles
with his wrist, and almost as narrow as a monkey's.

Ahmat Naigul in turn outstretched his ungloved hand, from beneath his
cloak, and the leper deposited in it an object so minute that the Prince had
to press it firmly into the skin with his third finger lest he should lose it.

'The seven ways remain,' said the leper. 'And the easternmost is the way
of life. My gift, Highness, is but for remembrance's sake.' And without
more ado this saint of poverty swathed his miserable rags around his body,
and turned back towards the blossoming tree where he had been resting his
bones beside the waters of the lake.

Ahmat Naigul remounted into his coach, and the horsemen swept on.
Time passed unheeded while he sat bolt upright, finger still fixed to palm,
his lips like ice above his gums, and his eyes dark with the fear that had
clouded them.

And with daybreak, the forest by the roadside now withdrew itself a little.
Dark herbage scattered with flowers nodded its dews in the first rays of the
sun, as the eyes of the gentle unstirring one beside him opened, to gaze once
more at the companion of her journey; and her beauty was like a looking-
glass to the beauty of the morning.

'You have been gathering flowers,' she said; 'and the narrow air herewithin
is sweeter far than that of the country in which I have been wandering.'

'And what country was that?' whispered the Prince.

'I dreamed,' she said, 'that you were once a man, and a bird, and a serpent. And I dreamed, Ahmat Naigul, that you were once a scullion to the
Sages of the Most High. And that sometimes – forgive me, beloved – you
sipped of their wine-cups when the veil of the entering-in had hidden you
from their sight.'

She drew a warm hand from beneath her feathers. 'Why,' she said,
touching his, 'your lips are stained with it yet. They are like crimson

threads upon a honey ground. And what have you there beneath your finger-tip?'

She paused awhile. But Ahmat Naigul made no movement. 'And what have you there beneath your finger-tip?' she questioned him again, a remote accent of disappointment lurking in her voice.

'If, Princess, I had tasted the wine of that other sage whose glance none can resist, what would you say then?'

'Silence is golden, beloved. I would do just like this.'

And heedless of sunbeams, of strange eyes amid the thickets, of the birds wandering on their pathless ways from tree to tree, she bent upwards her fair face, and kissed Ahmat Naigul.

But not until the Prince's chief magician had toiled laboriously and for days together over his hoard of polished crystal was the Princess enabled at last to detect with clearness the speck that had lain so closely imprisoned beneath the finger of his hand; and this even though the magician had succeeded in so adjusting his workmanship that it enlarged it almost to the magnitude of a grain of mustard-seed.

So it was still by faith rather than by direct evidence of her gentle senses that she believed the frettings and mouldings on its infinitesimal surface resembled the features and hollows and fairnesses of a human face. And that, her own . . .

EN ROUTE

The mud houses at the western end of the vast city, crammed hugger-mugger together within its enormous sun-baked walls, showed no sign of life, even though the first frigid grey of dawn already showed in the eastern skies; even though from point to point in the distance the cocks crowed acknowledgment one to another of this mysterious though often repeated fragment of news. A peculiar odour lay heavy on the air, compounded of the sweet and the offensive. The beaten road wound out between the outlying huddle of houses, but was soon lost in the gloom that still overlay the desert.

The watchman at the slit of window in his turret, which looked inwards towards the city, muffled up in his sheepskin coat, his grey beard spread spadewise upon his chest, sat with so fixed and motionless an attention on the long vista of narrow street which stretched out beneath his eyes, that he was probably asleep. But one accustomed to sleep with caution can also wake with it. Not a hair of him stirred, except his eyelashes, at sound of a shuffling footstep approaching his eyrie.

A bent old man in the attire and with the symbols of a pilgrim dangling round his neck and affixed with a slender iron chain to his brow, was approaching the watch-tower. In spite of his feebleness and the cobwebs of age that seemed to hang about him even more visibly than the folds of his pilgrim's garb, a serenity, a gravity haunted his appearance which roused the watchman clean out of the last lingering fumes of sleep that yet hung over his senses, and brought him hastily down to the thick-barred door below. Thence his eyes – their whites just touched with the light that was rilling on and on into this country's dark – peered out at this untimely intruder.

News that a princeling, more gracious than Springtime in the wilderness, and yet of tender age, was now seated upon the throne of his father, had been the common property of the market-place the whole long day before. He had himself heard the High Officer of the Court, his retinue attired in silver and purple, read out for all to hear a proclamation announcing that father's abdication. Universal sorrow had been its effect, and universal gladness also that Fate had sweetened her medicine with a successor of such high promise.

The watchman continued to glare out of his window at the pilgrim in the street – who at length approached and was accosted. Pilgrims of any faith which the experience of life in this world may instil or fail to shatter, had long since been free to come and go without other question than could be answered by the symbols and relics which they bore.

Still, the watchman was human, and this particular pilgrim one of uncommon interest. None the less, the colloquy that followed in the murk of the deserted street and gate-house, was brief. The watchman was given to understand (though he had difficulty in distinguishing the quavering, muffled words) that the pilgrim had here expected to meet an acquaintance, a fellow-wayfarer, a friend. One of renowned punctuality, even though his assignations might be one-sided.

According to his own showing, the watchman could have slumbered never so much as a wink during the hours of his vigil, for he assured the old man that no human figure had entered or passed through under the gate-house during the whole of the preceding night. Feastings and junketings, he explained, even at this less ornate end of the great city, were over betimes. There was little need to enforce order where laws were so beneficent, and the people who obeyed them so content.

None the less, the old man persisted in assuring the watchman that this particular tryst was one impossible of failure. Could perchance the friend he looked for have concealed himself in the watch-tower? Was he, maybe, at this very moment surveying the street from the ancient battlements above – too far overhead for the discernment of his own faded sight? Could he have crept in under the shadows, secret and unseen?

The watchman's chin sunk deeper into his straggling beard. By the intensity of his scrutiny it might be guessed that he both desired and feared the increasing light which would enable him to pierce a little further under the peak of the pilgrim's hood. His next natural question concerned the appearance of the expected stranger. And at sound of the reply, the pupils of his eyes showed even a little more stonily in their sockets. With a hasty and furtive glance over his shoulder he perceived that the great door was securely barred. 'That being so, I can show you –' he muttered in the face of the old man pressing close against his barred window, 'I can show you the very likeness of him you seek.'

At this the pilgrim paused and looked gently and gravely around him. Nothing living, however, except a stray cur which had stretched itself up out of its dusty corner and now stood shaking the dried dung from its mangey slate-grey hide, appeared in view. He turned once more to the watchman, and explained that he would be able to recognize that likeness even at a glance.

The watchman withdrew and (his lamp having been extinguished) groped his way unsteadily up the narrow staircase, muttering what might be prayers or maledictions beneath his breath. There he paused awhile, consulting anxiously his hazy old wits whether or not he dare venture to betray his instant recognition of this august visitor. The lean black cat that shared his small earthen chamber in the turret stretched itself and yawned.

It was an omen, and he returned at last, carrying in his hand a platter of burnished metal, by means of which he was accustomed to trim his beard and hair when they were in urgent need of it. Between finger and thumb of both hands he held this mirror up to the window so that his own eyes over the rounded rim were only just able to watch its effect upon the pilgrim.

To free himself from any possible offence or discourtesy he explained rapidly that the features now reflected in the mirror answered as precisely as he could remember to the description which the old man had given of his friend.

The pilgrim gazed long and earnestly. 'Ah, my friend,' he said at last, 'you have a discerning eye, and an unflattering tongue. You have not only freed my mind of any mistrust of one whom I was prepared to find awaiting me here – lest, I mean, that he had perchance forgotten me; but you fill me with a happiness beyond even the voice of youth itself to express. I understand, as if he himself uttered it, that he and I are at one; and that I must forthwith continue my pilgrimage towards the Seventh Valley. Meanwhile, I pray you accept of me for his remembrance this most precious keepsake and relic. Guard it safely; and present it to him – press it into the very palm of his hand – when he shall himself come your way.'

The watchman drew down his blurred old mirror and thrust a horny hand close to the lattice. Into its palm the pilgrim pressed an object that appeared to have been carved out of ivory, but which in magnitude was whole worlds smaller than a pea. It was strange, too, that in these few moments the light of dawn seemed to have intensified to such a degree that it surrounded the bent old hooded head at the window with a vague radiance like that of a lunar rainbow. Having bowed a blessing, he was gone.

The watchman, being, as it has already been related, of an unusually cautious and sluggish brain, refrained from stirring for some few minutes afterwards. Having then for safety deposited beneath his tongue the relic he had received for keepsake, he stealthily ascended the deep worn stone steps of his staircase, and from well within the chamber peeped out across the flat roofs towards the desert.

By this time, slow though his progress had been, the figure of the pilgrim was almost out of sight; even though the first shoots of the gigantic sun had by now struck his garments, transmuting them to their own colour – that of red and gold. And when the watchman sat down to examine his infinitesimal gift, he gave thanks to his lucky stars that he had not broken into his visitor's confidence with any of the urbanities appropriate to converse between a subject and his king.

For though his faded sight was utterly unable to discern what similitude it bore, or his wits to skip from its fretted surface to the Queen Mother who now had no one but her son for inmost company, he realized that here was a jewel of great price. And he vowed within himself, too, that when the moment came for its presentation, he would do his utmost to secure that Bugghul Dur, his fellow watchman, should then be on duty.

Disillusioned *

Whenever Dr Lidgett's visitor paused in his monologue, so serene seemed the quiet in the consulting-room, so gently from its one high window rilled in the light, that these two strangers might have been closeted together in an oasis of everlasting peace. It was afternoon, and a scene of stillest life. The polished writing-table with its worn maroon leather, the cabinet over the chimney-piece, with its surgical instruments, and toy balances, the glass and gilt of the engraved portraits on the walls – everything in the room appeared to have sunken long ago into a reverie oceans deep. Even the faint fume of drugs on the air and the persistent tapping of water in a shallow basin behind the dark-blue screen only intensified the quiet. They were

* Printed with a number of manuscript alterations made by de la Mare in his copy of C (1926).

nothing more than a gentle reminder that our human frailty sometimes requires an anaesthetic, and that it is by moments life comes and goes.

'But I see I am detaining you,' the small yet penetrating voice began again out of the large leather-covered chair. 'I shouldn't have intruded at such a time.' The quick dark eyes of the stranger under the bony hollows of the brows were fixed on Dr Lidgett – as if he were a lighthouse looked at from a stormy sea. The face was pallid; the fingers twitched restlessly; there was an air of vigilant intelligence on the features – as if the spirit of which they were the mask had for some time been afraid of being frightened, and intent on realizing it when real cause for fear came.

Dr Lidgett sat with his back to the window, his chair turned a little away from the table, his right leg crossed over his left, showing a neat, well-cut boot. He remained perfectly still, his eyes downcast, his well-kept hands resting a little heavily on the arms of his chair. His attitude suggested indeed that to listen like this to what this untimely visitor was saying, and as heedfully and as sympathetically as possible, was, if anything, preferable, perhaps, to listening to nothing, to being, as he had been lately, so noticeably alone.

'Not at all,' he murmured reassuringly, glancing up at his visitor, 'please be quite comfortable about that, and go on with what you were telling me. As I say, this is not my usual consulting hour; and as a matter of fact my partner, Dr Herbert Scott, is attending to my patients for the next few days. You would find him this evening at Drayton House – No. 110 – a little further down the hill. But don't let that concern you now. You were complaining of physical lassitude, general malaise?'

His voice was low and unanimated, but he pronounced his words with precision, his rather full red lips moving beneath his square-cut beard. The eyes of the two of them met for an instant, and the doctor looked away.

'It's exceedingly kind of you,' his visitor demurred. 'And – well, that is really my trouble. But, as I was saying, it's not exactly physical. Indeed,' he added, as if in disappointment that there should be so little to tell, 'there appears to be precious little actually wrong with me; nothing much more, I mean, than what is usual in these days and at my age, I suppose. It is merely this detestable listlessness of mind; this loss of *mental* appetite. And I had a wonderful digestion once!' He smiled at this wintry ghost of a joke. 'The fact is I can't regain my grip on things. It is as though whatever I do or think or say – or feel for that matter – serves no purpose, is no manner of use – to myself, I mean. And yet, my friends talk to me much as usual. Nobody seems to have noticed anything wrong. They haven't said so. But then we don't, do we? I wonder at times, doctor, if it is not because we daren't. There must be many of us, surely, in much the same state.

'I am, as I say, a writer, an author by profession. I scribble a good deal for the magazines, fiction chiefly.' The dark eyebrows raised themselves above the intently dark and smallish eyes. 'As a matter of fact my name is Pritchard,' he explained. 'You may just possibly have come across it somewhere.'

'I know the name,' said Dr Lidgett discreetly, 'but I could not perhaps definitely connect it with anything I have actually read. But then I have little time for reading.'

'No, no, no, of course not,' his visitor hastened to reassure him. 'I didn't mean that; it was only that nowadays we can hardly help to some extent taking in one another's washing, so to speak. On the other hand, of course, fiction is read almost solely by women – a sort of stimulant, or sedative perhaps. I mentioned it merely because, I suppose, one's occupation *counts*. Not that I claim, thank heaven, to be a victim of the artistic temperament; as a matter of fact I'm not up to that standard. Far from it.' He smiled again, looking the while more haggard and lifeless than ever.

'But that's how I stand. What I mean is this – that, so far as I know, lungs, heart, liver, and all that, are sound enough – as sound at least as one would expect at my age. I was examined not so very long ago either. It's rather my nerves, my-*self*, you know. Not that there is anything definitely, organically wrong with my mind, I mean, either, I hope. At least I *hope* not.' He smiled – a smile almost lustrous in its intensity. 'Not at least in the usual meaning of the word.'

Dr Lidgett gazed steadily at this naïve yet receptive and highly-animated face. He too smiled, but as if at such moments it was customary to do so. 'It is exceedingly unlikely,' he agreed, 'that you would have come to me if that had been the case. Not at all. Were you recommended to see me – personally?'

'No, oh no. I haven't even that excuse. I was passing; I was walking along the street, not going anywhere in particular, of course; and I caught sight of the brass plate and the lamp. One is foolish perhaps to obey these vague impulses. It isn't quite fair. But...Somehow it seemed, *there's* your chance. I read the names – as I say – and my only fear was that this might be Dr Scott's. I wanted to see *you*, Dr Lidgett: I don't know why. But there, I am only worsening my case,' he stirred in his chair, groped for his hat, 'I see I *am* detaining you. Let me come again another time.'

If Dr Lidgett felt any impatience with so hesitant a visitor, his sober unmoving countenance showed not a trace of it. 'Please go on: I am anxious to hear,' he said, though his words sounded as if they were more unwilling than usual to come at the moment's call. 'Tell me precisely what these nervous or mental symptoms are. Is your memory fairly good for example – names, dates, words and so on? Do you find it difficult to fix your attention – to concentrate? Have you any worry? Is there any particular thing continually on your mind? Are your thoughts interrupted,

I mean, as if without cause?'

'I don't hear voices, or anything of that kind,' said his visitor. 'No more, I mean, than one *should* in doing my particular kind of work. My memory is remarkably good – for what I need. And I can concentrate on what I really want to do. What more do I ask?'

The blank face with which he put this question resembled Grimaldi's at his most melancholy; it was at the same time so empty, so forlorn and so ineffectual. 'Literally nothing, doctor, except to say that there is no purpose in what I do. It is lifeless, inert; the bottom's knocked out of it. No use at all; except, of course, for what it brings in – the merely practical side of it.'

'Have you – any family?' enquired the doctor. Indeed he almost blurted the question in his quiet fashion, as if it were one not entirely to his liking, too intrusive and personal.

'None whatever,' was the reply. Mr Pritchard in fact looked slightly astonished at being asked anything so commonplace, as if he had been unexpectedly presented with an aspect of life which he had never paused to consider. 'I live with my mother,' he said. 'She is an old lady now. Hale still, but a little deaf, and apt to repeat herself. We spend a great deal of time together. But lately she has not been so well as I could wish. Have you ever repeated that phrase – "failing health" – over to yourself? Tennyson, you know, used to say under his breath "*Alfred, Alfred, Alfred*" until he became like a shell with the wind in it – empty. But I say instead, "In failing health – in failing health – in failing health" – the meaning intensifies, doctor, the longer you brood on it. But that of course is not what you were asking. Besides, I doubt if any kind of responsibility – wife and children and so on – that kind of thing – would make much difference. I haven't noticed it in other men. It might even complicate matters, mightn't it?' But Dr Lidgett, on his side, appeared not to have considered this problem; and his visitor pressed on.

'To tell you the honest truth,' he said, 'I have come to the end of things. For me, the spirit, the meaning – whatever you like to call it – has vanished, gone clean out of the world, out of what we call reality. At least for me. It's nothing but a husk; and a dried-up husk at that. It may sound pompous and affected, but, try as I may, I can no longer see any purpose in it all, even if I ever did. You may retort,' he interrupted himself eagerly – 'you may retort: "But, then, who does?" But then, you see, there is all the difference between not seeing a purpose in life because you haven't looked for one; and being sure there is no purpose when you have.

'Besides, what right have we to assume there *is* a purpose? What justification? The palaver! I remember not many months ago – I had been in bed for a few days with a chill – I woke up one afternoon and found my eyes fixed on the window – autumn trees, a quiet blue sky, a few late swallows, twilight coming: and at that moment as if in divination I *knew* there was no purpose. I wanted nothing; so there was nothing to want...A tale told by an idiot – signifying nothing. What if Shakespeare himself *meant* that?'

Dr Lidgett glanced covertly away from his visitor. Nobody could have gathered from his quiet solemn eyes if he considered even Shakespearean convictions of final validity, or even if he needed any evidence in the matter. Their expression was absent and yet mournful, as if they were fixed on the ghost or spectre of some happy memory never to be retrieved, never to bloom again.

'It's difficult to explain these things,' his visitor was chattering on, almost vivaciously. 'But I wrote a bit of a story once, with something of that idea at the back of it – the changing points of view, I mean. It was about a man who buys a pair of spectacles – goggles – greenish glass, copper handles – at a shop tucked away under a row of lime-trees in a little cathedral town. Three steps down; very still and musty-fusty; owl in a glass case; antiques, all sorts; and a funny old shop-keeper with a goatee beard. That kind of thing. He asks the peering old creature if he has any glasses to shield his eyes from the glare outside. The thing's symbolic, of course. And when the customer goes out of the shop and puts them on, everything in the world is changed.' Up went the doctor's visitor's black eyebrows once more as if in the wildest astonishment at such an original idea: though apparently he was only waiting for a word of encouragement.

'Changed?' Dr Lidgett enquired. 'For the worse?'

'Oh no, the better! The other, surely, would be rather too much of a problem! I couldn't tackle that.'

'I fancied, Mr Pritchard,' the doctor patiently replied, 'you meant that the man who buys the spectacles was – well...'

'No, no, quite the reverse,' the visitor ejaculated eagerly. 'He puts them on in the street. And presto! his whole world is transmogrified. Grand transformation scene: everything around him becomes instantly irradiated with beauty and life and meaning – all that; dancing with happiness and light. Even the shop is an Aladdin's cavern: and the trees outside spread their boughs over him like green tents of enchantment, sighing with mystery and delight. The people in the street – creatures from another planet: Traherne, of course: all *colours* and beautiful forms intensified. They walk as if they had wings – head, shoulder, thigh, like the angels in Isaiah: "Each one had six wings; with twain he covered his face, and with twain he covered his feet, and with twain he did fly:" – just as if the fellow had been taking hashish or something. He sees a woman, with a basket – going shopping: she is fair as Israfel, wondrous as manna, shining – Botticelli. The buildings are marvellously transmuted, too. Even little common things changed: the dust, the cobwebs, the refuse, the manure in the streets, a sandy cat on a window-sill, the sparrows, a thrush in a cage, singing – "in the silence of morning the song of the bird".

'And he goes into the cathedral, in which only the day before he had yawned his way from tomb to tomb, to find it a shrine drenched with loveliness; as if some incomparable artist had spent centuries in cutting the stones, and as if the stones themselves had been quarried from some celestial quarry. There is a faint exquisite blue in the air. He can even hear, like a network of faintly shimmering strings, all the music, the Marbecke and Palestrina, the Bach and the Beethoven and the Purcell and so on, that had floated up and into silence and rest into the fretted roof century after century. I overdid it a little perhaps. You can't help yourself. But that's how my story ran. The spectacles, too, I agree, were a bit mechanical; but then for my part I could never quite stomach the physic trick in *Dr Jekyll and Mr Hyde*. But that's how it came; and the story was published all right. In fact I had one or two letters about it. People are very odd.'

Dr Lidgett had watched his patient steadily through this monologue – his alert gestures, his mobile features, his shining eyes. At this pause he recrossed his legs, closed his eyes very gently – much as a lion blinks at sight of a two-legged visitor looking at him through the bars of his cage.

'It's a story which I should think children particularly would delight in,' he remarked courteously, but with his usual reserve. 'I should like to have read it. How did it end?'

He made the question sound as free from mere civility as possible, but could not restrain the faint sigh which these last few days had been the completion of every other breath he breathed.

'Oh the end?' echoed Mr Pritchard a little dejectedly. 'That is always the difficulty. He begins to preach at the street corner and is shut up for a lunatic and they take his spectacles away and – and so on. It was only a tale. But you see my meaning. The curious thing is that *that* is what we all say about another world. We are haunted by this hope, even this divination of another state or condition of being that is beyond our mortal senses to realize. A place or condition where – well, after death, of course. And yet, I feel, if we are not capable of it here and now, how is the transition to be made? Where shall we find the spectacles? There are some people, of course, who seem never to have needed them – they *are* peace and happiness. But . . .'

He gazed at the doctor as if he were really and truly in need of enlightenment, and as if even possibly it might be included in the fee. 'Well, we don't come across wonder-working opticians under every lime-tree in every cathedral town. And supposing, as you suggested, the magic power of the spectacles had been reversed. What scene then would have met our friend's eyes!

'All I mean is, don't we all have to put up with what we ourselves, each one of us, can get? And the tendency — I remember another tale I read once, by a French writer – at least the name was French. A translation, I think. It was about a philosophical crank whose lifelong hobby had been to transmute knowledge, just as the old philosophers tried to transmute metals. Or rather to focus knowledge so that it became an intrinsic part of himself – as of course all true knowledge is to some extent; a genuine "common-sense" to the "nth" degree; a power of vision; almost, as one might say, another dimension. He sees things first through one aspect of knowledge and then through another in rapid succession, and realizes through a fleeting eternity of change reality's everlasting nothingness or somethingness, whichever way you like to put it.' Mr Pritchard smiled. 'In the end, my Frenchman decided he would have been a wiser and happier man if he had remained content with his own small natural instincts. He gave the game up – though that perhaps hardly sounds French. I have muddled the story, but that was the gist.'

The doctor nodded, as if in encouragement; but even an unobservant visitor could hardly have helped noticing that his attention and interest had begun to wane, had begun to resume their own natural channel. He had sunk a little lower into his chair, and a faint cloud of ennui or abstraction had settled on his features.

Mr Pritchard sighed. 'I don't mean, doctor, that that is in any sense my experience. Far from it. It's beyond me!' The animation died out of the pallid face. The wide forehead resumed its customary frown. The little black eyes fixed themselves on the pattern of the surgery carpet. 'All *my* knowledge only adds to the burden, the realization how helpless I am to contend against this settled conviction of my general uselessness and ineffectiveness. I realize, too, that it is only *my* knowledge, and that that being so, how am I to know that it has any true relation to – any bearing whatsoever on – the facts, on the reality? Please don't suppose that I am pretending to be an expert in anything. I have scarcely more than dabbled in subjects outside my own particular bent. But speaking of the little I have learned, and read, works of science and so on, and taking it for granted that even the novice, the mere man in the street, is free to come to his own conclusions, however partial and inadequate they are bound to be, it seems to me that all that too is nothing more than a general kind of human make-believe. It is merely what *they* – the experts – think, not regarding what really matters to the very self within but only outside material things.

'They work away – self-denyingly and modestly, too, for the most part – with their little scales and their instruments, their little scalpels and acids and batteries and retorts and all that paraphernalia. But whatever the result, however amusing and serviceable and ingenious, we all *know* that such evidence is only the secretion or excretion of their own senses. Senses that can tell us only what they are capable of being sensible *of*.

'And look at it! What – I ask you – is the instant's good of this enormous machine we call life – this treadmill, the moment you *question* whether there is any value or truth or purpose or what-not in what it grinds? Look at their chemistry – the beautiful water-tight jargon of it all. Look at their astronomy: their red star this and their green star that, and the waste of space and the curve to it, and their spectral analyses and their orbits, and their rules of thumb and their mileage – their mileage! As if, doctor, my being two or three yards from you now is a fact of the slightest *spiritual* importance! In itself, I mean.'

The doctor quietly eyeing his visitor, nodded once more. But even yet – though the faintest, dying spark of animation, even of remote amusement, had kindled in his quiet blue eye, it was hardly as though he took more than a merely courteous and friendly interest in what, with so much zest and conviction, his patient was *saying*. But that patient, as alert as any practised prima donna or conjurer in 'sensing' the responsiveness of an audience, had noticed this tiny ray of encouragement, and at once pressed forward.

'I went out last night: I went out into my garden. It's little more than a square green patch of grass, with a few old trees, an acacia and so on, but pleasant and secluded, and not much overlooked. We make a point of that, oddly enough: not to be overlooked! As if — It has a nice old wall, too – a fragment of flotsam left by the country when it receded from the filthy flood of London. And I looked up into what they call the starry void of space; splinters of light: Aldebaran, the rainy Hyades, the clusters, the nebulae – of the Pleiads, Orion and the rest – annular, elliptic, spiral; you know the delightful jargon. And then the Milky Way – the Milky Way! And Venus there in the west, the goddess of Roman love. And now and then, a gentle, soundless, silver curve of dying light – some meteor candling its way into oblivion. I agree you might call it solemn, beautiful, entrancing; significant, even, if you happened to be a young couple just fallen in love. But – for you and me, doctor! I looked, and my imagination simply refused to respond. The spectacle was there, punctual, brilliant, according to specification – but honestly this particular programme-seller was unable to applaud. It was like strumming on a dumb piano – a fake piano. It meant no more to me than a piece of paper over which some idiot in a moment of ill-temper has flicked a fountain-pen. Reverse the colour-scheme: make the sky silvery-white and the stars black dots. What interpretation should we put upon it then? Something sombre and profound and meaningful, not a doubt of it: and with as much and as little justification. The constellations: a child's scrawls! Doggerel!

'The *Goat* to Vesta we allot;
Juno prefers the *Water-pot*;
And Neptune has his *Fishes* got.

'Oh yes, amusing, romantic enough, if you're that way inclined. And I'm saying nothing against it for those who still happily are tinder to every scientific spark. But' – he shifted wearily in his luxurious chair – 'well, I went back into the house. As usual my old mother was sitting by the fire stooped up together in her easy chair in her silk shawl – one of those ugly old Victorian horsehair chairs, made for endurance. And I thought suddenly what a long time it had taken to make her old like that. I thought of what she had gone through – I'm not her only child – to come out *there*, like that. I thought I might perhaps have to survive her and grow old too – and only strangers to look after me. She was knitting. I don't know what she was knitting; but her hands are crooked now, and getting clumsy with her needles.

'I bawled, "It's a fine starry night, Mother."

'She said, "Eh, Charles?"

'I repeated the observation. She said she was glad it was fine. She is an old lady now. Very rarely goes out, you know; so weather hardly matters to her sitting cooped up indoors by the hearth. And upon my word, doctor, as I looked at her – my own mother – I seemed to see Death himself hooped together there in that chair huddling close down to the fire. It was as if the old villain had taken to that device to pass away the time in his old age! – knitting together a winding-sheet for the whole human race; for this complete ridiculous universe. Yet even as I thought it, I felt I was suffocating with remorse – the odiousness of such a feeling about *her*! But no. She wasn't to blame. *We* understand one another: mother and son. There's no need of any sense of proportion in that. One's heart almost breaks at the thought of its own impotence to express, and to comfort, and to tell... Those awful souls one sees in the streets. Awful. Good Lord, doctor, this whole stellar universe of ours may be no more than the bubbles in a bottle of champagne – or soda-water! And we humans the restless maggots in a rotting excretion of the sun. And yet – we go on breeding!'

The doctor drew his hand gently down over his beard. He coughed softly, glancing sidelong at his eloquent patient. 'Am I to understand,' he said, 'that you actually saw a physical change in your mother – I mean, that it amounted to anything in the nature of an hallucination?'

'That's just it,' said his visitor suddenly angling himself up in his chair as if someone had pulled the appropriate wire; 'that's just it. I *did* so see it: but only of course, with my inward eye. It was so because I saw it so: but I'm not pressing it as scientific evidence. No, doctor, I can manage the hallucinations all right, whenever I want to; and without trespassing too far over the border. In fact I should of course be a pretty poor scribbler of fiction – worse even than I am – if I couldn't.'

'But they don't persist?' persisted the doctor.

Once more Mr Pritchard's features seemed to collect themselves together into a point of intense vacuity; and Dr Lidgett looked away again. Beyond the surgery window was a patch of red-brick wall on which a young fruit-tree had been espaliered. It was in scanty leaf now, but though its flowers came punctually to the season, its fruit never ripened, for only the beams of a northwest sun ever peeped into this corner of the doctor's garden. His glance having wandered away from the occupant of his chair rested heavily on its vivid green. This valiant little plum-tree was an old friend of his. He had watched its miracle of revivification recur year after year: had noticed it while he had sat interviewing his patients one after the other, doing his best for them in his own solemn fashion before eagerly returning to that new life of his upstairs. And realizing that it was never likely to bear, he would go out in the evening and pluck a sprig or two of its blossom to bring in for a surprise. It showed greener than ever this particular spring, as if it had taken on an unprecedented verdure, had made the friendliest of efforts, for a particular occasion. And one could hardly blame it if the occasion had suddenly failed, or refused to keep its tryst.

His visitor, having shaken himself free of a momentary absent-mindedness, had followed the direction of the doctor's eyes, and himself gazed a moment at the leafing plum.

'It's a curious thing,' he said, 'but my mind – what they call the subconscious, I suppose – seems for some little time past to have been exploring in the very direction of the state into which I have been gradually reduced. One might almost suppose, I mean, that things and events of the outside world are only mere properties in the inward scene – farce or melodrama – in which one is the only *unquestionably* living actor. Not that I am by profession a solipsist! That little tree, there, reminds me, for example, of yet another piece of fiction I managed to write a few months ago. I know I am boring you with all this stuff, Dr Lidgett; but it's only because it seems to me to be symptomatic so to speak; and I suppose even the smallest particular may be of service in arriving at a diagnosis.'

The doctor turned back his head again, shifted his elbows on the arms of the chair, leaned his chin on his fingers, and once more out of his calm settled eyes patiently surveyed his visitor. 'Certainly,' he said. 'We usually, you know, have to extract these things for ourselves. It is a help to have them volunteered. What is this other story you were referring to?'

'Why' – once more Mr Pritchard's pallid face lit up with inward animation and the gesticulations of his small long-fingered hands helped him out – 'why, in this story, it is Nature herself that dries up. Very gradually, of course. At first, indeed, almost imperceptibly. For a succession of autumns the harvests are slightly but cumulatively less abundant; now in this country, now in that. But steadily and incessantly the general average begins to dwindle all over the world. Then, here and there the deficit becomes acute. At first it is only the important – humanly important things, I mean – cereals, sugar, hops, vines, tea, coffee, and so on, that are noticeably deficient – the irony being that less vital though important things flourish. Rubber, cotton, hemp, for example, continue steady. And new gold and diamond mines are actually discovered. There is a positive glut of coal and petroleum. Transportation from one scene of growing desolation to another therefore remains easy.

'And then, doctor, the creeping shadow! First the cautious experts, the statisticians, the exchanges, the markets, and then on and on in ever widening circles of misgiving and panic. And ever more widely the rumour spreads. The merest patch of countryside reveals the secret at last – one glance at the straggling thinning fields, the wilting hedges, the famished cattle, the naked soil, gaping and grinning through the green – growing bald! And so the pinch grows steadily sharper until the world at large – at least the civilized part of it – begins to realize what it is really in for. There is an orgy of crises: changes of Government: International Conferences: ever more and more impotent and ineffectual. And then at last the newspapers fall on the scare like bluebottles on carrion.

'And the following spring the full realization comes. Things of age-long standing – the forests, the trees, the prairies and savannas – falter, pine, dwindle, fade, perish. And man realizes his final destiny. Even his beloved and trusty law of averages has gone to the deuce, and his just and equable old grandmother Nature is obviously playing the jilt. I can tell you this, doctor; the upshot of that little situation was a good deal worse than the European war. Society, of course, simply falls to pieces. Starvation; mobs; rioting; religious frenzies; fanatics; communities of suicide. You can imagine a starving Europe, a starving America – we have caught glimpses of a starving Asia. And in trouble like that the taking of sides is of comparatively little account. Even an imaginary situation such as that refreshes such dried up old problems as, What do we human beings really believe in? and, Exactly how much do we value posterity? For my part – provided that Nature kept things going just for aesthetic reasons, I cannot honestly see that it would be altogether a calamity if humanity did give up the ghost, or at any rate, if a very large proportion of our superabundant populations did. *I* am ready.'

The doctor spoke muffledly – through his fingers. 'The birth-rate *is*, I believe, actually falling in most European countries. And naturally there are many economists and eugenists who rejoice at it. You have a vivid fancy, Mr Pritchard, if I may venture to say so. But we may hope things won't reach such an extreme as that.'

His visitor smiled; candidly, almost eagerly. 'Perhaps not; and of course you are right about the birth-rate. But the death-rate's going down too – and so the tide is kept in genial flood. Isn't that so?'

But Dr Lidgett seemed to have as suddenly lost interest in the question as he had found it. He shut his mouth, unclenched his fingers, looked away. And once more the dark quick face opposite him also lost life and expression. Mr Pritchard indeed was stifling the rudiments of a yawn.

'Well, that was the story. A mere shocker, of course. It sold well, too. But I agree Nature has as yet ignored my hint.' He looked about him, as if in search of something lost long ago, as if searching had become little more than an automatic reaction. He appeared to be a little uneasy too, as if his conscience were at last chiding him for taking an advantage so extreme of a fellow-professional who merely happened to be at a loose end, and, kindly and tolerant enough to listen to him.

'But quite, quite seriously, doctor,' he began again apologetically, 'why *are* some of us singled out to realize the appalling trap we are all in? How many of us, do you suppose, do realize it: have the courage or the fatuity to face the question? And, as for the rest, what is the impulse, the impetus that keeps them going? Deceives them, if you like, but still keeps them going? Are we really to acknowledge that it is a purely physical thing? This fountain of life that keeps green our philosophical fallacies, keeps green our delight in things, our interest in our fellow-creatures, our faith in Hope, or, at any rate, in a decent courage, even though there is not the slightest logical justification for it – is it really and indeed nothing but a sort of physical well-being? If it's merely that, then I suppose treatment might put it right, Dr Lidgett? Treatment, at any rate, could prevent my concerning myself with it any longer. Say a fraction of a grain of prussic acid. But if it's mental, of the soul, well, my God, I shall keep a very silent tongue in my head when talking to anybody else than a man of your profession! On the other hand, if it *is* mental, why, somehow I feel I ought to try to fight it out. What do you suggest?'

Dr Lidgett having so long and so patiently (and so unenterprisingly) waited for this opportunity, asked his visitor a few sedate, commonplace questions concerning his actual health: his appetite, the hours he kept, how much he smoked, how badly he slept. But then, he had nothing else to do this long spring afternoon, nothing whatever except to look through a few bundles of discarded letters, to write a cheque or two, one in payment of a nominal fee to a specialist on cancer, another for services rendered by yet another kind of specialist – and then to leave his vacant, his incredibly vacant house, and to go away for a few days. He had indeed already once or twice during his visitor's jerky conversation seen himself pacing the deserted but 'bracing' esplanade of a small southern watering-place. This untimely creature would not detain him much longer. Besides, he was himself by nature and habit cautious and thorough. He submitted his patient to a close and exhaustive examination; heart, lungs, stomach, knee-jerk and the rest. Then he once more resumed his seat and looked out of the window.

Having no looking-glass handy, Mr Pritchard was now apparently taking particular care over the adjustment of his collar and tie, though the sidelong twist of his head at the moment suggested that of a bird past all care on a poulterer's hook. But his eyes meanwhile were busily exploring the neat efficient furnishings of Dr Lidgett's consulting-room. From object to object they darted, bright as fireflies on a summer's evening. They had become by long practice the willing servants of his craving for 'local colour'. It was a habit that would no doubt persist even when only a few minutes remained to him of his earthly existence. Indeed, though he must be even in an unusual degree the conscious centre of his own small universe, he was profoundly interested in his fellow-creatures – their absurd little ways and habits and eccentricities. Nothing human shocked or failed to concern him, except possibly most of his fellow-authors' fiction.

On the other hand, though his eyes and senses were at this moment as active as ever, his thoughts were otherwise engaged. Since it could lead to nothing, he was upbraiding himself again for giving all this trouble to the quiet sedate figure seated in the chair over there. He looked a good sort, if ever there was one – probably intensely kind to his poorer patients, even his panel patients, though, as probably, quite unable to appreciate what he himself had been saying, even if he had considered it worthy of attention. A general practitioner must often have to make allowances for patients that appear to him to be little better than freaks; women especially – with nerves rather than minds to pester them.

He had taken a liking to Dr Lidgett; he liked that placid, cautious manner – the reserve of the man. What kind of inward life did *he* lead, he wondered. What kind of home life? 'Have you – er – any family?' – the doctor's question recurred to him so amusingly that it brought the ghost of a smile into his mind. It must be an odd thing to spend one's days tinkering about with deranged human machines – deranged simply because the silly fool of an engineer has neglected or overworked them. On the other hand, the mere human norm must be as uninteresting as it is probably unprofitable. What 'family doctors' wanted were patients with plenty of money and small recurrent ailments. For his own particular purpose he himself preferred the human machine that was not running as smoothly as one of those ghastly electric dynamos with the huge buzzing fly-wheel. So much fuel; so much energy: so much lubricating oil; so much pressure to the square inch. Was it even possible to be fully and vividly conscious and physically sound and normal at the same time?

Apart too from the thoughts in Mr Pritchard's mind, dizzying themselves like wasps fluttering round a honey-pot, there lay only half-concealed beneath them the steady horrible conviction that nothing now was of the slightest account; that the spirit within him, past all hope of ease and happiness and reassurance, resembled a wretched fiend howling in the midst of a black cloud – darkness, and tempest. Once more leaning his head a little sidelong he glanced at his reflection in the glass of a picture, and buttoned up the last button of his waistcoat.

'I am afraid, doctor,' he murmured, 'I must have been the worst possible type of patient. And what is as bad, I ought not to have forced myself on you at this particular time – outside your consulting hours, I mean, which I confess to having seen on the doorplate. I gather too that just now you are actually taking a holiday. It was infamous. I hope you will forgive me!'

There was something curiously winning and amiable in the looks of the little man as the doctor glanced up at him and smiled, assuring him that there was no need whatever for such apologies. Indeed Dr Lidgett's one inward and unspoken regret was his incapacity to be of any real service to his patient. Only in the most rudimentary fashion could he minister to a mind diseased – even his own. *That* he knew. He knew too, only too well, that he could but potter around the problem which had been presented to him, and that even any practical advice he might give – a few little common-sensical directions regarding work, exercise, food, sleep and so on – would probably be ignored and forgotten as soon as his visitor was out of the house.

Was not Humanity itself for that matter habitually ignoring counsel and directions from mind and heart that were none the less sound for being instinctive and commonplace? The pity was that when so little was really wrong – for, so far as the mere circumstances of his visitor were concerned, there appeared to be absurdly little justification for complaint – there was no obvious handle to take hold of. These maladies of the spirit – what cure for *them*? Probably his best advice would be: Try the streets, my friend, for a week or two; without a halfpenny in your pocket and with your jacket for shirt. Or, Give away all you've got and get a dustman's, or stoker's, or fish-porter's job; and then come back to me in a month's time. Or, Take up some beastly philanthropic work – visiting cancer patients or syphilitic children. No doubt what Mr Pritchard was really in need of was a moral shock: something to 'larn him' to be a pessimist and a hypochondriac.

Nothing of all this showed on Dr Lidgett's tranquil and sober face, however. He went about what he was at with an almost feminine neatness and circumspection. And though his hand trembled a little as he held out the prescription he had written down, he talked quietly on awhile, specifying with precision the little things that might be of benefit, and assuring his visitor that the worst thing in the world was to look too closely at things. Except, of course, at things of nature, which after all (and in spite of his little extravaganza) had up to the present proved astonishingly faithful, and bore even the keenest scrutiny with triumphant ease. Provided you accepted its mute decrees and vetoes, with as much resolution as you were capable of.

He did not utter this last thought aloud, however. It had occurred to him merely because his eye had once more strayed to the young green leafing plum-tree crucified upon his garden wall. But the rest of his professional advice had not fallen on deaf ears, apparently. With a smiling reference to his 'pestilent' memory, his visitor had actually gone so far as to scribble down a few memoranda in his pocket-book while the doctor was speaking.

But when the pleasant suppressed voice had ceased, the merest glance at those restless eyes, as Mr Pritchard pushed back the tiny pencil into its place, and re-pocketed his pocket-book, would have perceived that once more the spirit within was circling like a coal-black swift over a gloomy and deserted waste of stones and brawling water – would have perceived, too, that the superficial mind of the creature was as active as ever over its own chosen trifles. He looked at the doctor, opened his mouth, hesitated: and even began again.

'The curious thing is,' he said, 'and oddly enough it has only just occurred to me – I once began a story with a situation in it very much like ours now.'

The doctor raised his head and lifted his eyebrows a little. It had at last occurred to his generous and unsuspicious mind that this scarecrow of a fellow was merely amusing himself at his expense, that he was making a butt of him. But at one glimpse again of that candid, darkly-hollowed face, the tiny flame of righteous indignation that had sprung up within him instantly faded out.

'How that?' he said kindly.

'Why, it was like this. The author – who was what is called for some God-forsaken reason a realist, which so far as I can make out merely means that he restricts his material (just like most of our men of science) to what ordinary human beings in their ordinary human moments would agree are "the facts of the case" – this author goes to a doctor. Neither of them was like ourselves. My author was a raw-boned, lanky fellow, with a shock of reddish hair; and the doctor was a kind of specialist, or rather consultant; a dark saturnine man with bristling black eyebrows – pallid. The author –

mainly in search of copy, of course – concocted some cock-and-bull story that his wife had suicidal tendencies. And what did the specialist advise?'

'And what *did* he advise?' enquired Dr Lidgett, but not as if with any particular curiosity.

'Well, you see, the doctor himself was at his last gasp, so to speak – had been speculating, and had lost all his money. And in addition, or in subtraction, whichever way one likes to put it, his own wife had run away from him. He asked his visitor a few questions, and the wretch, having a pretty quick invention and abundant *sang froid*, supplied him with vivid and convincing details of his wife's symptoms: how she had been dragged back angry and weeping from the very jaws of the grave.'

'And how did it end?'

The question was hardly audible even in the quietness of this habitually quiet room. The sound of the words indeed hardly interrupted the capricious little air which the restless water was tapping into its basin behind the screen. Mr Pritchard had leaned forward in his chair as if he were momentarily uncertain if the doctor had spoken at all.

'Oh,' he replied at last, 'it never ended at all. You see, when I was half way through, I came across a story by Anton Chekhov – the Russian writer you know – which has a somewhat similar theme. Near enough to mine, at any rate, to ensure that the reviewers would have accused me of plagiarizing if I had published it. But that is one of the amusing things about this deplorable life of ours – we are all incorrigible plagiarists, or, at best, parasites. We live on other people's well-being and happiness, our friends and relations. Even on their characters! Ask a father what he thinks of life when his son has gone to the bad, or – or anything of that kind. We can't help ourselves. Even to die and be free of it all is a woeful slap in the face to one's nearest and dearest. The curious detail in my story,' he pushed on almost gaily, 'curious, I mean, as things go – was that there was actually a photograph in a silver frame on the doctor's table very much like that one *there*. I mean the *frame*. But in this case my enterprising young Mr McKay could actually see the photograph itself – the photograph of a young woman – a lovely, seductive, dangerous-looking creature. It was a photograph, in fact, of the doctor's wife who had run away. And – as my ginger-haired friend compared the victim and victimized – he could hardly find it in his head to blame the gay seducer. As a matter of fact I hated the story.'

Dr Lidgett stirred heavily in his chair, and for the last time fixed intent eyes on his visitor's face. 'That was indeed a coincidence,' he said. 'For the portrait here on my table is also a photograph of my wife.'

He was now quite still and composed again, gazing fixedly but tranquilly at his visitor – yet as if only by keeping him well in focus would he be able to maintain his own professional calm and aloofness. Besides, in spite of the sharpest disinclination, he wished intensely to make the fleeting relation between them friendly and helpful to the end. 'However, it's a coincidence,' he added, 'that goes no further. I must some day read the story you mention – by the Russian writer. What did you say the name was?'

'Chekhov – he was himself a doctor, you know, and a devilish good one too, simply unwearying in doing good, besides being the finest writer of short stories, in my humble opinion, of any I know.'

With these words Mr Pritchard rose hastily out of his chair; and once more that awful vacancy spread up into his face. To look at that face now, it might be merely a cruel caricature of himself – dark, discoloured, null, without interest, hope or desire. He gulped – like a child after a long fit of crying – and held out his hand.

'Well doctor,' he said, 'you have been enormously kind to me; far, far kinder than I deserve. But you can have no notion what a help it has been just to – to have talked like this. Quite candidly, I doubt if any remedies can now be of much service; but I will do my best to follow your advice. Anyhow, I am not like that poor wretch's wife in my story: I shan't go to any extreme! In the first place I doubt if I have the courage to – to run away. And in the second, my own conviction is that there are so many people in this world in much the same state of mind as I am, that if any large proportion of us decided – well, to try elsewhere, the statistics would be positively alarming. That alone would solve the Malthusian problem.

'I suppose – to give it a fine-sounding phrase – it is the disease of our modern civilization: nothing definitely, tragically wrong, but just the general condition of things. Not that I am so foolish as to make any claim to being a thinker; I hardly even deserve the name of a feeler. I look on, chiefly. But it is this fate of being a human being at all, with this appalling power of watching ourselves suffer, that becomes at last almost intolerable. The power, too,' he smiled, 'of being actually able to describe our symptoms. And at considerable length, doctor. But there, I have had one supreme advantage this afternoon; for *you* have listened to me, whereas we humans in general in these days seem in the long run to have no one whatsoever to confide in. No one, I mean, in heaven or earth whom we really seem to trust any longer.'

He paused, softly drawing his hand round the brim of his hat; then once more smiled – that curiously childish ingratiating smile. 'Even at that,' he added, 'I feel you would be right in labelling me something of a fraud; for whatever happens – rest or no rest – I shall probably go on with my work all right. It's an odd thing, but, do you know, nothing seems to have the slightest effect upon that. I dare say that is your experience, too. My old mother sometimes tells our friends, "Charles thoroughly enjoys his work, you know...Charles thoroughly enjoys his writing." And Charles can't deny it. That alone should be almost enough to convince one that this is a mechanistic universe. Once wound up, and with enough ink and paper in the machine, one just goes on and on, like – well, even better than clock-work!'

Dr Lidgett took the hand stretched out to him and held it for the briefest moment clasped warmly in his own. His lips moved a little, as if in an attempt to express the inexpressible; or even to utter a syllable or two of kindliness concerning Mr Pritchard's old mother. But he made no further remark. He led the way to the door, then followed his visitor across the hall. A Sheraton barometer stood opposite the hat-stand. Something had gone wrong with its works. Its needle stood at 'Set Fair', whereas but one casual glance at the exquisite mackerel sky above the trees under the open porch was proof enough of the caprices of an English spring. Dr Lidgett stood holding the handle of the front door; and, looking out, watched his visitor until he had reached the gate.

For some reason, most of his patients, he had noticed, were punctilious in the matter of closing the gate after them, when they left his house. They did it firmly, scrupulously, finally, and without noise. This patient – Mr Pritchard – went even further. He once more turned, showing under his hard felt hat that dark white face – rather like a telescopic rendering of the landscapes of the moon. Then he raised that hat, and smiled. Dr Lidgett in response lifted his hand; and his visitor vanished behind the privet hedge.

These, of course, were but gestures of common courtesy. And yet, in the quiet damp air, in that darkening spring twilight, they seemed to be pregnant signals rushing to meet and to cross and to combine – like secret messages in the sphere of the telepathic.

Having bidden his visitor this almost solemn adieu, Dr Lidgett had then as gently and firmly shut his front door, and turned back into his surgery. He at once sat down at his desk and scribbled into his day-book a neat and methodical account of the interview that had just come to an end. He then shut the book, leaned back in his chair, folded his well-kept, competent hands; and his empty eyes, as if of their own volition, strayed towards the photograph on his table.

That too was the photograph of a young and lovely face, but not a 'dangerous' one. And its owner had certainly not 'run away'. She had merely 'gone' away, and for good, and very unwillingly.

The Nap[*]

The autumnal afternoon was creeping steadily on towards night; the sun after the morning's rain was now – from behind thinning clouds – glinting down on the chimney pots and slate roofs of Mr Thripp's suburb. And the day being a Saturday, across Europe, across England, an immense multi-tudinous stirring of humanity was in progress. It had begun in remote Australia and would presently sweep across the Atlantic into vast America, resembling the rustling of an ant-heap in a pine wood in sunny June. The Christian world, that is, was preparing for its weekly half-holiday; and Mr Thripp was taking his share.

As if time were of unusual importance to him, two clocks stood on his kitchen mantelpiece: one, gay as a peepshow in the middle, in a stained wood case with red and blue flowers on the glass front; the other an 'alarm' – which though it was made of tin had a voice and an appearance little short of the brazen. Above them, as if entirely oblivious to their ranting, a glazed King Edward VII stared stolidly out of a Christmas lithograph, with his Orders on his royal breast.

Mr Thripp's kitchen table was at this moment disordered with the remains of a meal straggling over a tablecloth that had now gallantly com-pleted its full week's service. Like all Saturday dinners in his household, this had been a hugger-mugger dinner – one of vehement relays. Mr Thripp himself had returned home from his office at a quarter to two – five min-utes after his daughter Millie and Mrs Thripp had already begun. Charlie Thripp had made his appearance a little before the hour; and James – who somehow had never become Jim or Jimmie – arrived soon afterwards. To each his due, kept warm.

But the hasty feeding was now over. Mr Thripp in his shirt-sleeves, and with his silver watch-chain disposed upon his front, had returned once more from the scullery with his empty tray. He was breathing heavily, for he inclined nowadays, as he would sometimes confess, to the *ongbong-pong*. He had remarkably muscular arms for a man of his sedentary pro-fession, that of ledger clerk in Messrs Bailey, Bailey and Company's counting house. His small eyes, usually half-hidden by their plump lids, were of a bright, clear blue. His round head was covered with close-cut hair; he had fullish lips, and his ample jowl always appeared as if it had been freshly shaved – even on Saturday afternoons.

Mr Thripp delighted in Saturday afternoons. He delighted in house-work. Though he never confessed it to a living soul (and even though it

[*] As printed in BS (1942).

annoyed Tilda to hear him) he delighted too in imitating the waitresses in the tea-shops, and rattled the plates and dishes together as if they were made of a material unshatterable and everlasting. When alone at the sink he would hiss like a groom currying a full-grown mare. He packed the tray full of dirty dishes once more, and returned into the steam of the scullery.

'You get along now, Tilda,' he said to his wife who was drying up. 'We shall have that Mrs Brown knocking every minute, and that only flusters you.'

Mrs Thripp looked more ill-tempered than she really was – with her angular face and chin, pitch-dark eyes, and black straight hair. With long damp fingers she drew back a limp strand of it that had straggled over her forehead.

'What beats me is, you never take a bit of enjoyment yourself,' she replied. 'It isn't fair to *us*. I slave away, morning, noon and night; but that's just as things are. But other husbands get out and about; why not you? *Let* her knock! She's got too much money to waste; that's what's the matter with *her*. I don't know what you wouldn't take her for in that new get-up she's got.'

Then what the devil do you go about with her for? were the words that entered Mr Thripp's mind; and as for slaving, haven't I just *asked* you to give over? Have reason, woman! But he didn't utter them. 'That'll be all right,' he said instead, in his absurd genial way. 'You get on along off, Tilda; I'll see to all this. I enjoy myself my own way, don't you fear. Did you never hear of the selfish sex? Well, that's me!'

'Oh yes, I know all about that,' said his wife sententiously: 'a pinch of salt on a bird's tail! But there's no need for sarcasms. Now do be careful with that dish, there. It don't belong to us, but to next door. She gave me one of her pancakes on it – and nothing better than a shapeless bit of leather, eether. Just to show she was once in service as a cook-general, I suppose; though she never owns to it.'

A spiteful old mischief-maker, if you asked me, was Mr Thripp's inward comment. But 'Oh well, Tilda, she means all right,' he said soothingly. 'Don't you worry. Now get along off with you; it's a hard day, Saturday, but you won't know yourself when you come down again.' As if forced into a line of conduct she deprecated and despised, Tilda flung her wet tea-cloth over a chair, and, with heart beating gaily beneath her shrunken breast, hastened away.

Mr Thripp began to whistle under his breath as he turned on the hot water tap again. It was the one thing he insisted on – a lavish supply of hot water. He was no musician and only himself knew the tune he was in search of; but it kept him going as vigorously as a company of grenadiers on the march, and he invariably did his household jobs against time. It indulged a sort of gambling instinct in him; and the more he hated his job the louder he whistled. So as a small boy he had met the challenge of the terrors of the dark. 'Keep going,' he would say. 'Don't let things mess over. That's waste!'

At that moment, his elder son, James, appeared in the scullery doorway. James took after his mother's side of the family. In his navy-blue serge suit, light-brown shoes, mauve socks and spotted tie, he showed what careful dressing can do for a man. A cigarette sagged from his lower lip. His head was oblong, and flat-sided, and his eyes had a damp and vacant look. He thrust his face an inch or two into the succulent steam beyond the doorway.

'Well, Dad, I'm off,' he said.

Oh, my God! thought his father; if only you'd drop those infernal fags. Smoke, smoke, smoke, morning to night; and you that pasty-looking I can't imagaine what the girl sees in you, with your nice superior ways. 'Right you are, my son', he said aloud, 'I won't ask you to take a hand! Enjoy yourself while you're young, I say. But slow and steady does it. Where might *you* be bound for this afternoon?'

'Oh, tea with Ivy's people,' said James magnanimously. 'Pretty dull going, I can tell you.'

'But it won't be tea all the evening, I suppose?' said his father, pushing a steaming plate into the plate-rack.

'Oh, I dare say we shall loaf off to a Revoo or something,' said James. He tossed his cigarette end into the sink, but missed the refuse strainer. Mr Thripp picked it up with a fork and put it into the receptacle it was intended for, while James 'lit up' again.

'Well, so long,' said his father, 'don't spoil that Sunday-go-to-Meeting suit of yours with all this steam. And by the way, James, I owe you five shillings for that little carpentering job you did for me. It's on the sitting-room shelf.'

'Right ho. Thanks, Dad,' said James. 'I thought it was six. But never mind.'

His father flashed a glance at his son – a glance like the smouldering of a coal. 'That so? Well, make it six, then,' he said. 'And I'm much obliged.'

'Oh, that's nothing,' replied James graciously. 'Cheerio; don't overdo it, Dad.'

Mr Thripp returned to his washing-up. He was thinking rapidly with an extraordinary medley of feeling – as if he were not one Mr Thripp, but many. None the less, his whistling broke out anew as though, like a canary, in rivalry with the gushing of the tap. After loading up his tray with crockery for the last time, he put its contents away in the cupboard, and on the kitchen dresser; cleansed the drain, swabbed up the sink, swabbed up the cracked cement floor, hung up his dish-clout, rinsed his hands, and returned into the kitchen.

Millie in a neat, tailor-made costume which had that week marvellously survived dyeing, was now posed before the little cracked square of kitchen looking-glass. She was a pale, slim thing. Her smooth hair, of a lightish brown streaked with gold and parted in the middle, resembled a gilded frame surrounding her mild angelic face – a face such as the medieval sculptors in France delighted to carve on their altar-pieces. Whatever she wore became her – even her skimpy old pale-blue flannel dressing-gown.

She turned her narrow pretty face sidelong under her hat and looked at her father. She looked at every human being like that – even at her own reflection in a shop window, even at a flower in a glass. She spent her whole life subtly, instinctively, wordlessly courting. She had as many young men as the White Queen has pawns: though not all of them remained long in her service.

It's all very well to be preening yourself in that mirror, my girl, her father was thinking, but you'd be far better off in the long run if you did a bit more to help your mother, even though you do earn a fraction of your living. More thinking and less face, *I* say. And all that — But 'Why, I never see such a girl as you, Millie,' he greeted her incredulously, 'for looking your best! And such a best, too, my dear. Which young spark is it to be *this* afternoon? Eh?'

'Sparks! Dad; how you do talk. Why, I don't hardly know, Dad. Sparks!' Millie's voice almost invariably ran down the scale like the notes of a dulcimer muted with velvet. 'I wasn't thinking of anybody in particular,' she went on, continuing to watch her moving mouth in the glass, 'but I promised Nellie Gibbs I . . . One thing, I am not going to stay out long on a day like this!'

'What's the matter with the day?' Mr Thripp inquired.

'The matter! Why, look at it! It's a fair filthy mug of a day.' The words slipped off her pretty curved lips like pearls over satin. A delicious anguish seemed to have arched the corners of her eyelids.

'Well, ain't there such a thing as a mackingtosh in the house, then?' inquired her father briskly.

'Mackingtosh! Over this? Oh, isn't that just like a man! I should look a perfect guy.' She stood gazing at him, like a gazelle startled by the flurry of a breeze across the placid surface of its drinking-pool.

Now see you here, my girl, that see-saw voice inside her father was expostulating once more, what's the good of them fine silly airs? I take you for an honest man's daughter with not a ha'penny to spare on fal-lals and monkey-traps. *That* won't get you a husband. But Mr Thripp once more ignored its interruption. He smiled almost roguishly out of his bright blue eyes at his daughter. 'Ask *me* what I take you for, my dear? Why, I take you for a nice, well-meaning, though remarkably plain young woman. Eh? But there, there, don't worry. What I say is, make sure of the best (and the best that's *inside*) and let the other young fellows go.'

He swept the last clean fork on the table into the drawer and folded up the tablecloth.

'Oh, Dad, how you do go on!' breathed Millie. 'It's always fellows you're thinking of. As if fellows made any difference.' Her glance roamed a little startledly round the room. 'What *I* can't understand,' she added quickly, 'is why we never have a clean tablecloth. How can anybody ask a friend home to their own place if that's the kind of thing they are going to eat off of?' The faint nuance of discontent in her voice only made it the more enchanting and seductive. She might be Sleeping Beauty babbling out of her dreams.

A cataract of invective coursed through the channels of Mr Thripp's mind. He paused an instant to give the soiled tablecloth another twist and the table another prolonged sweep of that formidable right arm which for twenty-three years had never once been lifted in chastisement of a single one of his three offspring. Then he turned and glanced at the fire.

'I wouldn't,' he said, seizing the shovel, 'I wouldn't let Mother hear that, my dear. We all have a good many things to put up with. And what I say is, all in good time. *You* bring that Mr Right along! and I can promise him not only a clean tablecloth but something appetizing to eat off of it. A bit of a fire in the sitting-room too, for that matter.'

'You're a good sort, Dad,' said Millie, putting up her face to be kissed – in complete confidence that the tiny powder-puff in her vanity bag would soon adjust any possible mishap to the tip of her small nose. 'But I don't believe you ever think *I* think of anything.'

'Good-bye, my dear,' said Mr Thripp; 'don't kiss me. I am all of a smother with the washing-up.'

'Toodle-loo, Ma,' Millie shrilled, as her father followed her out into the passage. He drew open the front door, secreting his shirt-sleeves well behind it in case of curious passers-by.

'Take care of yourself, my dear,' he called after her, 'and don't be too late.'

'Late!' tossed Millie, 'any one would think I had been coddled up in a hot-house.'

Out of a seething expense of spirit in Mr Thripp's mind only a few words made themselves distinct. 'Well, never mind, my precious dear. I'm *with* you for ever, whether you know it or not.'

He returned into the house, and at once confronted his younger son, Charlie, who was at that moment descending the stairs. As a matter of fact he was descending the stairs like fifteen Charlies, and nothing so much exasperated his father as to feel the whole house rock on its foundations at each fresh impact.

'Off to your Match, my boy?' he cried. 'Some day I expect you will be taking a hand in the game yourself. Better share than watch!'

Every single Saturday afternoon during the football season Mr Thripp ventured to express some such optimistic sentiment as this. But Charlie had no objection; not at all.

'Not me, Dad,' he assured him good-humouredly. 'I'd sooner pay a bob to see other fellows crocked up. You couldn't lend me one, I suppose?'

'Lend you what?'

'Two tanners; four frippenies; a twelfth of a gross of coppers.'

Good God! yelled Mr Thripp's inward monitor, am I *never* to have a minute's rest or relief? But it yelled in vain.

'Right you are, my son,' he said instead, and thrusting his fleshy hand into his tight-fitting trouser-pocket he brought out a fistful of silver and pence. 'And there,' he added, 'there's an extra sixpence, free, *gratis*, and for nothing, for the *table d'hôte*. All I say is, Charlie, better say "give" when there isn't much chance of keeping to the "lend". I don't want to preach; but that's always been *my* rule; and kept it too, as well as I could.'

Charles counted the coins in his hand, and looked at his father. He grinned companionably. He invariably found his father a little funny to look at. He seemed somehow to be so remote from anything you could mean by things as they are, and things as they are now. He wasn't so much old-fashioned, as just a Gone-by. He was his father, of course, just as a jug is a jug, and now and then Charlie was uncommonly fond of him, longed for his company, and remembered being a little boy walking with him in the Recreation Ground. But he wished he wouldn't be always giving advice, and especially the kind of advice which he had himself assiduously practised.

'Ta, Dad,' he said; 'that's doing me proud. I'll buy you a box of Havanas with what's over from the *table d'hôte*. And now we're square. Good-bye, dad.' He paused as he turned to go. 'Honour bright,' he added, 'I hope I shall be earning a bit more soon, and then I shan't have to ask you for anything.'

A curious shine came into Mr Thripp's small lively eyes; it seemed almost to spill over on to his plum cheeks. It looked as if those cheeks had even paled a little.

'Why, that's all right, Charlie, me boy,' he mumbled, 'I'd give you the skin off me body if it would be of any use. That's all right. Don't stand about too long but just keep going. What I can't abide is these young fellows that swallow down their enjoyments like so much black draught. But we are not that kind of a family, I'm thankful to say.'

'Not me!' said Charles, with a grimace like a good-humoured marmoset, and off he went to his soccer match.

Hardly had the sound of his footsteps ceased – and Mr Thripp stayed there in the passage, as if to listen till they were for ever out of hearing – when there came a muffled secretive tap on the panel of the door. At sound of it the genial podgy face blurred and blackened.

Oh, it's you, you cringing Jezebel is it? – the thought scurried through his mind like a mangy animal. Mr Thripp indeed was no lover of the ultra-feminine. He either feared it, or hated it, or both feared *and* hated it. It disturbed his even tenor. It was a thorn in the side of the Mr Thripp who not only believed second thoughts were best, but systematically refused to give utterance to first. Any sensible person, he would say, ought to know when he's a bit overtaxed, and act accordingly.

The gloved fingers, Delilah-like, had tapped again. Mr Thripp tiptoed back into the kitchen, put on his coat, and opened the door.

'Oh, it's you, Mrs Brown,' he said. 'Tilda won't be a moment. She's upstairs titivating. Come in and take a seat.'

His eyes meanwhile were informing that inward censor of his precisely how many inches thick the mauvish face-powder lay on Mrs Brown's cheek, the liver-coloured lipstick on her mouth, and the dye on her loaded eyelashes. Those naturally delicate lashes swept down in a gentle fringe upon her cheek as she smiled in reply. She was a graceful thing, too, but practised; and far more feline, far far more body-conscious than Millie. No longer in the blush of youth either; though still mistress of the gift that never leaves its predestined owner – the impulse and power to fascinate mere man. Still, there were limitations even to Mrs Brown's orbit of attraction, and Mr Thripp might have been the planet Neptune, he kept himself so far out in the cold.

He paused a moment at the entrance to the sitting-room, until his visitor had seated herself. He was eyeing her Frenchified silk scarf, her demure new hat, her smart high-heeled patent-leather shoes, but his eyes dropped like stones when he discovered her own dark languishing ones surveying him from under that hat's beguiling brim.

'Nice afternoon after the rain,' he remarked instantly. 'Going to the pictures, I suppose? As for meself, these days make me want to be out and in at the same time. It's the mustry, fusty, smoky dark of them places I can't stand.'

Mrs Brown rarely raised her voice much above a whisper. Indeed it appeared to be a physical effort to her to speak at all. She turned her face a little sidelong, her glance on the carpet. 'Why, it's the dark I enjoy, Mr Thripp,' she said. 'It' – and she raised her own – 'it rests the eyes so.'

For an instant Mr Thripp's memory returned to Millie, but he made no comment.

'Here's Mrs Brown, Tilda,' he called up the staircase. Good heavens, the woman might as well be the real thing, the voice within was declaring. But the words that immediately followed up this piece of news were merely,

'You'll be mighty surprised to hear, Tilda, Mrs Brown's got a new hat.' A faint catcall of merriment descended the stairs.

'Oh, now, Mr Thripp, listen to that!' whispered the peculiar voice from out of the little airless sitting-room, 'you always did make fun of me, Mr Thripp. Do I deserve it, now?'

A gentle wave of heat coursed over Mr Thripp as he covertly listened to these accents, but he was out of sight.

'Fun, Mrs Brown? Never,' he retorted gallantly; 'it's only my little way:' and then to his immense relief, on lifting his eyes, discovered Tilda already descending the stairs.

He saw the pair of them off. Being restored to his coat, he could watch them clean down the drying street from his gatepost. Astonishing, he thought, the difference there can be between two women's backs! Tilda's, straight, angular, and respectable, as you might say; and that other – sinuous, seductive, as if it were as crafty a means of expression as the very smile and long-lashed languishments upon its owner's face. 'What can the old woman see in her!' he muttered to himself; 'damned if *I* know!' On this problem Mr Thripp firmly shut his front door. Having shut it he stooped to pick up a tiny white feather on the linoleum; and stooping, sighed.

At last his longed-for hour had come – the hour for which his very soul pined throughout each workaday week. Not that it was always his happy fate to be left completely alone like this. At times, indeed, he had for company far too much housework to leave him any leisure. But to-day the dinner things were cleared away, the washing-up was over, the tables fair as a baker's board, the kitchen spick and span, the house empty. He would just have a look round his own and Tilda's bedroom (and, maybe, the boys' and Millie's). And then the chair by the fire; the simmering kettle on the hearth; and the soft tardy autumnal dusk fading quietly into night beyond the window.

It was a curious thing that a man who loved his family so much, who was as desperately loyal to every member of it as a she-wolf is to her cubs, should yet find this few minutes' weekly solitude a luxury such as only Paradise, one would suppose, would ever be able to provide.

Mr Thripp went upstairs and not only tidied up his own and Tilda's bedroom, and went on to Millie's and the boys', but even gave a sloosh to the bath, slid the soap out of the basin where Charlie had abandoned it, and hung up the draggled towels again in the tiny bathroom. What a place looks like when you come back to it from your little enjoyment – it's *that* makes all the difference to your feelings about a home. These small chores done, Mr Thripp put on an old tweed coat with frayed sleeves, and returned to the kitchen. In a quarter of an hour that too more than ever resembled a new pin.

Then he glanced up at the clocks; between them the time was a quarter to four. He was amazed. He laid the tea, took out of his little old leather bag a pot of jam which he had bought for a surprise on his way home, and arranged a bunch of violets in a small jar beside Tilda's plate. But apart from these family preparations, Mr Thripp was now depositing a demure little glossy-brown teapot all by itself on the kitchen range. This was his Eureka. This was practically the only sensual *secret* luxury Mr Thripp had ever allowed himself since he became a family man. Tilda's cooking was good enough for him provided that the others had their little dainties now and then. He enjoyed his beer, and could do a bit of supper occasionally with a friend. But the ritual of these solitary Saturday afternoons reached its climax in this small pot of tea. First the nap, sweet as nirvana in his easy-chair, then the tea, and then the still, profound quarter of an hour's musing before the door-knocker began again.

Having pulled down the blind a little in order to prevent any chance of draught, Mr Thripp eased his bootlaces, sat himself in his chair, his cheek turned a little away from the window, his feet on the box that usually lay under the table, and with fingers clasped over his stomach composed himself to sleep. The eyelids closed; the lips set; the thumbs twitched now and again. He breathed deep, and the kettle began a whispered anthem – as if a myriad voices were singing on and on without need of pause or rest, a thousand thousand leagues away.

But now there was none to listen; and beyond, quiet hung thick in the little house. Only the scarce-perceptible hum of the traffic at the end of the narrow side street was audible on the air. Within, the two clocks on the chimney-piece quarrelled furiously over the fleeting moments, attaining unanimity only in one of many ticks. Ever and again a tiny scutter of dying ashes rejoined those that had gone before in the pan beneath the fire. Soon even these faint stirrings became inaudible and in a few moments Mr Thripp's spirit would have wafted itself completely free awhile from its earthly tenement, if, suddenly, the image of Millie – more vivid than even the actual sight of her a few minutes before – had not floated up into the narrow darkness of her father's tight-shut eyes.

But this was not the image of Millie as her father usually saw her. A pathetic earthly melancholy lay over the fair angelic features. The young cheek was sunken in; the eye was faded, dejected, downcast; and that cheek was stubbornly turned away from her father, as if she resented or was afraid of his scrutiny.

At this vision a headlong anxiety darted across Mr Thripp's half-slumbering mind. His heart began heavily beating: and then a pulse in his forehead. Where was she now? What forecast, what warning was this? Millie was no fool. Millie knew her way about. And her mother if anything was perhaps a little too censorious of the ways of this wicked world. If you keep on talking at a girl, hinting of things that might otherwise not enter her head – that in itself is dangerous. Love itself even must edge in warily. The tight-shut lids blinked anxiously. But where was Millie now? Somewhere indoors, but where? Who with?

Mr Thripp saw her first in a tea-shop, sitting opposite a horrid young man with his hair greased back over his low round head, and a sham pin in his tie. His elbows were on the marble-top table, and he was looking at Millie very much as a young but experienced pig looks at his wash-trough. Perhaps she was at the Pictures? Dulcet accents echoed into the half-dreaming mind – 'But I enjoy the dark, Mr Thripp . . . It rests the eyes.' Why did the woman talk as if she had never more than half a breath to spare? Rest her eyes! She never at any rate wanted to rest the eyes of any fool in trousers who happened to be within glimpse of her own. It was almost unnaturally dark in the cinema of Mr Thripp's fancy at this moment, yet he could now see his Millie with her pale, harmless, youthful face, as plainly as if she were the 'close-up' of some star from Los Angeles on the screen. And now the young man in her company was almost as fair as herself, with a long-chinned sheepish face and bolting eyes; and the two of them were amorously hand in hand.

For a moment Mr Thripp sat immovable, as if a bugle had sounded in his ear. Then he deliberately opened his eyes and glanced about him. The November daylight was already beginning to fade. Yes, he would have a word with Millie – but not when she came home that evening. It is always wiser to let the actual coming-home be pleasant and welcoming. To-morrow morning, perhaps; that is, if her mother was not goading at her for being late down and lackadaisical when there was so much to be done. Nevertheless, all in good time he would have a little quiet word with her. He would say only what he would not afterwards regret having said. He had meant to do that ages ago; but you mustn't flood a house with water when it's not on fire. She was but a mere slip of a thing – like a flower; not a wild flower, but one of those sweet waxen flowers you see blooming in a florist's window – which you must be careful with and not just expose anywhere.

And yet how his own little place here could be compared with anything in the nature of a hot-house he could not for the life of him understand. Delicate-looking! Everybody said that. God bless me, perhaps her very lackadaisicalness was a symptom of some as yet hidden malady. Good God, supposing! . . . He would take her round to see the doctor as soon as he could. But the worst of it was you had to do these things on your own responsibility. And though Mr Thripp was now a man close on fifty, some-times he felt as if he could no longer bear the burden of all these responsibilities. Sometimes he felt as if he couldn't endure to brood over them as he was sometimes wont to do. If he did, he would snap. People *looked* old; but nobody was really old inside; not old at least in the sense that troubles were any the lighter, or forebodings any the more easily puffed away; or tongues easier to keep still; or tempers to control.

And talking of tempers reminded him of Charlie. What on earth was going to be done with Charlie? There was no difficulty in conjuring up, in seeing Charlie – that is if he really did go every Saturday to a football match. But Charlie was now of an age when he might think it a fine manly thing to be loafing about the counter of a pub talking to some flaxen barmaid with a tuppeny cigar between his teeth. Still, Mr Thripp refused to entertain more than a glimpse of this possibility. He saw him at this moment as clearly as if in a peepshow, packed in with hundreds of other male creatures close as sardines in a tin, with their check caps and their 'fags', and their staring eyes revolving in consort as if they were all attached to one wire, while that idiotic ball in the middle of the arena coursed on its helpless way from muddy boot to muddy boot.

Heaven knows, Mr Thripp himself was nothing much better than a football! You had precious small chance in this life of choosing which boot should give you the next kick. And what about that smug new creeping accountant at the office with his upstart airs and new-fangled book-keeping methods!

Mr Thripp's mouth opened in a yawn, but managed only to achieve a fraction of it. He rubbed his face; his eyes now shut again. It was not as if any of your children were of much practical help. Why should they be when they could never understand that what you pined for, what you really needed was not only practical help but some inward grace and clearness of mind wherewith they could slip in under your own thoughts and so share your point of view without all that endless terrifying argumentation. He didn't *always* give advice to suit his own ends; and yet whenever he uttered a word to James, tactfully suggesting that in a world like this – however competent a man may be and however sure of himself – you *had* to push your way, you had to make your weight felt, James always looked at him as if he were a superannuated orang-outang in a cage – an orang-outang with queer and not particularly engaging habits.

He wouldn't mind even that so much if only James would take his cigarette out of his mouth when he talked. To see that bit of stained paper attached to his son's lower lip wagging up and down, up and down, beneath that complacent smile and those dark helpless-looking eyes, all but sent Mr Thripp stark staring mad at times. Once, indeed, he had actually given vent to the appalling mass of emotion hoarded up like water in a reservoir in his mind. The remembrance of the scene that followed made him even at this moment tremble in his chair. Thank God, thank God, he hadn't often lost control like that.

Well, James would be married by this time next year, he supposed. And what a nice dainty pickle he was concocting for himself! Mr Thripp knew that type of young woman, with the compressed lips, and the thin dry hair, and the narrow hips. She'd be 'a good manager', right enough, but there's a point in married life where good managing is little short of being in a lunatic asylum between two iron-faced nurses and yourself in a strait waistcoat. The truth of it was, with all his fine airs and neat finish, James hadn't much common sense. He had a fair share of brains; but brains are no good if you are merely self-opinionated and contemptuous on principle. James was not like anybody in Mr Thripp's own family. He was a Simpkins.

And then suddenly it was as if some forgotten creature in Mr Thripp's mind or heart had burst out crying; and the loving look he thereupon cast on his elder son's face in his mind was almost maudlin in its sentimentality. He would do anything for James within reason: anything. But then it would have to be within James's reason – not his own. He knew that. Why he would himself marry the young woman and exult in being a bigamist if only he could keep his son out of her way. And yet, and yet; maybe there were worse women in the world than your stubborn, petulant, niggardly, half-sexed nagger. Mr Thripp knew a nagger of old. His brother's wife, Fanny, had been a nagger. She was dead now, and George was a free man – but drinking far too much.

Well, as soon as he could get a chance, Mr Thripp sitting there in his chair decided, he would have another good think; but that probably wouldn't be until next Saturday, if then. You can't think to much purpose – except in a worried disjointed fashion – when you are in the noise of an office or keeping yourself from saying things you have no wish to say. The worst of it was it was not much good discussing these matters with Tilda. Like most women, she always went off at a tangent. And when you came down to it, and wanted to be reasonable, there was so little left to discuss. Besides, Tilda had worries enough of her own.

At this moment Mr Thripp once more opened his eyes wide. The small kitchen loomed beatifically rosy and still in the glow of the fire. Evening had so far edged on its way now that he could hardly see the hands of his two clocks. He could but just detect the brass pendulum – imperturbably chopping up eternity into fragments of time. He craned forward; in five minutes he ought to be brewing his little private pot of tea. Even if he nodded off now, he would be able to wake in time, but five minutes doesn't leave *much* margin for dropping off. He shifted a little on his chair, and once more shut his eyes. And in a moment or two his mind went completely blank.

He seemed to have been suddenly hauled up helpless with horror into an enormous vacancy – to be dangling unconfined and motionless in space. A scene of wild sandy hills and spiky trees – an illimitable desert, came riding towards him out of nothingness. He hung motionless, and was yet sweeping rapidly forward, but for what purpose and to what goal there was not the smallest inkling. The wilderness before him grew ever more desolate and menacing. He began to be deadly afraid; groaned; stirred – and found himself with fingers clenched on its arms sitting bolt upright in his chair. And the hands of the clock looked to be by a hair's breadth precisely in the same position as when he had started on that ghastly nightmare journey. His face blanched. He sat appalled, listening to an outrageous wauling of voices. It was as though a thousand demons lay in wait for him beneath his window and were summoning him to his doom.

And all this nightmare horror of mind was due solely to a *conversazione* of cats! Yet, as with flesh still creeping he listened on to this clamour, it was so human in effect that it might be multitudinous shades of the unborn that were thronging about the glass of his window. Mr Thripp rose from his chair, his face transfigured with rage and desire for revenge. He went out into the scullery, opened the back door, and at sound of him the caterwauling instantly ceased.

And almost as instantly his fury died out in him. The cold evening air fanned his forehead. He smiled quixotically, and looked about him. There came a furtive rustle in the bushes. 'Ah, there you are!' he sang out gently into the dark. 'Have your play while you can, my fine gentlemen! Take it like your betters, for it's a sight too soon over.'

Above the one cramped leafless elder-tree in his yard a star was pricking the sky. A ground mist, too, was rising, already smelling a little stale. Great London and its suburbs appeared to be in for one of its autumnal fogs. A few of the upper windows opposite loomed dim with light. Mr Thripp's neighbours, it seemed, were also preparing to be off to the pictures or the music-halls. It was very still, and the air was damp and clammy.

As he stood silent there in the obscurity a deepening melancholy crept over his mind, though he was unaware into what gloomy folds and sags his face had fallen. He suddenly remembered that his rates would have to be paid next week. He remembered that Christmas would soon be coming, and that he was getting too old to enter into the fun of the thing as he used to do. His eyes rolled a little in their sockets. What the...! his old friend within began to suggest. But Mr Thripp himself did not even enunciate the missing 'hell'. Instead, he vigorously rubbed his face with his stout capable hand. 'Well, fog anyhow don't bring rain,' he muttered to himself.

And as if at a signal his own cat and his next-door neighbour's cat and Mrs Brown's cat and the cat of the painter and decorator whose back garden abutted his own, together with the ginger-and-white cat from the newsvendor's beyond, with one consent broke out once more into their Sabbath eve quintette. The many-stranded strains of it mounted up into the heavens like the yells of demented worshippers of Baal.

'And, as I say, I don't blame ye neether,' Mr Thripp retorted, with a grim smile. 'If you knew, my friends, how narrowly you some of you escaped a bucket of cold water when you couldn't even see out of your young eyes you'd sing twice as loud.'

He shut the door and returned to his fireside. No more hope of sleep that afternoon. He laughed to himself for sheer amusement at his disappointment. What kids men were! He stirred the fire, it leapt brightly as if intent to please him. He pushed the kettle on; lit the lamp; warmed his little privy glossy-brown tea-pot, and fetched out a small private supply of the richest Ceylon from behind some pots in the saucepan cupboard.

Puffs of steam were now vapouring out of the spout of the kettle with majestic pomposity. Mr Thripp lifted it off the coals and balanced it over his tea-pot. And at that very instant the electric bell – which a year or two ago in a moment of strangest caprice Charles had fixed up in the corner – began jangling like a fire-alarm. Mr Thripp hesitated. If this was one of the family, he was caught. Caught, that is, unless he was mighty quick in concealing these secret preparations. If it was Tilda – well, valour was the better part of discretion. He poured the water into the pot, replaced the lid, and put it on to the oven-top to stew. With a glance of satisfaction at the spinster-like tidiness of the room, he went out, and opened the door.

'Why, it's Millie!' he said, looking out at the slim-shouldered creature standing alone there under the porch; 'you don't mean to say it's you, my dear?'

Millie made no reply. Her father couldn't see her face, partly because the lamp-post stationed in front of the house three doors away gave at best a feeble light, and partly because her features were more or less concealed by her hat. She pushed furtively past him without a word, her head still stooping out of the light.

Oh, my God, what's wrong now? yelled her father's inward monstrous monitor, frenziedly clanging the fetters on wrist and ankle. 'Come right in, my pretty dear,' said Mr Thripp seductively, 'this *is* a pleasant surprise. And what's more, between you and me and the gatepost, I have just been making myself a cup of tea. Not a word to Mother; it's *our* little secret. We'll have it together before the others come in.'

He followed his daughter into the kitchen.

'Lor, what a glare you are in, Pa!' she said in a small muffled voice. She turned the wick of the lamp down so low that in an instant or two the flame flickered and expired, and she seated herself in her father's chair by the fire. But the flamelight showed her face now. It was paler even than usual. A strand of her gilded pale-brown hair had streaked itself over her blue-veined temple. She looked as if she had been crying. Her father, his hands hanging down beside him as uselessly as the front paws of a performing bear, watched her in an appalling trepidation of spirit. This then was the secret of his nightmare; for this the Cats of Fate had chorused!

'What's wrong, Millie love? Are you overtired, my girl? There! Don't say nothing for a minute or two. See, here's my little pot just meant for you and me!'

Millie began to cry again, pushing her ridiculous little handkerchief close to her eyes. Mr Thripp's hand hovered awkwardly above her dainty hat and then gently fumbled as if to stroke her hair beneath. He knelt down beside her chair.

For heaven's sake! for heaven's sake! for heaven's sake! a secret voice was gabbling frenziedly in his ear. 'Tell your old dad, lovey,' he murmured out loud, softly as the crooning of a wood-pigeon.

Millie tilted back her pretty hat and dropped her fair head on his shoulder. 'It's nothing, Dad,' she said, 'It's only that they are all the same.'

'What are all the same?'

'Oh, fellows, Dad.'

'Which one, precious?' Mr Thripp lulled wooingly. God strike him dead! muttered his monster.

'Oh, only young Arthur. Like a fool I waited half an hour for him and then saw him with – with that Westcliff girl.'

A sigh as voluminous as the suspiration of Niagara swept over Mr Thripp; but it made no sound. Half a dozen miraculous words of reassurance were storming his mind in a frenzy of relief. He paused an instant, and accepted the seventh.

'What's all that, my precious?' he was murmuring. 'Why, when I was courting your mother, I saw just the same thing happen. She was a mighty pretty young thing, too, as a girl, though not quite so trim and neat in the figure as you. I felt I could throttle him where he stood. But no, I just took no notice, trusting in my own charms!'

'That's all very well,' sobbed Millie, 'but you were a man, and *we* have to fight without seeming to. Not that I care a fig for him; he can go. But —'

'Lord, Millie!' Mr Thripp interrupted, smoothing her cheek with his squat forefinger, 'you'd beat twenty of them Westcliffs, with a cast in both eyes and your hands behind your back. Don't you grieve no more, my dear; he'll come back safe and sound, or he's less of a – of a nice young feller than I take him for.'

For a moment Mr Thripp caught a glimpse of the detestable creature with the goggling eyes and the suede shoes, but he dismissed him sternly from view.

'There now,' he said, 'give your poor old dad a kiss. What's disappoint-
ments, Millie; they soon pass away. And now, just take a sip or two of this
extra-strong Bohay! I was hoping I shouldn't have to put up with a lonely
cup and not a soul to keep me company. But mind, my precious, not a word
to your ma.'

So there they sat, father and daughter, comforter and comforted, while
Mr Thripp worked miracles for two out of a tea-pot for one. And while
Millie, with heart comforted, was musing of that other young fellow she
had noticed boldly watching her while she was waiting for her Arthur, Mr
Thripp was wondering when it would be safe and discreet to disturb her
solacing daydream so that he might be busying himself over the supper.

It's one dam neck-and-neck worry and trouble after another, his voice
was assuring him. But meanwhile, his plain square face was serene and
gentle as a nestful of halcyons, as he sat sipping his hot water and patting
his pensive Millie's hand.

Pretty Poll*

In her odd impulsive fashion – her piece of sewing pressed tight to her small
bosom, her two small feet as close to one another on the floor – Judy had
laughed out: and the sound of it had a faint far-away resemblance to bells
– bells muffled, in the sea.'You never, never, never speak of marriage,' she
charged Tressider, 'without being satirical. You just love to make nonsense
of us all. Now I say you have no right to. You haven't earned the privilege.
Wait till you've jilted Cleopatra, or left your second-best bed to – to
Catherine Parr – if she *was* the last. Don't you agree, Stella?'

The slight lifting at the corners of dark handsome Stella's mouth could
hardly have been described as a smile. 'I always agree,' she assented. 'And
surely, Mr Tressider, isn't marriage an "institution"? Mightn't you just as
well attack a police-station? No one gets any good out of it. It only hurts.'

'That's just it, Stella, it only hurts. It's water, after all, that has the best
chance of wearing away stones – not horrid sledge-hammers like that.'

From his low chair, his cleft clean-shaven chin resting on his hands,
Tressider for a moment or two continued to look up and across the room
at Judy, now absorbedly busy again over her needlework. Time, too, wears
like water; but little of its influence was perceptible there. The curtains at
the French windows had been left undrawn; a moon was over the garden.
It was Judy's choice – this mingling of the two lights – natural and artificial.

* First published in *London Mercury*, April 1925.

Hers, too, the fire, this late summer evening. She stooped forward, thrusting out a slightly trembling hand towards its flames.

'No, it isn't fair,' she said, 'there are many married people who are at least, well, endurably happy: Bill and me, for example. The real marvel is that any two ignorant, chance young things who happen to be of opposite sex should ever just go on getting older and older, more and more used to one another, and all that – and yet not want a change – not really for a single instant. I know dozens – apart from the others.'

'Oh, I never meant to suggest that "whited" are the only kind of sepulchres,' said Tressider. 'I agree, too, it's the substantial that wears longest. Second-best beds; rather than Wardour Street divans. But there are excesses – just human ones, I mean. It's this horrible curse of asking too much. Up there they seem to have supposed that the best ratio for a human being was one quart of feeling to every pint pot. I knew a man once, for example, who, quite apart from such little Eurekas as the Dunmow flitch, never even made the attempt to become endurably happy, as you call it. Simply because of a parrot. It repeated things. It was an eavesdropper: an *agent provocateur.*'

'What *do* you mean?' said Judy. 'Oh, how you amuse me! You haven't said a single thing this evening that was not ironical. You just love to masquerade. Did you ever know a woman who talked in parables? It's simply because, I suppose, men have such stupidly self-conscious hearts – I mean such absurdly rational minds. Isn't it, Stella? Don't be so reserved, you dark taciturn angel. Wouldn't he be even nicer than he is if he would only say what he thinks? A parrot!'

Stella merely desisted from shrugging her shoulders. 'My own opinion, Judy – judging, that is, from what Mr Tressider does say, is that it's far better that he should never say what he thinks.'

As if itself part and parcel of Stella's normal taciturnity, this voice of hers, when it did condescend to make itself heard, was of a low rasping timbre, like the sound of a strip of silk being torn from its piece. And it usually just left off, came to an abrupt end – as if interrupted. She turned her head out of the candle-light, as though even moonshine might be a refuge from the mere bare facts of the case. There was a pause. Judy had snatched her glance, and was now busily fishing in her work-basket for her tiny scissors.

'Well, that's what I say,' she said, staring close at the narrow hem of the ludicrously tiny shirt she was hemming. 'You men love to hide your heads in the sands. Even Bill does – and you know what a body *he* leaves outside. You positively prefer not to know where you are. You invent ideals and goddesses and all that sort of thing; and yet you would sooner let things slide than – than break the ice. I mean – I mean, of course, the right ice.

That can't be helped, I suppose. But what I simply cannot understand is being satirical. Here we all are, we men and women, and we just have to put up with it. In heaven,' and the tiny click, click, click of her needle had already begun again, 'in heaven there will be neither marriage nor giving in marriage. And poor Bill will have to – have to darn his socks himself.'

Her eyes lifted an instant, and glanced away so swiftly that it seemed to Tressider he caught no less fleeting a glimpse of their blue than that usually afforded of a kingfisher's wing. 'But what,' she went on hastily, 'what about the parrot – the *agent provocateur*? What about the parrot, Stella? Let's make him tell us about the parrot.'

'Yes,' concurred Stella. 'I should, of course, very much indeed enjoy hearing about the parrot. I just love natural history.'

'You ought really, of course,' said Tressider, 'to have heard the story from a friend of my sister Kate's – Minnie Sturgess. It was she who was responsible for the tragic – the absurd – *finale*. It was she who cut the tether, or rather the painter. The kind of woman that simply can't take things easy. Intuitions, no end; but mostly of a raw hostile order. Anyhow, they weren't of much use in the case of a man like – well, like my friend with the parrot.'

'We will call him Bysshe,' said Judy. 'It has romantic associations. Go on, Mr Satirist.'

'Bysshe, then,' said Tressider. 'Well, this Bysshe was a lanky, square-headed, black-eyed fellow. Something, I believe, in the ship-broking line, though with a little money of his own. A bit over thirty, and a bachelor from the thatch on his head to the inch-thick soles of his shoes. If his mother had lived – he was one of those "mother's boys" which the novelists used to be so fond of – Minnie Sturgess might perhaps herself have survived into his life, to keep, and, I wouldn't mind betting, even to prize the parrot. She would at any rate have learned the tact with which to dispose of it without undue friction. Minnie survived, in actual fact, to keep a small boarding-house at Ramsgate, though whether she is there now only the local directory could relate. As for Bysshe – well, I don't know, as a matter of fact, how long *he* survived. In Kate's view, the two of them were born to make each other unhappy. So Providence, to cut things short, supplied the parrot. But then Kate is something of a philosopher. And I have no views myself.'

'Did you ever see the parrot?' queried Judy, her left eye screwed up a little as she threaded an almost invisible needle. 'I remember an old servant of my mother's once had one, and it used to make love to her the very instant it supposed they were alone. But *she*, poor soul, wasn't too bright in her wits.'

'Oh,' said Tressider, 'Bysshe was right enough in his wits. It was merely one of his many queer harmless habits – and he had plenty of spare time left over from his ship-broking – to moon about the city. He suffered from indigestion, or thought he did, and used to lunch on apples or nuts which, so far as he was concerned, did not require for their enjoyment a sitting posture. He was a genuine lover of London, though; knew as much about its churches and streets, taverns and relics as old Stowe or Pepys himself. Possibly, too, if his digestion had been a reasonable one, Minnie and he might have made each other's lives miserable to the end of the chapter; since in that case, he would never have found himself loafing about one particular morning in Leadenhall Market; and so would never have set eyes on the parrot. Anyhow, that's how it all began.

'It was a sweltering day – clear black shadows, black as your hat, shafting clean across the narrow courts, and the air crammed with flavours characteristic of those parts – meat, poultry, sawdust, cats, straw, soot, and old bricks baking in the sun. He had meandered into one of the livestock alleys – mainly dogs, cats, poultry, with an occasional jackdaw, owl or raven. That kind of thing. And there, in a low entry, lounged the proprietor of one of its shops – a man with a face and head as hairless almost as a bladder of lard, and with eyes like a ferret.

'He was two steps up from the pavement, had a straw in the corner of his mouth, and was looking at Bysshe. And Bysshe was looking at one of his protégés, the edge of its cage glinting in a sunbeam, and the bird – or whatever you like to call it – mum and dreaming inside. Bysshe had finished his lunch, and was in a reflective mood. He stared on at the parrot almost to the point of vacancy.

' "Nice dawg there," insinuated an insolent voice above his head.

'He looked up, and for a moment absently surveyed the speaker. "Does it talk?" enquired Bysshe. The owner of the bird merely continued to chew his straw.

' "How do you teach them?" Bysshe persisted. "You clip or snip their tongues, or something, don't you?"

'An intensely violent look came into the fellow's eyes. "If you was to try to slit that bird's tongue,' he said, "you might as well order your corfin here and now."

'Bysshe's glance returned to the cage. Apart from an occasional almost imperceptible obscuring of its scale-like, shuttered eyes, its inmate might just as well have been stuffed. It sat there stagnantly surveying Bysshe as if he were one of the less intelligent apes. To start with, Bysshe didn't much like the look of the man. Naturally. Nor did he much like the look of the parrot. It was merely the following of an indolent habit that suggested his asking its price.

'He once more turned his attention from wizard-like bird to beast-like man. "What's the price of the thing?" he enquired; "and if I particularly wanted him to talk, could you make him?" The man rapidly shifted his straw from one corner of his mouth to the other.

' "The feller," he replied, "that says that he could make that bird do anything but give up the ghost, is a liar."

'Bysshe, when he told me about the deal, supplied the missing adjective. Still, such is life. The price was 25s. And as Bysshe had no more idea of the bird's value than that of an Egyptian pyramid, he didn't know whether he was getting a bargain or not. Nor did he attempt to beat the man down. He asked him a few questions about the proper food and treatment of the creature. Whereupon, squeezing one or two of his remaining lunch nuts between the bars, he picked up the cage by its ring, turned out of the shadowy coolness of the market into the burning glitter of Leadenhall Street, mounted on to the top of a bus, and bore his captive home.

'He had rooms in Clifford's Inn; and through the window the bird, if it so pleased, could feast its eyes on the greens and shadows of a magnificent plane-tree. The rooms were old – faded yellow panelling and a moulded cornice. It was quiet. Bysshe had few friends, and his pet therefore could have enjoyed – even if it wanted any – little company. Bysshe bought it a handsome new cage, with slight architectural advantages, and was as perfectly ready to enjoy its silent society as he expected the bird to be prepared to enjoy his.'

Stella gently withdrew her dark eyes from the moonlit garden, and stole a longish look at Tressider's face.

'I agree, Stella,' cried Judy breaking in. 'He *is* being rather a long time coming to what I suppose will be the point.'

'So are most little human tragedies,' retorted Tressider. 'But there's one point I have left out. I said "silent" society; and that at first was all Bysshe got. But I gathered that though there had been the usual din in the market the day of the bargain, it was some odd nondescript slight *sound* or other that had first caught his attention. A kind of call-note which appeared to have come out of the cage. Without being quite conscious of it, it seems to have been this faint rumour, at least as much as anything else, that persuaded him to invest in the bird.

'Well, anyhow, as he sat reading one evening – he had rather an odd and esoteric taste in books – there proceeded out of the cage one or two clear disjointed notes. Just a fragment of sound to which you could give no description or character except that it was unlike most of those which one expects from a similar source. Bysshe had instantly relapsed from one stage of stillness to another. Compared with what came after, this was nothing – mere "recording" as the bird-fanciers say. But it set Bysshe on the *qui vive*. For a while he listened intently. There was no response. And he had again almost forgotten the presence of the parrot when, hours afterwards, from the gloom that had crept into its corner, there softly broke out of the cage, no mere snatch of an inarticulate *bel canto*, but a low, slow, steady gush of indescribable abuse.

'The courtyard was as still as the garden of Eden. That less – that more – than human voice pressed steadily on – a low, minute, gushing fountain of vituperation. Bysshe was no chicken. He was pretty familiar with the various London lingoes – from Billingsgate to Soho. None the less the actual terms of this harangue, he afterwards told me, all but froze the blood in his veins. The voice ceased; and turning his head, Bysshe took a long and steady stare at the inmate of the cage. It sat there in its grey and cardinal; its curved beak closed, its glassy yellow eye motionless, and yet, it seemed, filled to its shallow brim with an inexhaustible contempt.

'There was nothing whatever wrong with its surroundings. Bysshe made quite certain of that. Its nuts were ripe and sound, its water fresh, its sand wholesome. As I say, at the first onset of this experience Bysshe had been profoundly shocked. But that night, as he stood in his pyjamas looking in at the bird for the last time – and he had omitted to throw over its cage its customary pall – the memory of it suddenly touched his sense of humour. And he began to laugh; an oddish laugh to laugh alone. The parrot lifted one clawed foot and gently readjusted it on its perch. It leaned its head sidelong; its beak opened. And then in frozen silence it turned its back on the interrupter.

'For days together after that the parrot was as mute as a fish – at least so long as Bysshe lay in wait for it. That it had been less taciturn in his absence he gathered one morning from the expression of his charwoman's face – an amiable old body with a fairly wide knowledge of "the world". She had thought it best, she explained, to shut the windows. "You never know, sir, what them might think who couldn't tell a canary from a bullfinch. I've kept birds myself. But I must say, sir, I wouldn't have chose to be brought up where *he* was." Something to that effect.

'And Bysshe noticed that though she had not refrained from putting some little emphasis on the "he", she had carefully omitted any indication to whom the pronoun referred.

' "He swore, did he, Mrs Giles?"

' "He didn't so much swear, sir, as extravastate. Never in all my life could I have credited there was such shocking things to say."

'Bysshe rather queerly returned the old lady's gaze. "I have heard rumours of it myself," he replied. "It looks to me, Mrs Giles, as if we should have to get the bird another home."

'The interview was a little disconcerting, but had it not been for this independent evidence, Bysshe, I feel sure (judging from my own reactions, as they call them) might easily have persuaded himself to believe that his experience had been nothing but the refuse of a dream.

'Minnie Sturgess's first appearance on the scene preceded mine by a few days. The two of them, so far as I could gather, were not exactly "engaged". They merely, as the little irony goes, understood one another; or rather Minnie seemed so far to understand Bysshe that we all knew perfectly well they would at last drift into matrimony as inevitably as a derelict boat, I gather, having found its way out of Lake Erie will drift over the Niagara Falls.'

'A very pretty metaphor,' remarked Judy. 'Then come the rapids, and then – but I'm not quite sure what happens then.'

'Don't forget, though,' cried Stella softly out of her moonshine, 'don't forget that meanwhile the best electric light has been supplied for miles around!'

'Ssh! Stella,' breathed Judy, thimbled finger on lip, 'we are merely playing into his hands. Let him just blunder on.' She turned with a mock-innocent smile towards Tressider. 'And did the parrot *swear* at Miss Sturgess?' she enquired.

'No. Miss Sturgess came; she contemplated; she admired; she was tactful to the last degree. But the bird paid her no more polite attention than if she had been a waxwork in the basement at Madame Tussaud's. It sat perfectly still on its perch, its eight neat claws arranged four on either side of it, and out of its whitish countenance it softly surveyed the lady.

'Naturally, she was a little nettled. She remonstrated. Hadn't Bysshe assured her that the creature talked, and wasn't it a horrid cheat to have a parrot sold to one for all that money, if it didn't? And Bysshe, relieved beyond words, that his pet had not even so much as deigned to chuckle, prevaricated. He said that a parrot that talked in season and out of season was nothing but a nuisance. Did she like its livery, and wasn't it a handsome cage?

'Miss Sturgess took courage. She bent her veiled head and whispered a seductive "Pretty Poll"; and then having failed to arouse any response by tapping its bars with the button of her glove, she insinuated a naked fore-finger between them as if to stroke the creature's wing or to scratch its poll. And, without an instant's hesitation the parrot nipped it to the bone. She might have read that much in its air: intuition, you know. But she was a plucky creature, and didn't even whimper. And no doubt for the moment this summary punishment may seem to have drawn these two blundering humans a little closer together.

'It was a few days after this that Bysshe and I lunched together at a restaurant in Fleet Street. And, naturally – in his reticent fashion – he told me of his prize. About three, we climbed the shallow wooden stairs up to his rooms, to see the bird. For discretion's sake – in case, that is, of chance visitors, he had shut it up in his bedroom, and rather foolishly, as I thought, had locked the door.

'No creature of any intelligence can much enjoy existence in a cage, and to immure that cage in a kind of cell is merely to add insult to injury. Besides, even eighteenth-century door panels are not sound-proof. We stole across on tiptoe and stood for a moment listening outside the bedroom.

'Possibly the bird had heard our muffled footsteps; or, maybe, to while solitude away, it was merely indulging in an audible reverie. I can't say. But hardly had we inclined our ears to listen, when, as if out of some vast hollow, dark and subterranean, a tongue within – unfalteringly, dispassion-ately – broke into speech. I have heard politicians, pill-venders and dema-gogues, but nothing even remotely to compare with that appalling eloquence – the ease, the abundance, the sustained unpremeditated verve! Nor was it an exhibition of mere vernacular. There were interludes, as I guessed, of a corrupt Spanish. There may have been even an Oriental leaven; even traces of the Zulu's "click" – the trend was exotic enough. But the words, the mere language were as nothing compared with the tone.

'Curates habituated to their duties tend to read the prayers in much the same way. The inmost sense, I mean, comes out the better because the speaker is not taking any notice of it. So it was with the parrot. I can't describe the evil of the effect. One stopped thinking. One lost for the moment even the power of being shocked. A torrent of outer darkness seemed to sweep over, dowse, submerge the mind, and you just floated like a straw on its calm even flood.'

'What was it swearing *about*? asked a cold voice.

Tressider seemed to be examining the Persian mat at his feet as if in search of inspiration. 'I think,' he said slowly, 'it was cursing the day of creation, with all the complexities involved in it. It was a voice out of nowhere, anathematizing with loathing a very definite somewhere. We most of us "bear up" in this world as much as possible. Not so the original owner of that unhurried speech. He had stated with perfect calm exactly what he thought about things. And I should guess that his name was Iago. But let's get back to Bysshe.

'At the moment he was holding his square, rather ugly face sidelong, in what looked like a constrained position. Then his eyes slid round and met mine.

' "Twenty-five shillings!" he said. "Any offers?" But there wasn't any-thing facetious in his look.

'The voice had ceased. And with it had vanished all else but the remembrance of the execrable *tone* of its speech. And as if all Nature, including its topmost artifice, London, had paused to listen, there followed an intense hush. Then, uncertainly, as if tentatively, there broke out another voice from behind the shut door, uttering just three or four low single notes – as of somebody singing. Then these ceased too.

'We had both of us been more or less prepared for the captive's first effort, but not I for this. This extraordinary scrap of singing – but I'll come back to it. Bysshe gently unlocked and pushed open his bedroom door and we looked in. But we knew perfectly well what we should find. The room was undisturbed, and, except for its solitary inmate, vacant. There stood Bysshe's truckle bed, his old tallboy, his empty boots, his looking-glass. And there sat the bird, motionless, unabashed, clasping its perch with its lizard-skinned claws. Apart from a slight trembling of its breast-plumage, there was no symptom whatever of anything in the least unwonted. It sidled the fraction of an inch towards its master, its beak ajar showing the small clumsy tongue, its bead-like eye firmly settled on mine; and with a peculiar aversion I stared back.

'I stayed on with Bysshe for an hour or two, but though most of the time we sat in silence, like confederates awaiting their crucial moment, nothing happened. A sort of absentness, a slight frown, had settled on his face. And when at last I hurried off to keep some stupid appointment, I might have guessed it was not merely to hear a parrot *swear* that he had pressed me to come. Afterwards, he was less eager to share his enchantress.'

'The voice, you mean?'

'Yes. Can you imagine the voice of the angel in the Leonardo Madonna? – Oh well, never mind that now. A few weeks afterwards Bysshe looked me up again, and for a while we talked aimlessly and at random. He was obviously waiting for me to question him.

' "Oh, by the way, how much did you get?" I enquired at last. He looked absolutely dead beat, his skin was a kind of muddy grey. It appeared that the tiny *motif* of *my* experience had been a mere prelude. Bysshe, it seems, had awakened a week or two after my visit in the very earliest of the morning, at the very moment when from underneath the parrot's pall had slipped solemnly out the complete aria. The words were not actually French, for he had detected something like "alone" and "grief". But here and there they had a slight nasal timbre, and Bysshe, drinking the fatal music in, lying there in his striped pyjamas still a little dazed with sleep, had simply succumbed.

'He had succumbed to such a degree that his sole preposterous object in life now seemed to be that of tracing the bird's ownership. Not his sole object, rather; for at every return from this preposterous quest, he spent hours in solitude, bent on the equally vain aim of discovering which in the divine order of things had come first: the invective or the charm. He had some notion that it mattered.

'There is a bit, you remember, in one of Conrad's novels about a voice –

Lena's. There is another bit in Shakespeare, and in Coleridge; in almost every poet, of course – but it doesn't matter. Four notes had been enough for me. And even if Melba in her dreams delights the listening shades on the borders of Paradise – even *they* will not have heard the best that earth can do. You see there was nothing bird-like in the parrot's piece, except the purity. It was the voice of a seraph, the voice of a marvellous fiddle (that bit of solo, for example, in Mozart's Minuet in E flat). A voice innocent of the meaning – even of the degree – of its longing; innocent, I mean, of realizing that life can't really stand – if it could comprehend it – anything so abjectly beautiful as all that; that there's a breaking-point.

'It's difficult even to suggest the effect. Absolutely the most beautiful thing in the world a cousin of mine once told me he had ever seen was from the top of a bus. He happened to glance into the dusk of an upper room through an open window, and a naked girl stood there, her eyes looking inward in a remote dream, her shift lifted a little above her small lovely head, as she was about to put it on. Well I suppose Bysshe's experience resembled that. But there; *I*, mind you, heard only four notes of it. And now there are no more to come. And my cousin, lost in stupefaction or remorse, had kept immovably to his bus.'

Judy's sewing lay for a moment idle in her lap; her downcast eyes were fixed on it as if suddenly it had presented her with an insoluble problem.

'But there was, of course, quite another – a farcical – side to the comedy,' Tressider pushed on. 'Poor Bysshe's pursuit proved as ludicrous as it looks amusing. When you come to think of it, you know, we make our own idols. A silence, a still look of the eyes, a crammed instant of oblivion, and we are what's called "in love". What Stendhal calls crystallization, doesn't he? Queer. But it's the same in everything. Not merely sex, I mean. And that, I suppose, is what happened to Bysshe.

'Those slowish internal creatures crystallize hardest, perhaps. Out of this lost wandering voice he made – well, he embodied it. And the result wasn't in the least like poor Minnie. There was no particular tragedy in that. For Bysshe, that is. But, just like him, he tried, as I say, to track the embodiment down. And how could he tell which he'd unearth first – angel or devil. Or – both together. Think of that. Anyhow, he completely failed. First, of course, he returned to the dealer in livestock, who extorted from him a larger sum than he had paid for the parrot, as a bribe to disclose where it had come from. After which Bysshe had at once hied off to a corn-chandler's at Leytonstone – a talkative man.

'This man had bought the bird from a customer to whom he sold weekly supplies of chicken-food and canary-seed – a maiden lady in a semi-detached villa neatly matted with *ampelopsis Veitchi*.'

'How nice!' said Judy in a hushed little voice – as if absent-mindedly.

'Yes,' said Tressider. 'When Bysshe at last asked her outright if the bird had ever talked while it was in her possession, a pink flush had spread over her face. She had herself tried to teach it, she told him, looking down her nose the while beneath her large gold-rimmed glasses: just "scratch-a-poll" or something of that kind. But she had failed. A seafaring nephew of some little naïvety, I should imagine. He had, she fancied, "picked it up" in Portsmouth.

' "It talks a little *now*," Bysshe had confided to her.

'And the lady had at once given her case away by retaliating that what it might do in the small hours, or with only a gentleman present, was no concern of hers.

'Then Bysshe asked if the parrot had ever engaged in song – "like a bullfinch, you know". And the lady's expression implied that his question had confirmed her suspicions of his sanity.

'Portsmouth turned out another bad egg. He tracked down the shop, but the proprietor had died of dropsy a week before. Still, his daughter confessed that if the parrot *was* the parrot she had in mind – though she had never heard it talking in particular – then it may have been resident in the shop for something under a year. At this a ray of hope struck down on the squalid scene, and Bysshe enquired if the late proprietor had ever indulged in "musical evenings".

'There was a young lady living not many doors down the street, he was informed, who taught the pianoforte, and who led a Mixed Methodist Choir. Bysshe had accordingly spent the greater part of that evening beneath the young lady's lighted window – providentially an inch or two ajar – while in successive keys she practised her scales. And for *bonne bouche* she had at last rewarded the eavesdropper with a rendering of "Hold the Fort"; but, alas, in tones of a pitch and volume which no mere mimic, feathered or otherwise, could hope to recapture.

'Bysshe could get no further for the present. As I say, he never did. His parrot's past had proved irrevocable. And apart from the hint of the pre-historic in all its species, even the age of this particular specimen remained a mystery. Destiny *may*, of course, have seduced it to that slum in Portsmouth from the Islands of the Blest. That would, at any rate, account for the critical side of its repertory. It *may* have taken flight clean out of a fairy-tale, leaving its rarer colours behind it. So at least one can imagine Snow-white singing over her bed-making in the house of the dwarfs. It *may* have had Belial for owner and then St Lucy; or *vice versa*. It may have been a fallen Parrot. But it doesn't matter.

'The only point worth bothering about is that Bysshe couldn't get its original out of his head – the original he had invented, I mean. Parrots don't learn to sing or to swear in an afternoon. Positive *months* of intercourse must have been necessary even for a fowl as intelligent as that. And so, poor Bysshe lived in constant torture. Where was she now – this impossible She? And where and whose the tongue that seemed to be vocal of the very rot to which all things living in this delightful world are – well – doomed, you know?

'Anyhow, Bysshe gave up the quest; and lived on in a furious, implacable dream. The one thing he couldn't do was to exorcize this ghost in him. He shut himself up in his chambers for days together, and the autumnal evenings rapidly lengthened. He existed in a condition of abject nausea of expectation; and in as abject a terror of having that expectation fulfilled. Nothing on earth would cajole or intimidate the bird, though Bysshe cursed it at one moment and at the next lavished upon it all the spices of the East. Cajoled it, I mean, to the extent of persuading it to embark on its programme unless the spirit moved it.

'It's an almost tragic thought too – for his loathing of the parrot now exceeded all bounds – that, far from returning these sentiments, the creature seemed to have fallen head over ears in love with his keeper. It would squat on its perch, muttering inarticulate endearments, or, sidling stealthily with beak and claw from base to keystone of its dome-shaped cage, would ogle him with an eye as amorous and amiable as the dumb thing could make it. And only dumb things of course can ever really be in love. There's a genuine pathos there, though Bysshe was immune to it.

'And now, when the old black Stygian flood set in anew, the bird no longer swore *at* him; it swore *with* him. And it so dispersed its favours that Bysshe up to the very last was never able to settle with any certainty which part of its programme came first – the paradisal aria or the other. You couldn't anticipate the creature. It chose its own moments – and these invariably unexpected. When gigantic storm-clouds were heaping themselves above the hill of the Strand, out of that menacing hush its amazing incantation would steal upon the air. In the balmiest hours of St Martin's summer, Bysshe would hurriedly spring to his windows to cut off the foul stream that came sliding out of that minute throat like the sluggish lees of a volcanic eruption.

'It was no good. You can't pin down human nature. Luckily Bysshe did not depend on his ship-broking. If he had, his parrot would have put him in the Workhouse. It's bad enough, so I am told, to fall in love with the tangible, with a creature owning a heart that you can at least believe in, or besiege, or at times hope to break. But to be infatuated by a second-hand voice and to share its decoy with the company of a friend possessing a tongue that might shock Beelzebub himself – well, that, I gather, is an even less pleasant experience.'

Judy raised the hand that held her sewing, and gently rubbed her left cheek. The air was close in spite of the open window, and in spite of the cool-looking vaporous moonlight in which Stella continued to sit and soak. But neither seemed inclined to interrupt the interminable yarn. Indeed Tressider himself appeared to have grown a little tired of it. He half yawned.

'There was nothing, you know,' he began again, with a more pronounced drawl in his voice; 'there was nothing of course extremely exceptional in Bysshe's parrot's powers, except possibly the collusion. There are numbers of historical parrots with a comparable repertory. There was the parrot for example, perfectly well accredited, that could recite a whole sonnet of Petrarch's. There is the Grand Khan's notorious cockatoo – though that was made of metal and precious stones. In France there are parrots that can reel off pages at a time of the academic dictionary. And there was the macaw that Luther despatched with his translation of the Bible. I'll bet, too, Catherine Parr had a parrot – with a five-stringed lute. Whether or not; the rest is silence.

'Minnie Sturgess naturally enough, poor thing, had been restless for weeks. The game in which she had never held any really decent cards she now saw slipping into fatuity. Bysshe was possessed. The assurance of *that* poisoned the very air she breathed. But possessed by what? By whom? She played on for a while, none the less, with all the courage and the skill she could muster. Bysshe indeed was even taking a tonic of her prescription – some patent food or other, when I saw him again towards the end of October. It didn't appear to be doing him much good. Knowing as I did the cause of this vacant somnambulism – that furtive vigilant stare of his as if from some living creature hiding far back in his eyes – the desperate change in his looks was almost ridiculous.

' "Why don't you drown the wretched thing?" I asked him. "It's a machine – an automaton: and half-devilish at that." But the face he lifted to me, its ears almost visibly pricked up towards the lair of his seducer, was – well, I suppose you know what unrequited passion can make of a man.'

'You really mean,' cried Judy suddenly, needle in the air, 'you really mean he was wasting away for the ghost of a voice?'

Tressider looked at her across the room. Even a stranger would have noticed the peculiar stridency of her shocked tones. Its bells were out of tune. To judge from Tressider's face, the telling of his story had tired him a good deal.

'I mean,' he said, 'things do happen like that. Though no doubt, as with John Keats, some "morbid affection" helped. What are we all but ghosts – of something? And who's telling this story for *you*, pray, but *your* ghost of *me*? All it comes to is that Bysshe kept on feeding his imagination, and the effort wore him down.'

' "Morbid affection!" ' echoed Stella. 'Why drag in the mortuary?'

'And what,' gasped Judy, 'and what did Miss Sturgess do? Finally, I mean? And apart' (and she added the words almost with a touch of bravado) 'apart from the food, or patent medicine, or whatever it was?'

'Miss Sturgess?' Tressider echoed. 'She played her last card; and it was a poor card, played like that. You see, poor thing, her only possible hope was to discover *somehow* exactly how she stood, since Bysshe had become little but a sullen recluse. She scarcely saw him now, even though so far as I can tell, there had been no open rift or quarrel between them. One may assume she had been awaiting her opportunity; and I'm not attacking her intentions. And one evening – and, mind you, as the colder weather approached, and possibly because Bysshe (though he lavished other kinds of dainties on his parrot) was incapable of showing it any *spiritual* sympathy, the creature was growing more and more stagnant and morose – well, one evening he had slipped out to fetch himself, I think, a bottle of wine. He was sinking into a sheer inertia – from being goaded on and on. And while on this errand he seems to have had some kind of fainting attack. Not the first of the kind. This had entailed his sitting for half an hour or so in the nearest pub; for in these later days of his obsession he had practically given up venturing further afield. All told, he couldn't have been more than an hour away.

'When he returned Minnie Sturgess was standing by the window in the further corner of his room. There was still a trace of twilight in the sky and it illumined her set face near the glass. And something in that or in her attitude set him shivering. He asked her what was wrong; then noticed that her left hand was bound up, and very inadequately, with a handkerchief – one of his own.

'She merely turned her head – and a stony one it must have appeared, I should imagine – and looked at him. He managed to repeat his question. He asked her what was the matter. I gathered that she didn't say very much in reply, only something to the effect that in future so far as she was concerned Bysshe was entirely at liberty to enjoy the delights of the company he had chosen, and which for some time past he had evidently preferred to hers. And that now at any rate he would no longer be taunted regarding it when it wasn't there. She had a raucous voice, and it was, I gathered, a bit of feminine sarcasm; something like that.

'And Bysshe knew pretty well what it meant. He knew that his voices, devilish and seraphic, were now for ever silent: that their murderess was there. He sat down without answering. Mad dogs' teeth are notoriously dangerous, Miss Sturgess went on to remark; did Bysshe know if parrots' were? And still, I gathered, he made no reply. He just sat there, paying no attention, as if almost he had taken lessons in endurance from his late pet.

'And then, his friend seems to have walked – or so at least I see her – in a kind of prowling semicircle round him, with eyes fixed on his face, and so out of the door. And then down the echoing shallow wooden staircase, and into the cobbled courtyard, and under the thinning plane-tree, and out into London – *en route*, at last, poor soul, for the boarding-house in Ramsgate.'

'And where did Bysshe bury the thing?' inquired Stella, as if sick to death of being satirical.

'I never asked him that,' said Tressider calmly. 'Nor, so far as I have heard, did he ever catechize the desolate one regarding which precise item of the two counts of the indictment had induced her to wring the parrot's neck. Probably the *bel canto*, for I don't believe myself that a woman much cares what company the man she is in love with keeps provided that it is not too good for *her*.'

At this, apparently, Judy had sat bolt upright in her chair, as if in sudden fear or anxiety. And at that precise moment heavyish footsteps were heard without.

'Hello,' inquired a bass, unctuous, yet hardly good-humoured voice, 'when shall you three meet again?'

It was Bill who stood in the doorway – Bill in his ineffable dinner-jacket and glossy shirt. And he all but filled it. He might almost have been a balloon, this Bill – tethered to the carpet there by his glossy patent-leather shoes – buoyant with gas.

'He has been telling us a story about a parrot,' said Judy in a low voice, 'who used very bad language.'

'*Has* he?' said Bill. 'Well, he ought to know better.' But his eye was almost as vacant as that of Bysshe's pet. It wandered off to rest on Judy's other guest, Stella. 'And what did *you* think of it?' he said; 'the bad man's tale?'

'Why,' said Stella, 'I am a little too grown-up for fairy-tales. And as for morals; I can find my own.'

'And you, Badroulbadour?' said Bill, widely smiling at his wife.

'Me, Bill,' echoed Judy firmly, her pretty cheeks flushed after her exertions. 'Why, I have been thinking that the tiny creature who's going to wear this shirt has ventured into a rather difficult world.'

'And who, may I ask, *is* the "tiny creature"?' drawled her husband, almost as though such a question could be a sarcasm.

Tressider's gaze was fixed vacantly on the scrap of sewing. He appeared to be entirely aloof from this little domestic catechism – seemed to have lost interest in the evening.

'It's for Mollie's little boy. He was born about three days ago,' Judy said.

But Stella, too, appeared to have lost interest. Though her face was in shadow, her eyes could still see the moon – a moon by its slightly cindrous light now betraying that it was soon to set. And to judge from her attitude and expression, this eventuality would bring her no regret, since, as it seemed in her darker moments, the moon of her own secret waters had long ago set for ever.

All Hallows*

'And because time in itselfe...can receive no alteration, the hallowing... must consist in the shape or countenance which we put upon the affaires that are incident in these days.'

Richard Hooker

It was about half-past three on an August afternoon when I found myself for the first time looking down upon All Hallows. And at glimpse of it, fatigue and vexation passed away. I stood 'at gaze', as the old phrase goes – like the two children of Israel sent in to spy out the Promised Land. How often the imagined transcends the real. Not so All Hallows. Having at last reached the end of my journey – flies, dust, heat, wind – having at last come limping out upon the green sea-bluff beneath which lay its walls – I confess the actuality excelled my feeble dreams of it.

What most astonished me, perhaps, was the sense not so much of its age, its austerity, or even its solitude, but its air of abandonment. It lay couched there as if in hiding in its narrow sea-bay. Not a sound was in the air; not a jackdaw clapped its wings among its turrets. No other roof, not even a chimney, was in sight; only the dark-blue arch of the sky; the narrow snow-line of the ebbing tide; and that gaunt coast fading away into the haze of a west over which were already gathering the veils of sunset.

We had met, then, at an appropriate hour and season. And yet – I wonder. For it was certainly not the 'beauty' of All Hallows, lulled as if into a dream in this serenity of air and heavens, which was to leave the sharpest impression upon me. And what kind of first showing would it have made, I speculated, if an autumnal gale had been shrilling and trumpeting across its narrow bay – clots of wind-borne spume floating among its dusky pinnacles – and the roar of the sea echoing against its walls. Imagine it frozen stark in winter, icy hoar-frost edging its every boss, moulding, finial, crocket, cusp!

Indeed, are there not works of man, legacies of a half-forgotten past,

---

* As printed in BS (1942), but also including manuscript alterations made by de la Mare in his copy of C (1926).

scattered across this human world of ours from China to Peru, which seem to daunt the imagination with their incomprehensibility? Incomprehensible, I mean, in the sense that the passion that inspired and conceived them is incomprehensible. Viewed in the light of the passing day, they might be the monuments of a race of demi-gods. And yet, if we could but free ourselves from our timidities, and follies, we might realize that even we ourselves have an obligation to leave behind us similar memorials – testaments to the creative and faithful genius not so much of the individual as of Humanity itself.

However that may be, it was my own personal fortune to see All Hallows for the first time in the heat of the Dog Days, after a journey which could hardly be justified except by its end. At this moment of the afternoon the great church almost cheated one into the belief that it was possessed of a life of its own. It lay, as I say, couched in its natural hollow, basking under the dark dome of the heavens like some half-fossilized monster that might at any moment stir and awaken out of the swoon to which the wand of the enchanter had committed it. And with every inch of the sun's descending journey it changed its appearance.

That is the charm of such things. Man himself, says the philosopher, is the sport of change. His life and the life around him are but the flotsam of a perpetual flux. Yet, haunted by ideals, egged on by impossibilities, he builds his vision of the changeless; and time diversifies it with its colours and its 'effects' at leisure. It was drawing near to harvest now; the summer was nearly over; the corn would soon be in stook; the season of silence had come, not even the robins had yet begun to practise their autumnal lament. I should have come earlier.

The distance was of little account. But nine flinty hills in seven miles is certainly hard commons. To plod (the occupant of a cloud of dust) up one steep incline and so see another; to plod up that and so see a third; to surmount that and, half-choked, half-roasted, to see (as if in unbelievable mirage) a fourth – and always stone walls, discoloured grass, no flower but ragged ragwort, whited fleabane, moody nettle, and the exquisite stubborn bindweed with its almond-burdened censers, and always the glitter and dazzle of the sun – well, the experience grows irksome. And then that endless flint erection with which some jealous Lord of the Manor had barricaded his verdurous estate! A fly-infested mile of the company of that wall was tantamount to making one's way into the infernal regions – with Tantalus for fellow-pilgrim. And when a solitary and empty dung-cart had lumbered by, lifting the dumb dust out of the road in swirling clouds into the heat-quivering air, I had all but wept aloud.

No, I shall not easily forget that walk – or the conclusion of it – when footsore, all but dead beat – dust all over me, cheeks, lips, eyelids, in my hair, dust in drifts even between my naked body and my clothes – I stretched my aching limbs on the turf under the straggle of trees which crowned the bluff of that last hill, still blessedly green and verdant, and feasted my eyes on the cathedral beneath me. How odd Memory is – in her sorting arrangements. How perverse her pigeon-holes.

It had reminded me of a drizzling evening many years ago. I had stayed a moment to listen to an old Salvation Army officer preaching at a street corner. The sopped and squalid houses echoed with his harangue. His penitents' drum resembled the block of an executioner. His goatish beard wagged at every word he uttered. 'My brothers and sisters,' he was saying 'the very instant our fleshly bodies are born they begin to perish; the moment the Lord has put them together, time begins to take them to pieces again. *Now* at this very instant if you listen close, you can hear the nibblings and frettings of the moth and rust within – the worm that never dies. It's the same with human causes and creeds and institutions – just the same. O, then, for that Strand of Beauty where all that is mortal shall be shed away and we shall appear in the likeness and verisimilitude of what in sober and awful truth we are!'

The light striking out of an oil-and-colourman's shop at the street corner lay across his cheek and beard and glassed his eye. The soaked circle of humanity in which he was gesticulating stood staring and motionless – the lassies, the probationers, the melancholy idlers. I had had enough. I went away. But is is odd that so utterly inappropriate a recollection should have edged back into my mind at this moment. There was, as I have said, not a living soul in sight. Only a few sea-birds – oyster-catchers maybe – were jangling on the distant beach.

It was now a quarter to four by my watch, and the usual pensive 'lin-lan-lone' from the belfry beneath me would soon no doubt be ringing to evensong. But if at that moment a triple bob-major had suddenly clanged its alarm over sea and shore I couldn't have stirred a finger's breadth. Scanty though the shade afforded by the wind-shorn tuft of trees under which I lay might be – I was ineffably at peace.

No bell, as a matter of fact, loosed its tongue that stagnant half-hour. Unless then the walls beneath me already concealed a few such chance visitors as myself, All Hallows would be empty. A cathedral not only without a close but without a congregation – yet another romantic charm. The Deanery and the residences of its clergy, my old guide-book had long since informed me, were a full mile or more away. I determined in due time, first to make sure of an entry, and then having quenched my thirst, to bathe.

How inhuman any extremity – hunger, fatigue, pain, desire – makes us poor humans. Thirst and drouth so haunted my mind that again and again as I glanced towards it I supped up in one long draught that complete blue sea. But meanwhile, too, my eyes had been steadily exploring and searching out this monument of the bygone centuries beneath me.

The headland faced approximately due west. The windows of the Lady Chapel therefore lay immediately beneath me, their fourteenth-century glass showing flatly dark amid their traceries. Above it, the shallow V-shaped, leaden ribbed roof of the chancel converged towards the un-finished tower, then broke away at right angles – for the cathedral was cruciform. Walls so ancient and so sparsely adorned and decorated could not but be inhospitable in effect. Their stone was of a bleached bone-grey; a grey that none the less seemed to be as immaterial as flame – or incandescent ash. They were substantial enough, however, to cast a marvellously lucent shadow, of a blue no less vivid but paler than that of the sea, on the shelving sward beneath them. And that shadow was steadily shifting as I watched. But even if the complete edifice had vanished into the void, the scene would still have been of an incredible loveliness. The colours in air and sky on this dangerous coast seemed to shed a peculiar unreality even on the rocks of its own outworks.

So, from my vantage place on the hill that dominates it, I continued for a while to watch All Hallows; to spy upon it; and no less intently than a sentry who, not quite trusting his own eyes, has seen a dubious shape approaching him in the dusk. It may sound absurd, but I felt that at any moment I too might surprise All Hallows in the act of revealing what in very truth it looked like – and *was*, when, I mean, no human witness was there to share its solitude.

Those gigantic statues, for example, which flanked the base of the un-finished tower, an intense bluish-white in the sunlight and a bluish-purple in shadow – images of angels and of saints, as I had learned of old from my guide-book. Only six of them at most could be visible, of course, from where I sat. And yet I found myself counting them again and yet again, as if doubting my own arithmetic. For my first impression had been that seven were in view – though the figure furthest from me at the western angle showed little more than a jutting fragment of stone which might perhaps be only part and parcel of the fabric itself.

But then the lights even of day may be deceitful, and fantasy plays strange tricks with one's eyes. With exercise, none the less, the mind is enabled to detect minute details which the unaided eye is incapable of particularizing. Given the imagination, man himself indeed may some day be able to distinguish what shapes are walking during our own terrestrial midnight amid the black shadows of the craters in the noonday of the moon. At any rate, I could trace at last frets of carving, minute weather marks, crookednesses, incrustations, repairings, that had before passed unnoticed. These walls, indeed, like human faces, were maps and charts of their own long past.

In the midst of this prolonged scrutiny, the hynotic air, the heat, must suddenly have overcome me. I fell asleep up there in my grove's scanty shade; and remained asleep, too, long enough (as time is measured by the clocks of sleep) to dream an immense panoramic dream. On waking, I could recall only the faintest vestiges of it, and found that the hand of my watch had crept on but a few minutes in the interval. It was eight minutes past four.

I scrambled up – numbed and inert – with that peculiar sense of panic which sometimes follows an uneasy sleep. What folly to have been frittering time away within sight of my goal at an hour when no doubt the cathedral would soon be closed to visitors, and abandoned for the night to its own secret ruminations. I hastened down the steep rounded incline of the hill, and having skirted under the sunlit expanse of the walls, came presently to the south door, only to discover that my forebodings had been justified, and that it was already barred and bolted. The discovery seemed to increase my fatigue fourfold. How foolish it is to obey mere caprices. What a straw is a man!

I glanced up into the beautiful shell of masonry above my head. Shapes and figures in stone it showed in plenty – symbols of an imagination that had flamed and faded, leaving this signature for sole witness – but not a living bird or butterfly. There was but one faint chance left of making an entry. Hunted now, rather than the hunter, I hastened out again into the full blazing flood of sunshine – and once more came within sight of the sea; a sea so near at last that I could hear its enormous sallies and murmurings. Indeed I had not realized until that moment how closely the great western doors of the cathedral abutted on the beach.

It was as if its hospitality had been deliberately designed, not for a people to whom the faith of which it was the shrine had become a weariness and a commonplace, but for the solace of pilgrims from over the ocean. I could see them tumbling into their cockle-boats out of their great hollow ships – sails idle, anchors down; see them leaping ashore and straggling up across the sands to these all-welcoming portals – 'Parthians and Medes and Elamites; dwellers in Mesopotamia and in the parts of Egypt about Cyrene; strangers of Rome, Jews and Proselytes – we do hear them speak in our own tongue the wonderful works of God.'

And so at last I found my way into All Hallows – entering by a rounded dwarfish side-door with zigzag mouldings. There hung for corbel to its dripstone a curious leering face, with its forked tongue out, to give me welcome. And an appropriate one, too, for the figure I made!

But once beneath that prodigious roof-tree, I forgot myself and everything that was mine. The hush, the coolness, the unfathomable twilight drifted in on my small human consciousness. Not even the ocean itself is able so completely to receive one into its solacing bosom. Except for the windows over my head, filtering with their stained glass the last western radiance of the sun, there was but little visible colour in those great spaces, and a severe economy of decoration. The stone piers carried their round arches with an almost intimidating impassivity.

By deliberate design, too, or by some illusion of perspective, the whole floor of the building appeared steadily to ascend towards the east, where a dark, wooden multitudinously figured rood-screen shut off the choir and the high altar from the nave. I seemed to have exchanged one universal actuality for another: the burning world of nature for this oasis of quiet. Here, the wings of the imagination need never rest in their flight out of the wilderness into the unknown.

Thus resting, I must again have fallen asleep. And so swiftly can even the merest freshet of sleep affect the mind, that when my eyes opened, I was completely at a loss.

Where was I? What demon of what romantic chasm had swept my poor drowsy body into this immense haunt? The din and clamour of an horrific dream whose fainting rumour was still in my ear, became suddenly stilled. Then at one and the same moment, a sense of utter dismay at earthly surroundings no longer serene and peaceful, but grim and forbidding, flooded my mind, and I became aware that I was no longer alone. Twenty or thirty paces away, and a little this side of the rood-screen, an old man was standing.

To judge from the black and purple velvet and tassel-tagged gown he wore, he was a verger. He had not yet realized, it seemed, that a visitor shared his solitude. And yet he was listening. His head was craned forward and leaned sideways on his rusty shoulders. As I steadily watched him, he raised his eyes, and with a peculiar stealthy deliberation scanned the complete upper regions of the northern transept. Not the faintest rumour of any sound that may have attracted his attention reached me where I sat. Perhaps a wild bird had made its entry through a broken pane of glass and with its cry had at the same moment awakened me and caught his attention. Or maybe the old man was waiting for some fellow-occupant to join him from above.

I continued to watch him. Even at this distance, the silvery twilight cast by the clerestory windows was sufficient to show me, though vaguely, his face: the high sloping nose, the lean cheekbones and protruding chin. He continued so long in the same position that I at last determined to break in on his reverie.

At sound of my footsteps his head sunk cautiously back upon his shoulders; and he turned; and then motionlessly surveyed me as I drew near. He resembled one of those old men whom Rembrandt delighted in drawing: the knotted hands, the black drooping eyebrows, the wide thin-lipped

ecclesiastical mouth, the intent cavernous dark eyes beneath the heavy folds
of their lids. White as a miller with dust, hot and draggled, I was hardly the
kind of visitor that any self-respecting custodian would warmly welcome,
but he greeted me none the less with every mark of courtesy.

I apologized for the lateness of my arrival, and explained it as best I
could. 'Until I caught sight of you,' I concluded lamely, 'I hadn't ventured
very far in: otherwise I might have found myself a prisoner for the night. It
must be dark in here when there is no moon.'

The old man smiled – but wryly. 'As a matter of fact, sir,' he replied, 'the
cathedral is closed to visitors at four – at such times, that is, when there is
no afternoon service. Services are not as frequent as they were. But visitors
are rare too. In winter, in particular, you notice the gloom – as you say, sir.
Not that I ever spend the night here: though I am usually last to leave.
There's the risk of fire to be thought of and . . . I think I should have detected your presence here, sir. One becomes accustomed after many years.'

There was the usual trace of official pedantry in his voice, but it was
more pleasing than otherwise. Nor did he show any wish to be rid of me.
He continued his survey, although his eye was a little absent and his attention seemed to be divided.

'I thought perhaps I might be able to find a room for the night and really
explore the cathedral to-morrow morning. It has been a tiring journey; I
come from B — '

'Ah, from B — ; it *is* a fatiguing journey, sir, taken on foot. I used to
walk in there to see a sick daughter of mine. Carriage parties occasionally
make their way here, but not so much as once. We are too far out of the
hurly-burly to be much intruded on. Not that them who come to make
their worship here are intruders. Far from it. But most that come are mere
sightseers. And the fewer of them, I say, in the circumstances, the better.'

Something in what I had said or in my appearance seemed to have reassured him. 'Well, I cannot claim to be a regular churchgoer,' I said. 'I am
myself a mere sightseer. And yet – even to sit here for a few minutes is to
be reconciled.'

'Ah, reconciled, sir:' the old man repeated, turning away. 'I can well
imagine it after that journey on such a day as this. But to live here is
another matter.'

'I was thinking of that,' I replied in a foolish attempt to retrieve the
position. 'It must, as you say, be desolate enough in the winter – for two-
thirds of the year, indeed.'

'We have our storms, sir – the bad with the good,' he agreed, 'and our
position is specially prolific of what they call sea-fog. It comes driving in
from the sea for days and nights together – gale and mist, so that you can
scarcely see your open hand in front of your eyes even in broad daylight.

And the noise of it, sir, sweeping across overhead in that wooliness of mist, if you take me, is most peculiar. It's shocking to a stranger. No, sir, we are left pretty much to ourselves when the fine-weather birds are flown... You'd be astonished at the power of the winds here. There was a mason – a local man too – not above two or three years ago was blown clean off the roof from under the tower – tossed up in the air like an empty sack. But' – and the old man at last allowed his eyes to stray upwards to the roof again – 'but there's not much doing now.' He seemed to be pondering. 'Nothing open.'

'I mustn't detain you,' I said, 'but you were saying that services are infrequent now. Why is that? When one thinks of — ' But tact restrained me.

'Pray don't think of keeping me, sir. It's a part of my duties. But from a remark you let fall I was supposing you may have seen something that appeared, I understand, not many months ago in the newspapers. We lost our dean – Dean Pomfrey – last November. To all intents and purposes I mean; and his office has not yet been filled. Between you and me, sir, there's a hitch – though I should wish it to go no further. They are greedy monsters – those newspapers: no respect, no discretion, no decency, in my view. And they copy each other like cats in a chorus.

'We have never wanted to be a notoriety here, sir: and not of late of all times. We must face our own troubles. You'd be astonished how callous the mere sightseer can be. And not only them from over the water whom our particular troubles cannot concern – but far worse – parties as English as you or me. They ask you questions you wouldn't believe possible in a civilized country. Not that they care what becomes of us – not one iota, sir. We talk of them masked-up Inquisitors in olden times, but there's many a human being in our own would enjoy seeing a fellow-creature on the rack if he could get the opportunity. It's a heartless age, sir.'

This was queerish talk in the circumstances: and after all myself was of the glorious company of the sightseers. I held my peace. And the old man, as if to make amends, asked me if I would care to see any particular part of the building. 'The light is smalling,' he explained, 'but still if we keep to the ground level there'll be a few minutes to spare; and we shall not be interrupted if we go quietly on our way.'

For the moment the reference eluded me: I could only thank him for the suggestion and once more beg him not to put himself to any inconvenience. I explained, too, that though I had no personal acquaintance with Dr Pomfrey, I had read of his illness in the newspapers. 'Isn't he,' I added a little dubiously, 'the author of *The Church and the Folk*? If so, he must be an exceedingly learned and delightful man.'

'Ay, sir.' The old verger put up a hand towards me. 'You may well say it: a saint if ever there was one. But it's worse than "illness", sir – it's oblivion.

And, thank God, the newspapers didn't get hold of more than a bare outline.'

He dropped his voice. 'This way, if you please'; and he led me off gently down the aisle, once more coming to a standstill beneath the roof of the tower. 'What I mean, sir, is that there's very few left in this world who have any place in their minds for a sacred confidence – no reverence, sir. They would as lief All Hallows and all it stands for were swept away to-morrow, demolished to the dust. And that gives me the greatest caution with whom I speak. But sharing one's troubles is sometimes a relief. If it weren't so, why do those Catholics have their wooden boxes all built for the purpose? What else, I ask you, is the meaning of their fasts and penances?

'You see, sir, I am myself, and have been for upwards of twelve years now, the dean's verger. In the sight of no respecter of persons – of offices and dignities, that is, I take it – I might claim to be even an elder brother. And our dean, sir, was a man who was all things to all men. No pride of place, no vauntingness, none of your apron-and-gaiter high-and-mightiness whatsoever, sir. And then that! And to come on us without warning; or at least without warning as could be taken as *such*.' I followed his eyes into the darkening stony spaces above us; a light like tarnished silver lay over the soundless vaultings. But so, of course, dusk, either of evening or day-break, would affect the ancient stones. Nothing moved there.

'You must understand, sir,' the old man was continuing, 'the procession for divine service proceeds from the vestry over yonder out through those wrought-iron gates and so under the rood-screen and into the chancel there. Visitors are admitted on showing a card or a word to the verger in charge; but not otherwise. If you stand a pace or two to the right, you will catch a glimpse of the altar-screen – fourteenth-century work, Bishop Robert de Beaufort – and a unique example of the age. But what I was saying is that when we proceed for the services *out* of here *into* there, it has always been our custom to keep pretty close together; more seemly and decent, sir, than straggling in like so many sheep.

'Besides, sir, aren't we at such times in the manner of an *array*; "marching as to war", if you take me: it's a lesson in objects. The third verger leading: then the choristers, boys and men, though sadly depleted; then the minor canons; then any other dignitaries who may happen to be present, with the canon in residence; then myself, sir, followed by the dean.

'There hadn't been much amiss up to then, and on that afternoon, I can vouch – and I've repeated it *ad naushum* – there was not a single stranger out in this beyond here, sir – nave or transepts. Not within view, that is: one can't be expected to see through four feet of Norman stone. Well, sir, we had gone on our way, and I had actually turned about as usual to bow Dr Pomfrey into his stall, when I found to my consternation, to my con-sternation, I say, he wasn't there! It alarmed me, sir, and as you might well believe if you knew the full circumstances.

'Not that I lost my presence of mind. My first duty was to see all things to be in order and nothing unseemly to occur. My feelings were another matter. The old gentleman had left the vestry with us: that I knew: I had myself robed 'im as usual, and he in his own manner, smiling with his "Well, Jones, another day gone; another day gone." He was always an anxious gentleman for *time*, sir. How we spend it and all.

'As I say, then, he was behind me when we swepp out of the gates. I saw him coming on out of the tail of my eye – we grow accustomed to it, to see with the whole of the eye, I mean. And then – not a vestige; and me –well, sir, nonplussed, as you may imagine. I gave a look and sign at Canon Ockham, and the service proceeded as usual, while I hurried back to the vestry thinking the poor gentleman must have been taken suddenly ill. And yet, sir, I was not surprised to find the vestry vacant, and him not there. I had been expecting matters to come to what you might call a head.

'As best I could I held my tongue, and a fortunate thing it was that Canon Ockham was then in residence and not Canon Leigh Shougar, though perhaps I am not the one to say it. No, sir, our beloved dean – as pious and unworldly a gentleman as ever graced the Church – was gone for ever. He was not to appear in our midst again. He had been' – and the old man with elevated eyebrows and long lean mouth nearly whispered the words into my ear – 'he had been absconded – abducted, sir.'

'Abducted!' I murmured.

The old man closed his eyes, and with trembling lids added, 'He was found, sir, late that night up there in what they call the Trophy Room – sitting in a corner there, weeping. A child. Not a word of what had persuaded him to go or misled him there, not a word of sorrow or sadness, thank God. He didn't know us, sir – didn't know *me*. Just simple; harmless; memory all gone. Simple, sir.'

It was foolish to be whispering together like this beneath these enormous spaces with not so much as a clothes-moth for sign of life within view. But I even lowered my voice still further: 'Were there no premonitory symptoms? Had he been failing for long?'

The spectacle of grief in any human face is afflicting, but in a face as aged and resigned as this old man's – I turned away in remorse the moment the question was out of my lips; emotion is a human solvent and a sort of friendliness had sprung up between us.

'If you will just follow me,' he whispered, 'there's a little place where I make my ablutions that might be of service, sir. We would converse there in better comfort. I am sometimes reminded of those words in Ecclesiastes: "And a bird of the air shall tell of the matter." There is not much in our poor human affairs, sir, that was not known to the writer of *that* book.'

He turned and led the way with surprising celerity, gliding along in his thin-soled, square-toed, clerical springside boots; and came to a pause outside a nail-studded door. He opened it with a huge key, and admitted me into a recess under the central tower. We mounted a spiral stone staircase and passed along a corridor hardly more than two feet wide and so dark that now and again I thrust out my fingertips in search of his black velveted gown to make sure of my guide.

This corridor at length conducted us into a little room whose only illumination I gathered was that of the ebbing dusk from within the cathedral. The old man with trembling rheumatic fingers lit a candle, and thrusting its stick into the middle of an old oak table, pushed open yet another thick oaken door. 'You will find a basin and a towel in there, sir, if you will be so kind.'

I entered. A print of the Crucifixion was tin-tacked to the panelled wall, and beneath it stood a tin basin and jug on a stand. Never was water sweeter. I laved my face and hands and drank deep; my throat like a parched river-course after a drought. What appeared to be a tarnished censer lay in one corner of the room; a pair of seven-branched candlesticks shared a recess with a mouse-trap and a book. My eyes passed wearily yet gratefully from one to another of these mute discarded objects while I stood drying my hands.

When I returned, the old man was standing motionless before the spike-barred grill of the window, peering out and down.

'You asked me, sir,' he said, turning his lank waxen face into the feeble rays of the candle, 'you asked me, sir, a question which, if I understood you aright, was this: Was there anything that had occurred *previous* that would explain what I have been telling you? Well, sir, it's a long story, and one best restricted to them perhaps that have the goodwill of things at heart. All Hallows, I might say, sir, is my second home. I have been here, boy and man, for close on fifty-five years – have seen four bishops pass away and have served under no less than five several deans, Dr Pomfrey, poor gentleman, being the last of the five.

'If such a word could be excused, sir, it's no exaggeration to say that Canon Leigh Shougar is a greenhorn by comparison; which may in part be why he has never quite hit it off, as they say, with Canon Ockham. Or even with Archdeacon Trafford, though he's another kind of gentleman altogether. And *he* is at present abroad. He had what they call a breakdown in health, sir.

'Now in my humble opinion, what was required was not only wisdom and knowledge but simple common sense. In the circumstances I am about to mention, it serves no purpose for any of us to be talking too much; to be for ever sitting at a table with shut doors and finger on lip, and discussing what to most intents and purposes would hardly be called evidence at all, sir. What is the use of argufying, splitting hairs, objurgating about trifles, when matters are sweeping rapidly on from bad to worse. I say it with all due respect and not, I hope, thrusting myself into what doesn't concern me: Dr Pomfrey might be with us now in his own self and reason if only common caution had been observed.

'But now that the poor gentleman is gone beyond all that, there is no hope of action or agreement left, none whatsoever. They meet and they meet, and they have now one expert now another down from London, and even from the continent. And I don't say they are not knowledgeable gentlemen either, nor a pride to their profession. But why not tell *all*? Why keep back the very secret of what we know? That's what I am asking. And, what's the answer? Why simply that what they don't want to believe, what runs counter to their hopes and wishes and credibilities – and comfort – in this world, that's what they keep out of sight as long as decency permits.

'Canon Leigh Shougar *knows*, sir, what *I* know. And how, I ask, is he going to get to grips with it at this late day if he refuses to acknowledge that such things are what every fragment of evidence goes to prove that they are. It's *we*, sir, and not the rest of the heedless world outside, who in the long and the short of it are responsible. And what I say is: no power or principality here or hereunder can take possession of a place while those inside have faith enough to keep them out. But once let that falter – the seas are in. And when I say no power, sir, I mean – with all deference – even Satan himself.' The lean lank face had set at the word like a wax mask. The black eyes beneath the heavy lids were fixed on mine with an acute intensity and – though more inscrutable things haunted them – with an unfaltering courage. So dense a hush hung about us that the very stones of the walls seemed to be of silence solidified. It is curious what a refreshment of spirit a mere tin basinful of water may be. I stood leaning against the edge of the table so that the candlelight still rested on my companion.

'What is *wrong* here?' I asked him baldly.

He seemed not to have expected so direct an inquiry. 'Wrong, sir? Why, if I might make so bold,' he replied with a wan, far-away smile and gently drawing his hand down one of the velvet lapels of his gown, 'if I might make so bold, sir, I take it that you have come as a direct answer to prayer.'

His voice faltered. 'I am an old man now, and nearly at the end of my tether. You must realize, if you please, that I can't get any help that I can understand. I am not doubting that the gentlemen I have mentioned have only the salvation of the cathedral at heart – the cause, sir; and a graver responsibility yet. But they refuse to see how close to the edge of things we are: and how we are drifting.

'Take mere situation. So far as my knowledge tells me, there is no sacred edifice in the whole kingdom – of a piece, that is, with All Hallows not only in mere size and age but in what I might call sanctity and tradition – that is so open – open, I mean, sir, to attack of this peculiar and terrifying nature.'

'Terrifying?'

'*Terrifying*, sir; though I hold fast to what wits my Maker has bestowed on me. Where else, may I ask, would you expect the powers of darkness to congregate in open besiegement than in this narrow valley? First, the sea out there. Are you aware, sir, that ever since living remembrance flood-tide has been gnawing and mumbling its way into this bay to the extent of three or four feet *per annum*? Forty inches, and forty inches, and forty inches corroding on and on: Watch it, sir, man and boy as I have these sixty years past and then make a century of it. Not to mention positive leaps and bounds.

'And now, think a moment of the floods and gales that fall upon us autumn and winter through and even in spring, when this valley is liker paradise to young eyes than any place on earth. They make the roads from the nearest towns well-nigh impassable; which means that for some months of the year we are to all intents and purposes clean cut off from the rest of the world – as the Schindels out there are from the mainland. Are you aware, sir, I continue, that as we stand now we are above a mile from traces of the nearest human habitation, and them merely the relics of a burnt-out old farmstead? I warrant that if (and which God forbid) you had been shut up here during the coming night, and it was a near thing but what you weren't – I warrant you might have shouted yourself dumb out of the nearest window if window you could reach – and not a human soul to heed or help you.'

I shifted my hands on the table. It was tedious to be asking questions that received only such vague and evasive replies: and it is always a little disconcerting in the presence of a stranger to be spoken to so close, and with such positiveness.

'Well', I smiled, 'I hope I should not have disgraced my nerves to such an extreme as that. As a small boy, one of my particular fancies was to spend a night in a pulpit. There's a cushion, you know!'

The old man's solemn glance never swerved from my eyes. 'But I take it, sir,' he said, 'if you had ventured to give out a text up there in the dark hours, your jocular young mind would not have been prepared for any kind of a congregation?'

'You mean,' I said a little sharply, 'that the place is haunted?' The absurd notion flitted across my mind of some wandering tribe of gipsies chancing on a refuge so ample and isolated as this, and taking up its quarters in its secret parts. The old church must be honeycombed with corridors and passages and chambers pretty much like the one in which we were now concealed: and what does 'cartholic' imply but an infinite hospitality within prescribed limits? But the old man had taken me at my word.

'I mean, sir,' he said firmly, shutting his eyes, 'that there are devilish agencies at work here.' He raised his hand. 'Don't, I entreat you, dismiss what I am saying as the wanderings of a foolish old man.' He drew a little nearer. 'I have heard them with these ears; I have seen them with these eyes; though whether they have any positive substance, sir, is beyond my small knowledge to declare. But what indeed might we expect their substance to *be*? First: "I take it," says the Book, "to be such as no man can by learning define, nor by wisdom search out." Is that so? Then I go by the Book. And next: what does the same Word or very near it (I speak of the Apocrypha) say of their *purpose*? It says – and correct me if I go astray – "Devils are creatures made by God, and *that for vengeance*."

'So far, so good, sir. We stop when we can go no further. Vengeance. But of their power, of what they can *do*, I can give you definite evidences. It would be a byword if once the rumour was spread abroad. And if it is *not* so, why, I ask, does every expert that comes here leave us in haste and in dismay? They go off with their tails between their legs. They see, they grope in, but they don't believe. They *invent* reasons. And they *hasten* to leave us!' His face shook with the emphasis he laid upon the word. 'Why? Why, because the experience is beyond their knowledge, sir.' He drew back breathless and, as I could see, profoundly moved.

'But surely,' I said, 'every old building is bound in time to show symptoms of decay. Half the cathedrals in England, half its churches, even, of any age, have been "restored" – and in many cases with ghastly results. This new grouting and so on. Why, only the other day... All I mean is, why should you suppose mere wear and tear should be caused by any other agency than — '

The old man turned away. 'I must apologize,' he interrupted me with his inimitable admixture of modesty and dignity. 'I am a poor mouth at explanations, sir. Decay – stress – strain – settling – dissolution: I have heard those words bandied from lip to lip like a game at cup and ball. They fill me with nausea. Why, I am speaking not of dissolution, sir, but of *repairs*, *restorations*. Not decay, *strengthening*. Not a corroding loss, an awful *progress*. I could show you places – and chiefly obscured from direct view and difficult of a close examination, sir, where stones lately as rotten as pumice and as fretted as a sponge have been replaced by others fresh-quarried – and nothing of their kind within twenty miles.

'There are spots where massive blocks a yard or more square have been *pushed* into place by sheer force. All Hallows is safer at this moment than it has been for three hundred years. They meant well – them who came to see, full of talk and fine language, and went dumb away. I grant you they meant well. I allow that. They hummed and they hawed. They smirked this and they shrugged that. But at heart, sir, they were cowed – horrified: all at a loss. Their very faces showed it. But if you ask me for what purpose such doings are afoot – I have no answer; none.

'But now, supposing you yourself, sir, were one of them, with *your* repute at stake, and you were called in to look at a house which the owners of it and them who had it in trust were disturbed by its being re-edificated and restored by some agency unknown to them. Supposing that! *Why,*' and he rapped with his knuckles on the table, 'being human and *not one of us* mightn't you be going away too with mouth shut, because you didn't want to get talked about to your disadvantage? And wouldn't you at last dismiss the whole thing as a foolish delusion, in the belief that living in out-of-the-way parts like these cuts a man off from the world, breeds maggots in the mind?

'I assure you, sir, they don't – not even Canon Ockham himself to the full – they don't believe even me. And yet, when they have their meetings of the Chapter they talk and wrangle round and round about nothing else. I can bear the other without a murmur. What God sends, I say, we humans deserve. We have laid ourselves open to it. But when you buttress up blindness and wickedness with downright folly, why then, sir, I sometimes fear for my own reason.'

He set his shoulders as square as his aged frame would permit, and with fingers clutching the lapels beneath his chin, he stood gazing out into the darkness through that narrow inward window.

'Ah, sir,' he began again, 'I have not spent sixty years in this solitary place without paying heed to my own small wandering thoughts and instincts. Look at your newspapers, sir. What they call the Great War is over – and he'd be a brave man who would take an oath before heaven that *that* was only of human designing – and yet what do we see around us? Nothing but strife and juggleries and hatred and contempt and discord wherever you look. I am no scholar, sir, but so far as my knowledge and experience carry me, we human beings are living to-day merely from hand to mouth. We learn to-day what ought to have been done yesterday, and yet are at a loss to know what's to be done to-morrow.

'And the Church, sir. God forbid I should push my way into what does not concern me; and if you had told me half an hour gone by that you were a regular churchman, I shouldn't be pouring out all this to you now. It wouldn't be seemly. But being not so gives me confidence. By merely listening you can help me, sir; though you can't help *us*. Centuries ago – and in my humble judgement, rightly – we broke away from the parent stem and rooted outselves in our own soil. But, right or wrong, doesn't that of itself, I ask you, make us all the more open to attack from him who never wearies in going to and fro in the world seeking whom he may devour?

'I am not wishing you to take sides. But a gentleman doesn't scoff; you don't find him jeering at what he doesn't rightly understand. He keeps his own counsel, sir. And that's where, as I say, Canon Leigh Shougar sets me doubting. He refuses to make allowances; though up there in London things may look different. He gets his company there; and then for him the whole kallyidoscope changes, if you take me.'

The old man scanned me an instant as if inquiring within himself whether, after all, I too might not be one of the outcasts. 'You see, sir,' he went on dejectedly, 'I can bear what may be to come. I can, if need be, live on through what few years may yet remain to me and keep going, as they say. But only if I can be assured that my own inmost senses are not cheating and misleading me. Tell me the worst, and you will have done an old man a service he can never repay. Tell me, on the other hand, that I am merely groping along in a network of devilish *delusion*, sir – well, in that case I hope to with my master, with Dr Pomfrey, as soon as possible. We were all children once; and now there's nothing worse in this world for him to come into, in a manner of speaking.

'Oh, sir, I sometimes wonder if what we call childhood and growing up isn't a copy of the fate of our ancient forefathers. In the beginning of time there were Fallen Angels, we are told; but even if it weren't there in Holy Writ, we might have learnt it of our own fears and misgivings. I sometimes find myself looking at a young child with little short of awe, sir, knowing that within its mind is a scene of peace and paradise of which we older folk have no notion, and which will fade away out of it, as life wears on, like the mere tabernacling of a dream.'

There was no trace of unction in his speech, though the phraseology might suggest it, and he smiled at me as if in reassurance. 'You see, sir – if I have any true notion of the matter – then I say, heaven is dealing very gently with Dr Pomfrey. He has gone back, and, I take it, his soul is elsewhere and at rest.'

He had come a pace or two nearer, and the candle-light now cast grotesque shadows in the hollows of his brows and cheekbones, silvering his long scanty hair. The eyes, dimming with age, were fixed on mine as if in incommunicable entreaty. I was at a loss to answer him.

He dropped his hands to his sides. 'The fact is,' he looked cautiously about him, 'what I am now being so bold as to suggest, though it's a familiar enough experience to me, may put you in actual physical danger. But then, duty's duty, and a deed of kindness from stranger to stranger quite another matter. You seem to have come, if I may say so, in the nick of time; that was all. On the other hand, we can leave the building at once if you are so minded. In any case we must be gone well before dark sets in;

even mere human beings are best not disturbed at any night-work they may be after. The dark brings recklessness: conscience cannot see as clear in the dark. Besides, I once delayed too long myself. There is not much of day left even now, though I see by the almanac there should be a slip of moon to-night – unless the sky is over-clouded. All that I'm meaning is that our all-in-all, so to speak, is the calm untrammelled evidence of the outer senses, sir. And there comes a time when – well, when one hesitates to trust one's own.'

I have read somewhere that it is only its setting – the shape, the line, the fold, the angle of the lid and so on – that gives its finer shades of meaning and significance to the human eye. Looking into his, even in that narrow and melancholy light, was like pondering over a grey, salt, desolate pool – such as sometimes neighbours the sea on a flat and dangerous coast.

Perhaps if I had been a little less credulous, or less exhausted, I should by now have begun to doubt this old creature's sanity. And yet, surely, at even the faintest contact with the insane, a sentinel in the mind sends up flares and warnings; the very landscape changes; there is a sense of in-security. If, too, the characters inscribed by age and experience on a man's face can be evidence of goodness and simplicity, then my companion was safe enough. To trust in his sagacity was another matter.

But then, there was All Hallows itself to take into account. That first glimpse from my green headland of its louring yet lovely walls had been strangely moving. There are buildings (almost as though they were once copies of originals now half-forgotten in the human mind) that have a sin-gular influence on the imagination. Even now in this remote candlelit room, immured between its massive stones, the vast edifice seemed to be gently and furtively fretting its impression on my mind.

I glanced again at the old man: he had turned aside as if to leave me, unbiased, to my own decision. How would a lifetime spent between these sombre walls have affected *me*, I wondered? Surely it would be an act of mere decency to indulge their worn-out hermit! He had appealed to me. If I were ten times more reluctant to follow him, I could hardly refuse. Not at any rate without risking a retreat as humiliating as that of the architec-tural experts he had referred to – with my tail between my legs.

'I only wish I could hope to be of any real help.'

He turned about; his expression changed, as if at the coming of a light. 'Why, then, sir, let us be gone at once. You are with me, sir: that was all I hoped and asked. And now there's no time to waste.'

He tilted his head to listen a moment – with that large, flat, shell-like ear of his which age alone seems to produce. 'Matches and candle, sir,' he had lowered his voice to a whisper, 'but – though we mustn't lose each other; you and me, I mean – *not*, I think, a naked light. What I would suggest, if you have no objection, is your kindly grasping my gown. There is a kind of streamer here, you see – as if made for the purpose. There will be a good deal of up-and-downing, but I know the building blindfold and as you might say inch by inch. And now that the bell-ringers have given up ringing it is more in my charge than ever.'

He stood back and looked at me with folded hands, a whimsical child-like smile on his aged face. 'I sometimes think to myself I'm like the sentry, sir, in that play by William Shakespeare. I saw it, sir, years ago, on my only visit to London – when I was a boy. If ever there were a villain for all his fine talk and all, commend me to that ghost. I see him yet.'

Whisper though it was, a sort of chirrup had come into his voice, like that of a cricket in a baker's shop. I took tight hold of the velveted tag of his gown. He opened the door, pressed the box of safety matches into my hand, himself grasped the candlestick and then blew out the light. We were instantly marooned in an impenetrable darkness. 'Now, sir, if you would kindly remove your walking shoes,' he muttered close in my ear, 'we should proceed with less noise. I shan't hurry you. And please to tug at the streamer if you need attention. In a few minutes the blackness will be less intense.'

As I stooped down to loose my shoe-laces I heard my heart thumping merrily away. It had been listening to our conversation apparently! I slung my shoes round my neck – as I had often done as a boy when going paddling – and we set out on our expedition.

I have endured too often the nightmare of being lost and abandoned in the stony bowels of some strange and prodigious building to take such an adventure lightly. I clung, I confess, desperately tight to my lifeline and we groped steadily onward – my guide ever and again turning back to mutter warning or encouragement in my ear.

Now I found myself steadily ascending; and then in a while, feeling my way down flights of hollowly worn stone steps, and anon brushing along a gallery or corkscrewing up a newel staircase so narrow that my shoulders all but touched the walls on either side. In spite of the sepulchral chill in these bowels of the cathedral, I was soon suffocatingly hot, and the effort to see became intolerably fatiguing. Once, to recover our breath we paused opposite a slit in the thickness of the masonry, at which to breathe the tepid sweetness of the outer air. It was faint with the scent of wild flowers and cool of the sea. And presently after, at a barred window, high overhead, I caught a glimpse of the night's first stars.

We then turned inward once more, ascending yet another spiral stair-case. And now the intense darkness had thinned a little, the groined roof above us becoming faintly discernible. A fresher air softly fanned my cheek; and then trembling fingers groped over my breast, and, cold and bony, clutched my own.

'Dead still here, sir, if you please.' So close sounded the whispered syllables the voice might have been a messenger's within my own consciousness. 'Dead still, here. There's a drop of some sixty or seventy feet a few paces on.'

I peered out across the abyss, conscious, as it seemed, of the huge superincumbent weight of the noble fretted roof only a small space now immediately above our heads. As we approached the edge of this stony precipice, the gloom paled a little, and I guessed that we must be standing in some coign of the southern transept, for what light the evening skies now afforded was clearer towards the right. On the other hand, it seemed the northern windows opposite us were most of them boarded up, or obscured in some fashion. Gazing out, I could detect scaffolding poles – like knitting needles – thrust out from the walls and a balloon-like spread of canvas above them. For the moment my ear was haunted by what appeared to be the droning of an immense insect. But this presently ceased. I fancy it was internal only.

'You will understand, sir,' breathed the old man close beside me – and we still stood, grotesquely enough, hand in hand – 'the scaffolding over there has been in position a good many months now. It was put up when the last gentleman came down from London to inspect the fabric. And there it's been left ever since. Now, sir! – though I implore you to be cautious.'

I hardly needed the warning. With one hand clutching my box of matches, the fingers of the other interlaced with my companion's, I strained every sense. And yet I could detect not the faintest stir or murmur under that wide-spreading roof. Only a hush as profound as that which must reign in the Royal Chamber of the pyramid of Cheops faintly swirled in the labyrinths of my ear.

How long we stayed in this position I cannot say; but minutes sometimes seem like hours. And then, suddenly, without the slightest warning, I became aware of a peculiar and incessant vibration. It is impossible to give a name to it. It suggested the remote whirring of an enormous mill-stone, or that – though without definite pulsation – of revolving wings, or even the spinning of an immense top.

In spite of his age, my companion apparently had ears as acute as mine. He had clutched me tighter a full ten seconds before I myself became aware of this disturbance of the air. He pressed closer. 'Do you see that, sir?'

I gazed and gazed, and saw nothing. Indeed even in what I had seemed to *hear* I might have been deceived. Nothing is more treacherous in certain circumstances – except possibly the eye – than the ear. It magnifies, distorts, and may even invent. As instantaneously as I had become aware of it, the murmur had ceased. And then – though I cannot be certain – it seemed the dingy and voluminous spread of canvas over there had perceptibly trembled, as if a huge cautious hand had been thrust out to draw it aside. No time was given me to make sure. The old man had hastily withdrawn me into the opening of the wall through which we had issued; and we made no pause in our retreat until we had come again to the narrow slit of window which I have spoken of and could refresh ourselves with a less stagnant air. We stood here resting awhile.

'Well, sir?' he inquired at last, in the same flat muffled tones.

'Do you ever pass along here alone?' I whispered. 'Oh, yes, sir. I make it a habit to be the last to leave – and often the first to come; but I am usually gone by this hour.'

I looked close at the dim face in profile against that narrow oblong of night. 'It is so difficult to be sure of oneself,' I said. 'Have you ever actually *encountered* anything – near at hand, I mean?'

'I keep a sharp look-out, sir. Maybe they don't think me of enough importance to molest – the last rat, as they say.'

'But *have* you?' – I might myself have been communicating with the phantasmal *genius loci* of All Hallows – our muffled voices; this intense caution and secret listening; the slight breathlessness, as if at any instant one's heart were ready for flight: 'But *have* you?'

'Well yes, sir,' he said. 'And in this very gallery. They nearly had me, sir. But by good fortune there's a recess a little further on – stored up with some old fragments of carving, from the original building, sixth-century, so it's said: stone-capitals, heads and hands, and suchlike. I had had my warning, and managed to leap in there and conceal myself. But only just in time. Indeed, sir, I confess I was in such a condition of terror and horror I turned my back.'

'You mean you heard, but didn't look? And – something came?'

'Yes, sir, I seemed to be reduced to no bigger than a child, huddled up there in that corner. There was a sound like clanging metal – but I don't think it was metal. It drew near at a furious speed, then passed me, making a filthy gust of wind. For some instants I couldn't breathe; the air was gone.'

'And no other sound?'

'No other, sir, except out of the distance a noise like the sounding of a stupendous kind of gibberish. A calling; or so it seemed – no human sound. The air shook with it. You see, sir, I myself wasn't of any consequence, I take it – unless a mere obstruction in the way. But – I have heard it said somewhere that the rarity of these happenings is only because it's a pain and torment and not any sort of pleasure for such beings, such apparitions, sir, good or bad, to visit our outward world. That's what I have heard said; though I can go no further.

'The time I'm telling you of was in the early winter – November. There was a dense sea-fog over the valley, I remember. It eddied through that opening there into the candle-light like flowing milk. I never light up now: and, if I may be forgiven the boast, sir, I seem to have almost forgotten how to be afraid. After all, in any walk of life a man can only do his best, and if there weren't such opposition and hindrances in high places I should have nothing to complain of. What is anybody's life, sir (come past the gaiety of youth), but marking time... Did you hear anything *then*, sir?'

His gentle monotonous mumbling ceased and we listened together. But every ancient edifice has voices and soundings of its own: there was nothing audible that I could put a name to, only what seemed to be a faint perpetual stir or whirr of grinding such as (to one's over-stimulated senses) the stablest stones set one on top of the other with an ever slightly varying weight and stress might be likely to make perceptible in a world of matter. A world which, after all, they say, is itself in unimaginably rapid rotation, and under the tyranny of time.

'No, I hear nothing,' I answered: 'but please don't think I am doubting what you say. Far from it. You must remember I am a stranger, and that therefore the influence of the place cannot but be less apparent to me. And you have no help in this now?'

'No, sir. Not now. But even at the best of times we had small company hereabouts, and no money. Not for any substantial outlay, I mean. And not even the boldest suggests making what's called a public appeal. It's a strange thing to me, sir, but whenever the newspapers get hold of anything, they turn it into a byword and a sham. Yet how can they help themselves? – with no beliefs to guide them and nothing to stay their mouths except about what for sheer human decency's sake they daren't talk about. But then, who am I to complain? And now, sir,' he continued with a sigh of utter weariness, 'if you are sufficiently rested, would you perhaps follow me on to the roof? It is the last visit I make – though by rights perhaps I should take in what there is of the tower. But I'm too old now for that – clambering and climbing over naked beams; and the ladders are not so safe as they were.'

We had not far to go. The old man drew open a squat heavily-ironed door at the head of a flight of wooden steps. It was latched but not bolted, and admitted us at once to the leaden roof of the building and to the immense amphitheatre of evening. The last faint hues of sunset were fading in the west; and silver-bright Spica shared with the tilted crescent of the moon the serene lagoon-like expanse of sky above the sea. Even at this height, the air was audibly stirred with the low lullaby of the tide.

The staircase by which we had come out was surmounted by a flat pent-house roof about seven feet high. We edged softly along, then paused once more; to find ourselves now all but *tête-à-tête* with the gigantic figures that stood sentinel at the base of the buttresses to the unfinished tower.

The tower was so far unfinished, indeed, as to wear the appearance of the ruinous; besides which, what appeared to be scars and stains as if of fire were detectable on some of its stones, reminding me of the legend which years before I had chanced upon, that this stretch of coast had more than once been visited centuries ago by pillaging Norsemen.

The night was unfathomably clear and still. On our left rose the conical bluff of the headland crowned with the solitary grove of trees beneath which I had taken refuge from the blinding sunshine that very afternoon. Its grasses were now hoary with faintest moonlight. Far to the right stretched the flat cold plain of the Atlantic – that enormous darkened looking-glass of space; only a distant lightship ever and again stealthily signalling to us with a lean phosphoric finger from its outermost reaches.

The mere sense of that abysm of space – its waste powdered with the stars of the Milky Way; the mere presence of the stony leviathan on whose back we two humans now stood, dwarfed into insignificance beside these gesturing images of stone, were enough of themselves to excite the imagination. And – whether matter-of-fact or pure delusion – this old verger's insinuations that the cathedral was now menaced by some inconceivable danger and assault had set my nerves on edge. My feet were numb as the lead they stood upon; while the tips of my fingers tingled as if a powerful electric discharge were coursing through my body.

We moved gently on – the spare shape of the old man a few steps ahead, peering cautiously to right and left of him as we advanced. Once with a hasty gesture, he drew me back and fixed his eyes for a full minute on a figure – at two removes – which was silhouetted at that moment against the starry emptiness: a forbidding thing enough, viewed in this vague luminosity, which seemed in spite of the unmoving stare that I fixed on it to be perceptibly stirring on its windworn pedestal.

But no; 'All's well!' the old man had mutely signalled to me, and we pushed on. Slowly and cautiously; indeed I had time to notice in passing that this particular figure held stretched in its right hand a bent bow, and was crowned with a high weather-worn stone coronet. One and all were frigid company. At last we completed our circuit of the tower, had come back to the place we had set out from, and stood eyeing one another like two conspirators in the clear dusk. Maybe there was a tinge of incredulity on my face.

'No, sir,' murmured the old man, 'I expected no other. The night is uncommonly quiet. I've noticed that before. They seem to leave us at peace on nights of quiet. We must turn in again and be getting home.'

Until that moment I had thought no more of where I was to sleep or to get food, nor had even realized how famished with hunger I was.

Nevertheless, the notion of fumbling down again out of the open air into the narrow inward blackness of the walls from which we had just issued was singularly uninviting. Across these wide, flat stretches of roof there was at least space for flight, and there were recesses for concealment. To gain a moment's respite, I inquired if I should have much difficulty in getting a bed in the village. And as I had hoped, the old man himself offered me hospitality.

I thanked him; but still hesitated to follow, for at that moment I was trying to discover what peculiar effect of dusk and darkness a moment before had deceived me into the belief that some small animal – a dog, a spaniel I should have guessed – had suddenly and surreptitiously taken cover behind the stone buttress nearby. But that apparently had been a mere illusion. The creature, whatever it might be, was no barker at any rate. Nothing stirred now; and my companion seemed to have noticed nothing amiss.

'You were saying', I pressed him, 'that when repairs – restorations – of the building were in contemplation, even the experts were perplexed by what they discovered? What did they actually say?'

'Say, sir!' Our voices sounded as small and meaningless up here as those of grasshoppers in a noonday meadow. 'Examine that balustrade which you are leaning against at this minute. Look at that gnawing and fretting – that furrowing above the lead. All that is honest wear and tear – constant weathering of the mere elements, sir – rain and wind and snow and frost. That's honest *nature*-work, sir. But now compare it, if you please, with this St Mark here; and remember, sir, these images were intended to be part and parcel of the fabric as you might say, sentries on a castle – symbols, you understand.'

I stooped close under the huge grey creature of stone until my eyes were scarcely more than six inches from its pedestal. And, unless the moon deceived me, I confess I could find not the slightest trace of fret or friction. Far from it. The stone had been grotesquely decorated in low relief with a gaping crocodile – a two-headed crocodile; and the angles, knubs and undulations of the creature were cut as sharp as with a knife in cheese. I drew back.

'Now cast your glance upwards, sir. Is that what you would call a saintly shape and gesture?'

What appeared to represent an eagle was perched on the image's lifted wrist – an eagle resembling a vulture. The head beneath it was poised at an angle of defiance – its ears abnormally erected on the skull; the lean right forearm extended with pointing forefinger as if in derision. Its stony gaze was fixed upon the stars; its whole aspect was hostile, sinister and intimidating. I drew aside. The faintest puff of milk-warm air from over the sea stirred on my cheek.

'Ay, sir, and so with one or two of the rest of them,' the old man commented, as he watched me, 'there are other wills than the Almighty's.'

At this, the pent-up excitement within me broke bounds. This nebulous insinuatory talk! – I all but lost my temper. 'I can't, for the life of me, understand what you are saying,' I exclaimed in a voice that astonished me with its shrill volume of sound in that intense lofty quiet. 'One doesn't *repair* in order to destroy.'

The old man met me without flinching. 'No, sir? Say you so? And why not? Are there not two kinds of change in this world? – a building-up and a breaking-down? To give strength and endurance for evil or misguided purposes, would that be power wasted, if such was your aim? Why, sir, isn't that true even of the human mind and heart? We here are on the outskirts, I grant, but where would you expect the enemy to show himself unless in the outer defences? An institution may be beyond saving, sir: it may be being restored for a worse destruction. And a hundred trumpeting voices would make no difference when the faith and life within is tottering to its fall.'

Somehow, this muddle of metaphors reassured me. Obviously the old man's wits had worn a little thin: he was the victim of an intelligible but monstrous hallucination.

'And yet you are taking it for granted,' I expostulated, 'that, if what you say is true, a stranger could be of the slightest help. A visitor – mind you – who hasn't been inside the doors of a church, except in search of what is old and obsolete, for years.'

The old man laid a trembling hand upon my sleeve. The folly of it – with my shoes hanging like ludicrous millstones round my neck!

'If you please, sir,' he pleaded, 'have a little patience with me. I'm preaching at nobody. I'm not even hinting that them outside the fold circumstantially speaking aren't of the flock. All in good time, sir; the Almighty's time. Maybe – with all due respect – it's from them within we have most to fear. And indeed, sir, believe an old man: I could never express the gratitude I feel. You have given me the occasion to unbosom myself, to make a clean breast, as they say. All Hallows is my earthly home, and – well, there, let us say no more. You couldn't *help me* – except only by your presence here. God alone knows who can!'

At that instant, a dull enormous rumble reverberated from within the building – as if a huge boulder or block of stone had been shifted or dislodged in the fabric; a peculiar grinding nerve-wracking sound. And for the fraction of a second the flags on which we stood seemed to tremble beneath our feet.

The fingers tightened on my arm. 'Come, sir; keep close; we must be gone at once' the quavering old voice whispered; 'we have stayed too long.'

But we emerged into the night at last without mishap. The little western door, above which the grinning head had welcomed me on my arrival, admitted us to *terra firma* again, and we made our way up a deep sandy track, bordered by clumps of hemp agrimony and fennel and hemlock, with viper's bugloss and sea-poppy blooming in the gentle dusk of night at our feet. We turned when we reached the summit of this sandy incline and looked back. All Hallows, vague and enormous, lay beneath us in its hollow, resembling some natural prehistoric outcrop of that sea-worn rock-bound coast; but strangely human and saturnine.

The air was mild as milk – a pool of faintest sweetnesses – gorse, bracken, heather; and not a rumour disturbed its calm, except only the furtive and stertorous sighings of the tide. But far out to sea and beneath the horizon summer lightnings were now in idle play – flickering into the sky like the unfolding of a signal, planet to planet – then gone. That alone, and perhaps too this feeble moonlight glinting on the ancient glass, may have accounted for the faint vitreous glare that seemed ever and again to glitter across the windows of the northern transept far beneath us. And yet how easily deceived is the imagination. This old man's talk still echoing in my ear, I could have vowed this was no reflection but the glow of some light shining fitfully from within outwards.

We paused together beside a flowering bush of fuchsia at the wicket-gate leading into his small square of country garden. 'You'll forgive me, sir, for mentioning it; but I make it a rule as far as possible to leave all my troubles and misgivings outside when I come home. My daughter is a widow, and not long in that sad condition, so I keep as happy a face as I can on things. And yet: well, sir, I wonder at times if – if a personal sacrifice isn't incumbent on them that have their object most at heart. I'd go out myself very willingly, sir, I can assure you, if there was any certainty in my mind that it would serve the cause. It would be little to me if —' He made no attempt to complete the sentence.

On my way to bed, that night, the old man led me in on tiptoe to show me his grandson. His daughter watched me intently as I stooped over the child's cot – with that bird-like solicitude which all mothers show in the presence of a stranger.

Her small son was of that fairness which almost suggests the unreal. He had flung back his bedclothes – as if innocence in this world needed no covering or defence – and lay at ease, the dews of sleep on lip, cheek, and forehead. He was breathing so quietly that not the least movement of shoulder or narrow breast was perceptible.

'The lovely thing!' I muttered, staring at him. 'Where is he now, I wonder?' His mother lifted her face and smiled at me with a drowsy ecstatic happiness, then sighed.

And from out of the distance, there came the first prolonged whisper of a wind from over the sea. It was eleven by my watch, the storm after the long heat of the day seemed to be drifting inland; but All Hallows, apparently, had forgotten to wind its clock.

The Wharf*

She gave a critical pat or two to the handsome cherry bow, turning her head this way then that, as she did so; pulled balloonishly out its dainty loops; then once more twisted round the small figure with its dark little face and dancing burning eyes, and scanned the home-made party frock from in front.

'What does it *look* like, Mother?' the small creature cried in the voice of a mermaid: then tucked in her chin like a preening swan to see herself closer. The firelight danced from the kitchen range. There was an inch of snow on the sill of the window, and the evergreen leaves of the bushes of euonymus beyond bore each its saucerful of woolly whiteness.

'Please, Mother. What do I look like?' the chiming voice repeated; 'my frock?'

With that wearer within it, it looked for all the world like the white petals of a flower; its flashing crimson fruit just peeping out from beneath. It looked like spindle-tree blossom and spindle berries both together. And the creature inside danced up and down with the motion of a bird on its claws, at sight, first, of the grave intentness and ardour and love in its mother's eyes; and next, in expectation of the wonderful party, which was now floating there in the offing like a ship in full sail upon the enormous ocean.

'Then I look nice, Mother, nice, nice, nice?' she cried. And her mother smiled with half-closed eyes, just as if she were drinking up a little glass of some strange far-fetched wine.

'You do my precious one,' she said, still gazing at her. 'And you will be *very* good? And eat just a little at a time, and not get over-excited?'

'Oh dear, oh dear,' cried the mite, her dark face turning aside in dismay like a tiny cloud from the sunrise; 'they won't never, never be done dressing.'

'There, now, be still, my dear,' her mother pleaded. 'You mustn't excite yourself. Why, there they are, you see, coming down the stairs.'

And when the three – the two elder fair ones and this – were safely off,

* As printed in *The Picnic and Other Stories* (1941). First published in *The Queen*, November 1924.

she returned to the fire, knelt down to poke it into a blaze, and then reclining softly back upon her heels, remained there a while, quite still –
brooding on a distant day indeed.

Something had reminded her of a scene – a queer little scene when you
came to think of it, but one she would never forget, though she seldom had
even the time to brood over it. And now there was one whole long hour of
peace and solitude before her. She was with herself. It was a scene, even in
this distant retrospect entangled, drenched, in a darkness which, thank
Heaven, she could only just vaguely recall. To return back even in thought
into that would be like going down into a coal-mine. Worse; for 'nerves'
have other things to frighten one with than merely impenetrable darkness.
The little scene itself, of course, quite small now because so far away, had
come afterwards. It shone uncommonly like a star on a black winter night.
And yet not exactly winter; for cold wakens the body before puttting it to
sleep. And that time was like the throes of a nightmare in a hot, still, huge
country – a country like Africa; enormous and sinister and black.

And so, piece by piece, as it had never returned to her before, she
explored the whole beginning of that strange experience. She remembered
kneeling as she was now, half sitting on her heels, and looking into a fire.
A kitchen fire, then, as now; though not this kitchen. And not winter, but
early May. And behind her the two elder children were playing, in their
blue overalls, the fair hair gently shimmering in the napes of their necks as
they stooped over their toys. It was, of course, before this house, before
tiny Nell had come – dark and different from her two quiet sisters. And yet
– good gracious me, how strange things are!

As now at this moment, she had been alone in that kitchen, even though
the children were there. And alone as she had never been before. It seemed
as though she had come to the end of things – a vacant abyss. Her husband
had gone on to his work after having been with her to the doctor. She
remembered that doctor – a taciturn, wide-faced man, who had listened to
her symptoms without the least change of countenance, just steadily fixing
his grey eyes on her face. Still, however piercing their attention, and whatever the symptoms, they could only have guessed at the horror within.

And then her husband had brought her home again, and after consoling
her as best he could, had gone off late and anxious to his work, leaving her
in utter despair. She must go away at once into the country, the doctor had
said, and go away without company: must leave everything and rest. Rest!
She had hated the very thought of the country: its green fields, its living
things, and the long days and evenings with nothing to do; and then the
nights! Even though a farm was the very place in the world she would have
wished to have been born in, to live in, and there to die, she would be more
than ever at the mercy there of those horrors within. And country people

can stare and pry, too. They despise Londoners.

The extraordinary thing was that though her husband had reeled off to the doctor, as if he had learned it all by heart, as if he wanted to get rid of it once and for all, the long list of her symptoms, the one worst symptom of them all he had never had the faintest glimpse of. His pale face, that queer frown between his eyebrows and the odd uncertain way in which he had moved his mouth as he was speaking, though they showed that he was talking by rote – or, rather, talking just as men do, with the one idea of making himself clear and business-like, were yet proof too of what he was feeling. But not a single word he had said had touched her inmost secret. He hadn't an inkling that her awful state, body and soul, was centred on *him*.

She could smile to herself now to think what contortions the body may twist itself into when anything goes wrong in the mind. That detestation of food, those dizzying moments when you twirl helplessly on a kind of vacant devilish merry-go-round; that repetition of one thought on and on like a rat in a cage; those forebodings rising up one after the other like clouds out of the sea in an Arabian tale. Why, she had had symptoms enough for every patent medicine there was. She smiled again at thought of her portrait appearing in the advertisements in the newspapers for pills and tonics, her hand clutching the small of her back, or clamped over a knotted forehead.

Still, though she quite agreed now, and had almost agreed then, that it had been wise to see the doctor, and though she agreed now beyond all telling that she owed him what was infinitely more precious even than life itself; still she hadn't breathed to her husband one word about that dream; not a word. And never would. Not even if she lay dying, and if its living horror came to her then again – though it never would – in the hope of crushing her once for all, utterly and for ever.

It was something no one could tell to anybody. There were vile things enough in the world for every one to read and share, but this was one not even a newspaper could print, simply because she supposed no one could realize except herself how abject, how unendurable it was. Perhaps this was because it was a dream, she wondered. Dreams are more terrible than anything that happens in the day, in the real world.

A gentle quietude had descended upon her face lit up by the firelight there. It was as if the very thought of a dream had endued it with the expression of sleep. Nor, of course, was there anything to harm her now. This was yet another mystery concerning the life one's spirit lives in a dream, in sleep. The worst of haunting dreams may lose not only its poison, its horror, it may even lose its meaning, just as dreams of happiness and peace, in the glare and noise of day, may lose the secret of their beauty.

Not that *this* particular dream had ever lost its meaning. It had kept its meaning, though what came after had completely changed it – turned it outside in, so to speak.

And now, since she was sane and 'normal' again, just the mother of her three children, with her work to do, and able to do it – the meanings did not seem really to matter very much. You must just live on, she was thinking to herself, and do all you have to do, and not push about or pierce too much into your hidden mind. Leave it alone; you will be happier so. Griefs come of themselves. They break in like thieves, destroying as they go. No need to seek *them* out, anticipate *them*!

But what a mercy her husband had been the kind of man he was – so patient over those horrible symptoms, so matter-of-fact. It was absurd of the doctor to try to hurry him on, to get testy. Clever people are all very well, but if her husband had been clever or conceited he would have noticed she was keeping something back – might have questioned her. And then she would have been beyond hope – crazy.

And that, of course, put one face to face with the unanswerable question: was what she had seen real? *Was* there such a place? Were there such dreadful beings? After all, places you could not see had real existence – think of the vast mountainous forests of the world and the deserts and all their horrors! And perhaps after death? ... For a while the white-faced clock on the wall overhead, hanging above the burnished row of kitchen tins, ticked out its seconds, without so much as one further thought passing in her mind. The room was deliciously warm; all the familiar things in it were friendly. This was home. And in an hour or two her husband would return to it; and a little later their three girls: the two fair ones, with the little dark creature – tired probably and a little fretful – between them. And life would begin again.

She was happy now. But thinking too much was unwise. That had really been at the root of her Uncle Willie's malady. He could not rest, and then had become hopelessly 'silly' – then, his 'visitors'! What a comfort to pretend for a moment to be like one of those empty jugs on the dresser; or, rather, not quite empty but with a bunch of flowers in one! And a fresh bunch every morning. If you remain empty, ideas come creeping in – as horrible things as the 'movies' show; prowling things. And in sleep, too, one's mind is empty, waiting for dreams to well in. It is always dangerous – leaving doors ajar.

And so – she had merely come round to the same place once more. But now, and for the first time since that visit to the country, she could afford to face the whole experience. It was surprising how its worst had evaporated. It had begun in the March by her being just 'out of sorts', overtired and fretful. But she had got better. And then, while she was going up to bed that night – seven years ago now – her candle had been blown out by a draught from the dark open landing window. Nothing of consequence had happened during the evening. Her husband had been elated by a letter from an old friend of his bachelor days, and she herself had been doing needle-work. And yet, this absurd little accident to her candle had resembled the straw too many on the camel's back.

It had seemed like an enemy – that puff of wind: as if a spectre had whispered, 'Try the dark!' And she had sat down there on the stairs in the gloom and had begun to cry. Without a sound the burning tears had slowly rolled down her cheeks as if from the very depths of her life. 'So *this* was the meaning of everything!' they seemed to tell her. 'It is high time you were told.' The fit was quickly over. The cold air at the landing window had soothed her, and in a moment or two she had lit her candle again, and, as if filled with remorse, had looked in on her two sleeping children, and after kissing them, gone on to bed.

And it was in the middle of that night her dream had come. After stifling in her pillow a few last belated sobs, lest her husband should hear her, she had fallen asleep. And she had dreamed that she was standing alone on the timbers of a kind of immense wharf, beside a wide sluggish stream. There was no moon, and there were no stars, so far as she could remember, in the sky. Yet all around her was faintly visible. The water itself as if of its own slow-moving darkness, seemed to be luminous. She could see that darkness as if by its own light: or rather was conscious of it, as if all around her was taking its light from herself. How absurd!

The wharf was built on piles that plunged down into the water and into the slime beneath. There were flights of stone steps on the left, and up there, beyond, loomed what appeared to be immense unwindowed buildings, like warehouses or granaries; but these she could not see very plainly. Confronting her, further down the wharf, and moored to it by a thick rope, floated on the river a huge and empty barge. There was a wrapped figure stooping there, where the sweeps jut out, as if in profound sleep. And above the barge, on the wharf itself, lay a vague irregular mass of what apparently had come out of the barge.

It was at the spectacle of the mere shape of this foul mass, it seemed, that she had begun to be afraid. It would have horrified her even if she had been alone in the solitude of the wharf – even in the absence of the gigantic apparition-like beings who stood round about it; busy with great shovels, working silently in company. They, she realized, were unaware of her presence. They laboured on, without speech, intent only on their office. And as she watched them — She could not have conceived it was possible to be so solitary and terrified and lost.

There was no Past in her dream. She stood on this dreadful wharf, beside this soundless and sluggish river under the impenetrable murk of its skies, as if in an eternal Present. And though she could scarcely move for terror, some impulse within impelled her to approach nearer to discover what these angelic yet horrifying shapes were at. And as she drew near enough to them to distinguish the faintly flaming eyes in their faces, and the straight flax-coloured hair upon their heads, even the shape of their enormous shovels, she became aware of yet another presence standing close beside her, more shadowy than they, more closely resembling her own phantom self.

But though it was beyond her power to turn and confront it, it seemed that by its influence she realized what cargo the barge had been carrying up the stream and had disgorged upon the wharf. It was a heap, sombre and terrific, of a kind of refuse. The horror of this realization shook her even now, as she knelt there, the flames of the kitchen fire lighting up her fair blonde face. For, as if through a whisper in her consciousness from the companion that stood beside her – she knew that this refuse was the souls of men; the souls not of utterly vile and evil men (if such there were; and no knowledge was given to her of where *their* souls lay or where the blessed) but of ordinary nondescript men – 'wayfaring men, though fools'. Yet nothing but what seemed to be a sublime indifference to their laborious toil and to its object, showed on the faces of the labourers on the wharf.

Perhaps if there had been any speech among them, or if any sound – no more earthly than echo in her imagination – of their movements had reached her above the flowing of that vast, dark stealthy stream, and above the scrapings on the timbers of the shovels, almost as large as those used in an oast-house, she would have been less afraid.

But this unfathomable silence seemed to intensify the gloom as she watched; every object there became darker yet more sharply outlined, so that she could see more clearly, up above, the immense steep-walled ware-houses. For now *their* walls too seemed to afford a gentle luminosity. And one thought only was repeating itself again and again in her mind: The souls, the souls, of men! *The souls, the souls, of men!*

And then, beyond human heart to bear, the secret messenger beside her let fall into consciousness another seed of thought. She realized that her poor husband's soul was there in that vast nondescript heap; and those of loved-ones gone, wayfarers, friends of her childhood, her girlhood, and of those nearer yet, valueless, neglected – being shovelled away by these gigantic, angelic beings. 'Oh, my dear, my dear,' she was weeping within. And, as with afflicted lungs and bursting temples she continued to gaze, suddenly out of the nowhere of those skies, two or three angle-winged birds swooped down and alighting in greed nearby, covertly watched the toilers.

And one, bolder than the rest, scurried forward on scowering wing, and leapt back into the air burdened with its morsel out of that accumulation. The sight of it pierced her being in this eternity as if that morsel were her own. And suddenly one of the shapes, and not an instant too soon, had lifted its shovel, brandishing it on high above his head, with a shrill resounding cry – 'Harpy!'

The cry shattered the silence, reverberated on and on, wharf, warehouse, starless arch, and she had awakened: had awakened to her small homely bedroom. It was bathed as if with beauty by the beams of the nightlight that shone on a small table beside her bed where used to sleep her three-year-old. It was safety, assurance, peace; and yet unreal. Unreal even her husband – his simple face perfectly still and strange in sleep – lying quietly beside her. And she – lost amid the gloom of her own mind.

Tell *that* dream – never, never! But yet now in this quiet firelight, so many cares over – and, above all, that dreary entanglement of the mind a thing of the past – what alone still kept the dream a secret was not so much its horror, but its shame. The shame not only that she should have dreamed such a dream, but that she should as it were have seen only its horror and should have become its slave.

To have believed in such a doom; to have supposed that God . . . But she could afford to smile indulgently now at this weakness and cowardice and infidelity. She could afford it simply because of Mr Simmonds, the farmer. That was the solemn, the really-and-truly amusing truth. It was that rather corpulent, short, red-faced Mr Simmonds who had been responsible for the very happiest moment in her life: who had saved her, had saved far more even than her 'reason'.

Her husband, of course, knew how much they owed to his kindness. But he did not know that he owed Mr Simmonds her very heart's salvation, if that was not a conceited way of putting it. And yet it was this Mr Simmonds – she laughed softly out loud as she gazed on into the fire – it was this Mr Simmonds who had at first sight, in his old brown coat and mud-caked gaiters, reminded her of a potato! Of a potato and then an apple, one of those cobbled apples, their bright red faded a little and the skin drawn up. His smile was like that, as dry as it was sweet, like cider.

What an interminable Sunday that had been before her husband and the two children had said good-bye to her at the railway station. How that man in spectacles had stared at her over his newspaper. Then the ride in the trap, her roped box behind, and Mrs Simmonds, and the farm. Two or three times a day at least she had rushed out in imagination to drown everything in the looking-glass-like pond among the reeds not very far from the farm. And yet all the time, though Mrs Simmonds knew she was 'queer', she could not possibly have guessed, while she was talking to her of an evening in the parlour, the things that were flaring and fleering in her mind like the noises and sights of a fair.

The doctor had said – looking at her very steadily: 'But you won't, you must remember, be really much alone, because you will have your home and your children to think of. You will have *them*. Think as little as possible about everything else. Just rest, and be looked after.'

The consequence of which had been the suspicion that she was being not merely 'looked after' but watched. And she would openly pretend to set out from the farm in another direction when she was bent on looking once more at her reflection in the pond. None the less she had remembered what the doctor had said, had held on to it almost as if it had been a bag she was carrying and must keep safe. And by and by in the hayfields, in the lanes by the hedges, she had begun to be a quieter companion to herself and even glad of Mrs Simmonds's company, and of talking to her plump brown-haired daughter, or to the pale skimpy dairy-maid.

It was curious though that, while passing the opening in the farm-wall she had never failed to cast a glance towards that dark distant mound with its flowers beyond the yard, she had yet never really noticed it. She had seen it, even admired its burden, but not definitely attended to it. It had taken her eye and yet not her attention. She had been far less conscious of it, for example, than of the pretty Jersey heifer that was sometimes there, and even of the tortoiseshell cat, and the cocks and hens, and of the geese in the green meadow.

All these she saw with an extraordinary clearness, as if she were looking at them from out of a window in a strange world. They quieted her mind without her being aware of it, and she would talk of them to Mrs Simmonds partly because she was interested to hear about them; partly to keep her in the room; and partly so that she might think of other things while the farmer's wife was talking. Of other things indeed! – when first and foremost, like a huge louring storm-cloud on the horizon of a sea, there never left her mind for a single moment the memory and influence of her dream. It would sweep back on her, so much distorting her face and clouding her eyes that she would be compelled to turn her head away out of the glare of the parlour lamp, in case Mrs Simmonds should notice it.

And then came that calm, sunlit afternoon. She had had quiet sleep the night before. It had been her first night at the farm untroubled by sudden galvanic leaps into consciousness and by the swarming cries and phantom faces that appeared as soon as her tired-out eyes hid themselves from the tiny radiance of the nightlight.

She had been for a walk – yes, and to the reed-pond – and had there promised her absent husband and her two children never to go there again unless she could positively bear herself no longer. She had promised; and, quieted in mind, she was coming back. She remembered even thinking with pleasure of the home-made jam that Mrs Simmonds would give her for her tea.

There was no doubt at all, then, that she had been getting better – just as before (when the dream came) she had been really, though secretly, getting worse. And as she was turning in home by the farm-gate, she saw Nellie, the heifer, there; the nimble young fawn-haired creature, with its delicate head and lustrous eyes with their long lashes; and she had advanced in her silly London fashion, with a handful of coarse grass, to make real friends with her. The animal had sidled away and then had trotted off into the farmyard, and she had followed it with an unusual effort of will.

The sun was pouring its light in abundance out of the west on the white-washed walls and stones and living creatures in the yard; midges in the air, wagtails, chaffinches in the golden straw, a wren scolding, a cart-horse in reverie at the gate, and the deep black-shadowed holes of the byres and stables.

Still eluding her, Nellie had edged across the yard; and it was then that, lifting her eyes beyond the retreating creature, she had caught sight of that mound, now near at hand, and had realized what it was. She had realized what it was almost as if because her dream had instantly returned with it, almost as if the one thing were the 'familiar' of the other. But the horror now was more distant. She could not even (more than vaguely like re-flection in water) see those shapes with the shovels simply because what she now saw in actuality was so vivid and lovely a thing. It was a heap of old stable manure; and it must have lain there where it was for a very long time, since it was strayed over in every direction, and was lit up with the tufted colours of at least a dozen varieties of wild flowers. Her glance wandered to and fro from bell to bell and cup to cup; the harsh yet sweet odour of the yard and stables was in her nostrils: that of hay was in the air; and into the distance stretched meadow and field under the sky, their crops sprouting, their green deepening.

And as she stood, densely gazing at this heap, she herself it had seemed became nothing more than that picture in her eyes. And then Mr Simmonds had come out and across the yard, his flannel shirt-sleeves tucked up above his thick sun-burned arms, and a pitch-fork in his hand. He had touched his hat with that almost schoolboyish little gentle grin of his; then when he noticed that she was trying to speak to him, had stood beside her, leaning on his pitch-fork, his glance following the direction of her eyes.

For a moment or two she had been unable to utter a syllable for sheer breathlessness, and had turned her face aside a little under its wide-brimmed hat, stammering on, and then almost whispering, as if she were a mere breath of wind and he a dense deep-rooted oak-tree. But he had caught the word 'flowers' easily enough.

There must have been at *least* a dozen varieties on that foster-mothering heap; complete little families of them: silver, cream, crimson, rose-pink, stars and cups and coronals, and a most marvellous green in their leaves, all standing still together there in the windless ruddying light of the sun. And Mr Simmonds had told her a few of their country names, the very sounds of them like the happy things themselves.

She had explained how exquisitely fresh they looked – not like street-flowers – though she supposed of course that to him they were mere waste – just 'wild' flowers.

And he had replied, with his courteous 'ma'ams' and those curiously bright blue eyes of his in his plain plump face, that it was no wonder they flourished there. And as for being 'waste', why, they were kind of enjoying themselves, he supposed, and welcome to it.

He had been amused, too, in an almost courtly fashion at her disjointed curious questions about the heap. It was just 'stable-mook'; and the older that is, of course, the better. It would be used all right some time, he assured her. The wild flowers, pretty creatures, wouldn't harm it; not they. They'd fade by the winter and *become* it. Some were what they called annuals, he explained, and some perennials. The birds brought the seeds in their droppings, or the wind carried them, or the roots just wandered about of themselves. You couldn't keep them out of the fields! That was another matter. 'You see there you had other things to mind. And with that charlock over there! ...'

And still she persisted, struggling as it were in the midst of the dream vaguely hanging its shrouds in her mind, as if towards a crevice of light to come out by. And Mr Simmonds had been patience and courtesy itself. He had told her about the various chemical manures they used on the crops. That was one thing. But there was, she gathered, what was called 'nature' in *this* stuff. It was not exactly the very life of the flowers, for that came you could not tell whence, it is the 'virtue' in it. It and the rain and the dew was just as much and as little their life-blood – their sap – as the drink and victuals of humans and animals are. 'If you starve a lad, ma'am, keep him from his victuals, he don't exactly flourish, do he?'

Oh yes, he agreed such facts were strange, and, as you might say almost unknowledgeable. A curious thing, too, that what to some seems just filth and waste and nastiness should be the very secret of all that is most precious in the living things of the world. But then, we don't all think alike; ''t wouldn't do, d'ye see?' Why, he had explained and she had listened to him as quietly as a child at school, the roots of a tree will bend at right angles after the secret waters underneath. He crooked his forefinger to show her how. And the groping hair-like filaments of the shallowest weed would turn towards a richer food in the soil. 'We farmers couldn't do without it, ma'am.' If the nature's out of a thing, it is as good as dead and gone, for ever. Wasn't it now the 'good-nature' in a human being that made him what he was? That and what you might call his very life. 'Look at Nellie, there! Don't her just comfort your eye in a manner of speaking?'

And whether it was Mr Simmonds's words or the way he said them, as if for her comfort – and they were as much a part and parcel of his own good nature as were his brown hairy arms and his pitch-fork and the creases on his round face – or whether it was just the calm, copious gentle sunshine that was streaming down on them from across the low heavens, and on the roofs and walls of the yard, and on that rich brown-and-golden heap of stable manure with its delicate colonies of live things shedding their beauty on every side, nodding their heads in the lightest of airs; she could not tell. At that very moment and as if for joy a red cock clapped his wings on the midden, and shouted his *Qui vive!*

At this, a whelming wave of consolation and understanding seemed to have enveloped her very soul. Mr Simmonds may have actually seen the tears dropping from her eyes as she turned to smile at him, and to thank him. She didn't mind. It was nothing in the world in her perhaps that he would ever be able to understand. He would never know, never even guess that he had been her predestined redemption.

For a while they had stood there in silence, like figures in a picture. Nellie had long since wandered off, grazing her way across the meadow. She had now joined the other cows, though she herself was but a heifer, and had not yet calved or given milk. How 'out of it' a Londoner was in country places! Her very love of it was a kind of barrier between herself and Mr Simmonds.

And yet, not an impassable one. Knowing that she was 'ill', and being a 'family man', and sympathetic, he had understood a little. She had at last hastened away into the house; and shutting her door on herself, had flung herself down at her bedside, remaining there on her knees, with nothing in the nature of a thought in her mind, not a word on her lips; conscious of no more than an incredibly placid vacancy and the realization that the worst was over.

The kitchen fire had lapsed into a brilliant glow, unbroken by any flame. Her lids smarted; she had stared so long without blinking into its red. She must have been kneeling there for hours, thus lost in memory. Her glance swept up in dismay to the clock; and at that instant she heard the scraping of her husband's latch-key in the lock – and his evening meal not even so much as laid yet!

She sprang to her feet and, stumbling a little because one of them had 'gone to sleep', met him in the doorway. 'I am late,' she breathed into his shoulder, putting her arms round his neck with an intensity of greeting that astonished even his familiar knowledge of her. 'But there were the children to get off. And then I just sat down by the fire a minute. Jim: don't think I'm never thankful. You were kind to me that time I was ill. Kinder than ever you can possibly think or imagine. But we won't say anything about that.'

Her arms slipped down to her sides; a sort of absentness spread itself over her faintly-lit features, her cheeks flushed by the fire. 'I've been day-dreaming – just thinking: *you* know. How queer things are! Can you really believe that that Mr Simmonds is at the farm *now*, this very moment?' Her voice sank lower. 'It's all snow; and soon it will be getting dark; and the cows have been milked; and the fields are fading away out of the light; and the pond with the reeds ... It's still; like a dream – and now ...'

And her husband, being tireder than usual that afternoon, cast a rather dejected look at the empty table. But he spoke up bravely: 'And how did the youngsters get off? They must have been a handful!'

He smoothed her smooth hair with his hand. But she seemed still too deeply submerged and far-lost in her memory of the farm to answer for a moment, and then her words came as if by rote.

' "A handful"? They *were* – and that tiny thing! – I am sometimes, you know, Jim, almost afraid of those wild spirits – as if she might – just burst into tiny pieces some day – like glass. It's such a world to have to be careful in!'

The Lost Track

8 Ranley Street,
S.W.2.

My Dear James,

You remember that night we stayed up talking – a week or two before Christmas, wasn't it. Anyhow, not very long after I came back from America. It was a good talk – the kind that always reminds me of old sherry and Bath Olivers (yours the Amontillado); but there came a moment in it when – well, bubbles began to rise. It was soon after Bettie had looked in – tilting us that queer half-derisive glance women always reserve for men surprised in their natural haunts and habits. She gave us up in despair, said good-night, and went off to bed. At that moment, I remember, you were humped up over the fire and knocking out your pipe on the bars of the grate; and you remarked between the two halves of a yawn: 'So you didn't have any actual adventures, then? Worth talking about, I mean?'

I smiled to myself as I looked at you through the smoke. Worth talking about! Perhaps, if you had been the least bit less complacent and insular you would have noticed that I made no reply. Your taken-for-granted was, of course, first, that I am not the sort of creature to whom anything worth happening happens, and next, that in any case things worth happening are not in the habit of happening 'over there'.

But in this particular case, you were wrong on both counts. At least, so I think. And from the moment when – as we steamed gently on – half-suffocated with home-sickness I caught my first glimpse of the low-lying lovely emerald of the Isle of Wight through a placid haze of English drizzle, I have been pining to share with you what I am going to tell you now. It sounds a little absurd to say that a promise given in America made this impossible until the day before yesterday; but so it is. But now that is done with. The whole episode is over and done with – so far at least as *anything* can be done with in a world where even the whirr of a grasshopper never ceases to echo.

I suppose the smile with which I met your question was a sort of a lie – a colourless one, I hope. But even if I had answered you with the bare facts – you wouldn't have believed me. Probably you won't believe me now, though you are bound to confess human nature rarely writes a letter of this length merely to deceive without gain! And as you are off on Tuesday, and I shan't see you for weeks, this had better not wait.

Then again, it's a pretty little habit of yours to assume that life in these days is all but played-out and that the only things worth much consideration are of the mind or by way of books. In other words, that the really raw material of life is fit only for the newspapers, the police-courts, and the 'movies'. In a way I agree with you. I agree, I mean, that events are only of importance in relation to our Selves. If they make *no* appeal to the imagination, that is, they are mostly null and void. Now the amusing thing (at least, I suppose it is amusing) is that my American adventure is as raw as pickled cabbage. It is precisely the stuff that films and shockers are made of. I can see – for I have returned from their fountain-head – the appropriate newspaper headlines. I believe you will agree too that it is of the 'twopence coloured' variety, rather than the 'penny plain'; and it continues to haunt me.

I don't see how things without any 'meaning' – whatever that may mean – can do that. On the other hand, I can't be quite sure even of what I mean by its meaning. Still, there are things in life that drop like stones into a dark subterranean pool. One leans over, listens to the reverberations, hears them die away, looks up – and the grass is of a livelier green than ever, the sky of an incredible blue, and the butterfly on a tuft of thrift nearby a miracle.

What follows then is merely a plain and precise account. It is not intended to titillate your fastidious taste in style. You need not even bother to read it if you feel disinclined. But if you do read it, I should like a word later on concerning one or two points in it that will suggest themselves; and this, by the way, is the first word I have breathed on the subject to a living soul...

Time: Late-October; Scene: U.S.A.

By a piece of real good fortune I had been staying a day or two a little south – south of Washington, at any rate. For I saw the country. I had then been in America about seven weeks. If I use the phrase 'American hospitality' you will probably shrug your thick shoulders and smile. The actual fact is, though, that that hospitality is (*a*) sincere; (*b*) boundless; and (*c*) may set one speculating a little closely on the English variety. From out of the bosom of one family into which I had been welcomed without the smallest hesitation or forethought I had sent on a letter of introduction to yet another American friend of English friends of mine: the usual kind of letter with the usual kind remarks concerning the bearer.

The answer came by return of post. In brief: Would I give the signatories – husband and wife – the inexpressible happiness of remaining their guest for the rest of my days on earth. I had discovered from a map that they were living thirty miles or so beyond a fairly large town across country still further south and west – I am not going to mention any names yet. I set out. And as I was still only a novice in the land where a twenty-four hours' railway journey is looked upon as a jaunt one can enjoy between tea and supper, the novelties were for me novelties still.

The green-upholstered armchair in the vast metallic Pullman car, for example; the sound of the voices; the cut of the faces; the ecstatic bill of fare in the dining-car – you write your order on a slip – Turkey and Cranberries, Chicken Pie, Six-inch Oysters, Corn on the Cob (eaten monkey fashion), the divinest Scallops in the world: and Prices to match! Then, too, the courteous white-laundered waiters with hands and faces ranging from blackest ebony to creamiest cream; the ice; and, of course, the landscape. On and on.

Rather neglected-looking woods and fields; suggesting that they are still scared by the encroachments of civilization; maize ('corn') in stook; pumpkins (punkins) in heaps; running water; wooden houses; and the occasional town – with its ancient buggy; its drug-store; its Fords (early fourteenth-century); and the dread knolling of one's engine's bell – surely, apart from that monster's prehistoric trumpetings, the saddest sound in Christendom – as one's huge metallic caravan edges slowly through Main Street.

I am an excellent traveller, for throughout any journey in unknown parts I am in a continual effervescing state of anxiety and foreboding. I invariably expect to go astray, and as invariably hope, yet dread, that I shall. But you can't (any more than your baggage) go far astray on any American railway, provided you can understand what the 'conductor' says.

All went well. The black fellow, smiling on me like Friday's long-lost father, gave me my 'brush-off' (not brush-up or brush-down, you will notice), and I (a little shamefacedly) gave him a quarter. He took out my suit-case – my grip – he let down the clanging steps, and deposited the wooden stool beneath them. I descended. And there, with open arms and angelic faces, stood two strangers who, as quickly as you can switch on an electric light in a dark room, were at once my friends – and for life, I hope. We got into their car; it was latish afternoon; and in about half an hour were at their house. I had been talking so hard to my hostess that I had caught scarcely a glimpse of the view, though I had absorbed it through my pores, none the less.

It was rather a queer meal, that first dinner that evening. I remember talking nineteen to the dozen and noticing how unusually brilliant a sparkle the silver and glass had, and also how much more violent my headache was than it had been in the train. I recalled the heated frequency of my visits to the little ice-water reservoir in the railway carriage. You drink it out of a small envelope. I got to bed, however, without saying anything. But next morning there was no disguising the fact that I had a rollicking temperature, pains in the limbs, aching at the back of the eyes and so on: all the usual symptoms.

Did my host and hostess tack me up instantly in a piece of old sacking, replace me in their car, and dump me down on the nearest goods platform? Not a bit of it. Nor did they pour oil and smuggled wine into my wounds and pass me on with twopence to the nearest innkeeeper. They stood on either side of the bed, irradiated with delight. Now, if a stranger from over the seas were taken ill in my house, I should first assure him what an exquisite privilege and joy it would be to nurse him back to health again. And then I should go downstairs and muse gently how pitiful it is that mortality may be subject to ills so inconsiderate.

Not so my friends in America (and no names yet, so we will call them Flora and John). They were enraptured. Their eyes shone with triumph as they brandished the thermometer. If you'd only die, they all but assured me, we'd give you a costlier funeral than ever was on sea or land. Bricks, both of them.

The doctor – the doc – came, saw, and sent me a bottle of medicine. It was 'flu, of course, and for days together I lay there, in Luxury's ample lap, looking out from my bed through a window over the countryside, reading

Isabel Ostrander, Freeman Wills Crofts, with interludes of O. Henry, nibbling grapes, and imbibing beef-juice – not to speak of oysters and champagne (think of it) in due season.

I had come for a week-end. It was six days before I was up again. On the eighth I was 'down'. Even then, said the doctor, I must not yet attempt to go on my travels. He knew his patrons. His veto was followed by a chorus of delicious 'Surelies!' from Flora and John. By the Wednesday of that week I was horribly normal, and being taken for walks and drives. The following Friday, my host and hostess were booked for a visit themselves. Did they speed the parting guest? Not they. They insisted that I should stay on at their house until they came back. Was I quite, quite sure that I should be perfectly happy and comfortable? The servants were, with one exception, black, but comely. Did I really mind being left alone? It was hateful of them to have to go; they would never forgive themselves, but...I hesitated, languished, and gave way.

Allons, once more. Now, in the first place, I suppose you suppose there isn't any 'country' in the United States? There are excuses for you, because I myself had read a good many American novels without fully realizing what country there is; and till then I had seen chiefly cities. But, gracious heavens, what country! There it was a little like a beautiful kind of Wiltshire or Somerset; but vaster, stretching leagues and leagues away to Columbus knows where, and still all but virgin: virginally free, virginally romantic.

It was October, you will remember, and I had chanced on one of the loveliest falls since the *Mayflower* landed its pilgrims on Plymouth Rock. I was by this time as right as a trivet again, though still conscious of the queer sense of novelty and unexpectedness in things which even a slight illness produces, especially 'flu. Every mere man supposes, of course, that a rising temperature is a summons to the grave. Mine had proved only a *caveat*, and I was at once roving around in the little two-seater that Flora and John had handed over to me for my special recreation.

They left the house on a Friday afternoon, and on the next my adventure began. I must have trundled on at haphazard about fifteen or twenty miles or so, having turned off from the State road perhaps ten minutes after I left the house, and having clean forgotten that the area of the two Virginias is more than half as large as England. The lane or by-road in which I then found myself had grown steadily more and more like a cart-track, and ever wilder and lovelier. Apart from the incessant multitudinous rasping of the grass-green katydids and crickets – some brilliantly coloured, that fly for a few yards at a stretch – the air was marvellously still over those low hills of fading woods. Above them hung a pale blue afternoon sky, brimmed with sunshine of a gentle and mellow intensity, its shafts eddying silken soft through the dells and dingles around me; shafts, discs, splashes, gilding the very marrow in my bones, surfeiting my eyes and bathing me with delight – a satisfaction, by the way, not discounted by the thought of the weather you were probably enduring at home.

And the colours! Our English autumn, poor beloved sweetheart, is a comparative child in such matters. Here the trees – oak, dogwood, maple, hickory, sumach – masquerade for weeks together in coats that would have made Jacob weep aloud: amber-yellow, coral-pink, a wondrous rose, blood-red – Bluebeard red. Mounting in cones and domes and triangles above the greyish grass and the sand-colour of the soil, they draped the hills around me, while the track steadily edged off out of civilization, and I went bobbing over its boulders and chasms like a Jack-in-a-box or a monkey-on-a-stick. The only fellow human I had passed – and that was miles behind – was an old negro with a grizzled head who was leading a long-eared mule attached to a low, faded, red-and-green farm-cart.

I had come to a patch of flattish ground just wide enough to afford me turning room. I got out, intending to push on a few paces beyond a turn in the track in order to get a glimpse of what lay beyond. And, looking down from there into the gully below, I saw – now what do you think? – not a dryad, not a Sioux camp counting its scalps, not a chorus of blackamoors around a keg of rum – but a fragment of abandoned railway line – a phrase, by the way, that amuses our American cousins. There were but twenty yards or so of it in sight, and it was not exactly in spick-and-span order. The gauge was narrow. The steel rails had been torn up. Only the rotting sleepers remained, matted with weeds and bordered with Queen Anne's lace, golden rod and Michaelmas daisy. A row of telegraph poles (never neat and spruce like ours, but ungainly and crooked) held only one cross-bar each, and that adorned with two bright-green twinkling insulators.

In that country of distances, netted over by scores of thousands of miles of railroads (see *Whitaker* or *The World's Almanac*) on which for ever pound monsters that would set an antediluvian pterodactyl gaping, this narrow derelict strip looked immeasurebly aged, forlorn, and romantic. I was a bit tired, too; and of course that helps. One's fancy grows a little greedy after illness. Having glanced round for traces of poison-ivy, I sat down on a hump of rock to look at it.

The line, as I say, led out of a gully and into a gully. And anything, my dear James, which, like Life itself, emanates from no discernible whence, and vanishes out into no detectable whither, is – well, you notice it. My heart leapt up when I beheld that derelict below. And gently, without any warning, as I sat staring downward, there entered upon it, as if moved by clockwork, a man in a cloak and a hat. The eyes under that hat's brim were bent upon the sleepers as he stepped rapidly on from one to another. He was not tall; the inch of cheek I could see was waxy pale; and his hands were out of sight. He just glided on from sleeper to sleeper: was gone. The clockwork had removed him out of my sight again. It reminded me of a toy I had as a child.

Why this commonplace spectacle interested me to such a degree I can hardly say. He might have been a phantom. The sun shone on. The katydids continued their courting and their concert; though come but one touch of frost and as if at the flick of a conductor's baton, that annual harvest festival instantly ceases. Death no more than wags once an icy finger.

The only other sound was that of shallow running water, and the cry (I think) of mocking-birds. Two things instantly occurred to me: first, I at once badly wanted to follow up the track in the direction from which the human just gone had appeared; and next, I felt a curious apprehension at doing so. There was something in the effect of him oddly exotic and dubious. He stirred urgent remembrances of the 'movies' and – now I come to think of it – of no less a man of genius than Mr Charles Chaplin. Have you ever noticed, by the way, how singularly appropriate a name Charles's *Chaplin* is for that inexhaustibly melancholic and unworldly Joy of the universe? Whatever he wears, he always *appears* to be in dead black, and his face looks out like a Child of Mercy from fold upon fold of dingiest crape. What a Hamlet, what an Iago awaits his enterprise! Anyhow, the sight of that cousin of his twenty-times-removed down there, stepping between the flower-bushes under the emerald-studded poles and blood-red branches, had a slight flavour of the preternatural.

The warmth of the sun was beginning to dwindle and evening was coming on. That afternoon I ventured no further – merely waited until my phantom was well out of hearing before I got into John and Flora's two-seater again and started up the engine.

All that evening – windows wide open with their gauze casing to the lofty pillared porch of the house, I sat reading and at the same time thinking of that strip of railroad-track and the odd creature in the gully. I rather fancy I dreamed of him most of that night.

Happy and copious as ever, the sun rose again next morning, and by two o'clock in the afternoon I was well on my way to my trysting-place. A little reflection had washed out the grotesque apprehension of the day before. None the less, when I got to the end of the wheel marks left by my car on the previous day, I had a good look round before I ventured down into the gully. Once there, on I went. It was impossible at any moment to see more than thirty yards in front of me, because of the winding of these narrow valleys between their hills. The line had evidently been laid for the conveyance not of animate but of inanimate matter.

I had gone about a mile or so when a little clicking noise in the distance broke the hush. I at once scrambled off the track into the cover of the trees, and waited. It may have been the dislodging of a stone or the crack of a dry stick I had heard, for in a while two figures appeared: my friend of yesterday and an old stooping negro with a sack on his back. Age has particularly tragic effects on the black: his almost greenish cheeks were sunken in, his lamb's-wool hair was nearly white, he had a hump on his back, and his long flat feet brought him along with a sort of shuffling trot, for his companion was making no allowances.

He himself was in the cloak and hat of yesterday; a man, I should guess, of about thirty-eight to forty, sallow, beardless, with a high nose and a stoop. His eyes were unflinchingly fixed on the ground, and I wondered if he would notice any signs of a trespasser. While within hearing this oddly matched pair exchanged not a single word. I watched them out of sight and went on.

The track at last twisted almost at a right angle, and I found myself surveying what might have been a natural break in the hillside, and what were clearly the relics of an abandoned quarry. And a little this side of its further horn I saw a house. Like all solitary houses, it stood up there in the silence under the blue-bowled sky mute with its own story. Its front side was at an angle with me: it was sideways on, I mean. The few windows I could see were shuttered; its timbers dangled with leafy wisps of brilliantly-dyed creeper – vines as they are called more picturesquely over there.

It was a house of three stories, rather lanky in look; its blue paint was faded, though it showed no traces of decay. None the less, it had a deserted, almost forlorn appearance. Indeed with that semi-precipitous background, and beneath its fringes of gaudy woodland, it was exactly the species of house one would expect to find as the terminus of a dismantled railroad – a railroad obviously intended for the conveyance of the stone, or whatever it might be was quarriable, among these hills.

There was a something else in the aspect of the house a good deal more difficult to describe, though this effect may in part have been retrospective. It looked (I can't quite explain it) as if it were the headquarters of Somebody or Something. It looked like an old woman with vanishing tinged-up traces of the beauty she once enjoyed – as if it had had a past. Indeed I should guess it was well over a hundred years old. Apart from that – as if the lady still insisted on dressing to her past – the flat ground in front of it was densely carpeted with convolvuluses ('Morning Glory'): a living mat of a myriad tiny silent trumpets; bright blue, red, purple, slashed, striped, parti-coloured. A ravishing sight to see!

I stayed there, drawn back a little out of view of the windows, watching the house for some little time. A few large, black heavy birds, of the crow kind apparently, were circling sluggishly over the trees above. There was no particular reason to hesitate to go on, and 'Trespassers will be Prosecuted' is a sign that one sees far less rarely in America than 'Live Wire: Keep Off!' But if the four last words had been scrawled up in paint on the nearest tree they would not have seemed inappropriate. Indeed if I had supposed the gentleman in the cloak was within, I should have turned back. *He* looked inhospitable. But he was safely 'out' it seemed, and for at least half an hour or so. So at length I went on.

Taking into consideration what I am going to tell you in a minute or two, it is proof of the solitude and isolation of the house that when I came round to the further side of it, past the main porch, there was an open door; and just within, on a table, were a few pieces of old silver and of Oriental porcelain that would have made a Duveen's mouth water. They looked singularly incongruous, somehow. And still there was no symptom or rumour of life whatever, though nearby stood a shed containing an immense heap of pumpkins, beside which lay an old bridle and a bill-hook.

There could be no harm in enquiring my way and asking for a drink of water. I rapped on the open door, and waited. Beyond it was a narrow staircase; but not a picture on the walls, not a shred of carpet on the boards. After waiting a few minutes I edged in a little, and peeped into a room. That, too, was empty, except for a rusty stove and a bowlful of brilliant fairy-like miniature gourds on the chimneypiece, as gay as a child's paint-box. Curtains, quite clean, and yet as if they had come from Nottingham twenty years ago and had been undisturbed ever since, hung at this window. This was evidently an entrance seldom used.

Not a sound came from within, and at last – it was my first attempt at housebreaking, and I still blush for it – at last I could resist the temptation no longer. After one hasty glance outside to make sure that master and man were not returning, I crept rapidly up the stairs. To this moment I can't conceive what induced me to make such a venture. The call of the wild, I suppose!

The first flight gave only on to shut doors, and for the moment I dared not risk opening any; but continued the ascent instead. And at the top of the next flight I came to a room that was evidently a man's room. It contained some old bits of rather uncouth but pleasant Colonial furniture, and a good many books. If the house had any central heating apparatus it was evidently not yet in use; the room was coldish. Shutters were over one of the windows, and it smelt stuffy and of old cigar smoke.

It was neverthless a pleasant and well-proportioned room with a curious air of serenity in spite of the gentleman who some sixty or seventy years ago had painted the portraits on the walls and had achieved only daubs and caricatures. There were four or five of them at least, and they looked across at me with a fixed unsmiling astonishment, and a mute 'And who are you?'

Some primitive embroidery and Indian beadwork lay here and there, and over the fireplace another strip of it. At the further end of the room was a door ajar. This evidently led off to the rest of the house, but at this – at my – end of the room, and not three paces away, was yet another door opening inwards and partially concealed by a sort of old dresser with a few books and knick-knacks on its shelves. This had been drawn aside and not replaced. My heart gave a thump or two at sight of it, for as likely as not someone might be sitting within – and what reception would he be likely to give an interloper like myself? Still innocence is innocence all the world over, and can be brazen at that. Again I listened, then stepped across the faded carpet, tapped, paused, and looked in.

I found myself on the threshold of a room in area about six yards or so by four, and low-ceiled. Its walls were roughly whitewashed and there was but one half-obscured window, over which gauze mosquito frames were fixed. It was cold, still, and empty: except that in each of the four corners of the ceiling a small gilded seraph in rough carved wood hung suspended with outstretched wings. The bowed heads of these seraphim were directed inwards towards a gilded image of the sun in the midst of the ceiling, its rays radiating outwards, like the design on a mariner's compass. There was but one piece of furniture in the room – a table, and in the centre of it was what appeared to be a plain ebony box inlaid with silver and ivory.

I stood in that twilight with eyes fixed on this small box – the distant whirring of the grasshoppers in the flowers and sand below the only sound to be heard. The secret, the kernel, the meaning of these peculiar surroundings must lie concealed in this box, I thought. It fascinated me.

Influenza (have you ever noticed it?) is apt to leave behind it a phlegmatic audacity. One does not seem to mind much what happens next; because, I suppose, one's nerves are fatigued and yet excited after its dose of poison. But this situation in any circumstances was out of the common – that abandoned track, the exotic details, the huge fall of rock, the faded ungainly house amid its marvellous carpeting of convolvulus. And last, this shrine.

Remember, too, that I was a stranger and that this was Virginia; the old old Virginia of Raleigh and the plantations, of Old Joe and the minstrels; of the aristocratic, defeated, gallant, romantic Southerners! A nobler spirit than mine would, of course, have at once withdrawn in shame and regret at such a trespass, such sheer effrontery. Instead, still intent on the slightest whisper of sound in the house beneath me, I stepped over, laid my fingers on the ebony case and lifted it.

It was as though at a gesture I had pushed aside a tiny shutter between this world and Paradise. Instantly the room in which I stood was suffused to its uttermost angles with a gentle unsurpassable radiance – a radiance of

a faint lovely lilac-blue, resembling in colour the flickering summer lightning one occasionally sees in our English thunderstorms. How much of this
effulgence was its own and how much a condensation of the twilight from
the muffled window I cannot tell; but it proceeded, at any rate, from a
diamond that now lay revealed in the middle of the table on its low carved
ebony stand. It was a diamond in size and shape rather like a flat-ended
apple – flat at the base, I mean; and in its cutting a blunted cone.

Well: I never hope to make you realize the curious solemnity of this
experience. Without much 'fire' or coruscation this marvellous gem icily
burned there – burned there with its own imprisoned radiance and with
borrowed reflections of the waning day. It shone so softly it might have
been asleep. And as I watched it there in the midst of the wooden table, not
a thought entered my mind except that of its surpassing beauty in this plain
whitewashed setting, mused over by its guardian seraphim and plumb
beneath that raying outspread sun. Maybe, apart from the fact of its mere
actuality, there was nothing very remarkable in this; even a green field in
sunshine wears an almost incredible radiance, and human faces now and
then seem to be illuminated as if from within. Even the plainest and commonest object is capable of a seemingly miraculous metamorphosis, given
the moment of insight.

However that may be, without realizing it, I must for a few moments
have slipped into a kind of trance or daydream in mere contemplation of
the thing. *Sum-m-ject* and *om-m-ject,* as Coleridge used to say: here we
were: *en rapport.* Neither then nor since, I may as well tell you, have I for
an instant coveted to possess that object. There is a limit even to the instinct
of acquisitiveness. You might as well plot to embezzle the evening star.

Well there I stood, all but lost to my surroundings, and lost to shame;
and, in this condition, low and soft yet quite distinct, I heard the sound of
a voice near at hand yet as if out of nowhere. It was addressing *me.* It had
said, 'Hands up!'

On my honour, I assure you, just like that. In a low, even, unaffected
tone: 'Hands up!' Almost as perfunctorily as one might call softly to a
child, 'Take care!' or to a friend (if one were less fastidious in the use of
English than you are), 'So long!' For an instant I suspected that the conscience which makes cowards of us all had been the victim of an illusion.
And then, still with the wooden case between my fingers, I turned my head
over my shoulder and saw a woman standing in the doorway. *Saw* her,
indeed! – in that light!

She looked rather taller than she actually was, maybe because the faded
blue dress she wore with its full skirts fell to her ankles. Her face was long
and narrow, with high cheekbones; her hair, smooth and parted in the
middle, was of a dull gold and tied in a knot at the back. Beneath it, over

blue eyes steadfastly fixed on mine, arched unusually dark eyebrows. These, too, and her eyelashes had a little gold in their dark, like that of her hair.

For moments together we gazed at each other eye to eye – utter strangers, yet sharing the common memories of all humanity. And in her hand – and quite in the approved fashion of the 'golden remote wild west' – she held a small but effective-looking revolver.

It is curious how flatly one reads of these lethal weapons – Brownings, Colts, and suchlike – in a newspaper. As a literary device they were long since exhausted, but yet no melodrama, no movie, is complete without them. I remember one even in one of Henry James's stories, and incredibly odd it looked in the environment of his style. None the less, when such things actually come poking into one's private life, the novelty is complete.

On the other hand, I can honestly say that I was not in the least dismayed or alarmed. I suppose the summons of those quiet lips had conveyed to my mind no active meaning – and that in part maybe because that summons had been so remote from my personal vocabulary. But only in part, for immediately after that prolonged exchange of looks between us, there was in a sense no need to understand it. Our spirits, our revenants, our secret sharers, or whatever one means by such words, had exchanged greetings in *their* secret tongue; and further explanations would be without need.

There we were, we two human beings, in by far the loveliest place I have ever seen on earth, beyond change, beyond decay, its beauty awakening only incredulity and wonder in the presence of this miracle of serenity and light. What on earth at such a moment could anything *practical* matter – even a bullet in your stomach? Mere self – that horrible Ego one talks about, perched inside one, like the blackened anatomy of a crow – seemed to be of no importance. I was hardly even thinking. I glanced at the sinister little round black hole of the revolver and then looked straight up again into this stranger's face, and knew I was smiling.

The one thing I hesitated to do, queerly enough, was to hide the thing between us from view. I realized instinctively that any such action would put the two of us on an entirely different footing. At present we were quits, so to speak; discoverer and discovered; hunter and quarry; pilgrim and priestess. *Then* she would have the supreme advantage. For after all, mine was the most abjectly contemptible 'case'.

Instead, I put the box down on the table beside the precious stone, and began to explain myself. I told her precisely how I had come to be found there in these – compromising circumstances. I nodded, still smiling, at the jinnee on the table. It was unlikely I should wish to run away with *that*, I explained. I was completely at her mercy, of course, and under her orders. But...

Remember, too, that she too was *there* – in that particular place, and in those particular circumstances; and therefore of a curious loveliness, though she was no longer young. Indeed any object, living or inanimate, rare or common, could not but be transmuted, essentialized in that gentle lustrous light. And I realized not only that she was not now thinking of the situation in itself, but also that my account of myself was now of minor importance. Even further– she was not in the least concerned, I could see, with what I should like to call the sanctity of the place. An odd word to use, perhaps; but still, I stick to it. Yet as for me, so for her, this experience was something entirely unforeseen; even though she must again and again have rehearsed in fancy a similar eventuality. But it had never been one quite like this. In that at least we were at one.

'You are not an American?' she questioned me – her first question. And she still kept the revolver in true alignment. 'You are English?'

This surprised me, for I had not yet observed in any of my remarks to her that anything was 'nice' or 'awfully jolly'. And most English visitors in America suppose that such little peculiarities as these bewray them.

I explained that I was on a visit; that I had come along the little railway. 'What for?' she said.

My shoulders shrugged themselves of their own volition, but I managed to suggest that my presence there was chiefly due to curiosity – to curiosity and delight in the beauty of the American countryside as it showed to an English visitor who had never so much as dreamt of its existence. Then again the derelict track and this house – her house; its effect, its atmosphere. It had resembled the experience, in the grey of night at sea, of looking up across dark dawn-lit tumbling water, and there! an abandoned ship floating above its shadow, almost within hail; appealing, mysterious. I agreed that this was chiefly because I was a stranger to her part of the world; and added, a 'queer kind of stranger, too'. Then I remarked once more that the house was fascinating.

'Fascinating!' she echoed, listening to me with intense attention; and there was more in the cadence and timbre of the word that a whole sheet of this notepaper could express. It suggested to me that she was desperately sick of the place; that she longed to be quit of it; that she loathed this secluded life; that she was all but beyond being delighted or surprised by anything. At least, that is how it seemed to me at the time. And it filled me with dismay. I realized at once that *her* light, at any rate, had for years been unintermittently concealed and (as she supposed) wasted. All this, of course, passed only vaguely through my mind at the moment, but it was true, none the less. Her square masterful hand dropped to her side, and the full faded blue skirt at once concealed it, and what it held.

'If my husband had found you here like this,' she went on in restrained and slightly trembling tones, 'I doubt if you would have got away again. So far as I know – apart from ourselves and our two old negro servants – there isn't a living creature on earth who has seen *that*.' A barely perceptible shrug indicated what she referred to. 'He does not wish it to be seen.' She said it as if it were an edict of the Caesars. 'I don't see why you came here at all. What right have you? But never mind. He hasn't seen you yet. And I shall take the risk of not telling him. And you meanwhile – well, I am assuming that you, on your side too, will say nothing of all this; of what you have seen. But that being so, we must – I must – talk to you again. No visitors ever come here; though occasionally we go into the town. But when I was small, just the first eight years of my life, I lived in England. And so —' She took a deep breath and broke off – a blank desolation had swept gently over her face. Her eyes looked at me almost as if she were frightened.

These were not her actual words, of course; they are only the nearest I can get to remembering them. But I remember *her*. We had remained in the same position while we had been talking – she in the doorway, I at the table, the wooden creatures above us concentrating their gaze upon us both. I remember how low we kept our voices, and the queer physical and mental restraint that seemed to have come over me, due in part, no doubt, to her unusual personality.

But only in part, for meanwhile the unwasting radiance of that other inmate of the room seemed to be conferring a curious saliency and meaning on even the commonest object within its 'sweet influences'. It was as if the light it shed were a kind of divination. For after all, the meaning and beauty of anything depends on who is looking at it. Imagine an intelligence resembling in its serene lucidity that stone! Imagine what this life on earth would be to us humans if never sun or moon or star had been in heaven to stir its dark. I can't put into words what I mean; but in a sense surely the light of the mind and that of the world without are in definite relation one with the other, and in a sense interdependent?

Whether or not; this particular radiance patterned the rough distemper of walls and ceiling behind the pendant images with the loveliest of coloured shadows, softly transmuted their faded gilt, revealing even the knots and graining of their wood, and that of the painted window-frame. It glowed softly on every several thread of a spider's web that hung from tip of seraph's wing to cornice. All this – the very texture of that threadbare blue dress – seemed to be symbols of an indecipherable yet enthralling message. As for the wearer of that dress, I seemed to be gazing at her far rather as though she were a work of art than one of nature – the tiny arch of her lip, the curve of her nostril, the line of eyelid and temple, the sheen of her eyelashes, and every facet of the cut-steel brooch of coloured gems she wore at her breast. They had become manifest and significant in a fashion that – well, only Rembrandt could tell you how.

No portrait I have ever seen bears comparison in memory with that solitary figure. Yet it was not her own beauty that was the marvel. My eye travelled in fascination up and down the double row of little pearl buttons that decorated the border of her bodice, and I sighed. Even the criss-crossed cotton with which they had been sewn on seemed to be letters of some secret rune.

Smile on, sardonic creature; but you'll agree that it's difficult to describe a state of mind. We went on talking after that almost like casual visitors at a religious ceremony, and, on my part, not wholly unconscious of the indecorum in so doing. She was asking me questions, chiefly, I fancied, to gain time while she continued to reflect on other matters. Anyhow, she showed little interest in my replies to them. At last there came a pause. She turned her face away towards the gauze-blurred window – the marvel of merely watching her there: the translucent eye-ball, the capable hand now visible again, the arch of the head, the golden separate hairs! The very thought of interruption at this moment of utter serenity filled me with dismay. But there! – however closely I try to put the experience into words, something remains that evades me. I can merely hint at it. An unknown power or presence was between us compared with which we were objects no more if no less meaningful than were those dangling wooden seraphim compared with our own sensitive and miraculous humanity. My God, how we have debased and defiled even the fountains of our nature. What fools we humans are in our anxious restlessness of mind and body. Only still waters reflect the skies.

'I think perhaps you had better go now,' she said presently, as if half to herself. 'Would you please cover the thing up, and we will arrange when and where we are to meet again.'

She turned back on me. 'You see, it would at least be as well for you to hear definitely if my husband finds any evidence of your having been here.'

It was sheer bravado, of course, but there was nothing to reply to that except that I was perfectly willing – even eager – to await his return. She looked fixedly at me, and gently shook her head.

'Better not,' she said, and for the first time smiled. 'That would be four to one.' The words haunt me.

But then so too do those of 'O Keith of Ravelston, the sorrows of thy line!' and so too do 'Bare ruined choirs where late the sweet birds sang', and so too do 'Cover her face; mine eyes dazzle; she died young'. What are we to make of ourselves while we are the slaves of such incantations as these?

There was no need to argue the question. And yet, I wonder. I replaced its ebony hood over the diamond as you might place a rusty extinguisher on a guttering tallow candle; and in that moment it seemed as if all interest, life and reality had vanished out of the room. In the dingy blur of the window the gilded images still showed faintly, but their office was gone, and the ceilinged sun became slightly Frenchified and vulgar in effect. We ourselves had returned to the condition of just two ordinary human beings, self-conscious, slightly compromised, so to speak, who yet seemed to have passed through an overwhelming experience together. That at least was my impression. I cannot even guess how much of it she shared.

I followed her out of the room, shut the door, pushed back the old dresser into its place, and she led the way downstairs. At the foot she bade me stay where I was for a moment, and went out. The melodrama was over; the limelight had been extinguished, and these were the jaded wings.

I stood there looking out of the doorway. A change had passed over the scene in my absence. The sun was gone; it must by now be nearly set. The matted carpet of convolvulus showed only a surface of sombre green and grey; every gaudy little trumpet having wreathed itself into an everlasting silence, its day ended. It was absurd; but at sight of them (their beauty gone but their true creative service beginning) a sort of disillusionment and regret came over me – that I had ever been decoyed not only into trespassing in these particular wilds, but into the world at all.

I got back to John and Flora's before nightfall; meeting not a single human being on the way. My solitude seemed insipid and fatuous. I loafed from room to room in a fit of mental and spiritual indigestion. What I wanted of course was to talk to somebody, but my only company was the black butler, and he met every attempt I made at conversation with little more than an inexhaustibly genial but vacant grin.

John was nothing much of a bookman, and Flora confined her reading chiefly to fiction; and I searched their shelves in vain for any monograph on precious stones. But since then I have read the subject up a little. It is worth while solely for its own sake. The giants of the species have had alluring names, and many of them such bloody and romantic histories they might well have been the creation of the evil one.

But I might as profitably have remained resigned to my native ignorance. Not one of my specialists made any attempt to *explain* the human lust and infatuation produced by such baubles. It cannot be merely on account of their beauty and rarity? Hardly. Burton, as usual, blows hot and cold in turn. ' "That stones can work any wonders let them believe that list ... for my part I have found no virtue in them." ' On the other hand, ' "They adorn kings' crowns, grace the fingers ... defend us from enchantments ... drive away grief, cares, and exhilarate the mind." ' He mentions in his inimitable fashion the sapphire, too, that mends manners; and the cheledonius (found in a swallow's belly) that makes lunatics amiable and merry. But concerning the diamond he is mum.

Browne is even more disappointing, merely citing (in order to dismiss it) the vulgar error that a diamond may be 'made soft, or broke by the blood of a goat'. Charming speculations; but alas, the mystery remains. Personally I detest diamonds. They are hard and showy. They give any young and lovely human creature an air of meretriciousness; and merely serve to disguise and conceal the old and ugly. They price their wearer, and only the evil come alive in their baleful company. But I must cut this cackle – with the warning, a trifle late, perhaps, that this adventure of mine is nothing of a story. Like life itself, it will come to a full stop, but not to be continued in our next. Never mind. I want to get through with it.

In the small hours that night – and my windows were thickly curtained – I discovered myself lying wide awake in bed, the room an oven, my mind swept and garnished, my body in a cold sweat. I lay staring up into the dark, and the enormity of the evening's adventure swept over me. Like a cadging thief I had crept into what I believed to be an unprotected house, had made an impudent attempt to explore it, and had been caught in the act by an armed female. Vanity writhed within me like a wounded worm. The whole experience in those few hours of sleep had withered and rotted away like Jonah's gourd; had become utterly vulgarized.

In cowardly self-defence I began to consider the motives of my strange lady; and to speculate on the value of her charge. And once you invite the spectre of money, or of distrust, into your drowsy mind, not only sleep but the most precious ghost that's in you at once decamps. The very hint of money is in some degree destructive of one's peace and poise of mind. So at least it seems to me. Pay a man in kind – do you find him *gloating* on his earnings. Would the Hope Blue Diamond – that fragmentary frozen lump of violet light – have sent quite so many victims to a quick end if all that could be got in exchange for it had been beef and potatoes?

The Young Man in Holy Orders, for example, stooping in ecstasy over the dewy mould under that bottle-glassed wall that wondrous summer morning – was his soul's quarry only what the Rajah's heirloom would bring in hard cash? Didn't his aspirations reach out from cash to kind, from symbol to substance, and then on to symbol again? Not that R.L.S. was much concerned with such niceties in that particular context. That's what I enjoy in him. He tells *stories*; and he is only off and on a casuistical Scot. He amuses himself.

Let us get back to Virginia. For hours that night I tossed about in John and Flora's swans'-down guest-bed, prostrated with humiliation and chagrin. How much simpler, how much more restful an eventuality it would have been if my 'armed female' had been the kind of 'vamp' one would cheer to the echo in a detective story – a vamp decoying me on in order to give that wide-hatted husband of hers and the old negro a chance of digging my last resting-place under that tangled mat of wild convolvulus? But no; a cemetery with more headstones even than geraniums is likelier to be my final goal.

In actual fact she had accompanied me a few hundred yards beyond the house, to see me on my way. Not a breath of wind had stirred between earth and evening sky. And apart from the chorus of grasshoppers the only sound that broke upon us, shrill and liquid – was the voice (I suppose) of the old negress singing in the backward parts of the house over a tub of washing. It was like a scene from a book, from an old Kentucky ballad. At times I wonder if the whole thing is not merely the memory of a dream. I wish it were.

My companion, during the few brief moments of our walk together, had seemed to be thinking – closely and rapidly. Now and again she turned as if to look at me or to speak to me, but desisted. I realized how anxious she was that I should keep my appointment with her; and yet just then was baffled to see why. It was not, I feel sure, from any want of confidence that her secret was safe with me. And on my side – well, my midnight ruminations were made none the happier by my implicit trust in her.

We arranged that she should put a couple of stones in a certain position near the furthest wheelmarks of the car. 'Turn back at once,' she insisted, 'if they are not there.' This was her last injunction. She looked me steadily in the face without offering her hand – her eyes as serenely clear with inward depths and distances as the evening sky itself – and we parted.

I had failed to tell her how little time was now left to me. John and Flora would be back on the Tuesday morning. In decency I could not stay beyond the Wednesday. Think of it! – to have to pack up my grip, go off on my travels again, and become a normal sociable being in a black bow and a Tuxedo after such an experience as that! It was mortifying to the last degree.

It is still more mortifying to realize now that this experience is to all intents and purposes *finally* over, that I haven't the faintest desire to see the place again – the house, I mean. I am not sure if I should even have wished to think of her there – growing old, growing listless, resigned. My mind becomes stupid and useless the moment I begin to reflect on this. Nor is it only because of what has happened since. The whole thing has slipped into my imagination, I suppose; and the imagination, as you yourself once observed, retains essences, not mere tinctures. And yet the whole experience remains not only a mortifying but a horrifying memory. If it is not absurd to say so – it terrifies me with its perplexity. I could never be 'happy' about it, even if – but wait.

I started off the next afternoon – it was a Sunday, of course – some hours later than before. This bothered me a little because it would entail my returning after dark. And though my road by now was fairly familiar, it would be none too easy for me to pick it out in the dark. As you know, I am little short of an idiot at finding my way. It would be nothing but a nuisance just then to have to spend the night in the woods, and there were excellent reasons for not converting the car into a travelling pharos on my return journey. So I kept a sharp eye on the road's turns and twistings, and having left the car some little distance down the hill, I followed the path past the track in the ravine, found the pre-arranged signal, and pushed on until I came to a semi-circular break in the woods, well above the precipitous descent at the foot of which was the house. By craning forward a little under a weeping willow I could now get a glimpse of one corner of its roof.

The evening was twin-sister to its predecessor – as quiet as a peep-show. Another sun-drenched day was drawing to its end – a day that throughout its course had remained so serene and still that one could with ease have counted the leaves that had fallen since its dawn. It was fascinating to stare at that edging of roof, realizing that beneath it was concealed a magnet potent enough to enslave every desperado and cut-throat this wicked world contains.

The lady was late but made no comment on that. She appeared quietly at my side and must have ascended the ravine by some path unknown to me. For a moment or two in her odd way she looked at me without speaking while she recovered her breath. She was without a hat, and wore the same faded blue gown that had haunted my miserable dreams in the dark of the night before. She was naturally pale, though her skin was slightly tanned; and she held herself upright as if by conscious habit. And if she looked at one at all, she turned her head completely to do so – never glancing out of the tail of her eye. Throughout her brief talk I detected no single wile or trick or hint of the ancient feminine – which is intended neither as a compliment nor the reverse. One merely gets accustomed to things.

Even in that dying twilight she looked a good deal older than I had assumed her to be. Her face was one you find yourself speculating about – exploring – even while you are actually talking to the owner of it: those dark, straight eyebrows; the wide, light, open eyes; the gold-streaked hair. A longish face, and not easily 'read', explored, analysed.

It seemed, too, to be strangely, incredibly familiar to me. It was as if we had lived together, she and I, for years at a stretch, had parted and had now met again after a prolonged absence; and yet as if that meeting had been a bitter disappointment and disillusionment. I cannot account for this except by supposing that into a moment of acute sensibility – some sudden drop of the mind into the deeps – one may condense a prolonged experience.

Imaginatively exhaust it, so to speak. That few instants' intimacy had been too much for human nerves and hearts. I felt desperately listless, yet afflicted and aggrieved. Circumstances had betrayed me; I had turned from the first to the last chapter of my tale of mystery and somehow its glamour had gone. How can I explain myself?

Circumstantially all had been well. Her husband had noticed nothing amiss. 'And even *live* men sometimes tell no tales, it seems!' she faintly smiled at me. 'I believed you would come, and yet – well of course I could not be certain if I should ever see you again.'

We sat down awhile in that tepid air, beneath the brilliant but now darkened autumnal branches, and she told me her story in her own languid, uninterested, broken fashion; our voices falling lower yet when, presently after, we rose again and wandered on a little further up the hill until at last we could actually see through a crevice of the trees (though we ourselves remained hidden) the window of the sanctuary itself.

It was an outlandish story, and, like the one I am telling you, of the 'shocker' variety. But I have no reason to disbelieve it. It would never occur to me indeed to mistrust a single word she uttered. There was a tinge of the sleepwalker in all she said and did.

The house, it seemed, had been built by the grandfather of the present owner, a quixotic creature who had fought – and fought fiercely – in the Civil War. He was killed early in 'sixty-five, leaving an only son, a boy of sixteen or so, though how this youngster had himself escaped being roped into the army even at that early age I don't know. Until then he had been left in charge of faithful negro servants at home. The family was old and well-to-do if not wealthy, but even before the war had been slipping into the shade.

The boy's grandfather had formerly owned a large property further south with its usual complement of slaves, but had lost most of it by sheer neglect and by reason of his habit of wandering off on long and apparently aimless journeys over the countryside. He seems to have been a natural vagrant – in search of Mecca, maybe.

On one of these expeditions he had chanced on this ravine. Its beauty and isolation alone might have been fascination enough, but there was also apparently something in the soil that attracted his attention, and he discovered too that this particular 'desirable site' had once been the scene of a violent convulsion of nature, during which it welcomed a visitor more alarming (though less extensive in effect) than Columbus himself.

An enormous meteorite had found here its earthly abiding-place. I suppose such things are not so rare as one supposes. There must be scores of them in the oozy bed of old Ocean. There is a famous one, isn't there, in the wilds of Arizona? It was his son, who, some time in the 'eighties, succeeded at last in blowing a huge fragment of this meteorite to smithereens with a stick of dynamite. No one seems to have had an inkling of what he hoped to discover in its entrails. What he did discover, however, brought his labours in this world to an end. Up till then the ravine had been used in a modest way as a stone quarry; hence the low-gauge railway. After the night of that explosion the industry ceased – for the owner of it had disinterred from amongst the slag and refuse left by his experiment the diamond down below. It must have been a queer and shattering moment. The effect on him seems to have resembled that of a wild Southern love-affair; it changed his complete existence.

At that time the lady's husband must have been a boy in his early teens, and had already as a child been initiated into the company of this peculiar prey in what I gathered was little short of a religious ceremony. I can see it, too, the narrow, dark, pallid boy open-eyed in that radiance, and the father (to judge from one of the portraits I saw) of the Old Abe type – an early 'highbrow', with a beard. Oddly enough I heard nothing of the mother, but whether or not she or any one else knelt there with these two at that ceremony, I wish Vermeer could have been there to paint it. This boy, no doubt as time went on, came to think of the stone as a kind of symbol of the Lost Cause – and of *his* lost cause. Some ghastly shock to nerve and mind during the war had intensified an hereditary bent and left him a prey to intense melancholy and depression. It was he who had found for the gem its wooden sentinel seraphs and had hung up that sun in the shrine I have described. It seems to have become a refuge for his tormented spirit, the holy place not only of this indestructible emblem and of the ravaged South, but of his own half-broken insatiable spirit and possibly much else besides.

I can just imagine how in these surroundings and with his temperament it must have vivified and infatuated that languid and rich Southern imagination which even to this day has never broken fully into flower. Fantastic, I admit. But remember that this thing was literally ex-terrestrial, a visitant from the wilds (or the serene) of 'space', of the unknown, of the dreamed of. Nowadays we rap on a table and are presented with ectoplasm and similar evidences. On the other hand all pioneers, surely, in their exploitations even of the material world have had *some* twist and contortion of fantasy in their minds. This one's delight and desire were not in the gross world of the senses but in the regions of the mind. He had turned contemplative. It is easy to mock at him shut up, up there, in the silence with his talisman for whole nights together – the solitude, the intense heat of summer, the icy gales of winter, in that aloofness from most of what we mean by life. But in such times as ours is it worth while?

That black-haired creature then in saturnine cape and hat whom I myself had seen glide like an automaton into view and glide out of it again on the abandoned track, had sucked in his father's superstitions with his milk. *His* mind had been doubly dyed. He still secreted an implacable abhorrence of the North – an attitude, surely, nowadays only very faintly shared by any other living creature. But this was but one peculiar ingredient in the make-up of his extraordinary consciousness. Some day I will tell you a little more about him; but I doubt if my informant for an instant realized how queerly many of her intimate confidences that evening fell upon that cold, calm Englishman's ear.

While she talked, I listened and mused. It would be agreed I suppose that the winning side in that cruel and bloody Civil War has not hidden its own bright particular gems under a bushel. It has surged on from strength to strength. It has more diamonds to show than Beelzebub has flies. None the less even to-day in that vast half-ravished country of theirs there must be scores of half-hidden Koh-i-noors still waiting to be shared around – natural resources eagerly expecting the rap of some millionaire Moses's rod to pour out their abundance into the lap of these Nordic adventurers. Our own potentialities are now less abundant. It is a remarkable phenomenon. It sets one thinking – the problem, I mean, of hoarding versus exploiting; the problem of spiritual intensity versus material enterprise; of imaginative intuition versus man's mere reasoning powers. It sets me thinking of my own part in that afternoon's adventure. That inescapable law – the immutability of one's past!

Down there (as we sat in our moment's peace together), down there under cover of this shag of dusky woodlands lay concealed this incredible bauble which, if it emerged into our civilized world, would instantly knock the bottom out of the diamond market, and would awaken in scores of human hearts the vilest passion of which they are capable. There may be nothing much in that. But why should the mere memory of it have affected the very life and light of *me*, have sunk deep down into the depths of consciousness wherein all our 'longings, dreams, and aspirations lie'? What strange inward radiance had shone on me that solemn hour? The problem – absurd though it may sound – continues to enthral me.

I stirred and looked round at her. For the moment I had not been listening. Perhaps that dark Edgar-Poe-like creature was even at this moment at his orisons! Night had been advancing while we talked and a stealthy moon-pale radiance lay over the wooded landscape spread out beneath us. And still this lady's low uneven voice in her peculiarly tortuous manner continued telling me her outlandish story, though I knew in my heart that she was sick to death of the whole business. For her its interest had long since worn through and was now worn out. The situation had become an unendurable burden and obstacle.

On the other hand, her mind was still obviously dominated by the presence and influence of her husband; though I rather doubt from what she said – mere inference, of course – if she had ever been for more than a little while in love with him. The momentary bonfire had burned itself out or been swiftly extinguished, and she had slipped apparently into the part of the childless mother, with this egocentric fanatic for *protégé*.

That is the position as it seemed to me then, as on reflection it seems to me now. Not that her husband was stark staring mad, only a little crazy. There are too few of his kind in this world. I wish there had been an opportunity of meeting the creature. Like nature with her sunsets, life, it seems, is beginning to mimic men's movies. The more I think of it, the more melodramatic the situation becomes. I hate fingering over, as Keats says, other people's domesticities. But it was plain from what she told me that for many years past a silent, continuous, but none the less embittered war of the spirit must have been raging between these two poor human derelicts.

Maybe she herself was a pace or two over the borderland. Like most people who are accustomed to solitude she would now and then forget as it were to go on talking, her eyes fixed meanwhile as if in reverie or in contemplation of some thought or feeling which she was anxious but loth or unable to express. Her eyes indeed had that half-vacant look in their beauty of those who day-dream. They seemed to divine rather than observe. And though she uttered no word to suggest she was unhappy, the tones of her voice, every instinctive gesture of her hands, told the same tale. There are sorrows and misgivings in every mind which we as human creatures shrink from revealing – that of growing old, for example; of falling short of one's poor best. But this was a canker much nearer home even than these. It was at her heart. She had been 'confined into a cage' and had long since begun to realize what that means – even though freedom might prove nothing but a treachery and a delusion. Then, suddenly, had appeared this interloper from the great Outside – and had reminded her of her childhood and of England.

I see as I write the troubled simplicity that lightened her face as she spoke of it. The very ghost of childhood returned into it. Her own small daughter, if she had ever had one, might have looked like that – the young moon in the old moon's arms. Not, I suppose, that I am to blame for that, any more than the executioner's axe is to *blame* for the mute head in the basket of sawdust.

She has had her revenge, too; for now as I sit here, wasting my time and all this ink, and return in fancy to her Virginia, 'my heart aches and a drowsy numbness fills my sense, As though of hemlock I had drunk'. It is useless to attempt to follow the inward workings of one's mind. All may seem quiet, and in repose there; and then you realize – by the weedy flotsam, the rollers, the screaming of the birds and the wreckage – the storm that is now over. However that may be, it is nothing but the truth to say that the faintest memory of her Virginia – the mere sound of the word makes me as homesick as a cat. Homesick, and I know not what else besides.

She can't have foreseen that. I must have appeared repulsively cold and indifferent – but I hope not mistrustful. You appear what you feel, feign as you may. I had butted in, then; unforgivably if you consider how. But apart from that, and far worse, it became clearer and clearer to me while we talked or sat silent that she had seen in me her long-deferred opportunity to escape. I was the fate-ordained saviour come to rescue her from the island on which she had been so long marooned. Even to suggest the faintest consciousness of such a thing may seem incredibly raw and ugly, if not worse. But there it is. Remember too, that the actual rights and wrongs of the problem did not so much as even arise. Maybe I should not now be loathing myself like this if they had. Yet it was not exactly cowardice that kept them back. All I can say is that I listened to these undertones in a fever of disquiet and perplexity.

I listened; but after all, the thread that skeins up even the most sophisticated heart is tied only with a slip knot. And how I wish I could give you the faintest notion of the marvel of that scene and night. The first thin silver of a crescent moon had come into the sky low down in the west and was being dogged by a planet glassy as a raindrop by candle-light. The blue above our heads was of a depth and brilliance that no Chinaman even has succeeded in putting on paper or clay. And there was I – the doors of understanding, of compassion, even of mere humanity shut and bolted – gently, insistently temporizing; and she zigzaggedly insinuating her long-suppressed desires, aspirations and anxieties into my mind.

'What is he going to do with the thing when he goes?' I croaked at last. Can you imagine a more idiotic question in the circumstances? Think how it might have been taken! But the faintest subterfuge was impossible to her. She did not 'take it' at all; she replied as simply as a child that the diamond was to be buried with him: 'interred with his bones'! He had long since arranged, it seems, that the two old servants who from his infancy had watched over him as closely as guardian angels, were to dispose of his body so that not even the privy wolves of Hatton Garden could dig it up again. And Providence itself had made this possible.

There was a crevasse a few hundred yards beyond the valley beneath us. The meteor had at its impact split earth's shallow, brittle crust, and this was the scar. Drop him and his charge into that, down there – well, it would be a final exit for them both.

Time was flitting by and darkness had come before we rose from where we had seated ourselves at the edge of the track. The thick dust muffled our footsteps; the languid sweetness of the autumnal air was still resonant with the clashing cries of tiny ardent creatures exulting in their brief moment of life. My companion seemed to be in no apprehension of being missed from the house. It was her custom to wander in these solitudes alone in the evening.

I think of her there in the earlier days when love and marriage, when that tranquil shrine of light and loveliness, and these hills and unravished valleys were still new to her and still seemingly inexhaustible in romance and delight and promise. But now... For twelve solid months, she assured me, but one single stranger, and he only an enterprising hobo, had come their way; and hoboes prefer a different welcome from the one this particular hobo received. Twelve months: to her of waste and weariness; and I – I would all but sell my soul for but one week of it!

Well, there is no more story left. She asked me, she seemed to expect me, to come again the following evening. And I hadn't the courage to tell her it would be my last. I half-promised to do so, realizing none the less, I know, that it *was* only a half-promise and without much genuine intention behind it. What could I do? What purpose would there be? I have asked myself the question a thousand times. I am sick of it.

You yourself, I am sure, would vouch for my staidness and respectability even to an Income Tax Inspector. But then you are a seasoned sophisticated wretch. You enjoy looking at life steadily, especially when its back is turned. But what, say, of Blanche? What would she have said, do you think, if, like the Good Samaritan, I had brought the lady home in my hold-all? But that, yet again, does not arise. The one and only question that does is this: What kind of *me* was there for porter? My old jaded mind is utterly incapable of anything that America would recognize as ordinary hospitality. And there is a hospitality of the spirit.

You will notice I am facing the delicate situation not exactly with *sang froid*, but with a hideous insensibility. I am not intending that. I am trying not to excuse, not even to explain, but to express my feelings *then* – the most obvious being that I hadn't the faintest wish in the world to enter that secret shrine again and to stand beneath that gilded sun. The mere thought of it was distasteful to the last degree. It had been an 'event' in my uneventful existence – an initiation, a mystery, if you like; and it was over.

But apart from that, I see now (though not then, I swear) that other hidden door, ajar: that other shrine and gilded sun; enraying the secrecy of this desolated creature's mind and heart. Whatever, too, I may have said to the contrary, her company was strangely moving, strangely exciting. And I mean the company not merely of her mind and personality, but of her body. There was something in her face, her talk, her presence, that suggested an infinity of interest and suppressed activity. Some human beings are not merely intensely life-giving; but one realizes that the mystery of them is infinite – their reserves. You never get to the end of them. They may say the same thing a thousand times and it is always different. A Will-o'-the-Wisp or a Kindly Light, whichever it may be, leads you on.

I guessed too, vaguely, the hoard of day-dreams and speculations which she was keeping back, which she could not express or had not the heart to express; which yet, given the opportunity, might have found their ease and happiness. Let me, at risk of banality and worse, be even more explicit. It was as if we two, for the century of a passionate moment, had been in love, and that in that moment I myself had exhausted that strange and terrifying experience. And then so far as I was concerned – then, not now – only ashes, ennui, disillusionment. And yet, I blame it less on myself than on the stone – its dream, its nightmare. And how could I justify that – say, to an English jury? It's monstrous I should be writing like this; but it must stand.

'You will be going back to England soon?' she said to me after a long pause, and when we were about to say good-bye. I nodded, listening on and on to the broken syllables of that *England*; and once more silence edged in between us. Her face was close to mine in the dark. I was conscious of her breathing, that tears were in her eyes; conscious too of that other vision of her during the few minutes that had transcended these as manna transcends unleavened bread. If only the sister-meteorite of that ravished visitor below could at that instant have descended out of the intense inane and blotted me out.

We parted. I did not go back. There was no opportunity unless I had positively wrenched one out of the preposterous circumstances in which I was placed, and at instant risk of discovery. She would have bitterly resented any suggestion that I should share her confidences, however trustworthy the confidant. That was certain. I could not even send her a word of explanation or of apology. There was no address. What she thought of me during the weeks that followed I can only guess. It does not much matter now, does it?

As a matter of fact, it was only by chance I ever heard of her again. The day before yesterday there came by post, from Flora, a newspaper already a fortnight old. She had marked in it a column containing the account of a tragedy that had recently taken place 'not many miles distant from us'. She thought I might be 'interested' in it, as the people concerned, though unknown to her personally, were neighbours of hers – as neighbours go, that is, in Virginia. Interested!

There is no mistaking who these neighbours were. Having paused over its headlines, read the cutting I enclose and tell me what you think of it, and even what you think of me too if you feel inclined and have the patience. I can only assume that the one death was not self-inflicted, assume that – well, as I say, read it.

To me the worst horror of the account is not so much that my visit may have been the occasion of some fatal quarrel, but that that old, hump-backed, greying negro was all but lynched on account of it, and that he died of the shock. But not, I gather, before he had consigned his master and his miserable talisman to the abyss prepared for them. I see it, shining there through the ages with only those mouldering bones on which to waste its paradisal radiance – that eyeless skull. But there is an eye of the mind, and mine is still awake. Centuries hence, when we and all we stand for may in turn have become 'prehistoric', other 'humans' may find it there. What will those humans be like, I wonder – mind and body? What will be *their* reactions to the fire and lustre and communings of the thing?

But, as I say, I am sick of the whole experience and of its faintest remem-brances. It has been an inexpressible relief even to rid memory of it like this, to express it as plainly as I can. At thought of it my mind becomes liked a sucked orange. ' "*Traditore!*" ' Do you remember the old gentleman in *The Pavilion on the Links*? '*Traditore!*' And yet, Why? What actually did I do or leave undone that sickens me so? What was there in this unin-telligible ordeal that still eludes me?

Three or four evenings ago a friend of mine nearly suffocated me with the strains of a gramophone record. It was Alma Gluck who was singing; accompanied by a male chorus resembling molasses and rum. And the tune was:

'Carry me back to Old Virginny,
    Dat's where de cotton' [*and the words
      elude me*] 'grow,
Dat's where de birds warble sweet in de
    Spring-time ...'

But then, I was never in Virginia in the spring-time ...

UNCOLLECTED STORIES

UNCOLLECTED STORIES

*Kismet**

The man in the cart, when he reached the top of the long hill up which the old mare had been steadily plodding, was rejoiced to spy against the whiteness of the road beyond the figure of a man walking. For, although he was of a taciturn disposition, and cared little for company, yet on this night he felt lonely. At times, even, he had peered timorously between the trees that overshadowed the roadway, and had started in affright when the ring of the hoofs on the frozen ground had roused some bird from sleep, and the sound of its swift flight could be heard, growing gradually fainter, till hushed in the distance. Uncanny stories had flocked up from forgotten stores of memory, and, with the creeping of his flesh, haunting fancies had come that grim shapes were gathering behind him. With a shudder at the dread thought, he had pulled the collar of his heavy coat about his ears, and so had sat, almost fearful to breathe.

But now, as he leisurely drove down the steady decline, the sight of the lonely figure in the distance restored his usual stupidity; defiantly he hummed under his breath a song brimming over with blasphemy against all midnight loiterers other than those of the flesh, to which song the mare put back her ears, and hearkened in astonishment.

As he drew slowly nearer to the traveller, suddenly a great, deep voice came leaping through the cold air, roaring out the swinging chorus of some song of the sea; the man in the cart stopped dead in his crooning, and listened in amazement to the intense happiness that rang in every note. The music in the song seemed to run in his blood – a shudder shook him from head to foot. The song ceased as suddenly as it had begun; the traveller had heard the noise of the approaching cart, and was now waiting at the side of the road till it should come up with him.

The driver pulled up near at hand, and eyed the stranger with some curiosity; the mare also turned her head to gaze wonderingly at him for a

* First published in *The Sketch*, 7 August 1895, 'by Walter Ramal'; revised for publication in Beg (1955), but omitted at the galley-proof stage; later published in *Eight Tales*, ed. Edward Wagenknecht, Sauk City, Wisconsin, 1971. The late revised version has been used here.

moment, then shook herself, till every scrap of metal on her harness rang again. The stranger startled the man in the cart when he spoke, so intent was his stare.

'How far might it be to Barrowmere?' inquired the man on foot.

'Nigh on seven mile,' replied the driver, with wonder in his brain at a man possessing the courage to walk alone at midnight through the still country lanes.

'Thanks,' said the stranger shortly, in a bluff, hearty voice, then turned as if to continue his tramp.

The driver watched him a few paces. 'He's a seaman,' he muttered to himself, 'and I don't make no doubt but he's going home,' after which reflection he was about to gather up the reins to continue his interrupted journey, when his whole face lit up at the brilliant charitable idea that, as he was taking much the same way as the other, he should offer him a lift in the cart. His plump cheeks grew hot with virtuous pride as he shouted, 'Hi! Was it Barrowmere you said?'

The man wheeled round smartly. 'Barrowmere it was!' he sang out in answer.

'I be going to Barrowmere,' said the driver. 'There's room enough behind if you want a lift.'

The stranger with the joyous resonant voice strode back, and swung himself into the cart with a muscular jerk.

'P'raps you'll sit there,' said the driver, pointing with the butt of his whip to a tarpaulin-covered box at the bottom of the cart.

There the stranger sat himself down. 'Thankee,' he said.

A peculiar smile sped over the driver's face as he shook the reins and drove on without another word.

By degrees he grew morose and sulky. He blamed the traveller for accepting his hospitable offer.

The stranger, who was muffled to the chin in a thick pea-jacket, made a vain attempt to converse with the driver, but finding him both unwilling and witless, he turned his attention to his more pleasant thoughts. His sun-tanned face beamed at the thought of the meeting with his wife soon to come about, he chuckled audibly as he imagined her surprised delight, and he rubbed his hands for the twentieth time when the full subtlety of his little joke in not letting her know the day of his return was again forced upon him.

The full moon flooded the fields with light, making them appear even colder than in reality they were; a very slight fall of snow and a sharp frost had clothed the trees and hedges in a shimmering glory of sparkling white. Not a sound was in the air save the buzz of the cart's wheels, the steady beat of the hoofs, and an occasional shuddering snort from the mare. The cold was severe, at times compelling both men to beat their arms upon their bodies to restore the running of their blood.

Maybe it was the intense silence, maybe the lonely hour of the night, that oppressed the spirits; but there slowly crept over the traveller, who until now had been in so genial a humour, a stern sobriety, a vague presage of impending disaster, an unreasonable mistrust of his former jollity, so that he sat dumb and perplexed on his seat in the cart, watching the sharp-drawn shadows of the trees upon the white road flit silently by, eyeing with stealthy suspicion the burly, bowed body of the driver, and the while ardently desiring the eager arms of his wife.

The traveller got upon his feet in the cart and peered over the driver's shoulder. He could see, in the hollow ahead, the first outlying cottage of the village, and the blood surged up in his body as one by one the well-remembered landmarks of home came into view.

His heart yearned for the shelter of his house, for the kiss of the loved woman: he reminded himself of the mate of his little craft, who knew no friend in the world to give him welcome.

The driver looked back over his shoulder at the stranger, and muttered huskily, 'That be Barrowmere yonder.'

The stranger paid him no heed; at the same moment the notion had come into his head that he would get down from the cart and travel the remainder of the journey on foot; he had no mind that his surly companion should witness his meeting with his wife. So he tapped him on the shoulder. The man turned sulkily; he was bidden pull up, and obeyed with sullen tardiness. The seaman leaped out at the back, tossed a coin to the man, who pocketed it with a nod of thanks and drove on again; the peculiar smile reappeared as he muttered to something between the ears of the old mare.

'I do hope, now, he finds it easy.'

And the man of the sea was trudging slowly along the country lane towards his home; he was rejoiced to be free from his unfriendly companion; his good spirits began to return to him; when, on a sudden, the piteous, wailing howl of a dog struck upon his ears – terror seized upon him for a moment, so that he gasped for breath and trembled as he walked. Bitterly he cursed the land; he vowed he would carry his wife away to the sea and never touch England again.

With almost unwilling footsteps, he approached the bend in the road where his cottage would come into view; every tiny twig in the hedgerows was its own self in glass, not a cloud obscured the living heavens, only the pitiless, cold stare of the moon upon all and the silence of death. It ate into the heart of the man as he walked; he feared greatly, though he knew not why nor what manner of thing he feared. With bated breath, he turned the corner; there lay his home, peaceful under the white moonlight; but his surprise was great at seeing the cart he had journeyed in at a standstill before the little rustic gate. The man, apparently, had entered the house, for the horse was standing with hanging head, its reins tied to the gate-post, awaiting its driver. He walked quietly towards the house, with that strange misgiving at his heart. When he reached it, he feared to enter. He looked into the cart; the box he had used as a seat had gone. He made a weak attempt to laugh his fears down, but failed miserably.

The windows facing the roadway were in pitch darkness; no sign was there that life was within. The seaman crept with muffled footsteps to the back of the house, and there rose into the night again the desolate howling of a dog. He leant over the rough wooden rail and called softly. The dog – his dog – whined joyously, straining at its chain to welcome its master.

He leapt over the low fence; the idea crossed his mind that he was using his own house like a thief in the night. He paused for a moment, perplexed at the sudden beam of light which had dazzled his eyes. He glanced up to discover whence it came; the curtains had been drawn across one of the windows, but had not met, thus leaving a narrow space through which the bright rays of light were streaming out upon the night from within – it was the window of his bedroom.

With fitful breath he crept over to the dog, and fondled it for a while, but still keeping his eyes fixed upon that lonely beam of light. The dog licked its master's hand in unrestrained joy at his return.

And there came into the man's mind a fervent desire to look in through that window. He struggled with himself to restrain the impulse, and to knock boldly at the door, but his wild forebodings and fears of unknown evil conquered him. He looked round for some means by which he might reach the window.

A large tree grew a few yards from the house, a bough of which jetted out towards the window; he remembered that, when he had lain awake on summer nights gone by, he had heard it tapping against the pane. With reluctant steps, he crawled to the tree, clasped a projecting knot, and began to climb the weather-worn trunk. With much labour he scrambled on till at last he reached the bough that ran out towards the house. His hands were numb with the frost and cold. Slowly he crept on, trembling and panting. One last painful effort, and he lay on the branch, with his face toward the window, the light beaming out into his blue eyes.

Gradually he grew accustomed to the glare; he saw plainly into the room.

He saw the bed shrouded in a white sheet; he saw the mother of his wife, kneeling at its head, bend over and gently lift the sheet; he saw the still, pallid face of his dead wife; he saw the driver of the cart pass across the rift between the curtains, carrying the coffin on which he had sat in his joyous ride to his home. A rush of blood blinded his eyes and sang in his ears; he clawed madly at the bough of the tree with his stiff fingers. As he swung in the air, his breath shook him, his teeth chattered and bit into his tongue. He heard with strange distinctness the whispering voices of the night, the stealthy movements in the little room; he saw all things as he stared.

Gradually his clutching fingers relaxed; the whole firmament seemed to reel. In his struggling flight through the air his skull struck and cracked against a bossy branch; his body turned limply, and fell motionless upon the turf beneath.

The dog crawled nearer, shivering and dismayed: it licked the bloody hand of its master, then threw up its head to give tongue to a long-drawn howl of terror.

The Hangman Luck *

I woke at the sound of the voice with such a jerk of chin upon chest as seemed to rattle the brains in my head. I leapt from the bench with a shiver. The heavy meal and the old ale after long hunger had sent my wits wool-gathering. Blinking my eyes in dazed fashion, I turned my head slowly and discovered the breaker of my slumbers, and at the sight was assured of safety. He stood with a glass of spirits before him, laughing and talking loudly with the landlord. My head was giddy, and my legs heavy, so that in trying to get on my feet and go – for it was not a wise thing to be seen by strangers – I stumbled and fell back with a crash. The fellow turned sharply, and clutching his glass, came and took a seat at my side of the bench. A spasm of terror shot through my body, and perhaps I squirmed from his touch, for he shouted heartily, 'Eh! man, I've got room enough for my carcase; it's my good spirits that be difficult to tie up.'

I was sick and weary, and devilish thoughts kept flashing through my head. I stared at his glass; this also he noticed.

'Not *them*,' said he, and dropped his voice to a whisper; 'for 'tween you and me and old Strong's deaf ear I cannot abide spirits; but I make it a pleasure if they do smack of a black draught. Beer is too cheap for the day. Surely!'

'What is the fool chattering about?' thought I angrily, and made a move to go. He clutched me by the arm; I turned swiftly.

* First published in *Pall Mall Gazette*, 4 November 1895, 'by Walter Ramal'; revised by de la Mare in a few places, and published in this version in *Eight Tales*, ed. Edward Wagenknecht, Sauk City, Wisconsin, 1971. The revised version has been used here.

'Lord!' says he, 'ye're white as chalk.'

'And what the devil — ' I started, my stomach heaving with fear.

'Man,' said he solemnly catching my hand, 'pride's out of season with me. When the world treads on a man, it uses muddy boots. You have seen fairer days; tramping it, I can see. Thank God you have got bread and cheese and a pair of eyes. If rum's to your taste – why — ' His hand delved into his pocket and hauled out a canvas bag.

'Rum!' he shouted.

In came the landlord – yes, for twilight was gathering fast, and the dusty road looked blue-grey outside the open door. A string of geese went strutting pertly by as I looked. My eyes smarted. I was weak as water, for I had been nearly starved before tasting my bread and cheese. I would have liked to sleep.

The landlord clapped the rum on the table – forgetting manners, I took a gulp. The neat spirit pelted hot as fire through my veins and roused my courage for a trice. I turned upon the stranger and open-mouthed landlord (the last at a loss whether to crow at my appreciation of his spirits or to frown upon my mongrel manners), and said with a smack of the lips, 'To the hangman, Luck!'

My fellow customer burst into such a roar of laughter at this that it brought down dust and bits of plaster from the oaken beams above.

'I like your pluck,' said he, and the landlord grinned approval.

This reception to my toast in some unaccountable fashion displeased me greatly. Placing my hand on the table, again I tried to rise. As my knees straightened beneath me, I discerned in the half-light a patch of sullen red upon my hand. I stood, a fool, struck senseless, staring down upon my hand, and first the landlord and then the stranger followed my eyes.

'Ah, a nasty tear,' said stranger, almost as softly as a pitying woman; but the landlord eyed me under a forest of eyebrow, and went away into his parlour, without a word.

As for me, I smiled in sickly fashion, and collapsed upon the bench for the third time.

'A thorn in the hedge?' suggested the stranger.

I stared at him and hid my hand in the folds of my ragged coat.

He turned his face towards the door, and looking out, began softly to whistle. The cuckoo clock clucked on its shelf above the two Delft fat men, with good bellies full of tobacco. I sipped my rum with feigned good comfort, eyeing the loose-sitting stranger over the brim. Even in my rags and full of horrid fear, for the rum had added fuel to the furnace, I felt myself to be his better – he was heavy-limbed and ruddy, uncouth in carriage, and wore a-tilt on his head a hat of an old-fashioned brim.

The curve of his cheek, seen dimly against the planks of the wall, was

gentle as an infant. His bag of money sat upon the table, squat, for all the world like a surfeited hunchback. I looked at the bag and grinned. The melancholy tone of the fellow's whistle fell suddenly into a galloping jig.

A wagon and team of lusty horses came journeying past the door.

'Hi!' shouts my man.

'Gee wo-a!' chanted the old fellow plodding at the side and put his head in at the door just as the wheels screeched and came to a standstill.

'A pint of beer!' shouted my man.

The landlord drew it foaming from the tap, peering askance at me the while. The lean old crony blew off the froth, clucked in his throat, and guzzled the beer, then, with a tremulous nod of approval, turned to go.

'If you see the old mother as ye pass by, maybe she's watching, I be coming on,' sang out my man.

'Maybe I will,' twittered the old fellow, and shuffled out. Away went the team and crunching wagon wheels. Down the hill they would go tardily, and along the winding lane under the oaks, and on past cottages, and past women gossiping at garden gates in the twilight, and past homeward harvesters – and by fields of standing corn, thought I – fields of corn.

'You come from the town?' said my man, when the sound of the wheels was low in the distance.

'Yes,' I said.

'Cities are the devil's works,' said he.

'A man pelts down to hell never seeing a gleam of a star; look at me,' said I, all my hopelessness and misery boiling in my heart, nearly choking speech. 'What chance have I had? Maybe I am weak-kneed and a lounger. But if I had been no sinner, maybe I should have been a saint! And now' – my tongue was running on, oiled into freedom by the rum, when suddenly I caught a glimpse of the landlord lurking in the shadow. I pulled up short.

'Why, man, God won't shut heaven's gates in your face because your coat is in holes.'

'Ay,' said I, and hugged my hand closer.

There was a short silence, then the fellow's whistle chirruped forth again. Suddenly it ceased; he turned a red face to me, and laid his hand upon the money bag.

'All in a month,' said he, vain as cock on a wall. 'I am taking it home. Perhaps you are wondering why I am not up and on my way, and you'd wonder well, if you did, for my feet ache to run. But, think you of the pleasant *waiting*, here, looking forward; drinking a good harvest and dreaming in this quiet room – the flower-garden, and the cottage windows all of a sparkle in the sun. That's why I sit here shuffling feet; d'ye see, man?' He lurched forward with a wink of delight. 'And p'raps the old lady is dancing on thorns, all the time thinking I'll not be coming tonight. And

I expects she listens to the belly of pork grumbling in the pot. It's more than a month and it's less than a minute since she put her two hands on my shoulders and, high on her toes, kissed me on the cheek. God bless me – this cheek, man!'

He leaned forward, speaking softly. 'You shall come with me, and bide a bit by the hollyhocks whilst I go in; then I'll come back and bring ye in to the bacon and ale – that I will. How the honeysuckle do swim about the place!'

He sniffed in delight, took a sip of his spirits, shuddered, and turned a dancing, roving eye on me.

I sat, looking out upon the purple shadows of the roadway; a cricket was chirruping and a glow-worm greening in the gloom. 'Ah, God!' said I, and hid my face in my hands.

'Eh! now, what's the matter, lad?' said the fellow, laying his hand upon my shoulder.

'I have no wife waiting for *me*,' I said, knowing nothing else to say.

'Then you're in luck,' says he, laughing loudly. 'I thought you were quarrelling with your Maker, not giving Him praise. It ain't a wife I go to, it's my old mother, she's grey and feeble...my old mother.'

I leapt in a flash from my chair – the landlord put his head in at the parlour door at the sound.

'You startled me, you did,' said the stranger rising. 'Are you going on?'

I nodded. Walking softly to the door I looked to the right, under the painted signboard, up the hill, where only the rabbits skipped and nibbled in the gloaming under the overhanging trees; and to the left, down the hill, westwards, where the dying red of the sunset painted blacker the woods, and the fields lay quiet under the faint stars. A mist was creeping up from the weedy pond and the low hedge-ditches – a soft mist obscuring the distant fields, creeping up stealthily from the fields towards me. I stood in the porch looking westward. Far back there...My teeth chattered; I couldn't face the night alone. Not yet.

The thickset fellow came out after me.

'I am thinking you're sick. Would you now be coming on with me where my old mother will see to you and physic you? It would be a pleasure.'

'Why do you force yourself upon me?' said I, in a fury.

' "Force!" ' said the landlord, indignantly.

'No, man, you did not mean that, I know,' said the stranger consolatorily. 'You are sick of hedgerows, eh? and haystacks...you are sick of life. Maybe you are too proud for your old clothes, you are. And I – I am an old fool who is crazy for his mother, and who would bring a patch of colour into your cheeks, if you would give us a chance. We're wayfaring men, both of us, after all, and she'd open her arms to you if you followed me in. An apple pasty after the bacon! Ay? Think of it! She's been every-thing to me since I was so high; she'd die for me. Lord alive, I nearly make a woman of myself at the end of every long month. Now you'll come; give me your hand on it. I mind not the blood, I mind not the past; an empty stomach cannot thrive – it takes its right.'

No, he wasn't, maybe, quite sober; but so he spoke, with his great face beaming; and the landlord snuffled in confusion behind us. All the horrors of the coming night welled up at his touch, and away went care for my safety. A man stood with me who would realize my need, I thought, who perhaps for his mother's sake would listen, and might even give me a word of pity. The quiet evening mocked my hopes, and evil things threatened me out of the dense foliage of the trees.

'There'll be a heavy dew,' I said. 'I will come with you.'

So he paid the landlord, cracking his joke, while I waited on the road-way shaking in the cold of the night. Soon the fellow strode out of the house. I turned my face eastwards.

'No,' says he, with wondrous cheerfulness in his voice, 'our way lies towards the sun.'

I turned upon my trying vainly to speak. But what did it matter; near or far; everywhere fear stalked, and worse than fear – a vile hatred of self, a sickening of life. I buttoned my coat about me (the mists were upon us) and walked away at his side.

As we turned the corner under the pine tree I caught a glimpse of the landlord almost hidden in the gloom of the porch, watching our departure with suspicious eyes. We spoke little for nearly half a mile, I should say. And each step was nearing us to the cornfield, each step was retracing the way by which I had come. I had thought those few hours since to be safe if I kept my wits and nerve rested. And now I didn't care.

I only followed my friend without speaking as a child might its mother. He made the silence crow at the sound of his laughter, and he made it sigh with stories of his childhood here. He even told me the names of the flowers in his mother's garden and of those in the old lady's cap! He would rattle his money gleefully at me one minute and as suddenly pocket it, remembering my empty pockets, the next. And we drew nearer to the corn-field.

'I know a little pond,' he said, 'near the watercress beds, where you may wash your hands.'

He led me by a by-path to a place in the shadow of the trees, where there was a shallow pond. I bade him sit down, and with my hand in the water and the blood being washed away, I told him I was afraid.

'I have been walking all day,' I said. 'In the late afternoon, being worn and hungry, I drew near to a village. At each house I asked for milk and food; at every one I was refused. The children of the place ran after me in the roadway, hooting and throwing dust. The men in the fields stayed for a moment to shout a jest to their neighbours at my coming. The loony of the place spat on me under the rectory wall, and a dog snapped at my heels when I had left the village behind.

'By-and-by I came to cottages, solitary in vast gardens and hemmed with fruit trees – there also the people refused me food.' My companion at last interrupted my story.

'Let us hasten on,' he said. 'The bacon is boiling, friend, and the old mother waits. You shall finish your story in the chimney corner, behind a pipe of tobacco.'

I shook my head. 'At last,' I said, going on with my story, 'an old woman answered to my knock. She all but screamed at me, called me a thief and a tramp. She told me' (even at the moment I wondered at my calm memory and my cool words) 'she told me that the pigs had all she did not want, and they should always have it. They were cleaner beasts than some she knew of.

'I stood listening in silence for a while; madness of hunger and thirst and heat and anger and hatred of God mounting in my brain. Then, I lifted the heavy stick I carried and struck the old woman down; and when she fell I struck again till she was silent. And there she lay – an ugly old crone – without life. I carried her out through the garden and hid her in a field. I stole some bread, cheese, and some coppers, and ran off.

'And then you came.' So I said, and finished my story.

The blood was washed from my hand; I dried it on the grass. My companion had never stirred. Then, after a long silence, 'Well,' he said, 'you were hard driven. I'll bring something out to you, and a mug of beer.' He fumbled in his bag – 'And here's a bit of money. You'll be safe for the time hiding here. I fancy I know the woman; she's a long talker, and of a shrill temper. Stone dead! A bloody death, too. You must fly, man – soon. But first something to eat.' He drew back a little from me. I saw his face in the early starlight.

Once more we paced the roadway, but he had stopped chattering. The spirit had gone out of him and he stalked on, solemn and silent at my elbow. And I – I cared not, so long as I had his companionship! I simply could not face the night alone, with the eyes of the old woman staring up at me from low down deep in the corn.

'Here lies a shorter way,' says he, jumping a fence.

'So the body will be left unfound,' thought I, and noticed a pool of deep cool water. I would live till he was gone, and then I would come back. And before I had looked round me again, he and I were skirting the field of corn.

He heard my low cry, and turned his head.

'My old mother!' he said.

And he said no more, and I couldn't run away, but led him to where she lay low there, huddled up half-hidden in the corn, with open eyes.

He put some pieces of money into my hand; and I left him sitting there in the corn and the poppies, the grey old head of his mother resting on his hands.

I ran off away to the pool – stayed hesitating there, and, being a fool and a coward, I shuddered, and ran on.

A Mote*

I awoke from a dream of a gruesome fight with a giant geranium. I surveyed, with drowsy satisfaction and complacency, the eccentric jogs and jerks of my aunt's head. Dozing in her basket chair, she reminded me of an Oriental doll decked in a bunch of gaudy fabrics. Her cap squatted unsafely and awry upon her pendulous curls; her yellow, glossy-skinned, emerald-ringed hands lay loosely upon her silken lap. I sat in my chair like some gorged spider surveying his grey expanse of web, more placid than malevolent concerning this meagre fly. The sleepy sun leered upon the garden with blowzy face. I turned from my aunt to the black cat. The luminous green of his eye glowered with lazy spitefulness upon the manoeuvres of a regiment of gnats. Him too, with sleepy amusement, I wove into the tapestry of my dreams. Presently, beyond measure vexed, the beast sprang into the air and buffeted right and left with his forepaws. I turned towards my uncle to enjoy with him a smile at his behaviour, and thus on a sudden perceived his odd posture. His bald mauve head was propped upon his right hand, and his elbow was supported by his chequered knee. He seemed to be watching with minute attention a sun-beetle diligently labouring between the stubborn grass-blades. His attitude was conventional, but his gaze was extraordinary; for he was looking at the beetle with the whites of his eyes.

So that there might be no doubt in the matter, I dropped cautiously upon my knees and peered up at his face from underneath. His mouth was open, just wide enough to betray the glint of gold between his teeth; a faint, infantile flush reddened his cheeks; his lids were uncommon wide apart, disclosing, not two grey pupils, but simply two unrelieved ovals of yellowish white. I was amazed. In my amazement I forgot discretion; I stayed upon my knees in the soft turf – thus becoming an insurmountable

* First published in *Cornhill Magazine*, August 1896, 'by Walter Ramal'; later published in *Eight Tales*, ed. Edward Wagenknecht, Sauk City, Wisconsin, 1971.

obstacle to the beetle – and thought hard. Perhaps my fixed attention troubled my uncle; perhaps he heard me breathing. For, on an alarming sudden, his orbs revolved as it were on greased hinges, and his two pale grey pupils, with an unwonted glitter in them, gazed full into mine. The pink flush upon his cheek deepened into an unwholesome ruddiness. His teeth clicked together. He fastened an icy finger and thumb upon my wrist, and, stealthily craning his neck, looked back upon my aunt. Audibly satisfied with her serene helplessness, and still bent almost double, he beckoned me over the lawn towards the apple trees. This obscure conduct in a man of transparent respectability – the admiration of every comfortable widow of the neighbourhood, a man of ponderous jollity and bellicose good-humour – gave me not a little satisfaction. I congratulated myself on his lapse from sobriety. It had always seemed to me a misfortune that so potential a Falstaff should be a saint. Under cover of the apple trees, with red cheeks made ruddier by the belated beams of the sun through the twinkling leaves, he looked as bibulous a sinner as one might wish. I was to be disappointed.

'What were they like?' said he anxiously.

'All white,' said I laughing.

'Ah! don't giggle, my boy!' said he. 'I see, you are yet in your veal. Drunkenness and women are the whole duty of the twenties. I am not drunk.' (His manner defied incredulity.) 'One minute's silence, my boy. I must see the end of this. The place is black under the pines, and soon the moon will be swallowed up by the drift. Two minutes!' Whereupon he rolled back his pupils, and with white blind eyes stood gently swaying to and fro in a yellow ribbon of sunlight. Through the green of the trees I could see the unrhythmic flutter of my aunt's lavender ribbons. Patiently, and with some alarm, I awaited the return of Uncle's pupils. Presently they again revolved, and returned to their normal position. 'Trouble is brewing,' said he, blinking at the sun, 'but yet he stalks on inscrutable.' He heaved a prodigious sigh, and clutched at my wrist. 'My heart will knuckle under some day,' said he. 'Feel that!' He placed my hand upon a piston-rod just above his watch fob. Blue had mingled with the red in his face. I deemed it better to be dumb. 'You see, my boy,' he continued in an asthmatic voice, 'if your aunt knew of these things, it would be farewell to quiet. She would never cease to worry. Besides, your aunt is not fanciful. Why should she be?' he asked himself strenuously.

'Can I be of any help?' said I. 'I have skimmed a few medical books. I know a chap in Guy's. I might, you know — '

'Medical books be damned!' said my uncle. This I took to be a reassuring symptom. 'I am not a monstrosity,' he added irritably; 'my carcase is my own. Hang it! I'll tell you, Edmond. Let me tell you all from the beginning;

the burden grows irksome upon my back. Only the night shares it with me. He is on his trackless travels even now, and I am not there to see. Scoff if you please, but do not preach. Sit down, my boy; your aunt is good for ten minutes.'

His gravity astonished me even more than his eccentricity. I sat down at the foot of an apple tree and leaned my back against its whitewashed trunk. My uncle did likewise.

'I remember,' said he, wrinkling his lids, 'I remember a dream frequently dreamed when I was about six or seven years old; I used to wake wet and shaking. It was a simple dream of an interminable path between walls of white smooth stone. By that way one might walk to eternity, or space, or infinity. You understand?'

I nodded my head.

'Remember, my boy, I find it hard work to prose – I would sooner be watching. The dream never came back to me after I was twelve years old, but since then I have had other dreams, as false to the Ten Commandments. I have seen things which Nature would spit out of her mouth. Yet each one has been threaded, each has been one of an interminable sequence. There's a theory written under the letter D in a little book I used to keep when I first entered the bank, "A Theory concerning Dreams Expressed Algebraically" – the result of mental flatulency. So far you are clear?'

'Yes,' said I.

'Well, last autumn, towards the end of October, a time of strong winds, I was troubled with many sleepless nights. Being retired from the bank I could not occupy my mind with mental arithmetic, so, having no dry goods to carry in my head, I simply gave unlimited rope to my thoughts. Now *I* wear the halter. On 5th November, Guy Fawkes' Day (I remember that your aunt complained of a strong smell of gunpowder in the bedroom), at a quarter to two, by St Simon's clock, I was lying flat upon my back and wide awake. My eyes were naturally attracted by the white circle of light thrown by the gas globe upon the ceiling. Your aunt will not sleep without a glimmer of light in the room. Without danger of lying I may say that I was thinking absolutely of nothing. It is a vulgar but discredited practice. However, let it be agreed that whatever thoughts I had lay between my retina and the end of my optic nerve. Theory is easier than science. Suddenly, as I watched idly, a little figure – a tiny insect-like figure crawled in at the left of my eye, and slowly traversing a small segment of the luminous disc upon the ceiling crawled out at the right. In my astonishment my lids blinked rapidly, my eyes moved of their own volition in an odd, perplexing manner. Please to mark that it was precisely at that moment when I discovered that my eyes had tricked me. Perhaps they had revolted from the uncommon and disagreeable fixity of sleeplessness and had revolved upon their axes inward. Perhaps I do not know the reason. Whatever it may have been, I know now that I had been looking under the bows of my eyebones into my skull. In all likelihood the grey circle of light which I had seen was the natural stored light of my eyes glowing in the darkness. If this was so, I had mistaken the personal, perhaps imaginary, light of my eye for the actual light of the gas-globe. It's not science, but it's common sense. Such, I say, were my conclusions some time subsequently, after many nights' experience. Try as I pleased in my wakefulness, the creature would not walk again upon the ceiling, for the very excellent reason that in my excitement and ignorance *I was looking in exactly the opposite direction.* But invisible, unfelt, undreamed, there it was, there it had always been, and there it will be until – Heaven knows.'

My uncle patted his brow, eyes, and cheeks with his bandana handkerchief, and (in a manner not unlike that of the black cat) gazed up at the patches of blue between the green boughs. 'The boom of that bee seemed to make the scent of the blossoms stronger, didn't it?' said he, with his handkerchief poised on the top of his head.

'What happened then?' said I.

'Upon the next night,' continued my uncle, 'as I purposely lay in the same position, I fancy that I almost fell asleep. So it seemed, although all the time I could hear your aunt snoring – 'twas time reckoned by a dream-clock. There was the circle of light; there was the gas-globe, the venetian blind, the embroidered watch-holder. But almost imperceptibly the light circle was becoming blurred at the circumference; it still possessed the same shiver, but now there were faint marks upon it, permanent stains in its whitest places; it was not without shadows. I gripped the bed-clothes and strangled my thoughts. And again, again, Edmond, the tiny figure walked out of the east into the west. I watched. The dim shapes in the centre moved and trembled, but took no nameable form. Again I saw the transit of the figure, but now it toiled more slowly. Soon the circumference seemed to widen. The figure took bulk and distinction. At the base of the disc a flatness became discernible encompassed by a huge bow of grey (my skull, perhaps) lightening and deepening into white and pink. A white thread suddenly crept out of the obscurity at the base, crept and wriggled between masses of black (masses like flour seen through a microscope). Presently the black masses caught colour and motion. Sudden glaring spots pricked my eye, and slow-moving blotches writhed into being with a dull pain as though my eyeballs were bringing them forth. Then I perceived slender lines and tassels of elegant grace and wide expanses of smooth, restful green, lit by jewels and trills and spears of yellow light. I seemed to be striving rather to remember than to see. If I am not deceived, albeit my eyes watched the process with curiosity, yet I clearly foresaw the result. The dimness and distortion fell away like smoke. And now, I was looking at a white, caked, trampled path, over which a black-green army of trees stood sentinel. I was round-eyed at gorgeous birds on the wing, and flowers waxen, gaudy and gleaming. My boy, there are none such here. There huge monsters wallowed in heat, and unimaginable wee things leapt and scrambled and minced from bough to bough. The whole air shook with their chirrup and purr and drone; the baked earth sweated a dry scent. Monstrous bat-winged insects speckled profusely the black boughs. Honey scent whetted the tongue and the tartness of resinous bark cried out from beneath the honey scent. Deep in the lazy foetid green of the underwood sparkled quick eyes, and smooth, glossy skins shimmered. There was an atmosphere of ages over the place, and a distressing suggestion that all upon which my eyes looked was of me and in me – my own creatures and creations. But this I know, that myself magnified the scene. The heavy sky, the trees, and all the living things, were a picture painted on a pin's head. God knows more than a German philosopher. So, too, my dear boy, as in a dream of Job, a figure naked and familiar (although his face was turned from me) stalked upon the trampled path. And that figure of a man brought me very near to the terror of my babyhood's dream. I turned to your aunt for comfort, and could not see her. Nor did I awake. Then the awful thought clawed me that I was alive and awake, and with that thought the vision was blinded (so sudden was its going). Then followed a slow easy movement of my eyes, and immediately I was looking upon your aunt's face, bland and young in sleep. I hid my face in her sweet laces, and like any dipsomaniac sobbed loudly. 'Why, John,' said your aunt sleepily, 'you've had a bad dream!' Again my uncle paused. 'This wholesome cleanliness of air is admirable,' he added under his breath, sniffing the evening.

I looked at my uncle uneasily. 'More of a nightmare than a dream,' said I.

'It's getting chilly for your aunt,' he replied. Then, after spying through the trunks upon the old lady, he came close to me, and, on tiptoe, whispered this in my ear: 'In eight months that wee creature has walked through centuries. Would dreams be so vile and consistent? Would I, the manager of a bank, cry like any girl at night if every living thing, every tree, rock and cloud of the world in my skull were not of mine own image? That mote of a man – although he will never turn and show his face to me, try as I may to peer round – that mote of a man is me – me, your uncle. Quick, she's stirring.'

I hastened at his heels to my chair. My aunt woke from her nap, a little peevish. She complained of the dampness. But my uncle, giving her tongue no opportunity to wag nor her mood to fester, taught me how to snare a woman into smiling. Quick to profit, he wrapped a knitted shawl of gaudy wool about my aunt's shoulders, lifted her from the ground with a prodigious puff and a coy scream from the little lady, and trotted away with her into the house. I followed with two basket chairs.

Of course I entitled my uncle's fable *Nerves*. Eccentric would be far too polite a word with which to tell the truth if I were so minded. But as I was brushing my hair, I came to the conclusion that it would be undesirable to betray my uncle's confidence to any, least of all to a physician. If his nerves were the progenitors of his visions, a dose or two of valerian might timely teach them their duty. If he was mad, no finical physician could better his condition, and a strait waistcoat would probably kill my aunt. Thus it will be seen that I laughed. Like Sarah, I was afterwards reproved. It surprised me how that in the past odd trifling actions and movements of my uncle must have escaped my attention. For instance, during dinner, as he was poising a wine-glass and testing the colour of his claret in the light of the lamp, he shut his eyes quick, and laid down the glass in confusion. When offering my aunt some tapioca pudding, his smiling pupils suddenly disappeared; he dived under the table, presumably for his napkin. Not only; but also now and again he would mutter a few words, or swear perhaps, or twist his fingers, thereby greatly discomposing a timid, colourless parlour-maid. Such accidents, or their like, must have frequently happened before. To all these drolleries, however, my aunt paid no attention, but nibbled serenely and smiled placidly. When dinner was over, my uncle and I took a turn in the garden. We chatted in a desultory fashion, but it was apparent that only my uncle's tongue was with me; his thoughts were busy with his dreams. At last he began anxiously to question me regarding his behaviour at dinner. I told the truth.

'My dear boy,' he answered bitterly, 'I have tried to look on the tragedy as a farce, but it is useless. I am getting into clammier bog each step I take. My eyes refuse to obey me. I want above all things to spend my life watching. The climax is speeding to a conclusion. I have spied upon the gambols of my hairy ancestry – perhaps Darwin! – and each godless ape was in mine own image. Each transmigration of my eternal – think on't, my boy – eternal self has passed before my eyes, is now. This brood of creatures, of which I am the god and maker, are multiplying like worms in offal; cities teem with ugly and deformed, with lame and vile. Every thought of the past takes human shape. Here one incites to lewdness, here one taints the air with foulness. Here a white-clad, meagre creature struggles and pants for the light. And ever goes that one mite of a man, stalking unheeding and alone under sun and moon. Through sleep and waking, its horrid minuteness, its awful remoteness troubles my skin; I grow sick. I remember Farquharson, the cashier, took hysteria. (Too much life, my boy.) We twitted him and embroidered him a sunbonnet. A sunbonnet! See this!'

My uncle stopped dead upon the gravel with his face towards the garden. I seemed to *feel* the slow revolution of his eyes.

'I see a huge city of granite,' he grunted; 'I see lean spires of metal and hazardous towers, frowning upon the blackness of their shadows. White lights stare out of narrow window-slits: a black cloud breathes smoke in the streets. There is no wind, yet a wind sits still upon the city. The air smells like copper. Every sound rings as it were upon metal. There is a glow – a glow of outer darkness – a glow imagined by straining eyes. The city is a bubble with clamour and tumult rising thin and yellow in the lean streets like dust in a loampit. The city is walled as with a finger-ring. The sky is dumb with listeners. Far down, as the crow sees ears of wheat, I see that mote of a man in his black clothes, now lit by flaming jets, now hid in thick darkness. Every street breeds creatures. They swarm gabbling, and walk like ants in the sun. Their faces are fierce and wary, with malevolent lips. Each mouths to each, and points and stares. On I walk, imperturbable and stark. But I know, oh, my boy, I know the alphabet of their vile whispering and gapings and gesticulations. The air quivers with the flight of black winged shapes. Each foot-tap of that sure figure upon the granite is ticking his hour away.' My uncle turned and took my hand. 'And this, Edmond, this is the man of business who purchased his game in the city, and vied with all in the excellence of his claret. The man who courted your aunt, begot hale and whole children, who sits in his pew and is respected. That beneath my skull should lurk such monstrous things! You are my godchild, Edmond. Actions are mere sediment, and words – froth, froth. Let the thoughts be clean, my boy; the thoughts must be clean; thoughts make the man. You may never at any time be of ill repute, and yet be a blackguard. Every thought, black or white, lives for ever, and to life there is no end.'

'Look here, Uncle,' said I, 'it's serious, you know, you must come to town and see Jenkinson, the brain man. A change of air, sir.'

'Do you smell sulphur?' said my uncle.

I tittered and was alarmed.

Subsequently I looked up my uncle's man, and had an earnest chat with him, telling him nothing save that my uncle was indisposed and needed attention. Moreover, I did my best to prevail upon my uncle to sleep by himself for a few nights. I thought it safer. But (poor old gentlman!) he seemed to have an unrighteous horror of loneliness. 'Only to be able,' said he, 'only to be able to touch her hand. No sceptic doctors, my boy, let me die wholesomely,' he replied to my earnest entreaties that he should see a physician. I determined to obey him.

The next day he seemed to have recovered his usual excellent spirits, and although he sometimes fell away into vacancy, his condition in the light of my experience was undoubtedly different from that of many months past. 'I have an idea that I gossipped a good deal of nonsense in the garden yesterday,' said he, buttonholing me after breakfast. 'The sun was hot, very hot. Between ourselves? – that's all right. I had a better night; no nightmares. Eh! E – ay?' In a flash he hid his eyes with his sleeve. 'Er – bless the midges! Come into the garden, my boy,' said he, and forthwith denied his denial.

On Wednesday afternoons when my aunt was upon her parish-visiting, and also at any time that we might snatch, my uncle and I would steal away into the woods or conceal ourselves in a crazy, musty summer-house near the gooseberry bushes. There we would sit for hours together while he narrated to me the doings and adventures of the fantastic creatures which he professed to see. I acted foolishly, perhaps, in consenting to his absurdities, but who would have done otherwise? The charm of his narrations was irresistible. To listen to him as he sat there, with his white eyes, his ragged straw hat upon his head, in the midst of the summer, was fine. Sometimes he would return to the experience of past dreams; sometimes he would look in upon his world, and tell me what he saw there. Whatever he affected to see, moreover, he made me see too. For even, perhaps, gave he not every detail, yet myself by his seeds could raise my own crop of visions of an exact likeness to his. This, too, he was ever at pains to insist upon – that the many beings, the uncouth cities, all that which he had described to me possessed an atmosphere of himself, an intellectual colouring peculiarly his own. He was the unwitting creator, but responsible for his creations. How mad a theory it seems! This, too: 'I see that the end is coming; he treads solitary paths. O that he would flee, and seek for hiding! And the scattered thousands come round about him; they sneak upon his footsteps; they net him in on every side. He passes through villages (which I think I have seen in dreams). The people mock in the streets, and the dogs bark. He journeys through cities that are familiar and yet unknown to me. Danger hides under every leaf. There is a clangour in the air of terror and disaster.' My uncle would carry me away with his enthusiasm, and I would grow with him as eager as a boy, and though it was easy to see that his sickness was serious and that the consequences might be dire, yet with the gentleness of a mother and the intuition of a child he kissed away my aunt's occasional anxieties. He kept the mellow roundness of his cheeks, the vigour of his voice; he neither advertised his pain nor trumpeted his woes. He consistently reviled the doctors. If his perpetual hilarity was sometimes maudlin, he never turned tail or lacked a pun to the end.

On 15th July my aunt came by herself into the breakfast-room, and immediately rustled to me who was sitting in the window-seat, basking in the sun. The sunlight seemed to caress her frailty, to cling to her old laces, her muslins and her trinkets. 'I am afraid, dear Edmond, your uncle is not quite the thing today,' she said affably. 'He seems a little feverish, I think. He tossed in the night, and this morning he was so impatient with his clothes. He alarmed me, dear.'

Just then my uncle walked into the room. He walked in jerks, and collided brutally with the table. When the sunlight fell upon him, I noticed a sullen bruise upon his forehead. His arms swung in time to his legs, his left to his left, his right to his right. He lurched directly towards me. I dodged deftly. He sat down upon the corner of the settee, in the place which I had vacated. A fly was buzzing upon the hot windowpane. My aunt stood at my side with her left hand over her mouth. My uncle's head was wagging slowly to and fro. The sun blazed upon his face and scanty hair.

'Like a sunbeam,' said he. 'Like a sunbeam in winter swift and keen. That stone thudded. Another beacon! The city is bloody with flames. No moon tonight. Run, run, run! He'll be met by those mouldy faces. A twist. By the throat!' My uncle's hand clenched upon the blind-cord and relaxed.

'Edmond, Edmond,' chirruped my aunt.

The venetian blind crashed down upon my uncle's skull. He hauled it up without a word, turning fleeting, red, flaming eyes upon us. My aunt knelt down at his feet and set to slapping his hands. I broke the bell-cord, and dashed cold milk into his face, for there was no water.

'The thunder is breaking. The heavens belch their fires; see – like a worm, like a wasp. He'll escape them; he must, he must. Oh God! in their thousands they leap, they scurry, and flee like dead leaves in my garden. Savage and crazy, and implacable as ice. Ah! the granite griffin! He is under, he is under. See the hag, the lewd hag. The air is pitch and bespattered. The wind shivers. Now growls the thunder, their feet are oats rustling. Oh me! Twist, double, under!'

The maid entered, carrying a dish of kidneys. She stood in the doorway looking at my uncle. My aunt continued to slap his hands and to call plaintively, 'John, John!'

'Lo!' he screamed with gaping mouth. 'He is caught, he is trampled upon and wounded. I am caught. Oh! where the white men with kindly white faces? Are there no white men? None? The granite towers wriggle in their seats. My boy Edmond, my boy, he has turned his face – poor white dead face. He is hand in hand with death...he is away, he climbs. They are many as swarming bees. See, hurrah! hurrah!' (His cheer was thin as the song of a wire in the wind.) 'The white men! My boy, very few. Every thought lives for — We are careless, we are careless. Clutch tight to thy seat, wan mote of a man. Do not heed their savagery. Kiss the cold stone, mote of a man, look to heaven through the lightning-rents. Lucy, your hand, your kind hand. All is ungodly tiny.'

The maid went away.

'Now they fight – in their thousands they gather. Their growl frightens the night. Wan and lurid, mouldy and green and lascivious. He crouches and shakes and sweats on his perch. The smell of blood is sharp to the tongue. The white men fall. They are trampled down. The sky is shaken. The swift tongues of flames are black, for the sky is open – opens wide. It is the light of day. I heard the sound of many — It is just. Oh, mote of a man!' My uncle's tongue clucked in his throat. He grew silent. His whole body shook spasmodically. The fly buzzed in the sun and danced. Presently my uncle rose to his feet. With neck outstretched (as though led by a halter) he walked across the room. Out by the glass doors into the conservatory he went. The hot, heavy scent of his housed flowers rallied behind him and fought with the smell of the kidneys. On my uncle walked between the red pots, and out into the garden where the birds made clamour in the dappled leaves and the earth was alive with insects. He stepped down gingerly upon the gravel and immediately set to running, and as he ran he cried out and flung his arms into the air. The door-frame shut him from me. My aunt and I followed quickly after him. My aunt came first into the garden. When I skipped into the sunlight I saw him again. He was running amuck in the orchard, maddened by blows from the tree trunks and the low-hanging swaying boughs. He frisked hither and thither, to and fro. My aunt hung upon my arm, and with a wee scream greeted every dull blow. I heard the maids sobbing in the kitchen. There was no cloud to hide the sun. Wounded and battered and panting, all sudden in the midst of a blind rush he stopped still and stark. He clasped his hands about his neck. Then with child-steps he laboured patiently toward us. Without doubt or fear he walked over grass and flower-beds until he came to my aunt. He sat down on the low garden seat, saying 'Lucy, Lucy.' Then he was silent.

The Village of Old Age*

Far away from the noise and fret of men's business I had lived, content to find new joys in the passing days, and to welcome, year by year, with unfailing serenity, the placid monotony of fair days and foul, the coming and the flying of the swallows, the springing and the falling of the leaf.

And it was with the sad farewells of the summer that my mother bade me goodbye. With her falling to sleep the world in some dim fashion was changed to me. Strange and sombre tints sobered the autumn; the birds piped a softer note of melancholy; the dawn came but to prophesy the

* First published in *Cornhill Magazine*, September 1896, *New York Evening Post*, September 1896, and *Living Age*, 31 October 1896, 'by Walter Ramal'; later published in *Eight Tales*, ed. Edward Wagenknecht, Sauk City, Wisconsin, 1971.

twilight. In the wish to rid myself in some degree of a growing distaste for my fellows, an ever-increasing moodiness of mien, I set out from my haven of rest into the busy tideways of the world. 'Surely,' thought I, 'friends are many, and welcome will be freely given me. I will die laughing, and die then of over-ripeness.' But soon I found that men forget and seldom wish to remember; that friends once so charming and so flattering see the world through keener eyes; that tongues once mellifluous taste the bitterness of life, and that ready hands have too great labour to wave greetings to one risen from the silence of the past. Vexed and disappointed, with sore heart and ill at ease, I bethought myself of Basil. Thank God, cross-roads sometimes have the same goal. I was full of hot enthusiasm to meet him face to face. What a medley of wit and philosophy his name recalled to me! One who would choose a path of thistles to flout the gardener of roses. A fellow at whom death winked, of eternal youth and heartiness. 'I will go to him; he will understand,' thought I.

Hopeful as a child I set out to find him. Nor was I greatly disturbed to find his place empty. I made my way to the village whither report was that my friend had fled, and came to a sleepy place of ancient cottages, of silent, deserted streets, and of calm weather. I asked lodging of the grey landlord of the inn. He considered me with filmy eyes. He was a man shrunken and weak-kneed, with open toothless jaws. The days of summer he spent sunning himself in his garden of vegetables, and trembling over the log fire in his brick-floored hall in days of wintry weather.

'Aye, if Janie be within,' said he. 'The streets be damp, and, mebbe, a mouldy stench, by God a' mercy, thou'lt sleep no' the worse.'

'What of the waking, my friend?' said I gaily.

'Aye, what of the waking,' said he, 'if the slumbering be quiet and easy? Who'll heed the fret of the day? The graveyard for a', the graveyard for a'.'

I eyed him askance – this echo of a man – and rallied him with a loud laugh and in bluff manner.

'Nonsense,' said I, ' 'tis a place in which to crow, is the graveyard. Pshaw! we are live men. We go one better than the mouldering bones with their scanty record, that is not a moment's thought. I sit on a tombstone and see a cheerier sun and a blither day for the stuffing of my seat.'

'I would no' doubt thou'rt a stranger to these parts,' said the old man with weary lids. 'Ye canno' know the place.'

He rose from his straw cushions and tottered on feeble knees into the shadow of the narrow courtyard of lichen-grown stones which led to the house. And at his going the place seemed wondrous cheerless and quiet. The sky was blue almost to purple, and not any cloud showed in the vast expanse. The trees wore the green of spring in this month of July; but the hum of insects, the twitterings of birds, were not on the air. An empty kennel, from which crawled a rusty chain, stood in the shadow of the high wall, and a crazy dovecot leaned against the red bricks, over which climbed a cherry-tree in rich profusion of leaves. The fragrance of the flowers, the rich scent of the earth, sluggishly intermingled in the faint wind. 'Surely a sweet place of repose,' thought I. 'I will purchase pigeons and a crowing cock, and I will keep bees.'

Footsteps sounded hollowly on the stones, and the old man, followed by a feeble crone, came out of the cool shadow into the sunlight. I was mistaken. A young girl followed the old man, but pale, and bent, and hollow-cheeked, with fettered limbs and scanty hair. A beldame of ninety was the old man's niece of sixteen.

'My uncle says, "Get ready a bed," ' said she in a weak, monotonous voice.

'Yes,' said I, boisterously, 'I would like to make a meal, too. Gracious me, lass, my hunger is a savage monster bellowing for meat.'

The old man was gone back to his chair.

'There be cheese and ale,' said she.

'And a pretty maid to smile over the froth,' said I.

'A pretty maid,' said she, as though it were the refrain of some doleful ballad.

'Have you no meat – a fat leg of mutton or a red sirloin of beef, eh! with brown Yorkshire pudding?'

'There be bread and cheese,' said she with a quaver. Her head almost rested on her shoulder.

'Then Hunger shall wake Fancy,' said I. 'Fetch out for me some bread and cheese – I will eat it here, in this sunny place, with the landlord – and a good tankard of ale. That's it, my dear.'

I bent and kissed her cheek, giving her arm a little pinch. I am past the fopperies of youth, and it grieved my heart to see the maid so feeble and woebegone. She simply turned without quip or toss of head, and went back into the house, out of the sunlight over the cobblestones. An old crow came cawing high up in the sky. I watched him with eagerness until my eyes could see him no longer. Then I turned to the old man, thinking to take my seat at his side. But seeing no chair, I went after the maid. The air in the courtyard was cool, and pleasant, and cleanly, breathing the fresh scent of malt and a not unpleasing mustiness as of a wine cellar. Behind an open casement I caught sight of a maid washing dishes. I popped my head in at the window.

'Now, my pretty, would you give me a plump, easy chair?' said I. 'I would keep your master company in the sunlight.'

The pallor and the weariness of her face astonished me. I withdrew my head rather ungraciously, and hastily climbed the steep stone steps, and so into the house. Fearing to pry or to intrude myself upon the secrecy of the place – secrecy! however absurd such an attribute be for a tavern open to wayfarers – I took the first chair that I saw, a chair with stiff wooden arms. With some pother and groaning I carried it back to the old man by the way I had come. I sat down beside him, and lazily set to smoking. Surely the blue smoke of a reverend pipe was no desecration to the placid place. Yet the old man's slow turn of head and his unobtrusive sick glance of wonderment, and of curiosity, and of entreaty even seemed a plaintive remonstrance; and almost unthinkingly I watched the smoke as it was bandied to and fro and swallowed up by the thin air, and let my pipe grow cold as it hung between my lips. We sat silent in the mellow sunlight. The shadow of the inn crawled over the garden until it encroached even upon us sitting there; until the old man's hair was half-burnished silver and half-dull lead.

Eagerly had I come to the inn, full of enthusiasm at my search for my friend Basil being come to an end; now, notwithstanding, I lolled there in my chair without a word of inquiry, without the desire to speak or to know, in lethargy serene, and well content to sit with the old clown in the silence till night should come down and the twinkle of candles in the windows of the inn should call us to rest. Presently, however, came the maid, carrying a tray upon which was spread my meal. She brought to my knees a low three-legged table and set the tray thereon. The sight of the brown bread and the yellow cheese richly enlivened me, and when the maid, having gone again to the house, returned with a pint tankard of old ale I almost laughed aloud. I rose, and, with a pretty bow to the maid and a wink to the landlord, took a long pull at the stuff, gazing over the froth as I did so at the weathercock upon the inn top, all of a glitter in the reddening sun. When I replaced the tankard upon the table the maid had already tottered a few steps towards the house. I called loudly. The sound of my voice seemed as sudden as a clap of thunder in the quiet place.

'No, no, my dear,' said I, 'you must give a tired traveller your pretty company and chat with him. There are some few questions I wish to put ye.'

She turned about with her right hand upon her bosom and her red hair falling in wisps upon her wrinkled forehead. She came very slowly and stood a few paces distant. I slashed at the loaf with excessive zest.

'Poor soul!' whimpered the old man. 'A right eno' lassie was Janie, ruddy as a winter apple; aye, full of trickins and jollity. Dear God! and a wisp, dear God, the graveyard for a', the graveyard for a'.'

'But, sir,' said the maid, facing the sun, 'here it do seem a wearisome long journey to the yard. Most of us be old folks e'en at fifteen, but in the yard not a one under ninety. I do miss me fayther's farmyard. I look for the jangle of bells and the baa of the sheep. And my fayther had a daw. Here the day is always noon, and the night la! a wearyin' hour for the spirits to walk.'

'Tut, tut, you want a holiday,' said I, chewing my bread and cheese, for I was very hungry. 'The neighbours should wake a clamour in this mossy place, should rummage and drive away the silence. 'Pon my word, you shall take a walk with me this very sunset.'

The old man smiled at his apple trees, heavy with young fruit. 'Thou be'st a stranger for sure – naybours!'

Then I remembered with new surprise how barren and deserted was the high road, how empty were the fields, and how desolate the gardens.

'The lassie shall take a walk on my arm,' said I, 'and see that God made the world.'

'I would no' think that God might be so cruel,' said the maid.

I jumped in my chair. 'Will you drink with me, sir?' said I with pomposity to the landlord, but I could not otherwise than stare at the red-haired, meagre girl in the sunlight.

'Nay,' said the old man, 'I'll not drink with thee. Jollity eno' for the morn, a gaudy dizened jollity, but for what is t' end of 't? – a rainbow in sleeping-time. And then the going down of the red sun. Sure we play wi' our toys, and a lean wisdom clucks i' the throat and calls 'em bubbles. Mebbe God's i' the bubble. Who knows? He drives us all into the pen. The day be late. The dew falls very heavy at times.'

I was sick of speech, and set to my victuals with poor simulation of relish. When I had finished my joyless meal, I spoke again. Try as I would, my voice was bereft of its ring; weariness was again stealing upon me. 'I have come a long distance to find a friend. Men have pointed me out this village, have told me that here I shall find him. Pray, sir, do you know my friend, Mr Basil Gray?'

The old man never turned his palsied head. He peered at me vacantly out of the corners of his feeble eyes. 'I know none o' the name,' said he.

'He lives in the Grey House,' said the maid; 'an old man wi' beautiful silver hair. I know him, sir, in the Grey House, where the owls hoot o' nights, and ivy bursts in at the windows.'

'Silver hair!' said I, in dismay. 'His hair is black, and his voice loud and full. Good people, you live in this remote nook out of the world, and you look at all things through an old man's spectacles. Silver hair!...Now, my pretty maid, you shall show me the house. I am tired of being alone. Fancy this, I have not a friend alive but Mr Gray. In the midst of a hale, hearty life to be alone! Fancy it! Now, little maid, come away.'

I thought the old man smiled faintly at something in my speech. I cannot say. I spoke very tenderly, for a sudden pity and a new sympathy had come into me for the frail child. Perhaps some day I shall need the like, thought I. So I put my arm round her waist, and we went together into the house. When we reached the steep steps I saw upon the topmost a little child. This pleased me greatly. 'And whom does this mite, this flower-maiden belong to?' said I. 'Now, little one, come and play with me. Many years have gone by since I was a little child. Come along. Put on the bonnet, and we will gather pretty posies and weave daisy-chains. Dear me, it seems that my mother taught me but yesterday.'

I talked like a pantaloon. The little child climbed up and stood in the doorway, its tiny thin finger in its mouth, and its round grey eyes looking into my eyes, and looking out at something far away, something which seemed to catch my breath, to lay an icy finger upon my heart.

'I am tho tired,' lisped the little creature; 'and mummy thayth the pothieth 'll die in my hot hands.'

I said never a word, but still with my arm round the maid's waist, for she seemed to have become an unwonted comfort to me, we passed into the house. The maid led me through the tiled passages upon which the red sun shone. The reflected ruddiness of the bricks prettily reddened her cheek. Together we went up the wide and twisted staircase and into a little room, clean and white, which overlooked the old man sitting solitary in the garden. Far away in the soft blue haze were the ruinous tower of the church and the beckoning gravestones.

'A pretty white room, lassie,' said I.

'Sure it be very quiet,' said she, 'and sometimes I think there be talkers in the air, and sometimes, as it were, birds at sundown. When I be lying wake i' the long nights, I do think the blackness will some day come down upon me, and cover me up out o' sight.'

I sat on the little bed and looked at the ceiling, and I saw night frowning upon the child.

'But God is with you,' said I, and when I had said it I looked for Him at my side and found Him gone. I turned to the maid, and knew the child's solitude, and heard the echoes of the talkers and the hovering winds. I pined to see her lips blossom into smiles. And, as in languid negligence she smoothed her hair before the open casement, I bethought me of a precious jewel – one which I had set great store by – a gem of lustre and elegance, a delight for young eyes. I searched my wallet and found the gem. This I fastened at the throat of the maid. My heart grew sick at its lack of lustre. The smile of the maid was the smile of autumn in a garden of flowers.

'Oh!' cried I, 'jewels glitter brightest at dawn. Wait till the sun like a giant comes out of the east. Wait for the lark and the new flowers of dawn. Then we will be gay, you and I.'

'After the night, sir,' said the maid.

I looked out upon the dolorous garden, upon the lazy crone, upon the gilded fields.

'After the night,' said I, taking the maid's hand in mine. She put on her white bonnet and we went out of the room. Opposite to us was a door ajar. Of late inquisitiveness had grown upon me. I had much difficulty in refraining from pampering the habit. I pushed the door a little wider and peeped in. I looked into a darkened room; I saw in the gloaming a tumbled bed. A still sick man eyed me with glassy eyes. I felt that one more wrinkle was scrawled upon my face.

The sun was ripe for setting as the maid and I set out upon the white road between the hedges. The doors of the cottages were shut. The flowers in the gardens were in rank disorder and choked with rank weeds. Only one man we saw. He sat outside his cottage door with his grindstone in front of him – a very old shrunken man, busily grinding his scythe. But his fingers were so weak that the steel scarcely grated upon the stone, and made only a low humming sound, soft as the hum of bees in a distant hive.

''Tis Simon, the mower,' said the maid; 'he be for ever grinding his scythe, but, la he'st too weak to snap a twig,' she smiled compassionately.

The grinder never turned his bent head nor stayed his profitless labour.

'All day long,' said the maid, 'all day long sings the drone of his scythe; and the childer used to sit quiet at the window watching wi' their eyes of mice for the sparks to skip fro' the stone. Their yellow hair was just golden in the green. But the childer a' gone back fro' the window, and all the white summer day the buzz shakes i' the air. Ay, and i' winter. Oh, sir, the sun climbs up sick and sulky, and crawls lik' a fat snail i' the blue, and goes down by the Black Mill, and the darkness eats him up. I do feel that my heart is o' glass and be nigh to breaken' when the chill night sneaks in at the keyhole. I do miss the cluck'n' hens in the sunny dust and the douce-smell'n hay.'

I spied furtively at the glazed windows, but no children looked out upon us thence, and the forsaken nests of birds in the thatch were draggled and in wisps like a widow's weeds. Not long after the maid and I came to the village well. The hoary stones were green in patches. The brown shreds of a broken pitcher lay in the dust at our feet. There I was fain to sit and muse, looking into the still black waters, which seemed to have in hiding the silence of the dead. But my friend called me, and we journeyed on together hand in hand. With each step upon our way I seemed to draw nearer to the thoughts of the antiquated maid at my side. Myself was not left behind, for the pleasure and lustiness of youth took a new colour. Feeble knees and waning courage were carrying me out of the ken of the world. Yet my mind's calm was rather the calm of a child's awakening to the morn than the lazy ease of falling to sleep at the slow coming of night. We climbed a steep and rocky way, full of ruts and holes, and upon our eyes, when we turned an angle of the road and came out from under the gloomy cedars, suddenly shone the red windows of a house standing gaunt and solitary and watchful upon a crest of the hill.

'There be the Grey House,' said the maid, kneeling down amidst the long green grass.

The evening was glorious.

Here was left behind the toil and fret of men's business. And while I was looking under my hand towards the brightness, a strange company of men defiled between the iron gates of the house, carrying a burden upon their shoulders. I sat down with the maid by the roadside, and waited until the procession should come up with us. When they were come near I shouted, 'Is Mr Basil Gray at home?'

The weedy men paused. They put down their burden in the dust. They shot furtive glances the one to the other.

'Ay, sir, "at home" that he be,' shrilly laughed a wizened little man who led the way with a lighted lantern and a mattock.

The maid turned to the west. I bent over the box, and read my friend's name upon the lid. Death took me by the hand. Presently the little band proceeded on their way. The maid and I followed afar off... When darkness was come I tottered to my musty snowy chamber in the little inn. The wan child led the way, carrying a candle. I sat at the open window. For a long time I watched the sexton labouring by the stilly light of his lantern and the yellow crescent moon in the graveyard of the 'Village of Old Age'.

The Moon's Miracle *

As when, to warn proud cities, war appears
Waged in the troubled sky, and armies rush
To battle in the clouds; before each van
Prick forth the aery knights, and couch their spears,
Till thickest legions close; with feats of arms
From either end of heaven the welkin burns.

Paradise Lost, Book II, 533

How the Count saw a city in the sky and men in harness issuing thereout – Of the encampment of the host of the moonsmen – Of how the battle was joined – The Count's great joy thereat and of how the fight sped.

* First published in *Cornhill Magazine*, April 1897, 'by Walter Ramal'; selected for inclusion in R (1923) but finally omitted; later published in *Eight Tales*, ed. Edward Wagenknecht, Sauk City, Wisconsin, 1971. It is the earliest printed 'Count' story: cf 'The Almond Tree' and 'The Count's Courtship' (R (1923)), and 'A Beginning' (Beg (1955)).

The housekeeper's matronly skirts had sounded upon the staircase. The maidens had simpered their timid 'Good-night, sir,' and were to bed. Nevertheless, the Count still sat imperturbable and silent. A silence of frowns, of eloquence on the simmer; a silence that was almost a menace.

'Bed-time, Count,' I suggested.

His thinking had dishevelled his hair. He peered at me with wrathful disapprobation. 'How glum,' he muttered, 'how desperately glum!' and again fell silent.

'I fancied that it was getting late,' said I.

'Late, late?' he grunted, 'Am I the slave of the clock? Bed for old women.'

'May I ask what is wrong, sir?' said I.

The floodgates were opened.

'I am in the blues, boy, unfathomable. All is wrong: that I am old and full of wear, that Life, the sorceress, is wearying of me; soon she will play the jilt. And here I sit, cudgelling my jaded brains for to evade the one event. But even the Count is mortal, and his palace of youth evanished in a golden mist of memories. Now the worms' banqueting hour is at hand, now wails the Banshee.' The Count was smiling and frowning. He limped over to me and sat down beside me, under the candles at the window.

'I am in the blues, boy; call it what you will – indigestion or homesickness of soul. The green of the past is out of sight, the pitiless sands of old age stretch out to the brink – and a certain Bird is patient.' He leaned forward and tapped me upon the knee. 'I will fight,' said he between his teeth, 'fingers against beak till the white bones show.'

Then back was flung his head with his familiar guffaw. 'Tut! here am I lavishing my hoarded experience on a raw youth who sucks at his book as though it were the fruit of the tree of Life. Laughing, are you? So am I. It is the candles, the candles, the candles. They conjure up musty shrines and greedy heirs. Shut your book, raw youth, and draw aside the curtains; we will hob a nob with the moon.'

The moon was high above the housetop, so that only a faint twilight trickled into the room; but, upon the grassy stretch of common, whose skirt was twinkling fair with distant lamps, she shone cold and bleak. The trees, indecorously clothed this autumn-time, feebly shivered in their rags. Upon the other side the common, over against the Swan Pond, the potboy was putting up the shutters of the 'Green Man'; and, as he drew to an end, one by one its lights went out as a man might shut his eyes. And when this landmark was thus silently withdrawn, it seemed that we were suddenly left the sole companions of the night.

The Count drew a deep breath. 'How good!' said he, 'how good! 'Tis a blue bowl of moonlight; let us drink to the dregs. 'Gad! a mere eyeshot of my Wimbledon is a recompense for all our woe. A lovable rogue is life, but a jilt, a jilt.' He surveyed the world with a mother's eyes. One by one, in the silence, our neighbour's cocks began to crow. The Count's face grew merry again.

'Now the cocks do shout the midnight,' he chanted. 'How quiet is the air! but yet I'll wager to a keener ear a thousand fairy harps are rippling. And mark you that crook-backed elm; what a pose, a personality she has in her tattered petticoat. You would think – but Dryads are out of fashion in this age of gilt.' (I was listening now with little attention.) 'Sing hey for shrewd Mrs Grundy though she see no farther than the Ultimate Plumes. Down soul, down! and out of the drawing-room. So the gaffer's tongue wags, for equivocation must drown doubt; yet had I a tittle of certainty (just the glimmer of a ghost) I would ecstatically die and my hearse should be a veritable Car of Triumph. Alas! many an old comrade have I seen swagger into eternity, but never a one has bugled clear to me from his shadowy bourne.'

('It is an optical delusion,' I muttered.)

'Are their eagle spirits snuffed out into blindness and silence? Do they — ?'

Out of the misty far away rose the mere echo of a cockcrow.

'Whist!' said I, 'whist!'

The Count's rhapsody was cut short. We stood agape at the window.

The north-west brought it forth. In this direction alongside of the road-way, is a row of poplars. And it was just here, above their topmost twigs, that, when the Count was in the midst of his talking, I saw the first sign in the sky. 'Mirage,' said the Count curtly, polishing the glass with his sleeve. His aged grey eyes were wide-open as a child's at a Christmas tree. 'A thing common enough, common enough, but — '

A policeman loosely sauntering on the pathway overlooked by the house, to my astonishment, seemed to notice nothing uncommon. I was near calling out to him as street boys call to one another at the appearance of a balloon. But in the weighing of the matter in my mind I let him saunter on, out of hearing. When he was well gone I was glad to have kept silence. The intense stillness of the city's surreption of the night-sky for a while assured me of its unreality; but soon it was impossible so to think. Out of space the city had risen upon us. Out of the night she sallied forth like a bride.

'Look, look!' said the Count hotly.

The city was now hovering at a span above the Home for the Dying. A sudden light shone in a window to the north. Maybe it was set shining by a mother fetching milk for her baby or by some one awakened out of night-mare, for soon it was extinguished.

'The silence is like a wary beast,' said the Count. 'D'ye think, is it the

dust of the air (my eyes are dim), or do I see men moving upon the ramparts
and busy about the gates? That pinnacle grows clearer every minute; it
pricks the sky. Really it is very odd. What? What says the boy? And yet,
mark you, not an inch of it is moonlit. Some inner light glimmers upon the
stone, or a sister moon is prowling in her rear.'

'Men, men!' said I.

Very slowly the world's circumference dipped in the sky until the city
hung free of all earthly excrescences, as though she were swinging by a
cord, as swings a seagull, out of space. Like a huge, still summer-cloud
lazily lolling on the horizon near before sunset was the city, save that upon
her walls and buildings was the light of a wintry dawn fluttering.

Presently winged men in a multitude were to be clearly seen, and also
upon the right of the main gate flanked by smooth turrets, a multitude of
horsemen likewise with outstretching wings. Again I searched the common
that I might point out the wonder to some chance passer-by and be convinced. To me it seemed a traitorous deed to extinguish the candle of
science in a breath, to trample Newton's grave. A woman upon a seat near
at hand was inert and asleep; none stirred anywhere. But while my eyes
went vainly roaming the extremities of the common they lighted upon slow
moving blotches in the darkness of the northeast. These I pointed out to the
Count.

'My field-glasses in the green leather case,' said he.

'In the old cabinet,' said I.

But neither of us stirred a pace from the window.

'Horsemen? Yes, horsemen!' said I. 'How they ride!'

'Like secrets,' said the Count.

Soon, it was a difficult matter to keep watch on all these things. The
concourse of people about the city's gates was increasing. Mustered in rigid
order, they stood like an army prepared for battle. For a little while I was
apprehensive lest a trumpet should sound and should wake the world,
fetching men and women, all in a panic, in nightcap and gown, from the
warren of houses into this open place.

But no sound fell. The vast assemblage was silent. The horsemen upon
the sky's verge were making stealthy progress. Clearly some tumult was
toward.

'Such business means the devil to pay,' said the Count. 'No peaceable
city that, my friend. See how tense is the bustle, even the watching of it
clenches the fists. I know the heart-gnaw, the rat at the pit of the stomach.
Chut! My pension for new blood. Every man of 'em writes hazard in every
movement. If that be an outflanking ruse,' he continued, pointing a
ludicrously gaunt finger towards the left, 'the enemy must be encamped in
mid-sky. They go the pace. Mettlesome beasts they be. And observe the

order, line upon line, with nice interspacing. Mark the ease of their seat, horse and man – one, like a hawk, confident of every wrought muscle. Line upon line they ride, hugging the shadow. A fit body of men – and the beasts!'

'Ay,' said I, 'you are right, Count, it is a rear attack. They are making profit of the earth's shadow. Their accoutrements are dull too. Are they not purpureal, sir? 'Cute enough!'

'In night khaki,' said the Count, like one inspired.

'Yes,' said I, 'you are right. The enemy must be in mid-sky, overhead.'

We turned quickly, the one towards the other. 'Round about the moon!' we shouted together.

Pretty certainly we were to be justified of our surmise, unless far westward, out of the world's ken, lay their goal. The Count was already hurrying out of the room. In his heat and boisterous haste he overstrained his leg, but, careless of the pain, and leaning upon my arm while he flourished the candle on high in his left hand to light our way (and assist the placid scrutiny of his ancestors), he pushed forward down the passage. The eyes of the pictures were exceeding dull painted it seemed to me. ('I owe them this night,' was the Count's rebuke of my levity.) On our way, because of the bend in the hallway, we saw the dwarf city speed, as it were, across the fanlight of the door.

'Ha! d'ye see, a manoeuvre to the sou'-west, too!' said the Count.

In our anxiety to shoot back the bolts of the door, we much incommoded one another, whereupon the Count fiercely swore at me in a flurry of anger. He was another man. With the forethought that is sometimes twin with excitement, I seized a mackintosh which hung upon a peg at the doorway, and with this followed near after the Count, who, impatient of my help, with never a step without a groan, was wrathfully hobbling down the steps into the garden. In our short absence, the walls and towers of the sky-city had waxed plainer yet. But, though nearer at hand – the very war men's faces were discernible – yet the utmost limits of the city I could not see, since round about her the stars were obscured; for there hovered London's smoke. And now we were free of the shadow of the house. By clambering upon the stone pilasters nearby the yews where lies the stableyard, we could sight nigh the whole firmament. Here, simultaneously, we bleated amazement at the tents of the army encamped about the moon.

The tents were of divers pale colours, some dove-grey, others saffron and moth-green, and those on the farther side, of the colour of pale violets, and all pitched in a vast circle whose centre was the moon. I handed the mackintosh to the Count and insisted upon his donning of it. 'The dew hangs in the air,' said I, 'and unless the world spin on too quickly we shall pass some hours in watching.'

'Ay,' said he in a muse, 'but it seems to me the moon-army keeps infamous bad watch. I see not one sentinel. Those wings travel sure as a homing bird; and to be driven back upon their centre be defeat for the – lunatics. Give *me* but a handful of such cavalry, I would capture the Southern Cross. Magnificent! magnificent! I remember when I was in — '

For, while he was yet deriding, from points a little distant apart, single, winged horsemen dropped from the far sky, whither, I suppose, they had soared to keep more efficient watch; and though we heard no whisper of sound, by some means (inaudible bugle call, positively maintains the Count) the camp was instantly roused and soon astir like seething broth. Tents were struck and withdrawn to the rear. Arms and harness, bucklers and gemmy helms sparkled and glared. All was orderly confusion.

It was just now that a little breeze moved, lifting the hair upon my head and letting it fall. By and by it came again, fluttered, and fell; and again, like the breath of a Polar bear. Soon it blew briskly and steadily. 'Put up your collar, Count,' said I. 'Fortune defend us from rain!'

So gently was the city ascending that it seemed she was being wafted onward by the gentle wind. In a little while she emerged quite out of the haze and revealed to us her remoter pinnacles and towers, fair and lucid, and of gossamer airiness. Her course was not the moon's course, and at no time did she rise many degrees above the skyline. Her progress (whither, who can say?) must have been very slow, so much my bones on the morrow painfully testified, but zest is time's sharpest rowel, and when morn came, putting out the vision, the night seemed only too soon to have come to an end.

This while the Count, in his own conceit, was Commander-in-Chief of the celestial aliens. He growled commands, stormed, and soliloquized. He squandered his virile vocabulary upon trembling *aides-de-camp*. His pose was heroic. In his dun mackintosh, at attention – so far as his leg would permit him – upon his own gatepost he cut a figure droll enough.

In some measure his isolation warranted his boast. As fortunate as inexplicable was our solitude. Even the woman to whom we were now come near, was not at all disturbed, but lay fast asleep, her face upturned to the pale sky, quite regardless of the miracle, grossly unabashed by these 'minions of the moon'. Perhaps she entertained in her dreams other visitors – silks, and ease, and plenty – as rare and as pleasing.

Upon the Count and the sleeper, however, I wasted little attention. Troop after troop of horse, of somewhat gloomy equipment, were defiling between the gates of the city; some to join the main body, now distent in a crescent, some to spread fanwise on either flank of the moon-army. It chanced, moreover, that while I was watching there fell a lull in the procession; those horsemen who were just beyond the portal looked back and sharply drew in against the wall; and, presently after, a rider with cloak astream, bearing despatches (perchance) from one in authority or from council convened in secret debate, burst solitary and precipitate out of the shadow, curved upward, dwindled to a spark under the sprawling Bear, went out – and the horsemen trooped on orderly between the city gates.

The contingents despatched before, whom we had espied on the horizon, had seized the south, and with tight rein were stretching in towards the centre, driving before them isolated stragglers ('scouts,' said the Count) of the moon-army. This latter, constantly being recruited by these few and others from above, was now swollen to quite formidable bulk.

'How are the chances, Count?' said I.

'I like it not, I like it not,' said he, astutely wagging his head. 'I wonder,' he continued, 'if a cockcrow would reach their ears! England expects! *Ma foi*, what city is this of marvellous architecture? Now it minds me of a black pearl, now of a dreamed Babylon. I say, I say!'

'What now?' said I. A troop of horse was wheeling in the black north in stealthiest fashion.

'See you there? See you the main gate?' said the Count, with antic gesticulations.

'The main gate?' said I. One of my men had fallen headlong.

'Yes,' said the Count; 'yes; well, look back, fifty yards or so, to that sheeny dome where the grey birds are fluttering; now to the right a little – ken ye a turret? It is the king; it is the king.'

I left watching my troop, and followed his directions. Nearby the ramparts, in full view of the battlefield, upon a turret, was a little gorgeous company, with heads sapiently inclined each to each, gossiping together with restrained gestures; and a little afore them upon that turret, alone, a man, very sombre and regal and elect. Whether king or city mayor or grand vizier. 'Ho!' bawled the Count, 'old lamps for new.' No answer came. 'Sky wolves,' he howled in a frenzy, 'birds of battle, show us of things. Turn your faces agleam. Whence came you out? Is time there? Passes the night? Ho, Ho, Ho!'

We waited for but the stir of a finger to betray them; but, even did they hear, they took no heed. Indeed, it seemed that all the combatants were clean without knowledge of the earth. Theirs only was the universe. If I may again quote the Count: 'Why, sir, even the camp followers are Napoleons' – which is fanciful, but this is just. 'I have walked the world this three-score and ten, and tonight see soldiers.'

Soldiers indeed they were; their callous persistency, their vigorous order and array, and their trim machinal manoeuvres alarmed me (down here in safety) not a little. But this not so much as the silence. For not until near break of day did the wind grow turbulent, and bluster and grumble at the chimney tops, and shrill in the bare twigs. Meanwhile the small voice of a cricket in the stable-wall sounded continuously in my ear, although my eyes were dazzled and giddy, and my wits in a maze with watching of the ever-moving host. I wondered at the Count's temerity. 'Ah,' said he, 'my uncle the Major would have enjoyed this! Their wings beat in my heart. Do but put out a finger, it would touch them. Bah, blockheads! Blockheads! Stretch him against a wall. I will have 'em all court-martialled. Skirted misses! Weanlings! Ha, a devilish fine fellow! He knows his business, he knows his business.' Thus the Count dittied, now to the skies, now to me.

Slowly, in an icy silence, the armies drew together. Of a thousand warriors of old, spent, heart-sick Sisera alone came to my mind and Deborah's Song of Victory – 'They fought from heaven; the stars in their courses fought against Sisera,' thrilled down the centuries to the clap of timbrels, as though I had been the traitress Jael herself. Indeed, myself was fanatical, up in arms. Doubtless our cramped position, the cold, the solitude, and the seeing of nought earthly but here a tree-top, now a glossy roof, in some measure cut us off from life's corporeity, gave us wings; it is, nevertheless, remarkable that these extramundane noctivagators should have so convinced us that (as the Count said) this fat, palpable, complacent world suddenly grew spectre-thin and stalked out of reality into a mist of dreams. We were like flies upon the ceiling of a ballroom watching the motley festivities, save that the feet of the dancers (the celestial hosts) trod our air. How vast seemed the circuit of the skies.

'I give them twenty minutes to get into action,' said the Count.

The minutes passed by exceeding slowly. The night was wind-swept and very clear; everything plotted to assist and entrance our observation. Hitherto, we had been quite undisturbed, but when a half of the Count's twenty minutes was gone by, suddenly I heard a loud shouting. I looked with some vexation across the common; a man with his hands clapped upon his head was violently running over the grass, crying out shrilly as he ran. 'Here's a wretch at last who calls "Fall on us,"' said the Count. The intruder came on with many a stumble and now and then a fall, for the moon played tricks with her shadows upon the unequal ground.

'Hollo,' I shouted, 'hold your tongue – hold your tongue!'

The intruder threw back his head with a gasp (he was then twenty paces distant), and seeing that the sudden voice was human and not, as he might think, from the clouds, quickly trotted towards us and soon was cowering at the pedestal, his hand upon the Count's boot. The Count was on a roar, and roared the louder when the woman, awakened by the fellow's clamour, put back her head to yawn, and saw the sky. She waited not to scream, but lifting her skirts that they should not impede her, whipped round and in a wink was nimbly footing it over the grass towards this, the only haven, like a startled bat. When she reached us, she hid her face in a corner of her ulster and gabbled incessantly, like a woman possessed.

'Chut! hold your tongue, ma'am,' said the Count testily, 'you desecrate the silence.'

Her voice fell to a low continuous moaning. The street musician, for such was the first-comer, after the first flush of terror, quickly recovered his wits. In high feather he perched himself upon the stable-wall, and thence commanded a wider view to the south than ourselves. This he used to advantage, crying us news when detachments thereabouts swooped out of our sight. Nor were we the only watchers: the walls of the night-begotten city were black with still onlookers viewing the battle from afar off.

Now the last moment was come. My heart stood still in panic expectancy. Even the Count henceforward held his peace; even things inanimate seemed to bow beneath the burden of the silence; and the trees crouched under the moving skies like huddled beasts at the thunder. All sudden the blood gushed warm in my body. All sudden a weltering wave of horsemen rocked against the stars. Then the armies of the sky met.

Now at full speed, in silence, the nightsmen swept down upon the moonsmen, surging in their onslaught almost within touch of the moon. Now steadily with grim stubbornness, in silence of deep seas, the moonsmen drove back their assailants and falling and leaping, leaping and falling, regained their magic circle. The sky was rimpled over with galloping horsemen as foam rides in on wind-beaten waves. The spark-spitting hoofs, the pulse of moonlit wings, the fury of brandished weapons, though without sound, rang in my inward ears. All this night the moon wended her steep way in a girdle of glittering warriors.

Albeit here was the very acme of the battle, yet to me the outlying troops of horsemen far down in the heavens until they almost grazed roof, were more engrossing. Sometimes in one of these petty fights most ingenious tactics were evident. Like falcon and heron, two would flutter, swoop, hover, fall; in a trice, without a sound. Such a duel as this took place immediately above our heads. Even the woman, seated upon the Count's mackintosh, left her wailing and thereafter gave little rest to her small quick eyes.

Now a vehement squadron sped higher, highmost until the sight yearned in vain. Now a luckless horseman in the full heat of fight fell like a meteor into our unfriendly air and silently, like a meteor, disappeared. Fleet soaring skirmishers, slow compact regiments, disarrayed frenzied fugitives, hither and thither, to and fro, put out the stars and filled the air with lightnings. Without sound, undaunted, and more gloriously ablaze in their swift decadence, a thousand fell out of silence into nothingness. And if a legion in grim magnificence should in its tactics droop from on high to within some few spire-lengths of the earth, then a giant shadow would sweep the moonbeams from the dewy grass, and would transiently dull the glitter of the Count's round eyes. I noticed, also, more than once, that at some extreme point of vantage the troops would muster innumerably until, like a wolf-harried flock, a tangled tumultuous mass would rear itself fantastically upon the horizon, and ere long, trembling, would sink out of sight.

Once, a bird, out of the ivy of the house, with low chirrups of dismay, went fluttering from tree to tree – it seemed like a voice from the dead. Ever and anon, the eye, debauched with movement, returned to that silent city, black with her people upon her walls, whom every accident of the fight, whether of victory or defeat, visibly moved. ('Alack, the brave mothers!' said the Count.) The king, too, austere and motionless, with finger upon cheek – his brain, I wager, on an itch to be doing – was a sight for young eyes.

'My friend,' afterwards said the Count, 'I almost wept that I was not a boy!'

All the night through the battle waged and the moon fell lower towards her setting: all the night through silent battalions sped and met and scattered: all the night through the 'pedestalled' Count, and the woman, and the street musician, and I myself, in a little company, watched the wonder. Throughout the night we kept our watch while our good neighbours, orthodox and sceptical alike, on the other side their shining windows snored in comfortable and decorous ignorance, slumbered then and slumber now – I doubt if death himself shall open their eyes.

It may be debated if this prodigy were visible outside of the Count's Wimbledon. At some miles distant the horsemen might appear like clouds, the city a cloud, and would call for little attention. Maybe (and the Count thinks it) some solitary astrologer at a window wielded a telescope; some boy watching, ate apples. But, of all men, none could have deeper joy of the thing than the Count. Perhaps it were not amiss to the military reader here to be presented with the Count's full diagrams, and technical utterances, relating to the event; but so abstruse were his explanations, so voluble and incoherent (and so drastic) his censures and approofs, his charts so profoundly 'impressionistic', that I despaired even of understanding them, far more of fitly and authoritatively setting them down. Wherefore this account is brief and merely my own. The end of the matter I may not know; even the cause of the battle is hid from me. The Count was afterwards cocksure of the city's victory. It is better known to them who blackened her walls and kept watch; to her king himself.

The vision faded with the stars in the east-south-east, and was put out at the coming of day. At the first doubtful peep of dawn's grey eye the city seemed to tremble and the horsemen to wax pale, as a cheek grows pale with fear. We sorrowfully watched their passing. Ere long the tyrant sun, preceded by a garish retinue, rose in the east, and the city with her history and her people and her wonder, as she had come out of the night, went forth into the day, and we saw her no more. Maybe the combatants fought on, and the world left them behind; maybe they are superior inhabitants of far places and will appear to us no more; but perhaps, if like monsters in the deep seas we shall watch in patience for the repassing of such craft sailing in silence our long nights, our expectations will be not altogether vain. Now, however, morning smoke was rising; London was out of bed; and moonsmen and nightsmen had disappeared as if they were mere creatures of the imagination.

The Count was very cold and nigh helpless. 'I have seen the sign,' said he anagogically. 'What heroes! what a fight! My brothers in arms in the to be.' He chafed his gouty fingers and continued with emotion. 'We have seen – you and I. Valhalla! Dust to — ? Ha! that Rascal besashed, that Press-gangsman.' He fetched a deep breath. 'Now, ma'am, and you, sir,' he added, with kindly nods to our fellow-watchers, ' 'tis nipping and raw, pray walk in.'

We entered the house together. The Count walked in upon the musician's arm, deploring as he went the silence of the night. 'What did it lack say I? – a band, my friend – a skyey drum-and-fife band. Think on't – drum-taps like cowards' teeth, a brazen war-blast out of the sky deeps.'

'Fireworks without the pop,' replied the musician, more than confident after his fears.

'Ah, sir, I perceive you are a man of the world,' said the Count.

The musician tittered.

The Count's visitors were hospitably regaled with rum-and-water. The musician, before his departure, entertained us with a tune. Soon they were gone away with a bit of silver in their pockets, not bound, I trust, for a lunatic asylum. The Count and I tried vainly to converse upon topics befitting the breakfast table. We eyed each other askance, each suspicious of the other's credulity. Conversation was flat and unprofitable, and the ingressive sun a sorry mockery. Optimism is not unfrequently the harbinger of pessimism.

At the first stir of the housekeeper's rising the Count made morosely for bed.

The Giant*

Peter lived with his aunt, and his sister Emma, in a small house near Romford. His aunt was a woman of very fair complexion, her heavy hair was golden-brown, her eyes blue; on work days she wore a broad printed apron. His sister Emma helped her aunt in the housework as best she could, out of school-time. She would sometimes play at games with Peter, but she cared for few in which her doll could take no part. Still, Peter knew games which he might play by himself; and although sometimes he played with Emma and her doll, yet generally they played apart, she alone with her doll, and he with the people of his own imagining.

The rose-papered room above the kitchen (being the largest room upstairs) was his aunt's bedroom. There Emma also slept, in a little bed near the window. For, although in the great double bed was room enough (her aunt being but a middle-sized woman), yet the other pillow was always smooth and undinted, and that half of the bed was always undisturbed. On May-day primroses were strewn here, and a sprig of mistletoe at Christmas.

On a bright morning in July (for not withstanding the sun shone fiercely in the sky, yet a random wind tempered his heat), Peter went to sit under the shadow of the wall to read his book in the garden. But when he opened the door to go out, something seemed strange to him in the garden. Whether it was the garden itself that looked or sounded strange, or himself and his thoughts that were different from usual, he could not tell. He stood on the doorstep and looked out across the grass. He wrinkled up his eyes because of the fervid sunshine that glanced bright even upon the curved blades of grass. And, while he looked across towards the foot of the garden, almost without his knowing it his eyes began to travel up along the trees, till he was looking into the cloudless skies. He quickly averted his eyes, with water brimming over, it was so bright above. But yet, again, as he looked across, slowly his gaze wandered up from the ground into the dark blue. He fumbled the painted covers of his book and sat down on the doorstep. He could hear the neighbouring chickens clucking and scratching in the dust, and sometimes a voice in one of the gardens spoke out in the heat. But he could not read his book for glancing out of his eye along the garden. And suddenly, with a frown, he opened the door and ran back into the kitchen.

Emma was in the bedroom making the great bed. Peter climbed upstairs

---

* First published in *Pall Mall Magazine*, May-August 1901, 'by Walter Ramal'; later published in *Eight Tales*, ed. Edward Wagenknecht, Sauk City, Wisconsin, 1971.

and began to talk to her, and while he talked drew gradually nearer and nearer to the window. And then he walked quickly away, and took hold of the brass knob of the bedpost.

'Why don't you look out of the window, Emmie?' said he.

'I'm a-making the bed, Peter, don't you see?' said Emma.

'You can see Mrs Watts feeding the chickens,' said Peter.

Emma drew aside the window blind and looked out. Peter stood still, watching her intently.

'She's gone in now, and they are all pecking in the dust,' said Emma.

'Can you see the black-and-white pussycat on our fence, Emmie?' said Peter in a soft voice.

Emma looked down towards the poplar trees at the foot of the garden.

'No,' she said, 'and the sparrows are pecking up the crumbs I shook out of the tablecloth, so she can't be in our garden at all.'

Emma turned away from the window, and set to dusting the looking-glass, unheeding her grave reflection. Peter watched her in silence awhile.

'But, Emmie, didn't you see anything else in the bottom of the garden?' he said. But he said it in so small a voice that Emma, busy at her work, did not hear him.

In the evening of that day Peter and his aunt went out to water the mignonette and the sweet-williams, and the nasturtiums in the garden. There were slipper sweetpeas there, also, and lad's love, and tall hollyhocks twice as high as himself swaying, indeed, their topmost flower-cups above his aunt's brown head. And Peter carried down the pots of water to his aunt, and watered the garden, too, with his small rose-pot. Yet he could not forbear glancing anxiously and timidly towards the poplars, and following up with his eye the gigantic shape of his fancy that he found there.

'Aren't the trees sprouting up tall, Auntie?' said he, standing close beside her.

'That they are, Peter,' said his aunt. 'Now some for the middle bed, my man, though I'm much afeared the rose-bush is done for with blight: time it blossomed long since.'

'How high are the trees, Auntie?' said Peter.

'Why, surely they're a good lump higher than the house; they do grow wonderful fast,' said his aunt, stooping to pluck up a weed from the bed.

'How high is the house, Auntie?' said Peter, bending down beside her.

'Bless me! I can't tell you that,' said she, glancing up; 'ask Mr Ash there in his garden. Good-evening, Mr Ash; here's my little boy asking me how high the house is – they do ask questions, to be sure.'

'Well,' said Mr Ash, narrowing his eye, over the fence, 'I should think, ma'am, it were about thirty foot high; say thirty-five foot to the rim of the chimney-pot.'

'Is that as high as the trees?' said Peter.

'Now, which trees might you be meaning, my friend?' said Mr Ash.

'You mean those down by the fence yonder, don't you, Peter?' said his aunt. 'Poplars, aren't they? That's what he means, Mr Ash.'

'Well,' said Mr Ash, pointing the stem of his pipe towards them, 'if you ask me, the poplars must be a full forty foot high, and mighty well they've growed, too, seeing as how I saw 'em planted.'

Peter watched Mr Ash attentively, as he stood there looking over the fence towards the poplar-trees. But his aunt began to talk of other matters, so that Mr Ash said no more on the subject. Yet he did not appear to have descried anything out of the common there.

Now the evening was darkening; already a lamp was shining at an upper window, and the crescent moon had become bright in the west. Peter stayed close beside his aunt; sometimes peeping from behind her skirts towards the trees, glancing from root to foliage, to crown, and thence into the shadowy skies, whence the daylight was fast withdrawing. By and by his aunt began to feel the chill of the night air. She bade Mr Ash good-night, and went into the house with Peter. Soon Peter heard Mr Ash scraping his boots upon the stones. Presently he also went in, and shut his door, leaving the gardens silent now.

At this time Peter was making a rabbit-hutch out of a sugar-box; but tonight he had no relish for the work, and sat down with a book, while Emma learned her spelling, repeating the words to herself.

'Auntie,' said Peter, looking up when the clock had ceased striking, 'If Satan was to come in our garden, would he be like a man, or is he little like a hunchback?'

'Dearie me? what'll these stories put into his head next? Why, Peter, God would not let him come up into the world like that, not to hurt His dear children. But if they are bad, wicked children, and grown-up folks too for that matter, then God goes away angry, and the Spirit is grieved too. Why, my pretty, in pictures he has great dark wings, just as the angels' are beautiful and bright; but the good angels watch and guard little children and all good people.'

'Then he's just as big as a man in the pictures, like Mr Ash, not a —'

'Aunt Elizabeth has heaps of pictures of him in a book, Auntie, with all the wicked angels crowding round,' said Emma; 'but he's much taller than Mr Ash, like a giant, and they are all standing up in the sky, and —'

'Yes, Emmie, that's in the book, I daresay,' said her aunt, frowning at Emma, and nodding her head. 'But come and sit on Auntie's lap, dearie; why he looks quite scared, poor pigeon, with his stories. Auntie will tell you about little Snow White, shall she? – about little Snow White and the dwarfs?'

Peter said nothing, though his lip trembled; and albeit he asked no more questions, yet he did not attend to the story of Snow White.

At the beginning of the next day, Peter woke soon after the dawning, and getting out of bed peered through the glass of his window, down the garden. The flowers were not yet unfolded in the misty air. There was no movement nor sound anywhere. The trees leaned motionless in the early morning. But towering implacable against the rosy east stood that gigantic spectre of his imagination, secret and terrific there. And Peter with a sob ran back quickly to bed.

However, he mentioned nothing of his thoughts during the day, eating his breakfast, and going to school as usual. But when he reached school he had forgotten his lessons, and was kept in. Even there, alone in the vacant schoolroom, he could not learn his returned lessons because of all his vivid fears passing to and fro in his mind. As the afternoon decreased, hour by hour, towards evening, he began to hate the memory of night and bedtime. He lingered on, seeking any excuse for light and company, until Emma spoke roughly to him. 'Leave off worrying, Peter, do! How you do worry!'

At last, when even his aunt grew vexed at his disobedience, Peter begged her for a light to go to bed by. At first she refused, laughing at his timidity. But, in the end, with importunities he persuaded her; and she gave him a piece of candle in his room, to be burned in a little water, in order that when he was asleep, and the burning wick should fall low, then the water would rush in and extinguish it.

It was far in the night, just when the flame of the candle leapt out into darkness with a hiss, that Peter woke from a dream, and sat up trembling in his bed. He had dreamed of a street in the distance, whither a giant became a speck, and the eye was strained in vain. Even yet he saw its undimmed length retreating back unimaginably. And, as if impelled by an influence inscrutable, he got out silently and drew back the muslin window-blind. In the clear, dark air he saw the row of poplar trees; he saw that gigantic shade of fear abiding there, uplifted as with a threat, and the trembling stars of the heavens about him for a head-dress.

Peter cried out in terror at the sight, hiding his eyes in his hands. And while he stood sobbing bitterly, scarcely able to take breath, his ear caught a sound in the room like the wintry shaking of dry reeds at the brink of a pool. At this new sound he caught back his sobs; his scalp seemed to creep upon his head. He looked out between his fingers towards the bed; and he saw there an Angel standing, whose face was white and steadfast as silver, and whose eyes were pure as the white flame of the Holy Ones. His wings were to him as a covering of perfect brightness, his feet hovering in the silentness of the little room. Peter, his tears dried upon his face, could not bear to gaze long upon that steadfast figure angelical; yet it seemed as if he was now indeed come out of a dreadful vision into the pure and safe light of day; and when presently the visitant was vanished away, he went back into his still warm bed, his fear more than half abated, and fell asleep.

In the morning, when he looked out of the window, a gentle rustling rain was falling, clear in the reflected cloud-light of the sun. He could hear the waterdrops running together and dripping down from leaf to leaf. He heard the sparrows chirping upon the housetop, the remote crowing of a cock. And the poplar-trees were swaying their leafy tops in the cool air, as if they also had awakened refreshed from the evil perils of a dream.

De Mortuis*

There is a graveyard by a solitary wayside, with many an antique tomb in the seclusion of umbrageous yews and willows. A rude wall of flint, the glittering target of the sunbeams, is its barrier against the wild, unconsecrated moorland; a dark tower its ancient sentinel. It is an abandoned garden where flowers meet together without favour – rosemary and nettle, myrtle and lily, and yellow charlock. Green unweeded paths are the waste avenue of its dead. It is the resort of wild bees and yet wilder birds, whose murmur and melody cease only with the twilight, the hour of the owl and the nightjar. There is no sound of lamentation in all its silent ways. A quiet company, country people all, is laid here, who have in stealth departed, and do not return. 'O Death, O Time,' cries one, 'the wicket and the approach!' The wicket in due season has been unlatched to each; and now none comes: theirs is the wild vacant solitude, theirs the thicket of elder and crimson hawthorn. Moss, and lichen, and stringent ivy weave ever upon their names and legends the immortal web of oblivion.

They found death no unwholesome theme for rhyme, these country people; they knew him of old – a strange whimsical figure enough with his great key, silent yet eloquent, austere, capricious. To die was but to make an end, the ruddy sun on the stubble, the dark wintry staircase to bed; and the tombstone being narrow at best, and transient after all, they did not daub it with flattery, but they put much in little space:

> Here lieth alone John Alfred Mole:
> He hath burrowed now so deep, poor soul.

---

* First published in *Pall Mall Magazine*, September-December 1901, 'by Walter Ramal'; later published in *Eight Tales*, ed. Edward Wagenknecht, Sauk City, Wisconsin, 1971. See also 'Lichen' and 'Winter' (DDB (1924)), which have epitaphs in common.

the final jest of all, and not quite heartless. You may see 'Mary Alice Gilmore' very clearly in her muslin gown:

> She came with her garland all in the May morning,
> Her face shining fair as the milk in the pail,
> But Death walked behind her with yew and with cypress,
> And hath lured her away to his house in the vale.

A rain-darked stone, a pace or two beyond, echoes shrilly that desperate cry in the *Urn Burial* – 'Even such as hope to rise again . . .':

> Dig not my grave o'er-deep,
> Lest in my sleep
> I strive with sudden fear
> Towards the sweet air.
>
> Alas! lest my dim eye
> Should open clear
> To the depth and the weight –
> Pity my fear!
>
> Friends, I have such a wild fear
> Of depth, and space,
> And heaviness, O bury me
> In easy place!

He has a friable soil for his rest – too easy, perhaps, if his fear quicken also against the 'wolf with nails'. Nearby, a vacant man is interred, whose dull ear would scarce have caught the clangour of his own elegiac bells:

HERE LIES THOMAS MATTHEW DALE,
aet: 81

> He lay like to a simple child,
> So stealthily old Death drew near;
> His intellects were all too dim
> T'acquaint his soul with fear.
>
> White as the blackthorn bloom his head,
> His voice like a far singing bird,
> His hands they trembled like a leaf
> By southern breezes stirred.

He seemed a stranger to his frame,
He seemed his spirit was elsewhere gone,
Nor found not any selfsame thought
Of what he gazed upon.

Like jargoning bells blown out of tune,
Yet with a sweetness on the wind,
God leads us young and old about
Just as He hath a mind.

The alien grave of the sailor is in the morning shadow of the low wall,
dense with flowering nettles, sated with dew:

Here sleepeth a poor mariner,
And only silence him to cheer:
He pineth for the roaring sea,
Who must in earth so quiet be:
There seemed a voice in the deep sea,
That strange and winsome haunted he.

But the deep sea is beyond the hills, and the wind faint only with the
inland sweetness. It might be the quavering voice of Darby McGraw himself complaining of exile.

Thomas Small, a miller, fusty yet of meal, who died in dark February,
keeps him company:

Here lies a Miller;
Each working day
He went as white
As blossoming May:
A goodly thing enough to be
If thy soul do keep thee company;

and a philosophic warrior, his field of valour undecipherable:

This quiet mound beneath
Lies Corporal Pym,
He had no fear of death,
Nor death of him.

Close to the footpaths, so that children must often have fingered the two
long ears rudely carved at the upper corners of its leaning stone, is the grave

of a mute. Beneath his pollard window of an April evening, Pan pipes luringly – and in vain – as if the blackbirds were singing.

> Step soft, good friends, for though a mute,
> Silence doth best the sleeper suit.

A mute cares little for the sound of his name: there is scored deep only 'A.A.'

Under a mound that now scarce would harbour a cherub, a comrade of Falstaff gluts his great body with an intolerable deal of slumber:

> Here lies the body of Andrew Haste,
> Now in the ground doth go of waste,
> If Mr Haste you e'er did see,
> Ye'll know what a terrible waste it be.

Laid a little out of line, three strangers, who could go no farther, solace themselves; the first a rhymeless traveller in a cloak.

> Here lies a stranger to this place;
> 'Twas a windy eve he came upon,
> At dusk he opens the tavern door
> And with a few words climbs up to his bed;
>
> The red cock up in the morning crew,
> But neither he nor the chambermaid
> Might rouse the stranger where he lay,
> Wrapped in his cloak there still and grey.

The second, a needy fellow with two very memorable 'e'e,' serves for the celebration of his benefactors a meek and not unusual office of poverty:

> Mistress Mellor hemmed a shroud
> For this stranger beggar man;
> Peter, Sexton, digs his grave
> Comforting as ever he can;
> Just rags and bones and greenish e'e
> Were all this begger was pardee!

In the dazzling fervour of the summer sun stands an obelisk, evidently a public purchase. Yet, despite its unseemly pallor, it is not out of place, for the unstable earth has fallen away, proving it a very trivial thing. Its legend is certainly not the work of its mason:

> Here rests in peace, and security,
>   Ann Fell, who was
> Cruelly, and foully done to death
>   In Milton Fields,
> Snow lying deep upon the ground.

>   Sleep without fear, sweet Ann,
>   Thy murderer cometh not
>   To wreak his vengeance
>   In this quiet spot.

>   Hid in the silver clouds
>   The sworded legions move:
>   What shall his hate
>   'Gainst legions prove?

>   Like glouts of summer dew
>   Thy blood shall be,
>   Rubies celestial
>   For the blest Mary.

The wind ever hums along the jagged flints where lies a leper uncontagious:

>   Toll ye the Bell, a Leper now is come
>   To the gate merciful of his long Home;
>   Like a Paule's scales his filthy Sores shall be
>   When heaven's glory he doth blinking see;

>   Whiter than Snow his body's Skin shall shine,
>   As Moses' face in Israelitish eyne;
>   But, when old Dives knocketh, black with Sin,
>   D'ye think Saint Leper will invite him in?

Time has shown. At the foot of the quiet, windy tower in the deeper grasses is the dust of 'Elizabeth Page, Spinster':

>   Here sleeps a maiden who deceased
>   On the even before her marriage feast;
>   All put with sprigs of lavender

Lieth the gown she'll never wear;
Idle and quite untenanted
Her gloves, her shoes; her nosegay dead;
Yea, even her smock her shroud now is,
And rosemary for love's caress.
Ah! Wo is me poor piteous bride,
Would we were lying side by side!

One vault there is, stared upon by the attentive gargoyles of the tower. It is large and lichenous, and echoes the note of the bird in its depths.

Fall down upon thy bended knees, O man,
And 'twixt thy restless finger and thy thumb
Roll but a fragment of this crumbling earth,
And know that ev'n to this thou shalt come!

Put thou thy naked hand upon this stone,
Compose thy heart, and in thy fancy see
A form without friend, or comeliness, or power;
Even to this thou too shalt come with me.

For thy bright candle but the dim night worm,
For music the lone hooting of the owl,
The baseness of thy end for reverie:
Oh, in thy pride, consider with thy soul,

While yet thou sojournest 'neath the tree of Life,
Viewing its fruit of evil and of good,
Lest the bright serpent of earth's rank desire
Be thy companion in this solitude.

Ev'n in this solitude of leaf and flower,
O, lonely man, on thee dark Satan gloats;
Let him not, triumphing at the deep Trump's blast,
Urge thee to exile with his drove of goats.

One looks up abashed from reading, and far across the purple moors passes a visionary flock with bleatings and cloven tramplings.

A narrow mound of pebbles set in cement, as it were pearls in a brooch, has for its memorial a slab sunken in the wall:

Here lieth our infant Alice Rodd;
　　She was so small,
　　Scarce ought at all,
But just a breath of sweetness sent from God.

All on her pillow laid so fair,
　　White in her clothes,
　　Eyes, mouth, and nose,
She seemed a lily-bud now fallen there.

Sore he did weep who Alice did beget,
　　Till on our knees
　　God send us ease;
And now we weep no more than we forget.

This is the merry gallery of the grasshoppers; they laugh perpetually all day here from blade across to blade, and in the dark evening their cousin, a cricket, creaks prudently from the wall. Perhaps the following is of these three also:

Dear Mother, happy be,
　　Thy toil is over,
Thou liest with thy infant,
　　And thy lover.

All, all, branch, bud, and root,
　　Gold hair, and hoary,
Husband, and wife, and babe,
　　Singing in glory.

It was by chance I came upon the 'natural's' tomb, for his oval stone is matted with ivy. I had pursued a flight of magpies into the dense bushes, and so threw the sunlight on his mouldering inscription:

Here lieth a dull natural:
The Lord who understandeth all
Hath opened now his witless eyes
On the sweet fields of Paradise.

He used to leap, he used to sing
Wild hollow notes; now angels bring
Their harps, and sit about his tomb,
Who was a natural from the womb.

He'd whistle high to the passing birds,
With so small store of human words;
He found i' his own rude company
The peace his fellows would deny.

He'd not the wit rejoiced to be
When Death approached him soberly,
Bearing th' equality of all,
Wherein to attire a natural.

A long narrow stone had fallen a little asunder in an angle of the wall, and through its crevice bindweed (whose roots strike marvellously deep for so delicate a thing) has sprung up. It puts forth its pale blossoms upon weed, stalk, and stone.

Here lies the body of Madeleine
Wrapped to the throat in a shroud of green;
Daisies her jewels here and there,
A bud at her foot, a bud in her hair;

Her eyelids close, her hands laid down,
Her sweet mouth shut, her tresses brown
On either side her placid face:
Christ of His mercy send her grace!

Three others.

Ruth
V.V. MDCCCXV

Bright eyes of youth look softly on this stone:
Let but a name suffice to character one
Whose earthly beauty was so piercing sweet
It brake the hearts of them that gazed on it:
Here, as if all her Aprils to one end –
The beautifying of her face did tend,
Sleeps she at last where neither flattery
Nor tears nor singing may distinguished be:
And from its lovely and so delicate house
Is passed the spirit: all that ravished us
Lies here at end, even her loveliness,
And the sweet bird cometh to songlessness.

The last of a Spaniard:

> Laid in this English ground
> A Spaniard sleepeth sound.
> Death heedeth not man's dreams,
> Else, friend, How strange it seems,
> This alien body and soul
> Should reach at last this goal.
> Well might the tender weep
> To think how he doth sleep,
> Strangers on either hand,
> So far from his own land.
> O! when the last trump blow,
> May Christ ordain that so
> This poor Spaniard arise
> 'Neath his own native skies:
> How bleak to wake, how dread a doom,
> To cry his sins so far from home.

To the living:

> What seek ye in this old Churchyard?
>   The dead are we,
> The forgotten dead who, dead long since,
> Close together in silence laid,
> Find death sweet we once thought sad,
> And peace the last felicity,
>   The dead are we.

> What shall we find in this sad Churchyard?
>   Cypress and yew,
> Dark shadows upon Time and signs
> Of death by day, how many days!
> How many starry nights they raise
> Their gloomy branches grey with dew
>   Cypress and yew!

> Why will ye leave this still Churchyard?
>   Here is sweet rest.
> On earth there is no rest for man.
> Love is not rest, nor toil, nor faith;
> But only faith will sweeten death

When the heart pants in the tired breast
For death and rest.

The briefest of all, upon a dark vault, ancient and gaping, without date or name: 'O Aprille month!' A great house for such a little body.

It is a faithful servant of the seasons, this untended graveyard. In spring the almond and the resinous elder hang over against the grave of the natural, with an extraordinary alertness, like an archer with bow bent; in summer the wine-sweet wild rose, the echoing cry of the bird; and so to autumn and winter-brown leaves, and twigs, and snow. Time will efface all record soon. Its narrow wall is ruinous, scarce hindering even now the wandering sheep from trespass, and surely no obstacle to pucks and gnomes that hoot and squeal above its recumbent stones. Perhaps, but for its abundance and its solitary tower, it will presently be at one again with the wild and broomy moor.

The Rejection of the Rector*

Mr Wilmot was of too indolent a temperament to be an acute observer of Nature; indeed Nature was the more active of the pair, and influenced him in her various moods more intimately than he himself imagined or would have cared to confess. April was come with lilac and chestnut, and as the Rector returned at evening to his solitude, a serene melancholy took possession of his mind, bending his thoughts on two matters similar yet remote. He was in spirit gone back to the youthful days of the past and to the memory of his first love, yet at the same time he was considering the present also in the matter of taking a wife. The sentiments were strangely in harmony one with the other, the one perhaps as befitted his age (a very practical thing), the other deep-rooted and intense beyond decline.

Fortune favours the ductile as well as the strong, and after many years of difficulty and effort she had steered him into a tranquil haven. He had faced laborious days with placid courage, but without zeal, so intent had been his rather weak desire for ease; and now that his desire was attained, he was able to enjoy it to the full.

His living was not affluent, yet ample for a man of moderation and solitary habits. The poor of his parish were few and docile; the wealthy equable and staid. His churchwardens were meritorious institutions, whom Time would remove only when successors should be rife. The little town was built on the incline of a hill; on its elevated outskirts stood the houses

* *Black and White*, 5 October 1901, 'by Walter Ramal'.

of the wealthier members of his congregation, amid green trees and orchards, in imperturbable somnolency. It seemed the children of these families must be merely importations by request. It is true a sleeping infant in its fleecy bassinet might sometimes be seen along the sunny chestnut walks, and in June boys would be met with in the fields; else the daughters of the place were for the amelioration of invalid widowers, and its young men rather ladylike. It was a parish where it seemed always afternoon, where the six week-days were but a torpid preparation for a demure Sabbath.

The Rector was a tall, slender man, not yet quite grey, somewhat dainty of speech, yet not insipid of matter; a writer of pleasing verse, a preacher who deemed his congregation of more importance than his prejudices, a graceful listener when in the company of men of the world; and beside these things, he was gifted as only Genius and Indifference and Felinity are gifted – he was almost unconsciously erudite in the sex.

He opened his gate and entered his garden. Its walks lay along between daffodils and tulips. A lofty pear-tree was the punctual resort of a thrush. All the swift magic of spring was in that quick budding garden of flower and fruit tree. He had debated the eligible spinsters, one and all, with his customary hesitation, and now resumed what was rather a mood than a memory – the memory of the days of his youth, of his first wife Hannah.

Notwithstanding the discretion of his parishioners, gossip had long been busy with the former subject. His poorer matrons found in it tattle ever new and animating. His crabbed sexton shook a crazy head. And the little clean girls of the Sunday-school looked pleased and askance, and each talked over the chances of her particular teacher, with sneers for every rival. Quite young and somewhat anaemic girls fretted with wildest daydreams, and quaked with stifled heart at his approach. Of these Rebecca Mills adored him candidly, without fear, retaining meanwhile a butcher in her service, quite unjealous, and slaughtering busily for the sake of a wife and home. Strangely enough it was she who most quickly perceived the secrets of her elderly and patrician rivals. She had them one and all by rote, and every detail of her passion, prospects and prosperity. She was love's most obedient weathercock, nor ever wavered in pointing whither his influence bade. Moreover, she was the eldest and favourite pupil of Miss Alice Seymour, and her allegiance and ardour were beyond reproach. It was her desire and assurance that since herself was fated butcherwards, Miss Seymour should become the Rector's second wife.

The Rector had been not quite so sure as he seated himself in his ivied arbour. His bow had many strings: only polygamy would secure him from all sympathetic regret. The purple silks of Miss Pugh, her cheerful, spectacled countenance, and perennial banter; Miss Minto, pale, austere, antique, fine in wit, elegant in mien, caustic in criticism; Miss Daw, a little

round widow, like a dove in her pleasant house: all were variously excellent
– one only of these ladies, alas! was allowable. Moreover, all were similarly
excellent in the primary matter of means. The Rector was not a mercenary
man, but the one passionate and tragic influence in his life had dulled his
eyes and secluded his heart from all other remembrance of romance. He
was intended to be a duteous and cockerel husband: it was his vague intention to take a suitable lady to wife.

Miss Seymour lived rather beyond her neighbours and their gardens, a
lonely and somewhat sequestered life. She might walk over her little garden
bridge across a brook into a great wood of primroses, and here she would
seat herself these warm spring mornings to work or to read or to muse. She
was unaccustomed, perhaps would have deemed it a somewhat vain and
vulgar act, to analyse her emotions. She was content rather to enjoy being,
than to vex herself with questions of becoming. Yet as she sat gazing with
clear blue eyes, not by any means without insight, on the April prospect of
green and blossom, a faint wonder was wafted through her mind, of her
own strange sense of felicity. She was inclined rather to attribute it to a life
mercifully suffered to be spent in compassion and patience than to any
more trenchant and disturbing cause.

Rebecca Mills came through the wood gathering primroses in a little
wicker basket, and in hope to find Miss Seymour there alone. She liked
nothing better than to perch herself upon the margin of that perilous
subject, perilous alike to herself and to Miss Seymour, less perilous, perhaps, to the dogged, thrifty butcher. To-day she soon perceived a facility in
the conversation that was seldom vouchsafed her. Her words moved easily
to the rhythm of her thoughts, she yearned in deep unselfishness to aid her
friend and teacher to the bliss she might not share, and so turned as quickly
as possible to matters cordial and ecclesiastic.

'Tom says he wants me soon, Miss,' she remarked wistfully. 'He's so firm
I can't gainsay him having his own way.'

'But don't you wish to be married soon, Rebecca?' inquired Miss
Seymour gently.

'It's a blow, Miss,' Rebecca answered. 'Castles in the air is a pleasant
way o' spendin' the time, but they're not for wedded wives with children
to bring up. Leastways, if you never think of no one else.' She let fall one
by one a handful of primroses into her basket.

'But, my dear girl, you must not marry if you do not love your husband;
it would be very wrong and very indiscreet.'

'O, it's not that, Miss! Why, he doesn't love me neither, leastways not
love – how could he? But when we're settled down we shall rub along
nicely, I warrant. Him and me was meant to come together I do believe. I
do believe every heart has its mate: only the spirit yearns.' She came rather

vacantly to an end, but continued with head a little sidelong. 'Was the Rector's first an invalid lady, Miss, because I couldn't fancy him weddin' a *robust* girl?'

'I never met Mrs Wilmot,' Miss Seymour answered, faintly.

'It does seem strange to think of him livin' so lonely. I do think he wants a body's care. And he wouldn't need to look far. He's just the way of seein' thro' us. I mean, Miss, he knows that where he seeks he'll find sure enough. Men's love's so different.'

'Why, how, Rebecca?' murmured her companion without stirring.

'They loves with the body, Miss, and ladies wi' their souls. They ax for comfort and usefulness, and just blind idolatry: but wi' women – it's like flowers.'

Rebecca sat dismayed at so strange and unconsidered a statement. She paled a little as she turned to her companion in fear of laughter or rebuke. But Miss Seymour's face was turned away, she was looking furtively into the green deeps of the silent wood. 'What strange ideas you have, child!' she said, sharply.

'I fancy, Miss,' continued the girl as if impelled by truth itself, 'I fancy when a man has once loved a young woman, whomsoever it be, it has gushed out all like a water-spring, and ever after it's just mockery and make-believe. He do look so cast down at times. It would be a mercy, I'm sure, poor soul.'

Miss Seymour rose rather awkwardly and smoothed out her skirts.

'My dear girl, you must not indulge these notions: they lead nowhere, they are idle. A woman has a long way to go, Rebecca, and you must make up your mind to be a true wife to your husband.'

'O, yes, Miss,' the girl answered, opening her large eyes. 'We shall rub along like a greased wheel: it's the leaving the other I was thinkin' on.'

'But what other, Rebecca?' Rebecca's cheeks flamed scarlet.

'Why, it's only my silly fashion o' talk. I'm just playin' at supposin', I do declare.'

She walked with her teacher to the brook and left her standing there, herself taking the way along the edge of the wood into the lanes.

Miss Seymour had listened to her talk, scarcely remembering the shame of it. She gazed gravely at her reflection in the gliding waters. Her sad, shamed eyes and trembling lip spoke out when herself had long equivocated. She withdrew softly, drawing her skirts tight to her side, and returned into the sunny garden. The birds' high songs were strained and mad, the fragrance of the spring flowers oppressive. She struck her cheek petulantly. Her self-deception vexed her beyond measure; her humiliation showed her herself and all things else in a bleak clear light that only truth vouchsafes to unconquerable eyes. The Rector dwindled to the elderly, refined, and rather pathetic gentleman he was; the covert gossip and glances of her neighbours were now without sting for very remorse at their justification. 'My own pupil!' she whispered bitterly. This chit of a girl had read the man from preface to finis. All the world had perceived the comedy, the comedy of what was to her a grand treachery. Her glorious love of freedom, her glorious independence and unsullied history – no blemish or shadow of man upon it – girlishness came back to her with its swift, easy stride and lofty carriage. The Rector was then a very light thing.

She rested awhile in the afternoon, listless and rather peevish, and fell asleep. She woke overcome with ennui and took her Keble into her parlour lest red flannel for potential infants should become irksome or her fancies rebellious. To church and meeting she went as punctual and persistently as ever. She met the Rector with graciousness, quite regardless of the shameful tumult in her heart; even began to be amused at those more strenuous neighbours, and learned in all their wiles.

With this new aspect of affairs the Rector vacillated no longer. It was after a meeting of the Girls' Friendly Society that he accompanied Miss Seymour on her evening way to her house.

'Your influence over these young girls is remarkable,' he said. Miss Seymour glanced sidelong at her companion. He was blinking his eyes rapidly and moistening his lips, as was his habit before announcing his text.

Her heart flagged like a bird in her breast. 'They shall grow up strenuous, brave girls; the future is in their own hands,' she answered breathlessly, 'That is what I try to impress on them.'

'Certainly their future is in their own hands,' said the Rector. 'It used to be in mine.' The epilogue was so melancholy and chastened, the lady battled with her distress. 'You see, Miss Seymour, time reduces us to a timid level;' the 'timid' might have been a word chaunted in the Psalms. 'We push and struggle in youth for a landing-place, and there we remain until the end.'

'The memory of the struggle is not apathy,' said his companion firmly.

'I grant you it.' He turned swift and sure, and before the house was reached had made his proposal, and submitted gracefully to rejection.

'I would answer yes, Mr Wilmot, if I dared,' the lady said, bravely, 'but marriage, I think, is not a compact of convenience, nor even of affection. It is a compact of love, I feel sure. I am past the days when such a thing is possible, or – or seemly. I do not think it would be honourable to omit this explanation. You will not think me ungracious... Thank you, thank you!' She hastened awkwardly towards the house, humiliated at her haste. She sat down on a garden-seat in the still warm night. The brook filled the silence with perpetual warbling; the air was sweet and pure. She folded her gloved hands in her lap and remained motionless, until beyond the poplars rose the moon, and with the moon a chill, gentle breeze.

The Rector absently returned home, pensively enjoying the calm of the evening. It seemed the memory of an irksome duty had been lifted from his mind. This question of a second wife had troubled him more than he had supposed. Now that the question was temporarily removed he felt free and renewed – an exorcized Hamlet. Nor was this at all an affair of pride. He admired Miss Seymour very tenderly, as one admires an old friend. She had even quickened the poignancy of the past in him, had drawn it out of ways conventional. The beauty of the night inspired him. He lingered under the trees of his garden, gazing vacantly at the pale night of stars, and murmured in a strange, deep, tremulous voice –

> 'Lead, kindly light, amid
> the encircling gloom,
> Lead thou me on.
> The night is dark, and I
> am far from home,
> Lead thou me on...'

Strangely enough, with the morrow, all idea of seeking consolation of his loneliness, and betterment of his fortunes, from any other of the excellent ladies, whose caps were at his feet, passed out of his mind. The thought of marriage simply evaporated. He met Miss Seymour with unaffected pleasure and sincerity. He suddenly became perfectly content to remain the widower adversity had brought him up – even smiled gently at remembrance of his former enterprise. And with this new contentment he became even more charming, more robust in his opinions, and in the conduct of his church and people, yet more tender in his affection for the girls with flaxen hair, and for texts taken from the Book of Ruth. He played a remarkable, albeit brief, innings in the local cricket match, raced an elderly and boyish visitor from his pear-tree to his garden gate for the stake of a new hat, and purchased a bicycle.

Despite this activity, his lonely thoughts of his 'own dear lady' more frequently brought vacancy into his eyes and sharp and difficult pain into his heart. He was more often abroad, yet more often in perfect seclusion with his Donne, and his gold pencil, and a scrap of paper for occasional verse.

The Match-Makers*

'No, Herbert,' repeated my aunt firmly, 'when a man reaches your age, has a comfortable income – a fact I assume mainly from your expenditure – and, possibly, prospects, it is his *duty* to marry.'

'But who – I mean whom – my dear aunt, whom?' said I. 'No one will have me.'

'How many,' inquired my aunt crisply, 'have you asked?'

'Oh! two or three,' I said, somewhere between modesty and shame.

'Two *or* three?' repeated my aunt.

I counted them wildly over, conscious of that ruthless glance on my face.

'I think three, Aunt,' I said.

'Who, then,' said my aunt cheerfully, 'who shall be the fourth?'

'I suppose,' I murmured apologetically, '*you* mayn't?'

My aunt obviously brightened.

'Don't be facetious, Herbert! Tell me the names of *all* you'd *like* to have.'

'*All,* Aunt!' I gasped.

'To select from,' said my aunt severely. 'And please, Herbert, be less indolent; I have a mission-meeting at seven.'

'But, my dear kind lady, you don't expect me to get married in an hour?'

'I do not expect, I insist,' said my aunt. 'Now, then!'

I placed one leg deliberately over the other, leaned finger on finger, and said:

'There's Zannie Treves, there's Betty Hamilton, there's – there's —'

But at that precise moment the maid tapped on the door and admitted Rose Saumarez. I own I started; I would own, if pressed, I blushed.

'There, Herbert,' said my aunt triumphantly, 'how very propitious!'

'Who? Me?' said Rose, smiling from one to the other of us.

'Yes, my dear,' said my aunt; 'and when my bachelor nephew desists from his dumb-crambo, I'll tell you why. *Which,* in your deliberate opinion, would make the better wife for him: Betty Hamilton or Zannie – I think you said Zannie, Herbert? – Zannie Grieves?'

'Treves, Aunt,' I said gently, 'not Grieves yet.'

'Zannie Treves,' said my aunt.

Rose narrowed her lids and looked rather oddly, I thought, at me.

'Don't you think,' she said suavely, 'that after a lady has tried so many, it's almost impossible for one to say which she's at last likely to – to select?'

'You refer —' said my aunt.

'Oh! to dear Zannie,' said Rose, rather sweetly.

---

* *Lady's Realm,* December 1906, 'by Walter de la Mare'.

'You mean —?' said my aunt.

'I mean, dear Miss Mittenson, she's so *frightfully* fascinating, you know, and so of course has heaps —'

'And Herbert?' suggested my aunt rather gloomily.

'Oh, yes, he's quite one,' said Rose. 'Aren't you?'

'Quite,' I said.

'You mean —?' said my aunt inquiringly.

'Rose means, Aunt, Zannie's no zany. She means I'm a rank outsider.'

'I gather, my dear, from his shocking language,' said my aunt, 'that we can dismiss Miss Treves.'

'But doesn't that depend a little on – on our client, Miss Mittenson?'

'Speak up, Herbert!' commanded my aunt.

'Very well,' I said firmly; 'I dismiss Miss Treves.'

'That leaves, then, only —' began Rose, and tried in vain to recall the name. 'Oh yes, Betsy Hamilton!'

'I fancy no *s*" I said.

'Betty – Betty Hamilton,' said Rose. 'I *beg* your pardon. Now, Betty's a thoroughly nice, homely, unsophisticated – girl; and I think *any* man could be immensely happy with her. I congratulate you, Herbert.'

'Thank you, Rose, immensely!' I replied.

'Then,' said my aunt acidly, 'you have decided on Betty Hamilton?'

'No,' I said, 'not decided, Aunt; but Rose is thinking of my thinking about her?'

My aunt turned sharply.

'Age?' she said.

Rose reflected with a beautiful smile.

'Thirty, would you think?' she said.

'Twenty-four,' I said, 'on May the first.'

'Age, twenty-seven,' said my aunt. 'Means?'

'I *believe* Mr Hamilton is something in the City,' said Rose rather vaguely.

'Hardware,' I said, 'and £200 a year in her own right.'

'Twenty-eight, merchant's daughter, £60 per annum,' said my aunt. 'Domesticated?'

'Oh yes!' said Rose eagerly. 'You should see her home-made hats, Miss Mittenson! – and boots!'

'A man doesn't marry hats and boots,' I said sententiously.

'No!' said Rose, 'one *must* think of the contents.'

'Twenty-eight, merchant's daughter, £60 per annum, thrifty,' summed up my aunt once more. 'Brains?'

Rose stooped to stroke the cat on the hearthrug, and the flames played in her hair quite strangely with the gold.

'Brains?' repeated my aunt sternly, and this time gazed at me.

'Well,' I said, 'Rose says she makes her own boots, that's —'

'I never!' said Rose, looking indignantly at me over Selim's white fur.

'Miss Hamilton would never say "I never!"' I said frigidly; 'she'd say, "Excuse me, dear Herbert"; or, "Forgive me, sweet, such was not —"'

My aunt repeated for the third time: 'Brains?' but in so half-hearted a fashion I wondered if it had been intentional.

Then, it seemed, a most awkward silence followed.

My aunt shook out her skirts.

'It's a quarter to seven, Herbert,' she said.

'I'll put my bonnet on. Be prepared for me when I return.' She glanced shrewdly, and yet I fancied almost tenderly, at our visitor. 'And do please aid the poor man!' she added.

I waited till the door was quite shut.

'My aunt,' I said, 'did not mention another name.'

Rose did not stir.

'But really – really, Herbert,' she said, 'Betty Hamilton would make —'

'My aunt,' I said, 'did not mention another name.'

She stroked Selim with one finger-tip from his nose to the extremity of his tail.

'Whose?' she said suddenly, lifting her clear eyes on me.

'Yours, Rose,' said I.

The Budget*

A Matter Of Domestic Finance

I scanned the unspeakable thing patiently and soberly, and then took Nancie's hand.

'You won't be cross?' I said.

'Cross? Of course not, silly boy.'

'Or – or hurt?'

'Hurt! How could I be, dear, after all your *immense* kindness?'

'Oh, nonsense!' I said; 'but still – there – well, it's a *tiny* bit stiff, eh?'

Nancie looked not the least bit hurt or cross – simply astonished.

'I don't mean so much the individual items – each separate thing, you know: it's the total – the whole thing together. You see, dear, we're not so very rich – we're not the Duke of Westminster, are we?'

'No, I suppose not,' said Nancie ruminatingly; 'but what exactly do you

* *Lady's Realm*, June 1907, published anonymously.

mean, dear – the total?'

I felt the faintest suspicion of dizziness, but I passed my hand over my head and rather gingerly took up the bill again.

'I am perfectly well aware,' I said candidly, 'perfectly well aware I may seem just like any other ordinary husband, dear – I mean the kind of thing you see in plays and all that. I've seen it myself, and perhaps it is very funny on the stage; but, you see, we don't quite catch the drift sometimes.' I playfully brandished the bill. 'Why so much bait when the trap's sprung, eh?'

'Oh, please, Harry! You seem to think I'm so awfully clever. What *do* you mean? What trap? I am sure Madame Lalingerie is *immensely* scrupulous. I have sometimes wondered even if she can be really French, for that very reason.'

'Oh!' I replied hurriedly, 'I didn't mean that, a bit. I dare say she's as honest as day, and the name's simply a decoy; but she's a dressmaker – a bonneteer, isn't she? And they know an extra when they see one, don't they, dear?'

'An extra?' said Nancie, unfathomably perplexed.

'I mean they take care of the pence; they prefer guineas to pounds, which is much the same thing.'

'But *you* are paid in guineas, Harry; and aren't lawyers? and I know dentists are, and that kind of thing. I don't *quite* see the harm in that, *really.*'

I sighed, and as negligently as possible surveyed the list again.

'Now there's one, two . . . five hats,' I said. 'I dare say it sounds like a silly question in one of those idiotic dialogues one reads sometimes; but honestly, dear – five hats?'

'But it isn't five, dear; there's two more at the bottom there, and they were *much* the prettiest: it's seven, Harry.'

'Well, seven, then.' But the brilliance of the question seemed to have evaporated somehow. 'Leave the hats, then,' I cried, 'and just tell me this: what the – why on earth, when a woman buys a hat, does she rip out all the trimming?'

'Rip – out – all – the trimming!'

'You must have, Nancie! Just look at all these gimcracks – flowers and ribbons and chiffons. Good heavens! That's trimmings, isn't it?'

'*Is* it?' said Nancie. 'I thought there seemed so few just pretty little things. I suppose, dear, it's having dolls when one's a child. I'm sure they make *huge* mistakes when one's a child. One gets used to little things like that – but they're cheap, that's one blessing.'

I searched frantically for the faintest symptom of anything cheap anywhere; but it was no use losing my case on trifles. I advanced boldly and firmly on the main position.

'Not at all, not at all; that was only a little pleasantry, dear, merely that. It's the frocks and the gowns, you know, blouses, and – er – all that. Now, would you believe it, Nancie, your evening things alone – alone – would have paid the rent, rates, and taxes – yes, and gas!' I added, catching a wild and terrifying glimpse suddenly of an infinitesimal P.T.O.

'But I thought you *said*, Harry,' replied Nancie, the least bit injured – 'you said you had got the house rated *much* lower than that; is that the word? Besides, we never burn a bead of gas at night, though it does seem dangerous in case of burglars, and only lamps in the drawing-room.'

'My dear, dear child, we must really keep to the point, and I honestly, deliberately think three tea-and-coffee gowns a bit stiff. *I* never saw *one*. Besides, what would you think of a *man* who bought a Bass jacket, or a whiskey waistcoat, or a —?'

'As for your not seeing one, Harry,' said Nancie, and I knew I had lost again, her eyes shone as dim and lovely as an April sky before rain, 'you never looked. And I do think if you are going to be hard and angry and unjust, it's not a bit nice to make fun of me, too. You know perfectly well men don't wear Bass jackets; then what is the use of saying they do?'

'I am not angry, Nancie. I try not to be hard or unjust and I'll bolt the coffee-things and all that with pleasure; but I must say, frankly and finally, Madame Lalingerie may fit like an angel, and be as French as Marie Antoinette, but she's deucedly expensive – deucedly. I have had sisters, you must remember, and I think that for just last year's bill, and considering we scarcely went out at all because of your grandmother, poor soul! I think it's – it's a sheer atrocity.'

Something began to sparkle behind Nancie's tears, I couldn't for the life of me say why. 'Now isn't it?' I demanded cheerfully.

'But it isn't,' she said, smiling.

'Not five guineas for a flimsy frock of chiffon that's ruined by the steam of a cup of tea?'

'I mean it isn't last year's bill,' said Nancie, with infinite forbearance. 'You paid that, dear, in February.'

'Do you mean to tell me,' I said, profoundly moved, 'that this monstrous acre of extortion is only for three months?'

'Please, please don't, Harry! You've no idea how funny you look when you're serious. It's not a bill at all, dear.'

'An I.O.U., a deed of gift, then?' I remarked ascetically.

'No, dearest boy; it's just a silly little list I made out, just so as to be frightfully economical, dear, so that you could *see* – don't you understand? – before I ordered *anything*. Just so that you could suggest any little something extra, Harry, you thought, living in such a cheap house, we might be able to afford.'

'You mean,' I said, vainly trying to hide an immeasurable relief, 'you mean it's only a kind of try-on – an estimate?'

'Yes, dear; how well you put it!'

'Oh!' I said.

We paused, and I suddenly became aware that Nancie was looking as intently at me as I at her.

'And you will? And I *may* go to just a tiny scrap more? I mustn't look dowdy, Harry, and you so famous, dear.'

I stared vaguely forward to a February that seemed centuries away.

'Of course,' she continued exquisitely, 'I won't, dear, if —'

'You could never look dowdy, Nancie,' I said brokenly. 'I thought it was last year's, that was all.'

'That's just it,' said Nancie magnanimously. 'I *thought* you thought that. I knew you didn't realize what bargains I was going to get...Poor Madame! you did say very horrid things about her, now didn't you, Harry?'

'Eh?' I said, rather vacantly.

The Pear-Tree*

A Cornish Idyll

The northern parts of Cornwall, next the sea, are very destitute of shade for the traveller. And all one summer's afternoon the tinker, so he told me, had been trundling his wheel along a white and arid road towards the sea village of Treboath, when at a meeting of the ways his ear was arrested by the noise of the grinding of an axe. This sound, it appeared, issued from a long green garden over against a sheep field.

Treboath was still a dusty league away; the afternoon refused the least hint of evening; the tinker was tired and thirsty. He pushed his grindstone through a gate in the slate wall, which is substituted for hedges in these parts, and footed it as quickly as the sandy turf would permit towards shade and ease.

Moreover, the odd familiarity of the summons – the whistle, as it were, of decoy to bird on wing – set him thinking of good company, perhaps a convivial chat on hard times over an amicable mug of ale.

He wheeled his grindstone close against the wall, and being a little man, stood on tiptoe, scrambled up, and looked over. It was a garden, very rich, for the locality, in leaf and flower. Yellow stonecrop flared bright against the dark sweet-william and fuchsia bushes; a hive in one corner was populous with bees; and near at hand lay cool shadows about an old grey well, where water dripped scarcely faster than the long sunny minutes. These

---

* *Lady's Realm*, July 1907, published anonymously.

and the apple and plum trees the tinker took in at a glance, but he more closely scrutinized what seemed to be the owner of the pleasant garden.

He was a lean cadaverous old man, with a large head, and dressed in a white linen jacket. His beard was white and bushy, and as he angrily confronted the tinker, his eyes gleamed singularly clear and keen. He had lifted his axe from the revolving stone at first sound of an intruder, yet it seemed to the tinker just as serviceable so to hold the axe as to whittle the hours away in useless labour; for his stone was old and crazy, and his axe blunted and rusty in the extreme. But the tinker's best policy, as he thought, was to conciliate the old man, for he wanted a rest in the garden and a drink from the well, if not from a yet pleasanter source. So he called out loud, in case the old man were as deaf as he looked, that he would sharpen the axe willingly and for love, if he so desired it; or better yet would lend him a brand-new one, an axe he carried by chance (and had acquired 'by mistake') in his little cupboard.

The old man drew down his brows, and without making reply returned the more vehemently to his grinding. But the tinker was familiar with Cornish whims and graces, and waited patiently and pleasantly till the uselessness of his toil should put the old man into a more complaisant frame of mind. This presently came to pass, for he threw down his old axe beside the wheel and hobbled, with his great head bent, towards the tinker. The tinker thus, as it were, invited, scrambled over the wall in a twinkling with his axe, and at a venture requested the old man to point out the tree he proposed felling.

The old man peered curiously at him, with his hands in his jacket pockets and his head sidelong.

'What's the price of your axe, or the loan of it?' he said.

'Sir,' replied the tinker, 'my axe is not for sale, and it's not for hire. But it's none the less at your service till nightfall, when I am looked for in Treboath. Perhaps it is merely a little chopping on hand; or a stake or two? For the sake of the green and the shade after these godless roads, I will spare your years and – your ignorance, sir. Point the job out! For, to tell the truth, sir, wheeling a grindstone through Cornwall is not a task congenial to a Christian.'

The old man, so the tinker said, brooded long over this rather glib invitation. There was silence between them – with the bleating of sheep and the sound of bees and waterdrops. Presently he lifted his head, and suddenly, as if in a rage, wheeled round and pointed his finger at a lofty pear-tree growing some fifteen paces from the house along the garden.

' 'Tis him!' he said, 'and I'll lay him low before sundown.'

The tinker glanced shrewdly at man and tree. 'Why, and that's a pity,' he said, 'it's thick with fruit; 'twill soon be stooping with it.'

'What's the fruit!' said the old man with a kind of flashing contempt.

'Down him comes leaf and branch and his fruit like buttons on him.' He spoke softly, with suppressed rage, and, to the mind of the tinker, with a tremor of fear in his voice.

'Tish, sir! I don't gainsay ye,' he answered easily. 'I did but see the little fruit: and a morning of sun and dust makes the sight of such like Dives' crumbs, though it's a longish day to October yet, sir. I couldn't catch like at the purpose,' he added casually.

'Be easy o' that,' said the old man gloomily – 'purpose enough for me if he roost no more up there o' these sevenths of June.'

'It's a pest, and no mistake,' remarked the tinker cordially.

The old man eyed him. And at that the tinker leered knowingly, but discreetly held his tongue.

'What have they been telling ye?' demanded the old man.

'It's my trade, sir,' said the tinker, 'to tinker and grind. My wits are but passable, and my ears useful as ears go. But as for my tongue, sir, he asks his wages and says thankee. Else, like most of his kind, he's a wastrel and good-for-nothing.'

The old man fumed in thought. 'Look'ee here, Mr Tinker,' he said, 'it's better to know all than part. Hoist yourself up into yonder pear-tree and cry what you see!'

The tinker concealed his surprise, and climbed up as quick as might be into the upper branches of the old tree, and thence looked about him.

'What do ye see?' called the old man up through the foliage.

The disblossomed fruit smelled faintly sweet around and above the tinker.

'I looks across to the sheep, hundreds of 'em, on the hillside,' said the tinker; 'and, bless me, there's Grey Tor!'

'Turn the man round, turn the man round!' cried the old man impatiently, 'what now, what now?'

'Now I sees a little old church with a spire in the trees, and there! the blue ocean, calm as a duckpond behind,' began the tinker.

'Farther, farther,' shouted the old man.

But now the tinker answered not at all, for he was looking betwixt the boughs clear into a window of the old stone house, where sat sewing a woman pale as Death himself, yet young and marvellously lovely, between her dimity curtains, her brown hair braided on her head.

'Well,' began the tinker slowly, 'why, now I see your daughter sewing at the window: and as like a heavenly angel as ever I did behold,' he added, so he told me, under his breath.

'Come down, come down again!' bellowed the old man in a rage; 'it's my wife you're looking upon from the tree.'

And at that the tinker looked again at the lovely creature stooping, so young, sad, and patient, over her needle; and then slid down again to the foolish old man below. And he stood there staring into the tinker's face, as grey and gloomy as a winter's mist. Till at last the tinker said, catching as best he could at the clue:

'Oh, now, then it's from *this* tree, then, the young vagabond whistles these moonlit nights?'

The old man clutched the tinker's sleeve.

'Down with him, down with him, I beseech ye; have him down before nightfall! I could not bear to see his shape again.'

'Shape, shape!' repeated the tinker to himself, and looked at the old man a little aloof.

And thereupon the old man led him to a bench, so the tinker said, and told him the story from the beginning. It seemed then, the young man he spoke of had been from childhood the playmate and sweetheart of his wife. But, when come to manhood, he had proved of too adventurous and unprofitable a temperament in her parents' estimation to be accepted as a suitor. Yet they had met again and again, these two, William and his sweetheart, on the lonely stretches of the seashore, in the country lanes, anywhere where love may imagine the world far distant, and facts are but fancy, until the girl was betrothed and speedily wedded to this old moneyed man some seven years ago. His sweetheart gone, the young man William went from bad to worse, and left the village far easier for his absence. But back he comes again in a while, rash, bitter, and unscrupulous; and with such a contemptuous hatred of the old man as almost smothered his love for his wife. Every means he tried to reach the poor girl. But she was lonely and timid, afraid of him and of herself; and the old man was always alert.

But one May evening the old man was sitting in his kitchen reading his chapter of the Bible, and she in her bedchamber, when he thought to hear voices whispering. He got up from his chair, burning and trembling, and stole out to his garden-door ajar, to listen to this same William hidden above on high in the pear-blossom, tempting and cajoling, and pleading with the young wife as never serpent wooed Eve to the apple.

The old man listened on in a kind of helpless patience, doubtless recognizing, thought the tinker, the awful justice of youth and beauty coming together, and remembering, too, the May moon and all the spring flowers ascending in perfume to his unhappy young wife at the window. Yet he listened on in patience, for she made no answer to the wild and passionate words. Still William argued and pleaded, and his voice rose and fell softly in the silence of the night like a bird's singing in the tree to one so eager, yet so loth to listen and heed. Until at last, and her voice seemed to echo in and out among the motionless trees – at last the poor child answered that she did indeed love her lover, and ever would, and besought him to go and come no more.

And then the old man broke out, and snatching up his gun from behind the door, ran down like a beast to the pear-tree, brandishing it and calling on the young man to come down. Without the least fear of him William leapt down out of the tree, not knowing that the old man was armed. And before he could turn to defend himself, the butt of the gun descended on his head, blinding and half-stupefying him.

He reeled aside in terror and astonishment. But the old man pursued him, and when he came to the well, sightless and giddy, the poor fellow tripped and fell headlong into its deep and narrow waters.

'It wasn't murder, by no law of man,' agreed the tinker sagely, 'neither in fact nor deed; and even if murder, as things go, why, justifiable homicide,' the tinker considered. Yet remembrance of it lay heavy and unabsolved on the old man's heart, 'as well it might'. And though the body of the young man was fetched up out of the well and decently buried 'in consecrated ground'; and though the well was fed by a never-failing, clear-as-crystal spring, the old man used its waters no more, not even for watering his flowers. Nor did he upbraid his wife – said nought, and drew apart brooding over her confession ('that, after all, was no news to him,' said the tinker), and thinking of the unhappy dead and the May night and all.

But, strangely enough, it was not in the month of May when the ghost of the young man first appeared, but on his own birthday – the seventh of June, a day the people thereabouts remembered as that whereon, when boy and girl, these two children had plighted their troth in the hay-fields. The old man, sitting in his kitchen before his open book, heard his wife in the room above leap up and run weeping to the window. And he himself went out, a fine rain falling in the grey light (a moon stood over behind clouds), and there in the branches of the pear-tree he saw the ghost of William, white as the fallen bloom, his hand clasped round the bough.

The old man stood still in dismay, his heart drawn up, hearing the small rain rustling on the leaves, regarding the spirit of the young man in the gloomy light of the moon, speechless and still.

And so afterwards, as returning spring broke and bloomed and faded into June, so this same awful fear came upon him of this seventh night, until now, worn-out, lonely, beaten down, and not too clear in his wits, he was bent on felling the tree once and for ever and daring all.

But yet at the last (the tinker told me), his courage failed him. For the tinker, being by nature glib and persuasive, enlarged vividly on the revenges which the injured spirit might take on the old man in this world and the next for such a retaliation. And this he did because he was burning curious to see the ghost in the pear-tree with his own eyes. 'For my mother saw a ghost once, but a little before I came into the world, and here's the mark of it yet,' the tinker said.

So the tinker and the old man sat down together beside the kitchen door. It was a dark and moonless night. A window had long since been wide-opened to the night above them; and now all was perfectly still for the cricket to be whistling.

They waited on in silence, watching a pear-tree still and empty but for its foliage and newly-set fruit. And though ever and again the old man would shrink back and mutter, opening wide his light-grey eyes, so as almost to seem a ghost himself in his white jacket, all was still and solitary, and the cricket shrilling clear above the croaking of the frogs the only sounds to be heard.

And the tinker began to grow ashamed and fretful at losing his evening's entertainment in Treboath. But about ten o'clock by the distant chimes, and they still watching silent in the misty garden, he heard a faint yet wonderfully clear voice cry, 'Ellen, Ellen!'; but yet no spirit appeared. The cricket ceased awhile. And then a low and dreadful cry sounded above their heads – 'as if her heart was broken', said the tinker.

At that the old man rose up without a word and went into the darkness of the house.

The tinker waited, but he heard and saw nothing more. Then feeling rather sick and giddy, he cautiously climbed up into the pear-tree again, not fearing the coming of the ghost now at all, he told me, and looked across at the window. It was wide open, he could see, and he heard the old man sobbing and crying like a child; but he could distinguish nothing in the inner darkness; there was no light in the room.

Leap Year*

'But you are, aren't you?' said Judy.

'It depends on the *kind* of question,' said I.

'I mean about what one ought and ought not to do; propriety, conventionality, and all that!'

'Ethics, my dear young lady, is every man's speciality!'

'But is Leap Year ethics?' asked Judy rather forlornly.

' "Leap Year"!' I echoed; 'you didn't say anything about Leap Year. Oh, no! That's not in my line at all!'

Judy put her hands together, and leaning forward in her chair, stared into the fire.

* *Lady's Realm*, May 1908, 'by W.D.L.M.'.

'What I mean is this,' she said: 'could any really *nice* woman – really, really nice, mind – propose?'

'Propose what?' I inquired stubbornly.

'Well,' said Judy, drawing her hands back softly and leaning still more forward, 'to a man.'

'If you are not very careful, Judy,' I pleaded, 'you'll topple over into the fire. Propose what – to a man?'

'Propose *what!*' repeated Judy scornfully. 'You're simply being stupid on purpose.'

'Never,' said I firmly, 'it's second nature.'

'Well, could one?' repeated Judy gravely.

'One *could*,' I said.

'*Should* one?'

'It depends, I think,' I said reflectively, 'partly on the man. What's his income?'

Judy very gently lifted the tiny poker she was so fond of spoiling the fire with.

'Don't, please, be quite horrid,' she said.

'First "dull",' I said, 'now "horrid".'

'Because, you see,' said Judy, plunging in her tiny weapon almost to the knob, 'I feel I ought to: and that's flat!'

I stirred, I hope, never so much as a hair's-breadth.

'I'll have nothing – absolutely nothing – to do with other people's "oughts" ',' I said firmly; 'not even with yours, my dear child.'

'My dear grandmother,' said Judy.

'Well, anyhow, I won't,' I said.

'You see,' continued Judy quietly, almost cowering over the glowing coals, 'I feel to some extent that if he thinks I have been – well, pretending; you know what I mean, *pretending* – it would be only right of me to give him the chance of – of having his revenge. Please do try and understand.'

'Revenge?' I repeated, 'revenge? What ridiculous rubbish! Who *is* this precious "he", may I ask? He must be a deuced poor chap, if he thinks you haven't a perfect right to pretend whatever you please. And what's more: why on earth did he ever give you the chance?'

'What chance?'

'Of pretending,' I answered, perhaps not quite without bitterness.

'When so many questions come all at once,' replied Judy, 'I never answer any. Besides, you haven't answered mine.'

'What *is* the use?' I expostulated; 'what is the use of asking *me?* I'm not your guardian; I'm not a Court of Love; I'm not a Correspondence Column; I'll hear nothing about the conceited fool. Is it likely I should advise one way or the other? You must use your own – discretion, my dear —'

'Grandmother!' interposed Judy. And there was a rather strained pause.

'You see,' began Judy again, abandoning her little poker to its glowing chasm of cinders, 'he's so too awfully shy – not shy, modest – oh, no, not modest – I mean he has such an absurdly, wretchedly small opinion of himself.'

'So long as it's true,' said I, 'I don't see that it matters.'

'But it isn't,' said Judy, casting me a fleeting glance of shining eyes.

'*I* should if it were me.'

'If what were "me"?' asked Judy curiously.

'Why, if *I* had philandered like that, or taken it into my head that a pretty girl, and a straight, "really, really nice girl" too – for you are, Judy' (I heard myself speaking rather sadly) 'in spite of being pretty – if I thought that such a girl as that hadn't the right to turn the head of any fool she pleased — Why shouldn't she? I suppose the silly chap enjoyed it. And as for thinking her to be in earnest, he must be the most insufferable prig that ever breathed. And you haven't absolutely the remotest reason for considering him at all. Hang Leap Year!'

'I see,' said Judy, and sank into silence again.

'How's Jack?' I inquired politely, after a protracted and rather arduous pause.

'Oh, it isn't Jack,' said Judy, speaking muffledly through her fingers.

'I don't suggest it,' I said mildly. 'You see, I didn't gather that this *was* a guessing game. It would take far too long. Besides, I'm "horrid" as well as "dull" – how could you expect it of me?'

'You mean, I suppose, by "far too long" ', said Judy tonelessly, 'that I have had *scores*.'

' "Scores"?'

'Of "Jacks".'

'Honi soit qui mal y pense.'

'But you said just now it wasn't "mal",' said Judy.

'Only in excess.'

'Well,' said Judy, sitting suddenly back, and turning to me her fire-flushed face in the gloaming, 'you'll let the chance go by, then?'

'What chance?' I managed to ask rather thickly, staring blankly into those eyes of childlike sincerity, and could say no more.

'The chance of telling him that I am not a co — a worthless humbug – a mere, silly, selfish, odious every-man's – flirt!'

'He's an utter blackguard, if he thinks a tenth of it.'

'But *does* he? You said just now "only in excess".'

She continued to confront me with shining eyes that yet were not shining only, but still and calm and brave and truthful.

I stooped down, and rather gingerly removed the tiny poker from its absorbing environment.

'Who?' I all but spluttered.

'Who? What?' said Judy, still unstirring.

'Oh, who's the man?' said I, tired out. And then it seemed the glowing fire, everything, went black, and only by sheer blindman's intuition I had found and seized her hand. 'If you do ask him,' I said, 'as sure as you're a heartless, hopeless hypocrite, I'll blow his brains out.'

She never stirred; and gradually the darkness thinned away, and left me utterly sick and cold. I tried in vain to withdraw my hands.

'Harry, Harry,' she said very quickly, as if to race eternal silence, '*won't* you understand? Won't you, dear? *That* would be *suicide*.'

Promise at Dusk*

A doctor hears many strange stories, which must for ever remain a secret confidence between himself and his patients. But the story that my old friend, whom we will call Purcell, told me cannot, I think, be so considered. We were sitting one evening in his long garden, just after the fall of dusk, smoking together. His wife had been dangerously (but quite triumphantly) ill; and this was a few evenings afterwards.

'You know, of course,' he said half apologetically, 'that she has always been very nervous and high-strung; at least —' He broke off and puffed softly on, narrowing his eyes, his hands resting one over the other on his knee. A robin was chattering in the lilac bushes. 'I don't think I ever told you how we actually met. There's no harm in telling...Is there?'

'Well, that's best answered when I've heard,' I replied. And we laughed.

Well, you remember – oh, years ago – when I used to live with my mother at Witchelham? It was an absurdly long journey from town. But she liked the country; and so, nearly two hours every day of my life, except Saturdays and Sundays, were spent in rumbling up and down on that antediluvian branch line.

I believe they bought their carriages second-hand. We had an amazing collection of antiques. The stations, too, were that kind of stranded Noah's ark in a garden, which make it rather jolly to look out of the window in the summer, with their banks of flowers, and martins in the eaves. A kind of romance hung over the very engines. You felt in some of the carriages like a savant confronted with a papyrus he can't read. It was all very vague,

* First published in *English Review*, January 1919, and *Living Age*, 8 February 1919, where it was called 'The Promise'; later published in *Argosy*, August 1956.

of course. But there it was.

One evening, a Tuesday in December, I left my office rather later than usual. There had been a lofty fog most of the day; all the lights flared yellow and amber, and the traffic was muffled to a woolly roar. The station was nearly empty. An early train, the 5.3, coming in late, had carried off most of the usual passengers, and only just we few long-distance ones were left.

I walked slowly along the platform, past the silent, illuminated carriages, and got into No. 3399 – a 'Second'. The number, of course, I noticed afterwards. It was cushioned in deep crimson, lit unusually clearly with oil; half a window-strap was gone, and the strings of the luggage bracket hung down in one corner – like a cockatrice's tent. It was haunted, too, by the very faintest of fragrances, as if it had stood all the summer with windows wide open in a rose garden.

I sat down in the right-hand corner facing the engine, and began to read. Footsteps passed now and again; fog signals detonated out of space; a whistle sounded, and then, rather like an indolent and timid centipede, we crept out of the station. I read on until I presently found that I hadn't for quite some little while been following the sense of what I was reading. Back I went a page or two, and failed again.

Then I put the book down, and found myself in this rather clearly-lit old crimson carriage alone – quite curiously alone. You know what I mean; just as one is alone in a ballroom when the guests have said good-bye after a dance; just as one's alone after a funeral. It pressed on me. I was rather tired, and perhaps a little run down, so that I keenly welcomed all such vague psychological nuances. The carriage was vacant then, richly, delicately, absorbingly vacant.

Who had gone out? I know this sounds like utter nonsense. I assure you, though, it was just as it affected me then. There was first this very faint suggestion of flowers in this almost sinister amber lamplight; that was nothing in itself; but there was also an undefined presence of someone, a personality of someone here, too, as obviously reminiscent of a reality as the perfume was reminiscent of once-real flowers.

The 5.29 did not stop near town, loitered straight on to Thornwood, missed Upland Bois, and launched itself into Witchelham. All that interminable journey – for the fog had fallen low with nightfall – I sat and brooded on this curious impression, on all such impressions, however faint and illusory. So deep did I fall into reverie that when I came to myself and looked up, I was first conscious that the train was at a standstill, and next that I was no longer alone. In the farther and opposite corner of the carriage a lady was sitting. The air between us was the least bit dimmed with fog. But I saw her, none the less, quite clearly – a lady in deep black.

Her right hand was gloveless and lay in her lap. On her left hand her chin was resting, so that the face was turned away from me towards the black glass of the window. Whether it was her deep mourning, her utter stillness, something in her attitude, I cannot say. I only know that I had never seen such tragic and complete dejection in any human creature before. And yet something was wanting, something was absent. How can I describe it? I can only say it was as if I was dreaming her there. She was absolutely real to my mind, to myself; and yet I knew, by some extra-ordinary inward instinct, that if I did but turn my head, withdraw my eyes, she would be gone.

I watched her without stirring, simply watched her, overwhelmed with interest and pity, and a kind of faint anxiety or apprehension. And suddenly, I cannot more exactly express it, I became conscious that my eyes were out of focus, that they were fixed with extreme attention on – nothing at all.

I cannot say I was alarmed, nor even astonished. It was rather vexation, disappointment. But as I looked, glancing about me, I became conscious of a small, oblong, brown-paper package, lying partly hidden under the arm-rest of the seat only just now so mysteriously occupied, and as mysteriously vacated.

Directly I became aware of it, it seemed, of course, extraordinarily con-spicuous. Could I by the faintest chance in the world have overlooked it on first entering the carriage? I see now that it must have been so. But at the time I was convinced it was impossible.

I took up the package, felt it, shook it, and then, without the least excuse or compunction in the world, untied the string and opened the plain wooden case within. It contained a small six-chambered revolver. It was inlaid with mother-of-pearl – a beautiful, deadly little weapon. I scrutinized it for a moment almost in confusion, then I flung down the carriage window, just in time to see the face of the station-master momentarily illumined in the fog as we crept out of Thornwood. I hastily shut the box and packed it, paper and all, into my pocket.

It was entirely intuitive, simply the irresistible caprice of the moment, but I felt I could not surrender it; I felt certain that I should sooner or later meet with its owner. I would surrender it then.

The next day seemed interminable. Fog still hung over the city. I longed to get back to my haunted carriage. I felt vaguely expectant, as if some very distant, scarcely audible voice were calling to me, questioningly, appealingly. I was convinced that my ghost was really a ghost, a phantasm, an appari-tion – not an hallucination. Surely an event so rare and inexplicable must have a sequel.

Out into the misty street (which, in the mist, indeed seemed thronged with phantoms) I turned once more that evening with an excitement I cannot describe – such an excitement as one feels when one is about to meet again a long-absent, a very close and intimate friend.

Again the 5.3 had befriended me. The platform was nearly empty when the 5.29 backed slowly into the station. I had expected no obstacle, had encountered none. Here was my 3399, its lamp, perhaps, not quite so lustrous, its crimson a little dimmed.

I entered and sat down in my corner, like a spider in its newly-spun web. What prompted such certainty, such conviction, I cannot conceive. The few minutes passed, passengers walked deliberately by. Some glanced in; one old lady, with a reticule and gold spectacles, peered hesitatingly, peered again, all but entered, and, as if suddenly alarmed, hastily withdrew. We were already late.

And then, just at the last moment, as the doors were beginning to slam, I heard with extraordinary distinctness what it seemed I had for long been waiting for – a light and hurried footfall. It paused, came nearer, paused again, and then (although I simply could not turn my head to look) I knew that there, looking in on me, searchingly, anxiously, stood framed in the misty doorway – my ghost.

Still she hesitated. But it was too late to retreat. She entered, for I heard the rustling of her gown. And then, at once, the train began to move. At last, when we were really rumbling on, I managed to turn my head. There she sat, completely in black, her left hand in her lap, her chin lightly resting on the other, her eyes gazing gravely and reflectively, yet with a curious fixity, out of the window. She did not stir. So slim, so unreal, she looked in her dead black, it seemed almost that this might be illusion, too – this, too, an apparition. *Almost,* but how surely, how convincingly, not quite.

It sounds absurd, but so absorbed again I grew in watching her, so lost in thought, I think I sighed. Whether or not, she suddenly turned her head and looked at me with startled eyes and parted lips. And, I think, the faintest red rose in her cheeks.

I leaned forward. 'You won't please misunderstand me – my speaking, I mean. I think, perhaps, if I might explain...you would forgive me...' I blundered on.

She raised her eyebrows, faintly and distantly smiling. But I felt vaguely certain that somehow she had foreseen my being there. 'I don't quite see why one should *have* to explain,' she said indifferently. 'You could not ask me to forgive anything that would need forgiveness. But tonight, you must please excuse me. I am so very tired I don't really think I could listen. I know I couldn't answer.'

'It's only this, just this,' I replied in confusion. 'Something has happened: I can't explain now; only if I should seem inexcusably inquisitive – horribly so, perhaps – you will understand when I do explain...You need but answer yes or no to three brief questions – I cannot tell you how deeply interested I am in their answers. May I?'

She frowned a little, and turned again to the window. 'What is the first question?' she asked coldly.

'The first is – please don't suppose that I do not already know the answer, instinctively, as it were, en rapport – have you ever travelled in this carriage before, No. 3399?'

Could you imagine a more inane way of putting it? I knew that she had, with absolute certainty. But, none the less, she feigned to be unsure. Her eyes scrutinized every corner, but indifferently, and finally settled on the broken netting. 'Yes,' she said simply. 'But as for the number – I don't think I knew railway carriages *were* numbered.' She turned her eyes again directly on mine.

'Were you alone?' I said, and held my breath.

She frowned. 'I don't see —' she began. 'But, yes,' she broke off obstinately. 'It was the night before last. I was alone.'

I turned for a moment to the window. 'The last question,' I went on slowly, 'could only possibly be forgiven to one who was a very real, or hoped to be a very real, faithful friend.' We looked gently and calmly, and just in that curious instantaneous way, immortally as it were, into each other's eyes.

'Well?' she said.

'You were in extreme trouble?'

She did not at once reply. Her beautiful face grew not paler, more shadowy. She leaned one narrow hand on the crimson seat, and still looked with utterly frank, terribly miserable, desolate eyes into mine. 'I think – I had got beyond,' she said.

What sane thing could I offer for a confidence so generous and so child-like? 'Well,' I said, 'it's the same world for all.'

She shook her head and smiled. 'I remember one quite, quite different. But still,' she continued gravely, as if speaking to herself, and still leaning on her hand, 'it is nearly over now. And I can take an interest, a real interest, in what you might tell me; I mean, as to how you came to know, and why you ask.'

I told her simply of my dream, the hallucination, psychic experience, or whatever you may care to call it.

'Yes,' she said, 'I *did* sit here. It is very, very strange. It...' and then, she stopped as if waiting, as if fearing to go on.

I said nothing for a moment, knowing not what to say. At last I took out the little wooden case just as it was. 'I cannot ask forgiveness *now*,' I said, 'but this – is it yours?'

She nodded with a slight shudder. Every trace of colour left her face.

'You left it in the train on Monday?'

She nodded.

'And today' – it was a wild, improbable guess – 'today you came to town to look for it, to inquire about it?'

She did not answer, merely sat transfixed, with hard, unmoving eyes and trembling lip.

'I can't help what you may think, how you may resent my asking. I can't shirk responsibility. I know this is not an accident. I cannot believe it was an accident which sent me here last night. I cannot believe God ever meant any trouble, any grief, to have *this* for an end. If I give it you, will you promise me something?'

She did not answer.

'You must promise me,' I said.

'*What* am I to promise you?' she said, her eyes burning in her still, white, furious face.

'Need I say?'

She leaned her elbows on her knees, did not look at me again, merely talked, talked on, as if to her reflection, in that dim crimson, fronting her eyes.

'It is just as it happens, I suppose,' she said. 'It's just this miserable thing we call life, all the world over. You hadn't the ghost of a right to open it – not the faintest right in the world. It is all sheer inference, that is all. As for believing, there's not the faintest proof – not the faintest. Who *can* care *now?* But, no; somehow you got to know, without the least mercy or compunction. Who would believe you? It is simply a blind, pitiless ruse, I suppose... And so... you have compelled me, forced me to confess, to explain what no one on earth dreams of, or suspects – you, a complete stranger. Isn't my life my own, then? Oh yes, I know all that. I know all that... I refuse. You will understand, please, I will *not* promise.

'Who,' she cried, flinging scoffingly back her head, 'who gave *you* my life? Who gave *you* the right to question, to persecute me?' And then, suddenly, she hid her face in her hands. 'What am I saying, what am I saying?' she almost whispered. 'I don't know what I am saying.'

'Please, please,' I said, 'don't think of me. It doesn't in the least matter what you think, or say, of me. Listen, only listen; you must, you *must* promise.'

'I can't, I can't!' she cried, rising to her feet and facing me once more. The train was slowing down. Here, then, was her station. Was I, after all, to be too late? I, too, stood up.

'Think what you will of me,' I said, 'I am only, only your friend, now and always. I do believe that I was sent here. I don't understand why, or how: but I cannot, cannot, I mustn't leave you, until you promise.'

Something seemed to stoop, to look out of her eyes into mine. How can I possibly put the thought into words? – a fear, a haunting, terrible sorrow and despair, simply, I suppose, her soul's, her spirit's last glance of utter weariness, utter hopelessness; a challenge, a defiance. I know not what I prayed, or to whom, but pray I did, gazing blindly into her face. And then it faded, fainted, died away, that awful presence in those dark beautiful eyes.

She put out her hand with a sob, like a tired-out, beaten child.

'I promise,' she said...

My friend stopped speaking. Night had fallen deep around us. The garden lay silent, tree and flower obscure and still, beneath the feebly shining stars. We turned towards the house. A white blind in an upper window glimmered faintly in the darkness. And we heard a tiny, impatient, angry, inarticulate voice, crying, crying.

'Well,' I said, taking his arm, and waving my hand, with my best professional smile, towards the window, 'she has kept her promise, hasn't she?'

Two Days in Town*

Katie and I gazed steadfastly at Katie's aunt; and Katie's aunt blinked gently and benignly in reply.

'Our plan is, you see,' I proceeded concisely, 'to make as much of the time we have at our disposal as we possibly can. It's so short to do all in.'

Katie's aunt smiled again, and shook her head.

'You mustn't speak so thickly, Jimmie,' said Katie, 'and shouting's not a bit of good unless you speak clearly too – like this... What Jimmie is trying to say, Auntie, dear,' began Katie, with an energy that astounded me in so frail a body, '*is*, that as you only have two days in town to see everything, we must go everywhere as soon as *ever* we can.'

'Yes, yes,' said Katie's aunt.

'But "everywhere", Katie!' I murmured.

'Please don't quibble,' said Katie.

'The only difficulty,' I continued with unabated decision, turning to Katie's aunt, 'is where to go *first*.'

'Yes, yes,' repeated the old lady, and we looked most intelligently at one another. 'Well,' I said, taking out my 'proposals', 'I have just jotted down the most important, the essential points of interest... Points of interest.'

* *Sphere*, 13 November 1920.

' "Points of interest?" ' cried Katie, generously.

'Yes, yes,' said Katie's aunt.

'First, then, there's St Paul's, the Bank of England (the Old Lady of Threadneedle Street, you know – practically impregnable), and the Mint.'

Katie repeated most of the list without a mistake.

'Yes, yes,' said the old lady, 'but tell me, Mr James, do they abut?'

' "Abut?" ' I exclaimed.

'She means, poor dear, are they within a cab-drive?' explained Katie. 'You must remember, Jimmie, Auntie has never stirred out of Meadowsham; how can she know anything about London? – I mean, that isn't in histories, and that kind of thing.'

'Well, yes,' I said cheerfully, nodding my head at Katie's aunt, 'practically, they do.'

'Ah,' said Katie's aunt steadily, 'I fear I am but a very indifferent walker, and ... '

'You shan't walk a step,' I shouted.

'And,' continued the old lady imperturbably, 'very alarmed at strange horses.'

'A taxi,' I cried, waving my list, as if with a cheer.

'For goodness sake, Jimmie,' said Katie, 'have some sense! Auntie would faint dead off in a taxi. And don't wave like that, it will only intimidate her.'

'Pray, my dear,' said Katie's aunt with unexpected lucidity, 'let Mr James have his way. I am quite willing to entrust myself, sir, to your wonderful knowledge of London. Is a taxi an open carriage?'

'It's a motor-cab!' I said.

'Ah,' said Katie's aunt, and seemed to fall into a reverie.

'Well, that will be for to-morrow,' I continued, rapidly, 'and if time allows we could take in the Imperial Institute, the British Museum, and the National Gallery.'

'The National ... ?'

'Gallery.'

'Yes, yes,' said the old lady, 'I have frequently read of the National Gallery. I greatly enjoy pictures.'

'Lunch somewhere up west,' I turned to Katie, 'and home to tea. How would that do?'

Katie looked at me very solemnly. 'Have you really all that down on your list, Jimmie?'

'Of course I have,' said I.

'For one day?'

'Of course,' I cried, bending double towards Katie's aunt, 'if pressed for time we could perhaps *cut* St Paul's.'

She raised a mittened hand. 'Do you know, I fancy, sir, you intend my visit to be *very* gay?'

'London's a big place,' I explained magnanimously; and, why I know not, turned hot all over beneath Katie's quiet eyes.

'And so – home to tea,' I added weakly, pretending to blow my nose.

'Certainly, "home to tea" ,' said Katie's aunt, with extraordinary apprehension, 'that would be very pleasant.'

'In the evening,' I proceeded carelessly, consulting my list again, 'we have quite an *embarras de richesses*.'

Katie's aunt smiled softly and questioningly at Katie.

'He means,' she said, gently stroking her aunt's hand, 'he means there are crowds of decent plays on.'

The old lady raised a mild and silvery eyebrow, and a distinct pause ensued. 'He means,' Katie added explanatorily, with a rather red face, 'quite nice, jolly, old-fashioned plays, Auntie.'

'Ah,' remarked the old lady with splendid tact, 'I so very rarely visit a place of amusement, Mr James.'

'In that case,' I replied with decision, 'you will enjoy *Archie's Mermaid*.'

'*Archie's Mermaid*?' breathed Katie into space, 'my dear Jimmie!'

'I hope, I hope,' suggested the old lady, glancing feebly from one to the other of us, 'there are no fire-arms in the piece. I have,' she continued, with delicious confidentiality, 'such a horror of powder, sir.'

'No,' I insinuated reassuringly, 'I don't think there's any powder in *Archie's Mermaid* – at least, not gunpowder.' I looked in vain for encouragement to Katie.

'Perhaps, Auntie dear, you were thinking the double journey would be rather a strain; there's the bazaar at St Ethelreda's?'

'I think, do you know, my dear, and with all respect to Mr James, I should perhaps prefer the bazaar. I have never been to a religious bazaar.'

'So much for Tuesday, then,' I concluded, again consulting my list. 'On Wednesday' – in spite of every effort I could not raise my voice without suggesting a shopwalker – 'on Wednesday we have the Coliseum, Madame Tussaud's, the Zoo, South Kensington (and, of course, the Albert Hall and Memorial), the National Portrait Gallery (unless, as your aunt is fond of pictures, we could squeeze that in to-morrow), Kew Gardens, Hampton court, the Crystal Palace (cat-show), the White City, and, say, a little bus jaunt through the West End – *shopping*, you know.'

Katie's aunt gazed on in happy unconsciousness. Katie was eyeing me with either chastened amazement or immeasurable reproach; it was impossible to say which. And, at one of those cold inspirations that well into the minds of the best of men at crucial moments, I compelled myself to add, 'Moreover, with half an hour to spare there's the old site of the Royal

Aquarium and the Thames Tunnel.'

'I think,' murmured Katie's aunt with the faintest trembling, 'I think, perhaps, sir, I had better avoid *tunnels*. Some of the other places of interest which you have kindly proposed for Wednesday I did not quite catch, but if it could be in any way arranged – without, of course, inconvenience to you and to my niece – I should so very much value a sermon from Mr Spurgeon, and – I daresay you will be amused at the notion – may I see the Woolsack? My dear father used to talk so much of the Woolsack when I was a girl; I suppose it is still in use?'

'Poor Mr Spurgeon is dead, Auntie dear,' said Katie gently. 'It was in all the papers. He has been dead some time.' And I – I refrained from committing myself regarding the Woolsack.

Katie's aunt sat thinking over her loss; at least, so I suppose, though, indeed, her mild, reflective eyes were fixed rather disconcertingly on me.

'Even now, Jimmie,' said Katie, biting her lips, 'you have forgotten Bedlam and Woking.' She glanced fierily up, and added rapidly, 'you've simply been poking fun at the poor old thing the whole time; it's mean, mean!'

If Katie's aunt would have removed her eyes from my face only for the merest instant I could have made a complete defence in a glance. As it was, I rose with concentrated indignation and bowed deferentially over the old lady's hand. 'To-morrow, then, at 9.25,' I shouted soothingly, 'a comfortable four-wheeled cab to the railway station – then taxies, taxies all the way !'

'Thank you, my dear sir, thank you,' said Katie's aunt; 'it will prove, I foresee, a veritable orgy of diversion.'

I bowed as distantly as I could to Katie's muslin shoulder, and with a somewhat funereal dignity made for the door.

'Jimmie dear,' called a clear and cloudless voice as I turned the handle, 'did you say 9.25, or 9.26?'

I choked back my sorrow, and went out...

My cabman (for I had practically made him mine by a process of drastic elimination) drew up to the minute at Katie's, and with dignified promptitude I stepped out and knocked crisply at the door.

Katie herself opened it so immediately I was a little disconcerted by her morning beauty so suddenly breaking out on me.

'Where is your aunt?' I inquired, after a rather tepid greeting. 'It is exactly nineteen minutes past nine.'

'She's gone,' said Katie, glancing at her watch; 'she must have just reached home by now.'

'Home?'

'Yes,' said Katie, 'she caught the 6.31.'

'What for?' said I.

'My dear Jimmie, "why" indeed! Look at your list!'

I looked instead at her bright lovely face under the lawn of her hat, and I tried in vain to be tart. 'I did my best,' I said with a gesture.

'You did so,' said Katie warmly, pushing her hand through my arm. 'She thinks you the polishedest, attentivest, man-about-towniest, real old-English-gentlemenliest creature that ever wore sulphur-coloured gloves. And she's given me a ten-pound-note to take you to the Zoo with. Come along! I adore you both. You're just a pair.'

BIBLIOGRAPHICAL APPENDIX

The entries under the eight main collections, R (1923), DDB (1924, 1936), Br (1925), C (1926), OE (1930), LF (1933), WBO (1936) and Beg (1955), which have been used as the framework for *Short Stories*, include all the known information about:

(a) the serialization of stories and their
publication in book form before they appeared in
those collections, and
(b) their later inclusion in other collections of
de la Mare works during his lifetime.

It has occasionally been difficult to establish definitely whether serializations and appearances in book form were before or after the publication of a main collection (e.g. *Lispet, Lispett and Vaine* (1923) and some of the stories in Br (1925)), and in such cases they have been listed under (a), even if some of them were a month or two later. They have also been assumed to be earlier in the footnotes to the stories for the sake of convenience. Except where there are indications to the contrary, all the books mentioned were published in London. Finally, where texts other than those in the eight main collections have been used in *Short Stories*, they have been asterisked (*). For abbreviations, see page x.

Story and Rhyme (1921)
A selection of his writings de la Mare made for schools and colleges. It included 'The Almond Tree' and 'The Riddle' that were collected in R (1923).

Lispet, Lispett and Vaine (1923)
Published by itself in a limited edition of 200 signed copies, with wood-engravings by W.P. Robins. The story was collected in R (1923) and later included in CT (1950).

The Riddle and Other Stories (R) (1923)
De la Mare's first volume of short stories, published in May 1923. It contained fifteen stories:
'The Almond Tree' (originally written in or before 1899)
(a) *English Review*, August 1909
Story and Rhyme (1921)
(b) SEP (1938)
BS (1942)*
The Almond Tree (1943)
CT (1950)
'The Count's Courtship' (originally written in or before 1899)
(a) *Lady's Realm*, July 1907

'The Looking-Glass'
'Miss Duveen' (originally written in or before 1907)
(b)   SSS (1931)
      SEP (1938)
      The Picnic and Other Stories (1941)
      BS (1942)*
      CT (1950)
'Selina's Parable'
(a)   *New Statesman*, 1 November 1919
      Living Age, 6 December 1919
(b)   *The Nap and Other Stories* (1936)*
'Seaton's Aunt' (originally written in or before 1909)
(a)   *London Mercury*, April 1922
(b)   *Seaton's Aunt* (1927)
      BS (1942)*
      CT (1950)
'The Bird of Travel'
(a)   *Lady's Realm*, October 1908
(b)   SSS (1931)
'The Bowl' (originally written in or before 1904)
(b)   *The Nap and Other Stories* (1936)*
      CT (1950)
'The Three Friends'
(a)   *Saturday Westminster Gazette*, 19 April 1913
(b)   SEP (1938)
      The Picnic and Other Stories (1941)*
      CT (1950)
'Lispet, Lispett and Vaine'
(a)   *Yale Review*, January 1923
      Bookman's Journal, February 1923
      Lispet, Lispett and Vaine (1923)
(b)   CT (1950)
'The Tree'
(a)   *Century*, August 1922
      London Mercury, October 1922
(b)   SSS (1931)
      CT (1950)
'Out of the Deep'
(b)   GS (1956)
'The Creatures'
(a)   *London Mercury*, January 1920
(b)   CT (1950)
'The Riddle' (originally written in or before 1898)
(a)   *Monthly Review*, February 1903
      Story and Rhyme (1921)
(b)   SEP (1938)
      The Magic Jacket and Other Stories (1943)

CSC (1947)*
CT (1950)
'The Vats'
(a) *Saturday Westminster Gazette*, 16 June 1917
(b) BS (1942)*
CT (1950)

Ding Dong Bell (DDB) (1924, 1936)
The original edition, published in April 1924, consisted of three short stories
written round groups of epitaphs. It had a wood-engraving by Reynolds Stone.
A fourth story was added in the 1936 edition. (See also 'De Mortuis' on page 444,
which has epitaphs in common with 'Lichen' and 'Winter'.)
'Lichen'
(a) *Lady's Realm*, September 1907
(b) SEP (1938)*
' "Benighted" '
(a) *Pall Mall Magazine*, July-December 1906
'Strangers and Pilgrims' (1936)
(a) *Yale Review*, March 1936
(b) CT (1950)
'Winter'

Miss Jemima (1925)
Published by itself at Oxford, with illustrations by Alec Buckels. The story was
collected in Br (1925), and later included in *The Magic Jacket and Other Stories*
(1943) and CSC (1947).

Broomsticks and Other Tales (Br) (1925)
The first volume of short stories for children, with designs by Bold, the second
being LF (1933). It had twelve stories, of which three were omitted from CSC
(1947): 'Pigtails, Ltd.', 'The Thief' and 'A Nose'.
'Pigtails, Ltd.'
(a) *Atlantic Monthly*, August 1925
'The Dutch Cheese'
(a) *Lady's Realm*, May 1908
(b) *The Dutch Cheese* (New York, 1931)
The Dutch Cheese and Other Stories (1946)
CSC (1947)*
SSV (1952)
'Miss Jemima'
(a) *Number One Joy Street* (Oxford, 1923)
Miss Jemima (Oxford, 1925)
(b) *The Magic Jacket and Other Stories* (1943)
CSC (1947)*
'The Thief'
(a) *G.K.'s Weekly*, 21 March and 4 April 1925

'Broomsticks'
(a)   *London Mercury*, October 1925
      Yale Review, October 1925
(b)   *The Scarecrow and Other Stories* (1945)
      CSC (1947)*
'Lucy'
(a)   *Number Two Joy Street* (Oxford, 1924)
(b)   *Lucy* (Oxford, 1927)
      The Dutch Cheese and Other Stories (1946)
      CSC (1947)*
'A Nose'
'The Three Sleeping Boys of Warwickshire'
(a)   *Virginia Quarterly Review*, October 1925
(b)   *The Dutch Cheese and Other Stories* (1946)
      CSC (1947)*
      SSV (1952)
'The Lovely Myfanwy'
(b)   *The Dutch Cheese* (New York, 1931)
      The Scarecrow and Other Stories (1945)
      CSC (1947)*
'Alice's Godmother'
(b)   *The Dutch Cheese and Other Stories* (1946)
      CSC (1947)*
'Maria-Fly'
(a)   *G.K.'s Weekly*, 19 and 26 September 1925
(b)   SSS (1931)
      The Nap and Other Stories (1936)
      The Old Lion and Other Stories (1942)
      CSC (1947)*
'Visitors'
(a)   *Forum*, October 1925
(b)   *The Scarecrow and Other Stories* (1945)
      CSC (1947)*

Two Tales (1925)
This was published in July 1925 in a limited edition of 250 signed copies, and had the first printed versions of 'The Connoisseur' (C (1926)) (full version) and 'The Green Room' (OE (1930)). See C (1926) and OE (1930) below.

The Connoisseur and Other Stories (C) (1926)
Contained nine short stories, and was published in May 1926. Two sections of 'The Connoisseur', the title story, called 'The Seven Valleys' and 'En Route' that had appeared in *Two Tales* (1925) were omitted in C (1926). They were restored in CT (1950), probably with de la Mare's approval, and they have been retained in this volume.

'Mr Kempe'
(a) *London Mercury,* November 1925
    Harper's Magazine, November 1925
'Missing'
(b) SSS (1931)
    SEP (1938)
    BS (1942)*
    CT (1950)
'The Connoisseur' (without 'The Seven Valleys' and 'En Route')
(a) *Two Tales* (July 1925) (full version)
    Yale Review, July 1925 (full version)
(b) CT (1950) (full version)
'Disillusioned'
'The Nap'
(b) SSS (1931)
    The Nap and Other Stories (1936)
    The Picnic and Other Stories (1941)
    BS (1942)*
    CT (1950)
'Pretty Poll'
(a) *London Mercury,* April 1925
'All Hallows'
(b) *The Nap and Other Stories* (1936)
    BS (1942)*
    CT (1950)
'The Wharf'
(a) *The Queen,* November 1924
(b) SSS (1931)
    The Picnic and Other Stories (1941)*
    CT (1950)
'The Lost Track'

Seaton's Aunt (1927)
Reprinted by itself from R (1923) with wood-engravings by Blair Hughes-Stanton.
It was also included in BS (1942) and CT (1950).

Lucy (1927)
Reprinted by itself from Br (1925) at Oxford, with illustrations by Hilda T. Miller.
It was also included in *The Dutch Cheese and Other Stories* (1946) and CSC
(1947).

Old Joe (1927)
At different times, this story had no less than four different titles. After appearing
in *Number Three Joy Street* (Oxford, 1925) and being printed by itself at Oxford
in 1927, with illustrations by C.T. Nightingale, as 'Old Joe', it was included in LF
(1933) as 'Hodmadod'. In *The Scarecrow and Other Stories* (1945) it became 'The
Scarecrow or Hodmadod', and in CSC (1947) 'The Scarecrow'.

At First Sight (1928)
One of de la Mare's longest short stories, it was published by itself in New York in 1928 (in a limited edition of 650 signed copies) before being collected in OE (1930). The 1928 version had the sub-title 'A Novel'. The story appeared again in SEP (1938).

On the Edge: Short Stories (OE) (1930)
It contained eight short stories (with wood-engravings by Elizabeth Rivers), one of which had been serialized in 1905 ('An Ideal Craftsman'); and it came out in September 1930. See also Unpublished Stories in *Short Stories 1927-1956*.
'A Recluse'
(a)   *The Ghost Book*, ed. Cynthia Asquith (1926)
'Willows'
(a)   *Blackwood's Magazine*, September 1929
     Virginia Quarterly Review, October 1929
(b)   CT (1950)
'Crewe'
(a)   *London Mercury*, July 1929
     Shudders, ed. Cynthia Asquith (1929)
     (where it was called 'Crewe Train')
(b)   BS (1942)*
'At First Sight'
(a)   *Forum*, June-September 1927
     At First Sight: A Novel (New York, 1928)
(b)   SEP (1938)*
'The Green Room'
(a)   *Two Tales* (July 1925)
     Bookman's Journal, September 1925 (where it was called 'The Green Room: A Bookshop Story')
(b)   SEP (1938)*
     GS (1956)
'The Orgy: An Idyll' (for Part II of the story, see Unpublished Stories in *Short Stories 1927-1956*)
(a)   *Blackwood's Magazine*, June 1930 (where it was called 'The Orgy')
     Yale Review, June 1930 (where it was called 'The Orgy')
(b)   SEP (1938)
     BS (1942)*
     The Orgy (1943)
     CT (1950)
'The Picnic'
(a)   *Criterion*, April 1930
     Virginia Quarterly Review, April 1930
(b)   *The Picnic and Other Stories* (1941)
     BS (1942)*
'An Ideal Craftsman' (originally written in or before 1900; and, according to de la Mare's introduction to OE (1930), it 'has not merely, like the rest, been revised, but has been twice re-written: once by myself and once by my old friend

Mr Forrest Reid, who also went over it again in proof').
(a)   *Monthly Review,* June 1905
(b)   *The Nap and Other Stories* (1936)
      BS (1942)*
      CT (1950)

Seven Short Stories (SSS) (1931)
A selection of seven stories published in collections that was illustrated by John
Nash. They were 'Miss Duveen', 'The Bird of Travel' and 'The Tree' from R
(1923), 'Maria-Fly' from Br (1925), and 'Missing', 'The Nap' and 'The Wharf'
from C (1926).

The Dutch Cheese (1931)
Published in New York, this contained two children's stories from Br (1925), 'The
Dutch Cheese' and 'The Lovely Myfanwy', together with illustrations by Dorothy
P. Lathrop. It should not be confused with *The Dutch Cheese and Other Stories*
(1946).

The Lord Fish (LF) (1933)
De la Mare's second volume of short stories for children. It was illustrated by Rex
Whistler, and contained seven stories. In a note at the end, de la Mare wrote as
follows: 'Four of the stories included in this volume appeared in print for the first
time some years ago in *Joy Street,* but they have been revised – titles and all.
"Dick and the Beanstalk", "The Old Lion" and "Sambo and the Snow
Mountains" are new.'
'The Lord Fish'
(a)   *Number Four Joy Street* (Oxford, 1926)
      (where it was called 'John Cobbler')
(b)   *Animal Stories* (1939)
      The Old Lion and Other Stories (1942)
      CSC (1947)*
'A Penny a Day'
(a)   *Number Five Joy Street* (Oxford, 1927)
      (where it was called 'Wages')
(b)   *The Dutch Cheese and Other Stories* (1946)
      CSC (1947)*
      SSV (1952)
'The Magic Jacket' (in LF (1933) and SSV (1952)
it was called 'The Jacket')
(a)   *Number Six Joy Street* (Oxford, 1928)
(b)   *The Magic Jacket and Other Stories* (1943)
      CSC (1947)*
      SSV (1952)
'Dick and the Beanstalk'
(b)   *The Magic Jacket and Other Stories* (1943)
      CSC (1947)*
      SSV (1952)

'The Scarecrow' (in LF (1933) it was called 'Hodmadod')
(a)   *Number Three Joy Street* (Oxford, 1925)
       (where it was called 'Old Joe')
       Old Joe (Oxford, 1927)
(b)   *The Scarecrow and Other Stories* (1945)
       (where it was called 'The Scarecrow or Hodmadod')
       CSC (1947) (where it was called 'The Scarecrow')*
'The Old Lion'
(b)   *The Old Lion and Other Stories* (1942)
       Mr Bumps and His Monkey (Philadelphia, 1942) (the story
       was given this title here)
       CSC (1947)*
       SSV (1952)
'Sambo and the Snow Mountains'
(b)   SEP (1938)
       The Old Lion and Other Stories (1942)
       CSC (1947)*

A Froward Child (1934)
The story that was collected in WBO (1936) was published separately in 1934.

The Wind Blows Over (WBO) (1936)
Contained eleven short stories (with an illustration by Barnett Freedman), of
which two, 'In the Forest' and 'The Talisman', had been serialized in 1904 and
1907 respectively. In a note at the beginning of the book, de la Mare states that
'both have been revised'. WBO (1936) appeared in October 1936.
'What Dreams May Come'
(a)   *John O'London's Weekly*, 1 December 1934
(b)   BS (1942)*
'Cape Race'
(a)   *Yale Review*, September 1929
(b)   *The Picnic and Other Stories* (1941)*
       CT (1950)
'Physic'
(a)   *Nash's Magazine*, June 1936
       Harper's Magazine, August 1936
(b)   *The Picnic and Other Stories* (1941)
       BS (1942)*
       CT (1950)
'The Talisman'
(a)   *Lady's Realm*, March 1907 (where it was called 'The Talisman of
       Weisshausen')
(b)   CT (1950)
'In the Forest'
(a)   *Black and White*, 27 August 1904
(b)   SEP (1938)*

'A Froward Child'
(a) *Times Weekly Edition*, 10 November 1932
      A Froward Child (1934)
'Miss Miller'
(a) *Story-teller*, August 1930
(b) *The Picnic and Other Stories* (1941)
      BS (1942)*
'The House'
(a) *Observer*, 25 December 1932
(b) BS (1942)*
      GS (1956)
'A Revenant'
(b) SEP (1938)*
      GS (1956)
'A Nest of Singing-Birds'
(a) *Yale Review*, December 1933 (where it was called 'Parleyings')
      Lovat Dickson's Magazine, January 1934
      (where it was also called 'Parleyings')
(b) SEP (1938)*
'The Trumpet'
(a) *Virginia Quarterly Review*, October 1936
(b) BS (1942)*
      CT (1950)

The Nap and Other Stories (1936)
A selection of six stories published in collections that was done for the Nelson
Classics. They were 'Selina's Parable' and 'The Bowl' from R (1923), 'Maria-Fly'
from Br (1925), 'The Nap' and 'All Hallows' from C (1926), and 'An Ideal
Craftsman' from OE (1930).

Stories, Essays and Poems (SEP) (1938)
Thirteen short stories were included in this selection of his writings that Mildred
Bozman prepared in close collaboration with the author for Everyman's Library.
They had all been published in collections, and were as follows: 'The Almond
Tree', 'Miss Duveen', 'The Three Friends' and 'The Riddle' from R (1923),
'Lichen' from DDB (1924), 'Missing' from C (1926), 'At First Sight', 'The Green
Room' and 'The Orgy: An Idyll' from OE (1930), 'Sambo and the Snow
Mountains' from LF (1933), and 'In the Forest', 'A Revenant' and 'A Nest of
Singing-Birds' from WBO (1936). There was an introduction by the author. See
also the Introduction on page vii.

Animal Stories (1939)
A volume of stories about animals for children, with wood-cuts from Edward
Topsell's *Historie of Foure-footed Beastes* (1658). One story, 'The Lord Fish' from
LF (1933), was by de la Mare. The rest he had collected together, re-writing some
of them.

The Picnic and Other Stories (1941)
A selection of eight stories already published in collections. They were 'Miss
Duveen' and 'The Three Friends' from R (1923), 'The Nap' and 'The Wharf' from
C (1926), 'The Picnic' from OE (1930), and 'Cape Race', 'Physic' and 'Miss Miller'
from WBO (1936).

Best Stories of Walter de la Mare (BS) (1942)
This selection of sixteen stories published in collections was made by de la Mare
himself. It contained: 'The Almond Tree', 'Miss Duveen', 'Seaton's Aunt' and 'The
Vats' from R (1923), 'Missing', 'The Nap' and 'All Hallows' from C (1926),
'Crewe', 'The Orgy: An Idyll', 'The Picnic' and 'An Ideal Craftsman' from OE
(1930), and 'What Dreams May Come', 'Physic', 'Miss Miller', 'The House' and
'The Trumpet' from WBO (1936). No stories for children were included.

The Old Lion and Other Stories (1942)
A selection of four stories from the children's collections, illustrated by Irene
Hawkins. They were 'Maria-Fly' from Br (1925), and 'The Lord Fish', 'The Old
Lion' and 'Sambo and the Snow Mountains' from LF (1933).

Mr Bumps and His Monkey (1942)
Dorothy P. Lathrop did the illustrations for this edition of 'The Old Lion' (LF
(1933)), published in Philadelphia in 1942.

The Magic Jacket and Other Stories (1943)
A selection of four stories for children from R (1923) ('The Riddle'), Br (1925)
('Miss Jemima') and LF (1933) ('The Magic Jacket' and 'Dick and the Beanstalk').
It was also illustrated by Irene Hawkins.

The Orgy (1943)
Reprinted by itself with an illustration by Frank R. Grey. In OE (1930) the story
was called 'The Orgy: An Idyll'.

The Almond Tree (1943)
Reprinted by itself with an illustration by Frank R. Grey. The story originally
appeared in R (1923).

The Scarecrow and Other Stories (1945)
Another selection of four stories from the two children's collections, illustrated by
Irene Hawkins. They were 'Broomsticks', 'The Lovely Myfanwy' and 'Visitors'
from Br (1925), and 'The Scarecrow' from LF (1933) (called 'The Scarecrow or
Hodmadod' here).

The Dutch Cheese and Other Stories (1946)
The fourth selection of children's stories illustrated by Irene Hawkins, containing
five this time: 'The Dutch Cheese', 'Lucy', 'The Three Sleeping Boys of
Warwickshire' and 'Alice's Godmother' from Br (1925), and 'A Penny a Day' from
LF (1933).

Collected Stories for Children (CSC) (1947)
Brought together in one volume all except three of de la Mare's stories for children in Br (1925) and LF (1933), and also 'The Riddle' from R (1923). The three omitted were 'Pigtails, Ltd.', 'The Thief' and 'A Nose' in Br (1925). It contained seventeen stories in all, and was illustrated by Irene Hawkins. The second edition (1957) was illustrated by Robin Jacques. See also the Introduction on page vii.

The Collected Tales of Walter de la Mare (CT) (1950)
A selection published in New York of twenty-four out of the forty-seven stories in R (1923), DDB (1924, 1936), C (1926), OE (1930) and WBO (1936). It was edited by Edward Wagenknecht. 'The Connoisseur' (C (1926)) was given complete. The stories were as follows. R (1923): 'The Almond Tree', 'Miss Duveen', 'Seaton's Aunt', 'The Bowl', 'The Three Friends', 'Lispet, Lispett and Vaine', 'The Tree', 'The Creatures', 'The Riddle' and 'The Vats'; C (1926): 'Missing', 'The Connoisseur', 'The Nap', 'All Hallows' and 'The Wharf'; OE (1930): 'Willows', 'The Orgy: An Idyll' and 'An Ideal Craftsman'; DDB (1936): 'Strangers and Pilgrims'; and WBO (1936): 'Cape Race', 'Physic', 'The Talisman', 'In the Forest' and 'The Trumpet.

Selected Stories and Verses of Walter de la Mare (SSV) (1952)
This Puffin included six of de la Mare's stories for children: 'The Dutch Cheese' and 'The Sleeping Boys of Warwickshire' from Br (1925), and 'A Penny a Day', 'The [Magic] Jacket', 'Dick and the Beanstalk' and 'The Old Lion' from LF (1933).

A Beginning and Other Stories (Beg) (1955)
De la Mare's last major published work before his death in 1956. It came out sometime after June 1955. It contained thirteen short stories, and of these 'The Quincunx' had been serialized in 1906, 'Odd Shop' in 1937 and 'The Guardian' in 1938. Others too had originally been written years before, e.g. 'A Beginning', the title story, which dates from before 1900. But some were recent.
In his introduction, de la Mare wrote as follows: 'Most of (the stories) have passed through changes – seldom rich, alas, but occasionally strange. Some of them are middle-aged. And, worse, may only too clearly look it. Most have been revised repeatedly; while some were born all but spick and span, only a springtime or so ago. One of them, cut down by half, actually came into being when Queen Victoria was still on the throne. Some of them, finally, in a different shape, have been "on the air", and many have been serialized...' See also the Introduction on page vii, and Unpublished Stories in *Short Stories 1927-1956*.
'Odd Shop'
(a) *Listener*, 31 March 1937 (where it was called 'Odd Shop: A Dialogue for Broadcasting')
'Music'
(a) *Adelphi*, April-June 1952 (where it was called 'Music from the Sea')
'The Stranger'
(a) *London Magazine*, September 1954 (where it was called 'The Stranger: A Dialogue')
'Neighbours'
'The Princess' (two notes on the TS read '13.3.37' (the day on which it was

broadcast by the BBC) and 'revised again Jan. 1954')
(a)   *Good Housekeeping,* October 1952
'The Guardian'
(a)   *John O'London's Weekly,* 10 June 1938
        The Best British Stories of 1939, ed.
        Edward O'Brien (Boston, 1939)
        Second Ghost Book, ed. Cynthia Asquith (1952)
'The Face'
(a)   *World Review,* December 1950
'The Cartouche'
(a)   *Encounter,* December 1954
'The Picture'
(a)   *Argosy,* February 1955
'The Quincunx'
(a)   *Lady's Realm,* December 1906
(b)   GS (1956)
'An Anniversary' (originally written in or before 1945)
(a)   *Saturday Book,* No. 12 (1952)
(b)   GS (1956)
'Bad Company'
(a)   *Listener,* 1 April 1954
(b)   GS (1956)
'A Beginning' (originally written in about 1900)

Walter de la Mare: Ghost Stories (GS) (1956)
A Folio Society selection of seven de la Mare ghost stories, edited by Kenneth
Hopkins and with lithographs by Barnett Freedman. It included 'Out of the Deep'
from R (1923), 'The Green Room' from OE (1930), 'The House' and 'A Revenant'
from WBO (1936), and 'The Quincunx', 'An Anniversary' and 'Bad Company'
from Beg (1955).

Eight Tales (1971)
This was a selection of eight very early de la Mare stories, all of them serialized
(except possibly 'A:B:O.') but none later collected, that Edward Wagenknecht
embarked on in about 1952 with de la Mare's approval. They were 'Kismet'
(1895), 'The Hangman Luck' (1895), 'A Mote' (1896), 'The Village of Old Age'
(1896), 'The Moon's Miracle' (1897), 'The Giant' (1901), 'De Mortuis' (1901) and
'A:B:O.' (dated 1896 or earlier according to Theresa Whistler). Wagenknecht
wrote an introduction and the volume was published by Arkham House, Sauk
City, Wisconsin. See also the CT (1950) entry and the Uncollected Stories sections
in *Short Stories 1895–1926* and *Short Stories 1927–1956.*

The Dutch Cheese and Other Stories (1988)
A new selection of eight children's stories, published in the Puffin Classics series. It
had six stories from Br (1925), 'The Three Sleeping Boys of Warwickshire',
'Alice's Godmother', 'The Dutch Cheese', 'Broomsticks', 'Miss Jemima' and 'The
Lovely Myfanwy', and one from LF (1933), 'The Lord Fish', and one from R
(1923), 'The Riddle'. It was different from the volumes published in 1931 and 1946.

CHRONOLOGICAL LIST
OF EARLIEST KNOWN
PRINTED VERSIONS*

1895

Kismet	uncoll	7 August 1895	*The Sketch*
The Hangman Luck	uncoll	4 November 1895	*Pall Mall Gazette*
A Mote	uncoll	August 1896	*Cornhill Magazine*
The Village of Old Age	uncoll	September 1896	*Cornhill Magazine*
The Moon's Miracle	uncoll	April 1897	*Cornhill Magazine*

1900

The Giant	uncoll	May-Aug 1901	*Pall Mall Magazine*
De Mortuis	uncoll	Sept-Dec 1901	*Pall Mall Magazine*
The Rejection of the Rector	uncoll	5 October 1901	*Black and White*
The Riddle	R	February 1903	*Monthly Review*
In the Forest	WBO	27 August 1904	*Black and White*

1905

An Ideal Craftsman	OE	June 1905	*Monthly Review*
'Benighted'	DDB	July-Dec 1906	*Pall Mall Magazine*
The Quincunx	Beg	December 1906	*Lady's Realm*
The Match-Makers	uncoll	December 1906	*Lady's Realm*
The Talisman	WBO	March 1907	*Lady's Realm*
The Budget	uncoll	June 1907	*Lady's Realm*
The Count's Courtship	R	July 1907	*Lady's Realm*
The Pear-Tree	uncoll	July 1907	*Lady's Realm*
Lichen	DDB	September 1907	*Lady's Realm*
Leap Year	uncoll	May 1908	*Lady's Realm*
The Dutch Cheese	Br	May 1908	*Lady's Realm*
The Bird of Travel	R	October 1908	*Lady's Realm*
The Almond Tree	R	August 1909	*English Review*

1910

The Three Friends	R	19 April 1913	*Saturday Westminster Gazette*

1915

The Vats	R	16 June 1917	*Saturday Westminster Gazette*
Promise at Dusk	uncoll	January 1919	*English Review*
Selina's Parable	R	1 November 1919	*New Statesman*

---

* Dates are given in italics for stories that were not serialized or published separately before they appeared in collections.

1920

The Creatures	R	January 1920	*London Mercury*
Two Days in Town	uncoll	13 November 1920	*Sphere*
Seaton's Aunt	R	April 1922	*London Mercury*
The Tree	R	October 1922	*London Mercury*
Lispet, Lispett and Vaine	R	January 1923	*Yale Review*
Miss Jemima	Br	1923	*Number One Joy Street*, Oxford
The Looking-Glass	R	*1923*	
Miss Duveen	R	*1923*	
The Bowl	R	*1923*	
Out of the Deep	R	*1923*	
The Wharf	C	November 1924	*The Queen*
Lucy	Br	1924	*Number Two Joy Street*, Oxford
Winter	DDB	*1924*	

1925

The Thief	Br	21 March 1925 and 4 April 1925	*G.K.'s Weekly*
Pretty Poll	C	April 1925	*London Mercury*
The Green Room	OE	July 1925	*Two Tales*, Bookman's Journal, London
The Connoisseur	C	July 1925	*Two Tales*, Bookman's Journal, London; *Yale Review*
Pigtails, Ltd.	Br	August 1925	*Atlantic Monthly*
Maria-Fly	Br	19 September 1925	*G.K.'s Weekly*
Broomsticks	Br	October 1925	*London Mercury*
The Three Sleeping Boys of Warwickshire	Br	October 1925	*Virginia Quarterly Review*
Visitors	Br	October 1925	*Forum*
Mr Kempe	C	November 1925	*London Mercury*
The Scarecrow	LF	1925	*Number Three Joy Street*, Oxford
A Nose	Br	*1925*	
The Lovely Myfanwy	Br	*1925*	
Alice's Godmother	Br	*1925*	
A Recluse	OE	1926	*The Ghost Book*, London
The Lord Fish	LF	1926	*Number Four Joy Street*, Oxford
Missing	C	*1926*	
Disillusioned	C	*1926*	
The Nap	C	*1926*	
All Hallows	C	*1926*	
The Lost Track	C	*1926*	
At First Sight	OE	June and Sept 1927	*Forum*

A Penny a Day	LF	1927	*Number Five Joy Street*, Oxford
The Magic Jacket	LF	1928	*Number Six Joy Street*, Oxford
Crewe	OE	July 1929	*London Mercury*
Willows	OE	September 1929	*Blackwood's Magazine*
Cape Race	WBO	September 1929	*Yale Review*

1930
The Picnic	OE	April 1930	*Criterion; Virginia Quarterly Review*
The Orgy: An Idyll	OE	June 1930	*Blackwood's Magazine*
Miss Miller	WBO	August 1930	*Story-Teller*
A Froward Child	WBO	10 November 1932	*The Times Weekly Edition*
The House	WBO	25 December 1932	*Observer*
A Nest of Singing-Birds	WBO	December 1933	*Yale Review*
Dick and the Beanstalk	LF	1933	
The Old Lion	LF	1933	
Sambo and the Snow Mountains	LF	1933	
What Dreams May Come	WBO	1 December 1934	*John O'London's Weekly*

1935
Strangers and Pilgrims	DDB 1936	March 1936	*Yale Review*
Physic	WBO	June 1936	*Nash's Magazine*
The Trumpet	WBO	October 1936	*Virginia Quarterly*
A Sort of Interview	uncoll	November 1936	*London Mercury*
A Revenant	WBO	1936	
Odd Shop	Beg	31 March 1937	*Listener*
The Guardian	Beg	10 June 1938	*John O'London's Weekly*

1940–1949   No new stories printed.

1950
The Face	Beg	December 1950	*World Review*
Music	Beg	April-June 1952	*The Adelphi*
The Princess	Beg	October 1952	*Good Housekeeping*
An Anniversary	Beg	1952	*Saturday Book,* London
Bad Company	Beg	1 April 1954	*Listener*
The Stranger	Beg	September 1954	*London Magazine*
The Cartouche	Beg	December 1954	*Encounter*

1955

The Picture	Beg	February 1955	*Argosy*
The Miller's Tale	uncoll	3 December 1955	*Time and Tide*
Neighbours	Beg	*1955*	
A Beginning	Beg	*1955*	

Marvin Banks
4 - 4 - 02